# The Guineaman
## *and*
# The Privateersman

D0635047

Richard Woodman is the author of over twenty novels. He has spent over thirty years at sea, serving in a variety of ships, from apprentice to captain. A member of the Society for Nautical Research, the Square Rigger Club and the Navy Records Society, in his spare time Richard sails an elderly gaff cutter with his wife and two children.

# The Guineaman

*and*

# The Privateersman

Richard Woodman

Pan Books

*The Guineaman* first published 2000 by Severn House Publishers
*The Privateersman* first published 2000 by Severn House Publishers

This omnibus edition published 2001 by Pan Books
an imprint of Pan Macmillan Ltd
Pan Macmillan, 20 New Wharf Road, London N1 9RR
Basingstoke and Oxford
Associated companies throughout the world
www.panmacmillan.com

ISBN 0 330 39877 6

Copyright © Richard Woodman 2000

The right of Richard Woodman to be identified as the
author of this work has been asserted by him in accordance
with the Copyright, Designs and Patents Act 1988.

All rights reserved. No part of this publication may be
reproduced, stored in or introduced into a retrieval system, or
transmitted, in any form, or by any means (electronic, mechanical,
photocopying, recording or otherwise) without the prior written
permission of the publisher. Any person who does any unauthorized
act in relation to this publication may be liable to criminal
prosecution and civil claims for damages.

1 3 5 7 9 8 6 4 2

A CIP catalogue record for this book is available from
the British Library.

Printed and bound in Great Britain by
Mackays of Chatham plc, Chatham, Kent

This book is sold subject to the condition that it shall not,
by way of trade or otherwise, be lent, re-sold, hired out,
or otherwise circulated without the publisher's prior consent
in any form of binding or cover other than that in which
it is published and without a similar condition including this
condition being imposed on the subsequent purchaser.

# The Guineaman

*'Until the lions have their own story-tellers,
tales of hunting will always glorify the hunter.'*
African Proverb

# Part One

## Blood

# The Fugitive

His breath was rasping painfully in his throat now. The effort to run, to raise one foot after another, seemed too much for his failing strength, and still the ground continued to rise, a sharper incline it seemed to his numbed mind, for the sparse grass had given way to a treacherous scree and he sent stones tumbling down behind him. Instinct and a long familiarity with the wild countryside surrounding the lakes had brought him up on to the Black Fell. He began to slacken his pace, feeling his leg muscles trembling with the effort of escape, the thunderous pain of his beating heart and the fogging of his brain. Sweat poured into his eyes and soaked his clothes. He was close to fainting now, as he almost fell headlong, for he had no idea how long he had been running, only that his whole world had suddenly contracted in this effort of escaping his pursuers.

He slowed to a stumbling lope, gradually reclaiming the use of his faculties. He became aware, dimly at first, that night was coming on, and of a sharp chill in the air that presaged rain. He raised his eyes and saw, at last, the summit of the fell. Now that it seemed attainable, it failed to bring him the security he hoped for. Breathing ponderously he stopped, trying to think. He bent over, gasping, hands on knees, his throat raw, his leg muscles cramped, the moisture on his exposed skin suddenly chilled.

Then he heard a shout and the baying of the dogs, and fear leapt again in his guts. Lifting his head with a strangled cry he began to run once more.

He knew his pursuers could see him against the sky as he crossed the ridge, but it was only as he felt the scree begin to fall away, treacherously inducing his exhausted legs to falter, that he realised how foolish he had been to expose himself. Had the effort of escape not dominated him, his normal ready intelligence would have prevented so foolish a mistake, but it was too late now. For perhaps another five minutes he blundered on, increasingly uncertain of his footing, his arms flailing, his will ebbing with his

3

stamina. Then he slipped, the moment of lost control coinciding with a sharp declivity in the ground, and his shoulder glanced against a rocky outcrop. The impact spun him half round so that his left leg tripped over his right and he tumbled at the foot of the rock.

He fell full length, splashing into a cold pool of water lying under the outcrop. Face down, he swallowed the brackish stuff, then, in a last reflex, he raised his head, gasped at the air and crawled, like a terrified child, along some ten yards of what felt like a magically soft landscape of green. Then he slowly subsided, lying down in the bed of the stream, his head to one side as he lapsed into complete unconsciousness. The water trickled into and out of his open mouth but the lush landscape of his imagination, which was in fact nothing more than tall flanking grasses and some patches of moss, concealed him in the twilight.

Some moments later, when his pursuers reached the rock, they had lost the trail. In the gathering darkness they stared down into the valley beyond, and one of them pointed to something bounding down a slope half a mile away. The two men bent, like their victim a little earlier, their hands on their knees, gasping for breath as they tried to make out their distant quarry. The hounds slumped on the ground, flanks heaving and tongues lolling from their slobbering chops as they panted like their masters. One lapped water from the pool, the other shook foam from its muzzle. Neither were good coursers, and both men and dogs were badly winded.

"Th' bugger always could run on the fells," one of the men said to the other between gulps of air, nodding at the dark shape still just visible below.

"He'll be back," responded the other. "Then we've got 'un."

At that moment the rain began. A few tentative drops at first, followed by a sudden, sleeting downpour that hissed at them, bouncing off the scree as a squall drove it up the valley and over the brow of the open moorland. Twilight turned suddenly to the onset of night.

"Come on, Phil, time we got back home. We'll get the justice's men after 'im and have 'im in a noose in Carlisle by next quarter-day!"

The man called Phil did not follow his brother at once but continued to stare down into the valley. Rain streamed down his face. "Billie Kite!" he roared into the wind. "I haven't finished with you, you bastard!"

Then he turned, and was gone, following his brother back the way they had come, swallowed by the darkness and the torrential rain. Far down the side of the abandoned valley, the frightened goat ran in its sure-footed way.

\* \* \*

The fugitive recovered consciousness a few minutes later. The cooling sweat of his exertion and the chill of the downpour woke him to a shivering cold. Slowly he raised his head, and for several long minutes he remained thus, listening with the keen attention of a hunted animal. All he could hear was the hiss of the rain on the stones and the low moan of the rising wind. The loom of the rock outcrop startled him for a moment, but then he realised not only what it was, but where he was. He had run near enough to five miles from the lake, up the steep incline of the Black Fell, far up beyond the trees and beyond even the high pasture where the flocks of sheep grazed. He had given the Hebblewhite brothers a good run for their money, to be sure! For a moment he thought it was time to return home and then the ghastly events of the early evening flooded back to him, along with the dark realisation that he was a damned soul.

By running away he had compromised his innocence. No one would now believe he had nothing to do with the girl's death!

Oh, God, that it should be his poor Susie . . .

The impact of this terrible realisation caused him to void his stomach in pure fear: he could never go home again. Never. He could only run on, away down the far valley after the goat.

# One

## The Whore

William Kite walked south by night, hiding up during daylight. He sheltered in a succession of barns, in a churchyard where the sexton had made a small bower to keep his pick, shovel, sickle and scythe, and, as he neared Liverpool, under the wreckage of an old boat he found on a beach on the southern shore of the River Ribble. At first he had been terrified, but once south of Lancaster, with no hue and cry obvious behind him, he began to feel more confident of escape. He was innocent of the charge the two brothers had screamed at him when they saw the body of their sister, but there was sufficient confusion and guilt attached to his relationship with the dead girl to prick his own conscience. That and the long-standing enmity of Susie's brothers goaded him with the very spurs of the devil himself.

All his fear and irresolution translated into the desire to put many miles between himself and the Hebblewhite farm and the bloody scene upon which he had stumbled that dreadful afternoon. Exhaustion induced sleep, but when he woke, cramped and cold, he sprang instantly to his feet and pressed on southwards. He drank from streams and scavenged what food he could. He caught and cooked a rabbit as he had often done in his carefree boyhood, a youth which now seemed an age away, golden in its fading insubstantiality. Yet, out of the conflicting conviction of innocence and guilt by association, he found the will to press on, to escape, to survive. And as time passed, and no one challenged him and there was no sound of bloodhounds borne on the wind, the eviscerating panic gradually faded. He found that he could think again.

As he walked, only hiding from another night traveller who rode north on a steaming horse with the fugitive air of a highwayman, Kite learned that the ability to think brought with it a train of terrors. The shadow of the gallows fell constantly across his path; the horror of execution, of the disgrace he knew capture, trial and execution would bring upon his father and sister; the impossibility of establishing innocence in an England lusty for death in this year of

6

Grace 1755, spurred him ever southwards. His fear combined with a natural solitary disposition and the cunning born of a boyhood and youth amid the lakes and fells of Cumbria, to enable him to avoid other humans, and in due course he formulated a strategy, just as he had seen his father formulate a specific in the little workshop filled with the mysteries of the pharmacopoeia. It chilled him to think that he would never see his father again, nor his own sister, but the circumstantial evidence condemned him for ever. Only the dry logic of his father's profession of apothecary sustained him. Perhaps he could go for a soldier and lose himself in the ranks of a regular battalion sent on duty overseas . . . perhaps . . . But there were few opportunities that he could think of, although a thousand mad schemes came and went as he walked, burning his mind with the one searing certainty that somehow he must live to let his father know he was innocent.

And it was then that he thought of his cousin Francis, and the Liverpool merchant to whom he was apprenticed. Kite recalled the address on the letter his father had last written to Francis, for Kite's widower father had brought up Francis as well as his own two children. Mr Kite had stretched his influence to the utmost to secure the young man employment which would remove the necessity of feeding him from the slender profits from the apothecary's trade.

During the fourth day, as Kite settled beneath the old boat on the bank of the Ribble, he spread out his coat and, having rinsed his shirt and hose in the sea, laid them to dry. If anyone saw them while he slept exhausted beneath the split tarred planking, nothing came of it and he felt better when he pulled them on again that night, for all the clamminess of the salt in his shirt. At the end of his fifth night's march he approached Liverpool. Intending to rest for only an hour or two, he fell deeply asleep, awaking towards evening in a state close to panic. He wandered utterly confused amid the crowded and noisy streets of the waterfront. Worn out with anxiety and exertion, he failed to locate his cousin's lodging. But on finding he had sufficient money to do so, he secured a night's sleep in a cheap lodging house near the river.

The landlord looked him up and down, shifted the quid of tobacco and remarked, "You'll likely have to share before the night's out, but a young man of your quality'll have to get used to that if you lodge here."

Kite was too tired to grasp to what the landlord alluded, aware only of the warmth of the alehouse and the smell of some sort of gruel or stew cooking within the tavern. An hour later, having removed his coat and shoes, he was stretched on a flea-ridden mattress, half covered by a stained blanket.

Some two hours later he woke suddenly, sitting up in bed with a start. The door to the room was open and in it loomed a man bearing a candle in one hand. His other was about the waist of a young woman. Her stays were loose and she and the man were obviously drunk.

"There's a young feller in the bed already, Jimmy. I didn't know youse was after having one of them nights—" and she broke off into a giggle, staring at Kite as he hurriedly reached for his coat and shoes, recalling the landlord's warning. He was confused. It was dark, he should have been marching; the young whore reminded him of Susie. The same wet and open mouth, the same disorganisation of dress, the same damp stink of sexual intent.

He thought only of escape again, thrusting his feet into his shoes, grabbing his coat and making for the door, to shove past the swaying seaman and his hussy. The seaman reeled back with an oath as Kite pushed past. Kite stumbled on the stairs, recovered and then descended into the taproom. Behind him the seaman, having made an attempt to grab Kite, was drawn back into the bedroom by his whore and the door slammed.

The taproom was crowded now, the air thick with tobacco smoke and raucous conversation. The variety of men, men of colour, men with red hair, men of sallow complexion and jet-black hair, even a Chinaman with narrow eyes that Kite had only ever heard of in a story, were interspersed with the shabbily gay dresses of the common drabs who sought to service them. Pots of ale and flip were borne hither and thither by the pot-boys and a lass or two and the whole thick atmosphere seemed instantly recognisable to a young man catechised from childhood. "I am in hell," he muttered, seeking the door to the street.

It was an ill-chosen and in the event a fateful moment for, as he made for the entrance and the cool night air beyond, two men rose in front of him. Already in heated argument over a smirking trollop who lolled back on the adjacent bench, one shoved at the other and he in turn, recovering, lunged back at his assailant. In an instant, they were fighting.

Kite recoiled from this further manifestation of devilment as the yelps of encouragement and amusement went up all around him. The crowd egged on the contestants until after only a few moments one fetched the other a heavy belt on the jaw and the luckless victim subsided with a crash against the bench.

The victor turned to the woman who was eyeing him with an excited gleam in her eye and held out his hand. "C'mon, you!" he said, breathing heavily.

"You sure youse can manage her after all that fisticuffs, Tommy-boy?" someone called out and the excited company roared once more.

Tommy-boy ignored the ribaldry, tugged the girl to her feet and pulled her roughly to him, embracing her and planting a kiss upon her wet and ready mouth. The company lost interest and Kite made to pass the couple when suddenly the defeated man rose to his feet. Kite saw the flash of steel and shouted a warning, but he was too late. The knife, thrust upwards, was driven to the hilt into the woman's buttocks so that she screamed and arched her back, her would-be lover staggering under the impact. In the next second a bottle descended upon the head of the seaman with the knife and he fell a second time to the floor.

Kite's exit was now blocked as the other women screamed and gathered round. He caught a glimpse of stocking and a pink thigh pouring with blood and then, amid the wails and the screams and the shouts of the men now crowding about the wretched trollop, he reacted in a way that he could never quite explain. Perhaps it was the earnest desire to prove he was not capable of the murder of which, in distant Cumbria, he stood accused. Perhaps some unconscious urge drove him to prove his innate goodness, that he might, at some desperate future moment, call these low-born seafaring folk and their dockside whores to stand as witness to his character.

"Clear a table," he said, his voice loud and commanding. He swept an arm and sent pots and bottles to the sawdusted floor, adding, "Stretch her out here, and quick, for she loses blood."

Amid the hubbub, a face or two turned towards him. It was clear from his coat and neckcloth that, modest though they were without any pretensions to fashion, he was not a man of the seafaring stock that filled the alehouse. His pallid complexion alone set him apart from them, but the impression of his being a gentleman was lent credibility by his assumption of authority.

"Lay her out upon the table," he said again, eager to staunch the haemorrhage that reminded him so painfully of the bleeding Susie. Perhaps he sought to make amends, perhaps he accepted that this scene, with its terrible echoes of a late afternoon only a few days earlier, was a fatal repetition from which there was no escape. All he was aware of in that unpleasant moment was that from an unnerved young man intent on escape from a dockside alehouse, he had become again the youth who could set bones and stem the flow of blood. He had done it for Susie's pet rabbit after a fox had savaged it, he had done it for his sister's puppy after Philip Hebblewhite's hound had mauled it, and he had set the wings of birds caught in nets, including a beautiful peregrine falcon. He had been trying to help Susie herself when her brothers found him and raised the cry of 'murderer!'

"I can help her," he said now, staring about him and dismissing the suspicion in the faces round him.

"Do as he says," said the man Tommy suddenly, his face pale under his sunburn, the stink of liquor overlaying that of stale sweat. "Get her up on the table!"

Kite turned, caught the eye of one of the serving girls and said, "Get me some clean water and a clout . . . And a needle and thread . . ."

The wounded woman had fainted as Tommy lugged her unceremoniously on to the table. She lay face down, a large, buxom woman of some twenty-three or -four years of age, unlovely in her unconscious state. Kite carefully raised her filthy skirt and her soiled petticoats as the sailor's knife fell from her. He bent and retrieved it, regarding the wound as the crowd round about fell silent with an intent curiosity. The thrust had been upwards, and the blade had begun its incision in the upper portion of the thigh, reaching its greatest penetration in the subcutaneous fat covering her left buttock. If the cheated and would-be lover who stabbed her had been intending to wound her private parts, he had mercifully missed. The woman's ample figure had saved her from certain death. A momentary yet bitter reflection about the capricious nature of fate crossed Kite's mind: the drunken seaman had escaped a certain charge of murder while he himself, caught in a moment of extreme compromise, yet innocent of any harm to Susie, was sought as a murderer.

Kite shook off the thought and addressed the business in hand. The woman's wound was not as serious as it at first appeared from the steady flow of blood. She wore no drawers, but Kite used the knife to cut away a fold of her petticoat that had been driven into her flesh and then carefully withdrew it from the gash. A portion of muscular tissue obtruded in its wake and, calling again for water, Kite pushed it gently back and drew the two edges of the wound together.

The girl brought him water and he repeated his request for a needle and thread.

"'Ere you are, love," another trollop said, tugging the drawstring of a small cloth bag and withdrawing a rolled hussif. Kite swabbed the wound while the woman threaded the needle. A few moments later he had closed the gash with a half-dozen sutures. Cleaning the drying blood from round the neat stitches, he pulled the woman's petticoat back over her rear. Looking up at the man called Tommy he said, "She needs to sleep quietly on her front. Can you see to that?"

"Aye, I think so, sir." Tommy looked crestfallen. Someone in the crowd cheered as Kite rinsed his hands in the bowl and wiped them on a grubby towel the serving girl held out to him.

"You a surgeon, sir?" the woman with the hussif asked. Kite smiled. He was too tired to laugh at the ridiculous notion, and too tired to deny it. At their feet the wounded whore's felled assailant stirred, but no one took any notice of him. Then the landlord was shoving forward through the press.

"Let's be having your pots, damn you all! Get ye all off to your beds, and as for you, sir, please to follow me, I'll see to it you have a quiet night after all this botheration."

Kite slept until late and woke to descend to the now stale air of the noxious taproom. A woman was swabbing the tables with a filthy clout and a pot-boy was eating what looked like oatmeal and water beside the fire. The woman looked round at the boy and nodded, whereupon the lad put down his bowl and scampered out, returning a moment later, followed by the landlord.

"You'll take some breakfast, sir?" the Landlord asked and Kite looked dubiously at the boy's bowl. A fierce hunger gnawed at him and he nodded.

"I'll see to it," said the woman, bustling off to the kitchen while the landlord addressed the boy.

"You be off and tell the Cap'n, like I told yer, lad." And again the boy disappeared, on a second errand.

Kite sat at the table which last night he had used to stitch up the slashed jade. Hot coffee and fresh bread were soon filling the taproom with a welcome and surprising aroma. In the chimney, the landlord eased himself on to a bench and lit a small clay pipe, eyeing his guest over the flame which leapt and subsided at the end of the spill.

He shook out the spill and blew a cloud of smoke from his mouth. "We don't often get the gentry staying with us," he said. "I s'pose you'll be looking for a ship . . ."

Kite looked up with a start. The idea had never occurred to him, but it suddenly offered him a solution to his problem. He could write an affidavit, have it properly sworn and post it to his father. The time which would elapse during a voyage would allow the hue and cry to subside and the real cause of Susie's death to be determined by the magistrates. When he came home again, the whole affair would have blown over.

"You've the right trade for these parts and Captain Makepeace is hard pushed to find what he wants for the *Enterprize* . . ."

"Right trade?" quizzed Kite as it dawned upon him that he knew nothing of ships and therefore had nothing to recommend him as a potential seaman.

The landlord nodded. "You're not the first barber's 'prentice we've seen here, familiar enough with lifting a doxy's skirts. Happen you've done it once too often and now there's a puddin' in the basin when all you wanted was to dip yer little wick, eh?" A leering wink and a chuckle that rumbled deep in the landlord's belly accompanied this comforting reassurance.

Kite, frowning, was in the process of working out what the landlord meant when the door flew open and a well-dressed man swept into the taproom, spun on his heel and, thumping the heels of both hands on the table in front of Kite, peered under the forecock of a silver-laced tricorne hat into Kite's eyes.

"I have heard you can suture a trollop's arse, Mister . . ."

"Kite, sir," said the startled Kite, instantly regretting betraying his name, but rising slowly to his feet under the intimidating gaze of the stranger.

"I am Captain Makepeace of the *Enterprize*," the stranger said, still leaning forward on his hands, but raising his head and following Kite's elevating figure. "A Guineaman sir, perhaps the best in Liverpool, though I shall not claim it so myself." He paused, regarding Kite with a cold eye. "I want you to ship out with me as my surgeon."

Kite suddenly made sense of the landlord's reference to his being a barber's apprentice, thinking Kite to be the indentured assistant to a barber-surgeon.

"Look, I have no—"

Makepeace drew himself up and stuck out his chin. Under the shadow of the hat, Kite saw him to be a man of some thirty years of age. The captain's features were handsome in a squared way, the skin swarthy and weather-beaten. Notwithstanding this, his jaw was already dark with the shadow of his beard, while his hair was his own and was drawn back into a clubbed queue. The captain's dark grey eyes bored into Kite's. He felt a sensation of unease so palpable that it silenced his protest, but this vanished as Makepeace clapped him on the shoulder with a charming smile.

"Come, Mr Kite, say you'll sign articles and I assure you of a profitable voyage which will set you up for life. A bounty of a hundred guineas on top of your pay will not displease you, eh? A man would be fool to pass up such an offer and stay an instant longer in a hell-hole like this." Makepeace gestured at the tawdry surroundings, rapidly hurrying on, "Well, then, the matter is settled." He swung away, fished some coins from his waistcoat pocket and, flicking a copper penny to the boy and a gold half-sovereign to the landlord, concluded his business.

"Thank you, Young. I trust I am no longer in debt to you." The landlord caught the coin and rose to his feet. "Not at all, Cap'n. As usual, 'tis a pleasure to do business wid yer."

Kite felt Makepeace's hand under his elbow. "We shall find," Makepeace dropped his voice to a confidential and intimate tone, "a more congenial breakfast aboard the *Enterprize*."

And having just time to seize his own hat, Kite felt himself propelled out into the street.

# Two

## The Journal

*My Dear Helen*, Kite wrote, his borrowed goose quill spluttering as he formed the letters in his quick hand,

> I cannot Write without the Strongest Emotions almost Suffocating me with their Intensity. You will have heard, no doubt, of my now being a Murderer and that I was Responsible for the Death of Susan Hebblewhite. It is Not True, and I should be there to defend my Good Name had not the Two Brothers Hebblewhite Come Upon Me in the Most Difficult of Circumstances. I Write now that you may lay the Facts before Father and make him acquainted with them in the Most Emphatick manner possible, as you Love me.
>
> I was, upon Friday last, coming through the Village from Mr Watkins' place, whither I had gone, you may recall upon an errand of Father's . . .

The normality of that quiet, late afternoon walk imposed itself upon Kite's imagination. He paused in his scribbling to recall the prelude to disaster. It seemed inconceivable that life should lurch round so abrupt and terrifying a corner, precipitating him into so desperate a situation and threatening his sanity. A sense of utter panic rose in him; he felt he was on the verge of madness as he attempted the task of letting his sister and father know what had happened. A cry almost choked him, but he recalled his present surroundings, that he was safe for the moment, and while the confinement of the cabin seemed like a cell, it was not so. After a moment, he grew calm and bent to his task again, once more resolute.

Watkins was a rich and retired old West India merchant who kept a rambling house just beyond the environs of the village and between which lay the Hebblewhites' farm. Kite had been in the act of passing the rickety gate of the mired farmyard when the scream that rent the quiet afternoon had so quickened his heartbeat that he scarcely remembered running from the lane, across the

14

pebbled and muddy yard towards the whitewashed stone house. As the piercing shriek came again he swung aside, running full tilt into the adjacent barn.

Hearing a Scream from the Hebblewhites' barn, yet not seeing any Person about the yard, I gave a Shout that I was coming and Pulled aside the Barn Door. It was Dark inside and I heard a Rustling and Whimpering. Stumbling forward into the Gloom I came upon the most Hideous Sight. Susan, all uncovered, her Womb running Blood and Gore into the Straw and Filth, her Belly Pierced by a pitchfork which I withdrew Whereupon there went up a Great Shout, as of Joy, I thought in my hopeless Confusion, for I was so Shaking and Almost Weeping, when from Behind I felt Hands Laid upon me and turning, so Full of Fury was I Suddenly Infused that I wielded the Bloody Instrument of Death and Phil. Hebblewhite and his brother Colin fell back and sent up the Cry MURDERER! MURDERER! as if I had been caught in the very Act of Committing the Bloody Deed.

Instantly sensing that the Implication of Guilt was Strongly Laid Upon Me by the holding of the Pitchfork, I Stabbed Twice at the Brothers that they might Let me Pass and began to Run. Oh, Dearest Sister, how I now Regret this Impetuous Action and the Subsequent Flight. They Assumed Guilt lay Upon Me, and Knowing that I had some Affection for Their Sister thought the Worst – That I had got her with Child and was Intent upon Concealing my Crime with One more Heinous by Far. They set their Hounds upon me, but, As if the Devil Himself possessed Me, I outran Them and so, after Many Days Trial, Came to this place and have now Taken Ship for the Coast of Africa.

My Only Object in Fleeing, was to Avoid the Murderous Intentions of Colin and Philip Hebblewhite who, You Know too well, Bear no Love for me. I durst not write to Father, but Plead with You that You will Lay these Desperate Circumstances before Him to Establish My Innocence. That this Matter May be Laid before the Justices is Something that I Devoutly Hope, but Whatever may befall I Affirm My Innocence . . .

Kite laid down the quill and buried his head in his hands. The headlong rush to express himself left him feeling drained. He wanted to write more, to express his stupefied gratitude to Captain Makepeace for his generosity in advancing sufficient funds for him to buy himself a few garments and necessaries, for his ready friendship in taking him up and his own guilt that, in his own eagerness to escape, he had so far obscured from the good captain the fact that he was not a surgeon. It had seemed that luck favoured his innocence as the day of departure arrived but then his anxiety had redoubled. Hardly had they warped out into the stream of the River Mersey than a blinding fog had descended and they had been trapped for two days.

The only merit in this delay was the opportunity to write home, an endeavour he had at first considered too risky until he recollected that no defence was tantamount to an admission of guilt. When he had casually, or as casually as his beating heart permitted, asked Makepeace, the *Enterprize*'s commander had assured him the pilot would take the letter and post it, that being a part of his duty in seeing ships clear of the dangers of the estuary. As for the rest, Kite's anxiety, his need to acquire a few personal effects and the strangeness of his own confusing surroundings had swallowed the slow plod of time. He vacillated between periods of profound depression that led him to fearful and terrifying moments, but the instinct to survive and the strong restorative certainty of his own innocence pulled him back from the brink. He turned aside from contemplation of the dark river and its promise of eternal oblivion, thrusting himself into the business of the ship with a fervid activity. Apart from brief encounters, Captain Makepeace became an increasingly aloof, preoccupied or absent figure while, unfortunately, the society of his fellow officers had been denied him in the hurried preparations for departure and the apparent mayhem that prevailed. Any notion of matters on shipboard being well regulated seemed wildly inaccurate as stores, cargo and trade goods poured aboard the *Enterprize*. Kite, personally distracted, confused and neglected, had no hope of understanding the distinction between the artefacts, consumables and goods of singular description that were salted away below, even had he had a mind to. All about him sounded an alien tongue, replete with lavish use of shipboard expressions and a proliferation of oaths. This was much conducted at the shout, so that he derived no information from it, other than a certainty that the crescendo in its general intensity seemed to rise as the moment of departure drew closer. When the decks were suddenly cleared and the teeming mass of seamen and longshoremen drew apart, a strange, almost silent order did in fact descend upon the *Enterprize*'s decks. These were suddenly less cluttered, festooned instead by carefully coiled ropes, so that the business of their warping into the river, a shred of canvas dangling above their heads until the anchor was let go as the fog settled, seemed almost peaceful.

There had been some small duties thrust Kite's way. Makepeace, after his brief and generous solicitude in advancing him ten guineas, had hardly spoken to him. Another man, the ship's first officer, known not as a mate but as a lieutenant, as if he were a King's officer, had introduced himself as Thomas Gerard. Gerard had shown him a small cubby-hole in the bottom of the ship. Where exactly this was in relation to those parts of the vessel with which Kite was better acquainted, it took him three days to determine. This cubby-hole was his store, in which lay several small wooden chests that contained his pills, tablets and other bottled specifics, a set of ghastly chirurgical tools, a pestle, a mortar and an assortment of dirty, glass-stoppered bottles. Having made a short trip ashore, constantly looking over his shoulder for fear of apprehension by constables, to fit himself out with some small clothes and a new pair of shoes, he occupied himself in a desultory attempt to make an inventory of his gear. He spent long hours at this task, reliving those dreadful moments in the Hebblewhite barn over and over again, suddenly coming to himself when some noisy oath obtruded and woke him with a start from his obsessive trance. Thus he filled his days and afterwards could remember little beyond the overwhelming confusion prior to departure. He slept but fitfully, disturbed by dreams of Susie and her torn belly, confusing reality and spectre so that he could scarce recall what he had really seen from the grotesque inventions of his fevered imagination. As is the way with nightmares, Susie's death agonies became confused with the stitching up of the whore's backside, the agony of pursuit and the slavering hounds of the Hebblewhite brothers.

The fog caused moisture on every rope and spar so that water dripped so persistently upon the ship's deck that it seemed like rain. As the *Enterprize* swung in the tideway, snubbing at her cable in this pervading damp, Kite completed his letter to Helen. Why he wrote to her in preference to her father, he was not certain, except that it seemed less likely that her correspondence would be suspect while he imagined every letter addressed to his father would be subject to scrutiny by the shadowy, yet persistent agents of the law. Despite the ease of his escape, his over-wrought imagination conjured up a constable or a sworn citizen skulking behind every cottage in the village, eager to pounce upon evidence leading to the location of his whereabouts, a tension heightened by their fog-bound delay. This seemed a cruel and fateful prolongation of his agony; a certain indicator that he would be caught, to dance at the end of the hangman's noose after due process in the Carlisle Assizes.

But it was not so, for on the ebb coming away that very afternoon, the fog vanished as quickly as it had appeared and the *Enterprize*, with equal speed, weighed her anchor. The stirring and the capstan shanty woke Kite, and he went on deck, to be first shoved out of the way by a stream of bawling men walking the bars of the capstan round, and then shouldered aside by cursing seamen as they manned the halliards and sent the yards aloft to another rousing and discordant song. He succeeded, however, in passing his letter and a half-sovereign to the pilot, lingering on deck long enough to wonder at the downright insolence of the words of the shanty. These blackened the name of the commander and his officers in an orgy of insubordination, but neither Makepeace, standing aft by the helmsman and pilot, nor Gerard, staring aloft at the ascending yards, seemed to take any notice, and when the lieutenant bawled "Belay!" the words and rough tune ended abruptly, the men easing the ropes to the leading hauliers, who smartly turned them up on the pins and fell to coiling them neatly. The moment of near-mutiny had apparently passed. It took Kite some time before he understood this had been merely a ritual, a meaningless chanting to co-ordinate effort and only an expression of the crew's unity for a specific task; that of hoisting the heavy yards, not of overthrowing established order. With a half-comprehending shrug, he went below, resigning himself to fortune.

Here he hesitated a moment then, drawing out from one of the crude deal shelves that lined his nook a ledger left from a previous voyage, he tore out half a dozen pages of records and began a journal.

*In my Extremity*, he began under the date and making the only reference to his private misfortune,

> I Commence this Journal of my Voyage to Sea in the *Enterprize*, Brig, of Liverpool, Captain Makepeace commanding. We are bound for the Coast of Guinea and I know not what Future Events shall befall us, but I am Determined that they shall find in these Pages a Faithful Recorder, that these Events, whatsoever they be, shall stand against my Good Intentions in This World.

He sat back; *against* his good intentions, or *towards* them? He thought of crossing the first word out and substituting the second; then he abandoned the idea. What did it matter? He was writing a journal for his own distraction. No one would ever read it; he would probably never read the words again himself, but it might prove a vehicle for his despair and help him bear the burden of his new life.

The wind, giving them a slant to the south and west, was light enough to rock the *Enterprize* with a gentle motion and Kite slept soundly for the rest of that night. When he woke and went on deck the world seemed transformed and the moment suddenly lifted his spirits. By nature he was a cheerful, if thoughtful soul, not much given to fits of the blue devils, even during the most tedious days of his young manhood. Sunshine danced upon a sea which was thereby transformed into a bright and sparkling green. Gulls abounded, with black auks, their wings thrumming in a blur of effort, skimming the sea as they beat their way shorewards where the stacks of Holy Island rose on their larboard quarter. Beyond, he could see the mountains of Carnarvon, upon which the winter snow still lay. The poignant sight of those distant summits, so like the pikes and fells of his native Cumbria, both cheered and depressed him. The notion of departure was born heavily in upon him, of an uncertain future and of what he was leaving for ever. Yet he took comfort from the sight, seeing in it a valediction, almost a blessing from fate, and he recalled again his innocence. Whatever perversion of the truth the Hebblewhites had peddled, and, he thought in the security of the outward-bound *Enterprize*, whatever fate held in store, he *knew* he was guiltless. At this point in his reflections he staggered, fetching up against the lee main pin-rail, feeling for the first time the growing discomfort of the ship's motion as she met a heavier swell rolling up from the south west.

"You've yet to get your sea-legs, Mr Kite," a voice called, and he turned to see Captain Makepeace on his quarterdeck.

"Yes, sir," Kite replied, making his way gingerly across the deck as a patter of spray swept aft from the weather bow.

"You will. In a day or so you will be rolling with the gait of a hardened sea-jack, as comfortable with the motion as the rest of these lubbers." Makepeace paused, studying the *Enterprize*'s newest officer, as if for the first time. "Has Gerard told you of your duties as surgeon?"

"Well, Captain Makepeace, he has acquainted me with the fact that I am to attend the sick and to hold a daily meeting for those of the company wishing to consult me with their ills, but so far . . ." Kite felt a strange queasiness and a prickling sweat break out on his skin.

"Well, you'll be among the sick yourself for a while, I dare say," Makepeace broke in, "and then you will be called upon to provide mercury and potassium permanganate for the lues and clap." Makepeace gestured forward. The men of the watch were hauling the foretack down to the weather bumpkin as Gerard supervised them trimming the yards to an alteration of course. "Several of these wasters will have poxed themselves in Liverpool, Devil take it . . ."

"Captain Makepeace," Kite broke in with a sudden urgency, "you should know that I have no certificate . . . . I am not a proper surgeon . . ."

Makepeace stepped towards Kite and took his arm, turning him to leeward and propelling him none too gently to the rail, bending to his ear. "Mr Kite, you should know that I am sufficiently persuaded that you can accomplish the duties of a surgeon well enough. A man who can stitch up a woman's backside and pop mercury into a sailor's gob will do the duty of a surgeon in a Guineaman tolerably well. Besides, I myself was once a surgeon – yes, yes, don't look so damned surprised, 'tis a necessary qualification, like that of sailing as mate, for a man to command a Guinea-bound ship. Providing you have sailed your two voyages as mate or sawbones, you may yourself become master. You will have papers enough then even if Surgeon's Hall has no present recollection of your existence. Besides, Mr Kite, a guinea or two will suffice to obtain the papers you seek and the Custom House in Liverpool is not aware that yours cost that sum."

Kite frowned, comprehension dawning upon him slowly. "You mean you have lodged false papers to the effect that I am a surgeon . . ."

"I would not put it quite that strongly, Mr Kite," Makepeace said drily, "you will be competent enough when this voyage is over, that is for sure. Provided you survive it, of course."

Later, in the small lobby off which the cabins of the *Enterprize*'s officers led and which served them as a wardroom, he quizzed Gerard. The first mate, or lieutenant as he was styled, for the *Enterprize* bore a dozen guns and had been a privateer during the last war, belched discreetly behind his fist, dabbed at his lips with a napkin and regarded his questioner over a glass. They had dined well on fresh provisions and Gerard was in an expansive mood. He was not prone to the megrims that bedevilled sea-officers just fresh from the shore where they had left the ordinary comforts of life which even the meanest cottager took for granted. On the contrary, he viewed the coming voyage with some relish, seeing in it both peril and opportunity. Of a somewhat mercurial temperament, Mr Gerard was, at that moment, inclined to be friendly.

"Well, Kite, you are a stranger among us indeed, I suppose you know what a Guineaman is?"

Kite shrugged. "A vessel destined to trade upon the coast of Guinea, which I had supposed was somewhere in Africa."

Gerard nodded. "Well done. You are not a *complete* ignoramus.

And what then?" The emphasis on the adjective suggested Gerard suspected Kite's phoney status and he faltered in his response.

"Well, er, we return home with the produce of the country. Elephant's teeth, I imagine, spices, jewels and, er, the skins of tigers. What else can net a humble surgeon the one hundred guineas that Captain Makepeace assured me? Come, sir, you are laughing at me! You have the advantage, damn it. Have I speculated foolishly?"

"Only moderately so," Gerard said, leaning forward and refilling Kite's glass. "There are no tigers in Africa, though you might stumble across a leopard should you prove unlucky, but the chief error is to suppose that we return home. First we go to Brazil or the Indies with the, er, the freight we take aboard on the coast . . ."

"That is the Guinea coast?"

"Just so."

"And this freight consists not of elephant's teeth, but of something else?"

"Well, we shall almost certainly ship a quantity of tusks, but no, this is not the chief commodity from which your profit of one hundred guineas arises. Your principal task, and hence the importance of every Guineaman carrying a surgeon, is not to minister to the lubbers forward who ship as seamen, though you will be expected to lose as few of the fellows as possible, but to act in behalf of the blackamoors who come aboard."

"Blackamoors?" Kite frowned. "You mean — slaves." The truth dawned upon him. His preoccupation had prevented his enquiring the reason for the quantities of chains, shackles and leg-irons that he had seen about the ship, vaguely supposing them to be object of export, but now Gerard nodded.

"Blackamoors, Negroes, men as well as women — " Gerard leered unpleasantly — "and their welfare, my dear Kite, will be your sole concern. Furthermore, may I be permitted to add, solicitude for the preservation of all of them is paramount. You will find them well treated aboard the *Enterprize*, not, as you may have heard happens in other bottoms, abused and beaten and thrown overboard. They are a most valuable commodity and the captain will have had to purchase them with a not inconsiderable laying out of money, trade goods and rum. Moreover, my dear Kite, and of the utmost significance to you as surgeon, the dues payable to the majority of our ship's company will be dependent upon the highest number reaching the markets in the Brazils or the Indies."

"So the burden of this enterprise falls upon me?" Kite's pun was involuntary.

Gerard tossed off his glass and rose to his feet. "Squarely, if not fairly, my dear Kite, though as you will discover Captain Makepeace takes a very great – no, a very *personal* interest in the welfare, if indeed that is the absolutely correct term, for the preservation of the blacks. And now forgive me, I have but three hours before being on deck and must get a little sleep."

The following evening, somewhere to the north and west of the Isles of Scilly, the *Enterprize* ran into a gale. For Kite the experience was numbingly humiliating. The incipient queasiness, felt since the ship rounded the Skerries off Anglesey, now burgeoned into a violent succession of retching upheavals so persistent that his throat was rasped raw and the muscles of his gut seemed incapable of anything but a furious gagging. He was revolted by his own stench, yet was powerless to overcome his lassitude and lay prostrate as the motion of the ship made his head spin. In his lonely agony, he was reminded of once having been made drunk. He had been only ten years old when Colin Hebblewhite had forced ale on him and reduced him to an intoxicated stupor from which he took two days to recover. His father had been uncensorious, and treated him as though poisoned, remonstrating with old Hebblewhite to little avail.

"'Twas but a prank, Maister Kite," the farmer had laughed, "boys will be boys, d'ye know."

Mr Kite had told his son not to keep the company of the Hebblewhites, but it was they who constantly pressed themselves upon William Kite, seeing him as fit for guying and bullying. Kite had been of the same age as their own young sister Susan, and had sat beside her at the little dame school they were favoured with in the village. Susan was the first girl he had kissed and later, the first his questing and curious hands had fondled when she possessed growing breasts. They had other things in common. Both their mothers had died in childbed, Susan's at her own and Kite's at Helen's birth. Kite and Susan were equally sensitive to this loss, but the subtle distinctions of class obtruded. Joseph Hebblewhite successfully farmed rented land, held learning cheap and needed his children, particularly his strapping lads, to work his land; Jaybez Kite practised his quasi-profession amid a small library of battered volumes, patiently acquired, some in payment for simples, others bought at Carlisle, or Cockermouth. The Hebblewhites maintained a rough claim to social distinction, though it was the Kite children who played at the vicarage.

At puberty the lives of Susan and Kite had divided. He had gone to the grammar school at Cockermouth, she had continued her work in her father's dairy, where she had found her charms useful not merely to pleasure her old classmate. Jealous, but at the same time growing away from the narrow confinements of the village, Kite had sought a new purpose in life. Friendless and lacking invitations, he found himself unable to participate in the social life of Cockermouth. Cousin Frank, older and more cocksure, had done better, though he had not won any great distinction in the little town and, in any case, left the grammar school before William. In due course Kite returned to the village, content with his own company and interests, if somewhat introverted, and relatively untroubled by his solitary existence. The village had not changed in his absence, but it seemed to the metamorphosed Kite that it had. Susan was a comely and confident young woman, her brothers prospering boors who fell to their old ways of taunting the now lettered Kite. The bullying that he had forgotten or cast aside amid the remnant memories of childhood, was now insufferably insulting to him. Wanting employment he had found himself a half-hearted unindentured apprentice to his father's trade, a runner of errands and messages, still living off his father's charity though it was assumed that in due course he would be as competent an apothecary as his parent.

Kite's lack of interest in his assumed career was well known to his father, but the older Kite was too conscientious and attentive a man not to fill his entire day with his own business, never quite understanding a son who seemed, to his well-ordered mind, more than a trifle wayward. The senior Kite was also unable to remonstrate with his son, for the youth possessed too disquieting a likeness to his dead mother for the widower to unleash anger in the empty house. Kite's father mourned ceaselessly, figuring the lad would come round in the end, while Kite himself suffered a long, if well-meant, neglect.

Insofar as son was like father, the younger Kite's enthusiasm was for the natural world. But it was not the ground-foraging botanising of the apothecary's necessaries that drew the young man to his native fells. He loved the open air of the uplands and the soaring flight of the buzzards. He loved the bottled screech of the moorland grouse and the upward whirr of the brown wings; he felt his heart thunder whenever he saw the lordly peregrine stoop like a Jovian bolt and shatter the fat bird into an explosion of feathers. He was a good shot too, with a long-barrelled musket of uncertain manufacture and had once sent a ball whistling damnably close to the head of Philip Hebblewhite whom he had met one day on the western slopes of Dander Pike. Kite's motive had been more than fury at the insults offered him by the lout; rather, a fierce objection to the oaf's presence in that high and lonely place. For the fells were where Kite sought solace, and he had tramped thither on an expedition that had lasted a week and had had a search-party trudging through a night's mist after him when he learned of Susan's first unfaithfulness. Not that Kite had entertained any right to her fidelity, but the unspoken bond of their first trembling sexual questing had, it seemed to him, united them. He felt Susan's spurning with an acute pain.

Beyond the vague notion that he would succeed his father, Kite's life became aimless. Only his odd ability to bind up wounded animals was regarded with any wonder by the few people who witnessed it. For the most part, he was regarded as a disappointment, a feckless and idle waster, slowly but surely acquiring the reputation of being the young man who first turned Susan Hebblewhite into the trollop she had since become.

Such rumours feed on bird seed in a small community and Kite knew that there would be those that would readily believe he had killed Susan. The incident when he had shot at Phil Hebblewhite would be adduced as evidence of a violent nature. That the young woman had been pregnant was beyond doubt, that she had been killed by a jealous lover was also likely. Circumstantially, William Kite was known to roam the moors for unrequited love of her, after he had received an education in Cockermouth and become too grand for the village. They had all heard how he had been seen tending her little dog, making calf's eyes at her all the while, though she was no better than the male members of her family, growing up without a mother. She had had it coming to her, of course, but that did not make the matter right, and someone should swing for it.

Kite had done it, no doubt about it. He had skidaddled, had he not? It had to be him; that it should be someone else, someone still at large in the village, was unthinkable.

But Kite had had no hand in the affair. He had fondled Susie, as she him, but not for more months than it takes to make a child, and the tending of her dog almost a year earlier had been the last time they had spoken at length. Not quite, though; a week or so later, some ten months ago now, he had caught her in the churchyard with a man who had made off in the dusk.

She had laughed at him, reminding him that he too had played with her, though he had lacked the courage to fulfil matters – "like," she taunted him, "a real man". He had blushed foolishly. Susie had been the first and only woman to grasp his eager manhood and the first to hold the sticky results of her motions as she stirred him to uncontrollable passion. And though he had probed her in a reciprocal act, her ministrations to him, pleaded for for months afterwards, increased her power over him. Thus the wounding she had given him later in the churchyard stung him the more. It seemed she had matured and, where once she had been so unlike them, had grown up with the offensive character of her brothers. Angry, he had shunned her for months before that last, tragic encounter in her father's barn.

As he lay reeking in his cot, watching the deckhead and the beams swing about him and feeling the endless churning of his heaving gut, he remembered again the events of that dreadful afternoon. It was strangely as if he had never recalled it before with such precision, as though his earlier terrors had missed some details in the overwhelming inflammation of mental anguish. It was as if the images that now came back to him had in some strange way been withheld, frozen by the wild reflexes of action, of self-preservation and escape. He now knew that he had run not merely from a scene of brutal and bloody murder, but from a place of unimaginable horror.

Now, with perfect clarity, he recalled that between Susie's white thighs there had been something other than the blood of her apparent evisceration. The vertical pitchfork had not been planted in her voided belly or in her spread legs, but had transfixed the thing that lay between them.

Kite had run not so much from the bloodily bespattered and twitching corpse of the murdered woman, but from the monster she had given birth to.

# Three

## The Egyptians

It was three days before Kite made his renewed appearance on deck and then he endured a last humiliation, being told by Gerard, who popped his head into Kite's tiny cabin, that only a surgeon would have been suffered to lie in vile indolence for so long. Had he occupied any other station in the ship, Gerard explained with heavy emphasis, he would have been turned out to keep his watch.

Yet Kite, finding himself so much better, bore the jibe without protest. He was, after all, a neophyte and although the wind remained strong and the ship laboured with a creaking and a groaning, he now knew his condition was not fatal and he seemed to be as durable as the ship herself. The certainty overwhelmed him with relief. The very vastness of the heaving Atlantic, when he finally stared out over it, was too immense a thing to be affected by the hue and cry of a handful of Cumbrians. Even the notion of the island of Britain with its bewigged judges and slavering jurymen seemed faintly ridiculous, somehow so small as to be insubstantial amid this eternal, undulating greyness. He felt at last that the matter of Susan Hebblewhite's unhappy end belonged far astern, beyond the horizon in a world whose very existence was now doubtful. So full of the unknown was the foreseeable future that it too offered no identifiable threat to him. He was young enough not to be fearful of the thought of death and saw only boundless possible opportunities. He had run away to sea, and the security of that trite phrase now struck him with an accuracy that he had never before considered.

Bracing himself against the working of the brig, he clasped a rope that led upwards amid what appeared to him a tangle of other such ropes, to be lost against the grey and racing scud as the brig's two masts and their yards crossed and recrossed the sky in a dizzying series of arabesques. As he stood in his shirtsleeves, he muttered his triumph to himself. "I have run away to sea."

As if sensing this lightening of the surgeon's mood, though in fact merely reacting to his obvious recovery from seasickness and his appearance on deck, Captain Makepeace called out to him.

"Mr Kite!" Kite turned. Just for a moment he realised his escape was compromised by the fact that Makepeace knew his name and had presumably used it to obtain the false papers declaring him a surgeon. But the thought failed to dampen his mood as he crossed the deck, almost sure of his footing, to pay his respects to the master.

"Good morning, Captain," he said, and recalling Gerard's remark, added, "I apologise for failing in my duty—"

Makepeace cut him short. "No matter, Mr Kite, there is little duty for you to attend to at the moment and that is why you may stand your watch on deck with Mr Gerard. 'Twill be useful for you to acquire a working knowledge of the ship," Makepeace said, fixing his eyes on Kite and giving his next remark significance. "You never know when you might find it expedient to become a proper sea-officer."

If Makepeace guessed anything of Kite's predicament, and the gravity of his utterance suggested to the susceptible Kite that he not only guessed but could see into his very conscience, the captain's expression was not unsympathetic. Instead of holding over him the Damoclean sword of exposure, Makepeace seemed to offer a friendly, almost disinterested complicity. As if underwriting this unspoken bond, Makepeace went on, "At sea, Mr Kite, one never knows what will happen. You have joined a fraternity whose fates are inextricably linked. We are, forgive the abject pun, all in the same boat."

Makepeace was smiling with that charming air that Kite had first noticed in the Liverpool taproom. He smiled back. "I take your point, sir, and will do my utmost to acquire some sea-sense, if that is what you call it."

"Very well, Mr Kite. That will do splendidly."

As if to set its seal of approval upon this accommodation, the overcast broke and the sun suddenly shone down, transforming the world, turning the under-crests of the grey and breaking seas to a remarkable pellucid green. From one of these there suddenly leapt a pair of bottle-nosed dolphins, whose course for some moments lay parallel with that of the *Enterprize*.

That evening, after standing his first watch with Gerard, Kite wrote in his journal:

> Today, thro' the Kindness of Capt$^n$ Makepeace, I Kept the Deck with the First Lieutenant, M$^r$ Gerard. He was civil enough to Inform me the Names of the Spars and Sails and of the Principal Ropes which Controul them. He also appraised me of the Difference between the Standing and the Running Rigging, and How the Helm Works, Promising, should circumstances permit, to advance my Knowledge by

Degrees until I have a Perfect Understanding of Matters
Nautical.
I found his Instruction Interesting and Diverting . . .

To those last words, Kite owed an untroubled night's sleep.

Not that it was what he would have called a full night, for the
*Enterprize*'s officers worked watch-and-watch, four hours on and
four hours off duty. Having perhaps foolishly delayed climbing
into his cot until he had made the entry into his journal, Kite
found himself roused out again, after less than three hours' rest.
But he rose willingly enough, and stumbled on deck to be put
on the wheel until daylight, an old seaman standing near him to
admonish him every time he tried to correct the course by chasing
the lubber's line.

"No, no, Mr Kite. That'll never do, sir. See – " the man took the
helm and with a swift half turn stopped the brig from swerving out
of her track and throwing all her sails aback – " see, the lubber's
line there, that marks the heading of the ship, and while it looks
like the compass card swings in the bowl, 'tis really the ship that
be swinging. Though in truth," the man conceded, "the motion of
the ship does make the compass card turn about a bit."

It took a moment for the laws of physics to sink in at such a chilly,
dark and unsociable hour, but when Kite had grasped the fact that,
despite appearances, the compass card effectively remained station-
ary and the ship revolved around it, he had little trouble holding
the *Enterprize* on her headlong course to the south-westwards. That
morning established a pattern for all the days they ran south. Kite
quickly picked up the rudiments of sailing a ship and even began to
tackle the greater challenge of understanding the art of navigation.
By the time Makepeace backed *Enterprize*'s maintopsail off Funchal
and sent a boat thither for fresh fruit and some casks of Madeira wine,
Kite could work a traverse, box the compass in quarter-points, join
two ropes in a short splice and lay an eye splice, and he knew a dozen
common knots and hitches. He had, moreover, taken his place on the
yards when shortening down and knew the perils of passing gaskets.
All this raised his status in the eyes of the crew so that they were
less free with their comments and began to recognise that, while he
remained a neophyte, he nevertheless possessed the qualities of a
potential officer. Not that Kite appreciated any of this, he was far
too self-conscious of his shortcomings and ignorance. But he was
keen to learn and discovered for himself that here was something
that, all unknowing, he had an aptitude for. However, while the
crew might approve of him, they had yet to test him, and on the

fifteenth night at sea, a few moments after he had gone below and was in the act of undressing, a soft knock came at his cabin door.

Opening it, Kite was confronted by a young able seaman named Thomas. He was a short, wiry man, not much older than Kite himself but with the sunburnt skin of an experienced sailor.

"Beg pardon, Mr Kite, but I've got a problem. Not the first time, but I've caught a dose of the clap."

"Ah . . ." said Kite, conscious that he had been saved the ignominious task of attempting a diagnosis. "You've had it before, then?"

"Scarce rid of it, sir, to be truthful, but a body can't pine for ever an' there always are them promptings by way of nature, sir."

Kite frowned, caught between genuine interest, fear of the infection and of being exposed as a fraud. "It is an, er, intractable condition," he bluffed, aware only of the pertinacity of the infection. "Er, what did the last surgeon prescribe for you?"

"That purple stuff . . ."

"Permanganate of potassium," Kite said hurriedly, keeping his voice matter-of-fact as he grasped the passing straw. "And you, er, did the application yourself?"

"Oh yes," Thomas said leering, "bit awkward to get another feller to do it, even aboard this bleeder, eh? But it works out all right when we get the blackamoors aboard . . ."

"You mean . . ."

"You know, Mr Kite," Thomas confided with obvious relish, "ask one them black wenches to get it up and you can pour the stuff down dandy-oh. We make a joke of it, telling them they'll all beget mulatto pickaninnies and the perm . . . the purple stuff is white magic."

Kite dismissed the disturbing image Thomas's words conjured up. "What do you use – to apply the solution?"

"There's plenty of straw in the manger forrard . . ."

"You *must* clean it first," said Kite with sharp authority, in his first original contribution to this one-sided medical discussion. It was a fundamental principle he had learned from his father, that no object should be introduced to any subcutaneous part, wound or orifice of the human body that had been in any contact with another such place. Using a straw from the filth of the live animals' manger as a pipette to insert drops of specific into the canal of the male member seemed a most disquieting method. "Salt water will do, but don't neglect this precaution and neither use the straw twice, nor neglect this whenever you take up a piece of the stuff. I shall make you up a preparation in the morning. Now, you had better let me see . . ."

The tone of Kite's short lecture to Thomas obscured any early havering on the former's part, while Kite's inspection of the errant seaman's organ convinced Thomas of Kite's professional ability. Kite's own morbid fascination threatened to keep him awake after Thomas had gone. Terrible things, it seemed, lurked between the thighs of human beings. But he forbore commenting upon his first medical task and instead, as he lay back in his cot, he forced himself to enumerate the ropes that controlled the foretopsail. Before he had followed through the procedure for taking in a double reef, he was fast asleep.

Thus passed Kite's days as the *Enterprize* sailed southwards from Madeira. Passing the magnificent peak of Tenerife she skimmed before the north-east trade wind under a sky of unsurpassable blue. The puff-ball clouds that accompanied their passage were unthreatening, but a metaphorical cloud was growing in Kite's mind. The dominating terror of Susie's death and its aftermath had disposed him to imaginings of deep-seated worry. He had become an obsessive, and had had to develop techniques to divert his mind to prevent himself dwelling upon the horrors he associated with those terrible few moments in the Hebblewhite barn. Thus the trick of going over Gerard's lessons to superimpose his own memories had helped him manage this inclination to worry, but also acted as a maturing process, moulding the turn of his mind into deep ruts of preoccupation. Thus Thomas's crude reference to 'the blackamoors' and 'those black wenches' combined with certain oblique references of Gerard and others to prompt him to consider the next few weeks, when they would arrive 'on the coast' and take up their lading of slaves. The notion of slavery was one that he considered biblical, most naturally associating the state of enslavement with the Israelites. This historical plight seemed remote, so remote that it involved the active participation of the Jewish God who was, most emphatically, on the side of his unfortunate if occasionally wayward children. Jehovah's rescue of the Hebrew tribes was the triumph of good over evil and their delivery out of the hands of the Egyptians a satisfying confirmation of ultimate justice.

*If we are to take on Board Numbers of Slaves, that they are Black seems not to be the Matter for Consideration,* he wrote in his journal.

*That they are not Free and are to be Sold into Servitude seems the Chief Concern in this Age of Enlightenment. That we Traffick in Them places Us in the like Case as that of the Egyptians who, for Their Wickednesses, were afflicted by Seven Plagues and Drowned in the Red Sea.*

\*   \*   \*

Life, it seemed then to him, had every prospect of being one long series of moral dilemmas compared to which the acquisition of a sea-officer's skills was a simple matter, and moreover a far more enjoyable one. Therefore he threw himself into an understanding of meridian altitudes, parallel sailing and stellar recognition. He learned how to determine the latitude by the elevation of Polaris and, it has to be said, entirely specious methods of determining the ship's longitude. Despite this progress, Makepeace made no attempt to share the secrets of command, to show Kite, or any of his officers, the *Enterprize*'s progress on a chart. The descending value of the parallels of latitude therefore meant little to Kite, who could not relate them to their progress across the earth's sphere, no matter how much he longed to as he recalled the large globe in the grammar school at Cockermouth. Nor did Gerard or his colleague in the second lieutenant's berth evince the slightest curiosity in this regard. For them the swift progress of the ship was all that mattered, and while they took those observations that were necessary, they seemed to work the figures out as a matter of rote, handing them to Makepeace for inscription upon the chart in the privacy of the commander's cabin. Kite was somewhat confounded by this apparent secrecy; it was only long afterwards that he discovered that the chart, such as it was, was Makepeace's private property and bore all the secret notations of the captain's collected experience. Indeed, the printed chart was almost valueless without these superscriptions, bare of any but the most basic geographical information and produced speculatively by a company of self-styled cartographers in the city of London.

But these esoterica did not concern Kite in those last weeks of their outward passage to Guinea. Among a few sprains, bruises and one rupture, he dealt competently with a number of cases of venereal infection. His patients reported relief from the painful symptoms of the infliction by the lavish application of permanganate of potassium. Kite caught them once, a circle of half-ashamed, half-amused seamen, squatting by common consent within the amphitheatre of the coiled anchor cables on the orlop platform, their pipette-straws applied to their private parts. They had a guard, designed to keep out the mockery of their unaffected shipmates, though Kite himself was suffered to pass, as the *Enterprize*'s medical officer. Despite this privilege, he beat a hasty retreat, musing on the willingness of the men to share their common misfortune in so public and demeaning a way.

Rather shocked, he mentioned this to Gerard, while they stood upon the quarterdeck that afternoon as the *Enterprize* doubled Cape Verde, distant somewhere far to the east. Gerard merely chuckled.

"There are few secrets in a ship, Kite, that is why we maintain the social distinctions of rank, or all would soon tumble down." His face became serious and he turned towards his younger companion. "You may find greater surprises in store for you. You should not judge us. Just as you will find the ways of the blackamoors curious because of the country in which they dwell and the tribal society in which they live, you must regard seamen in a similar fashion. We are, after all, circumscribed by the limits of our ship, cooped up upon the raging main and subject to all the powerful vicissitudes of nature . . . Well, you shall see and you are not now a man apart; you are now – well, almost – " Gerard grinned again – "one of us."

Kite only partially understood these oblique remarks, but he was pleasantly surprised by the acceptance of the *Enterprize*'s second-in-command, who, despite his earlier sarcasm, had proved a willing instructor and an affable companion.

"Oh, by the way," Gerard went on, "are you much of a shot?"

For a second Kite was drawing imaginary sights on a lofting grouse rising above his native fells. "I can shoot, yes," he said.

"Good. Fencing is not required, but can you handle a blade?"

"Well, I was tolerably able with the single-stick."

"A hack and slash man, eh?" grinned Gerard. "That will do nicely, I dare say."

The following day, at the change of watch at noon, Makepeace summoned all hands. By a process of elimination, with all the seamen shooting at empty wine bottles hauled out to the lee foretopgallant yardarm, a platoon of 'marines' was enlisted from the most able shots. These were placed under the command of the second lieutenant, Francis Molloy, a heavily built Liverpool Irishman whose acquaintance Kite had hardly made, since he was on the opposite watch.

The officers too, including Kite, enjoyed a few shots by way of target practice. On completion, Makepeace told the mustered company that within a few days they would arrive off their destination, the coast of Guinea. "We shall anchor off York Island," he announced, "in the mouth of the Sherbro River, and determine the state of trade. It is not my intention to linger if we can complete our lading, though I must seek the best prices for the goods we have brought with us. In the meantime I shall not countenance any drunkenness among you. Most of you know well the native liking for liquor and most of you indulged yourselves to excess in Liverpool. Any man found half-seas-over runs a great risk from apprehension by the Negro chiefs, whose kings are not only important to themselves but to the prosperity of our trade. Therefore I consider any man among you who loses himself to drunkenness to be opposed to the profit of our voyage and he can expect little mercy from me. I can always ship mulattoes as seamen . . ." Makepeace paused to let the inference of abandonment sink in and the men shifted uncomfortably; Kite knew from his associating with Gerard and the men that Makepeace was both admired and feared.

"As for licentiousness," Makepeace resumed, "I cannot properly ask you to be continent, but I can advise you to be wise. As you indulge yourselves in liquor in Liverpool, you are best to whore in the Indies . . ."

"Where the dagos have poxed all the women?" a voice queried loudly from the crowd. "Not me, Captain, nor you if I know your liking . . ."

A laugh passed through the old hands and it was Makepeace's turn to look discomfited as he braced himself and called for silence.

"Belay there! D'you mind my words!"

"Aye," murmured someone behind to Kite, "not thy deeds."

Makepeace called out: "Now dismiss!"

Kite turned and caught Molloy's eye as the men dispersed. The big Irishman was shaking his head. "What did—?" Kite began, but Molloy cut his question short.

"He shouldn't moralise on *that* score," Molloy muttered.

"The commander is a womaniser?" Kite asked, stealing a glance at the figure of Makepeace as he descended the companionway to his cabin.

"Womaniser, profligate, whore-master, bugger, but a most successful slaving commander withal. So, my friend, our Cap'n Makepeace is not altogether a bad fellow."

This news shocked Kite. Up until this revelation he had assumed Makepeace to be a gentleman, if engaged in a trade of some moral dubiety. Exposure to the world beyond the lakes and valleys of his former life suggested to Kite that the extent of human activity and endeavour was almost incredibly diverse. Much might run contrary to one's private opinions, but that did not arm one with an incontrovertible righteousness. *Judgement and Vengeance*, Kite confided to his journal later, *are matters for the Divine Disposer of All Things.* It was not for him to do more than make the best of his circumstances. In the eyes of parts of the world, he recalled with a shudder, he was himself far beyond the moral pale. But Molloy's confidence deprived Captain Makepeace's invitation to dinner of any pleasurable anticipation.

It was difficult to square Molloy's evaluation of Makepeace's character with his host. The *Enterprize* was heading south-east, parallel with the Guinea coast, and the captain presided at his table with the westering sun gilding the heaving seas astern of the ship. Occasional twinkling points of light stabbed the incautious eye as it was drawn beyond the dark outline of the captain to the mighty ocean beyond the glass of the windows. The wake streamed out, a marbled roil of water given a curious personality, Kite thought inconsequentially, by the groaning of the rudder beneath them. It was odd that although the passage of the ship seemed stately from the vantage point of the quarterdeck, the escape of water running out from underneath the stern was surprisingly fast.

"Well, gentlemen," Makepeace said, raising his glass to his guests, Kite and Gerard, "to your continuing healths, I'm sure."

The guests reciprocated and they fell to their meat with alacrity. The two capons had had their necks wrung only that morning, and were exceedingly tasty to Kite, who enjoyed a young man's appetite. After a short pause for assuaging their hunger, Makepeace said, "So, Kite, Mr Gerard tells me you have taken to the business of a sea-officer with commendable alacrity, diligence and understanding."

"That is generous of Mr Gerard, sir," said Kite, smiling at the first lieutenant.

"'Tis no more than the truth," confirmed Gerard. "You were like a fish to water, Kite."

"It was not entirely disinterested tuition, Kite," Makepeace went on, "the dangers of the coast, due mainly to marsh ague, but with a score of subsidiary maladies, take any one of us at any moment, and sickness, or even death, may ensue. It is therefore prudent to ensure that as many of us as possible are competent to manage the ship." Makepeace paused on this solemn note. "Now to other matters," he resumed cheerfully. "When we arrive in the Sherbro I shall require your close attendance upon myself, Mr Kite. Both as surgeon, in which capacity you have not yet been overtaxed, and also as my assistant. In this capacity, you will assist me in the trafficking which will occupy me for a few days. As few days as I can possibly contrive at a profit, of course, eh, Gerard?"

"Indeed, sir, only that which is commensurate with the satisfaction of your partners . . ."

"One of the advantages, Mr Kite," Makepeace explained with a condescending air of confidence, "of being no mere master, but a part-owner in the *Enterprize*."

"I see, sir. Well, then, may I offer my best wishes for the voyage." Kite politely raised his glass. Both Makepeace and Gerard joined the toast, but Kite was uncomfortable, feeling the captain's eyes upon him and with Molloy's words lingering in his ears.

As if divining Kite's train of thought, Makepeace asked with a disarming candour, "Are you fond of women, Mr Kite?"

"Er, as, er fond as the next man, sir," responded Kite quickly.

"But you are a young man . . ."

"Though well enough acquainted with the pox, I hear," added Gerard.

"The clap, Mr Gerard. Mercifully I have not yet encountered a case of the pox." Kite recalled an embarrassing evening in the serious company of his father when that worthy attempted a cautionary explanation of the diseases of Venus. Kite had most certainly not yet encountered the horrors, as taught to him by his parent, of the 'foreign disease', attributable it seemed to loathsome intercourse with the French and Spanish.

"But you have had a wench, or two, I dare say?" queried Makepeace with a disquieting persistence.

Kite faced his interlocutor, a little flushed with the captain's wine, and skilfully turned the question. "Surely, Captain Makepeace, you will recall our introduction was occasioned by my familiarity with the parts beneath a woman's skirts."

"So it was, my dear fellow," said Makepeace smiling his charming smile and raising his glass, "so it was."

When he returned to his cabin, Kite was more than a little drunk. He drew his journal towards him, then rejected the idea of making an entry. He would be required on deck shortly and instead he lay down in his cot.

"I fear I am to become an Egyptian," he murmured as he sank into sleep.

# Four

## The River

A cross the entrance to the Sherbro River lay a bar which, even on
a day of light winds, caused the Atlantic swell to rear up and
roll over upon the shallows with a menacing and forbidding roar.
To Kite's horror and, he noticed, to no little anxiety upon even
the suave Gerard's experienced face, Makepeace held *Enterprize*'s
course boldly east, heading towards the line of roaring breakers,
behind which the low, jungle-clad coast of Guinea could be seen.
Makepeace stood beside the two helmsmen, from time to time raising
his hand as if to restrain them from nervous or faulty movements of
the helm, commanding them to keep their eyes upon the compass
as he took *Enterprize* over the Sherbro bar. At that moment, Kite
admired Makepeace's coolness, glimpsing the degree to which a man
must cultivate nerve and command over himself before he was fitted
to command a ship. The evidence of danger became suddenly obvious
as the swell steepened and heaved beneath them, lifting the vessel and
speeding her forwards, before dropping her in a hollow with such
precipitation that Kite thought she surely must strike the bottom.
Hardly had his conscious mind recognised the proximity of the sand
beneath their keel from the thick sediment swirling about them, than
the *Enterprize* was borne up on the succeeding swell. Propelled
forward they now seemed to hurtle on the very crest of a toppling
wave which broke with a roar, setting the ship down again and filling
the clear warm air with a mist of spray. The breaking water rushed
past them, disintegrating in a welter of white foam which slid ahead,
overrunning the blue-green surface of the shoal water beyond the
obstruction of the sandbar. Birds dipped into the turbulent shallows,
picking off the bounty of the ocean, and then the *Enterprize* broke free,
clear of the bar, breasting the seaward flow of the Sherbro itself.

The boatswain, standing in the starboard fore chains, swung the
lead rhythmically, steadily calling out the soundings as Makepeace
sought the deeper water of the river's channel. All about him Kite
noticed the relaxation apparent in the men; the smiles and resumption
of suspended tasks. A man who had paused in coiling down a rope

finished it off with a twirl about its belaying pin; another, taking off the cover of the longboat, pulled the last lashing clear and withdrew the canvas, to roll it on the deck. Gerard looked at Makepeace and grinned, while the captain, unconsciously betraying his own anxiety, removed his hat and flicked a linen kerchief across his brow.

Beyond the confusion of the bar, the outward flowing Sherbro darkened the sea water with its brackishness and the random flotsam of the interior jungle of the great dark continent of Africa. Slowly they left the roar of the breakers behind them, the green line defined itself as dense and swampy jungle, and then the pale shallows also fell astern and they entered the river itself.

Instantly the fresh sweetness of the ocean wind left them, though a breeze still filled their upper sails. A heavy heat fell upon them like a blanket, palpable in its weight. The air filled with the harsh whirr of insects and the occasional screech of a bird; Africa embraced them as the men clewed up the courses and went aloft to furl them.

York Island lay some twenty miles upstream, a low place, clear of the denser vegetation, though covered with palms. At its inner extremity it subsided into a marsh, at its seaward end it bore the ruins of a fort which, built in the previous century, had for a score or more years been abandoned when the trade in slaves fell off. A recent revival had reinvigorated the place, so that as the *Enterprize* dropped her anchor, after a slow passage upstream against the green current of the river, she found herself in the company of four other Guineamen. Three of these ships were from Liverpool and all were swiftly recognised by the ship's company.

"There's the *Lutwidge* . . ."

"Aye, and the *Nancy* . . . and the *Marquis of Lothian* . . ."

Hardly had the *Enterprize* brought to her anchor than Makepeace called away the longboat. Kite made ready to join him and, as the majority of her hands went aloft to put a harbour stow in her canvas, the grinning boat's crew began to ply their oars and drive the boat shorewards through the anchorage. It was blisteringly hot, and Kite felt his skin prickle with sweat. Though Makepeace and Kite were both in shirtsleeves, their tight neckcloths felt uncomfortably like hangman's nooses.

Makepeace looked at the anchored Guineamen, raising his hat to one man on the stern of the *Lutwidge* as they passed. "This is not a good sign," he remarked to Kite, sitting beside him in the sternsheets of the boat. "It argues delays in loading, which in turn means either the coastal chiefs have not brought down sufficient Negroes, or the damned lançados are asking too high a price for my fellow commanders to agree upon."

"The lançados . . . ?"

"Oh, men of mixed blood, mulattoes, quadroons, a very devil's brew of half-castes, fathered by seamen from the slaving vessels and born to women of the country. They all want to trade and act as go-betweens and agents. Most merely make fools of themselves, comic characters posing as self-styled white gentlemen who possess only the worst attributes of their fathers: they drink like fishes and whore like dogs." Makepeace dismissed the human results of miscegenation and slapped at a mosquito that landed upon his bare wrist.

A few native canoes passed them, and Kite stared with unconcealed curiosity at the gleaming figures of the black men bending to their paddles. Their unfamiliar physiognomy struck him at once and Makepeace, noticing his fascination, chuckled. "Ugly devils, ain't they? They're gromettos, free blacks who are useful to us here as we await our lading. You'll become used to them, even find their women capable of rousing your lust!" The captain exchanged a complicit grin with the seaman pulling stroke oar, a small, wiry Welshman. "Eh, Jenkin. You love 'em, do you not?"

"Aye, sir." Jenkin grinned back and winked at Kite; he was one of what Able Seaman Thomas had ironically named the Cable-Tier Rangers. Kite suppressed a shudder.

The broken-down ramparts of the ancient fort fell astern and a low and sandy strand, backed by wooden buildings and grass-roofed hutments, came into view. "Behold the true coast of Guinea . . ." murmured Makepeace, half to himself.

In the ensuing hours, for all that he kept Makepeace constant company, Kite had only the haziest notion of what was going on. In the largest house on York Island, a clapboard, daub and wattle structure roofed with long grass thatch, they sat and spoke with a strange white man whose name, Kite learned, was Thomas Lorimoor. He traded in all manner of goods and, in what Makepeace afterwards facetiously called a 'palaver', exchanged information with them about the availability of slaves and other commodities. Although born a Scotsman, Lorimoor used English mixed with a strange argot, a mishmash of English, Portuguese and native words taken from the languages of the Mandingo and Bulum tribes. Since Makepeace was familiar with this lingua franca, Kite could make little of the substance of the conference. He was left to bring himself to eat from a calabash of what appeared to be revolting worms, but which Lorimoor called *bul* and which Makepeace assured him were good eating. Indeed the commander endlessly picked at the contents of the calabash until it was emptied, whereupon a native woman suddenly appeared, silently barefoot upon the floor of beaten dirt to refill it. She was flat-faced and bore about her neck a thick silver ring that Kite at first took for a necklace but later knew for a thrall-ring. Her large body was ungainly under the loose, brightly coloured cotton wrap she wore about it. She seemed to be a sister, in all but colour, to the sad trulls that had inhabited the dark dockside tavern in which Makepeace had found him, except that she moved with a motion that Kite could only describe as dignified. That she was Lorimoor's native concubine was confirmed as they pulled back to the ship, an hour before sunset.

That evening Kite confided the day's events to his journal.

The Scotch trader Lorimoor lived with a Black Woman. He is a Sick Man, much taken with a Fever which, in the Season of Tornadoes, becomes Quotidian. His Pallor is Severe, his Eyes are Bloodshot and marked by Empurpled Shadows. Though having the Appearance of Age, his long Sojourn in this Countrie has Aged him far beyond his actual years which, I understand are about Forty. His Woman, whom he calls Elizabeth, Captain Makepeace Informed me, had lived with him a Slave for nigh Twenty Years and certainly All the Years that the Captain hath known Mister Lorimoor which is about half that time. Our Palaver lasted for five Hours in which we ate a Species of Worms of Disgusting Appearance but which Owned a taste not unlike Fresh Mutton and Quite Delicious after One has overcome a Natural Disinclination to Swallow them. We Drank also what I supposed to be Palm Wine which I was told is taken directly from the Bark of that Tree which grows well upon York Island. I am Disposed to suppose this some sort of Joke played against Persons without Experience in the Ways of the Countrie.

I was much Mystified as to All the Deliberations entered into by the Captn and Mister Lorimoor, but the Captn was solicitous enough to offer me a Full Explanation which I but imperfectly understood, not being Conversant with the Manner of Trading in this Countrie.

There is somewhat of a Currency which for Convenience is called a Barr. The Value of a Barr varies as to whether it be a Ship's Barr, or the Trader's Barr, thus a Quantity of Goods hath Two Values, a Matter of Speculation apparent to those familiar with it, but from which I could Derive no Satisfaction other than that it be a Method of Extracting a Profitt, at least upon invoice. This is more than Somewhat of a Mystery to Me. This Barr equates to the Value of Iron which is much Prized Hereabouts and which we have in Quantitie in the Hold.

There was also some Discussion of the Countrie which I better understood, Mr Lorimoor spoke of a Native Chieftan whose Name translated meant the Great Son of a Woman on Account of him being a Bastard. This Chieftan who is styled in this Place a King, is of the Mandingo Tribe, a Warlike and Mahomettan People who reside some Distance from the Sherbro River, but who Seek to Convert the Bulum Tribe to their Religion. Since the Bulum are Pagan, Lorimoor spake as though Their Society would derive some Benefit from this Civilising Influence, and though I suppose it Better than to be Bound to Superstition, I cannot pass up the Opinion that it would be more Desirable that they should know the Gospel of Christ than the Teachings of Mahomet.

This Mandingo King is waging War in the Interior of the Countrie and Delaying the Sending down to the Coast, of the Slaves. This Accounts for the Number of Guineamen waiting at Anchor Here. But there is another Reason, Capt$^n$ Makepeace Opines, and that Mr Lorimoor put into his Mind with the Rumoured News of a Greater War. This is said to have Broken Out between England and France and Spain, tho' how this is Known hereabouts but was not Known at the time of our Departure from Liverpool, I am at a Loss to Comprehend, as is Capt$^n$ Makepeace. Perhaps the Turbulence with the French in North America has Precipitated Hostilities.

But the Capt$^n$ says with a Perfect Logick that, Mandingo War or Not, such Rumours, Whether or Not they become Proved by Time, are often Employed by the Traders, the Lanchadoes and Even the Native Chiefs, to Delay the Delivery of the Slaves to the Coast. This Raises the Price, Particularly as the Hurricane Season in the Indies Approaches and the Anxiety increases among the Commanders of the Various Ships to Depart. Such a Delay, in the Present Case, gives Time for the Enemy, if there be one, to Send down his Men-o'-War to Cruise in the Offing and to Trap Us in Leaving the Guinea Coast, whereby all our Endeavours may be Brought Swiftly to Disaster.

I am Not Certain but that Capt$^n$ Makepeace is not going This Evening to Concert his Intentions with his Fellow Commanders, Most of Whom are Liverpool Men and can thus be Depended upon.

Kite set down his quill and slapped at the buzzing mosquito who flew about him. Sweat poured liberally from his body, and as he raised his left hand from the pages of his journal he left a damp stain upon the paper. A score of flies and moths fluttered and buzzed around the candle flame. He went on deck. In leaving Lorimoor's house, he had caught sight of the trader's bed, a stout framework of camwood over which hung a tent of plain calico; he wished now he had some such thing to drape above his own cot to protect himself from the infernal pestilence of insects.

Molloy, a pale shape in the darkness, had the anchor watch and straightened up from where he had been leaning on the rail.

"Not asleep, then, Billy?" he asked.

No one had called Kite 'Billy' since he had been a boy and the familiarity caught him aback. Molloy seemed unaware of the impropriety.

"Too hot for you, I imagine. Still, you'll become accustomed to it." A few lights showed on York Island, like small eyes piercing the blackness surrounding them. The chafing rasp of unnumbered cicadas filled the air, giving voice to the heavy oppression of the tropic night.

"'Tis a little hellish," Kite ventured, leaning on the rail beside Molloy. Both men stared out over the dark swirl of the river rushing by below them. Over the water wraiths of mist coiled, at once both sinister and yet unreal.

Molloy chuckled. "Sure, you are a real Englishman, Billy. Tch, tch, a *little* hellish. Now how can that be? Yes, it's Hell, but put your conscience aside, Billy; see it as a little bit of God's good earth for you to profit from. Hasn't that stingy bastard Makepeace told you your interest?"

"My interest?"

"Your share; your dividend under the provisions of the articles. He might be a part-owner in the *Enterprize*, but surely you've seen the agreement?"

Kite had seen no agreement, though he did not like to admit it; all he had agreed, and that by word of mouth, was to sail with Captain Makepeace on the promise of a profit of a hundred pounds or so.

"I suppose you didn't read the damned thing and took it all on trust. How very *English* of you. Well, Billy, as the surgeon you're entitled to one shilling per head on the blacks that are discharged on two legs in the West Indies . . ."

Kite supposed that his profit of one hundred pounds derived from this source and, embarrassed he said quickly, "Oh yes, yes, I knew of that."

"But did you know of your right to ship a quantity of scrivelloes?" Molloy asked, mocking him.

"Er, no, I confess I did not, nor do I comprehend what scrivelloes are."

"Well, then, let me tell you. They are the teeth of elephants. You will learn that elephant's teeth, which some call tusks like a boar's, are a commodity much beloved in London. You'll not be permitted to ship large tusks, since they hold the greatest value, but the smaller teeth, which we call scrivelloes, may be traded by you an' me and Mr Gerard, God bless him."

"I see." Kite had no idea what profit might be made on these scrivelloes, nor how he might raise any credit to purchase them, let alone whether he would be permitted the liberty to sell them if he ever reached British shores again. As he put these disquieting riders aside, trading in elephant's teeth seemed to his conscience far less reprehensible than trading in human beings, notwithstanding the fact that they were black.

"But that isn't all, Billy-boy," Molloy went on, "the best is yet to come."

"The best . . ."

"Oh, indeed it is. You are also allowed, on your own account, two slaves. If you're smart you'll pick strong ones, but the balance of all the private slaves chosen by Makepeace, Gerard, yourself, myself and the gunner, must be equally men as women. I don't, for the life of me, know why that regulation is insisted upon, unless it is to keep the breeding stock provided for, for if I had my way we'd trade only in hefty big fellers, but the captain'll insist upon it."

"I see." Kite's heart sank. While he could reconcile receiving twelve pence per head on delivery, which he was content to see as an incentive to keep as many of the unfortunate blacks in good health, the thought of directly profiting from the seizure and sale of individual persons seemed a great and terrible sin. Whatever the world thought of his culpability in the matter of Susan Hebblewhite's death, he knew he was innocent. Fate, it seemed, would have him a mortal sinner by alternative means. For a moment a dark and terrible horror overhung him, then he threw it off with a question to Molloy.

"I, er, I was ashore with the captain, but I could not understand where the slaves come from and where they are now."

Molloy gestured at the jungle, a gunshot away. "Out there somewhere, in a stockadoe or a barracoon guarded by the warriors of the local chiefs . . ."

"Then blacks sell us blacks?"

"Oh, yes. Did you think we went into the countryside and *stole* them?" Molloy laughed. "No, no, 'tis a very well-regulated trade, Billy, very well regulated. You'll see, you'll see." Molloy straightened up and yawned. "Enough of this! You can take over the watch, if you wish. It wants only a while until we turn the glass. Let the infernal mosquitoes dine off you for a few hours. I'm for my cot."

Despite Makepeace's insistence that he had 'no intention of hanging about awaiting the convenience of a dying slave-dealer' and the delivery of several ultimata to the wasting Lorimoor by a deputation of all the masters of the Guineamen lying off York Island, a month passed and, to Gerard's frustration, species of grass grew on the white stuff payed upon the brig's bottom. The weed would slow them on their passage to the Antilles and, Kite learned, with the grass came the shipworm, an infestation of which could ruin a ship's hull in weeks.

The enforced idleness prompted the commanders of the vessels to adopt a practice of dining daily in each others' cabins, indulging in games of chance and once or twice quarrelling among themselves. Rumours circulated among the ships that, if matters were much delayed, they would sail upstream and bombard the barracoons until the recalcitrant chiefs released a sufficiency of their prisoners to complete the Guineamen's lading. No one apparently believed Lorimoor's claim that the Mandingo war had choked the supply of slaves and the experienced men freely voiced the opinion that it was all a device to raise the price of them.

*This has been done on Former Occasions*, Kite confided to his journal,

> but the Masters are Reluctant to carry this matter to a Precipitate Conclusion owing to the Revenge taken upon those who come afterwards. Much Mischief has been Caused on sundry Occasions by Dishonest dealing by Various Commanders, their Abduction of slaves without Proper Payment and their Cheating of the Blackamoor Chiefs. The Science of Justice in this Countrie is based upon Revenge, so while the Blacks and Lanchadoes will not Trouble the Ships of a Another State, they will Wreak Vengeance upon a British Vessel if they Conceive their Previous Wrongs to have been Inflicted by a British Vessel, and Upon a Dutch, or a Portuguese Guineaman, & C°, & C°.
>
> Moreover, it would not be Politick to Aggravate the Chiefs if War between England and France is Truly Imminent . . .

Kite was permanently relieved of his watch-keeping after a few days. His duties as surgeon now fully claimed him, for the first cases of fever began to appear aboard the *Enterprize*. Diagnosed by Makepeace and the other officers under the generic term 'marsh ague', two seamen named Noakes and Hughes were the first to die. They suffered an initial shivering fit and were sent to their hammocks, which, by Makepeace's orders, were swung forward above the manger, in a kind of quarantine. The two men were soon running high fevers, with terrible pains in their backs and heads. Their arms and legs were also afflicted and they became, as Kite noted, *taken by a Great Lassitude accompanied by a Deep Depression of Spirits and sense of Mortality*. Retching, vomiting and an insatiable thirst provoked mixed feelings of disgust and compassion in Kite, who found himself isolated and left alone to care for the two wretches. After a few days he was pleased to notice an improvement and an abatement of the fever. He expected the men to mend, at least in the manner of Lorimoor, who though profoundly affected, seemed able to continue living. In the gloom of the forward 'tween deck, the inexperienced Kite failed to notice the yellowing of the eyes and the skin, nor did he see the first sign of final decline that followed. Soon, however, the men submitted to the terminal stage of their disease by sudden copious eructations of blood which brought on a sinister cooling of the body.

*This morning,* Kite scribbled hurriedly, aware that circumstances compelled him to observe and learn from the two invalids, but drowning a greater and personal horror by this bloody climax,

> Hughes was as Cold as Death Itself and I noticed a Yellow Hue Suffusing his Skin. On Examination Noakes was the same, though to a lesser Extent. Both Men are Reconciled to their Fates . . .
> This evening, though Life was still discernible in Both Men, I could Determine no Heartbeat and Their Bodies are already Cold to the Touch . . .

By next morning both men were dead and were conveyed ashore for burial beneath the ruined ramparts of the fort. The following day three men from the *Marquis of Lothian* were laid to rest, followed in the subsequent ten days by eight more from among the crews of the waiting Guineamen. These sad events, though failing to surprise the experienced seamen in the combined company, nevertheless had a demoralising effect, prompting a restlessness and a desire among the assembled ship's companies to get away. In fear of their lives, they increasingly spoke among themselves of sailing upstream to bombard the Bulum townships and coerce the chiefs to trade. They resolved to urge their commanders to do this before more of them died, but before any deputation approached Makepeace and his colleagues, the *Cleveland* arrived. She was from Bristol and her master, Captain Burn, soon spread the news that the rumours of a European war were confirmed.

This further depressed the crews spread among the waiting ships but in fact acted as the spring for their release. For weeks Makepeace and his colleagues had advertised the wares they had brought to trade. The Manchester checks and Osnaburg cottons so beloved by the natives, the gin and so-called brandy, the musketoons, flints and gunpowder, the knives, soft iron bars and metal trinkets had all been shown to the lançados and the gromettos. But the inhabitants of the coast viewed these products with some disdain; they had satisfied their immediate wants and now craved novelties, aware that the musketoons they were sold were inferior to the muskets the white men kept for themselves. Moreover, the lançados, affecting the dress of white men, had created a desire among the envious chiefs for cocked hats and even boots of soft leather, such as the Arabs of the far distant desert interior sometimes, and these white interlopers of the coast often wore. Lorimoor had shaken his head and the palaver had descended into a complex and apparently irreconcilable variation between what Makepeace and his fellow commanders, and Lorimoor on behalf of the chiefs, regarded as a negotiable barr.

Captain Burn's news, however, spiced up this game of supply and demand. By good fortune Burn had a few tricornes, trimmed with silver braid that he had brought out to sell to a hatter in Antigua. Under pressure from his fellows, he agreed to trade these at once, enabling the deadlock to be broken. Makepeace also counselled his colleagues to threaten to withdraw without further delay, arguing that the presence of French cruisers in the chops of the Channel would deter other Guineamen from sailing and the slaves would be left in the stockades, an ever and increasingly hungry liability to the chiefs.

Humbert of the *Marquis of Lothian* thought that, on the contrary, a delay would bring down the price, but Makepeace poured scorn on 'so meanly Scottish a proceeding', arguing that a debilitated and ill-fed black would not survive the middle passage to the West Indies or the Brazils and what was saved in the initial purchase price would be lost to mortality on the voyage. Besides, Makepeace reasoned, their ships had already been affected with the dreaded yellow jack; as every master knew, if they cleared out promptly, the infection would likely subside and those not yet affected would escape with their lives.

"Once let the sickness take a hold and it will be crews we will all be wanting, not cargoes! Aye, and more, what crews are left may want commanders . . ."

Makepeace delivered this logic and stared about him. Humbert finally turned his palms upwards and shrugged. The difference of opinion being thus resolved, the masters agreed to send word of their resolve to Lorimoor and to make ostentatious preparations for departure; meanwhile the lançados were shown the silver-laced hats. The ruse worked. The following day Lorimoor passed word that the chiefs would send down the first canoes on the morrow and so *Enterprize*, with her sister Guineamen, prepared to receive her lading.

# Five

## The Cargo

The hands were turned up next morning as soon as the first canoes were sighted coming downstream. They gathered at the rails of all the assembled Guineamen like excited children as fortune and opportunity approached them in the form of abject misery and degradation. As he came on deck, Kite was immediately aware that changes had taken place about the ship. One of the *Enterprize*'s six-pounder carriage guns had been run inboard, moved amidships and swung round. Now the breech was quoined up, so that the black muzzle pointed down into the waist through the rail, a deterrent to insurrection. The seamen designated marines were paraded with their muskets under Mr Molloy who, with a piratical air, bore two pistols in his belt and wore a hanger on his hip. Further aft, lounging on the taffrail, Makepeace and Gerard were similarly armed, while several of the crew bore whips or canes.

To the watching and waiting Kite, it was the smell that first turned his stomach, for although only a few dozen slaves arrived aboard the *Enterprize* from the initial consignment of twenty or so canoes which dispersed about the anchorage, it was clear that the distant barracoons were little better than overcrowded sties. Perceiving that the slaves' own ordure clung to their legs and their breechclouts, Kite was moved to approach Gerard and request that they were all soused down as they came aboard, and allowed to rinse out their flimsy clothing.

"You're not a prating Quaker, are you, Kite?" a high-spirited Gerard asked, with a leer.

"No, I am not, Mr Gerard, but you would not put a horse in a stable in so filthy a condition." Kite, remembering his father's odd conviction that dirt lay disease, a theory based largely on some observations that purulent infection and uncleanness were not uncommon neighbours, added, "And we have so recently buried our shipmates. We'd be damned stupid to admit another fever to the vessel."

"Tut, tut, Kite, the heat hath made thee damned touchy." Apeing the speech of the Quakers, Gerard turned with a grin to Makepeace who, surprisingly, nodded his approval. "I concur. Let the men give them a wash down. It may ease their minds before we send them below." Makepeace straightened up and called along the deck to where the boatswain, a man called Kerr, stood upon the rail.

"Mr Kerr, where the devil is my linguistier? Ask one of those damned gromettos if he has come down as arranged . . ."

A tall mulatto lançado, who bore a striking resemblance, Kite noted later in his journal, to pictures he had seen of Sir Francis Drake, came over the rail in response to Kerr's enquiry and walked insouciantly aft. The man wore an ancient red velvet jacket, frayed knee breeches and silk stockings from which the bottoms had been cut, leaving his feet bare. Stuck into his belt, like an old-fashioned rapier, was a long-handled whip, the tail of which was coiled neatly round the staff. As he approached Captain Makepeace he doffed a new silver-laced tricorne and, sweeping the deck with it, footed an elegant bow.

"Captain, my name is Golden-Opportunity Plantagenet and I am at your service. I bring you forty-two fine blackmen according to Sir Lorimoor's instruction."

Makepeace graciously inclined his head and responded in an ironic tone. "Honoured, Mr Plantagenet, deeply honoured. I wish you to tell the forty-two fine blackmen that my surgeon will not examine them unless they wash their arses and their breeches. My surgeon is, you see, Mr Plantagenet, like yourself, a gentleman of refinement," and turning to Kite, Makepeace added: "You may concert with him, Mr Kite, he will act the interpreter for you."

Plantagenet bowed to Kite who, embarrassed and awkward, scarce able to make out to what extent Makepeace was guying him, the interpreter, or both of them equally, followed the mulatto forward. As the first of the slaves clambered aboard, the whites of their eyes wide with terror, there began a pantomime of shouting and misunderstanding, of flung buckets of water, of moans and cries of humiliation and shock until, after about fifteen minutes, the seamen had grown fed up with inflicting this mild cruelty on their victims and the terrified slaves realised what was expected of them.

*I am Surprised how Willingly They Acquiesce to being thus Treated*, Kite wrote later that evening, after a second shipment of male slaves had arrived.

> Indeed, left to Sit about on Deck until their Clouts dried under the Hot Sun, there Seemed nothing very Terrible about their Circumstances, tho' Molloy and his armed Mariners were in Continual Attendance. But then, at about Noon, more Canows

Arrived and the First Party were taken below and Secured Between Decks. Here they were each Allocated a Space and Compelled to Lie Down. Then the leg-irons were Placed about their Ankles, at which Terrible and Piteous Cries, which Rent the Breast, went up. This Stirred no Compassion among my Companions and I thus take it to be the Sad Manner of carrying on this Trade.

The Lanchadoe who brings the Unfortunate Blacks down the Sherbro from the Barracoons Rejoices under a Most Extravagant Name. Mr Gerard Informs me that it derives in part from the Ship on which his Father probably served, Thus is he Called Golden-Opportunity by way of a Christian Name. His Surname is Plantagenet, but his Mother cannot have known of the Plantagenets and Gerard says the lanchadoes often take a Name they Conceive to be of Noble Blood. Such Names are supplied by the Factors or the Commanders of the Vessels, who think it a Great Joke to thus saddle the Half-Castes with Pretentious Names. In this Manner we have a Mr Duke Attending the 'Lutwidge', and even a Mr Emperor aboard the 'Nancy'. Such Conceits, Vastly Amusing the Masters & Officers of the Various Ships, are carefully Observed in All Propriety. I took notice that the Factor, Mr Lorimoor, is Dignified hereabouts, with the Title of a Knight.

Kite paused, thinking of his own part in the day's proceedings.

I hope my Examination did not much Distress the Slaves. I am Obliged to Establish they are All Sound in Wind and Limb, and Free from Infectious Disease.

He stopped writing again, unsure of whether or not to commit all his private sentiments to paper and then, with a shrug, bent again to the lamp-lit page.

At first, I supposed them all to be the same, finding in their Features a Similarity of Flattened Noses, Thickened Lips and Black Hair covering their heads in a close matting of Curls. The Deep Brown of their Skin admits no Differentiation, unlike our own Pallid Countenances with our Individual Colouring, and only the Whites of the Eyes seems to indicate a Lack of Spirits, while their Teeth betray Evidence of Age, as do other clear Differences. However, the Similarity soon Disappears and one can mark Distinctions in their Individual

Appearance, Indications of Character that mark them as they would Ourselves. Some I hold to be Possessed of a Rebellious and Contrary Spirit, which is Unsurprising, while Others gave every Appearance of Submission to their Captivity. For the Main part, they were in Good Condition, if Tired and Hungry, and even the Boldest, not a little Affrighted.

It is very Hot Tonight, and it seems our Peace is Over, for the Moans of the Slaves in the Slave Rooms between decks are Terrible, accompanied as they are by the clink of their Fetters.

In five terribly similar days, as the hot sun beat down from a cloudless sky upon the ships anchored off York Island, the slaves arrived in canoes under the convoy of Mr Plantagenet and his fellow lançados. It was a grim business, but Kite became inured to it, even in that short period of time. Only once did he hear the treatment of the natives spoken of in any critical sense when Mr Kerr remarked that it was 'a brutal necessity'. Kerr's comment, propped up by assertions that Kite had already heard, assertions claiming the blackamoors would be far better treated by white masters in the Indies or the Brazils than ever they were under their native chiefs, was provoked chiefly by the arrival of the first women, which occurred on the third day of loading. In retrospect it sounded like an excuse for what was about to happen and which was anticipated by everyone except the inexperienced Kite. Perhaps Kite's acceptance of the fate of the blacks began at that same moment, when the women were sighted and the word passed through the waiting men like a gust of wind through dry grass, for he was not insensible to the prickle of expectant lust that the news provoked.

Like the men, the women were all young and strong, the oldest still capable of breeding. Although they climbed up on to the decks nimbly enough, once there they huddled in a group, heads together, occasionally turning in anticipation of torment: nor did they have to wait long. Mr Plantagenet strode in amongst them, his long whip in his hand, pulling the huddle apart and roaring instructions that they were to remove the loose, gaily coloured but now filthy cotton wraps from themselves. Here and there he gave a helpful indicator of his requirements by tearing garments off, exposing the women's bare backs. They screamed, the seamen cheered and from below there arose a howl of pain and rage from their fettered menfolk.

Intimidated by the muskets of the marines, the women stood and gasped as the remaining seamen plied their buckets and the sunlight sparkled on flashes of flung water. Hurriedly, the wretched women washed themselves down, a sight which infected Kite with an almost overwhelming lust. The sight of breasts and thighs, of the gleam of light upon wet skin and, most shocking of all, the feathered pudendae showing beneath the buttocks of the women as they squatted in the scuppers to pummel their besmirched clothing, sent a physical shock through him. It struck him that despite or perhaps because of their humiliation, their brown skin held a potence absent from the discomfited white flesh of the Liverpool whore. In his arousal, he shunned all thoughts of poor, bloody Susan Hebblewhite. He could not yet admire these Negro women as beautiful, for his sensibilities were suspended and his lust was tormentingly mixed with a self-loathing that he could even contemplate coupling with what, despite his natural compassion, he regarded as not fully as human as himself. This and his natural reserve held him back from any precipitate action, prompted by raw and primitive instinct, but in this he was almost alone.

As the first two boatloads of women finished their washing and hung their clothing in the rigging to dry, they squatted together, crying and wiping the tears from their faces with the palms of their hands, staring fearfully about them. Circling them, their jibes ended, the watching ring of seamen seemed poised for some act of violence. Then this momentary spell was broken. Mr Plantagenet's whip cracked in the air and he roared something in the native tongue. The women began to stand uncertainly when from the quarterdeck, Makepeace's voice called out, "Your examination, Mr Kite, and make it speedy, sir, make it speedy!"

The captain's impatient tone was reinforced by a murmur of anticipation from the men and a shuffling, instinctive recoiling from the women. Kite was suddenly confronted by the first woman, unaware of crossing the deck. He motioned her to stand and ran his eyes over her as the sweat poured from him and his lust lay half formed in his breeches. He twirled his hand and Plantagenet gave an order. The woman revolved and, at another barked command, she obediently opened her mouth. Kite peered at her teeth and looked into her eyes, touching her only to draw down the lower lid.

He was about to tap her shoulder and pass on to the next woman, when Makepeace said from just behind him, "Look at her cunt, Mr Kite. We want no trouble from that source."

Kite turned, his face pale beneath his tan. Makepeace was close beside him, his face flushed, and Kite could smell a sourness on his heavy breath. Kite thought of the 'trouble' the Cable-Tier Rangers would bring to the women.

"Captain Makepeace," Kite began, but Makepeace cut him short.

"Do as I say, Mr Kite," he said, his voice purposeful as a sword-blade.

Abashed, Kite looked at the woman as her eyes flickered from his own to Plantagenet's. The mulatto was saying something to her, at which she gasped and her gaze came back to Kite. He felt the hatred in their slight but telling contraction, saw the ripple of muscle settle along her jaw and then her hands drew his own eyes downwards. She parted herself and he stooped to peer into her.

"Properly, man, properly!" Makepeace commanded. "An examination, for God's sake! Not a damned sniff!" Kite hesitated, then felt himself shoved aside while Makepeace bent in his stead, handling the women with his intrusive fingers, opening the red vulva with a coarse gesture, then standing, slapping her thigh and, moving to the next, to repeated the humiliating procedure. The first woman hurriedly squatted, her thighs so tightly pressed together that the muscles trembled and tears poured down her face as her whole body began to shake. Having examined the second woman, Makepeace straightened up and confronted Kite. "There, Mr Kite, I don't intend to keep a dog and do all the barking, but that is how you attend to the matter. Look for a discharge, or sores . . ."

"Yes, sir, I understand," said Kite, shaking himself, partly from rage, partly from his own humiliation, but his words were lost in the cheering of the men. He motioned the next woman and she turned and he touched her, briefly, with his fingertips, seeking to reassure her of his own innate kindness, shocked by the hatred in the woman's eyes, hatred that was aimed exclusively at himself. Then, in emulation of his commander, Kite stooped.

As he worked his way down the line, he heard Makepeace say, "Put aside any with their lunar bleeding, Mr Kite," and in this way several woman were moved to one side. When he had finished, he felt no trace of the priapic urge that had quickened him at the start of his appalling task; he felt filthy, hot and begrimed, somehow paralysed by the experience and Makepeace's nastiness. He despised himself for not having remonstrated with Makepeace that the very least they could have done for the poor creatures was to carry out the examination behind a screen of canvas, but he had only thought of the notion when he had almost finished the work. Another time, perhaps, if God forbid, there ever was another time.

What happened next he wrote down that night, when he could not sleep and the noises from the slave decks was not that of distress alone, but of lust and horror and degradation.

When I had Completed my Examination those Women taken by their Lunar Periods were Removed below, the Seamen handling them with a Palpable Disgust. Then our Captain came forward and, Seizing Two Women he had Selected during the

Examination, Withdrew to the Privacy of his Cabin. At this,
as at a Signal, each of the Men who felt Inclined to Lust,
took a Woman, According to the Precedence of Rank. Those
Assigned to Guard, which Constituted Half of the Marines,
Each Marked a Woman by placing a Hand upon her, and
these were left on deck until those Occupied in Satisfying
Themselves in Copulation returned to their Duty.

I noticed a Few of the Men did not Avail themselves
and Submit to Temptation, though for whatever Reason was
not Apparent. Molloy Abstained, which much Surprised but
Gratified me, but Gerard also removed Two Women once
Captain Makepeace had gone below.

This Event put me out of all Sympathy with Capt$^n$
Makepeace, for where the behaviour of the Men did not
Shock me, that of the Capt$^n$ most assuredly did, for he
speaks often of his Wife and Three Children in Liverpool
and his Character as a Gentleman seemed at Variance with
this Unspeakable Display of Lust . . .

A cry rent the hot and foetid air in the ship. It was not a scream,
for there had been enough of those earlier; this was a plaintive wail
of despair which was somehow the harder to bear than the shrill
objections of the victimised. But it was the last noise of that noisome
day. The ship became silent at last and most on board slept, the
ravished and the ravishing sharing the slumber of the damned.

Kite could not sleep. Silently he went up on deck, noticing the
creeping stench that now began to pervade the interior of the
vessel. About the deck the handful of guards were pale shapes
in the starlight. Molloy had the watch and Kite wondered if he
had forborne from rape in order to keep his watch, and that by
some devilish arrangement in this 'well-regulated' trade, his turn
would come later.

"Not sleeping, Billy-boy?" Molloy asked wearily.

"No I am not!" Kite answered with a vehemence that surprised
himself.

"Tch, tch, you *are* touchy. Gerard said you looked as if you could
have murdered our gallant commander. The women upset you, eh?
Well, if it's any consolation, it's always the same. When you were a
little lad back in England, Englishmen were out here doing the same
thing. And if it ain't Englishmen, it's Dagos, Portugooses, Frogs,
Danes or square-headed Dutchmen."

"But not Irishmen, I take it," Kite said with a withering sarcasm.

"Oh, yes, Irishmen, Scotchmen, Welshmen," Molloy responded quickly, "and what difference does it make, eh?"

"Difference?" Kite spluttered. "Why, do we treat our own women like that?" But he knew his protest was hypocritical, his mind's eye had already conjured up the dead Susie and the stabbed whore.

"B'God, Billy, you're a touchy devil. Why, certainly we may precede matters with a little flattery, or a financial agreement, but the substance is the same. And mark you, man that is made in God's image, don't forget, is prompted by ungovernable lusts at such times of extreme provocation. Think now how long it is since we saw a woman. Surely we are allowed these little moments of creation . . ."

"You were not so tempted," Kite responded swiftly, "unless you hold yourself in readiness for tomorrow."

Molloy chuckled. "Well, Billy, 'tis either that, or you'll think the worst of me."

A dark and terrible thought crossed Kite's mind and he looked sharply at the ghostly figure beside him. Molloy seemed unaffected by the turmoil of the impressionable young man beside him. Kite said, "I hope I will not have to think the worst of you . . ."

"Let me give you a word of advice," Molloy said kindly, turning towards him. "Mark my words well, Billy. You will spend the next few weeks in an agony of temptation. Whether or not you succumb to the beast within you remains to be seen but do not, I beg you, make this an issue with Captain Makepeace. These people may seem to you to be piteous, and perhaps by our own standards they are, but ask yourself what circumstances brought them here? Why, nothing but war, war between their own chiefs and the Mandingos, or the Ashanti, or the Wolofs. These are powerful tribes who bring the spoils of their victories to trade on the coast, from Sierra Leone all along this benighted bloody country, to the Bight of Benin. If the captured blacks are not cattle themselves, then they are treated as cattle, no worse than others in other places. The Guinea coast now is no worse than the Irish coast a century ago and perhaps even the English coast before you were conquered by the Norman duke." Molloy paused and blew the air out of his puffed cheeks. "Pah, I sound like a damned dominie, do I not, eh? But surely it is all the work of God, Billy, foreordained and made by His Hand."

"You are a Papist?" Kite asked.

Molloy chuckled. "Does the notion of a Papist officer at sea surprise you?"

"No, no, I have never knowingly known one before."

"Never known a Papist, eh? Well, well. I shan't catechise you. If it suits you to see God's Hand as providential, then so be it. You see, Billy, in company with most of my fellow creatures, Francis Molloy is incapable of untangling many mysteries, to be sure, but heed me in one thing. Do your duty by Captain Makepeace, Billy, as I have no doubt but that you will, and in due course you will earn your pay and an easy conscience."

Kite felt the touch of kindness in Molloy's words. He had not expected such concern from so unusual a quarter. Mumbling his thanks, though unconsoled, he turned away and went below.

The next day the slaves arriving were a mixture of the sexes, clearly a sweeping-up of the emptying barracoons. Now there appeared a few older men and women and one could only guess how long they had been held prisoners before being shipped out. That afternoon a quantity of large elephant tusks and the smaller scrivelloes arrived, along with a floating raft of camwood logs which was manoeuvred alongside by half a dozen gromettoes armed with sweeps who skilfully used the river's current to assist them. More canoes arrived with woven baskets of manioc, food for the slaves during the middle passage, and Kite was compelled to remark that the trade was indeed well regulated. The enervating heat, the lack of sleep, the tormenting insects and the incessant groans and cries of the slaves, the noise of their fetters and the stink of their confinement, despite the ventilating ports purposely cut in the *Enterprize*'s sides, all combined to desensitise Kite. His task became a distasteful routine. His constant proximity to the dark bodies of the slaves utterly dispelled all thoughts of sexual congress, while the stares of fear and hatred he received as the most prominent and primary agent of their distress wore down his private sympathy.

Among the slaves he found cases of medorrhoea in both men and women and these were daubed with white lead by Kerr and shunned by the men. Otherwise the slaves seemed fit and, insofar as he could tell, healthy.

As he carried out his duty on the fourth day, he was aware of Makepeace's presence on deck. At the conclusion of his examination of the last of the slaves just brought aboard, the commander called him aft.

"Well, Mr Kite, you seem to have settled to your work most commendably." Makepeace spoke without sarcasm. Kite found it difficult to meet the captain's eyes, but he made the effort, coughing awkwardly. "I am not indifferent to your own sensibilities, Mr Kite, but caution you not to make judgements upon others. I do not require your respect, only your obedience. You are young, and doubtless proper, but I have never asked why you were, like a fish out of water, in that filthy tavern in Liverpool. Seek not the mote in the eyes of others, Mr Kite, and miss the beam in thine own. A man's eyes are the windows into his soul. Be sure there ain't a futtock timber or two stopping the clarity of thine own vision."

The sarcasm inherent in the use of the Quaker form of the pronoun gave sufficient of an edge to Makepeace's statement for Kite to know the geniality had vanished from the captain's attitude. Afterwards he wrote,

> Taken with Molloy's kind Caution, I Attribute Capt$^n$ Makepeace's Altered Attitude to a shift in Purpose now that we are to Embark on that Portion of our Voyage that we call the Middle-Passage.

Even as he waited for the ink to dry, re-reading the sentence he had just written, Kite failed to notice his own use of a significant pronoun. That he had written '*we* call' signified his unconscious acceptance of his integration into a well-regulated trade.

The oppressive conditions aboard *Enterprize* during those four days had so changed Kite that while he remained aloof from the moral turpitude of most of his fellow shipmates, he might still have followed them under the shadow of damnation and ended up indistinguishable from them. But on the last day of their loading, when the number of slaves embarked approached its final total of two hundred and eighty-five, Kite found himself staring into a face that caught his eye with a shocking intensity.

The curious, asexual propinquity that his duty had led him into seemed suddenly brought to an end by this particular confrontation. Kite had found it impossible to judge the age of the blacks, merely categorising them in his ledger as 'of about 20 y$^{rs}$', or 'about 25 y$^{rs}$', occasionally making an additional note, such as 'scarr$^d$, poss$^{ble}$ warrior' or, in three cases 'Woman with child', or to note seven females who were 'accom$^{pd}$ by suckling child'. These, unlike their menstruating sisters who were treated with a mild disgust, were almost tenderly handled by the seamen.

*Such Paradoxical Behaviour*, Kite noted in his journal, mitigating the conduct of his fellows with evident relief, *Argues some Influences of a Higher Civilisation amongst these Common Seamen, for here was a Manifestation of True Pity*. But his own attitude appeared to him to be less simple. Certainly he had noted some of the women possessed an attraction beyond others, just as some of the men were handsome and well set up, bearing themselves proudly. One or two of these males had imprinted their pride upon his consciousness and, in scrambling the dark and dreadful length of the slave deck, divided as it was into the male and female slave rooms, their eyes met with sparks of recognition. It was easier to accept the hatred of these young warriors than to acknowledge beauty in their women. The former was a direct consequence of the horrid confrontation brought about by the examinations, the latter was the antithesis to this intimacy, a result of luxurious contemplation and this he had been denied by the oppression and extent of his task.

But on the last afternoon, when the final canoe was awaited, Kite felt relief in the approaching end of his demeaning work and the prospect of returning to sea, clear of the green and foetid Sherbro with its insect-laden air. Perhaps, too, he had become a little blasé; nevertheless, he was sitting, sweating and uncomfortable, on the carriage of a broadside gun as the last batch of blacks clambered down over the ship's rail, fearfully regarding their destination. It occurred to him that the *Enterprize* must seem a most strange construction, beyond even their imaginings. It was then that he saw the young woman.

She was tall and slender, and stared about her in a manner that was not without fear but was utterly without any air of submission. It was this, rather than any inherent beauty, that first attracted Kite's jaded interest and as Plantagenet began to shout his instructions, Kite was suddenly, impulsively, up on his feet.

"All right, all right, Mr Plantagenet," Kite bellowed in so uncharacteristic an outburst that the men idling on deck, regarding this last consignment of slaves with satiated indifference, looked up and nudged each other. The linguistier turned and glared at Kite. "Tell them quietly, man, there is no need to bellow like that, and," Kite added sharply, "put that damned whip away!"

"Mr Kite," Plantagenet expostulated, tapping his breast, "I am the man in charge of bringing aboard the blackamoors . . ."

"And I am the officer responsible for seeing they are in prime condition, now tell them quietly what we require them to do . . ." He was looking at the girl and she was looking at him as he willed himself not to lower his eyes upon her bare breasts. Then she averted her gaze, and the merest suggestion of a relieved smile nervously twitched the corners of her mouth. It was an expression of such subtle sweetness, devoid of any coquetry, Kite felt, that his knees trembled and his guts churned with a powerful sensation of concupiscence. He swallowed hard and nodded at Plantagenet, who glared at Kite with hatred at his imagined loss of face.

Kite sighed, mastering himself. "Tell them *gently*, Mr Plantagenet, like a *gentle*man would . . ." Plantagenet received this instruction with a kind of confused comprehension. The allusion to gentleness in such a context led him to a concept he had not previously encountered, let alone considered. His curious social pretension led him to a ridiculously exaggerated assumption of what Kite required. In any other circumstances, he would have been thought sarcastically insolent, but Plantagenet's desire for a status he did not understand but only imagined made his delivery a model of moderation at which the surrounding seamen only gaped with astonishment.

"Will you please to be taking off your garments and washing yourselves, while the water is thrown over your heads," he insisted in their native tongue. "Then you must wash your nice clothes until they become all clean."

The women went through the business of washing and Kite conducted his medical examination. For the most part these last groups of women had boarded the *Enterprize* unmolested. The ship's company had slaked their sharp appetites of sexual deprivation and were, Kite learned in time, recoiling from their intimacies in a kind of disgust which was only partly directed at the slaves. As the numbers of these grew, and with the increase the risks of a rising, the seamen's duties associated with securing and tending them made them no longer objects of long-frustrated human desire, but mere parcels of cargo, representations of tasks to be done and duties to be attended. That so demanding a liability had also swiftly become a tiresome obligation distanced the white seamen from the acts of their immediate pasts.

"How could I have fucked that?" he heard Thomas say in self-disgust, though this sensation was manifested by an intimidating gesture at an adjacent male slave who barred his passage along the slave deck, seeking to shield the woman to whom Thomas referred from a further violation. The dismissal and dehumanisation implicit in Thomas's neutral pronoun, which robbed the wretched woman of gender, shocked Kite as he made his way below, following the last batch of slaves down to where Kerr and his gang were shackling them in the confined spaces allotted them.

The smell in what were now called the slave rooms was already foul. In the five days since they began loading their human cargo there had been little effort to clean the space. With no freedom to move around and a ban on any airing or exercise on deck until the *Enterprize* was at sea, the slaves had been induced to use buckets to defecate into, but the numbers of these were limited, nor were they emptied properly. Despite a primitive attempt at sanitation by Kerr, the sharp stink of urine and the heavier odours of human excrement permeated the air. Kite had learned from Molloy and Kerr that a strict and not inconsiderate regimen would begin once they had cleared the Sherbro bar, but in the meantime the restrictions made the slave deck a terrible place.

Kite saw the girl put her hand to her mouth as she descended into the darkness from the glaring sunlight on deck. The pity he felt for all of the blacks, which he was utterly powerless to extend in any practical manner to ameliorate their condition, he now felt he should offer her. But how? Any selection of a female was clear evidence of his desire and Kite even suspected his own motives, for the strong feelings the young woman had aroused in him were unequivocally possessive.

Captain Makepeace, who had already selected a pair of female slaves to grace his bed, had so far seduced them to his purposes that they were occasionally seen in tatty gowns, thoughtfully provided by the commander. It was clear that the tide of rape had ebbed, to be replaced during the middle passage by more regular relationships between most of the men and their chosen slave.

Not merely was the trade well regulated, Kite thought bitterly, it was remarkably democratic. And, he wanted to write in his journal but could not bring himself to do so, remarkably broad in its acceptance of human lust, for he had come across one of the able seamen in the act of buggering a young black male.

On the eve of departure, Makepeace gave a dinner in his cabin. On either side of the captain sat his black mistresses, awkward in their dresses, unused to being seated on chairs and eating with their hands. They were already half-drunk, a bizarre sight in their tawdry finery, giggling, curious and uninhibited.

"I take two, Mr Kite," said Makepeace seeing the discomfiture of his perspiring and red-faced surgeon, "because they are company for one another." Gerard and the other two officers round the table, sweating and stinking in the heat, slapping at the buzzing mosquitoes, drank immoderately and laughed dutifully. Kite had tried to avoid the invitation, volunteering to stand the anchor watch, but Gerard had told him his presence was insisted upon and that in any case, Molloy would stand the watch with his marines.

Although Gerard had taken his pleasure of the women, he had not retained any exclusively for himself and it was only the captain who used his privilege to sport his harlots so shamelessly. The remainder of the seamen were expected to keep their selected victims shackled, except when they were required for carnal purposes. Former experiences of the slaves getting their hands on the seamen's knives prohibited too great a freedom, even for those slave women who, for whatever reason, became compliant. During the middle passage, Molloy had told Kite, he would be surprised how many of the black women acquiesced to their circumstances and could be seen squatting washing their new masters' clothing in buckets of sea- or rainwater.

"Of course," Molloy had explained, adding detail to this picture of nautical domesticity, "we never let them on deck without leg-irons."

The dinner, which consisted of a deliciously baked pig, seemed set to end in riot, but Makepeace, despite appearances to the contrary, was far from being a man in the throes of unbridled lust. After about two hours, when the plates had been cleared and the company was slumped in amiable disarray, he ordered Gerard, Kite, Kerr and the gunner, a man named Mitchell, to fill their glasses. They dutifully drank a loyal toast to 'His Majesty King George' and, in view of the war, 'Damnation to His Majesty's enemies'. This done, Makepeace roused his drowsy mistresses and signalled to Gerard. Taking the hint, the first lieutenant rose and the officers clumsily and noisily withdrew.

"Until dawn, gentlemen," Makepeace said, "when we shall get under weigh, I wish you a good night."

Kite did not go immediately to his cabin, but as was his habit climbed on deck. Molloy, however, was not his usual friendly self. Piqued at not being able to indulge himself at the cabin table, tortured by his own confused feelings, the second lieutenant was short-tempered and a little in liquor.

"So, you've been enjoying yourself, eh? Sporting with our gallant commander and his black whores. Now you want to come and salve your tender conscience with old Frank Molloy, the dependable bog-Irish fool who'll stand a watch while you wallow in filth . . ."

"That's neither true, nor just . . ."

"Don't speak of justice aboard here," spat Molloy.

"Look, I volunteered to stand the anchor watch."

"Oh, go to the devil, damn you, Kite."

Kite stared at his friend. "The devil," he said quietly, "aye, 'tis surely hell below."

"Oh, for God's sake stop your prating, you pious bastard!" Molloy turned away, calling in a loud voice, "Sentries report!"

Kite made for the companionway as the voices of the dutymen responded in the darkness.

"F'c'sle; all's well!"

"'Tween deck forrard; all's well!"

"'Tween deck aft; all's well!"

Nodding to Thomas on guard at the grating, Kite waited while the sentry unlocked and lifted the wooden lattice, then descended into the greater darkness of the cramped slave deck. This was lit by the dim gleam of lanterns set at intervals on the stanchions, but these burnt fitfully in the mephitic air, failing to penetrate the gloom to any extent. The thick atmosphere was filled with the groans, snores and miserable whimpers of the sleeping slaves; occasionally a leg-iron chinked as a slave moved in his or her restless slumber.

Kite paused, his eyes slowly adjusting. The slight high-lighting of the lamps upon a sweat-moistened shoulder, thigh, breast or buttock created the impression that he gazed out over a calm sea on a dark and impenetrable night. The occasional stirring of the slaves added to this effect, looking like the slow movement upon the black tide's surface. The sentries' cries of 'all's well' echoed ironically in his ears; how in God's name could anything be well in this hell-hole?

He moved aft a little, drawn into the dark, confined space. So, by the lights of the times in which we dwell, he thought to himself, all is well in such a well-regulated trade. God help them all. That he was responsible for these wretches appalled him. The stink of their debased state threatened to overcome him, compounding the guilt he felt after his dinner. Why had he come here, he wondered? To tend his charges? To sharpen his own sense of fear for the future? Or just upon a drunken impulse? Suddenly, utterly dejected, he wished to be out of it, free of the stench of the place. He found himself some few feet from the ladder and turned, eager for the fresh air above. The low beams kept him at a crouch as he hurried back to the short ladder, where he paused but a moment before raising his hand to bang on the underside of the grating, to stare across that black sea of limbs and bodies.

Then he felt his leg touched. It was the merest sensation, offering no threat of seizure, so brief and so light that it might have been an insect bite. Looking down he thought he saw, though he could not be sure, the face of the girl looking up at him.

# Part Two

## Iron

# Six

## The Middle Passage

During the five days they had spent embarking the slaves, Kite's duties had kept him, if not constantly busy, then constantly preoccupied. Superficial and inept though his so called medical examinations had been, they had served to cast him more firmly in the role of the *Enterprize*'s surgeon and, coupled with his treatment of the Cable-Tier Rangers, established him credibly enough in his adopted profession, leaving only Captain Makepeace in possession of the truth. Moreover, while Makepeace had revealed a side of his character that Kite considered distinctly unpleasant, he had done so without lasting hostility to Kite himself. True, the captain had expressed himself with a veiled threat, but Kite found Makepeace thereafter resumed his usual smooth cordiality, even if he was accompanied by a black trull, a somewhat disconcerting sight on the quarterdeck.

Kite accepted the threat as little more than a rebuke, given like any other reprimand by the commander of a vessel maintaining his authority and the establishment of his will over that of his subordinates. If, Kite mused unhappily, there had been any real alteration in their relationship, it had been on his own part, for it was clear from the asides of Molloy and Gerard, that his own attitude had changed perceptibly: the nickname of 'Quaker' had stuck.

Oddly, Kite did not mind. In a sense it pleased him to stand against the slave trade, as a genuine Quaker would have done. Quaker opinion was not unknown in the Lakeland of Kite's boyhood; the roots of the philosophy lay in adjacent Lancashire and his father had spoken of them in admiration. But Kite could not claim any moral superiority; he was motivated less out of a general compassion for the mass of the unfortunate blacks, and more out of a specific pity for the young woman.

In the first days of the middle passage Kite found himself busy in the establishment and supervision of the regimen laid down for the slaves by Makepeace. Amid the stink of vomit and the groans of the chronically seasick, the adopted routine went some way to maintaining a semblance of cleanliness. The day began when those women who had become the concubines of the sailors, and were therefore to be trusted to a degree, went to the galley and brought the pots of manioc and rice to the slave deck where it was doled out under the watchful eye of Mr Kerr and his mates. These men were the immediate regulators of the slaves. Thereafter the deck was sluiced down and, if the weather was not too boisterous, the ventilating ports were opened. While this was in progress, the first batch of slaves were let loose and, still in leg-irons, allowed up on deck, where they walked in a circle round the waist, circling the chocked boats on the booms amidships. From the forecastle, they clinked aft along the larboard gangway, turned across the forepart of the quarterdeck and, passing the carriage gun aimed at their accommodation below, then went forward again, along the starboard gangway.

Having been specially constructed for the carriage of slaves, the *Enterprize* had a slightly elevated quarterdeck. This was raised at the hance and fenced with an athwartships rail which mounted two swivel guns. This arrangement gave a clear path across the beam of the ship to facilitate the exercise of the slaves, but, if an uprising were to occur, it provided a defensible position to be taken up aft by the ship's company. Standing at the forward end of the raised quarterdeck, his hands on the rail before him, Makepeace was able to review the condition of his cargo from a position of advantage. Makepeace undertook this duty seriously and never permitted the presence of his whores on deck at this time, which he would have considered improper. Instead he stood with his surgeon and the lieutenant of the watch, while the marines with loaded muskets, gunners manning the swivels and the midships carriage gun, and the watch on deck, all took up positions of vantage and vigilance. This show of force acted as a mild, ever-present act of passive, though potent, intimidation. Kite's dutiful attendance at these inspections filled the forenoon of every day as the *Enterprize* scudded westwards across blue seas and beneath a clear sky that sported the white and fluffy clouds of fine weather.

Each batch of slaves, their eyes downcast, shuffled four times round their circuit before passing below by way of the after companionway as the next group emerged on to the forecastle. From time to time Makepeace would stop the procession and pull a slave out of the line, concerned for the individual's condition. Commonly he bestowed this attention on a male who had been chafing his leg-iron until the man's ankles had bled. Such injuries were pointed out to Kite. A seamen named Wilson had been designated the surgeon's assistant. It was Wilson's duty to daub with white lead the right shoulder of any affected slave. After the last batch of slaves had gone below, Kite and Wilson followed them, applying tallow to their chafed ankles.

By the time this lengthy routine had been completed, it was

approaching apparent noon, when the vessel's latitude was determined. At Makepeace's suggestion, Kite took upon himself the task of acting for whichever of the two lieutenants was watch below, and thus, with Makepeace and the watch-keeping officer, was party to this navigational ritual. For this the *Enterprize* was well furnished with no less than four quadrants, each of the officers being required by the owners to provide their own, while Kite was loaned an instrument that had belonged to a former, long-dead lieutenant. The man had had no relatives and therefore his belongings were not auctioned off for the benefit of his widow; instead most were given away in trading deals with the lançados who were always eager for odds and ends of apparel and artefacts with which to dignify their persons. Makepeace had withheld the quadrant on account of its value and its uselessness to the ignorant.

On the fourth morning of the passage Kite stood beside Makepeace as the slaves disconsolately circled the deck. It was a fine day, the ship was making seven knots and Makepeace was in an expansive mood.

"Well, Mr Kite," he said waving his right hand over the passing slaves in, Kite thought, a gesture of devilish benediction, "I think you may take some credit for the condition of these blacks."

"Thank you," Kite replied in a subdued tone which caused Makepeace to turn and look at him.

"Come, sir, you are still not moping over the immorality of this trade, are you? I hear you are against it, and doubt its morality. If so it is really too depressing." Kite said nothing. The young woman had just emerged forward, where he had been watching for her, and he felt his heart quicken as she blinked in the sunshine and then stared straight at him. Though the slaves often looked about them as they came up on deck into the sunshine, by now only a few met the eyes of the white men who stood guard over them. They had long been accustomed to the presence of guards, whom they called vultures in their own tongue, and they had learned how to avoid drawing attention to themselves.

But Makepeace was unaware of Kite's preoccupation with observing the approaching woman, taking his demeanour for continuing disapproval. He let out his breath in a sigh audible above the clinking shuffle of the slaves and the moan of the wind in the rigging.

"You know, do you not, that these blacks were already prisoners long before we sought to buy them?"

The young woman had turned aft and was approaching the quarterdeck down the larboard gangway. He could not see her breasts, they were hidden by the shoulder of an older woman in front of her, but he noticed a ring was missing from her left ear.

"Their condition was abject before we took them aboard and, mark you, the women would not have been spared any horrors by the black tribes that captured them. What they are receiving now is a degree of care that they cannot have imagined possible when they were cooped up in the stockadoes of the King of Bulum . . . Why, Mr Kite, look at them; they are in the very pink!"

Kite did not hear the inept and insulting jibe, for just then the young woman turned and walked across the deck. Kite could see, so close and just below him, the glossy, upward sweep of her breasts and the slight, seductive movement of them as she walked. She had held his gaze all down the ship's side and only dropped it now, as she passed him, secure in the knowledge that he was watching her. Her long, delicate arms hung down and she lowered her head so that he saw the graceful line of her neck. She had worn a ring only in her left ear, and this was turned away from him, but as he stared down at her, he noticed the bloody graze on her ankle and, interrupting Makepeace said, "By your leave, sir . . . Wilson, daub this woman . . ."

Pausing, Makepeace regarded the object of Kite's solicitude. "There, you see, that is exactly what I mean: our treatment of these wretches is humane and decent."

Wilson quickly dabbed the woman's shoulder and she passed on. Her rump moved seductively under the cotton skirt and the curve of her back and the sharp, outward jut of her hips made Kite swallow.

"Now *she'll* fetch a good price," Makepeace remarked parenthetically before resuming his exposition. "The canting Quakers don't comprehend the realities of existence. They seek a perfect world, where food falls like manna from heaven and each man is reasonable unto his neighbour, where love reigns in some peaceable kingdom. Pah. 'Tis all flummery imagination. Can you conceive of a world where no one loses their temper or covets another's property, where passions are roused only to worship God and never to lie with a woman except it be ordained and sanctified by the Almighty? Huh! Would that it were true! But what does the Bible give us in its opening chapters, eh? A story of disobedience followed by a story of murder, a swift descent from petty to capital crime! Remarkably soon afterwards every form of vice runs riot with mankind unchastened even by flood, earthquake, fire and plague! By Heaven, Mr Kite," Makepeace almost roared, "does that not fill you with a certain pride in mankind: that he can *defy Omnipotence*?" Makepeace lowered his voice. "Why, sir, it is magnificent!"

Concluding his oration with this flourish, Makepeace turned to see the impact his manifesto had made on the young man beside him, but Kite was watching the young woman as she made her second circuit of the deck.

"So that is the way the land lies," Makepeace muttered to himself, a sly smile playing the corners of his mouth.

\* \* \*

Nervous of the forthcoming encounter, Kite left attending the young woman to last. Despite the quickening effect she had upon him and his growing desire for her, he was loath to commit himself and dreaded the contact he knew he would find irresistible; that much he knew about himself from his encounters with Susie. But now she was daubed and he was bound by his duty to approach her with his pot of rancid tallow, leaving Wilson to attend to the remaining male slave picked out that morning.

The young woman had seen enough of the routine to know what was required of her. Sitting quietly amid her fellow captives, she allowed Kite to ease her heavy leg-irons up her calves and to apply the sticky mess. It was odd, he thought as he knelt, that she had first touched him on the same spot. Her ankles were slim and the calves shapely. Her young skin felt smooth and cool, except where the cruel edges of the iron rings had scored and abraded her flesh. As he massaged the tallow he looked up and half-fearfully met her eyes, but there was no hatred, only the beginnings of a shy smile as she looked away. Beside her, her neighbour gave a grunt, distracting Kite so that he looked at an older woman he knew to be pregnant.

"Are you all right?" he asked, knowing the women could not understand him, but unable to think of anything else to say.

"Aw rye, aw rye, aw rye . . . !" the pregnant woman exclaimed, nodding her head as tears fell from her eyes and she held her swollen belly.

Kite returned his gaze to his patient. She was staring at him again, her head slightly turned away so that the light fell upon her left ear. The gold ring had been torn out. Kite put up his hand and, though she drew back, she allowed his fingertips to touch the torn lobe. The scab was only half formed, and still oozed blood.

"It's all right," he said again in a low, soothing voice. Then, his hand still extended, he turned and called, "Mr Kerr?"

One of Kerr's mates, Jonas Ritchie, approached. "Mr Kerr's on deck, Mr Kite, what d'ye want?"

"I want to know who did this?"

"What? Took the nigger's earring?"

Kite looked up at the smirking face. Many of the women wore rings in their ears, thin gold rings of little real value. Kite thought it might have been of some tribal significance, for even their black captors had left such paltry finery alone, though it was clear they had removed most valuable effects from their victims.

"Yes."

"How should I know?"

Kite stared at Ritchie. The man was not insolent, merely indifferent.

Kite turned to the woman, trying to see in her just a commercial object of flesh and blood, like a beast sent to market. Instead he saw a beautiful young woman who had begun to tremble at the presence of Ritchie and whose breathing set up a perceptible flutter about her wide, flared nostrils as if the smell of the boatswain's mate offended her.

"It's all right," Kite repeated, touching her scabbed ear. He caught her eyes again and he wanted to read thanks and gratitude for his intervention, the social obligation laid upon her by European culture. But of course she had no notion of this sensibility, merely twitching her mouth nervously, then looking up at Ritchie as he leaned over them. In that moment, Kite sensed the enormity of what he stood upon the brink of. The nearest he could do to rescue her from her future servitude was to do what Makepeace had done with his pair of trulls, to turn them into whoring dolls and claim some sexual rights over her. Could she be one of his allowed slaves? Could he buy her and give her her freedom? The notion was immediately appealing, but the difficulties made him angry. He felt the constriction in his throat, turned away and rose to a stoop to confront Ritchie.

"Be so good as to tell your mates that these women," Kite said, his voice cold as he gestured round at the figures lying on the deck, "are not to be molested in this way."

It was now that Ritchie became truly insolent, objecting to the younger man's appropriation of the tasks that were properly his and his mates'.

"Very good, Mr Kite," Ritchie said with a heavy sarcasm, "I'll ensure that these women are only molested in the usual way."

For a moment the two confronted each other, then Kite said, "Stand aside, if you please," and made for the companionway.

He did not see the parting kick Ritchie gave to the young woman, for his attention was diverted by a cry on deck and he began to run up the ladder.

"Sail ho! Broad on the windward beam, sir!"

For some time they had debated the likelihood of a French frigate lying off the Guinea coast, but there had been no sign of an enemy cruiser and they had escaped to begin the middle passage, hoping to get lost in the vastness of the ocean. They would run the greatest risk, Makepeace had given his opinion, as they approached the Lesser Antilles and the French possessions of Martinique and Guadeloupe. From these islands, the French naval cruisers and irregular privateers would lie in wait for the incoming slavers converging on the British possessions in the Leeward Islands. But a risk remained on the open ocean. An enemy man-of-war, either cruising opportunistically along the likely track of slavers from Guinea to the West Indies, or on her way south and bound for the Indian Ocean to prey on British Indiamen, might be encountered in these waters.

Such thoughts were uppermost in Makepeace's mind as he gave orders to clear for action and raised his glass to study the distant stranger. Hearing the order to prepare for battle, Kite turned about, his heart beating. His post was below, first seeing the slaves secured, so that no attacking enemy received a reinforcement from rebelling blacks. Ritchie was bawling out orders for the slaves to lie down, emphasising this by forcing backwards on to the deck a large Negro who had sat up. Fore and aft, additional chains were run through the wretches' leg-irons by Kerr's men, while a pair of seamen scrambled over the recumbent forms and closed the ventilating ports in the vessel's sides, shutting out a little light and seeming to seal the slaves in what might become their common, mass coffin.

It was Kite's duty to proceed below to the orlop platform once he was content with the security of the slave deck, and prepare his instruments for any surgery required on the wounded. Makepeace had presented him with an old treatise on the subject, but he had given it little attention. As he descended to the orlop, he heard the shouts of orders on deck and the rumble of the carriage guns as they were trundled out through the gunports to confront the enemy. In the semi-darkness of the lamp-lit orlop, just above the hold, he found Wilson.

The surgeon's mate was a middle-aged man whom Makepeace had appointed to the post shortly before the *Enterprize* arrived off the Sherbro. Wilson had served in the capacity on previous voyages and was familiar with the tending of the slaves, considerably easing Kite's burden as well as his conscience. Now the two of them sat in tense silence, waiting for the noise of the guns and the arrival of the first wounded to be delivered into their tender care by the fortunes of war.

The alarm proved a false one. The 'enemy frigate', converging upon them, turned out to be the ship-rigged *Marquis of Lothian*, their former companion from York Island. Relieved, the *Enterprize*'s company resumed their duties, watching the other ship as she bore down towards them, British colours at her peak. But the encounter was not entirely devoid of danger, for the *Marquis of Lothian* ran close to them an hour before sunset and her commander, Captain Ross, hoisted himself up on his rail, holding on to a mizzen backstay with one hand and raising a speaking trumpet with the other.

"*Enterprize*, ahoy," he hailed. "Cap'n Makepeace, d'you hear me?"

Waving aside Gerard's offer of a speaking trumpet, Makepeace took up a similar position. "Aye, I hear you, Cap'n Ross."

"Have you any sick aboard?"

"No, sir, my slaves are all fit and well."

"I do not mean among your slaves, sir, I mean among your crew."

"My men are all in hearty trim, sir. What is it that concerns you?"

"Be vigilant, Cap'n Makepeace, we have the yellow jack aboard . . ."

"Poor devils," said Molloy, standing close to Kite as all hands then on deck listened to the exchange and stared at the accompanying ship as if the sick would appear like a row of skulls along her rail.

"I am sorry to hear it," shouted Makepeace, turning to Gerard who had the watch and saying, "Keep us away, Mr Gerard, don't fall under his lee." And Gerard ordered a slight alteration of course, keeping the *Enterprize* from running too close to the infected ship.

"Well, perhaps you will be lucky, but there were four more dead aboard the *Lutwidge* before she sailed from the Sherbro," Ross continued.

"How many have you lost, sir?" asked Makepeace as the two vessels surged along on parallel courses, their diverging wakes slapping together in a white marbled confusion of water.

"Two yesterday, one this morning. I have seven men down with the damned fever and one on the cold threshold of eternity as we speak. Captain Makepeace . . ."

"What is it?"

"I should be obliged if you would keep me company . . . You will understand my reasoning."

Makepeace swore, then raised his hand and cupped it about his mouth, with evident reluctance. "I cannot well decline your request, Captain Ross, and will agree to it if you will undertake to keep a mile to loo'ard of me at all times."

"Very well, Cap'n Makepeace. I shall keep that station unless we are brought to action. Will you burn a lantern?"

"Aye, sir, we shall both do so."

Ross waved his arm in agreement and jumped down from his conspicuous stance on his ship's quarterdeck rail as Makepeace regained his own deck. "Hell and damnation," he swore, catching Kite's eye. "We don't want that damnable contagion aboard here. Is there any sign of the fever, Kite?"

"Not that I've seen, sir, but I'll keep my eyes open."

"Aye," Makepeace said and, embracing Gerard and Molloy in his remarks, added, "and pass the word that anyone with a touch of vomiting or nausea is to report the matter at once. Old Ross is scared he'll lose half his ship's company, if not worse . . ."

"You mean his slaves, sir?" Kite asked, his voice edged with irony.

"No, I do not mean his slaves, Kite," Makepeace responded sharply. Then in a reasonable tone, he went on, "For some reason the blackamoor don't take this particular ague with the same alacrity as the white man. 'Tis said the fever comes from monkeys and, I suppose, since the Negro is relative to the monkey, has become used to it; anyway, it seems not to kill them as it does us."

The simian comparison seemed oddly illogical to Kite, but he was thinking about how he could contain an outbreak of the Guinea marsh ague they called yellow jack. There was insufficient space to give a man quarantine in so crowded a ship as the laden *Enterprize*. God help them all if they suffered an outbreak; the white from the disease, and the blacks from the loss of the whites. Shackled in the ship with no one on deck, the miserable slaves would drift around until they all died of starvation.

Such a fate seemed too horrible to even imagine.

The first case occurred two days later, just before dark, with two seamen almost simultaneously struck down in violent shivering fits. Kite had their hammocks slung forward and by midnight both were vomiting and moaning deliriously. Makepeace immediately distanced himself, refusing Kite entrance to his cabin and ordering him to make it his business to see everything possible was done. The following morning, having the weather gauge, Makepeace ran the *Enterprize* down towards the *Marquis of Lothian* and informed Ross of the outbreak.

*I am at a Loss,* Kite wrote that night in his journal. *The Recurrence of the Disease may Kill us all and I, being in Close Proximity to the Infected Men, seem little likely to Avoid it.* He paused and stared into the gloomy corners of his tiny cabin. Then, in one of those rare moments a person may occasionally be vouchsafed, when a glimpse of some great purpose seems within the grasp of comprehension, and when reconciliation to fate is something to be embraced not feared, Kite suddenly began to write with rapid strokes of his scratching quill.

> I cannot Pretend to see Divine Purpose in this Event. Perhaps there is Retribution in a Fever that Strikes the White Man in Preference to the Black, but it seems more likely that this Ague, with all Other Plagues and Distempers, joins with those Evils Man himself Creates, to make of this World nothing more than a Vast Game of Hazard in which the many Lose but the Few, upon occasion, most Assuredly Win. Thus was I Singled out at Random for the Cruel and Fateful Circumstance of my being Forced Hither and being Placed in this Singular Position.

He paused a moment, then dipped his quill and went on.

And if I should Doubt that I am Nothing but a Pawn to be Played at the Whim of Fate, then There is that Private Matter which beckons me on to Further Folly. But Capt$^n$ Makepeace, Whom I Consider not to be a Gentleman may, in a World where a Gentleman counts for Nought, have Struck upon something Significant in saying that Man's Greatness lies in his Defiance of Fate. If therefore Death is soon to be my Lot as it must Assuredly be Someday, may I not Seek a little Joy now?

Providence . . .

But providence lay unamenable, beyond his grasp. He floundered uncertainly, irresolute, for the moment of insight had gone and he knew only that he was dog-tired. His head fell forward and his mind clouded over. He felt unable to make the effort to rise and slip out of his clothes before clambering into his gently swaying cot; instead his head dropped down upon the drying page. Suddenly the air was rent with a shriek, then another, quickly followed by a roar of rage. Kite was on his feet in an instant, and out of the cabin, fearing he knew not what. The underlying, ever-present thought of the horrors of a slave uprising quickened his heartbeat, but he moved instinctively, his perception still dopey with exhaustion.

Emerging into the gunroom he almost fell over the sprawling forms of the commander's two women, whom the crew had nicknamed Makepeace's Bedpans. They were a kicking, screaming welter of grubby petticoats, flailing limbs and flashing teeth. Makepeace had vanished, hidden behind the door of his cabin through which the two trulls had been ejected.

From a door opposite Kite's, Molloy stood yawning, staring indifferently at the two women as they fought together, crashing into the chairs set about the officers' dining table.

"Tooth and nail, Billy," he called out wearily, "Tooth and nail. 'Tis surgeon's business, not mine. You sort it out." Then Molloy retreated behind his own door. Kite stared at the spread of thrashing bare legs and buttocks as one wench got the other across her waist and laid into the black flesh with a series of smacks that sounded harsh and flat in the creaking air. As he stood there stupefied, Makepeace's door opened and, obviously half-drunk and wearing only his hastily drawn-on breeches, Makepeace roared for silence. Seeing Kite, Makepeace grinned. "You see the wisdom of keeping leg-irons on 'em now, Mr Kite, eh? Would you be a good fellow and call the after marine in."

The two women parted and fell into an instant truce, staring up at Makepeace. It was clear they were mutually considering pleading with their master, who, for his part, ignored them. Stepping over their disarray, Kite went forward, opened the door and called the guard.

The marine came aft into the gunroom and stopped, the women at his feet.

Makepeace called, "Take these two forward, Mason, get some leg-irons on 'em and get them out of my sight. Give him a hand, Kite . . ." The captain stood leaning on the door frame, bracing himself against the ship's easy roll and the unbalancing effects of the wine he had consumed.

As Mason grabbed one of the women, Kite wearily stooped to take the arm of the other. Suddenly, Kite felt himself struck across the face as the woman tore free and went for Makepeace with a reel of abuse.

Makepeace straightened. In a second his right arm shot out and he took the woman's throat with such a vicious grip that her eyes started from her head. Makepeace lifted her so that her feet danced upon the deck. "Take that bitch forward," Makepeace said quietly to Mason, "and then come back for this one." He looked at Kite. "Are you all right, Mr Kite? 'Tis not always amusing to be struck by a strong black woman."

Kite rubbed the side of his face. "No matter, sir. May I suggest you let her throat go, sir . . ."

"You may suggest what you like, Kite, but let these devils once think they can strike a white man and you'll have no end of problems . . ." Makepeace was now regarding his victim in a matter-of-fact way. She had ceased to struggle and merely tried to take her weight on her toes. Afterwards Kite recalled that despite the gloom of the gunroom and despite the woman's dusky skin, he could see her face empurpling.

Makepeace saw this too and let her go. She dropped to the deck like a sack of grain, inert and almost completely still. Then her body heaved, drawing air into her lungs and Kite saw that she was not dead. Makepeace grunted, then stepped over her and went forward, following Mason out of the gunroom into the gloom of the 'tween deck beyond the door. Kite stared down at the gasping woman, then knelt beside her with a sigh. Putting his hand on her back, he felt the heave of her lungs as instinct grasped at the life that had hung so perilously at Makepeace's whim.

He stayed thus, stooped over the woman as her breathing became normal again, unconsciously rubbing her back, waiting for Mason to reappear and conduct her forward, wondering if she would be capable of moving herself.

"Tie her to the damned table for the night." The commander's voice broke into Kite's thoughts and he looked up. Makepeace had re-entered the gunroom, pushing the young woman of Kite's fancy before him. His intentions were clear. Mason followed. "Oh, take *her* out, Mason," Makepeace ordered nodding at Kite's patient.

"Do what you like with the whore, though mind the dress . . ."

But Kite was not listening, he was staring at the terror in the young woman's eyes, aware that her plea could not be more eloquent than if she cried out in perfect English. What she thought of the events that had transpired in the gunroom he could only guess at, but his own complicity seemed so obvious as he squatted with his hands on the distressed and stirring female that Mason now stooped over. Kite stood up and Mason dragged his burden like a sack over the painted canvas on the deck, uncaring that her head and shoulders bumped and struck the chair legs as she passed.

Kite looked from the young woman to the leering Makepeace, then acted on an irresistible impulse to stop the captain from raping her.

He blocked the narrow space that ran down the length of the table and along which the captain and his prisoner would have to pass to reach the privacy of his cabin. "Not her, sir!" he said, head up, his shoulders hunched, anticipating the blow and aware now of the power in the captain's hands, one of which was ominously clasping the young woman's neck.

Makepeace looked at Kite. Slowly he turned his victim's head and regarded her. "And why not her, Mr Kite? Do you want her for yourself? Have you developed a taste for the black wench, then? The Quaker misgivings gone at the twitch of your prick, eh?" Makepeace was chuckling. Suddenly he thrust the young woman violently forward and she cannoned into Kite, who seized her. Kite was still staring incredulously at Makepeace whom, he realised, he had mutinously defied.

"I have seen you watching her," Makepeace said dismissively. "Go and take your pleasure of her. That is what women are for, Mr Kite. That and the perilous business of bearing offspring." And then Makepeace had somehow moved between them and only the bang of his cabin door marked his passing.

Kite stared at the young woman. Her face was inches from his; she was frozen in a rictus of fear.

"It's all right," he said urgently, never recalling that he had used those very words when soothing her abraded ankles. "It's all right," he repeated, then, putting up his hand to stroke her face, he gently drew her into his cabin and closed the door.

"Shhhh . . ." He let her go, his finger to his lips, casting about him, hurriedly closing his journal and stowing it away, along with the quill and ink-well. The young woman retreated to huddle into the forward outboard corner of the cabin, from where she stared up at Kite, her beautiful dark eyes round with apprehension.

Crouched down, her vulnerability struck him with a wave of lust.

# Seven

## The Negress

The blaze of sudden ferocity in Kite's expression ignited a responding terror in that of the trembling, crouching Negress. She shut
her eyes tight, screwing them up against his imminent assault, the
only defence she could offer. It stopped Kite dead. He felt the pang
of guilt as a physical wrench in his guts. Yes, he wanted the woman,
as a young man wanted a woman, but not in this manner! Instead he
squatted beside her and slid an arm about her shoulders, a gesture
of almost fraternal concern. He felt her shudder, as the captain's
half-strangled whore had shuddered, but he made no further move,
sensing that inaction would the quicker console her. After a while he
felt her trembling ease, and he bent and kissed the top of her head. At
this she looked at him and he gently withdrew, easing himself back
against the adjacent bulkhead and placing the tips of the fingers of both
hands on his breast said slowly: "Kite . . . I am Kite . . . Kite . . ."

She tried to enunciate the word, but her mouth was dry and she
had to swallow before she uncertainly formed his name. "Kite . . ."
she said.

He smiled and nodded. Then he extended his hand and without
thinking, still looking into her eyes, touched her breast, raised his
eyebrows questioningly and made as if to say a word. She frowned
and repeated, "Kite."

Kite smiled again and shook his head, touched his own breast,
repeated his own name, then her shoulder. She said something which
he failed to catch and he quickly cupped his right ear and bent forward.
She repeated the word which, if it was her name, he found himself
unable to grasp. Instead he sat back on his haunches and said, "I shall
call you Puella, which is Latin for girl." He repeated the name slowly.
"Puella."

Since he could not discover her real name, to confer some artificial
English substitute seemed but one more imposition; the Latin noun
seemed a not inappropriate expedient and, he hoped, temporary
substitute.

Rising, he slipped out of his cabin and reappeared with a handful of biscuits and some water from the gunroom, which he offered her. Eagerly she grabbed the carafe of water and upended it, swallowing quickly. When she had finished she gestured at her leg-irons and said something which he interpreted as a request that he should remove them.

He shrugged and shook his head. "I cannot," he said. Then, realising that if he said more, though she would be incapable of understanding it, she might comprehend that the matter was more complicated, he went on.

"Believe me, Puella, I would willingly remove those confounded irons if it was in my power, but they would only be replaced tomorrow." He saw the disappointment in her eyes and it suddenly occurred to Kite that although he, along with every man aboard the *Enterprize*, knew the fate of the Negroes, they themselves would have no idea of what lay in store for them. Thus his kindness, however partial, might seem to her not a temporary amelioration of her confinement, but the end of it. He fervently wished that this was so, but knew that the morning would present him with further problems. What, he asked himself, could he do to mitigate the poor creature's distress, to show her that although she must remain shackled, he meant no harm? Impulsively, he suddenly scooped her up and laid her out in his cot, pulling a sheet over her. Touching her lightly on the cheek, he wished her good night.

Then he spread a blanket on the deck and lay down to sleep.

When he woke it was still early. The faint clink of iron recalled the presence of Puella in his cot and told where she shifted uneasily in her sleep. He sighed, aware that he could do little to preserve Puella's privacy, yet dreaded her reaction to being returned to the women's room on the slave deck. He wished that there was someone on board who could translate between them, and express his intention of doing whatever he could to help her, but they had left Golden-Opportunity Plantagenet at York Island. He considered buying her himself; the notion had merit, for it offended no one and while he might be thought a damned fool, he could stomach that. But he presumed he would have to wait until the slaves were put up for sale, whenever and wherever they were landed. Then another idea struck him; so as not to wake her, he quietly slipped on his shoes and went on deck.

It was still dark and for a moment he stood in the chilly night air, staring at the first flush of the dawn to the east. Gerard had the watch and loomed up like a ghost. "Well, Mr Kite, what a surprise, I hear you have feet of mortal clay after all."

Kite opened his mouth to protest the innocence of his behaviour, but thought better of it, realising his continence would be as misunderstood as his own initial misunderstanding of Molloy's rectitude. It was preferable to meet his problems at a level others comprehended.

"I have taken a woman, yes. Is that so very remarkable?"

Gerard chuckled. "In your case it's remarkable, yes. Was she good?"

"I've had better," Kite riposted, pleased with the readiness of his glib reply.

"Have you now? Well, well. And I had you for a cock-virgin."

"We all make mistakes, Mr Gerard. Now, perhaps you will tell me something. How do I get her made into an assistant, as the other men's women have become? She would make a good assistant to Wilson and myself."

"Well . . ." Gerard appeared to consider the matter.

"Look, I understand I am entitled to profit from a slave or two. Why cannot I have this one . . . ?"

"In lieu of payment?"

"If necessary."

Gerard laughed. "Are you a fool? Have you any idea what a box of problems she'll bring?"

"Then I'll sell her on," Kite said with convincing brutality.

"Captain Makepeace doesn't favour . . ."

"Captain Makepeace thrust her in my face last night." As he uttered the words Kite was seized by a sudden suspicion and immediately voiced it: "In fact I'm not sure that he didn't intend to corrupt me by the act and prove my feet were of ordinary clay."

Gerard chuckled beside him. "Well, he seems to have achieved a degree of success. You now possess the zeal of the converted, Mr Kite. Only yesterday you moped about, utterly opposed to the trade, and now, here you are, up before the sun to ask me about buying a black whore."

Kite bit his lip at the insult, then said, "I thought perhaps you would approve. It would ease the burden on—"

"Beg pardon, sir."

"What is it?" Gerard turned as a man approached them in the gloom. "It's Holmes, ain't it?" Gerard peered at the figure who appeared bare legged, his shirt tails flapping in the wind. "What are you doing on deck?"

"There's trouble below, sir—"

"What, the slaves?" broke in Gerard, suddenly tense.

"No, no, sir, not them. That's Mr Kite, ain't it? It's more fever, sir. Johnny Good is shaking in his hammock, sir, damn near threw me out, and he's started to shout about his muvver."

"Dear God!"

"I'll go down, Mr Gerard," Kite said. "Take me below, Holmes."

In the next two days eight men were taken ill, including the gunner, Mitchell, the first of the *Spitfire*'s officers to be infected. The yellow jack, having lain dormant from its initial appearance among the crew of the *Enterprize*, had now incubated and struck in all its indiscriminate horror. It was only the beginning; by the end of a week one third of the ship's company were suffering, some in the preliminary stage, suffering terrible fits of uncontrollable shivering, wracked by pains in the head, the spine and the limbs, some already in the second phase, when an abatement gave the false impression of recovery before the final yellowing of skin and eyes. This was only a brief interlude, for the copious and bloody vomiting that followed was the prelude to the fatal chilling before death.

Like their consort, the *Marquis of Lothian,* aboard which the epidemic still raged, the work of the ship suffered. The morning exercise of the slaves was curtailed, then abandoned, for there were barely sufficient men fit to work the vessel. Instead a daily burial party mustered. Makepeace, a scented handkerchief held to his face, hurriedly mumbled the Protestant rites over the corpses, which had been sewn into their hammocks and were now sent to the bottom with a cannon ball at their feet.

For Kite the outbreak was not without ironic consequence, for he had succeeded in persuading Makepeace to strike off the leg-irons from a few of the women and these included Puella. They helped nurse the dying with a tender compassion that drew from the commander the observation that, "Such a thing seems scarcely possible and would doubtless prove so if they knew they were to be sold into a lifetime's servitude."

But that, it seemed to Kite, was increasingly unlikely, for the mortality among the crew threatened the continuation of the voyage. This fact formed the core of a shouted debate between Makepeace and Ross at the end of the twentieth day of the passage. Although the ships' route lay within the compass of the north-east trade winds which held steady, requiring little sail trimming by day or night, the loss of men seriously hampered the management of the slaves. That morning Molloy and Kerr were struck down.

Having compared the increasingly parlous state of his crew with that of Captain Ross, Makepeace clambered down from the rail to where Gerard and Kite waited. Kite had just reported the incapacity of Molloy, whose large frame shuddered below in the confinement of his cot.

"You know what is in my mind, Mr Gerard, if things get much worse?"

"I do, sir."

Kite looked enquiringly from one to the other, but it was clear that the obscure reference was to be kept from him.

"How many of the blacks are affected today?" Makepeace asked.

"Only five, sir," said Kite, "the same number as yesterday."

"How can this be?" Makepeace asked frowning, his expression desperate and fearful as he stared at Kite.

"They are a lower order of being," Gerard said, "their immunity proves it . . ."

"Aye, that may be true," said Makepeace, "but Kite here is so far unaffected and he has been in constant contact with the sick."

"Perhaps I too am of a lower order," Kite remarked. Black humour, he had observed, was a common means by which the seamen coped with the dread of their circumstances.

Makepeace smiled thinly. "I think that highly possible, Kite." He looked up at the foretopsail. "If this wind holds we shall sight land within the sennight; it remains to be seen whether we can win this race and keep sufficient men to work the ship into port."

"If we run into enemy men-of-war . . ." Gerard left the sentence incomplete, but Makepeace merely shrugged.

"Let us hope," he said, "we have a man left to strike the ensign."

"Kite will do it," said Gerard, half smiling.

\* \* \*

I have Little Inclination to Write these Lines.

Kite dipped his quill and stared across his cabin to the rumpled cot.

We now have over Half the Ship's Company sick with the Yellow-Fever. I am Deeply Perplex'd to know where this Contagion Arises. That it Comes from the Coast of Guinea is Clear, for the Negroes have grown Accustomed to it and are hardly Affected by it, but by what means, or from what Agent the Infection Comes, the Disease remains a Great Mystery.

He paused again, recalling the Sherbro and the dense jungle that crowded its banks, hemming in the grey-green water and depositing in its stream the detritus of its endless cycle of life and death. Did the slime-laden water contain some organism that bore the fatal disease? It was not dissimilar to the fever known in England as the marsh ague, endemic, he knew, in low, boggy and foetid areas. Although the deep and flowing Sherbro seemed at first to bear little resemblance to the marshes lying in the estuaries of many English rivers, he recalled the heavy miasma which, after nightfall, would descend upon the river like a thick and steaming fog. Was it this dense mist that, penetrating the opened ports and descending through the open gratings and companionways of the waist, introduced the deadly fever into the *Enterprize*?

Was it the river water, or the river-borne mist? Or both?

Then Kite remembered something with a start of horror and culpability. He himself had insisted the slaves were washed down with water from the Sherbro; had this sanitary measure actually imported the fever? "Oh, God . . ." he groaned, burying his head in his hands, shaking with deep sobs at his profound ignorance and the fatal events which had led to this tragedy.

"Kite . . . Kite?"

He looked up, wiping the moisture from his eyes. The Negress Puella had entered his cabin, barefoot and noiseless. She bore a bowl of steaming rice and he realised he had not eaten for hours. He nodded and expressed his thanks, taking the proffered bowl from her. She drew back to hunker down in the corner of his cabin, folding her arms on her drawn-up knees and staring up at him.

After swallowing a mouthful he said, "You are good to me, Puella. I thank you." He put the spoon in the bowl and extended his right hand, repeating, "Thank you."

She reached out and took his hand. It was the first mutual intimacy they had shared and they both smiled. "Kite may die, Puella," he said, "and God knows what will become of you, but if I live, I shall not abandon you." He cleared his throat and shook his head, adding in a firmer voice, "No, I shall not, upon my honour."

He knew she had no idea what he said as he made this compact with providence, but he sensed she derived some satisfaction from the sound of his voice, for she smiled again and he was beguiled by the curve of her full lips and the way a smile made her wide but not uncomely nostrils flare.

Scooping the bowl clear of rice he set it down, whereupon she rose to remove it. Standing close to him, swaying with the movement of the ship, she looked down at him, her breasts prominent, infinitely desirable and appealing. As she took up the bowl she gently touched his cheek. He resisted an impulse to put his arm about her and in the same instant she slid her hand about his head and drew his face to her. He felt the soft firmness of her breast, the erect tissue of her nipple, against his cheek and the soft touch of her lips on the crown of his head.

"Kite," she said slowly. Then she was gone, leaving him sitting like a loon, staring at the closed door of his cabin. He sighed, profoundly touched, then took up his quill again.

The Negresses have greatly Assisted in tending the Sick, among

them a Young Woman whom we call Puella and in whom I have
an Interest and Regard with Great Affection . : .

What did it matter what he wrote now? Who would read his
journal after his death? He crossed out the dissembling *we call* and
substituted *I call*.

On the following afternoon Gerard was taken ill, along with two other
men, including the gunner, and while Kite almost hourly expected to
begin a shuddering fit he remained strangely unaffected. Upon hearing
the news of the first lieutenant's incapacity Makepeace retired to his
own cabin and proceeded to render himself helplessly drunk. It was
Ritchie who brought both the news that Gerard had been carried
twitching from the quarterdeck to his cabin and that Makepeace had
taken to the bottle. Kite was then in the 'tween deck, binding up the
jaw of their most recent fatality, Francis Molloy.

Kite frowned, intent on his task, asking over his shoulder, "Who has
the deck? With Molloy dead, Captain Makepeace has no right getting
drunk."

"The steward says he's consigned the ship to the devil, Mr Kite."

Kite straightened up and looked at Ritchie. "I suppose he fears that
he'll be next."

Ritchie shrugged. "That's a risk we all run," he observed with
chilling logic, glancing at the pale form of Molloy. Then he confronted
Kite with an even colder piece of logic. "If the Cap'n goes, you'll be
the last officer left. I reckon you've a touch of luck about you, Mr
Kite. I've seen it before; Makepeace had it for years and maybe it ain't
deserted him yet – we'll see – but you've a winning way, sir and with
Mr Kerr gone . . . Well, sir, looks like you and Jacob Ritchie've got
a leg up in life, if you know what I mean . . ."

Kite frowned, then the penny dropped. "You mean you're the next
senior man?"

Ritchie nodded. "At the moment Mr Kite, it's Cap'n Makepeace,
you and me . . ." Ritchie waved his hand at Puella and another
Negress who were present, tending the sick seamen. "Along with
all this black ivory."

Kite saw the end of Ritchie's train of thought. The system of shares
upon which the rewards of the voyage rested accrued to those holding
the various stations at the conclusion of the voyage. "Yes," he agreed
hurriedly, "I see."

"I'm glad you do, Mr Kite. You and me haven't always seen eye to
eye, but then we can let bygones be bygones, can't we? I can work
the old *Enterprize*, sir, but I'll need you to navigate, like."

Kite nodded. The additional burden appalled him. "I'd better go and see the Captain, just the same. We'd be desperately short-handed without him."

Ritchie stood aside. "Oh yes, sir, quite so, but just tell him that Jake Ritchie's now his first luff, sir."

Kite left Ritchie laughing and made for the ladder. Ritchie watched him go, then still smiling, squeezed the buttocks of the nearer Negress.

"I Mister Thomas' woman . . ." she protested as she had been schooled to.

"Sure you are, sister, just as long as Mr Thomas can stand up and piss."


Kite went aft and knocked on Makepeace's door. "Go to the devil, whoever you are!"

"It's Kite, sir. Pray let me in . . ."

"To hell with you, Kite."

Kite hesitated only an instant before forcing the flimsy door. Makepeace rose to his feet. "Damn you!" Makepeace began, but Kite, seeing the quantity of bottle necks visible in the opened locker under the settee beneath the stern windows, over-rode him.

"Captain Makepeace, for God's sake recollect yourself. You are not sick and the ship requires you. If you submit to this meaningless debauch, do you think me capable of bringing the *Enterprize* into port?"

"I am in quarantine, Mr Kite," Makepeace began portentously, "to better preserve myself for precisely the purpose of bringing this brig into port . . ."

"And who do you expect to run the ship in the interval, sir? Are you aware that presently, with Mr Gerard like to die, your first lieutenant is Jacob Ritchie?"

Makepeace stared at Kite, frowned, then waved Kite's remark aside. "Well, you are an officer . . . haven't we taught you to take a meridian altitude?"

"I cannot tend the sick and—"

"Then give up tending the sick! The sick will die! The fever is fatal! Embrace your new opportunity with enthusiasm, Kite. It may not last long."

Kite was appalled, he was neither surgeon nor a sea-officer, but Makepeace's remark gave him a slight opening, for the commander was not yet completely inebriated.

"D'you want to bring the ship in, sir, because if so then I will willingly stand watch-and-watch with you? We cannot have many more days to run before sighting land . . ."

Makepeace stared at him, then he refilled his glass. "I shall consider your proposal," he said and Kite knew he had lost his argument. With a look of absolute contempt for Makepeace, he left the cabin, followed out by a bottle which flew through the air and smashed against the door Kite slammed behind him.

On deck Kite passed the word for Ritchie, telling him to take the watch until midnight when he himself would take over. Ritchie grinned and winked at him. "I told you, Mr Kite."

Kite turned away; he was desperate for some sleep. The prospect of even two or three hours away from the stench of vomit, blood and the last venting farts of the dead seemed to hold the promise of paradise.

Nothing mattered any more; the fell shadow of damnation that had fallen over his life in the Hebblewhites' barn, and against which he had struggled for so long, could no longer be opposed. He reconciled himself to death; it would come sooner or later and sooner now seemed preferable, for he lacked the will to fight the inevitable any more. Makepeace was neither a fool nor a coward, but Kite realised he had already capitulated. Makepeace had always known the enormity of the risks in his adopted trade. Perhaps these risks mitigated the cruelty of it and the mortality among the crews of the Guineamen paid in some part for those of the enslaved Negroes. Perhaps the constant presence of death prompted men of high temper and passion, such as Captain Makepeace, to take their pleasure of the black women while they still breathed . . .

With these dark certainties crowding his mind, Kite entered his cabin, intent only on falling fast asleep. Puella was crouching in the corner, whither she had run to escape Ritchie who, unwilling to antagonise Kite, had not followed her and had then been summoned to the quarterdeck.

"Puella . . ." he said thickly, swaying with fatigue. She stood hurriedly and caught him by the upper arms.

"Kite . . ."

Hesitantly, his hands went round her slender waist and ran down over her pert buttocks, slipping the cotton wrap from her. He felt the responsive pressure of her thighs against his and they looked at each other, she half smiling, half fearful as he bent and kissed her, losing himself in the sudden access of tremulous passion. Her nipples rasped against him as he tore at his breeches and then she was laying down before him, on the bare scrubbed planking of the deck, her knees drawn up, shielding the smooth and lovely brown expanse of her flat belly. As he exposed his throbbing and eager member she parted her legs and he tenderly knelt between them, pressing his loins down towards her black triangle of coiling pubic hair.

\*　　　\*　　　\*

Woken from a deep sleep, Kite disentangled himself from Puella's deliciously wanton limbs and clambered wearily up the companionway to the quarterdeck. His mind was a turmoil of contradicting thoughts. Love and desire mixed with self-contempt and despair; hope flowed through him, to be quenched by reality, while rambling and insane thoughts of defying fate and surviving against all the odds, were brought down to sea level by a dousing of cold spray sweeping across the brig's rail as he reached the deck.

The fog of sleep cleared and he stared about him, checking the course. The man at the wheel said nothing; the death-rate aboard the *Enterprize* had so altered everything aboard the brig that it seemed no longer odd that the surgeon was also the officer of the watch. Kite stared to leeward where, just abaft the larboard beam, he could see the *Marquis of Lothian* quite clearly in the starlight, a pale ghost of a ship, her waterline delineated by the faint trace of phosphorescence.

The beauty of the sight struck him, along with the incongruity of the sentimental effect the perception had on him here, on this stinking vessel with its cargo of death and misery. The strange, contradictory thoughts made his whole being tingle, like some late extension of the shuddering orgasm he had enjoyed with Puella. He sensed something of that triumphalism touched upon by Makepeace with his theory of providential defiance; he sensed too a brief connection between the wonder of creation that united the quickening of the life forces of Puella and himself with the dreadful, bloody death of his friend Molloy.

He was recalled from this introspection by a monosyllabic protest by the man at the wheel. Turning, he saw Puella beside him. "What are you doing here?" he began, stopping when he simultaneously realised she could neither understand him nor comprehend his hypocritical affront at the impropriety of her presence on the quarterdeck. Puella held out a twist of cloth containing something small and hard. Taking the tiny bundle, Kite thought it felt like irregular musket balls.

"Kola," she said, pointing at her mouth. "Good." She hesitated, then, pointing at his own mouth, added, "Kite . . . Good . . . Eat."

He opened the cloth, marvelling at her slow but sure acquisition of English words. She had learnt 'eat' from the curt commands of Ritchie and his men as they compelled the seasick slaves to consume their daily rations of manioc and rice. Kite recognised the nuts, which he had seen a few of the slaves eating. Makepeace had drawn his attention to them, explaining that they eased hunger and could drive away fatigue, even, it was claimed, dispel the symptoms of drunkenness and purify water. These, Kite deduced looking down at the handful he held, must have been preserved in the clothing of the blacks during their captivity in the barracoons. There could have been few left on board by now, and he assumed Puella had gone to some trouble to obtain them for his easement. He was touched by her solicitude and gratefully touched her cheek.

The man at the wheel sucked his teeth with whistling disapproval.

"Thank you," he said tenderly to Puella and she, sensing the solitary duty to which he must attend, left him alone. As she went below, the man at the wheel muttered something. When Puella had disappeared, Kite rounded on him. "Hold your tongue!" he snapped.

The man sniffed, but Kite let the insolence pass and, putting one of Puella's kola nuts into his mouth, he began chewing.

At dawn Kite went below and, crushing another kola nut with a pestle in his mortar, tipped the powder into a tankard and added water from the scuttlebutt. Then he went into Makepeace's cabin. The captain was in such a drunken stupor that Kite was unable to wake him. No longer tired, thanks to the masticated kola nut, Kite resumed the watch on deck, sending for the captain's steward and instructing him to give Makepeace the infusion as soon as he could.

But Makepeace made no appearance on deck during the forenoon. Kite, possessing an odd vitality and mental energy, left to his own devices, ordered all hands mustered aft at noon, when the next watch-change was due. Then, nervously giving the helm orders himself, he edged the *Enterprize* down towards the *Marquis of Lothian* and hailed Captain Ross. It was Ross's mate who made his appearance on the rail.

"Bad news, *Enterprize*! Cap'n Ross is struck with this damned plague! Where is Captain Makepeace?"

"Likewise unwell, sir," Kite replied, unwilling to explain further with a precise definition of Makepeace's condition.

"Our fortunes are on the ebb, sir. Our only hope is that we sight land. Until tomorrow!"

"Until tomorrow," Kite responded.

At noon, the men assembled at the break of the quarterdeck. There were sixteen of them.

"Mr Ritchie, pray take your station beside me." Ritchie swaggered up and stood beside Kite who turned his attention to the crew.

"Are there any among you who feel unwell?"

The men shuffled awkwardly and looked from one to another, but a negative mumble rose from them and Kite, standing behind the athwartships quarterdeck rail, nodded and cleared his throat. "Very well. We are in a desperate plight with Mr Gerard ill and Mr Molloy dead. But we are not yet entirely destitute. Captain Makepeace is unwell, but not from the fever . . ."

The aside provoked a laugh from the men and one shouted, "No sign of the yaws yet then, Mr Kite?"

Kite had no idea what the yaws were and merely smiled before resuming his address. "As the surgeon and the only officer fit for duty, Mr Ritchie here will assist me . . ." Ritchie grinned at his shipmates. "From eight bells we will take up new watches of eight men each," Kite went on. "For the next four hours, I want the slaves exercised and their decks mucked out." He saw a grin pass among the men at his use of a farming expression. "Now let's get on with it!"

By sunset Makepeace was sober and, still free of any signs of fever, somewhat contrite. Seeing Ritchie on deck he summoned Kite, who reported the events of the day.

"There's one other thing, sir," Kite said when he had finished, regarding his commander's dissipated pallor with disgust.

"Oh?" Makepeace looked up from the compass in the binnacle as if intent on finding an error in the brig's navigation greater than that of his own dereliction of duty. "Pray what is that?"

"We have had no new cases of yellow jack today."

"And is that significant?"

"That is for you to decide," said Kite, his voice coldly formal.

Makepeace stiffened and straightened up. "Have a care, Mr Kite, that promotion don't go to your head."

"Your solicitude is most thoughtful, Captain Makepeace."

Makepeace regarded Kite with a jaundiced eye. "You may go below, Mr Kite."

Kite footed a bow and wisely held his tongue.

Later that day, when the watch changed again and Kite came on deck, Makepeace was still pacing the quarterdeck. The captain said with his charming smile, "I have more than a reputation to maintain, Mr Kite, I have a name to keep."

"I'm sorry, sir, I don't understand," said Kite frowning, still fogged by sleep.

"My name; I have to live up to it. We are at odds, Mr Kite, and I have to make peace between us. I owe you an apology; you have done an uncommonly fine job and the knowledge that you are not properly a surgeon is set aside. We are quits, Mr Kite."

Was it that easy? That they were quits, and all dispute between them was set aside? Kite recalled the similarity of Ritchie's remark about bygones being bygones. Kite wanted to feel the weight of responsibility lifted from his shoulders, but this did not happen, though he was not one to maintain an ill-humour, even towards a man whose aberrations had for a while, threatened them all.

"It is a pity about Gerard, though," Makepeace said.

"Yes, and Molloy."

"Indeed yes; Molloy too, but Gerard and I had known each other a long time, and my wife is a relative of his."

"I see, sir. I am sorry."

"Well, we cannot weep long over the dead. Or the dying . . . We may yet join them in Hell."

"That is true, sir."

"But if our luck has improved, then we may yet turn this voyage to good account."

Kite grinned ruefully. "I think Mr Ritchie is somewhat sanguine on that score."

Makepeace frowned. "Ritchie? Oh, yes, I see, rapid promotion and an increased share. Well, much of that will be due to you." Kite demurred. "No, I am sincere," Makepeace insisted. "Mr Gerard and I had already concerted a plan if mortality had debarred the further passage of this vessel."

"I recall hearing you speak of it," said Kite, "though I took no meaning from your conversation."

"We are not yet out of trouble and it is as well if you know of it, Mr Kite. It is not unknown, in extremis, for the master of a slaver to jettison his cargo. The risk of an uprising increases with every death among the crew and it may yet be necessary."

"I do not understand, sir. Surely, to jettison means to throw overboard. Do you mean the scrivelloes and the camwood? Surely you cannot mean . . ."

"Of course I mean the slaves, Mr Kite." Makepeace looked at the young man beside him as Kite's astonishment changed to horror and outrage. "All of them," he added, "your paramour included." Then, with a sudden intensity Makepeace went on, "Like all intelligent young men, you judge your elders. You disapproved of my whoring and drinking, but when you have survived the yellow jack, and when you have to make a decision which may account for the deaths of nearly three hundred blackamoors, then you may not view me so harshly, Mr Kite. Life walks in constant companionship with death."

Kite considered Makepeace's strange half-apology, half-justification and, just for a second, recovered a fragment of the weird sensation he had felt that morning he had viewed the phosphor running along the waterline of the *Marquis of Lothian.*

"It is the Fates who direct us, Mr Kite," Makepeace concluded.

For Kite, the moment of magic vanished. He was again a murderer on the run, a man drawn to the contemplation of drowning almost three hundred blackamoors. "Of that I am only too well acquainted, Captain Makepeace."

"Aye, sir," Makepeace responded, his voice low. "You are in too deep now, Mr Kite."

Five days passed as they ran west and no further infections occurred; cautiously Kite came to believe the yellow jack had gone as mysteriously as it had arrived.

*I can only Conclude,* he wrote in his journal as Puella squatted in her corner and watched him,

> that the Mysterious Agent of Disease Possesses a Finite Lifetime and that this is now at an End. I now Believe that the Contagion was brought aboard by the Blacks. The first Infections were Probably caught from our Initial Contact with the Negroes in the Sherbro. The later Outbreak is Likely to have come from the Slaves held on board, which Spread after we had Sailed.

He reread his words, wondering if he had divined the actual means by which the fever infected white men. One or two of the seamen, he had heard, had voiced the opinion that the fever was caught from the bites of mosquitoes. They argued the mosquitoes lived in the salt-marshes in the Thames estuary where the marsh ague and dengue fever were widespread. But although one man claimed the ague killed many women on the coast of Essex, the man's description of the disease's progress indicated it to be a different sickness, more like the quotidian fever of Mr Lorimoor, than the yellow jack. Moreover, for the life of him Kite could not see how a mere fly could propagate a malady vicious enough to strike a fit man down so swiftly.

The remission of the fever, coinciding as it did with Kite's initiative in re-establishing a routine aboard the *Enterprize*, gave the surviving ship's company a new lease of life. In turn this compensated for their lack of numbers in the management of the slaves. The experienced Ritchie instituted a savagely oppressive regime over the increasingly resentful male slaves, whose women urged them to rebel as the voyage dragged on and they became more and more apprehensive over their future. Many among them were not as ignorant as Kite had supposed. They understood the vastness of the ocean and that their passage was to the westward where, they had heard, there lived terrible cousins of these white men who walked the earth like great kings.

With such stories the lançados had terrorised them as they had brought them from the stockadoes and the barracoons down the Sherbro to the waiting Guineamen.

# Eight

## The West India Merchant

They reached Antigua four days later, dropping anchor in the harbour of St John's on the north-west coast. Here they learned the rumours of war rife on the Guinea coast were unfounded. They had been based on the assumption that the attack by a British squadron under Vice-Admiral Edward Boscawen on some French men-of-war on the Grand Banks, resulting in the capture of the *Lys* and the *Alcide*, would lead to a declaration of war from Paris. Fog had dispersed the French fleet, and Boscawen's attack, designed to prevent a large reinforcement of troops under the escort of the Comte de la Motte reaching Canada, prevented neither the new Governor of Canada, the Marquis de Vaudreuil, nor the army commander, the Marquis de Montcalm, from reaching their destination.

Nevertheless, hostilities between the two colonising powers in North America, France in Canada and Britain in the thirteen American colonies along the Atlantic coast to the south, had been smouldering along the wild frontiers for some time. The first clash had come at Great Meadows on the Ohio, when a mixed force of colonial troops and Indians under a provincial major named George Washington had skirmished with French forces. But the previous summer the British had suffered disaster and humiliation when a British column under General Braddock was ambushed on the forested banks of the Monongahela. While hostilities had broken out in the backwoods, Boscawen's provocative attack on the French men-of-war failed in its objective of forcing the hand of King Louis XV into an outright declaration of war. Instead, so Makepeace and Kite now learned, a diplomatic tangle among the royal courts of Europe was embroiling the whole continent in opposing armed camps. Full-blown hostilities, it was sanguinely asserted, would come sooner or later.

But in the West Indies the remorseless workings of commerce ground on, untroubled by such considerations. Makepeace landed his slaves and they were sold at an average of nine pounds sterling, a price which furnished the *Enterprize*'s commander and his reduced company with a handsome profit. As for the miserable and fearful blacks, it was only now that their future became clear. Those who had not been seasick during the middle passage now found the strange island swayed under their fettered feet and that the irons round their ankles were not to be removed. Instead they were cruelly branded by their new owners and vanished into the country, or were transhipped to other islands in the West Indies. Over a hundred were purchased by a merchant from Havana, in Cuba. Makepeace was content, though his under-manned brig was incapable of touting her cargo beyond Antigua. He was keen to refit her, recruit more hands to man her for the homeward passage from among the human flotsam that accumulated on the waterfront of St John's, and load a cargo for Liverpool before war filled the chops of the Channel with French privateers.

In the hurly-burly of discharging the slaves, who left in a mournful, iron-bound column for the mastaba in the market to be pulled and prodded by the plantation owners prior to purchase, Kite's circumstances underwent a transformation. Nor was he insensible that his own fate was in a marked contrast to that of the majority of the slaves, for he had acquired slaves of his own. When the *Enterprize* had arrived at St John's, Kite had made clear to Makepeace his intention of securing the person of Puella and the captain had cynically charged him the exorbitant price of fifteen pounds for the privilege. On the morning that the slaves were roused for transfer to the slave market, she abandoned his cabin, and he found her cowering fearfully, her arm round a boy whose features, Kite realised, suggested he was a relative of Puella's. Kite recognised him as the victim of sodomy he had seen being abused at the beginning of the passage. Sighing, he had nodded, ordering Ritchie to release the boy's leg-irons and giving him into Puella's charge while he sought the captain.

"I am busy, Mr Kite," Makepeace said, waving him aside as he shuffled papers in his cabin. "You have your black whore, now indulge me and leave, I have to visit the agent and secure my homeward cargo . . ."

"Forgive me, Captain Makepeace, but I am determined to leave the *Enterprize,* sir. I doubt you will have need of a surgeon on the homeward voyage."

"But I need officers. You may have Molloy's berth, Mr Kite."

"I do not wish it, sir. Also, I wish to purchase a boy. He is, I think Puella's brother, or perhaps cousin or nephew."

Makepeace looked up. "You are a bigger fool than I conceived possible." He lay the paper he had been reading from on the table and confronted Kite, his expression hard and uncompromising. "You may go to the devil, Kite. You will tire of the wench and the boy will only prove mischievous unless you thrash him. Sell them . . ."

"No, sir, that I cannot do. I intend giving them their freedom."

"What, so that they can starve or prostitute themselves on the water-front?" Makepeace shook his head at Kite's lack of worldliness.

"No, so that they can live under my protection."

Makepeace shook his head. "I will not sell you the boy. I shall save you from your own folly."

"I am entitled to two slaves," Kite persisted. "I am resolved and shall buy him in the market. Surely you would rather profit directly without the auctioneer's fee."

Makepeace shook his head and regarded Kite with sudden interest. The young man who had sewn up a harlot's arse in Liverpool had become a strong character, a man it seemed impossible to reason with, who knew his own mind. And it was odd, Makepeace thought, that the affair with the black wench had somehow strengthened this impression; quite the reverse from his intention when he had dangled her enticingly in front of Kite.

"You are incorrigible . . ." Makepeace's handsome face took on a harsh expression. "Mr Kite, I had no idea, beyond serving my own ends, that taking you on board my ship would be the cause of her being saved from a plague of the yellow jack but such, I must confess, to have been the case. I – no, the whole surviving ship's company – are indebted to you. But I must warn you that within every man lie the seeds of his own destruction. You remarked my own distemper; yours is a foolish and wanton compassion. Compassion is not a vice found in the British sea services, thank God. We match our wits against a pitiless sea, against a pitiless climate and pitiless disease in a trade that better acquits itself by similarly being pitiless."

"That is why I cannot remain with you, Captain Makepeace."

A silence fell between the two men, broken by Makepeace, who expelled air through pursed lips and shook his head. "You are beyond me, Kite, beyond me. Whatever brought you aboard the *Enterprize* in Liverpool, I cannot think. But you may find employment here in Antigua. Do you wish me to speak to Mr Mulgrave, our agent? He is a well-known West India merchant with a large establishment here."

"I should be obliged and most grateful." Kite paused a moment, then said, "I, er, I mean you will make it clear to Mr Mulgrave that I have, er, a household."

Makepeace, who had resumed the perusal of his papers, looked up again, raising his eyebrows. "A household? My word, Kite, you have more than that, you have delusions of grandeur!" Makepeace laughed and nodded, smiling. "Yes, I shall speak to Mulgrave. I happen to know he is short of a clerk."

"That is kind of you, sir."

"We shall truly be quits, then."

"Truly, sir."

Makepeace suddenly held out his hand. "I cannot think that you were preserved from the yellow jack to waste your life as a counting-house clerk, but if that is what you want . . . You may have the boy for the price of a man, nine pounds . . ."

"I agree."

"In that case you shame me. You may have him for seven . . ."

"I shall pay you nine pounds, Captain Makepeace, and count myself the luckier man."

Makepeace pulled a face. "By Jupiter, Kite, you have the tongue of a preacher. In any case, you will have sufficient money from this voyage to subsist for a while on your own resources." Makepeace paused, then added, "If you keep that jade poorly shod and on short commons."

Kite left Makepeace, uncertain of his future. The immediate responsibility of Puella and the boy had diverted his mind from the problems of his past and their long shadow on the rest of his life. The legacy of his voyage on the *Enterprize* and his brush with death and disease was to mark him for life, but when he left the Guineaman in Antigua he did so with a reputation as an extraordinary and honest, if eccentric, young man.

William Kite was fortunate in finding himself employed by Joseph Mulgrave, then the leading and most influential merchant in Antigua. Mulgrave was a tall, cadaverous man whose skin had not been burned by the tropical sun, despite thirty years in the West Indies. Mulgrave avoided exposure during daylight whenever possible, but sat at his desk in a black suit more suited to the smoke of London, venturing out only after dark when his tall figure could be seen walking through the town, looking neither to right nor left, and acknowledging no one. An unconvivial and, insofar as respectable white society was concerned, solitary bachelor, Mulgrave's sole and absorbing passion was commerce and the amassing of capital. Aloof, dispassionate and apparently devoid of any human emotion, he was spoken of in reverential tones in the ports of the Antilles; the extent of his wealth was unknown, but rumoured to be enormous. His more accountable reputation derived from his scrupulous honesty in all his business transactions.

On their first encounter, Kite thought he had been delivered into the presence of a forbidding man of rigid views and severe habits, who would disapprove of Puella and the boy. But Mulgrave, having coldly addressed a few questions to Kite and having clearly gained from Makepeace an insight into the young man's character, proceeded to surprise him.

"You have two young blacks under your protection, I understand,

Mr Kite," Mulgrave said with dispassionate candour in a deep bass. The voice was surprising for one so slender, but was, Kite was to learn in due time, the most superficial of the surprises Mr Mulgrave would spring upon him.

"I do, sir."

"Do you intend to live in some intimacy with the young woman?"

"If that would not offend you, sir," Kite said cautiously, embarrassed and flushing.

The ghost of a smile flickered momentarily across Mulgrave's face and Kite saw the horizontal cicatrix of a scar that ran from the left cheekbone to the ear, the lobe of which was nicked. It added to the sinister image Makepeace presented as he formed his reply. "Not at all, but it would be best if you were to dwell under my own roof. I have adequate accommodation and we can better teach the two of them a smattering of English sufficient for your wants."

"That is most thoughtful of you, sir." Kite was only half-relieved; living under the same roof as Mr Mulgrave seemed to possess little attraction.

"Do you realise that consorting with a black damns you in the eyes of many of your fellow countrymen in Antigua? The fact that they fornicate and miscegenate themselves is a measure of their hypocrisy, but that does not alter the way they will regard an open liaison such as you have adopted. Your youth and opinions are contrary to what is regarded here as acceptable; recent arrivals may be treated like lepers, so you will not find yourself in great demand at Government House, or elsewhere, for that matter."

"I do not think that will greatly trouble me, sir."

"Well, we shall see about that in due course. But if you intend to keep her, you will burn your boats in respect of settling here. Do you understand?" Kite nodded; the prospect of surrendering Puella at this tremulously uncertain moment in his life filled him with horror.

"Now," went on Mulgrave, "pray tell me the young woman's name."

"I have called her Puella, sir."

Mulgrave raised an eyebrow. "And the boy?"

"I have not named him."

"Mmm. I like the Latin tag . . . Puella has a better sound to it than Puer, but we should keep the alliteration; let us call the lad Pompey." Again the faint trace of smile flitted across Mulgrave's face. "They will both wear their leg-irons until they have learned sufficient English to understand their circumstances. They may find that rather hard to bear, but it is for their own good. If they run away now and are caught out in the wild country near any of the plantations, they are like to be whipped, shot or savaged by dogs long before establishing their identity."

"I see, sir."

"You do not see, Mr Kite," Mulgrave said with cold finality, "but you will, in due course. Sometimes one must be cruel to be kind. St John's has many free men and women of colour. It will be difficult for Puella and Pompey, but they will come to understand in time. When they speak enough English, we may strike off their fetters. Perhaps by then you will be settled in your own establishment. While you are under my roof, Mr Kite, I regret to inform you that you will find yourself keeping your own company, I am not a sociable man and I eat alone. You may choose to do the same or to teach Puella her table manners, but that is your affair. I hope you read; I have a fair library and you are welcome to make use of it. Now, to business. My senior clerk is a Mr Wentworth, and his assistant has lately embarked aboard the *King George* packet, intending to return to England, hence the vacant post which is now, providentially, yours. In addition to your lodging, I can defray your living expenses and provide you with a small competence. In due course other opportunities may present themselves, but that will largely depend upon your own energy." Mulgrave's eyes remained fixed on Kite, who held their gaze steadily. "Now, Mr Kite, in return I require absolute loyalty, perfect probity and twelve hours a day of your attention. May I assume you still wish to take up my offer?"

"You may, sir."

And so Kite settled into the large rambling house that Joseph Mulgrave had built amid a tangle of dense thorn scrub on a hillside overlooking St John's, where Puella and Pompey began to learn English as they worked under the tutelage of Mulgrave's formidable house-keeper, a large, well-formed and handsome mulattess called Mistress Dorothea. Ignorant of the usual formalities of West Indian colonial society, yet seduced by its colourful manifestations on the waterfront that stretched along the quayside immediately outside the doors of Mulgrave's counting house, Kite fell easily into a routine. For the first time since he had stumbled into the Hebblewhites' barn, he was filled with the almost forgotten feeling of contentment. Now something like a future lay before him.

Mr Wentworth was a red-faced, perspiring, overweight and untidily dressed man whose appearance belied a keen intelligence and a considerable energy. Somewhat foppish in appearance and always a martyr to fashion in the tropical heat, he bore down upon the newcomer like a ship in full sail. An incorrigible talker, Kite soon learned that Wentworth possessed a driving ambition to rise socially. His origins were humble, for his father had been an indentured white, shipped out from England as a criminal and set to work on the plantations. His mother's origins were never referred to, so Kite assumed she had most probably been a prostitute, but the child had been seen by Mulgrave playing in the streets amid the children of free blacks, mulattoes and quadroons. Mulgrave was then a young man, newly arrived in Antigua with a livid scar on his cheek and a reputation, which was soon confirmed, as a crack shot with a pistol, suggesting a dark and, for the ladies of the island at least, a darkly romantic past. Taking the boy up, Mulgrave made the lad his servant. It was not long before Mulgrave had bought a share in an established business and was settled in St John's. By this time he had recognised the shrewd intelligence in his youthful valet.

"One morning, to my complete astonishment," Wentworth explained in a curious accent, "Mr Mulgrave said that I was to accompany him and he took me to a tailor then resident in St John's and outfitted me with a gentleman's habiliments. I already knew how to read and write and I was placed directly in the counting house. Of course," Wentworth said with a candid lack of modesty that Kite learned was a perverse copy of his benefactor's absolute honesty, "it was not long before it was clear that I was capable of more than merely making ledger entries . . ."

The disparagement of Kite's own present task was not, Kite felt, meant as an insult. There was a degree of affectation in Wentworth that caused unintentional irony and it took Kite sometime to realise that Wentworth's diction arose from his desire to copy Mulgrave's cool accent in what he assumed was the enunciation of the English aristocracy. Wentworth was aware that, however he got his own surname, it was that of one of England's grand families; this set his mind on ascending the social ladder. One day, he made it quite plain, when he had made his own or inherited Mulgrave's fortune, he would go to England and make his debut in what he referred to as 'polite society'. In the meantime, the lesser ladder of Antigua's colonial white establishment provided Mr Wentworth with a sufficient social challenge.

In the first few days of their acquaintance, Kite was bombarded with information about men and women of every station in the island's hierarchy. From the governor and his staff, by way of army officers, plantation owners, merchants, advocates, ship-masters, slave traders and overseers, Wentworth delivered himself of a discourse on the subtle social gradations, stressing, of course, the connections, alliances, divisions and pretensions among the white community. He grew salacious when referring to these men's wives, indicating the uses of making love to Mrs This or Mrs That; that the Misses The

Other were marriageable for their money, though not their looks, and that Kite, if he knew what was good for him, would make no moves to advancement without first consulting him.

"If you do that, Kite, you will not regret it." Wentworth concluded his introductory remarks with a smile that Kite found amusing. "Ah," he said seriously, "but I forgot, you co-habit openly . . ."

Despite the man's obsession, Kite did not dislike him. Had he personally entertained any desire for integration with Antiguan life he would have found Wentworth's patronising a mild irritant; as it was he merely recognised that Wentworth was warning a new clerk. Kite should not presume to tread on the preserves that Wentworth regarded as his own province.

"I understand," Wentworth said with a hint of disdain, "that you do not intend renouncing your blackamoor."

"No, I do not."

"I shall not hold that against you, Kite. Mr Mulgrave himself sets us an example not to be dismissed as mere licentiousness for indeed, my word, it is not in his case. For licentiousness you must look at the concubinage of Mr Lomax of the Crown Plantation! My word, sir, yes. And I feel so sorry for his wife, who is so kind a creature, or of George Radley from Willoughby . . . My word, they are hedonists alongside whom Mr Mulgrave is a perfect and most wonderful gentleman . . ."

"I am glad to hear it," Kite replied drily.

Setting aside this torrent of obsessive social pretension, Wentworth displayed a masterly grasp of the commercial activity not merely on the island of Antigua, but of the region, explaining the interrelationship between Antigua and Guadeloupe, the adjacent French possession; of the trade in slaves with Cuba; of the export of muscovado and sugar, of rum and molasses to Liverpool, London and Bristol; and of the importance of the trans-shipment of commodities to and from the Thirteen Colonies of North America. Under this general picture of a vigorous trade, Wentworth spoke of the necessary currency transactions, of the growing importance of banking and credit, supplying asides at every opportunity to demonstrate a coup here, a timely loan there, the swift taking up of a lading and the faster settlement of an advantageous freight rate made by the House of Mulgrave. Many, though Wentworth admitted not all, were entirely due to his own acumen. He stressed that of Mulgrave in the matter of investment, of the ships in which Mulgrave had a part, but never a whole interest. "Only a fool owns sixty-four sixty-fourths in a ship, Kite, only a fool . . . Oh dear, yes," Wentworth chuckled, emphasising this recondite wisdom.

He, like the obviously much admired Mulgrave, applied only three principles to commerce; the first was to keep one's word, the second was to be inquisitive and constantly seek out new opportunities, the third was never to place too many eggs in one basket.

It took three months, much of which was spent tediously at his ledgers, for Kite to begin to truly comprehend the complexities of his new employment. He wrote and copied out letters, pasting them in the company's guard books, he learned to draft bills of lading, becoming familiar with phrases such as *Bound by God's Grace*, and *Delivered in the like Good Order* and *Well Conditioned at the Aforesaid Port, the Danger of the Seas and Mortality only Excepted* . . . That by such documentation thousands of Africans were sent into hard labour in the sugar cane fields of the Indies and the plantations of the Carolinas faded from his perception as the middle passage of the *Enterprize* seemed more and more like a bad dream.

Wentworth patronised him, especially once he learned that Kite was from humdrum origins. It pleased him that Kite was not a name to set aside that of Wentworth or Mulgrave. But Kite found this tolerable. After the long and terrible weeks aboard the *Enterprize*, the steady routine of his life in the House of Mulgrave brought a great peace to him.

He no longer felt he was escaping, only that the dimming past was forgiven, if not forgotten. He was, of course, seduced by Puella; their relationship grew wonderfully and their self-engrossment grew daily as Puella's English improved. Mistress Dorothea proved a kind and tolerant teacher, and Kite learnt that although an Antiguan-born woman her situation was otherwise not dissimilar to Puella's. Like Wentworth, Dorothea had been picked up off the street and openly made Mulgrave's mistress. Shunned by the island's white society for this unholy admission of blatant concubinage, the naturally solitary Mulgrave had simply turned his considerable abilities to the despised opportunities offered by trade. In this he had become an institution and never, despite the disdain of formal convention, lost his romantic aura as far as the white ladies of the island were concerned. The men, many of whom overpopulated their estates with half-caste bastards, joked about Mulgrave's failure to beget 'pickaninnies' on his black mistress. The failure seemed to confirm the inadequacies of those who trafficked in mere 'goods', though there was not a man among them who would not have leapt eagerly into the beautiful Dorothea's bed had the opportunity offered. Their thin-lipped white-skinned wives, wilting in the heat or suffering vapid attacks in the heavy rains, envied Dorothea's indisputable beauty, marvelling at the uprightness of her carriage and the voluptuousness of her figure.

By the time Kite had familiarised himself with his new tasks, Puella had mastered sufficient English to exchange more than a minor daily dialogue with him. In another manifestation of his changing luck,

Kite learned that Dorothea's mother had belonged to the same tribe as Puella. It took some days before Dorothea had so far recalled the tongue of her childhood that the two could gossip freely, but thereafter her coaching of Puella was swift and sure, for the common origin quickly built a bond between the two women. For all his courtesy towards her, Dorothea never felt herself even a common-law wife to the austere and remote Mulgrave. He was a man for whom intimacy was something permissible only in his bedroom. Otherwise he stood quite alone in the world and although Dorothea knew Mulgrave, better than any other person living, for a truly kind and shy man, a man who had seen her cared for and secure long before he had taken her to bed, she mourned her lack of children. That, she thought in contrast to the white planters, was a measure of his power. Withholding the potence of his copious seed convinced her that she was loved by a white spirit too powerful to conceive like a simple man. By such reasoning Dorothea could explain his fabulous wealth and the respect Mulgrave commanded, and from it too she drew the secret empowerment of herself, for hers was, she knew, a position much envied, especially by the white women.

Though Puella and her young cousin could not compensate her for her lack of children, Dorothea was overjoyed to have them in Mulgrave's huge and gloomy house. She liked Kite too, about whom she knew a great deal, thanks to Puella's confidences. Kite was a handsome contrast to the sweating Wentworth, who always treated Dorothea with a confused mixture of fascination and terror.

The swiftly burgeoning friendship between the two women soon led to Puella being freed from her odious leg-irons. Pompey was similarly freed, but his was a less happy situation. Perhaps because of the abuse to which he had been subjected aboard the *Enterprize*, or earlier in the barracoons on the banks of the Sherbro, Pompey proved a simple soul. He was destined to remain no more than a barefoot house-boy for the rest of his life, soon passing from Kite's ownership to that of Wentworth.

Kite sold him for a nominal guinea to his new acquaintance and Wentworth was pleased with the bargain. It was not long before Pompey appeared in St John's in a livery devised, Wentworth was fond of saying, by Mrs Robertson, wife to one of the garrison's officers, whom he described as 'a particular friend'. Dressed thus, Pompey was seen everywhere his master went, holding Wentworth's hat and cane until he had drunk his dish of chocolate with his hostess. Mulgrave's misanthropy encouraged Wentworth to undertake all business errands between the House of Mulgrave and its clientele, errands which Wentworth, with his talent for flattery and admiration, usually succeeded in turning to some form of personal advantage.

Mulgrave did not object to this and Wentworth, having learnt much of his demeanour from his benefactor, never overstepped the limits of propriety. But his own natural sociability, a not unaffected subservience and the adroitness of his mind when considering matters of trade, made him generally welcome, for Wentworth had learned the benefits of giving disinterested advice. When this invariably proved beneficial, his stock rose and he acted as a magnet for business, a fact of which Mulgrave was not insensible.

Though Kite's work was dull, his presence and competence freed Wentworth to pursue a greater volume of business. One afternoon, after Kite had laboured at his desk for a period of some six months and the year drew to its close – when, incongruously, the community of St John's prepared to celebrate Christmas in insufferable heat – he was summoned by Mulgrave.

He was reading newspapers brought that day in the newly arrived packet and he set the broadsheet down with a rustle, to regard Kite above clasped hands. Upon these he rested his chin. It was a sign, Kite had learned, that Mulgrave was in an unbending mood. "I wish you to dine with me this evening, Mr Kite. An hour after sunset, shall we say?"

"As you wish, sir." Kite gave a half bow and withdrew. Shortly afterwards Wentworth returned from his daily visit to the harbour and the ships on whose behalf Mulgrave and Company acted or in which they had an interest. He too was swiftly summoned and similarly invited.

"I am to dine with Mr Mulgrave this evening," Wentworth said when he returned from Mulgrave's private office, a satisfied smile on his face.

"So am I," Kite countered, amused that the news put Wentworth's nose out of joint.

"That's odd . . ." Wentworth frowned and added, "I've only ever known him ask us to dine before on one occasion." Wentworth nodded. "Oh yes, it was the night he told Cornford, your predecessor, that he had been informed that Cornford had been left three thousand pounds a year and that in view of this fact it would be in neither Cornford's nor Mulgrave and Company's interest that he should remain in the company's employment."

"I see. Then Mulgrave knew before the beneficiary," remarked Kite.

"Well, that's his way," Wentworth said as if it were sufficient explanation for Mulgrave's apparent prescience. Kite saw that the single precedent was working on Wentworth's innate anxiety.

"Well, Mr Wentworth," Kite said drily, preserving the social distinction Wentworth insisted on in the counting house, "I am certain *I* am not to be told I have come into three thousand a year."

"Nor me, damn it."

"Perhaps our master is about to reveal the fact that he knows *you* to already have that sum on your own account," Kite teased.

"Would that it was true . . ." Wentworth said awkwardly.

Kite laughed. "You are colouring up, sir, I have heard it to be true."

"Who told you?" Wentworth snapped, taking the bait.

"Miss Cunningham."

"You do not know Miss Cunningham, Kite – do you?"

Kite shook his head. "No, sir, I do not."

"Then you tease me?"

"I fear I do. Will you fight me?" Kite grinned, slipping off his stool and putting up his fists. "Come fight me, Mr Wentworth, 'tis damned tedious here today."

Wentworth waved Kite aside. "Get on with your work, Kite, making money is never tedious if you engage your whole intelligence upon it, to be sure."

Kite sighed. "That is true, Mr Wentworth."

"I shall see you at dinner, Kite."

On reaching the house Kite repaired at once to the wing generously set aside for his accommodation. Apprised of his arrival, Puella quickly appeared. She wore a simple gown made of scarlet cotton, such as might have been worn by the wife of a comfortable shopkeeper in Cockermouth. She ran to him, kissed him and, as he sank into a chair, knelt and removed his shoes.

"Puella, you are a wonder."

"You like some lemonade?"

He nodded and she ran off, to return a few moments later with a glass of the cordial. He took it, leaned back and she kneeled again at his feet. Absently he tousled her hair as he drained the glass, then he smacked his lips and she took the glass from his hand and set it upon an adjacent table before sitting on his lap. After kissing, he said, "Puella, I shall not be dining with you tonight."

"Oh, Kite, I cannot dine with not you."

"Without," Kite corrected.

"Without you. What you eat tonight?"

Kite shrugged. "I don't know what I shall eat, Puella, but I know with whom I shall eat whatever I do eat."

She tapped the end of his nose, which she regarded as a curiously aberrant and pert proboscis. It was her way of responding when he teased her. "Kite, you horrible!"

Kite smiled and said seriously, "I am dining with Mr Mulgrave and, Puella, I think he has something important to say to me, and to Mr Wentworth." He frowned. "Has Dorothea said anything about him being unwell? I mean sick?" he added hurriedly.

Puella shook her head and lowered her eyes. "No, Kite. Dorothea told me Mr Mulgrave was still good for her," and she whipped up the hem of her skirt and rubbed herself with a giggle.

Kite frowned. "Puella, you must not do that. It is not what a lady would do . . ."

Puella slipped from his lap and stood in front of him, her hands on her hips. "Puella is not a lady; Puella is a black whore . . ."

Kite was on his feet in an instant, one arm round her waist, the other across her mouth. He was horrified. "Puella! You are not to speak those words! Never!"

Puella smiled triumphantly up at him. "Come then, Kite, you be good for Puella . . ."

An hour later Kite walked the length of the veranda, his footfalls creaking the timbers, the warm night air filled with the loud chirrup of a myriad of cicadas. He found Mulgrave sitting alone in a cane chair, sipping lemonade.

"Sit down, Mr Kite." A black servant emerged from the shadows and set down a glass alongside Kite as he lowered himself into one of Mulgrave's extraordinary wicker chaises longues. They had hardly wished each other good health when Wentworth arrived, puffing dangerously and clearly discomfited to find his junior already ensconced with their host.

Wentworth lived above the counting house and found Kite's residence under Mulgrave's private roof a touch irksome. He had, Kite thought, expected some alteration in his circumstances when he acquired a black servant in the person of Pompey, and his anxiety that Kite would replace himself in Mulgrave's plans seemed to have revived in recent weeks.

Perhaps Wentworth knew something of what was to transpire that evening. After a few moments' conversation about the affairs of the day, they went in to eat. The meal was sparse, the wine good but limited and the conversation non-existent. Mulgrave seemed unaffected, but both Wentworth and Kite felt the suspense intolerable. As the servants drew the cloth and Mulgrave selected a cigar from a humidor, he indicated they might join him in a smoke or help themselves from a decanter of rum. Wentworth accepted both, Kite neither. Mulgrave raised his eyebrow and waved the servants out. Having drawn upon his cigar and sent a feather of blue smoke across the table so that the candle flames flickered, he leaned forward on his elbows. Sitting on his left, Kite stared at the way the candlelight etched Mulgrave's features. The man was handsome, in a long-faced and lugubrious fashion, his grey hair swept back over his head into a tight queue at the nape of his neck where it was severely clubbed in a ribbon as black at the suit he habitually wore.

The jagged furrow of the scar which seamed his face supported the widespread rumour that Mulgrave had fought a duel. His opponent's ball had disfigured Mulgrave's face; his own, it was said, had found a more effective target.

"Well, gentlemen," Mulgrave said in his low bass voice, as he secured the undivided attention of his young colleagues, "you will be wondering at the meaning of all this joyless conviviality." He looked at the two young men and Kite thought he saw in the dark eyes a sardonic sparkle. "From time to time in a man's life, there come moments when matters shift their ground. One such moment has come to me and therefore to you also." He turned to Wentworth with his slight smile. "You, Wentworth, I have always regarded as a protégé. It is true that you are a somewhat out-of-elbows fellow, always running and puffing, but you have been a faithful servant, and while I know that from time to time you have accumulated on your own account, you have never cheated me . . ."

Kite watched Wentworth suffer under the ruthless assessment that was, it was obvious, all too true. It made Wentworth's earlier protestations over his acquisition of capital rather amusing. At least, Kite reflected, in his own case he had neither enjoyed so long an acquaintance with Mr Mulgrave, nor had anything more than a modestly gainful employment from him.

"So, Wentworth, it is my intention to pass the whole of my business over to you once I have secured such capital as I personally require."

Wentworth's eyes opened wide and he half-gasped, then his expression collapsed, like a man about to burst into guffaws of mirth, or howl at terrible news. With a kind of strangled cry, Wentworth buried his head in his hands, and his shoulders shook so that he seemed shaken either by great mirth, or great grief. Mulgrave merely glanced at his protégé and went on steadily – like a ship dashing aside a wave, Kite thought irrelevantly.

"One does not live for ever, and I have an account elsewhere that I wish soon to settle in a private manner." Those few words, it was clear to Kite, were all they were ever either going to have by way of explanation, but this thought had scarcely struck Kite than Mulgrave was speaking of him.

"As for you, Kite, Captain Makepeace said of you that you were an unusual young man, gifted as a surgeon and capable, he thought, of many things. Yet you remain a dilemma. You have made no effort to even promulgate the fact that you were a surgeon. I find that strange, unless you have reasons for concealing the fact."

Kite leaned forward to speak, but Mulgrave simply raised a hand and he remained silent.

"Whatever the reason for your singular conduct in this matter, I have observed you to be the man of principle that Makepeace said you were. I have known Captain Makepeace a long time. Although given to bouts of drunkenness, in which he is in no wise unique, he is an able sea officer and was, when in command of a letter of marque in the last war, a successful privateer commander. As a slaver he is astute, taking good care of his charges, and is a man who makes his own luck. I therefore value his opinion and have decided not to wait unduly long before prosecuting my own private affairs in order to verify his judgement. In short, Mr Kite, beyond what you have already shown of yourself, I am taking you on trust."

Kite murmured his thanks, though he was apprehensive now, certain that whatever Mulgrave was about to propose would disturb the tranquillity of his present life.

"In six months or so, I intend to return to England. War seems certain and my departure would be sooner, but matters cannot simply be dropped like a stone. In the mean time, having seen you, Wentworth, in possession of my affairs here, both as my successor and my agent, it is my intention to take passage for Carolina and afterwards Philadelphia and New York. I shall personally have relinquished my interest in all my ships and vessels in the Antilles in your favour, Wentworth, and I am moreover prejudiced against placing my person at risk at so uncertain a time. I am unwilling to sail in any vessel other than one in which I have a perfect confidence." Mulgrave turned to Kite. "I am therefore resolved to purchase an armed schooner in your name, Mr Kite, and, placing the vessel at least under your management if you do not feel competent to take the command, to request that you have her ready for sea by the end of January. Once purchased she will become not merely your property, but your domicile. Other details we will discuss in the coming days and I shall devote sufficient time to concert matters with each of you." Mulgrave paused, allowing his words to sink in. Wentworth, overjoyed at his new-found wealth and already contemplating the means by which he could announce it to Antigua in general and Miss Cunningham in particular, had emerged from behind his hands, a look of stupefaction on his broad face that belied the industry of his mind.

Kite's shift in fortunes were less spectacular, though more profound. That the schooner would become his own was clear and, Kite divined, somehow congruous with the way in which Mulgrave conducted his affairs. Like Dorothea, Kite found himself bound to

Mulgrave in a fashion akin in some small way to that of moral servitude. Of course, Kite could destroy that trust at his own whim, perhaps with little economic effect, but he half-guessed that in this way Mulgrave subtly secured the bonds that bound to him those people he selected as beneficiaries.

When Kite returned to Puella that night he was both elated and disturbed by the news that Mulgrave had given him. He had known that his idyllic existence would not go on for ever, but he fretted over Puella's fate, as he fretted over that of his father and sister in the distant lakes and fells of Cumbria. He was not a natural nomad, not drawn to the existence that Makepeace and others accepted as a means to a distant and uncertain end. Moreover, fate was moving him again, and this movement was inexorably towards England, where he was still regarded as a murderer.

Puella was fast asleep, replete from their earlier lovemaking, but Kite was too stimulated by the events of the evening to lie quietly beside her. He retired to the adjacent room and, finding his long-neglected journal, he lit a candle, and found pen and ink. Opening the book he regarded the single sheet of paper that lay inside. It was a half-completed letter to his sister, Helen, and was dated some weeks earlier.

> As for me, I am Well, as I Hope you and Father both are. You will Learn from this that I am in the West Indies, where Talk of War with all its Uncertainties, Prompts me to Write. I should like you to Write to me at the Address of Mulgrave & Co, St John's, Antigua, telling me the State of your Health, together with that of our Father's. I will

But he had never finished the unsatisfactory letter, unsure what to say, or whether the recipient would welcome it. With a sigh, he now lifted it up and held it in the candle flame. The paper curled then flared up, finally falling as black ash. Blowing the charred remnant on to the floor he took up his pen, dipped it in the inkwell and held it poised over his journal.

"Kite . . ." Puella stood in the doorway. She was naked and the candlelight fell upon the familiar curves of her beautiful brown body.

"I think I soon have pickaninny."

# Nine

## The Departure

In the weeks that followed, Wentworth reminded Kite of the contented peasant in the fairy tale who, through his own endeavours and with a little help from some magic entity, succeeds in winning the king's daughter and half the kingdom. Not that Wentworth had yet won any fair hand in wedlock, but his prospects were set fair, for he had gained not half but almost the entire kingdom. Mulgrave's extraction of capital nevertheless left Wentworth in command of a substantial sum, despite the fact that the older man intended to retain an interest in the business. As for the business itself, this was to pass into Wentworth's control, Mulgrave relinquishing it with a single remark that the new owner would do well if he did not succumb to drink. Within days of Mulgrave's announcement, Kite had abandoned his desk and his indoor existence to resume his intimacy with ships. Mulgrave sent to him a seafaring man named Da Silva, a man of Portuguese blood who had served in British West Indiamen as an able seaman, as a gunner to Captain Makepeace aboard the privateer *Firedrake*, and as boatswain aboard a slaver. In his last ship, the Guineaman, Da Silva had voyaged between the Bight of Benin and Cuba, from Ngola and Ouidah to Brazil, and from Guinea to Jamaica and the Carolinas. There was little he did not know about the mariner's art.

It was Mulgrave's suggestion that Kite assumed the title and dignity of 'Captain', while he appointed Da Silva to the post of sailing master. Such an expedient would compensate for Kite's lack of experience, while not detracting from the advantages to be had from Da Silva's expertise. Da Silva accepted this arrangement with apparent contentment, unsurprisingly proving another person whose life Mulgrave had influenced. He had been paid off the slaver with nothing, the master and owner having cheated the crew and disappeared. On hearing of this infamy, Mulgrave had taken up the entire abandoned crew and found berths for them in other vessels. It was a small enough kindness, perhaps due more to preserving the people of St John's from the rapacity of two score of distressed and desperate men, but, being the man he was, it obligated Da Silva. Kite took an instant liking for the man, who was twice his age and half his height, yet possessed shoulders of an extraordinary width, a powerful chest and strong arms. Da Silva's legs were bent with rickets and his teeth were broken and caried, but his aquiline face bore a pair of fierce mustachios, which twitched when he smiled and his eyes sparkled with a relentless cheerfulness. Gold rings in his ears and a habitual bandanna gave him a piratical air.

Word soon went round St John's that this oddly assorted pair were in search of a ship, but Da Silva turned up on the second morning of their acquaintance with a pair of mules, a skin of wine and the idea that they should proceed to Willoughby, where he knew of a smart schooner with a reputation for speed and which mounted a dozen guns.

Such a diversion pleased Kite. It seemed in tune with the increasing tempo of life in Antigua, for every ship arriving from Britain brought worsening news and the outbreak of war with France was clearly imminent and preparations for the outbreak were made throughout the West Indies. The news sharpened Mulgrave's desire to be gone and, for the first time he betrayed a side of his character in contrast with his hitherto calm exterior. In traces of an irascible impatience, Kite saw signs of a man who might have been provoked to fight a duel, and might well have shot an opponent in cold blood. The thought reminded him of the accusations laid against himself; the past seemed to increasingly penetrate his consciousness as the nearness of his own departure approached.

A day or so later Kite found himself registered at the Custom House as the owner, in full, of all sixty-four parts of the Cuban-built armed schooner *Cacafuego*. On Da Silva translating the meaning from Spanish, Kite renamed her *Spitfire*. As he took possession of the vessel and they prepared to move her round to St John's, he recalled Wentworth's remark about the folly of owning a ship outright. Well, Mulgrave would underwrite the running of the vessel, Kite consoled himself, so his ownership was little more than a technicality.

Of more legal consequence was the document he had requested Mulgrave to have drawn up to free Puella as soon as he arrived back at St John's with the *Spitfire*. Freedom was conferred upon Puella a week before Kite and Da Silva considered the *Spitfire* would be finally ready for departure. Kite asked Dorothea to explain the meaning of freedom and to make clear to Puella that it would leave her to chose her future life. On the day appointed, Puella was dressed in a new English gown of pale blue silk. To this Dorothea added a broad-brimmed feathered hat which swept about Puella's features in a captivating aureole, throwing her striking features into sharp and distinguished relief.

Holding herself with that natural elegance that had first attracted Kite's eye, Kite led her from Mulgrave's carriage that had brought the two black women into town. Passing through the counting house, Kite and Puella ascended the steps into Mulgrave's gloomy office, where Mulgrave and his attorney, a Mr Garvey, along with Wentworth, had the document drawn up for the principals' and the witnesses' signatures.

Dorothea had secretly coached Puella, so that when Garvey pointed to the place she should make her mark, Puella wrote in a sure, round hand, *Puella Kite-Mulgrave*. Kite could scarce hide his astonishment, both at Puella's ability to write, and to the grand name she had taken. Mulgrave's calm acceptance of the news was clear evidence that he had connived at it. Signed by Kite and Puella, witnessed by Mulgrave and Wentworth, and finally sealed by Garvey, Kite handed the instrument of manumission to Puella.

"With this, Puella, we strike the last iron fetters from you."

Puella curtseyed as she had been taught, and said, "I thank you."

Kite, having bowed over her hand, pressed a kiss on her cheek. Still holding Puella's hand, Kite turned to Mulgrave. "Sir, while it was long my intention to manumit Puella, I cannot conceive of any circumstances in which I could have done so without your assistance. We are both most grateful."

Mulgrave smiled and shook his head dismissively. "Mr Garvey had the burden of the task," he said, stepping forward and taking Puella's hand from Kite. His dark eyes glittered with pleasure as bent and kissed it. Mulgrave was followed by Wentworth and Garvey. Dorothea clasped her tribal sister, then Mulgrave led the company to a table where wine and sweetmeats were laid out. Later, as Kite followed Dorothea, Puella and Mulgrave into the carriage to return to the house, Garvey pressed into his hand a second paper with the words, "Mr Mulgrave is a great benefactor, sir. A great benefactor."

Settling himself in the carriage and smiling at Puella, Kite broke the wafer as the black coachman whipped up the horses and they jerked forward. When he had read the short letter, he looked up at Mulgrave sitting opposite, beside Dorothea. Mulgrave stared steadfastly out of the window and Kite felt a great affection from the graven features of this strange, aloof man.

He had settled an annuity of two hundred pounds upon Puella.

The departure of the *Spitfire* was subject to a number of delays, but finally decided upon for Lady Day, 1756. By that time the threat of war was impinging increasingly upon trade in the West Indies, where a naval presence was increasingly felt. The passage of frigates and sloops in and out of English Harbour was no longer the desultory occasion it had been a few months earlier. Already the idlers inhabiting the waterfront of St John's, Willoughby, Falmouth and Parham had been swept up by a hot press sent in ship's boats from the naval establishment at English Harbour. Here they had been found enforced employment in the small Leeward Islands Squadron.

From the window of Mulgrave and Company's offices one morning, Kite and Mulgrave were regarding a naval sloop lying-to off St John's, her main topsail backed against the mast while she waited to escort the dozen snows, brigs and schooners just then slipping their moorings and warping out to sea. Mulgrave remarked drily, "Now we shall see how assiduous our naval Johnnies are, Kite, for they have to choose between the lucrative pursuit of prizes and the dull, sober and routine duty of convoy escort."

He turned to Kite. "It is not my intention to sail in convoy, Kite, and I know Da Silva has taken aboard some powder and shot."

"Indeed he has, sir. But he is concerned that the, er, naval Johnnies have requisitioned the best and left us with inferior powder, of which there is little enough. I had hoped to load more."

Mulgrave smiled. "There is a store of it at the house, along with a quantity of small arms, which you may place on board. On an island with so many plantations there is a steady demand for powder and shot, and occasionally for muskets."

The following morning Kite and Da Silva, with a dozen of their crew of free blacks, mulattoes and white riff-raff happily scooped up by the Portuguese sailing master before the Royal Navy's ardent young midshipmen and their gangs, followed an overgrown path up the hill behind Mulgrave's house to where a brick bomb-proof store lay hidden by thorn scrub. The unlocked door revealed a small arsenal. Sixty kegs of fine-milled black powder were carefully transferred to the *Spitfire*.

The schooner was by now lying in the harbour, her standing rigging set up a-tanto, her topsides gleaming under a fresh application of turpentine and rosin and with new canvas lying furled along her spars. Following the powder, forty stands of arms and a dozen bundles of cutlasses and boarding pikes were carried on board, so that apart from the dress of her officers and the absence of a naval pendant at her mainmast truck, there was little to distinguish the *Spitfire* from a man-of-war schooner.

By Lady Day, the financially significant date upon which the formalities of Mulgrave and Company's transforming itself into Mulgrave, Wentworth and Company were completed, the *Spitfire* lay ready to leave. Powder, shot and small arms had been followed on board by the packing cases, trunks and personal effects of Mulgrave, Dorothea, Puella and Kite. Late that afternoon, having gone ahead of the others, Kite welcomed Mulgrave and Dorothea on board. The quayside was crowded with well-wishers and the merely curious. The brilliant colours worn by the free black women were in stark contrast to the black carriages of the island's gentry drawn up along the strand, amid which Wentworth held impatient court. A foot patrol of the garrison had been sent by Major Robertson to provide a guard of honour as Mulgrave, long an institution in Antigua, courteously raised his black tricorne as he stepped aboard the *Spitfire*. Along the waterfront a respectful cheer rippled.

The sun set as the schooner was warped out across the harbour, heading for the open sea beyond. The western sky flushed red as the halliards were manned and the sails rose up the masts, pink in the evening light. As the *Spitfire* cleared the outer limits of St John's, an unshotted gun boomed out from her bow. The concussion rolled round the bay, echoing in a long diminuendo, but this was not quite Joseph Mulgrave's final valediction to the place where he had made his name and his fortune; he had one more surprise for the Antiguans.

Amid the reverberations of the gunshot a lesser explosion went unnoticed until the first flicker of fire was seen from the quayside, prompting a gasp from the crowd. Growing indistinct in the gathering twilight against the shoulder of its hill, Mulgrave's house began to burn. It was the one thing he had denied Wentworth, though he had sold his enslaved household servants to his successor, and they now carried out their old master's last order.

As the *Spitfire* stood out to sea, her sails filling to the gentle *terral*, Mulgrave stood rigid at the taffrail, hands clasped behind his back, staring astern at the flickering light that was soon all that could be seen of the island where he had spent the greater part of his life.

The wooden structure had caught fire quickly and, long before *Spitfire* had passed beyond the horizon, the house had burned to the ground. As the last sparks faded, Mulgrave turned forward and went below.

"Good night, Captain Kite," he said and Kite, standing next to Da Silva at the foot of the mainmast, noticed the catch in the elderly man's voice.

"Good night, sir."

Da Silva coughed in the darkness. "The Senhor is tired," he said.

# Part Three

## War

# Ten

## The Schooner

During the next year and a half, Kite and the *Spitfire* enjoyed a varied existence. For the first quarter of that period the schooner acted as Mulgrave's yacht as he coasted slowly towards New York, spending weeks at a time visiting business associates and acquaintances among the merchants and trading houses of Savannah, Charleston, Norfolk, Williamsburg, Annapolis and Philadelphia. Before their arrival in the Savannah River, *Spitfire* had passed the bastions of the Moro Castle and called at Havana before dropping her anchor in Jamaican waters off Kingston. But her visits to these ports had been brief, for Mulgrave had come down with fever, a sweating and shuddering illness accompanied by delirium that reminded Kite and Puella of the terrible plague aboard the *Enterprize*.

The cramped conditions aboard *Spitfire*, where the stern cabin had been neatly but not spaciously divided for the two establishments of Mulgrave and Kite, forced a greater intimacy between the two men. The latter learned that like Lorimoor, Mulgrave had long suffered recurrent bouts of this sweating sickness, for it was not the bloody yellow jack that laid him low. Moreover, the affliction was one of the reasons he had maintained such a private life in St John's, and its incurable nature had persuaded him to effectively adopt Wentworth as his heir. Fear of the disease explained his apparent parsimony as a host, his abstemiousness and his avoidance of the sun, when he conceived he was at most danger from suffering a feverish attack. He confided that he believed that if he returned to England, he would throw off the disease, claiming, to Kite's considerable surprise, that he believed the malady to be spread by the bites of mosquitoes.

"If the little demons bite me and bite you, they will be biting every poxed rascal in St John's," Mulgrave gasped in a lucid moment as Kite visited him one morning. "God knows what contagions they spread between us." He gestured at the net that was tented above his bed and that he had ordered Kite to sleep under while in St John's. Kite had assumed the kindness to simply enable him to sleep undisturbed by the irritation of insects, whether mosquitoes or ants,

113

or to avoid the more serious attentions of snakes and lizards. "You must always cover yourself with such a bed-tent, Kite, while in these warm and humid latitudes," he had insisted.

Kite stared astern through the windows at the brilliant sunlight dancing upon the blue sea. The schooner lifted easily to the waves and the coast of Cuba fell astern, misty in the heat haze. He watched a bird dip into the wake, which drew out as a thin attenuated roil of disturbed water marking the passage of *Spitfire*'s hull, gradually fading as the greater power of the wind-blown waves overrode the schooner's temporary influence. Surely it was a kind of allegory of their own tiny existences, Kite thought, as Mulgrave closed his eyes; this small disturbance of the world, to be smoothed over after their passing.

Dorothea tended Mulgrave assiduously, making him concoctions which, though they could not prevent the fever, brought it swiftly to its climax and eased its passing. "She is clever," Puella whispered, as though in awe of Dorothea whom she loved and revered, "she know many things and Mr Mulgrave know she know."

"*Knows*, Puella, she knows many things and Mr Mulgrave knows she knows . . ."

Puella dutifully repeated Kite's correction. She never resented these and accepted them from Kite, Dorothea or Mulgrave, and all three, almost as a matter of concerted policy, corrected not merely her grammar, but her accent and diction so that she enunciated Mulgrave's title of 'mister' as if English were her native tongue, never falling into the cruder distortions of the lingua franca of the Antilles. The only occasion she complained of her tutoring was when she overheard some barbarous English used by Da Silva. Puella failed to recognise the coarse and rapid speech of the polyglot seamen as English, which in truth it scarcely resembled, but she comprehended that Kite addressed Da Silva in English, and that Da Silva responded incorrectly, mirroring her own mistakes without correction. This irritated her.

"Why do you not speak with him about his corrections, Kite?"

"About his errors, you mean, Puella . . . Well, it does not greatly matter that Mr Da Silva does not speak good English. I understand him, as do Mr Mulgrave and Dorothea and all the men in the crew. Besides, he will not need to learn any more now, for he is too old."

Puella frowned. "You confuse me, Kite."

"No more than you do me, my Puella," Kite laughed, caressing her swelling belly.

Puella was delivered of a son in Charleston, so the infant boy was called Charles, then Joseph William after both his benefactor and his father. The boy was the colour of creamed coffee, with his mother's dark, lustrous eyes and his father's straight nose.

"He could pass for an Italian," Mulgrave murmured as he regarded the baby in his arms. He had asked Puella to let him hold the tiny bundle in a request that seemed so uncharacteristic that Puella looked first at Kite, before acceding. "You must acknowledge him as your own, my boy," Mulgrave added, looking up at Kite, who stood proudly by. Mulgrave's eyes glittered with half-suppressed tears.

"Of course, sir."

"Good. That is as it should be. Do not be distracted by these tedious social niceties that speak against our siring sons on the country . . ."

They had already encountered social ostracism in Savannah, where Mulgrave was asked to leave an assembly on account of Dorothea's presence on his arm. The pretensions of English colonial society in the Carolinas, he afterwards remarked, were in odd contrast to those of the eponymous king after whom the colony was named. That the very men who asked Mulgrave to leave all had black mistresses, several of which openly paraded in grand coaches, only blackened Mulgrave's mood. The hypocrisy of Antigua was muted by contrast, an attitude fostered by a few and thus far less widespread than in Savannah. Unlike St John's, where although many of the blacks seen about the town were slaves, and though the disembarkation of slaves from the arriving Guineamen reminded everyone of the enthralment of the vast majority of the black population of enforced immigrants, the atmosphere in Savannah seemed unduly repressive. "Here," Mulgrave thought, voicing his observation to Kite in one of their moments of increasing friendship as the voyage advanced, "even the slaves themselves resent Dorothea's good fortune. Is a black never to rise from the shackles of serfdom as we have done? Why, Kite, you and I know these people are capable of all that we are. That their villainous chieftains and kings sell them into our custody should enable us to liberate them by degrees. Of course there can be no swift, revolutionary change, it would invite only the most savage repression, and the white must change with the black even more profoundly, for he must give up and share his advantages . . ." Mulgrave trailed off and Kite suddenly saw him as an ageing man, left weakened by his last bout of fever.

"Have you always thought thus?" Kite asked.

Mulgrave gave his pallid smile and shook his head. "No, of course not, and had Dorothea not treated my first bout of fever I doubt that I should have ever done so. But a man in exile, reduced to a sweating shadow, has to rediscover much and in doing so often finds matters are not quite as he had formerly thought them."

"You were . . . exiled?" Kite tried to draw Mulgrave, but the older man divined his intention. "You know Kite, curiosity about many things is a great virtue, without it mankind would never have advanced, but curiosity about each other is often a great bar to advancement of any kind."

"I beg your pardon, sir," Kite apologised hurriedly, "I meant no offence . . ."

"None was taken, I assure you."

In the succeeding months, as Charlie was weaned and began his first tentative crawls across the cabin floor encouraged by Dorothea and Puella, Kite himself learned much. Although the grander elements of society in Savannah shunned them, Mulgrave's wealth and mercantile power assured him of welcome elsewhere. Kite frequently accompanied him on his quasi-social visits as he called upon those he had traded with over the years. In this way the two men heard of the military and naval disasters befalling British arms. In the north of America, all along the border with French Canada, French troops and their Indian allies, brilliantly directed by the Marquis de Montcalm, raided and harried, shooting and burning the settlers in the backwoods, raping the women and tomahawking the men, scalping indiscriminately and carrying off children to feed their barbarous and perverse appetites in the fastnesses of their forest lodges. This frisson of fear and loathing rippled down from the dense woods of the north to the marshes and pine barrens of the south, increasing the natural apprehension of the outnumbered whites at the overwhelming numerical superiority of the natives whom their own commercial rapacity brought into their colonial economies. Between red skin and black there lay only the distinction of colour, it was argued; what a red warrior did to the whites at Oswego or Fort William Henry, a black might do to the white of the Carolinas.

The British armies in North America proved powerless to stem this flood and seemed destined to emulate the fate of General Braddock. New York, Boston and the towns of New England were said to be overwhelmed with settlers seeking refuge from the horrors of the frontier. This situation was exacerbated by the perverse folly of the colonial assemblies, who refused to join forces in raising troops, or to cooperate in any way. Mulgrave, commenting upon this, said that if the French gained a foothold in any of the British colonies, the assembly of that colony would probably seek an accommodation with the enemy, in defiance of the legitimate right of the British Parliament in London to decide such matters. The signal failure of British arms to prevent the encroaching raids of the French and Indians, Mulgrave claimed it would be argued in the assemblies, effectively removed the right of the Houses of Parliament in London to consider themselves the superior government of the American colonies, since they could not defend their own extensive and extended borders.

In Europe the story was much the same, with Admiral Byng failing to relieve the British garrison of Minorca. This surrendered ignominiously to the French, whereupon Byng fell victim to the malice of the Duke of Newcastle's ministry, which had him shot. The charge of alleged cowardice was proved to the government's satisfaction by their own suppression of half of Byng's dispatch, which laid out his reasons for withdrawal. The execution shook British society and led to a political crisis. The outdated newspapers Kite and Mulgrave read reported defiant and scathing attacks by William Pitt, and eventually contained the news that Pitt had consented to join a ministry if the direction of the war was placed in his hands. That the King hated Pitt only seemed to the two distant observers to play into the hands of the enemy, chief among which was France, though Russia and Austria were in the field against Britain's Continental ally, Prussia.

Pitt's position was unstable and, as the French overran King George's native electorate of Hanover, Frederick II suffered a humiliating defeat in Bohemia at Kolin. The heavy subsidies Britain paid to the Prussian monarch now seemed an inordinate waste and the national debt rose accordingly.

But in this same period, Kite learned that war, though it interferes with trade, prospers traders. Prices rose and Wentworth's letters spoke of great opportunities less, and of profitable deals more often. Nor were Mulgrave and Kite detached from this profiteering. Although the *Spitfire*'s voyage north was leisurely, consolidating the position of Mulgrave, Wentworth and Company as it progressed, she carried cargoes between her ports of call. These were often valuables, specie or bullion, payments placed on deposit and destined for other trading houses along the coast, or destined for the banks of Philadelphia, underwritten and guaranteed by Mulgrave's signature. Armed, fast and well manned as she was, *Spitfire* attracted this monetary traffic as merchant houses sought to salt away their gains before the impact of hostilities limited their freedom. Mulgrave's name for probity, and the fearsome appearance of the *Spitfire*'s crew, added to her growing reputation, which was discreetly spread among the commercial fraternity, so that she was almost as laden as a Spanish treasure ship. Not one shipment was accepted without an agreed percentage, deductible on safe delivery, and payable to 'the Said Master and Owner, and the Said Assigns of the Schooner *Spitfire* of St John's in the Island of Antigua'.

And as Mulgrave paid his respectful farewells to men he had often previously known only by the bond inherent in their signatures, he introduced them to 'the Said Master and Owner' of the *Spitfire*. Kite's reputation was enhanced by specious rumours that he had saved an entire slaver from the yellow jack, while his vessel was known to have been a fearsome privateer. This combination seemed to promise the smile of fortune upon the handsome young man's enterprises, a perception given greater weight by the endorsement of so shrewd and respected a man as Mulgrave.

For Kite, the progress northward had a great charm. The intensity of his love affair with Puella, the birth of his son, the fruitful association with the relaxing Mulgrave and his friendship with Dorothea, indeed the entire domestic atmosphere that prevailed aboard *Spitfire* in her guise as a private yacht, conferred upon him a period of almost blissful happiness. At the time he was unaware that, in their prolonged visits, he was establishing relationships with trading houses and merchants that he would afterwards prize; but he was aware of his growing mastery of all aspects of his adopted profession of ship-master, developing what Da Silva acknowledged was a hidden ability far outweighing his former clumsy attempts at surgery. Where this aptitude had come from, he could not guess, for he had never been told that his mother had been a Manx woman and her family had for generations fished the Irish Sea about the Isle of Man.

His basic understanding of navigation was brought to a practical competence by frequent practice and, unlike many masters formally but imperfectly instructed in the art, he never lost his sense of caution in conducting his ship. In mastering these skills he was helped not only by Da Silva, but by the curious loyalty of his oddly assorted crew. To man the *Spitfire*, the Portuguese sailing master had brought together some forty men whose paths had never previously crossed, other than from them being part of the casual, unemployed fraternity of the waterfront. They had never previously sailed together, nor shared a common place of origin, and this prevented them forming cliques, allowing their present common experiences to swiftly weld them together into an efficient crew. Da Silva had ensured they were well paid, and that they enjoyed a sufficiency of leisure in port so that the sight of Puella and Dorothea failed to stir them to resentment. Otherwise, Da Silva kept them hard at work. In port they toiled at cargo-handling or the general maintenance that *Spitfire* demanded and Mulgrave could underwrite; at sea, in the gruelling grind of watch-keeping. Nor was opportunity neglected to remind them frequently that it was wartime, and that their present employment might keep them from the clutches of the press gangs of the Royal Navy if they could evade trouble until they had obtained exemptions.

*     *     *

On their arrival at New York, Mulgrave disembarked. It had been his intention to cross the Atlantic in *Spitfire*, but at New York a number of considerations persuaded him to change his mind. The first grew out of his friendship for Kite, who proved to be a young man of great promise. Not only had Kite shown his ability as a ship-master in practical terms, but he had also demonstrated a firm grasp of the principles of commerce and, in their dealing with several American houses, had demonstrated an originality and independence of mind that suggested he would prosper on his own account. In particular, Kite had used his own money, mostly derived from his unspent pay-off from the *Enterprize*, to undertake a private speculation on a quantity of crocodile skins which he sold in Philadelphia at a profit. Mulgrave was therefore reluctant to deprive him of the opportunities thus offered by ordering the *Spitfire* to England, a reluctance that also took into consideration another factor.

One evening, on their passage from Annapolis to Philadelphia, when the *Spitfire* lay becalmed and rolling in a sluggish swell that promised a blow later, the two men had been enjoying a cigar after dinner. The women had withdrawn, as was their custom, to play with Charlie before he was settled to sleep, leaving the two men to discuss the completion of the voyage and their future plans.

"On completion of your affairs in New York," Kite said, uneasy about his return to his native land, "I know it to be your intention to sail for England, sir, so may I ask what port you would consider it best to make for?"

"Does it matter?" Mulgrave asked absently.

Kite shrugged, affecting a disinterest he was far from feeling. "Only insofar as I apprehend that a passage to London is better made with a landfall to the southward, whereas a passage to Liverpool is otherwise, and with the probability of French ships on the lookout, I take it they will congregate in greater numbers between the Caskets and the Wight than off Malin Head."

"You have been studying your charts, Kite. Where did you get them?"

"From a merchant in Charleston."

"Rawllings?"

"No, sir, Bigsby, he was but newly out from Bristol, where the slave trade is much fallen off."

"The war, I suppose . . ."

"Yes, and the fierce competition of Liverpool Guineamen, who run for lower wages than the Bristol ships."

"I see." Mulgrave paused. "Well, then, you recommend Liverpool as entailing less risk, I assume."

"The matter is yours to decide, sir," Kite replied, aware that much might depend upon Mulgrave's decision. Now he had Puella and Charlie to consider and in England he was still regarded as a murderer. "Though I should point out that despite the armament of our guns we have not fired them in anger and that one hopes it will never be necessary . . ."

"Amen to that," broke in Mulgrave, "but we cannot build assumptions on that score . . . That reminds me, we must obtain a letter of marque in either Philadelphia or New York. I was intending to wait until we arrived in England, but we need its protection to avoid our crew being poached by some damned over-zealous Johnny in an under-manned frigate off the Lizard . . ."

"So you're for London?" Kite asked quickly, visualising a passage up the Channel.

"Or Liverpool," countered Mulgrave swiftly. Leaning forward he ground out his cigar. As the last curl of smoke rose up from the plate, Mulgrave looked up at Kite. "I have never asked you, Kite, for I am not curious – you know my views on personal curiosity – but you have never spoken with any enthusiasm for England. Even now, I do not detect any great eagerness in your desire to return home. Do *you* have any preference whether I should land by way of Liverpool, London, Bristol or Falmouth?" Mulgrave paused a moment and then asked, "Tell me, would you rather perhaps remain here, on the American coast, or in the Antilles?"

Mulgrave sat back and Kite, his heart beating, responded. "Sir, I cannot at this moment tell you what I should perhaps have told you long ago . . ."

Mulgrave held up his hand. "I do not want to know anything about your personal affairs, Kite, life is too short and perilous and whatever mischief lies in the past, I have known you long enough to trust you. Only do me the honour of answering my question with an honest answer."

"Well, sir, I should like to go home, but for the present I cannot. If, however, I could prevail upon you to undertake one small favour in my interest, that of conveying privately a letter to my sister, matters may yet resolve themselves."

"That seems a trivial enough request, to which I can agree without reservation."

"It would ease my mind considerably, sir." ·

"Consider it done. There is, however, a favour which I must ask of you in return and which is another consideration persuading me to leave you and the schooner here, in the Americas. The present war makes a passage to England hazardous and to sail in this vessel, whether to Liverpool or London, might prove a risky or even a fatal enterprise. I am content, therefore, to take passage under convoy, perhaps in a man-of-war, if one can be found in New York. But I cannot take Dorothea. I am an old man and my health is failing; while the English air may cure my fevers, they will be otherwise to Dorothea, who frets during the rains in Antigua and complains constantly that our present northing is proving detrimental to her. Her culture and traditions belong in the tropics, don't you see, Kite; England would, I greatly fear, be fatal to her . . ." Mulgrave paused, then admitted frankly, "Besides, I have the impediment of another woman in England: my wife. She is still alive and I must provide for her old age. Not that I have quite failed to provide for her, despite her infidelities. Moreover, I doubt that I shall live long and leaving Dorothea on her own in England, at the mercy of rapacious relatives as well as the merciless climate, would be a cruelty I cannot contemplate."

"What would you have me do, sir?" Kite asked, awed by the confidence and the explanation that, were it known of in St John's, would stop the speculation of a whole generation.

"Keep always your own counsel, and ally yourself with no party. Find yourself a place, Kite, and build yourself a house from where, with your youth and wealth, you can command your own destiny. There, take Dorothea under your protection, she will be a companion to Puella and an undeniable asset." Mulgrave smiled. "And thereby please an old man."

Two months later, one evening some time after their arrival in New York following a passage of boisterous weather that had kept them at sea, Kite was summoned by way of a note brought by a boy from the tavern where Mulgrave had appointed their rendezvous.

*Come at Once without any Mention of myself. It is a matter of Business,* the note read, *but if you are Compelled to make known your Absence, say that an Accident has Occurred to me.* Kite knew Mulgrave well enough to perceive the man did not want news of the summons getting to Dorothea and could guess its meaning. He was right. Mulgrave sat in a private room; he was dressed in travelling clothes, booted and with a new cloak on the bench beside him. On the floor stood his portmanteau.

"We must say good-bye, Kite, but you have to write a letter for me to carry and I should be obliged if you would attend to it now." Mulgrave indicated pen, ink and paper on the table before him. His tone was as cold as when they had first met; this was indeed a business meeting, the abrupt conclusion of their partnership. Only the working of Mulgrave's face showed the emotion he was under.

Under the circumstances, Kite had some trouble writing his long-meditated but oft-postponed letter to his sister Helen. Now the time and manner of its doing were forced upon him, he made a poor job of it. Hurriedly he completed and folded it, adding the superscription and handing it to Mulgrave, who immediately stood up.

"There is a frigate leaving tonight with dispatches; the captain has kindly undertaken to give me a passage if I serve as a volunteer. I believe," Mulgrave added ironically, "my status lies somewhere above a midshipman and below a lieutenant. Tell Dorothea that I have gone to visit a ship in the harbour and that the boat was upset; she will believe you, having always feared such a thing. Sometimes these women have dreams that they believe to foretell the future . . ." Mulgrave smiled sardonically. "So, let matters fall out in that wise. She will not argue and there will be no corpse to bury or to grieve over. I am sorry to burden you with this piece of theatre."

Kite shook his head. "It is the least I can do, though I shall grieve your departure with Dorothea."

"You have a foolishly kind heart, Kite." Mulgrave looked at his watch and held out his hand. "If this war goes ill, as it seems it must, you may have to come home yourself, but in the meantime, I wish you well."

Just then a young man in naval uniform, the white patches of a midshipman on his collar, came into the room. "Mr Mulgrave?" he asked, looking from one to another of them.

"I am he," said Mulgrave.

"Henry Hope, at your service, sir." The midshipman gave a clumsy bow. "I have a boat at your disposal, but must urge you to hasten, sir. Captain Lasham is eager to get under weigh."

Mulgrave stood up and Kite rose with him. "Sir, you will send us word of your whereabouts?" he asked anxiously. "If and when I come home, I should like to pay my respects."

Mulgrave smiled and nodded. "Of course, Kite. Wentworth is your man. He will know my whereabouts. Recall I still retain an interest in the company."

"Of course." Kite felt stupid; events had moved too fast. How could he tell Dorothea? She would take it extremely ill.

"Goodbye, Kite." They shook hands.

"Goodbye, sir . . ." And Kite was left alone in the room as Mulgrave followed the midshipman out into the dark wintry night.

Dorothea was inconsolable and Kite sailed south for the sun and the warmth of the Antilles, bound for Antigua. The *Spitfire* bore a cargo of manufactured goods, New York gowns made 'according to the latest London fashions', wine and, despite the war, a small quantity of brandy. The schooner lay a month in St John's, a month during which Charlie first called for his mama, Wentworth bought the consignment of gowns, Da Silva bought a second schooner and Kite made plans for building a house. Between them, Kite and Wentworth debated ways of expanding their trade and, in due course, having rented a dwelling for his women and the boy, Kite sailed on the first of several voyages between Antigua, Jamaica and the Carolinas. He refused to make another Guinea voyage himself, partly from fear of contracting yellow jack and partly out of disgust for the trade, but he transhipped slaves between the islands, and bore cargoes of African manioc, camwood and scrivelloes to the American colonies.

Although French men-of-war and corsairs were at sea and active among the islands, Kite's now legendary luck held. They were chased several times, but such was the clean state of *Spitfire*'s bottom and the skill of her master and crew that the schooner escaped without having to fire a gun in her defence. Privately Kite grew anxious that when his luck ran out, as he felt sure it would, he would fail to live up to the valorous expectations of others. Moreover he was plagued by fears of being found a coward in the face of the enemy.

This feeling was encouraged by a stream of tales of French successes, stories which underwrote the creeping conviction of the inevitability of defeat. Ships with which they were familiar were captured by the enemy's corsairs and carried into French ports as prizes to the privateers now operating out of Guadeloupe and Martinique to the south of them. Meanwhile the main business of the war continued badly for the British. During the succeeding summer the capture of the French naval base of Louisbourg, on Cape Breton Island, though it had been successfully carried out in the last war by a handful of American colonists, was abandoned. The British fleet bound for the Gulf of St Lawrence had been delayed by contrary winds which in turn allowed the French to slip reinforcements across the Atlantic, but this did not excuse the fact that the matter was bungled. The *New York Gazette* railed that 1757 was 'a year of the most dishonour to the Crown, of the most detriment to the subject, and of the most disgrace to the nation'.

But the patient strategies of the remarkable Pitt, now re-established in government and with the conduct of the war in his capable hands, were beginning to tell. A story circulated from the naval ships refitting in English Harbour told of an admiral who confronted Pitt with the impossibility of his instructions. Pitt, it was laughingly recounted, had discomfited the admiral. Standing up to lean on his crutches, Pitt revealed his bandaged feet, grossly swollen by gout. "I *walk* upon impossibilities, sir," the minister was reputed to have said, whereupon the humiliated admiral left to obey his orders. Such yarns bolstered morale, coming as they did from sea officers, of which there were an increasing number in the island. The young lieutenants of the Royal Navy seen at assemblies in St John's seemed unaffected by the disasters raining down upon their colleagues in the army. At these same assemblies, local cynics marvelled at, and repeated the accuracy of Voltaire's alleged comment upon Byng's execution. "The English," the Frenchman was said to have remarked, "shoot an admiral from time to time, to encourage the others." Whatever the truth of this reported witticism, reinforcing cruisers augmented the Leeward Islands Squadron, and word began to circulate that the French could not long be left in possession of their West Indian islands. With every man present his own master of strategy and tactics, opinions were voiced as to the best method of wresting from them Guadeloupe, Martinique, St Lucia and Marie Galante.

"By Heaven," remarked Wentworth, rubbing his hands and discussing this matter over chocolate the following morning in the quayside office of Mulgrave, Wentworth and Company with a bunch of cronies, "think, gentlemen, what opportunities would be laid open to us with the French trade stopped!"

Then came news, by a schooner from Barbados which had had a brush with corsairs from St Lucia, that a fleet from England had arrived in the Windward Islands. The war in the West Indies was no longer to be a matter of mosquito bites, of enemy corsairs seizing British and colonial merchant vessels, or of British privateers retaliating by snapping up French inter-island traffic. Though British naval squadrons were maintained in the Antilles to protect trade and offer convoy, a major squadron had not yet made its appearance in the Caribbean Sea. In Antigua the news spread like wildfire.

Kite heard of it shortly after *Spitfire*'s anchor was dropped in the clear water of St John's and warps were run ashore. They had endured a chase for three days and he was dog-tired and wanted only to see Puella and his son before taking to his bed. Dorothea greeted him; tears poured down her cheeks and the exhausted Kite at first unkindly attributed her misery to yet another outburst of grief at the loss of Mulgrave. He had learned that the black and mulatto women set great store by what he thought of as dreams, but which they claimed to be the portentous visitations of spirits. Kite had seen them in trances and knew the contempt many of his fellow whites had for such 'primitive' behaviour, but his own intimacy with Dorothea had persuaded him that she did indeed possess powers of perception that passed his own understanding. Now, tired yet eager to see Charlie and Puella, supposing that Dorothea had had one of her spirit-trances, but irritated by her suddenly clinging to him, Kite took her shoulders and pushed her ungently away.

"Dorothea, I beseech you . . ."

"Mr Kite, oh, Mr Kite, Charlie is dead."

# Eleven

## The Attack

*Providence reached out its Cold Hand and Grasped my Very Heart*, Kite wrote of the death of Charlie, before he had to return to the affairs of men and could confide only to the blank pages of his journal. The keening and wailing of Puella and Dorothea had been terrible, their unhappiness at the Christian burial given to the little boy only compounding their grief. In his own sense of loss, Kite relived the personal horror of the death of his mother and, more shocking, felt the rebuke of fate at his former indifference to the grief of the blacks aboard the *Enterprize*. The extent to which the conditions aboard the Guineaman had hardened him, and the detachment he had felt from the Negroes as human beings, almost crushed him as he shared Puella's agony in those first few days. Though he wept when alone at night, after an exhausted Puella had fallen asleep, and though he smudged the pages of his journal with his tears, he was dry-eyed in her presence, a circumstance she failed to understand. It caused the first rift between them, for in grief Kite possessed no superiority over his dead child's mother and she beat his chest, her anger spilling from her in all the fulsome vituperation of her native tongue.

She slipped easily into this, abetted by Dorothea, who now viewed Kite with suspicion as a malign influence and not the natural heir of Joseph Mulgrave. Dorothea herself had seen things, and knew things that the white people could neither understand not believe. That her visions and visitations were utterly convincing to her only served to underline the gulf that existed between the white man and his black mistress. Kite and Puella could never be happy, and the loss of Charlie only served to emphasise the displeasure of the spirits. Though she was a product of interbreeding, Dorothea's strong belief in the spirits had grown from the childhood spent amid the black slaves of a plantation; this had produced instincts that were only distantly comparable with Kite's vague meanderings about 'the cold grasp of providence'. Both might have arisen from primeval fears, but the former was deemed primitive while the other had the sanction

125

of the assumption of superiority, and the demonstrable authority of overwhelming power.

Though Dorothea had submitted to her return to St John's in the train of her new protector, Captain William Kite, she had lost everything in the disappearance of Mulgrave. Her status, her house, her reason for living, had vanished in the night, caught up in the shadows of Joseph Mulgrave's cloak. She had seen that cloak only a few times aboard the *Spitfire*, for Mulgrave had bought it in Annapolis to combat the cooler air of the north, but she had seen its shadow several times since; in fact she knew now that Kite had not told her the truth, though she did not hold him a liar, for he may have himself believed what he had told her.

For her own part, Dorothea knew, like the disciples of the white man's Jesus-god, that her master and lover had not died in New York, but still lived. Or so she thought, until the night that little Charlie died. On that evening, as Kite crowded on sail to outrun a French privateer schooner from Marie Galante, Dorothea had heard the faint but memorable footfall of Mulgrave and, with a cry of joy, had leapt up expecting his embrace. So excited had she been, so certain that at last he was to return to her, that she ran quickly into the hall of the rented house, only to see the shadow of his cloak as he turned the corner of the stairs.

Dorothea rushed after him, to see the dark shape enter the bedroom in which little Charlie's cot lay. But it was not the Mulgrave whom Dorothea loved who turned at her intrusion; it was a Mulgrave with the dead white features of a drowned corpse, and he vanished before her eyes, taking with him the last breath of the little boy.

All this Dorothea told Puella, and all this was held to be the fault of Kite. Kite was a powerful man and Dorothea knew the white men cheated each other in business. Many times Mulgrave had explained to her with a wry smile the crooked transactions of his fellow traders in the Antilles; always he outwitted them, though she rarely understood how, only that he was invariably successful. Now, she thought, Mulgrave had been in some way outwitted by Kite. She had convinced herself that Kite had managed to abandon Mulgrave in New York. Perhaps, she excitedly argued to the receptive Puella, it had been Kite who had had the house burned; it would have been quite in character for Mulgrave to have said nothing, she claimed. Now Mulgrave, bereft and left far behind without Dorothea's support, had died. Even Dorothea's long-held conviction that her benefactor would finally drown seemed quite reconcilable with this imagined but convincing scenario. The vastness of the ocean and the complex geography of New York had convinced her that drowning was a not improbable fate for a man delirious from a sudden recurrence of his malaria. But such an impressive and convincing fulfilment of her prophetic visions had little impact on Puella.

For Puella, Kite was revealed as possessing those underlying vices of all white men: an insatiable greed and an indifference to the death of others.

For a week Kite attempted to comfort the grieving Puella. To him the death was at first a mystery; he imperfectly grasped Dorothea's garbled account, only registering the extent of her ridiculous superstition that Mulgrave had taken the spirit of Charlie out of some misplaced desire for revenge. Dorothea's references to the burning of the house made no sense, and for a while Kite thought the mulatto woman was deranged. Wrapped in his own distress he was unintentionally unkind and Dorothea noted his contempt; it only fuelled her misconceptions.

Mrs Robertson, whose attempts at offering consolation were largely motivated by a desire for the handsome young sea-captain at this vulnerable and pliant moment, did explain to him that infantile asphyxia was not unknown. That she added it was particularly so among children of mixed blood was pure mischief, intended to persuade the object of her scandalous lust that consolation and a greater satisfaction lay in her own embrace. Her visit failed to reconcile Kite to the loss of his son and only hurt Puella with its sinister suggestion of infidelity, for while Kite knew nothing of either Mrs Robertson's itch or her reputation, Puella was well aware of both. As for Mrs Robertson, she took back to her teatime cronies the intelligence that Captain Kite was a most sensitive young man who was still under the spell of 'that nigger witch'. With this demeaning opprobrium the garrison wives unconsciously acknowledged the universal beauty of the young African woman and Mrs Robertson hid the extent of her private disappointment.

But Puella's appearance in some respects justified this contemptuous description. She neglected herself, she went half-naked and unkempt about the house, she crouched in dark corners as she had once quailed in Kite's cabin aboard the *Enterprize*. Kite tried to draw her out, but after the first tender and consoling embraces of his return, Dorothea's words poisoned her against him and she shunned him with mounting passion. At first he merely thought that Puella's hostility was a passing manifestation of grief. She could not, Kite reasoned with himself, understand the notion of 'infantile asphyxia' and therefore the apparently inexplicable death must, in terms that Puella understood, lie within the malicious province of her pantheistic spirit world. She would come round in due course,

Kite felt sure; after all, the blacks lived close to death and had their pickaninnies by the dozen.

But Puella did not come round. Charlie had been for her something wonderful, something unique, joining her to the remarkable white man she had come close to idolising, as Dorothea had idolised Mulgrave. Bereft of children herself, Dorothea had told her the importance the white man vested in breeding a son, and that one son was better than many, for he would be a rich and powerful man, inheriting all his father's wealth. Moreover, despite the fact that the white men were indiscriminate as to where they rutted, their first wives were considered superior to all others and, even when they never shared their beds, they remained secure. The position of a first wife was assured, even when they were black. This assertion Dorothea based upon a lifetime's familiarity with the society of the Antilles and the promises made by Mulgrave. She had heard it was not the case in England, but there was no sun in England and it was a very different place to the islands.

Kite tolerated Puella's raging for a week then, one morning, he found her keening in a corner of the withdrawing room. She seemed quiescent, more as she had been on their first encounter, frightened, hurt and lonely. He knelt as he had once done aboard the slaver, and put out his hand. She bit it.

Kite recoiled with a cry of pain and astonishment. A moment later she was upon him, clawing and biting so that he had to strike her across her cheek with the flat of his hand. She reeled back and, wiping the back of one hand beneath her nose, displayed the stream of blood running down over her lips.

Kite was overwhelmed by shame and shook his head, stepping forward, his arms outstretched, uttering words of endearment. But Puella was gone, to hide behind a locked door. There she remained for two days, only taking food from Dorothea, whose expression of reproach haunted Kite like a spectre. When on the third day she refused to emerge or to speak to Kite, he resolved to return to sea without delay.

Word had come in that three ships from Falmouth and one from St John's had been taken by French corsairs. The news that several prominent St John's owners were abandoning trade, obtaining letters of marque from the governor and converting their vessels to privateers, appealed to Kite's mood. Consulting Wentworth, he put the matter in train with Garvey, the attorney. Then that same afternoon a message came overland from English Harbour. A Lieutenant Corrie of the hired cutter *Hawk* had arrived there from Guadeloupe. A British force consisting of six thousand soldiers under Major-General Thomas Hopson had some time since arrived from England. The naval squadron escorting them had combined with that of Commodore Moore at Barbados and the expedition had attacked Martinique. The attack had failed and Moore and Hopson had withdrawn to transfer their attentions to Guadeloupe. The ships' guns and the mortars of the bomb-vessels had bombarded Fort Royal on Basse Terre, silencing its guns, driving the garrison inland and setting fire to the adjacent town, where the year's harvest of sugar and rum burned furiously. Moore's ships had also bombarded and set afire Pointe-à-Pitre, the port on Grande Terre used principally by the enemy's corsairs, but by now fever and heat-stroke were seriously reducing the numbers of the unacclimatised troops. It had already killed the elderly and already ailing Hopson. The general's successor, Colonel Barrington, was now asking the colonists in Antigua to rally to the colours.

To Kite the opportunity seemed Heaven-sent. Privately, his evasion of French privateers by simply outrunning them might have enhanced his reputation and that of his speedy ship among the traders who had no wish to lose their valuable cargoes to the enemy, but not having exchanged so much as a distant shot with the French, not testing his mettle in battle, had secretly irked him. But now his son was dead and his love was repudiated. With, as he put it, the cold grasp of providence about his heart, he was indifferent to anything. He recalled Makepeace's defiant philosophy and heard it as a war cry; he was among the first to volunteer his services.

But Lieutenant Corrie brought other news and with it the whiff of disaster, for having appealed to the patriotism of the islanders, he now required preparations for the reception of six hundred sick soldiers. These, it was quickly rumoured, were but the worst afflicted; the real number approached two thousand, almost a third of the troops involved. The sick arrived in Antigua the following day, borne in two transports. Kite had spent the night aboard *Spitfire*, passing word among his crew that he wished them to muster that morning. Da Silva's ship was in port and he rejoined his old commander, "While we settle this bloody business," he said, shaking Kite's hand and offering Kite his condolences upon the death of Charlie.

That evening, several score of gentlemen-volunteers had mustered at Wentworth's premises where Mr Garvey appeared, offering to act as executor should any of them fall during the expedition. Though this might advance the glory of their country, several of the young bucks withdrew, declining to draw up their wills under Garvey's supervision.

"They prefer," remarked the son of a wealthy planter named Henry

Ranald, "to stick the sword of lust into their own property, than the sword of steel into King Louis's." The remaining men, laughing at this crude bravado, agreed to ship aboard *Spitfire* and the following morning they were at sea, stretching down towards the distant twin peaks of Guadeloupe.

The French West Indian possession of Guadeloupe consisted of two large islands so closely situated that the narrow strait between them was called merely 'the Salt River'. To the north-east lay Grande Terre, with Point-à-Pitre at the southern end of the debouchement of the Salt River into the great bay enclosed by the mountainous arms of the two islands. To the south-west lay the second island, divided into two areas by a mountainous spine running from north to south. On the eastern side of the mountains and opposite Point-à-Pitre, lay Cabes Terre; on the western was Basse Terre, with the island's principal town of that name at its southern extremity. Offshore, a few miles to the east of Basse Terre town, lay a cluster of small islands making up Les Isles des Saintes, beyond which, further to the east, rose Marie Galante. Off the north-east coast of Grande Terre was the smaller island of La Desirade, while off its narrow eastern point, the Pointe des Châteaux, between it and Marie Galante, lay the small island of Petite Terre.

The islands of Guadeloupe came in sight two mornings later, rising from the sea in the first light of the day like a firmly delineated cloud, taking on more substance as *Spitfire* approached and the sun burned the clinging mist out of the river valleys. The gentlemen-volunteers pressed forward, eager to see the goal that would soon, they felt certain, pass into the hands of the British and expose itself for exploitation by themselves, the legitimate heirs, they conceived, to the riches of the Leeward Islands. Guadeloupe they knew as far wealthier a territory than Martinique, an island from which it was said that sugar and rum worth more than the equivalent of one million pounds sterling were sent annually to France. There were, moreover, a hundred and fifty thousand slaves working on the plantations, a measure of Guadeloupe's value more readily comprehended by these young and eager men, for whom the figure of one million was beyond imagination.

Capture would divert some of this wealth their way, while the extirpation of the nests of corsairs at Point-à-Pitre and Marie Galante would release trade from the bondage of convoy. Even while they took passage in his ship and enjoyed his hospitality, many sniggered that such a change in their fortunes would 'cut the canter of Captain Kite', whose legendary luck while not sailing under convoy tended to create high freight rates for cargoes shifted by the *Spitfire*. Not that they greatly resented Kite personally, but there was an orthodox clique that suggested his taking a blackamoor woman to wife, while it might be condoned by fusty old Mulgrave, did not reflect well upon the sensibilities of younger gentlemen.

Gossiping in this wise, as the mountainous terrain of Guadeloupe grew in detail, pleasantly mantled from the sea by the brilliant green of lush tropical vegetation, they doubled Pointe des Châteaux and stood to the westward, along the southern coast of Grande Terre before a fair wind. Ahead of them rose the range of mountains bisecting Basse Terre and Cabes Terre, and tucked under the guns of Fort Louis, the toehold Barrington's reduced force had on the island, lay what appeared to be a squadron of British naval ships of war.

"So you gentlemen are from Antigua," Colonel Darrington, temporarily a general in the field, resplendent in his scarlet coat, the gorget of his commissioned rank gleaming at his throat, sat at a table in Fort Louis with one leg propped up on a stool. It was swollen with gout, and twitched curiously, each nervous tremor sending a shadow of pain across Barrington's perspiring features. He wiped his mouth and regarded Kite and Ranald, who had been deputed to wait upon the army commander.

"Have any of you any knowledge of the interior?"

"I have, sir. Before the war I was frequently here."

"But have you a knowledge of the *interior*, Mr Ranald? I am not interested in whether you drank tea with a French planter in Basse Terre or here, or anywhere else for that matter." Barrington exchanged glances with the young captain of foot who had attended Kite and Ranald on their visit.

"The coastal plains, where they are under cultivation, are clear, though the sugar canes can easily conceal a man. Otherwise it is rugged, sir, the higher ground split by ravines and watercourses, and covered with dense vegetation. You could hold up a column and harry troops trying to make progress through such a wilderness."

Barrington nodded. "So we discovered a few weeks ago," he remarked drily.

"You would have great difficulty moving artillery," Ranald added, to which Barrington agreed readily.

"*That* we discovered in Martinique, did we not, Goodley?" Captain Goodley agreed politely. "Well, gentlemen," Barrington went on, "I thank you. I am sure we shall be able to find something useful for you to do, for I am desperately short of men and, apart from the Highlanders and marines in this place and a garrison of the 63rd Foot holding the fort at Basse Terre, the enemy is at large in the island. We can scarcely claim to have subdued him by perching on the rim of these islands. Would you wish to serve together, or as guides to my corps' commanders?"

"I doubt whether we can all acquit ourselves as competent guides," Kite put in hurriedly, appalled at Ranald's presumption.

"But we wish to assume the character of officers," Ranald said.

Barrington sighed and flicked an ironic glance at Goodley. "Yes, I thought you might," he observed. "However, I should point out, gentlemen, that I have a thousand matters demanding my attention . . ."

"I have an armed schooner at your immediate disposal, General Barrington. You have only to command me," Kite put in hurriedly, wishing to dissociate himself from the clumsy, intemperate amateurishness of Ranald.

Barrington looked from Ranald to Kite, then smiled. "Well, perhaps before leaping so eagerly into the unknown, you should know the worst. We have had word of a French squadron off Barbados and Commodore Moore has withdrawn all the ships-of-the-line and the frigates towards Prince Rupert's Bay in the island of Dominica to cover us. Unfortunately sickness in the fleet necessitated the transfer of three hundred troops to assist the working of the ships. Apart from the transports and your own schooner, Captain . . . Forgive me, I have forgotten your name . . ."

"Kite, sir."

"Ah, yes. Well, we are effectively cut off, Captain Kite, for as we speak the French have crept out of the forest and are breaking ground beyond the walls of this fort." Barrington grasped a crutch and gingerly set his gouty foot down on the floor with a wince. Goodley stepped forward to help, but Barrington shook his head. His face was contorted with pain as he rose to his feet, his face glistening with sweat. He caught his breath sufficiently to resume. "Well, we cannot sit and await an outcome dictated by the enemy; we shall have to take matters into our own hands. Do you gentlemen prepare to land with your equipment . . . Have you your own victuals?"

"We have brought small arms, powder and shot," said Ranald, "but were hoping that you would—"

"I am able to victual the party, sir," put in Kite hurriedly, earning a relieved glance of interest from Barrington, who turned to the papers before him.

"You shall take up scouting duties . . . in a body, gentlemen, skirmish ahead of our advance. I trust that will suit your character as, er, officers."

"Splendidly, sir," Kite said, putting up a hand on to Ranald's shoulder. "Come Harry, the general has a great deal to attend to."

"How long d'you give 'em, Goodley?" Barrington asked as the adjutant returned from seeing the two men back to their boat.

"Oh, just long enough to draw the French fire, sir," Goodley laughed, adding, "though I must say the merchant master seemed devoid of the bluster of his friend."

"Captain Kite," mused Barrington. "Yes. Now pass the word for Brigadier Clavering and Colonel Crump, we must break out of this place and make the confounded French dance to *our* tune."

Ranald's eagerness to be in action was disappointed. Barrington spent a fortnight strengthening the defences of Fort Louis, working his garrison of Highlanders and marines hard. While Ranald and his fellow gentry lounged about the decks of the *Spitfire* or took one of her two boats and went wildfowling among the islands closing off the port to the southward, Kite and Da Silva better prepared the *Spitfire* for action.

They were ordered to be ready to move, but on the due day, towards the end of March 1759, Kite received a note from Goodley instructing him to send Ranald and the majority of his volunteers aboard the transports. *Spitfire* was to remain at anchor, but ready to proceed. The order however, did not come, and to the chagrin of those left aboard the schooner they remained behind when two of the transports weighed anchor and, in company, tacked offshore and stood to the east.

Word soon passed round that they had sailed to land raiding parties at St Anne's and St François, two towns along the coast of Grande Terre to the eastwards. But shortly before sunset two days later, Barrington himself came off in a boat. He had been preceded by Goodley, who arrived with a file of kilted Highlanders of the 42nd Foot and asked Kite if he had some method of 'embarking the General'. Kite roused out the canvas chair they had used to land the ladies on their northward progress the previous year and Barrington was brought on deck, to announce the *Spitfire* to be 'my flagship'. Asking for a chair to be placed on deck, he sat down, rested his gouty foot and ordered the schooner under weigh.

"Where are we bound, sir?" Kite asked.

Goodley stepped forward with a map and pointed. "Here, Captain, to Le Gosier, just beyond Grand Bay. There," Goodley indicated the two adjacent transports, "you will see the *Elizabeth Bury* and the *Orford Castle* getting under weigh. They have three hundred men embarked. We are going to attack Le Gosier—"

"I should like to serve with you, Captain Goodley," Kite said, abruptly breaking in.

"But your schooner?"

"Mr Da Silva, my sailing master and gunner, will tend to her."

Goodley shrugged. "As you wish, Captain Kite, as you wish. Now, sir, we shall stand offshore and lie to until daylight. We will land at Le Gosier at dawn."

Kite dined with Barrington and Goodley in the cabin, which had been expanded into one large stateroom after the American cruise of the previous summer. Then he went on deck, and in a state of extreme tension remained there for the rest of the night, dozing in Barrington's abandoned chair while the general occupied his own bunk. It was a moonless night, but the stars were bright enough to throw faint shadows across the deck as *Spitfire* lay hove to in the light trade wind. Astern of them they could see the pale sails as the transports rode easily in the low swell. To the north the mass of the Mornes Sainte Anne, dominating the island of Grande Terre, was dark against the star-spangled sky. Kite fancied that in the dark mass of the island he could discern Puella asleep beside him. He swore under his breath and took a turn up and down the deck, impatient for the first flush of dawn.

He must have fallen into a doze leaning against the taffrail, for the helmsman's cough woke him with a start. "Beg pardon, Cap'n Kite, but yon transport's hauled her main yard."

Kite shook the fog and the megrims from his brain. He could see the nearer transport, the *Orford Castle* he thought, had trimmed her sails and a pallid feather of water rose round her apple bow. Beyond her, the second transport was in the act of following suit.

Kite nodded. "Very well; let fly heads'l sheets and up helm!"

The helmsman acknowledged his order and the watch on deck stirred themselves into action. The schooner gave up holding the natural forces in balance, swung and began to make way again. A few moments later *Spitfire* was heeling to the breeze, standing after her consorts and rapidly gaining on them.

The eastern extremity of Grand Bay was separated by the inlet leading to Le Gosier by a headland called Pointe de Verdure. Further to the east, the inlet was bounded on its other side by a mass of rocks and islets which broke the surf pounding the beach. Into the gully between, the transports' boats, laden with soldiers and covered by the anchored schooner, made their way. Having dropped their anchor, a rope was hurriedly led up the *Spitfire*'s starboard side and seized to the anchor cable. With the spring secured, a little more cable was veered. The effect on the wind-rode *Spitfire* was to swing her broadside round, so that Da Silva had her guns directed on the sleeping village, the houses of which were showing in the dawn's early light. Sitting in his chair, Barrington stared through a glass, but the boats, grey shapes bristling with the dull sheen of bayonets and creeping like beetles over the dull purple-coloured sea, were almost within reach of the beach before the first puff of smoke told where a disturbed sentinel had discharged his musket in alarm. More puffs from widely differing spots followed before the sound of the first discharge reached the watchers offshore. Then the beetles merged with the shore. More cracks of musketry rolled towards them.

"They've landed," snapped Barrington, rising. "We shan't need your guns." Goodley and Kite saw him into his sling and then followed him over the side into the waiting boat. *Spitfire*'s seamen rowed them ashore in the wake of the troops and a few minutes later Kite splashed over the side of the boat into a few inches of water and turned to help Barrington.

"Forwards! Forwards!" Barrington insisted, waving them on.

A Highlander was left to assist the general, along with a corporal and two privates as a guard. Goodley, Kite and the other gentlemen volunteers ran after the file of Highlanders already tumbling ashore from *Spitfire*'s second boat. Passing a few local fishing boats drawn up on the beach, they made for a lane that rose steeply towards Le Gosier. From this position, all looked different. The horizon had closed in and the grand perspective of the view from the sea vanished. Now Le Gosier was a distant hint of roofs from which small clouds of smoke, some centred with a brief and fleeting flash of fire, produced an occasional whine as a spent musket ball passed them.

A few hundred yards up the rough lane, the intensity of the fire was focused. It seemed to have pinned down half the force of Highlanders, who lay sprawled on the ground, poking their muskets forward and seeking opportunities to return fire. A young officer grinned at them, "Lieutenant Macdonald's working round to the right, sir . . ."

"Very well," Goodley nodded to the subaltern. "Keep 'em occupied," then he turned and, ducking down, beckoned to his own file and the volunteers. "Follow me. Sergeant?" Goodley called to a large Scot with a tall mitre-shaped grenadier hat. The man looked up. "Follow me with your grenadiers . . ."

The party moved off to the left, taking shelter behind a low bank and then, moving on, a stony wall. At first they were unobserved, but then a ball struck a rock outcrop and whined past Kite's ear. Goodley raised his hat on his sword; a fusillade of balls spun it away and then in the wake of the discharge the adjutant was over the low wall, followed by the 42nd's grenadiers. Caught up in the breathless excitement of the swiftness of events, barely understanding what was going on and regretting his almost sleepless night, Kite followed. Armed with a ship's cutlass and a pistol, he was conscious that he was the only one of the Antiguan gentry that moved forward with the soldiers.

The rest, most armed with muskets, but without bayonets, threw themselves against the wall and gave the grenadiers supporting fire by firing wildly at the wooden buildings that appeared in their front behind a few trees. Kite found himself stumbling towards these and suddenly saw a face at an open window. The soldier was taking aim at him down the foreshortened length of a musket barrel. Running forward, he raised his pistol, but the soldier fired first. The flash and bang of his discharge were translated into a loud sucking of air as the ball passed Kite. He fired his own pistol. The next moment he crashed against the wall of the house and looked back. The heads of the Antiguan gentlemen volunteers bobbed where they reloaded, but the red tide of infantrymen had passed on and he seemed quite alone, leaning, gasping for breath against this alien dwelling. Somewhere in the distance, the crackle and rattle of small-arms fire rent the air, accompanied by shouts and screams. But it all seemed strangely remote.

Although temporarily deafened by the rapid and close discharge of the French musket and his own pistol, Kite thought he detected movement within the building. It struck him as faintly ridiculous that the two of them, intent on murdering one another, were separated by only the thickness of the planking. He looked at his pistol. The means to reload it were in his pocket, but the time taken would place him and his opponent back on an equal footing. Surely, the defending Frenchman would be occupied in reloading his own weapon now? Suddenly resolute, Kite jerked into action, moving along the wall to turn the corner.

Here the noise of the fire-fight was suddenly all about him. The whine and thud of ball was accompanied by the shouts of excited men, some calling for reassurance, some blaspheming, some shouting instructions.

"Watch yer flank, Dougal laddie!"

"Oh God, ma fuckin' leig!"

"Merde!"

"Eh bien, François, eh bien!"

The door to the dwelling swung half open on Kite's right. For a split second he saw the soldier in a white linen uniform with pale yellow facings, saw the astonishment in his eyes change to anger as the long gleaming barrel of the musket again foreshortened. But they were too close, almost stumbling over each other as the soldier made to fire. Savagely Kite swept the clumsy cutlass upwards, feeling the bite of the blade as it hacked halfway through the French infantryman's extended left arm. His right hand fumbled the trigger and the flint sparked. The weapon discharged itself alongside Kite's left ear.

Kite could hear nothing, but he saw his antagonist gasp with the pain of his wound. The French soldier dropped the musket with a clatter, reeling back into the darkness. Kite followed, the impetus of the heavy cutlass swing drawing him into the house after the collapsing infantryman. As the wounded soldier fell back, his companion, sharing the same billet and still in his shirt-tails, swung his own musket towards the intruder. The gun barked and the ball stung Kite's left shoulder with the searing sensation of a burn, but then the formidable horror of the extending bayonet stabbed at him.

Kite put up his hand, uncaring if the blade severed his fingers, eager only that the evil point was deflected from his face. By the greatest good fortune, the lunge of the enemy soldier took the muzzle of the musket past Kite's extended hand, and though the point of the steel nicked his left cheek, his hand struck the barrel and parried the thrust aside. Kite dragged his right hand back, trying to raise the cutlass for a cut; instead the back of the blade, two-thirds of which was blunt, drew up between the infantryman's legs. The unfortunate wretch gasped and dropped to his knees as Kite recovered his blade and drove it forward, running the soldier through. Gasping, Kite withdrew the cutlass and swung round, half aware of a movement behind him. The man he had first wounded had fallen back on to his haunches and squatted nursing his wound, watching the outcome. Seeking an opening to kill the Englishman, the Frenchman grabbed his dropped musket and thrust it between Kite's legs.

Kite stumbled, but now mad with blood-lust he flicked the cutlass blade by sharply pronating his wrist. The heavy blade caught the infantryman under the chin, driving his lower jaw upwards. Kite crashed into the wall as the Frenchman's head jerked violently backwards. Bracing himself against the wall, Kite swiftly extended his hand no more than an inch or two, and the cutlass point penetrated the Frenchman's neck. Blood poured from the soldier's throat as he scrabbled desperately at his punctured windpipe; Kite stepped past him and into the open air. Less than a minute had passed since he had sensed the faint movement of the enemy soldier through the wall.

Kite could see the red jackets and dark blue-black kilts of the bare-kneed Highlanders as they ran about, their claymores gleaming, or fired their muskets into dwellings along the street of the village as they flushed the defenders out. A few lay inert, alongside the dead and dying enemy in their white coats, corpses prepared for death long before by their master, King Louis, and his sepulchral colours.

He ran on, spurning the horror he had left in the house, yet eager for more blood. Turning a corner, he came upon the main street of Le Gosier and his way was blocked by a line of red-coated Highlanders, their backs to him, formed up in ranks three deep. Across the entire space of a small square beyond, Kite caught a glimpse of an opposing line, the now familiar white coats topped by black tricornes. As he came up behind the Highlanders, he heard Goodley's voice barking orders, then the almost simultaneous snap of flint on frizzen. The ripple of musketry from the white-coated ranks spewed flame and smoke. The balls smacked into the adjacent walls and gaps appeared in the ranks ahead, as the Highlanders fell backwards and the men in the rear, urged by the halberds of the non-commissioned officers, moved forward into the gaps. The Highlanders responded with rapid platoon fire, mowing down the French before they had discharged their second volley. The British musketry was relentlessly efficient, blasting the enemy line before rolling forward. Drawing their claymores as they cheered, the kilted Highlanders, grenadier and line companies, fell upon the wavering French. The white-clad infantry broke.

Kite ran with the Scots, and butchered with them, and chased the last remnants of the enemy from the square and in and out of a few houses until either they were dead, hidden, or had surrendered. Finally exhausted, Kite answered the call to re-form as Barrington hobbled into view on the arm of his attending soldier.

Goodley held out a sword taken from the dead officer command- ing the French garrison. "Le Gosier is yours, sir."

Barrington looked about him and nodded. "See the wounded are taken back to the ships, Mr Goodley. The rest form up in column of march with two platoons out ahead under Lieutenant Macdonald. I intend to take the French siege lines before Fort Louis in the rear. By the bye, where's Captain Kite?"

"Here, sir." Kite stepped forward.

"My God, Captain!" Barrington exclaimed, seeing the bloody state of Kite. "You've seen some service, by the state of you. Your fellows by the wall said you'd run off! Well, well, 'tis as well you are still with us. If you'd been taken the French might have shot you as a spy." Barrington laughed, and was joined by the officers and men round about him. "Upon my soul, they might indeed!"

# Twelve

## The Widow

Although Kite returned to *Spitfire* along with the wounded, who were withdrawn to the anchored transports, Barrington's little column set out to march back to Fort Louis overland. As they approached the fort to attack the besiegers, more British troops sallied out, nipping the French between two forces. Having thus relieved his own position at Fort Louis, taking a battery of enemy 24-pounders in the process, Barrington waited for the return of Clavering and Crump from their raids on St Anne's and St François. At this time there arrived in the road the remaining transports, which had been blown to leeward of Guadeloupe, bringing welcome reinforcements to the general.

Then Barrington learned of the death of the garrison commander at Basse Terre, the only other British toehold on Guadeloupe, on the other island. An accidental magazine explosion had killed several men, while the besieging French were in the final stages of erecting a heavy battery. Barrington immediately appointed an officer to replace the garrison commander, and to expedite his arrival Kite was asked to convey this officer aboard *Spitfire*. The schooner was got under weigh and stood south for Pointe du Vieux Fort as soon as the newly appointed officer clambered aboard. Rounding the headland and hauling her foretopsail yard, *Spitfire* made up for the Rade de Basse Terre. As she coasted into the anchorage she exchanged a few shots at extreme range with a French gun, an event which was attended by hardly any danger but a great deal of self-satisfaction. Kite, however, took little further part in the action at Basse Terre beyond making a demonstration before the enemy gun battery at closer range and firing a rolling broadside ashore. De Silva and his gunners cherished the moment long afterwards, but it did little damage beyond throwing up mounds of earth and stones along the beach, holing a fishing boat and killing three goats. This diversion was carried out in support of the sally made from Basse Terre, and though its tactical significance was negligible, the breakout of the garrison drove the enemy from their lines, took their heavy artillery and raised the siege.

Kite returned to Pointe-à-Pitre and waited upon Barrington in Fort Louis with the news of success. With the town of Basse Terre secured, Barrington went over to the offensive. Having relinquished the shoreline to the British, the French force on Guadeloupe was thinly spread and tied to the defence of strong points guarding the farms and plantations of the colonists, most of which lay in isolated valleys with rugged terrain between them. Barrington still retained a brace of bomb vessels by way of naval support and possessed the manoeuvrability conferred by the presence of the transports. He was therefore able to land his troops at will, advance into the interior and destroy the French positions at leisure.

The strongest of these lay above Mahaut Bay, where the French had been receiving supplies from the Dutch on the island of St Eustatia. Thirteen hundred men and six guns under the command of Brigadier Clavering were landed on the shores of the bay. Fighting their way through dense undergrowth and turning the French positions in rapid succession, the 4th and 42nd Foot drove after the enemy, the Highlanders wielding their claymores as they closed with their opponents, hand to hand. Clavering never gave his enemy a moment's rest, even at night, when his guns played on the French to keep them under constant pressure. Falling back, setting fire to the sugar-cane fields and breaking down bridges, the French attempted to delay Clavering's advance as he struck south, over the narrow quasi-isthmus that lay between the twin massifs. In an energetic pursuit that brooked no obstruction, Clavering's men outflanked the French, who again retired towards another strong defensive position at Petit Bourg.

Here, however, Barrington had sent a bomb vessel from Pointe-à-Pitre, offering Kite a contract as a hired vessel if he would take *Spitfire* in support. Kite declined the offer, since he would be obliged to submit command of his beloved schooner to a naval officer, probably a superannuated lieutenant transferred from the *Orford Castle* or one of the other transports, but he volunteered *Spitfire* on exchange for a new letter of marque, to be issued in due form at Antigua on the general's written instruction. Having attracted Barrington's notice at Le Gosier, the general was delighted to reach this economic expedient and placed marines aboard *Spitfire*, making her a naval auxiliary.

Thus Kite watched through his glass as the first shells began to burst among the lines and redoubts round Petit Bourg. The bomb vessel's huge 13-inch mortar, situated amidships, boomed out every few minutes and the shells could be clearly seen, arcing up into the air with their faint trail of sparks thrown off by the fizzing fuse. At first the shells burst prematurely in the air in the last split-second of their trajectory; then they landed and there was a brief hiatus before they blew apart. But after these ranging shots the fuses were cut to the correct length and the shells landed and blew up at almost the same instant, driving the unfortunate French from their positions. Under this distant bombardment, against which they were impotent, the enemy abandoned their entrenchments before they could withdraw their cannon.

Clavering arrived shortly afterwards and cleared Petit Bourg of the last tenacious defenders of the little town. Then he rested his men during two days of torrential rain. During the downpour Crump and a further seven hundred soldiers had been on the move. Following Clavering round to Mahaut Bay, they had completed the destruction of the French depôt there before joining Clavering. Waiting at Petit Bourg for the rain to ease, the reinforced Clavering prepared to move south again, along the coast of Cabes Terre towards Sainte Marie.

By now the entire French force on Guadeloupe had rallied at Sainte Marie, where a strong position had been prepared. But the French placed too much reliance upon the impassable nature of the river and the narrow paths leading round the inland flank of the redoubt and its outlying trenches. Having suffered continually from suddenly finding the enemy's red coats flitting through the forest in their rear a moment before opening their withering and rolling musketry, the French officers' improvident neglect proved fatal.

A large party was sent to turn the French position, while the British artillery was moved up to confront the enemy lines. The guns had fired only a few rounds when the French abandoned their position as the word spread that British infantry were once more in their rear. This retreat was less precipitate than at first appeared, for a second prepared position lay on the heights above the little port. This was flanked by ravines and dense rainforest, its approach congested by undergrowth, but the British moved their guns steadily forward, while once again flanking parties advanced on either wing.

Seeing the British making yet another encircling movement, and in an attempt to take advantage of the extended nature of Clavering's little force, the French left the shelter of their position and, covered by the fire of their own artillery, moved down the hill to engage the British centre and decide the matter. But Clavering was equal to this crisis and gathered the remnant of his troops. These were hurled against the French and drove them back towards their entrenchments, and then in disorder from their works. The following day the local planters, fearing their rich lands would be set on fire, asked for terms. Barrington granted the French inhabitants a liberal capitulation and the wealthiest French island in the West Indies transferred its allegiance, for the time being, to Great Britain.

Hardly had the instrument of surrender been signed, than a cutter ran into the bay with the news that General Beauharnais and French reinforcements had arrived at Martinique, but this did not prevent Barrington taking Marie Galante. He then secured the new colony, appointed a government and a few days later received word at Fort Louis that a discouraged Beauharnais had sailed away. Crump was appointed as governor and the troops redeployed: three battalions were left as a garrison, the others dispersed. Barrington took a further three back to England with him and the 42nd Foot, the Black Watch, were sent on to North America.

When Barrington and the transports left for England and the Highlanders embarked for America, Kite resolved to return to Antigua. It was the end of May and before the hurricane season was upon them, he wished to decide his future. Squaring the foretopsail yard and paying out the fore- and mainsheets, *Spitfire* headed for St John's. Astern of them the island of Guadeloupe was left in the possession of the British army. The soldiers, however, were yet to suffer from their most implacable enemy; in the remaining seven months of the year, eight hundred were to die of yellow jack.

Kite spent a month in Antigua after the capture of Guadeloupe. On their return the soldiers of the 38th Foot disembarked without Major Robertson; he had been one of eleven officers killed in the capture of the island and his widow plunged into a conspicuous and affecting mourning.

But Kite also returned to bad news. Dorothea lay dying, and when Kite went in to see her he was appalled. The once handsome, voluptuous and apparently ageless black woman was almost beyond recognition. Dorothea had metamorphosed into a shrivelled husk whose body hardly disturbed the clean white sheet laid over her.

Seeing her visitor, her eyes gleamed with alarm and she held out her hand for Puella. Kite regarded the two women, the one standing, the other lying inert, linked by their clasped hands. His heart filled with pity, sadness and regret.

"Dorothea . . ." he began, but Puella restrained his forward movement.

"She does not like you, Kite," Puella said with a flat finality.

"What is the matter with her?" he asked, overwhelmed by a sense of desperate inadequacy.

"She is dying, Kite; she stopped eating, she does not want to live any more, now that Mr Mulgrave is dead."

"But—" Kite began, then caught himself. For all his multiple kindnesses, Mulgrave had saddled Kite with a mighty obligation in return. He saw Dorothea watching him closely, saw the gleam of febrile intelligence in her eyes, and felt the conviction that Dorothea knew all about Mulgrave's deception. How could she then so hate him, if it was Mulgrave, her trusted and much admired lover who had, in the end, deceived her?

And then it struck Kite that, despite the protection and the advantage conferred by their association with himself and Mulgrave, these women hated their white men. He looked sharply at Puella.

"And Puella," he asked quietly, "do you hate me too?" Puella looked at Dorothea, as though for guidance, but the dying woman kept her eyes steadfastly upon Kite. It was clear Puella would offer him no comfort while Dorothea lived and he felt overwhelmed with weariness. "Well, Puella," he said, "you are a free woman, you have a competence upon which to live. You can afford this house upon your own account and Wentworth will protect you . . ."

A rasping came from Dorothea and Puella bent to hear her dying friend. As she straightened up, Kite asked, "What did she say?"

"She tells me that you will go away soon and that I may stay with you . . ."

"*May* stay, or *must* stay?"

"May stay, Kite."

"And when will you choose?" he asked, his voice cracking with despair. But Puella merely shrugged.

Kite slept aboard *Spitfire* and daily attended Wentworth's premises, where the two men sought to mature their plans for the future. Every evening, Kite returned to the house to pay his respects to Dorothea, but he exchanged no more than formal remarks with Puella, and the gulf between them grew wider.

On several evenings, after these depressing visits, he dined with Wentworth and attended an assembly or two. In the aftermath of the acquisition of Guadeloupe and the return of the island's soldiery, these were gay affairs, by no means confined to the white population, but embracing the better part of the wealthier townsfolk, many of whom were mulatto or quadroon. To her regret, Mrs Robertson was prevented from attending by the conventions of widowhood, but her chagrin was increased upon learning that the handsome Captain Kite had at last abandoned his 'nigger whore' and was making his way in polite society. Anxious to secure a new protector, Mrs Robertson fell victim to panic, becoming desperate to catch the eligible bachelor before some other schemer secured his affections. To this end she browbeat Wentworth and contrived to be at his rooms one evening when Kite was known to be calling. She had removed her black lace lappets and her black dress had fallen from her splendid shoulders so that her ample bosom was indecorously exposed to view.

"Captain Kite," she gushed, smiling and extending a hand to him, "what a pleasure." He bent politely over it and she seized his, drawing him down beside her, her features eager at his proximity. Despite his black servants, a sweaty and blushing Wentworth improbably pleaded a lack of lime juice to absent himself at this moment, and Mrs Robertson came swiftly to the point.

"Captain Kite," she said, boldly placing her hand between his thighs, "you are a most arresting man and I am deeply affected by you . . ." Her breath was hot on his face and the scent of her and the movement of her hand disturbed him. He felt the mounting flush of lust and twisted round. Relaxing, sure of her conquest, Mrs Robertson lay back, opening her legs and drawing up her skirt with a rustle of black silk, exposing petticoats and slender stockinged calves.

"I will do anything for you, William, anything . . ."

"Anything?" he whispered, stupidly wrestling with his conscience, longing to lose himself in her willing flesh and wash away the confusion in his soul. He half heard Makepeace's war cry as rising lust made him tug at himself.

"Anything," she repeated with breathless ardour, exposing herself naked above her stockings and looking down at him as he disencumbered himself of his breeches. "Oh, God . . ."

She sensed him hesitate, then quickly reassured him. "Wentworth will not trouble us, I have seen to that . . ."

Kite's member sprung free and he frowned. "What? How?"

She laughed and eased herself receptively. "Oh, my darling don't trouble yourself, come to Kitty. Here . . . here . . ." She reached down to guide him.

"But how," he insisted and she saw a dangerous gleam in his eye.

"Why, silly, like this," and she stroked his throbbing penis.

He looked at her, horrified. The extent of her scheming struck him at the moment of entry and he recoiled, priapic, foolish and half spending in his excitement and disgust.

"You are rejecting me?" Kitty Robertson could scarce believe the fact.

Kite had stood up. He was tucking his shirt tails in and settling his breeches. "No, I am not rejecting you," he temporised. "I am treating you like a whore . . ."

"But you like whores!" She was desperate in her disarrangement, but it was her mood that turned now. "Or are only nigger whores to your taste?" she snarled.

Kite swiped at her, but she evaded the blow with a grin of triumph, standing up with such a sudden motion that he fell back, still adjusting his clothing. Her skirt fell to the floor and she thrust her head forward, her expression furious.

"You nigger-loving *bastard*!" she hissed.

He regretted his attempt to strike her, it cancelled out her humiliation and made her the victim, sparking her spirited riposte. "And to think I considered you a gentleman! You are nothing but a—"

But Kite was provoked and a mounting anger overtook him. "Be silent!" he snapped. Then recovering himself before matters flew utterly out of hand said, "We have both behaved foolishly and impetuously . . ."

She was shaking her head. "Oh, no, you shall not say so! I will not have it! I will not have *you* make a fool of me, by God!" She would submit to no soothing; she was wildly indignant, outraged, a singular contrast to her wanton eagerness of a moment before. Kite stilled his protest, letting her have her head. What did it matter? If she and Wentworth kept their mouths shut, he was not going to gain any capital from the unhappy and awkward incident. He suddenly turned and picked up his hat. The unexpected retrograde movement caught her unawares and she paused.

"For God's sake, madam, make Wentworth happy!" Kite said. "He is rich beyond your late husband's competence and is probably sweating miserably below in an agony of disappointment that you should frig him, then offer yourself to me."

In the brief, calculating hiatus that followed, Kite hurried from the room and down the stairs where he ran into Wentworth. "Go to her, for God's sake, and take your pleasure; I love Puella and have no wish for her, she's as eager as an alley cat."

The regrettable encounter with Mrs Robertson brought to an end Kite's period of irresolution. He had been half-hearted and uncertain in his dealings with Wentworth, unsure of his objectives as much as his motives. After he had drowned himself in what he privately considered to be wanton murder at La Gosier, this further disquieting evidence of his own weakness acted like a slamming door. When, ten days later, Dorothea died and Puella agreed to accompany him wherever he went, he realised that her submission was the only thing that encumbered his mind. There was nothing beyond the considerations of business to keep him in Antigua, and even these lessened when Wentworth let it be known that his proposal of marriage had been accepted by Mrs Kitty Robertson. For propriety's sake, the wedding would have to be deferred until after a year's mourning, but Mrs Robertson could not entirely hide her satisfaction:

it would make her one of the richest women in the Antilles. As far as Kite was concerned, her triumph was unconcealed.

"She is a very bad woman for you, Kite," Puella remarked one evening after they had passed her carriage when out walking along the waterfront. Kite looked at Puella. He had mooted the evening walks as a means of attempting to re-establish some contact with her, though he had not returned to sleep under her roof. He had been pleased when she accepted, for he did not want to humiliate her in front of the townsfolk of St John's after the death of Dorothea, when the excuse that she was tending the ailing mulatto was at an end. Her comment about Mrs Robertson was the first remark she had made which showed any returning consideration for him.

"Why do you say that?" he asked.

"Because she wanted you. After the major died, she thought that you could throw over your black woman and marry her."

"How did you know that?"

Puella shrugged. "I know it."

"But I did not, and now she is to marry Mr Wentworth."

"He will make her rich and she will make him miserable."

"Like I make you miserable?" he asked tenderly. Puella walked, on saying nothing. "Tell me something, Puella," Kite went on, "why did Dorothea so dislike me? Did she attribute Mr Mulgrave's disappearance to me?"

"Of course. She believed you had tricked him and that he had to go back to England."

"I see. That is not what happened at all. Mr Mulgrave made me tell Dorothea that he had drowned. He said something about her having foretold he would drown and that it was best that she thought so." Puella said nothing, so he went on. "You see, Mr Mulgrave had to return to England, he went home to ease his fever and he had a wife in England. Did Dorothea know that?"

Puella shrugged again. "Perhaps she did, I don't know."

"The sad and stupid thing is, Puella, Mr Mulgrave is still alive . . ."

"No!" Puella shook her head. "No, Mr Mulgrave is dead," she said firmly. "He died in the water."

Kite held his peace. What did it matter? Dead or alive, Puella would believe what Dorothea had told her, such had been the mulatto woman's hold over her younger friend. Kite felt, with some sadness, that he had learned that whatever benefits of civilisation one conferred on these Africans, no matter how one sought to ameliorate their condition, no matter how much one was devoted to them, one could not make them anything other than Africans.

"I tell you something important, Kite." Puella broke into his unconsciously arrogant musing. He felt her draw closer to him as they turned and began to walk back towards the house. It was already dark, the last rosy flush of sunset in the western sky was already fading and the air had assumed the first slight chill of the night. "I am pleased that you have told me what happened to Mr Mulgrave. It is sad that Dorothea had to be left behind, but now Puella has said that she will come with you if you are going to England . . ."

"And if I go to America?"

"America, then, only you must take Puella."

"Do you love me, Puella?" he asked in a low voice, leaning towards her so that a passing couple remarked on their preoccupation.

"You must come to me tonight, Kite . . . but there is something important to tell you."

Kite chuckled, his heart lifting. "No, nothing is as important as what you have already told me."

"Yes, something is more important. You must be careful of Mrs Robertson. She will influence Mr Wentworth, especially after you have gone. She will try and ruin your business."

"You think she is that vindictive?"

"I do not understand 'vindictive', but I know she is your enemy."

Puella's warning crystallised Kite's intentions. The following day he called upon Wentworth and announced that he wished to realise his entire capital and that he intended to leave the island before the middle of June. Wentworth could not see Kite's logic until Kite explained there was none.

"I am resolved to leave the Antilles, my dear fellow, and not to return," Kite explained. "The place has too many unhappy memories."

Wentworth thought of Kite doting upon his late son and agreed. "It will reduce my ability to give credit, but . . ."

"Banker's drafts will suffice, though a quantity of currency and bullion will be necessary for contingent expenses."

Wentworth nodded. "I have moidores, specie and a little bullion upon which I can readily lay my hands," he said.

Kite smiled wryly. The 'little' bullion amused him. "That will do very well. The rest in drafts."

"To be drawn against Coutts' in London?"

"No," said Kite, "against Verhagen in New York."

Wentworth shook his head. "That is impossible. I have exhausted my credit with Cornelis until the next season's cane is in. He shipped me three large consignments of wine, timber, flax, notions and other fashionable fol-de-rols. The freight rates were ruinous and the underwriters' premiums exorbitant. I have yet to move much of the stuff out of my warehouse . . . I'm sorry. It must be London . . . Does that matter?"

Slowly, Kite shook his head. So, this was how fate finally compromised him. It was funny how the fatal blow came from a quarter from which it was least expected. He recalled Julius Caesar and the death blow from Brutus. He looked at Wentworth, but Wentworth lacked the guilt of Brutus; Wentworth was no friend turned political assassin, merely a man of commerce, venturing capital against an anticipated market. The risk made Wentworth sweat, Kite noticed, as his friend mopped his brow.

Kite wondered if he was seeing shadows, like Dorothea had; was it the vague umbral spectre of fate that, at that particular moment, lay behind Wentworth's lack of credit with the Dutch banker in New York? Kite shook his head again. "No; I was minded to go to New York, but I can as easily change my plans."

"You may have as much in moidores as you wish, William, I do not mean to discommode you."

"You don't discommode me," Kite said, smiling and rising to his feet. "Until tomorrow, then. And have Garvey here with a bill of sale for my shares in Da Silva's schooner. I shall offer them to him."

"No, let me buy her from you, you'll get nothing from the Portugoose."

"In gold, then."

"Yes," Wentworth nodded, "in gold. Sovereigns, if you wish."

"As you please." And picking up his hat, Kite left.

# Part Four

## Wind

# Thirteen

## The Hurricane

On the eve of his proposed departure for North America, Kite ran into Captain Makepeace and, inviting his old commander back to the rented house, agreed to embark a consignment of twenty slaves just then brought in by the *Enterprize* from Benin. The slaves were destined for Kingston, Jamaica, and Makepeace was not keen to delay loading molasses and rum for England, fretful that, already late in the season, he might be caught by a hurricane before he got clear of the islands.

"If you're bound for the American coast, I'd be obliged if you'd look favourably upon the task," Makepeace pleaded, as they sat in the small courtyard set behind a high wall separating them from the hurly-burly of the St John's waterfront. The sun was setting and the sky was suffused with a rich peach hue. Kite was disposed to be cordial and laughingly agreed as the two men drank glasses of mimbo. "You have done well, as I predicted," Makepeace said, watching Puella as she settled quietly beside them. "And you, Puella, are more beautiful than I could have imagined."

Puella lowered her eyes and remained silent; she was uneasy in Makepeace's presence, unable to adjust to the alteration in his relationship with either Kite or herself. Moreover, she did not want Kite to carry slaves in the *Spitfire*. The schooner was already loaded with a full cargo of muscovado and rum, some of which was bound for consignees in Savannah, where Kite intended replacing the discharged commodities with cotton. His returns would be modest, but with no personal contacts in Britain he did not wish to venture a speculation on a cargo which would be difficult to sell. However, despite his misgivings, he agreed to purchase a quantity of elephant's ivory from Makepeace.

"I hear you are a man of considerable substance," Makepeace said as they concluded their transaction.

"I doubt that I could match your own substance, Captain, but you did me a considerable service when you introduced me to Mr

151

Mulgrave. He was most generous to me as well as to Wentworth, his main protégé. I was quite undeserving."

"I daresay you will benefit further from his munificence, then," Makepeace remarked, helping himself to more mimbo from the jug.

Kite frowned. "Oh. In what way?"

"Why, have you not heard? Mulgrave is dead. I would have thought his attorney, what was his name . . . ?"

"Mr Garvey," put in Puella, sitting up and taking more than a casual interest.

"That's it, Garvey, I'd have thought he would have let you know. Well, no matter; Mulgrave has been dead for some time. Garvey will have the details. I'm surprised you knew nothing of it."

Kite looked at Puella. His expression was contrite; there was no need for words to pass between them: Dorothea had been right. "Do you know the manner of his death?" Kite asked.

"Yes, he was taking passage in a wherry on the Thames when it was overset by a passing squall."

"Then he drowned," said Kite, and Makepeace nodded, sipping the mimbo reflectively. "Well, I'll be damned," Kite said and Puella stirred and silently withdrew. The sun had set and the tropical night was swiftly descending upon them; Puella habitually sought her bed early, particularly if Kite was attending to his affairs.

Kite watched her leave, her tall figure upright and walking with that peculiarly fluid grace that suggested regal ancestry. He sensed her isolation and loneliness and his heart went out to her. He was about to make his excuses and hint that it was time for Makepeace to leave, when the captain poured himself another glass of mimbo and looked round the courtyard as the cool of the night eased the white men's discomfort.

"I am getting old, Kite, and am of a mind to settle soon. I have a place in Liverpool and I increasingly regret leaving it. So far I have avoided most of the plagues of Guinea, Benin and these infested islands, but a man always runs ahead of the fates. How I have avoided the yaws, I confess I don't know, but the devil, they say, looks after his own. I now own three ships besides the whole of the *Enterprize*: I acquired the *Adventure*, the *Endeavour* and the *Ambition* quite recently. The first is a fine frigate-built ship, the second a brig and the third a snow. They were all built as Bristolmen, but Liverpool has entirely eclipsed that port now, and they came cheap. They are all in good condition and now, run on Liverpool lines, are returning healthy profits. I was looking at your schooner today, she would make a small Guineaman it is true, but she would make a better privateer and I hear you already have a letter of marque and reprisal in her name."

Kite nodded, uncertain where this rather smug catalogue of success was leading them. He was not long left in suspense. Makepeace topped up his glass.

"Well now, Kite, I have a proposition to make to you. With your schooner and a portion of your capital, I wish to offer you a full half-share in the ownership of this little fleet. For myself the capital will secure me some retirement with my family and the peace of mind knowing that you, as a younger man, will continue the business to the mutual benefit of us both. In particular, of course, I shall seek assurances, drawn up by due process, that the inheritance of my children will be protected; in that I trust you implicitly. For you it would be a grand opportunity . . ." Makepeace paused. "Now, what do you say, eh?" Makepeace picked up his glass and drank deeply, watching Kite's reaction.

Kite nodded slowly. The news of Mulgrave's death, sad though it was, did not, he thought, have any further bearing upon his own life. If Garvey knew of it, it was certain Wentworth did. Why Wentworth had concealed it from him was a mystery, but not one that he, at this late moment, considered worth troubling himself with. He did not know how long Kitty Robertson had been intriguing with Wentworth, but he thought vaguely that she might have had something to do with the matter. It was quite possible, he thought, that she might have been manipulating the younger man for some time long before their betrothal. Wentworth was certainly not the most engaging of the island's potential lovers, but he was probably the most discreet. More certainly, he was the most liquid in terms of plunderable funds. Kite dismissed the train of thought. Despite the risks, he was wearied of St John's and felt the tug of England and the rain-swept hills of his native Cumbria. For a moment he thought of his father, and Helen, and how the letter he had written to his sister had probably never reached her, for he had received no reply, despite giving her the address of Cornelis Verhagen in New York, with whom Wentworth was in regular correspondence. But a shadow still lay over a return to Cumbria and now it confronted him.

"Well?" prompted Makepeace.

"I am attracted by your kind offer," Kite temporised, wondering how far he could trust this man whose worst excesses he had witnessed.

"Go on, something's troubling you. Don't you trust me? I am offering you a partnership, Kite, a partnership. I am inviting you to become an intimate at my house in the knowledge that you have opinions about my conduct, even evidence of my peccadilloes, that once known in certain places could blight my life – or what's left of it." Makepeace shifted in his chair and sat upright. He was a little drunk, but his thoughts were lucid and his voice only a trifle slurred.

"But consider, Kite, I *trust* you, upon my word I do." Makepeace paused, letting the import of his words sink in. Then he sighed and added, "So you may trust me and tell me what it is you fear by returning to England . . . Oh yes, I know of your intentions, you have touched upon the matter before, remember?"

"Well," Kite pulled himself together, "I should need a house in Liverpool, and it concerns me how Puella would be regarded there."

Makepeace waved aside the problems. "I shall see that you have a domicile befitting your standing as a wealthy sea-captain and merchant. As for Puella, if you don't become a fool and marry the girl, you may keep her as a mistress in quiet propriety in Liverpool. You have no children, so the matter may be managed, and since she is free, you will have little to concern you. I cannot speak for London, but Liverpool is a rising place and a man with money and standing is not too pressed if he is discreet and does not behave scandalously." Makepeace smiled. "And I have never seen you as a man likely to behave scandalously . . . Does that ease your mind?"

"A little . . ."

"There is still the matter of . . . what is it that ails you, eh?" Makepeace queried.

"A murder."

"Ahhh. I see." Makepeace nodded. He neither saw nor comprehended. "Would you care to elaborate?" he prompted.

Kite recounted the unforgettable moments of that afternoon, omitting only his revulsion at the monstrous-headed baby that had lain between Susie's shuddering thighs. It seemed so long ago, so detached from his present existence under the velvet, star-spangled tropical sky, and he had become so different from the long-legged youth who had run in terror from the Hebblewhites' barn.

When he had finished, Makepeace asked, "But you are in fact quite innocent?"

Kite nodded. "Oh. Yes. Though I dream sometimes, less often than in the past but still occasionally, that I *did* kill the girl."

"But that is merely an hallucination."

"Yes," Kite agreed, "of course it is."

"Then you have nothing to fear."

"How so?"

"Well, you are innocent in the first place and if, in the unlikely event that you are recognised, or the brothers hear of your presence in Liverpool, the matter is brought before the justices, you are now a man of sufficient means to defend yourself."

Kite considered the matter. "And does this confession not tempt you to withdraw your offer?"

Makepeace shook his head with a smile. "I know of few people less likely to commit murder than you, Kite. Your confession, as you call it, alters my proposal not one whit."

Kite sighed. Makepeace had not seen him butchering French soldiers at Le Gosier. "Very well. Though I must make plain that I shall not attempt any concealment. If my name is to be linked with yours, then I shall have perforce to take, as it were, the war into the enemy's camp and visit my father . . . If he still lives."

"Of course, of course. So we may conclude that to be the principle of our partnership, then." Makepeace held out the jug to refill Kite's glass. " 'Makepeace and Kite' has a certain ring about it, don't you agree?"

Kite smiled as the mimbo ran darkly into his glass. "Let me see how the land lies in Cumbria before we put up a shop sign in Liverpool," he said.

"As you wish, m'dear fellow. Now to the precise nature of the sum I am asking . . ."

Kite called for more candles and they discussed figures until late, but when Makepeace reeled out into the night they had shaken hands, each expressing his satisfaction at the proposed new venture.

When Kite woke late next morning, Puella had been up for some time. His head was furred from the rum and the sun beat remorselessly in through the open window. Slowly the events of the previous evening trickled back into his consciousness: the news of Mulgrave's death, the knowledge that it had been concealed from him, Makepeace's proposal, his own confession, his acceptance and then the agreed figure completing the transaction. It was also, he realised with a start, the day appointed for the departure of the *Spitfire*. He had much to do and would have to call on Garvey before sailing.

"Damnation!" He leapt from the bed.

Puella came into the room silently as he threw the last of his clothes into a portmanteau, hurriedly preparing to leave the rented house.

"Kite," she said, holding out a scrap of paper, her face a mask.

"What is it?" he asked looking up, but she merely waggled her hand impatiently, rustling the paper. The abrupt and almost monosyllabic nature of her communication with him marked the distances that remained separating them. Taking the folded note he opened it. It was written in a vaguely familiar hand that Kite could not identify; he looked at the simple date scrawled upon it.

"Where did you get this?"

"Mr Garvey."

Of course, now he recognised the attorney's script. "You called on Garvey at this time of the morning?"

"It is not early," she said flatly, waiting for the significance of the date to sink in.

Kite looked at the paper again, and then up at Puella. "This date," Kite began, feeling the lump in his throat, "this date . . . this is when Charlie . . ."

Puella nodded, her dark eyes filled with tears. "It is also the date that Mr Mulgrave died."

Kite recalled Dorothea's dark mutterings. "Well, I'm damned!"

From Jamaica, *Spitfire* made for Savannah where she discharged her part-cargo of sugar and loaded cotton bales. It was the height of the hurricane season, but Kite reasoned that he was sufficiently far north to miss the worst and sailed as soon as the schooner was ready for sea.

Clear of the estuary, they headed north-east, the *Spitfire* slipping easily through the blue water. Flying fish fluttered away from her advancing shadow as it raced over the gently heaving surface of the sea, while a school of dolphins gambolled under her bowsprit, riding the invisible wave of pressure that her thrusting bow forced ahead of her hull.

Kite came below after the morning watch to break his fast to find Puella vomiting copiously. "Ah, Puella, you were not seasick on the passage to Savannah, is the Atlantic too much for you, my love?"

Her brown skin glazed with perspiration, Puella looked up from the wooden bucket and shook her head. "I am with child," she said.

Three days out the steady breeze began to pick up during the early forenoon. The schooner was running with the wind and sea on her starboard quarter, the skies were untroubled, but a lumpy swell was building, running up from the south and inclining *Spitfire* to scend as she raced along. An anxiety began to gnaw at Kite. He cared little for himself or the ship and crew, they were stout enough, but Puella's condition worried him. She had carried Charlie serenely, but her present pregnancy seemed troubled. His ignorance reproached him; it seemed a lifetime ago that he had masqueraded as a surgeon and now his beloved Puella might well be in need of real help. She was the only woman on board and without Dorothea her isolation and vulnerability filled her with fear. Now the weather worsened and the battening down of the schooner only increased the staleness of the air below, trapping the sharp stink of vomit, so that both Kite and Puella were reminded of the slave deck of the *Enterprize*. Kite made Puella as comfortable as possible, but now the motion of the *Spitfire* and the mephitic air only added to the unfortunate woman's misery. It was not long before Kite was summoned on deck and compelled to leave Puella.

The *Spitfire*'s mate, a tall and powerful mulatto named Christopher Jones, drew his attention to the fact that there was an edge to the wind now and a rapid of darkening of the sky that presaged more than a mere gale.

"Hurricane coming, Cap'n," Jones asserted, "we should get all the sails down and let her run off before it." Kite stepped forward and looked from the windward tell-tale indicating the direction of the wind to the wildly swinging compass in its bowl. While he had been below with Puella the wind had begun to shift and they were already two points off their intended course. Kite bowed to the inevitable; at least they had sea room. He looked up at Jones and nodded. The mate was already raising his voice to make himself heard above the steady thrum of the gale in the rigging. The wind was not yet so strong that they would normally take in everything, but prudence dictated they should secure the schooner before the worst was upon them.

"Leave her a scrap of canvas forrard," Kite called in Jones's ear, "the clew of the foretopmast staysail! We'll luff her and call all hands!"

Jones nodded agreement. "Aye, aye, sir!"

Kite took his station beside the tiller as Jones called out the watch below. The *Spitfire*'s crew was smaller than during the Guadeloupe campaign, consisting of men willing to try their fortune with a long run across the Atlantic. The promise of prize-money inherent in the well-known letter of marque that converted *Spitfire* into a privateer had proved sufficient of a lure to both the feckless and the ambitious among the unemployed seafarers who idled their lives away along the waterfront of St John's, Willoughby and Falmouth. These idlers feared the appearance of the Royal Navy's cutters and launches, sent from English Harbour in search of such likely cannon-fodder. Besides, rates of pay aboard such private ships were better by far than the risks, dangers and uncertain pay in the men-of-war of His Britannic Majesty. Now Kite watched this motley band as it assembled on deck under the direction of Jones. The mate looked aft and nodded.

"Down helm," Kite ordered, lending his weight to the helmsman on the tiller. The *Spitfire* turned up into the wind, bucking wildly, her bowsprit stabbing first at the sky and then at the advancing walls of grey waves as they surged towards her. As they rose over the summits and the breaking crests roared and seethed past them in tumbling dissolution, they were exposed to the full strength of the wind. It tore at them with palpable force, howling in the standing rigging with a malevolent shriek as the sails flogged, rattling the swinging booms and gaffs so that the whole vessel trembled as they were lowered. Kite heard a faint scream as a terrified Puella, trapped below, thought the vessel was flying to pieces. Sheets of spray flew aboard over the bow, to be whipped aft in white streaks, so that the half-dry decks were sodden in an instant, and water streamed from every rope and spar above them. Caught in such a cascade, Kite felt his skin stung as from a lash, and he instinctively turned away.

Forward, each watch attending a mast, the gaffs came down and the reefed sails were slowly tamed by lashings as the crew bent to the task. The square topsails and the outer headsails had been taken in earlier and, after a few minutes, the schooner began to fall off the wind, rolling almost on her starboard beam ends as she swung away. Then the wind caught in the reefed staysail forward and added its power to the turning moment of the tiller. *Spitfire* crashed like a live and triumphant being over the crest and suddenly ran with the breaking sea, accelerating away from where the constraint of her master had held her for those few necessary minutes. Now, with only a scrap of canvas set over the stemhead, she tore away before the wind and Kite called for another man to be permanently stationed at the heavy tiller as it kicked in his hands.

"By Heaven, Mr Jones, she runs faster than a horse!"

"Indeed she do, sir!" Jones responded, affected by the exhilaration of the moment, with a broad grin. "Much faster!"

By now the sky was overcast, the scud lowering like a dark mantle, closing about them in their isolation. Beneath their keel they began to feel the *Spitfire* responding to the contrary and confusing influences of a cross-swell, at variance with the seas that rolled under them. Now there was another, sideways lurch, an arrhythmic and often abrupt roll that caused the following seas to catch up and strike the stern with a hammer blow that shook the hull from stern to stem. Once such a sea boiled over the rail, pouring forward in a torrent of water that swept two men from their feet and carried them forward so that they fetched up against the foremast fiferails in a swirling welter of water.

Half an hour after they had run off before the gale, just as Kite had decided he would relinquish the deck to Jones again and go and tend to Puella, the wind suddenly veered and began to roar with a deepening tone. The change was abrupt, the increase in force incontrovertible. Kite had never heard such a noise before, even when, two years earlier, he had been in St John's as a hurricane passed to the south of the island, sweeping through the cane fields of distant Martinique with destructive effect. But this was different, the booming roar seemed to contain an unimaginable power to which the former screaming shriek was an insipid prelude.

Jones caught his eye; he was no longer exhilarated. The mulatto's face was drained of colour, eloquent evidence of his fear. Jones hauled himself aft to where Kite stood clinging to the starboard main shrouds.

"Bad!" he shouted. "Big, big wind, Cap'n."

"Aye," Kite bellowed back.

"Bad hurricane, Cap'n! I'll put lifelines on the helmsmen!"

Kite nodded and let go of his handhold and plunged across the deck, fetching up against the binnacle. It took him some minutes before the spray allowed him to see clearly the relationship between the swinging card and the lubber's line, but it was obvious they were now headed north. Another such change in wind direction and they would be heading north-north-west.

He puzzled over this for some moments while Jones secured the helmsmen, but could make little sense of it. Perhaps the wind would veer when it next shifted, but something persuaded him otherwise. Fortunately they had sea room, and provided there were no other ships in the vicinity which they could run foul of, they would have an uncomfortable but not a fatal experience.

In the next quarter of an hour the wind backed another point. By now the booming roar had dulled their thoughts. Jones put the men on to the pumps to give them something to do, but Kite, as captain, could enjoy no such mind-numbing labour. He was left to try and think amid this awesome din. He became slowly aware that a subtle change was occurring. As the violence of the wind rose, the wild motion of the schooner lessened. It took Kite some time to penetrate this mystery until he realised that his vision was almost permanently obscured by the mass of water in the air. It was like a mist that moved with the speed and consistency of bird-shot, a tangible manifestation of the might of the wind. Eventually he realised that the wind in its rising had kicked up a heavy sea, but had now reached such a scale of power that it no longer did so. Now the wind simply excoriated the sea's surface, slicing it off it and carrying it to leeward. The air had become half liquid, salty, possessed of mass and density.

At first Kite thought this would ease the burden on the *Spitfire*, for her motion was far less violent, but in this he was deceived. It took a moment to register, but now she lay down under a constant pressure, and the forces impinging upon her were no longer air but air that was sodden with a weight of water. Even as the schooner continued to run off before them, the very forces that impelled her were conniving at her destruction, pushing her myriad component parts, those hundreds of scarphs and rebated joints, those butts, tenons and knees all held together with thousands of treenails, iron bolts and copper rovings, to the limits of their individual strengths.

On deck the men huddled unhappily and Kite had to lash himself to the weather rail, the thin line of the flag halyard cutting into him as the wind tried to pluck him from his perch. Even breathing became a labour, so choked was the air with salt water, so high the pressure of the wind upon his body. The mind fumbled through this chaos, and Kite found himself a living contradiction, with every instinct in his being telling him to lie down and curl up like a wounded cat, to make himself as small and insignificant as possible, to let the great wind pass over him in the simple hope that he would survive. Against this was an instinctive urge to reason, for survival depended upon the *Spitfire* remaining undamaged, providing the means of sustaining them upon the surface of this flattened, scoured and tormented sea. To achieve this it was not enough to let her go; she required nursing, helping through her ordeal in order that she could help them.

But Kite was tired and hungry, battered by the incessant noise, soaked by the wet and driving air, buffeted and bruised by the violent assault of wind and water. As hour succeeded hour he followed the crew, and slowly slipped into a half-conscious acceptance of the inevitable. He lost interest in their compass heading, for the whole world had contracted into this small circle of white and furious water above which the once vast and over-arching sky had shrunk into a dull limit of cloud-water, as thick and circumscribing as a fog. His mind seemed capable only of asking a simple and increasingly familiar question: What did it matter? What *did* it matter?

Nor was Kite the only man upon the *Spitfire*'s deck to be so afflicted. Those not hunkered down in the lee of some strong point to which they had lashed themselves stood at the tiller. The two men who struggled to keep the *Spitfire* before the wind were tiring rapidly; the compass bowl was difficult to see, so they steered by the tell-tales. But their concentration lapsed, their arms ached and they received no relief. Then a sea crashed at the stern and stove in the stern windows, canting the deck violently so that one of them lost his precarious footing. The *Spitfire* drove off to starboard with a heavy larboard lurch from which, as she broached, she did not recover.

Puella screamed as tons of water cascaded through the broken stern windows, smashing in the preventive shutters and filling the cabin with a sudden cold deluge. Perhaps it was Puella's shriek of terror, or perhaps it was the thin halyard cutting into his waist, that stirred Kite. He was vaguely troubled and roused from his catalepsy by the growing conviction that all was far from well. His mind swam, but he realised he had not heard the clunk of the pumps for some time; and then *Spitfire* protested again. The rigging to which Kite was seized suddenly jerked, and despite the roar of the wind the crack from aloft was loud enough to wake a dozing man. The maintopmast broke, snapping clean off above the doubling. The spar hung down, swaying and tugging at those ropes that still confined it. These jerked and strained under the load while the schooner fell farther over to larboard. From forward there came a report like the discharge of a gun: the shred of reefed canvas set on the forestay blew out.

Someone sent up a shout as *Spitfire* lay over on her beam ends and the deck heeled alarmingly. Kite lost his footing and hung from the weather pinrail like a sack of potatoes. The jerk finally alerted him to imminent disaster.

Kite had neither the experience nor the understanding of the great natural forces unleashed against his small schooner to comprehend that, by running off before the wind, his ignorance had contributed to their plight. Nor had Jones, notwithstanding his competence as the mate of an inter-island schooner, the faintest concept of the true nature of the hurricane. But both men, and several of the hands, knew the remedy for their present plight, and Jones's large frame was soon crouched over the weather rail, a grey silhouette against the sky forward, clinging for dear life with one hand and sawing at the rigging with the other.

The knife seemed to take an eternity to sever the first shroud, then the second was attacked. Meanwhile someone had found the axe and had jammed himself inside the main fiferails, from where he began to hack at the foot of the mainmast. Kite lugged out his own knife and turned to the tarred ropes that strained like iron bars under the load aloft, and all the while the delicate fabric of spars and rigging trembled and shook as the loose main topmast swung wildly hither and thither in reaction to the bucking of the schooner.

But the hull lifted less readily now, sluggish with the amount of water that had been taken aboard, assaulted by the wind and laid over at such an angle that the cunning of her hull lines contributed little to her survival. The beautiful and lively schooner was rapidly disintegrating into a derelict hulk. For several long and tremulous minutes, as the men hacked and sawed, the fate of the *Spitfire* hung, quite literally, in the balance. Then, with a mighty shudder and a violent windward lurch that nearly flung overboard the energetic seaman forward, the mainmast went by the board, followed by the greater portion of the foremast and the entire jib boom. The noise of this collapse was snatched away by the wind but the deck was covered by a spider's web of fallen and tangled rigging, all of it still secured or fouled in the mass of spars and wreckage now alongside. How it failed to entrap anyone was little short of miraculous.

Slowly the *Spitfire* adjusted herself to this new situation, seeking the equilibrium between the force of the wind and her own exposed surfaces. The drag of wreckage affected the leeward drift and slowly, as rope after rope was cut through by the labouring crew, the *Spitfire* spun round so that she stabilised with the wind on her larboard bow and the mass of spars and rigging streamed out to windward, still secured by a pair of unsevered larboard shrouds.

With this Kite bawled his relief. "Avast there! Leave that raffle for the time being." It was no longer banging against the hull and its drag helped hold the schooner almost head to wind, keeping her vulnerable damaged stern to leeward. Within a moment Jones had all hands turned up and the men at the pumps. The carpenter's sounding revealed four feet of water in the well. Kite swore; it was impossible that such an intake of water had not damaged the greater part of their spoilable cargo.

As if to reward them for their labour, the wind now began to drop. It died rapidly and the cloud cleared so that the sun shone and speedily dried up the deck. The sudden brightening raised spirits, and grins of relief were visible all round the deck. Kite went below to order the cook to dole out a measure of rum to everyone, then he sought to comfort Puella. He found her crouching sodden in a corner of the cabin, the deck of which was awash. Amid the water slopping up and down were personal effects; a pair of shoes, a fancy hat and a stocking belonging to Puella, some papers, a feathered quill and a shirt belonging to himself. Splintered wood from the window shutters that had been torn out of their frames added to the mess.

Despite the water washing about her, Puella was fast asleep. Terror and exhaustion had succeeded with her where they had failed with Kite. Bracing himself against the lurch of the schooner he tenderly lifted her and placed her, wet as she was, in the dry cot swaying above the mess on the cabin deck. Slowly the water was draining away, exposing great shards of the shattered crown glass from the windows which lay shining in the sunlight now flooding through the open frames.

Planting a kiss upon Puella's head Kite glanced out of the shattered windows as he withdrew. Conscious that the schooner was now bucking violently again he went back on deck to find the whole surface of the sea boiling. Flapping and exhausted seabirds were falling aboard, adding the quality of a nightmare to the scene. Kite noticed immediately that the wind had fallen almost dead calm and divined the reason for the chaotic state of the sea. It was liberated from the tyrannical driving of the wind and now flew first from one direction and then the other. It struck him that each incoming wave was the remnant of the wind's force, and if the waves appeared omni-directional it followed that the wind that had generated them must be omni-directional too.

How could this be? Especially as now there was little wind at all. He went aft, the deck bucking madly so that in a sense this wild and irregular motion was worse than the steady onslaught of the tempest. He managed to work aft and stood at the taffrail, and what he saw seemed like a seething madness as waves slapped into each other, sometimes throwing themselves high into the air and the *Spitfire* was tossed about betwixt summits and troughs, like a cork in a millstream.

A hint of a steady gust blew his disordered hair across his face, coinciding with a cloud crossing the sun. The passing shadow raced across the surface of the sea which had, in the sunlight, lost its grey aspect in favour of its customary blue. But he sensed no pleasure from this brief warning; he noticed that the direction of the wind was contrary to what it had been. Half understanding the mighty phenomenon, he felt the prickle of alarm. Stumbling forward he bent over the binnacle, peering at the swinging compass card to confirm his partial grasp of mighty events. Another gust of wind swept the deck and he glanced up quickly, but the tell-tale had gone with the mast. Then as if pressing its insistence upon him, the wind picked up and blew steadily. Spray lifted over the rail and pattered across the deck, laying a feather of wet planking as if to confirm its direction.

"By God," Kite muttered to himself, "there's more to come!"

Within the hour the sky was once more overcast and rain swept down in torrents, driving across the deck with an icy chill which was in sharp and uncomfortable contrast with the previous warm, wet salt-laden air. It was now growing dark as night fell. They had had nothing to eat since the previous day, but the wind was increasing all the time and the daylight had not quite faded behind the lowering scud, before the wind shriek had deepened to the booming roar of the returning hurricane.

They kept the pumps going all night as the *Spitfire* wallowed endlessly, her bow held off the wind by the remains of the wreckage, much of which tore free during the hours of darkness. Towards the end of the night the wind dropped, imperceptibly at first, so that it was some time before the exhausted Kite knew their ordeal was approaching its end as the hurricane finally passed them by. Dawn found the *Spitfire* left to her fate, wallowing, waterlogged in the trough of the sea.

No semblance of discipline haunted her decks. Men slumped where they fell after the toil at the pumps, or dragged themselves out of the way to lie inert, uncaring, only glad to be allowed to sleep to a gentle rocking. Dawn found them thus, and the forenoon was all but over before some, but not all, were wakened from their slumbers by a piercing shriek.

# Fourteen

## The Refit

It was already dark by the time they had eaten and turned-to to clear away the decks, recover from overboard what was useful, and contrive a jury rig. The *Spitfire* had been pumped out and, though she was still making water, it was not an overwhelming amount and Kite felt justified in setting half-watches and allowing the derelict schooner to drift throughout the night while below, her tired company slept.

They woke much refreshed. Although a fresh northerly wind chilled them and set up a sea that rolled the wallowing hull uncomfortably, they were spurred on by the invigoration of an urgent task. In this work Kite was ably assisted by Christopher Jones, who took upon himself much of the re-rigging. Jones proved a master of improvisation, knotting and splicing, setting up tackles and securely lashing the main boom to the stump of the mainmast. The remains of the foretopsail yard were then rigged as a boom. It was hard and tedious work, both helped and hindered by the roll of the vessel, but by nightfall two small masts were stayed rigidly and a party had begun work on roughly recutting the remaining sails. With these it was hoped that the following morning they would be under command again and heading for shelter.

For Kite the dilemma was where they should now make for. He had no idea where they were, and missed a meridian altitude at noon due to the continuing overcast. The only safe option was to return to the west and try and make an identifiable landfall on the coast of North America. In the interim he would probably be able to obtain at least one observation to determine their latitude and there was a strong likelihood that they would encounter other vessels as they drew nearer the land. But the wind was not favourable, shifting slowly in the wake of the hurricane, and having bent on their improvised suit of sails they spent another night hove-to.

Dawn the following morning found the wind settled again in its prevailing quarter of south-west and they set a course towards the north-west. For several days spirits remained optimistic, but then

164

matters began to deteriorate as their progress remained slow and uncertain. They were already on salt provisions, but these were now unalleviated by fresh food of any kind. Their livestock had been lost in the hurricane, their bags of limes swept overboard along with their fresh yams and other vegetables. As the days dragged into weeks it was not long before one or two of the men became resentfully lethargic. This mild insubordination, Kite soon realised, came with an inflammation of the gums and, after a further week, a loosening of teeth. The first to be affected were the disreputable beachcombers among the hands, men whose bodies had been subjected to neglect and excess. Rum, that sailors' soporific, plentiful in Antigua, was a poor diet to prepare men for an ocean voyage. The outbreak of sickness coincided with two cases exhibiting the eruption of the raspberry-like pustules of the secondary stage of what was colloquially known as button-scurvy. This initially masked the outbreak of that quite different, but similarly named disease, the common scurvy.

Jones recognised the affliction of the two sailors to be yaws, an infection indistinguishable at the time from the pox, and the consequent shunning of these men by their fellows, and the general horror of contagion, made those with sore gums and loosening teeth conceal their own symptoms, ignorant that they were suffering the seamen's greater curse, the common scurvy. But the reality was unavoidable. Unused to protracted passages, Kite again confronted all the horrors of being overwhelmed by disease, a depressing repetition of the middle passage of the *Enterprize*. Neither he nor Jones knew what to do and this lack of leadership told upon the moral state of the schooner. Her sluggish progress seemed an echo of the mood on board, a lethargic indifference to everything and a slow acceptance of the inevitable. Kite abandoned all pretence at command as the first symptoms of the malaise affected him, concentrating all his energies on preserving Puella, who had hardly risen from the cot into which he had placed her at the height of the hurricane. She seemed to sink into a morass of apathy, hardly recognising him as she succumbed to the disease, and her listlessness hurt Kite, further reducing his own spirits.

In this desperate state, the *Spitfire* sailed slowly to the north-west, the last shreds of common consent seeing her steered by a tired and half-reluctant remnant of her crew. Kite and Jones clung to their duties, the habits of responsibility dying less quickly than the sense of obligation among the hands, and it was Jones who first saw the blue smudge of land on the horizon ahead of them.

It was also Jones who recognised their landfall. In later years Kite was apt to descant upon their abrupt change of luck, telling the story with a certain amount of embellishment and reducing its real impact as it assumed, for his listeners at least, the character of a *deus ex machina*. At the time, however, it moved him to revive his journal entries:

> It seemed that Providence, having Passed us through the Most Extreme of Trials, had Equally Capriciously changed her Mind and, having Decided to Deliver us from the Evil of our Predicament, now Smoothed our Path. Mr Jones Recognised the Lighthouse at the Entrance to Narragansett Bay and we stood Inwards towards the Port, passing Castle Hill with our Ensign Flying.

Christopher Jones had visited Newport, Rhode Island, on several occasions when he had served in slavers, loading rum for export to the Guinea coast in exchange for imports of 'black ivory'. In the euphoria of arrival Jones took credit for having brought them into the shelter of its anchorage, to which a relieved Kite took no exception. The experience of the hurricane had reminded him of the severe limitations of his knowledge. His rise to command of the schooner had been too fast for him to acquire solid sea-sense, and too circumstantial for him to have submitted to the rigour of a real apprenticeship. Indeed so affected was he by their safe deliverance and the relief this would bring to Puella that he was content to let Jones himself act as pilot, and bring the limping, jury-rigged *Spitfire* up through the narrows between Dumpling's Rock and Brenton's Point, to the anchorage off Goat and Rose Islands. At the schooner brought up to her cable, he publicly thanked the mate and shook his hand. It was a spontaneous but inspired act; witnessed by all hands, it repaired the disintegrating morale of the crew at a stroke, reuniting them for the labour of repairing their battered vessel. In his journal, Kite briefly reflected this turn of events, generously concluding the day's entry with the remark that, *to Mr Jones goes not only the Honour of being the First to Sight Land, but of Conning the Vessel to her Anchorage off Newport.*

In the weeks that followed, *Spitfire* lay refitting in Roberts' shipyard at Newport. The men of the yard, though obliging and thorough in their work, made no attempt to offer Kite hospitality, nor a secret of their disapproval of Kite's way of life. Once Puella had been seen in town, taken by Kite to buy outer garments more suitable to a northern climate and in readiness for their eventual arrival in England, an unsubtle campaign had inveighed against them. Kite withdrew to the *Spitfire*, concerned for Puella and her unborn child.

He reconciled himself to this state of affairs insofar as it relieved him of the expense of social pretension, for he was committing much of his negotiable resources on the refit, leaving him little for further expenses. High among these was the payment of his crew. Several wished to sign off and abandon the voyage, and Kite had no desire to keep unwilling hands aboard by refusing them their wages until they reached Liverpool.

In the end he was fortunate in shipping three young New Englanders for whom Rhode Island was a place of little attraction. One, a former clerk named Whisstock, claimed to nurse ambitions only satisfied by living in London, where he thought he could make his fortune. Kite nicknamed him Whittington, after the optimistic youngster in the folk tale.

The condition of the schooner had caused Kite some anxiety but in fact she had weathered her ordeal better than he had anticipated. A portion of caulking had been dislodged by the straining of the hull, but the prompt cutting away of the vessel's top-hamper had prevented serious wracking. The *Spitfire* was first careened and the caulking renewed, after which the greater part of the work was in re-rigging her. In this Kite took the advice of the master-rigger, who suggested some modifications in tune with the schooners of New England, better fitting the *Spitfire* for a winter crossing of the North Atlantic. Inviting Jones's opinion, Kite found the mate supporting the master-rigger's views and so the work was put in hand. The only other modifications were the fitting of stoves in the crew's forecastle and the cabin, where the repair work to the stern windows was extended to incorporate some additional comforts for Puella's convenience. This latter work was done in a frosty atmosphere of severe disapproval, for Puella had nowhere to go while the carpenters laboured. Though quite indifferent on his own account, Kite was distressed at being unable to prevent this affecting her. She retreated into herself, and Kite, preoccupied with the affairs of the schooner, had little time for her during the day and often found her withdrawn by the evening. She would crouch silently in a corner of the cabin, sometimes muttering silently to herself, communing with her spirits and talking to Dorothea. It was a disquieting reminder of her ancestry, but Kite sensed it was her way of coping with her intense loneliness, against which he was unable to offer any comfort.

With the vessel in the hands of the shipyard, the schooner assumed the unpleasantly uncertain character of a camp on campaign. In the circumstances this was not entirely inappropriate, for during the sojourn in Rhode Island they learned the latest news of the war. The combined forces of General Sir Jeffrey Amherst and Admiral Boscawen had been successful in capturing the great French fortress at Louisbourg in July of the previous year. This was in marked contrast to the bungled attack of General Abercrombie on Fort Ticonderoga, which been ignominiously repulsed by General Montcalm. But the French military commander was in disagreement with Governor Vaudreuil and the rumours coming down from Canada, where the British were now concentrating their effort, suggested that matters there were coming to a head. Better news from Europe was already stale; the Duke of Brunswick had won a victory at Crefeld against the Austrians, but while the work on *Spitfire* was in hand, Kite heard that Brunswick had won a second, decisive battle at Minden, on the River Weser in Hanover. Reports that the British field officer in command of the cavalry, Lord George Sackville, had disgraced himself by refusing to advance, amused the Rhode Islanders. This interest in a scandalous and gloomy addendum to the news of Minden, a battle of distant irrelevance as far as the colonists were concerned, was, Kite noted, relished largely because cheering news came from Canada. Montcalm had been killed and Quebec taken by British troops under Major General Wolfe after a night landing and a scrambling ascent of the Heights of Abraham.

The brilliant young hero of Louisbourg, Wolfe, had also been killed, but the exploit had overturned the French position and now the future of Canada as a French colony seemed at an end. There was also heartening intelligence from the distant coast of Portugal. Here, it was learned, a French squadron, on its way to join forces with the fleet at Brest, had been destroyed by Boscawen after a chase from Gibraltar.

Then, one morning, as Kite stood shivering on the deck in the frosty December air, the master-rigger climbed aboard waving a newspaper. "See here, Cap'n, we have drubbed the French good and proper. This will sting them mightily," he remarked gleefully. Kite took the proffered copy of the broadsheet and read of Admiral Hawke's dramatic chase of de Conflans deep into Quiberon Bay.

Apparently bad weather had driven Hawke from his blockading station of Brest and the principal French fleet had escaped to embark troops intended to invade the English coast. The French Minister, the Duc de Choiseul, had planned to seize a number of coastal towns and hold them as hostage against the return of Martinique, Guadeloupe and Quebec. This project was known of in London and on learning of the departure of Conflans from Brest, Hawke had sailed in pursuit, catching the French fleet in a rising gale off the entrance to Quiberon Bay. De Conflans hoped to slip through a narrow, rock-girt passage into the shelter of the anchorage there, confident that his local knowledge would ensure success while the onshore gale would deter Hawke's ships from closing with his fleet on a dangerous lee shore.

De Conflans was wrong; Hawke's men-of-war fell upon de Conflans' in a pell-mell, running battle which continued until nightfall, as both fleets manoeuvred among the rocks. The French were overwhelmed, their fleet almost entirely annihilated in a victory which crowned a year already being described as remarkable.

"Our anxieties are at an end, it seems. Surely the French will sue for peace," Kite said, looking up from the paper.

"Well, the luck certainly seems to be running in our favour, Cap'n, that's for sure, and with winter upon us I guess you're right. But to business, Cap'n," the man pressed and Kite handed the newspaper back. "See here, Cap'n, I shall complete work today and we must concert arrangements to move you from here . . ."

"Yes," agreed Kite, putting the affairs of the greater world aside and returning his thoughts to the matter of the schooner. "We shall have to reload that portion of our unspoiled cargo which we discharged, and I have arranged a small lading from this place."

"We will be obliged, Cap'n, if you would haul off as soon as possible."

Kite noticed the shifting tone of the man's voice and followed his glance. Puella had come on deck, pulling a shawl tightly around her and regarding the steely cold waters of the harbour with distaste.

"As soon as possible, Cap'n," the master-rigger repeated as he turned away.

Kite approached Puella. She looked up at him, her face troubled.

"What is the matter, my dear?" he asked, touching her gently.

"I do not like this place, Kite. It is too cold . . . Why do you laugh at me?"

"I am not laughing," Kite suppressed his smile, "but you have a talent for understatement."

"I have?" Puella looked doubtful, but seeing she had Kite's attention she smiled back. "You have forgotten me, Kite. I am alone . . ."

"No, my darling, you are not alone, you are lonely and I am lonely and I too want to leave this place. We shall be gone soon."

"How soon?"

Kite looked at her, then said, "That I cannot promise, but within a week, perhaps a little less. It depends how long it takes to stow the cargo."

"Will we be long at sea?"

"Three weeks to a month."

"And is England as cold as this?"

"You should not be on deck. It is best that you remain in the shelter of the cabin . . ."

Accompanying Puella below and persuading her to remain there, Kite realised that his provisions for her were inadequate, despite the fitting of the stove. The prejudice he had encountered on their shopping expedition had shocked him, so inured had he become to the presence of black skins in the seething and vibrant waterfront of St John's. A kind of condescending tolerance existed alongside the hidebound gulfs of inequity in the Antilles. Here, in New England, the assumed equality of the northern colonies was characterised by this barrier against what he had heard euphemistically referred to as 'the race of Ham'.

For Kite, both were infinitely preferable to the stews of waterside Liverpool, where neither quality existed and dog ate dog in perpetual communal turmoil. Something of that littoral mishmash added a louche charm to St John's, set as it was amid the lush tropic vegetation, working a sinister yet seductive interplay between the throbbing passions of the dominant whites and the down-trodden blacks. Here in the north, where the leaves fell from the trees in riotous colour, the austerity created a chill as penetrating as the winter frosts riming the bare black branches. Kite shuddered to be off to sea. But in the meantime he had other ideas; smiling at Puella he made his excuses and went ashore.

He walked into town, heading for a furrier's he had seen on his previous visit, intent on purchasing some adequate furs for Puella. The woods of the back-country provided an abundance of wild animals, and he was able to buy a fine fox-fur coat. He was in the act of negotiating for a large bearskin when a woman's voice overrode that of the proprietor.

"My goodness, Captain, she must be a very worthy mistress that can command so rich a wrapping."

He turned as the proprietor, not a whit disaffected by the intrusion, bobbed a bow at the newcomer. She was young, tall and strikingly handsome in a plain grey riding habit about the shoulders of which was cast an elegant pelisse. Above dark hair a feathered hat was worn at a jaunty and improbable angle and her gloved hand held a riding crop with which she tapped her long skirt, beating quietly at the boot beneath it. Kite made a small, stiff bow. He was aware that he had coloured up, angry with himself for rising to the woman's obvious innuendo. It was quite clear that this stunning creature knew of his identity and the colour of his mistress. Having delivered her deliberate slight, she was smiling insolently at him. Her effrontery fuelled a sudden anger.

"You refer to my *wife*, madam," he lied with such emphasis that his sincerity carried an outraged conviction which struck her like a blow from her own crop. But she was equal to the occasion and even as her cheek paled, she replied with such a cool composure that she heaped insolence upon presumption.

"Indeed," she said, stringing out the word as though passing judgement on him. "Your wife."

The woman's hauteur made Kite realise that his falsehood had worsened the situation. The guilt of his own deception further infuriated him, notwithstanding the conviction of the vehement lie, for she had coolly regained the upper hand. Puella as wife was in her eyes clearly worse that Puella as whore.

"My name is William—"

"Kite," she interrupted cuttingly. "Yes, I know."

"Then you have the advantage of me, madam."

"I know that too, Captain." She smiled victoriously. Kite felt a strong impulse to strike her, but swallowed his anger and turned to the furrier.

"We are agreed, then," he said, ignoring the woman.

"Ten Portuguese moidores," the man said, returning his attention to his business.

"You should pay no more than eight," the woman's voice came from behind him.

"There, sir," Kite said, "are ten moidores for the bearskin and a further two for your courtesy. Pray send the goods down to my schooner before this evening."

The astonished furrier picked up the gold coins as Kite took up his hat from the table upon which the rich fur lay spread. He turned and jammed it on his head as he confronted the woman whom he saw he had succeeded in merely amusing by his rather childish largesse. Her smile, for it was not a smirk, he was annoyed to see, tripped his restraint.

"Should you wish to learn manners, madam," he said coldly, "my wife would be delighted to teach—"

But he got no further. The riding crop struck his cheek and he recoiled, catching his balance and raising his hand to his face. The rising weal was already bleeding profusely as their eyes met. Behind them the furrier's sharp intake of breath seemed to have been his last conscious act before immobility seized him.

Kite's shock and the beating of his heart were as nothing, he noted with a painful smile, to hers. Regret at the impetuosity of her rash act made her first blench and then colour. She staggered a little as if resisting an impulse to faint, but then her chin went up and her challenge was irresistible.

"To teach you over a dish of tea aboard the schooner *Spitfire*, lying at Roberts' yard," Kite finished his sentence disdainfully and stalked from the shop.

The refit of the *Spitfire* was now almost completed. As the winter afternoon drew on and the sun westered, a red ball in a cloudless sky of pale lavender, Kite was standing amidships, in final consultation with the master-rigger and Jones. The following day would see them ready to warp down to the jetty and complete their lading.

"What happened to your face, Cap'n?" Jones asked.

Instinctively Kite touched the crusty scab that marked his cheek. He looked at the master-rigger as he replied. "Oh," he responded, feigning indifference, "a white lady gave it to me for sleeping with a black lady. I cannot imagine why, can you, Mr Jones?"

Jones shook his mulatto head, embarrassed in front of the master-rigger, who could scarcely contain his interest. "Well, I'll be damned, Cap'n. They sure aren't too friendly hereabouts," Jones said.

"You'll have noticed it too, I dare say," Kite said pointedly.

Jones nodded. "Aye, I have."

The master-rigger coughed awkwardly. "If we could just keep to the business in hand . . . Say, is this the lady concerned?"

Kite and Jones turned to where the master-rigger was pointing. The woman from the furrier's was stepping gingerly over the rail, her grey skirt lifted and the black leather of her boots gleaming in the sunset. A workman was handing her down, holding a large bundle which she had obviously passed to him for safe-keeping while she negotiated the bulwarks.

Thanking the workman and recovering her parcel, she approached the three men. "Captain Kite," she said coolly meeting his eyes.

Beside Kite, Jones whistled under his breath and the master-rigger coughed again. "Thank you, gentlemen," said Kite, turning, raising his hat and footing a bow as the two men withdrew forward.

"Madam?"

She offered him the parcel. "I have brought your *wife*'s bearskin, Captain."

"Thank you." He took it and stared at her, angry that she had chosen to invade his small kingdom, and coldly formal in the hope that she would take the hint and leave at once.

"I thought perhaps I could take tea with your wife," she said, as if nothing unpleasant had passed between them and they had known each other for years.

"To what end, madam?" he asked with cold civility, masking his astonishment.

He saw her composure slip to the extent of her shooting a glance at Jones and the master-rigger. "I wish to make amends, Captain," she said, her voice low.

"And why would you wish to do that, madam? I cannot think that you act without a motive? Are you simply curious to see my wife, or are you intending to whip *her*?"

"*Please*, Captain Kite." Her voice was little more than a whisper, her face strained. "Do not humiliate me any more than I have already humiliated myself."

He sighed. His cheek burned and throbbed. How could he explain to Puella what he had already explained as a flying rope's end? How could he tell her that this elegant and beautiful white woman wanted to gawp at her as a black exhibit? Knowing Puella's jealousy, how could he stop Puella from jumping to the stupid conclusion that the rich creature had designs upon Kite himself, just as Kitty Robertson had?

"I am *apologising*, Captain Kite," the woman insisted. "And have brought you the bearskin as an act of contrition." She paused. "I *would* like to meet your wife, sir, if only to explain why I struck you."

Kite almost laughed, then he said, "I have explained this," he touched his cheek, "as the result of a rope fall flying from a block." He saw her frown with incomprehension. "It is no matter."

"But I should still like to meet your wife, Captain. She must be lonely cooped up aboard here." She gestured round the deck and he suddenly wanted to be rid of her. If she wanted an olive branch then so be it.

"I owe *you* an apology," he said, hurriedly going on to prevent interruption. "Puella – er, that is what I call her, for it seemed cruel to give her an English name when I cannot understand her native one . . ." Then his courage failed him as he found her face quite enchanting.

"Go on, Captain, I understand."

Kite swallowed. "Well, madam, she is not my wife. In the Antilles these things are not so important . . ."

"Quite so," the woman said, the hint of a self-satisfied smile playing around the corners of her mouth.

"But she is free, madam," Kite said with as much convincing emphasis as he could muster. "She is not a slave."

He started to edge back towards the gangway, but the woman moved aft, towards the companionway where Puella, with that disarming intuition that she seemed to have inherited from Dorothea, stood at the top of the steps leading below.

Seeing her, the woman stepped forward, smiled and held out her hand. "Puella," she said, "my name is Sarah Tyrell, I have brought you the fur Captain Kite purchased this morning. I am afraid I am also responsible for the cut on his cheek . . ."

Kite, trying to distinguish sincerity from condescension, wondered if she would have been so ready to make amends if Puella had been white. Confused, Puella took the proffered hand and bobbed a curtsey.

"Shall we go below?" Kite said, aware that he had been out-manoeuvred and the extraordinary tripartite encounter had brought all work to a standstill even before the sun set.

As he reached the foot of the steps and turned into the cabin, he asked coldly. "Is it Mrs Tyrell, or Miss, madam?"

"It's Mrs, Captain. My husband is a merchant and ship-owner in this town."

"A man of substance, I imagine," Puella said. She had drawn herself up and stood, perfectly composed, waiting for an opening into the conversation.

Mrs Tyrell looked at Puella in surprise. "Why . . . I suppose so, yes."

"Would you care for tea or chocolate?" Puella asked courteously.

"Tea would be perfectly splendid, thank you."

"I am afraid I shall have to attend to the matter myself," Puella explained, "there are no servants to wait upon us since the steward is otherwise employed at the moment."

"Of course . . ." Mrs Tyrell was clearly surprised at Puella's elegance, courtesy and cool self-assurance.

"Won't you sit down, Mrs Tyrell?" Puella indicated a chair beside the repaired cabin table as she withdrew to the adjacent pantry.

"We have just suffered in a hurricane," Kite explained awkwardly, "hence our presence in Newport."

"Yes," Mrs Tyrell said, removing her gloves. "I am, er . . ."

"I think it best, madam, in the circumstances, if we swiftly let bygones be bygones."

"That is kind of you, Captain." She paused, clearly gathering herself. "I behaved unforgivably. I had no idea your Puella was so, so charming. Please . . ."

Kite capitulated and smiled sympathetically. Sarah Tyrell's fine mouth was working with some emotion and there was the faint glint of remorseful tears in her eyes.

"The matter was between us," he said consolingly.

"You are very considerate, Captain." Her voice was husky and there was a pregnant pause before Mrs Tyrell coughed and asked with forced interest, "Where did you say you came from in the Antilles?"

"From St John's, in Antigua."

"Would you have known the late Joseph Mulgrave? He was long linked with my husband in commerce . . ."

"We knew him well," Puella said, bringing in a tray with cups and saucers. "I took his name, along with Kite's, when I received my manumission."

"I see . . ." said Mrs Tyrell, digesting this intelligence and further amazed at Puella's command of English.

As they waited for Puella to reappear with the teapot, Kite explained their connection with the house of Mulgrave, discovering that she knew of Wentworth and that a commercial connection still existed between her husband's enterprises and Mulgrave's successor.

"Do you trade in slaves?" Puella asked, pouring the tea.

"Well, er, yes, I'm afraid we do, Puella."

"And are you *afraid* that you trade in sugar and rum, Sarah?" Puella asked with disarming candour, looking up and handing the elegant white woman her tea.

Kite froze, suddenly, inexplicably, outrageously and confusingly sympathetic to both victims, but Mrs Tyrell rose to the occasion. "No, Puella, we are not apologetic about trading in sugar and rum, perhaps we should be, since they are directly linked with the trade in slaves."

"There are some who—" Kite began, but Puella broke in.

"Kite should be. He takes me because he finds he is in love with me but he still carries slaves."

Kite made a self-deprecating gesture. "I annoyed Puella, by taking a few blacks from Antigua to Jamaica . . ."

"Love makes people do extraordinary things," Mrs Tyrell said with sententious obscurity, sipping her tea.

"Like striking a man with a whip?" Puella asked.

"Puella!" Kite protested, astonished at how she knew. Had she overheard his remark to Jones and the master-rigger?

"No, she is right, Captain Kite, right to question me as to why I did it." Mrs Tyrell's hand went out to restrain Kite as Puella coolly sat down with her own cup of tea. "The trouble is, Puella, I am not certain that I can explain it. I had heard, of course, that there was a schooner at Roberts' yard and that the master had on board a Guinea woman. It is not unknown for such things to happen, even here in Rhode Island . . ." Mrs Tyrell paused with a sigh. "The plain truth is that I was bored. I encountered Captain Kite in the furrier's and confronted him with . . . with what I thought at the time was his outrageous behaviour. Now I feel foolish and contrite and regret what I did, the more so since making your acquaintance."

"Well," said Kite with relief, admiring Mrs Tyrell's considerable moral courage in confessing so handsomely, "there's an end to the matter, then."

"Perhaps I can make some amends," Mrs Tyrell said, placing her drained cup on the table before her and addressing Puella. "Tomorrow, please come and dine with us. I shall send a carriage and I shall not take a refusal. My husband will be pleased to meet you both and, Captain Kite," she turned to Kite, "who knows, this meeting may yet end happily with benefits for all of us."

Though Kite graciously accepted the invitation, Puella resisted it. Partly through jealousy, partly through fear and largely because of being pregnant. She had no wish to embark upon a social event so ill-prepared, in conditions of such local hostility.

But Kite put up contrary arguments; Mrs Tyrell's acceptance, no matter howsoever it had been gained, cocked a snook at the prejudice of the townsfolk. It did not take much intelligence, Kite said, to see that Mrs Tyrell was a woman of influence: only a woman of influence would have sought to make a scene in the furrier's. She was also a woman of courage, for she had needed nothing less, he argued, to come aboard and apologise. Moreover, he went on, warming to the subject of acceptance, the commercial advantages that might result from any association that sprang up from a dinner were worth cultivating for their own sake. Puella rejected this as an argument for her own presence at the meal.

"If you must dine with her, dine without me," she protested, "if you care so much about money, leave me here. I know she has her eyes on you; her husband will be old and she will be wanting you . . ."

"Good heavens, Puella, she's not Kitty Robertson . . ."

"No!" flared Puella. "But here you are arguing to increase trade and put money into Kitty Robertson's pocket!"

"Oh, for God's sake, Puella, if I see an advantage in trade it is to put money in *our* pockets," an exasperated Kite protested. They fell silent, then Kite rallied. "Look, Puella, I cannot pretend that any of this is easy for you, but when you get to England you cannot – no, by God, I *will* not let you – hide away. You will have to enter society and play your part as my . . . as my wife. You are carrying my child and I shall," he said with sudden resolution, "make you my wife." Then without waiting to see the impact his words had had upon her, for they had had too profound an effect upon himself, Kite blundered on. "Look, my darling, you astonished that woman with your composure and dignity. I saw it in her eyes. You held your head up in Antigua, and you can do it here. These people here are unaffected when compared with the wives of the merchants of Liverpool and London. See this as your entrance into society, it will not be so terrible."

"Suppose she is making some plan to, to . . ." Puella was weakening, Kite sensed, as she struggled to find words to express herself.

"To humiliate you?"

"Yes, to humiliate me."

"I cannot believe that. She is not that sort of person. She is passionate and quick-tempered, but I think not ungenerous and unkind."

"She would humiliate me if she made love to you and if she is passionate . . ."

"Puella," Kite said reproachfully, embracing her, "I love *you*. Only you."

"She is dangerous to me, Kite," Puella whispered. "I feel these things. You cannot understand."

"My darling," Kite soothed, "in three or four days we shall be at sea."

After a little they spread the bearskin on the deck.

Afterwards, Kite had to admit, the dinner was an undoubted success, and though it left him personally disturbed, it proved a triumph for Puella. Anyone who supposed the blacks ignorant and inferior to the whites would, had they known the astonishing transformation that Puella achieved, have instantly changed their mind. Puella rose from their extemporised couch transformed, invigorated and confident. Kite foolishly ascribed this to the intensity of their lovemaking on the bearskin.

When Jones informed them of the arrival of the Tyrells' carriage, Kite, who had often privately nurtured the conceit that Puella was a native princess, had no doubt of the matter as he led Puella ashore.

Puella's condition, though well into its term, was not yet obtrusive. She had readily assumed the character of the *grande dame* by hiding her burden under the ample elegance of one of Dorothea's dresses. Mulgrave had kept Dorothea expensively and, so far as Antiguan fashion allowed, fashionably dressed. Dorothea and the local dressmaker favoured the brilliant colours loved by the Africans, so Puella's skirt, while it paid due reverence to the wide mode of the day, was of a brilliant scarlet silk, which susurated over a petticoat of yellow. Puella had cinched in the laced bodice, sufficient to both accommodate her growing belly and to expose her increasing bosom in the fashionable manner, while her ebony shoulders rose from tulle trimming of the very latest manufacture. She set off Kite's blue broadcloth coat, buff waistcoat, white breeches and hose, and silver-buckled shoes to perfection. Overall she wore the fox skin coat, while he affected a caped cloak of heavy wool worsted.

Kite had been anxious lest the Tyrells had indeed meditated some ritual humiliation, but there were no other guests present and while it was possible that none had been invited in order to save their hosts from embarrassment, Kite thought not. It was clear from the outset that Sarah Tyrell sincerely wished to make amends, or at least to signal that as her disinterested intention. Equally clearly, her husband was too much a man of commerce to be unduly troubled over superimposed conventions when they ran contrary to business opportunities. Besides, to hide the fact that they were entertaining a black woman was impossible – the servants who waited at table would carry the news about Newport within hours, though they concealed their feelings well enough at the time. Tyrell, bending over Puella's hand as he courteously greeted her, set the tone within the hearing of his manservant by welcoming her as 'Mrs Kite'.

Tyrell was, as Puella had predicted, much older than his wife: a tall, soberly dressed man who wore a half-wig and, though far less taciturn and obscure, somewhat reminded Kite of Mulgrave. Grave in his deliberations, he had the same quality of measuring everything carefully before any commitment, knowing that once made, that commitment was permanent. Beyond the difference in their ages, he was an odd contrast to his wife; a man clearly used to being listened to and obeyed.

"Shall we go directly in to dinner?" he asked, though it was clear that he had no intention of doing anything else. It proved a shrewd move; the Tyrells were too polished to allow the conversation to become stilted. As the soup was swiftly served, Tyrell's question about the hurricane drew a general account from Kite. After this Sarah sought a few personal details of Puella's ordeal during the tempest, while Tyrell led Kite towards the subject of commerce by way of a concern for the *Spitfire*'s spoilt cargo. Having drawn his young guest and made his own assessment, Tyrell asked whether Kite would carry some documents, bills of exchange and debentures to London on his behalf.

"I am not certain when I shall be in London," Kite had said carefully, catching Sarah Tyrell's eye and colouring at her smile. "But I am certain that I can attend to the matter."

"I supposed, foolishly it seems, that you were making for London, but you are intending to land at Bristol, are you?" Tyrell asked.

"No, sir, it is my intention to return to Liverpool. I have an interest in a company there."

It was clear that as soon as Kite mentioned Liverpool and his partnership with Makepeace, Tyrell showed a greater interest in cultivating a connection with him. It transpired that on his return to England Mulgrave had intended to act as agent for a number of colonial trading houses, among which was Tyrell's. Tyrell now encouraged Kite to assume the task.

"Liverpool is a growing place, Captain, and is already eclipsing Bristol . . ."

It occurred to Kite, as Tyrell expatiated on the mutual advantages that could arise, that Sarah Tyrell had picked up some hint of an advantage in securing the friendship of Kite early in their tea-party aboard the *Spitfire*, but he did not judge her too harshly for it. Looking across the table to where she was listening to Puella, he found it easy to forgive her. She had clearly charmed Puella, for she was speaking animatedly and, though he was attentive to Tyrell, he caught the drift of Puella's discourse, a reminiscence of her early life up to the time of her captivity. She had never spoken of it to him, and the facility with which Sarah had drawn from her the story of her youth, distracted him from Tyrell's conversation.

When the women withdrew, Kite accepted the cigar Tyrell offered him "Would you take a small shipment of these?" Tyrell asked, rolling the tobacco leaf alongside his ear. "You see, Captain, I think we can do business." Tyrell passed the decanter. "Rhode Island is famous for its seamen and its ships, its rum and its slaves, but as it grows rich on these commodities there is a corresponding growth in demand for English manufactures. We produce much in the colonies now, but a pair of English pistols, or a fine hanger from Messrs Wilkinson, will command a higher price than a home-made article. As for London modes . . . well, you are a young but not an inexperienced man in the matter of woman, Captain."

Kite seized the opportunity. It was not that he warmed to Tyrell, but he sensed the man spoke the truth as he saw it. "You have been kind to us, sir. You will be aware that the presence of my, er, wife has caused some controversy."

Tyrell raised an eyebrow and smiled. "That is true, Captain Kite, but I am not entirely immune to the lady's attractions. Don't forget that I knew Mulgrave, knew him quite well . . ."

"And you visited Antigua?"

Tyrell nodded, adding, "And I knew Dorothea." He blew cigar smoke at the ceiling. "I also know my wife is responsible for the disfigurement of your face . . ."

"Please," Kite said hurriedly, "it is not important, Mr Tyrell. The matter is over and best forgotten."

"That is generous of you, Captain." Tyrell paused then, draining his glass, asked, "So may we join hands in business?"

"I see no objection, Mr Tyrell. You are already associated with Wentworth and he with me . . ."

"And I know Makepeace, though I have to confess I do not much warm to him." Tyrell smiled. "You had better call me Arthur," he said smiling and rising to his feet. "Shall we join the ladies?"

Following suit, Kite felt he had been granted an honour and inclined his head. "William Kite, at your service, Arthur."

On that they shook hands and left the dining room.

Only when they were returning to Roberts' yard did Kite feel any disquiet. He was not quite certain how it happened, for the food and wine had relaxed him, but he recalled that Tyrell had been showing Puella a small portrait of a Mohawk chieftain, which was said to be of some antiquity, when he had felt Sarah Tyrell's hand on his arm.

"Congratulations, Captain, on your good fortune," she breathed, and Kite looked down at her fine dark eyes and red mouth. He seemed perplexed. "Puella's anticipated confinement," she said.

"Oh, she told you."

"Of course not," Sarah chuckled. "I noticed."

"I see . . ."

"No, you don't, Captain, but no matter." She paused. "We shall meet again, I am sure."

"I, er, I hope so, madam . . ."

"Call me Sarah," she said, her finger reaching up and touching his scabbed cheek. "You will not forget me, I think, William."

Kite glanced quickly at her preoccupied husband and the attentive Puella. "No," he replied, his heart beating foolishly, "it would be very difficult to do that."

She smiled and he felt his response said more than he meant, and yet paradoxically, he wanted to say more.

"Until the next time," she whispered, drawing away from him and holding her hand out to Puella as she and Tyrell turned away from the little wooden panel that bore the image of the Mohawk sachem. "Arthur has been showing you his great, great, oh I forget how many greats, grandfather . . ." It was a statement, graciously made, a rounding off of the dinner by setting a light-hearted seal upon it. Perhaps, Kite thought in the confusion of the aftermath of his moment of intimacy with Sarah Tyrell, she had meant the occasion as much for Puella as for him, and as much for him as for her husband. It had been a great making of amends. But in the carriage going back to Roberts' shipyard, as he cradled Puella under his arm, there grew a conviction that it had been chiefly for herself. The conceit tormented him as he lay awake beside the sleeping Puella, possessed of unfaithful thoughts.

"Good night, Captain," she had said as they parted, "it was a fair wind that blew you hither."

Held from sleep he damned the woman who only yesterday had struck him with her riding crop, and whom he had viciously wished to strike across her lovely face. And he hoped the spirits would not be so unkind as to spoil Puella's new-found happiness.

# Fifteen

## The Corsair

During their last few busy days in Newport, Kite half hoped and half feared to meet Sarah Tyrell again. In the event, as Nantucket Island faded astern and resumed the blue insubstantiality that Jones had first sighted weeks earlier, he was glad that nothing further had passed between them. Arthur Tyrell had sent his clerk down with the papers he required Kite to take with him and later the same day, shortly before sailing, Kite had waited upon Tyrell in his counting house to enjoy a glass of wine and a fine view over the harbour. He had cleared *Spitfire* outwards at the Custom House and was enjoying the last moments of relaxation before he took the schooner to sea. It was Christmas Eve and a fine winter's morning. Tyrell had been in a cordial mood, solicitous that Kite would not remain in Newport over the festive season, but sympathetic to his anxiety to sail, so that Puella could be brought to bed in England, with the passage behind them.

"My wife will be disappointed," he remarked as they took their leave, an uncomfortably enigmatic enough remark from Sarah's husband to make Kite feel a shred of guilt at the warmth Sarah had kindled in him. But it was the closest he got to Sarah, and to his relief Puella gave no further signs of jealousy. In his self-conceit, he did not realise the extent to which Puella was a prey to fear. Nearing the time of her confinement, alone and bereft of the support of Dorothea that she had enjoyed during the birth of Charlie, she was as much worried over the approaching ordeal of a long ocean passage as over the uncertainty of her future and the arrival of her quickening child.

Kite was blissfully unaware of her acute anxiety. The final arrangements about the cargo, its stowage and the necessity of attending the Custom House filled his time and thoughts. As they slipped seaward in the last of the daylight of Christmas Eve, 1759, the land was already in shadow and Kite could not see the solitary horsewoman who, from the eminence of Castle Hill, watched the *Spitfire* turn east-south-east, heading south of the skein of islands beyond Buzzard's Bay.

181

They took their navigational departure the following day from the eastern extremity of Nantucket Island. Ahead of the *Spitfire* lay the broad expanse of the Atlantic. Taking a final glance at the low and misty shore, Kite could persuade himself that no such place as Newport existed, and no such person as Sarah Tyrell had ever smiled at him.

Only the flaking scab on his cheek reminded him otherwise.

The *Spitfire* ran east under her modified rig at a fine clip. It was cold, bitterly cold at times, and the west-north-westerly wind blew for nine days at gale force, but the schooner and her company were undeterred. The North Atlantic, even in her wintry mood, seemed disposed to treat them kindly. Those few of the hands who regretted leaving the warm climes of the tropics were seduced by Whisstock's glowing accounts of London and Liverpool, where, he affirmed, a man could live like a prince once he had made his fortune. So seductively did Whisstock descant upon the delights of these cities, so easily did he brush aside the actual mechanics of securing a fortune, that even Jones was persuaded there might be something in his claims. Consequently, one evening, as he handed over the watch to Kite, he raised the matter with him.

Kite laughed. "He is deceived, Mr Jones. Liverpool is a foul place, though London might be well enough, I wouldn't know, I have never been there. But Liverpool . . ." Kite pulled a face. "True, there are some elegant dwellings there," Kite went on, relying on Makepeace's assertions rather than any experience of his own, "but without any means, and I don't suppose Whisstock has any means, he will be reduced to seeking lodgings in low alehouses where the only things he can rely upon seeking him out are the drabs and the pick-pockets."

"It's the old choice between the pox, penury and an outward ship, then?" Jones queried with a grin.

Kite nodded. "I fear so, Mr Jones, but he may prove useful in a counting house and so avoid the first and last. As for the pox, that depends upon his continence."

"I supposed as much," Jones said, embarrassed at his temporary gullibility.

They laughed and Jones, having passed over the watch and relieved himself of his ignorance, went below.

As the days passed Kite felt an increasing confidence, for the clear cold weather enabled him to verify their latitude and it held until they approached the north coast of Ireland and ran along the parallel of Malin Head, a month out of Newport, Rhode Island. He continually made plans, revised, honed and discarded them in favour of new ones; so high were his spirits that Susan Hebblewhite's murder was only a faint shadow on his horizon.

The plain truth was that the land ahead was as insubstantial as the fading blue of Nantucket astern, and the joy of sailing in this crisp, fine weather, for all the icy blow that hurled itself at them from the north-west, was unalloyed. Time enough, he thought, to worry. Makepeace was right. If not rich, Kite possessed sufficient funds to stand trial with a good defence if matters reached that extremity.

Puella grew in girth and was warm in her bearskin. The brief social encounter with Sarah had persuaded her she could hold her own among white society and Kite was too ignorant himself to disabuse her. As a country apothecary's son he was incapable of making the distinction between the easy manner of the wealthy, meritocratic colonial gentility and the rigid hierarchies of his native land. Thanks to the influence of Mulgrave and his experiences in Antigua, Kite had matured into a genteel and courteous young man. His own manner was natural and uncontrived, but as far as England was concerned he lacked the sophistication or pretension to judge how England would regard himself, let alone his beautiful but black mistress. While his high mood and higher hopes were a measure of his new-found confidence, they were also a measure of his youth.

They sighted Malin Head on the horizon to the southward, and the island of Inistrahull a point or two on the starboard bow shortly before nightfall thirty-three days out from Newport. Kite bore up and hove-to for the night, unwilling to run down on so dangerous a coast in the dark. During the hours of darkness the wind dropped, and he came on deck at dawn to find them wallowing in a dense fog. What wind there was, was light and fluky, while the damp struck into their bones with far greater chill than the brisk cold wind of their passage. All about them lay a wall of damp and impenetrable vapour.

Kite swore, suddenly feeling the lonely burden of command after the jolly, light-hearted days of carefree running. He was again made abruptly and humiliatingly aware of his ignorance and lack of sea experience as the clammy fog insidiously depressed him. Lost in his thoughts he wanted to return to his cabin, to bury himself in the bearskin alongside Puella; he realised the temptation to give up and abandon matters was a strong and seductive compulsion to a man eager to conceal his inadequacy. Was this why men like Makepeace got drunk or drowned themselves in sensuality? Now vulnerable, bereft of self-confidence again, Kite felt the looming spectre of the gallows rise. He could put the future out of his mind no longer. His imagination conjured the loathsome and fearful image within the wraiths of fog, feeling again a sense of personal doom.

Fate was mocking him, chastising him for his weeks of satisfaction as *Spitfire* raced across the Western Ocean. He damned himself for his folly, for being seduced by Sarah Tyrell and agreeing to undertake her husband's commission; damned himself for listening to Makepeace and his plans for wealth and partnership. The fog was an omen, a certain portent that matters would not, *could* not, go well for him.

Kite swore again, the foul oath bursting forth with all the conviction his ardent and frustrated nature could muster. He regarded the deck ahead of him with distaste. It was now full daylight and he could see the planking sodden with condensation; every rope dripped and moisture ran in rivulets from the slatting, idle sails; even the helmsman could do little with the tiller as the rudder kicked back in the low swell. Kite fretted as the hours passed, frustrated and worried, the anxiety eating away at the pit of his stomach. He wondered whether waiting until the damned fog lifted was all he could do.

On this occasion Jones was of no use to him, for cold and fog were as unfamiliar to Jones as to Kite, and although Kite had known both since his boyhood on the fells of Cumbria, he had then borne no responsibility and he knew the country so well that he had never been lost.

Now Cumbria and its beloved fells lay not far away, beyond the narrow strait of the North Channel, through which he yet had to take the *Spitfire*. There was much yet to accomplish, and whatever happened to him, he *must* at least see his father and sister again. The decision brought him up with a round turn. This was no time for self-pity and he was suddenly contemptuous of the temptation to give in. If men like Makepeace could master situations like this, so could he. Then he suddenly recalled something Makepeace had said to him. It was almost his last remark, a friendly afterthought as he contemplated Kite's homeward passage.

"Don't forget, Kite, that if you are in home waters, you have to consider the run and the set of the tide. If you are lost in fog and in soundings, you should anchor."

He had forgotten about the tides! God, what a fool! At least he had had the forethought to put about the night before. He called forward to have a man set in the chains and to begin swinging the lead. As he waited for his order to be carried out and the leadsman's monotonous chant to begin, he resolved that once ashore he would leave Liverpool for Cumbria and proceed directly to his father's house. He would hire a carriage and make short work of the journey.

God willing he would find his father and Helen in good health. They would take Puella in, care for her and tend her during her labour. He could then return to Liverpool, wait upon Makepeace and try his luck or take the consequences. The resolution cleared his mind. It seemed easy enough and honest enough; he had not, after all, killed Susan. A doubt crossed his mind that his father might be dead and Helen married, but then the leadsman began to call out the soundings from the starboard chains.

"By the mark thirteen!"

Kite's heart hammered; it was not a great depth of water after the bottomless Atlantic. "Call all hands," he bellowed, "prepare to anchor!"

There followed half an hour of confusion as the cable was roused out and dragged forward to be bent on the starboard bower. This in turn had been released from its secure stowage, catted and prepared for dropping. By this time the leadsman was calling twenty fathoms and then twenty-five. Kite went forward and stared down into the water, telling the leadsman to leave the weight on the seabed for a moment, in order that he could estimate the speed and direction of their drift.

The line lay stubbornly against the ship's side. For a few moments Kite was deceived, then he had the lead cast again from the opposite side. The line drew rapidly away from the ship's side, out on the larboard beam. Kite hurried aft and peered into the binnacle.

"Is she steering?" he asked the helmsman.

"No, Cap'n," the man responded, as if he had been asked if the *Spitfire* had been flying.

"Damnation!" The schooner's head lay to the north, but according to the evidence of the leadline they were drifting east. Kite was mystified, then the leadsman's voice sang out shrilly: "By the deep four!"

"Dear Christ!"

"Let go, sir?" Jones called, his voice high pitched with fear.

"By the mark, seven!"

The temptation to relax was great. Was the depth increasing or not?

"By the mark, five!"

Then they all heard the echo, *"By the mark, five!"*

"Jeeesus Chris'!"

"Let go!" Kite shrieked, hearing the splash of the anchor, then the diminuendo of his fearful order bouncing back at them. The hairs on the nape of Kite's neck crawled as he felt the deck tremble slightly as the cable ran out through the hawsepipe. They must be close . . . So close.

"Nip it! Nip it!" Kite bellowed when he thought enough had run out to hold the *Spitfire*. Somewhere the unseen cliffs mocked him: "*Nip it! Nip it!*"

Kite hurried forward and peered over the side. The cable ran round the bow, rubbing against the stem, and he could see the tension in it as the anchor bit, then he felt the schooner's head snub round as the anchor brought up and spun the *Spitfire* head to tide. Now the cable ran down into the water at an angle, disappearing into the depths; the *Spitfire* was static, and not adrift on the bosom of the sea.

Kite felt the deep undulation of the incoming ocean swell and saw the velocity of the tide as it sluiced past them as if a mill-race. He felt his heartbeat subside and he swallowed, his mouth dry. Straightening up, he felt an immense relief that they were, for the moment at least, out of immediate danger.

As he composed himself, he sensed a change in the weather. The deck seemed to be less damp, the dankness of the fog diminishing, the vapour increasingly nacreous. Then, patchily at first, the limits of visibility began to extend as the fog began to thin. It took a moment to perceive anything, then slowly, with each man exclaiming at the sight, the echoes of their surprise bouncing back, the cliff reared upwards alongside them. It was huge and close, so close that the schooner was rocking to the backwash of the breaking swell as it met the vertical rock face.

"Good God!" whispered Kite to himself. He stared up at the fissured mass. The strata lay at a slight angle to the vertical. Here and there small ledges bore the stains of bird-lime, spring nesting places for guillemots, kittiwakes, razorbills and little auks. The dark purple of the striated rock reared above their mastheads and was shrouded in misty cloud and the swell broke in a ceaseless necklace of foaming water at its foot. Kite shuddered. Would the tide have swept them clear, or did sunken rocks lurk nearby, as the variability of the soundings suggested? He would never know. All that he could be certain of was that they had avoided disaster.

As the warmth of the wintry sun slowly burnt off the fog, the first whispers of a breeze began to ripple the water. Fortunately these airs came from the south-west, filling the sails so that, sheeted home, the *Spitfire* began to creep up tide, over their cable. Their situation was too precarious to tarry and Kite ordered the cable cut. They would lose an anchor but the slant of wind might be temporary and he could not wait to leave the proximity of that mighty cliff.

The *Spitfire* stood slowly to the west-north-west and the cliff disappeared astern in the mist. Kite could only suppose he had touched the coast somewhere near the Mull of Kintyre, or perhaps the coast of Islay, but he was never afterwards sure. All he knew at the time was that he must get away and stand back out into the Atlantic to wait for a final clearing of the weather before he attempted anything so foolish as to head for the North Channel and the Irish Sea.

It was two days before the visibility finally improved, and when it did, Kite saw a sail to the east. The stranger was a brig, standing close-hauled to the north-west, heading towards them.

"Outward bound," Kite remarked to Jones, who had come on deck to relieve him. The two vessels closed on reciprocal courses, the brig flying a bright new red ensign, prompting Kite to hoist his own colours.

"I suppose," Jones remarked, "she could be a naval brig sloop, come to take a look at us."

The strange vessel was edging down, and would pass close to them and Kite agreed, remarking, "I think you're correct. She appears to have her guns run out . . ."

The suddenly the two were approaching to pass close, a man standing atop the rail of the outward bound brig waving his hat and Kite, leaping up on his own rail and hanging on to the main rigging, waved back.

"Bloody hell!" Jones yelled. "Get down!"

The red ensign was descending in jerks to reveal the white and gold lilies of the Bourbon French. At the same instant a few puffs of grey smoke, accompanied by points of fire, rippled along the brig's gunwale. The shot tore over their heads. Holes appeared in both the main- and foresails and a ball hit the hull in a cloud of splinters which erupted with the impact. Then the brig's helm went over and her sails slammed aback. A second later first her main- and then her foreyard swung as she tacked and stood close across *Spitfire*'s stern.

"He's going to rake, sir!" shouted Jones, as the horror of their predicament struck them, ending their stupefaction. Kite heard Puella screaming but thrust the intrusion aside.

"Larboard watch, run out the larboard guns! Starboard, tend the sheets! Up helm!" Kite lunged at the helmsman, helping to push the heavy wheel over to windward.

It was as well they had met the brig at the change of the watch with the entire crew on deck. Kite had no very great chance of getting off a shot at the enemy, but he could run for it, at least gaining a small lead on his opponent, whom he rightly concluded was a French corsair. By turning the same way as the enemy, Kite succeeded in buying himself a few moments' respite, avoiding the catastrophe of the brig's broadside being poured into *Spitfire*'s stern where Puella was hiding.

But Puella was not hiding, she was on deck. "What is happening?"

In the cabin she had heard the discharge of the brig's guns and felt the impact of the shot, then the heel of *Spitfire*'s deck had caught her off balance as Kite turned towards the enemy. Frightened, she could remain below no longer. Kite was strangely glad to see her. She had wrapped herself in the bearskin and looked so incongruous that seeing her thus he smiled despite the circumstances.

"We are in trouble, Puella; that is a French privateer. An enemy ship. We must try and escape."

As the brig turned, so did *Spitfire*, frustrating the French commander as he tried to place his vessel so that his guns could fire the length of the schooner's deck. Instead Kite drew away to the north and east, running before the wind, with the brig swinging in *Spitfire*'s wake. Kite picked up the watch glass and levelled it on the brig. She had completed her turn in *Spitfire*'s wake and although Kite had opened up a lead, she was clearly able to overhaul her quarry. That she was well manned and ably handled he had no doubt. There had been sufficient insouciance in the ruse of the waving officer, and the smart execution of her turn under their lee to convince him of that. But having turned away, Kite could think of nothing further that could be done. He looked forward. The larboard watch were laboriously loading and running out the larboard battery, but he had insufficient men to work the guns on one side of the ship, let alone two, even supposing he had a crew of competent gunners. This he had neglected, despite the letter of marque and reprisal that *Spitfire* carried. It had not been intended that she operate as a privateer until after she had fitted out properly in Liverpool. As it was, she carried scarcely sufficient powder and shot to fire off a dozen guns, let alone fight with her broadsides. Besides, Kite thought bitterly, as a privateer *Spitfire* was supposed to act offensively, not in abject self-defence.

Looking astern again he could see the brig appeared larger as she closed the gap between them. He felt a desperate and sickening sensation rising in his throat. In Newport he had heard the French were beaten, on their damned knees and reduced to suing for terms, so what in the name of Almighty God was this bastard doing chasing him in British waters?

Kite cast a wild look around the horizon, as if his desperation would conjure up the arrival of a British cruiser, but all he could see were the distant mountains of the Scottish islands, and they were too far off to offer the slightest hope of refuge. Night too was some hours away, even in late January, and as for fog, well they had had their quota, Kite felt sure; it was not going to oblige him by shrouding them at this juncture!

"Bloody hell!" he ranted as Jones hovered anxiously.

"You'll have to strike, sir," Jones said unhappily.

"I will lose everything . . . No, damn it, I shall not! Not yet anyway!"

"Our rig is cut down . . ."

"But we've another jib below. Get it on deck!"

The men seized the idea and went at the labour with a will. Even Jones cast aside his misgivings and was soon at the head of the crowd as another jib ran aloft. Some light-weather kites used in the West Indies appeared, straining at their bolt ropes in the breeze as Jones boomed them out like studding sails. The repaying of their hull at Newport meant they had a clean bottom, and with the extra sails their speed increased perceptibly. The schooner was racing through the water, the white bone in her teeth fanning out on either bow and, although Kite hardly dared believe it, the brig seemed not to be gaining on them so fast.

"Puella," he said, "be so kind as to bring me my quadrant."

When she returned with the mahogany box, Kite removed the instrument, braced himself against the taffrail, set the index bar to zero and carefully subtended the image of the brig, measuring the angle between her plunging waterline and her main truck. Compelled to wait for some minutes before checking it again, he looked forward. Jones was adjusting sheets, carefully gauging how best to set each sail. What else could they do?

If only they could fight . . . But with little powder and shot, and an ineffective and small crew, Kite had little hope of anything more than discharging the guns to defend the honour of their flag before being compelled to strike it. If only . . .

The guns!

He could dispense with half of them without seriously prejudicing his chances of defending himself if he had to. "Mr Jones! Jettison half the guns on each side. No, just keep three in each waist . . . . And – and run one aft . . . See if you can get it into the cabin as a stern chaser!"

Kite saw Jones grin as he grasped the idea and waved his hand in acknowledgement. The excitement between the two men was almost palpable now as Kite turned back to his pursuer and raised the quadrant again. There was a change; he bent over the arc and saw that the angle had increased. The brig was still gaining, but she surely only had a very small advantage. Perhaps when the guns went overboard . . .

Puella was beside him. He had almost forgotten her in his excitement. She was remarkably calm, he thought, looking at her.

"*Spitfire* is a fast schooner, Kite," she said, her voice level.

"I hope so, my darling."

"What do you do with the quadrant?"

He explained. "I measure the angle . . ." He realised she would not understand the simple geometrical principle, so held thumb and forefinger close together, with only a small gap. Widening the gap he moved his hand closer to her face. "If the French ship gets closer she seems to get bigger." Then he withdrew his hand, closing the gap between the fingers again. "If we go faster than her, she drops backwards and seems to be smaller. This," he tapped the quadrant, "can quickly tell me of a very, very small change, so that I can see . . ."

A cheer followed by a splash told where the first gun had gone overboard.

"So that I can see," Kite resumed, "whether we are going faster than she is, or she is going faster than we are."

Puella crooked thumb and forefinger of her right hand together and moved her hand towards and away from her eye, nodding. "I understand," she said.

Kite looked at her and impulsively kissed her. Below them a widening ring of bubbling white dropped astern alongside the wake as the second gun sank to the bottom.

"Has the other ship come nearer?" she asked.

Kite raised the quadrant again, then bent over the arc. The angle was still opening, but the difference was tiny, a minute at the most. Nevertheless, the enemy was undoubtedly overhauling them. An idea occurred to Kite. "Puella, I must teach you how to fire a pistol."

"I know how."

"You do?" Kite was astonished.

"Of course. Dorothea showed me."

"Would you fight and kill Frenchmen?"

"Only if they are white," she replied, smiling.

"Would you kill me, Puella?" he asked, only half joking.

"Only when you stop loving me," she said, adding, "and love Sarah Tyrell."

"Don't be ridiculous," he stammered. "I will get you a pistol."

Puella put her hand out to restrain him. "No. I will get one myself – and Kite?"

"Yes?"

"I will not let those men in that ship take me. I will kill myself first."

He stared at her for a moment and then said, shaking his head, "I hope it will not come to that."

She shrugged and went forward to the companionway. Kite watched her go: she had a damnably uncanny knack of divination, he thought uneasily. Then he picked up the quadrant. There was no doubt, the enemy brig was gaining on them, slowly but no less surely.

As another gun went overboard, Kite went forward and spoke to Jones. Then he ordered the steward to issue a tot of rum and resumed his station aft, just abaft the helmsman straining at the tiller, while Jones made the preparations Kite had ordered. It was a damned long shot, but he had little left in his locker and he guessed the Frenchman would try winging them soon.

It was another half an hour before the enemy commander felt confident enough of his greater speed to sacrifice a little of his ground, and to swing off course sufficiently to try a shot from his larboard bow chaser. The brig was slightly off on the *Spitfire*'s starboard quarter, so she swung away a few degrees. The shot plunged into their wake, but it was only ten yards astern, slightly off on the larboard quarter. Another shot followed, about the same distance short, but directly astern. The wind caught the spray and carried it forward over the taffrail of the fleeing *Spitfire*.

Kite walked forward and ordered a slight alteration in course to starboard. It was just enough to bring the schooner more directly ahead of the pursuing brig and thus compel the corsair to swing even further off course for his next attempt. The enemy waited for a full twenty minutes, by which time Kite no longer required his quadrant to ascertain the sober fact that they were still slowly but remorselessly losing ground. He decided he could wait no longer and went below to arm himself. He had decided to fight.

A party of seamen under Jones' direction were in the cabin, gingerly easing a four-pounder into the centre of the stern window. "Captain Kite, I shall have to break down—"

"Yes, yes, of course; do what you must, but hurry, the sooner we can respond to his fire the better."

A moment later an axe bit into the wooden sill across the window transom, breaking up the carpentry so recently installed at Newport after the storm damage. The crude destruction would lower the level of the woodwork so that the gun could fire over it, while the angle of traverse would be wide. Jones was extemporising train tackles and a recoil line, which if the gun were much used would probably bring down the central pillars in the structure, but it was a small price to pay if it saved the schooner.

In a corner, Puella had wound a sash about her waist and had stuffed a brace of pistols into it. "Where did you get those?" he asked, already guessing the answer.

"From Dorothea," she said quietly, darting a glance at the seamen. "Mr Mulgrave let her keep a pair."

Kite hid his surprise. As he prepared his own weapons, he told her his plan, his voice soft. At first she stared open-mouthed and then she laughed. "If it happens, Puella," he said, "it will be a desperate gamble. You understand?"

"Yes, I understand. It will be all right."

"I hope so. You must stay in the boat. I do not want you involved in the fighting."

"I want our baby son to be born in England," she said simply. Kite felt a wrench of remorse that he had not once considered the delicacy of Puella's condition throughout the day, let alone in contemplating the desperate measure he was about to take. He could only nod dumbly before returning to the deck.

Once Jones reported the gun in the cabin ready, Kite called the hands aft and addressed them. They had one chance, he told them, and he had explained his intentions to the mate. It would only work if they cooperated, to which they assented.

"Very well, then. The cabin gun's crew had better be told off, Mr Jones, and we'll get to work—"

Kite never finished, for the French brig tried another shot. It passed through the starboard rail, not eight feet from where Kite was standing, and splinters sliced across the deck, catching one of the seamen in the face so that he fell back with a startled cry, blood pouring down his face.

Kite swung round. "Steady on the helm there."

"All steady, sir." It was the former clerk, Whisstock, and Kite walked up to him. "Now, Whisstock, try not to look astern."

"Very well, Captain."

But Kite did, just as the brig, noticeably nearer now, let fly another shot. It flew over them, so that he felt the wind of its passing suck at the air he was breathing. The ball buried itself in the larboard bulwarks with a thud. Whisstock swore and Kite remarked to no one in particular that the brig had their range. Fortunately the ball had missed the men working about the boat, set on chocks amidships between the masts.

Then there came a roar and a cloud of smoke rose over the taffrail as the gun in the cabin below was fired. The powder smoke wafted forward, carried by the following wind. Kite missed the fall of shot, but waited for the next. As he did so, the brig fired again, but either a yaw of her own or Whisstock's momentary inattention saved them and the shot plunged alongside, level with the mainmast, but ten yards to larboard of them.

Jones fired the stern chaser a second time; again Kite missed the fall of shot but a cheer came from the window below. He doubted that they had achieved anything, beyond encouraging each other. He did not want to allow the brig to get too close before putting his madcap plan into operation, for the longer she had to wing them, the more chance she had of inflicting real damage. But he was conscious of having only the one chance and that everything depended on the hazardous plan he had put in place. He looked forward again. The cover was off the boat amidships and he saw Puella helped into it by one of the men, the pistols at her waist.

Nearby, the scratch gun crews had knocked the quoins out on the remaining trio of starboard guns and were retreating to hide under the boat. The rest of the crew had disappeared forward, crowded into the forecastle space, with only the boatswain visible, his head poking out of the forecastle companionway. He saw the man nod, his teeth bared and grinning madly.

A ball from the brig tore overhead and passed through the mainsail. The enemy were getting damned close!

Kite could wait no longer; he resolved to act the moment he next saw the tell-tale puff of smoke under the brig's bow. He turned his head, and shouted, "Stand by the main peak halliards!" The two men posted at the mainmast threw the coiled ropes off their pins, and eased the turns belayed there.

As he saw the enemy fire again, he yelled, "Let go the peak!"

The able seaman at the peak halyard already had the rope singled up to a turn on the belaying pin and now he threw that off. The rope snaked upwards from its carefully coiled fall, but at the same moment the enemy ball struck the stern and Kite heard from the cabin below a second wounded man scream in agony below. Everything was now happening at once and Kite fought to keep his concentration on the elements he must remain master of. Above him and winged out to larboard the main peak had dropped and the gaff swung wildly, the ensign half struck as its halyard ran slack. Beside him at the mainmast the second seaman now let go the throat halyard and the whole mainsail came down, the boom end trailing in the water. This and the loss of driving power slowed the schooner, but at this critical moment the continual screaming of the wounded man below cut into Kite's consciousness like a knife. He swore as Whisstock fought the schooner's desire to swing, the trailing main boom acting as a drag, but already the seaman who had let go the halyard was hauling on the sheet, hauling the heavy boom inboard.

He hoped the ruse had worked and the enemy thought they had

shot the main halliards through, causing confusion aboard their quarry. Suddenly the brig was looming up closer. Another cloud of smoke blew over the stern and this time Kite saw their own stern chaser score a hit close to the root of the brig's bowsprit, near the gammoning. A cloud of splinters momentarily appeared and he thought he heard a shout, but he was standing close to Whisstock, his heart pumping, and he could almost sense the thundering of the helmsman's own pulse.

"Steady, my lad," Kite said in a low voice, quite oblivious to the inappropriate use of a term for a man at least two years older than himself.

The brig was overrunning them fast now, faster perhaps than her commander wished. Kite held his course as the stern chaser barked again below him, reloaded with creditable speed. He coughed as the powder smoke blew past them and waved the cloud aside, but then the brig discharged her own gun at point-blank range. This time there was no mistake. The ball thumped into the mainmast about five feet above the deck, almost severing it at a stroke. The weight of the gear to larboard was sufficient to cause it to crack. It swayed forward, the break working right through the spar with a rending split until it parted and dropped to the deck, to lean forward at a drunken angle, restrained by the shrouds.

The brig's bow was now ranging up on the starboard quarter. Kite could see several faces peering down at him. He glanced round. His own gun's crews had hidden behind the boat amidships, and the decks looked almost deserted but for Kite himself, the helmsman and the two hands still at the main sheet. It appeared, or at least Kite hoped it appeared, as though the schooner was short-handed and had concentrated all her efforts at self-defence in the manning of her stern chaser.

Kite turned again to stare up at the brig. He could distinguish an officer from several armed ratings, and saw the former turn and shout something aft, presumably to the brig's commander. Then the man cupped his hands and shouted at Kite.

"Capitaine, do . . . you . . . . strike . . . your . . . colours?"

Kite feigned incomprehension as the brig drew level, forty, thirty feet away. The larboard yardarms of her forecourse and foretopsail almost overhung the starboard quarter of *Spitfire*.

Then Jones defiantly fired the stern chaser again. He must have traversed the carriage, for the shot struck the brig amidships and Kite heard the cry of someone aboard the brig hit by a splinter. He could hear an oath, too, saw the grappling line thrown. The grapnel struck the *Spitfire*'s rail and held. He drew his cutlass and cut it adrift, but another flew through the air and then the brig was ranged alongside and Kite knew they were going to be boarded before they could do any more mischief.

The sea running between the two vessels slapped back and forth, the two wakes cresting and hissing in a roil of confused water as the gap closed. On the brig the topgallant halliards were let go, the course clewgarnets were hauled up as the sheets were started and she slowed to match the speed of the disabled schooner alongside her. Kite swung round.

"Gunners! Now!" he shouted. The appointed gun crews leapt from hiding behind the boat and in an instant touched their linstocks to the breeches of the three guns left in the starboard battery. At maximum elevation and double shotted, they discharged with a close sequence of booms so that Kite's ears rang. He saw the ball and langridge, composed for the most parts of carpenter's nails, rovings and scrap, tear upwards across the narrow gap. All along the brig's waist this iron hail struck indiscriminately at men, guns, ropes and the fabric of the brig's hull.

Amid the screams and shouts of fury, an order was passed and then the brig's helm went over, the yardarms loomed over the *Spitfire*'s deck and she dropped alongside with a jarring crash. The next instant the enemy boarding party were jumping and flinging themselves down into the schooner's waist.

"Whisstock!" Kite bawled, discharging one pistol at an officer who had just landed and turned aft towards him. Amidships the handful of men at the three guns were driven back and Kite saw one run through. A second had got his hands on a boarding pike and parried a sword thrust before a pistol shot blew out the side of his face. But the man still thrust, impaling an enemy boarder to the rail as he fell, mortally wounded.

Kite hefted his clumsy cutlass as a French sailor struck at him. He longed for a hanger, light and handy, to fight off the assault, but he slashed wildly and yelled with all his might, "Puella!"

Her screech was terrible; a hideous, high-pitched and attenuated shriek that tore through the air to rend the eardrums. Kite had never heard anything so dreadful as Puella rose from the boat amidships, the terrible cry ululating from her throat in a long exhalation. On her own initiative Puella had removed the shirt she had had on and emerged naked to the waist, levelling her brace of pistols at the mêlée below her.

The effect of her appearance was diabolical; the boarders paused for a vital instant, staring up at the voluptuous black manifestation which might have been from Hell itself, and then the *Spitfire*'s boatswain and the bulk of the crew swept aft. Their faces were blackened with soot from the galley and they howled in pale imitation of Puella but their weapons were bright as they wielded them with telling effect. During their wait they had helped themselves to extra rum, served out by Kite's steward whose need for Dutch courage now justified itself.

As the black-faced men swept aft, Kite despatched his attacker, the crude and heavy cutlass blade raking the man's ribcage so that he fell back with a gasp. In the *Spitfire*'s waist the blackguard crew were prevailing as Kite had hoped they might. Reassured, Kite looked up to the brig's quarterdeck and raised his second pistol in his left hand. Although the slightly lower freeboard of the schooner limited his view, he could see the French commander, just recovering from his surprise at Puella's appearance. Kite took careful aim and fired.

Kite's ball missed his target's head, but he caught the commander's shoulder and knocked him backwards. A moment later Kite was scrambling upwards, over the brig's rail, with the boatswain and his score of blackguards at his back, and Whisstock howling at his side. It was Guadeloupe and Le Gosier all over again. He cut and slashed with a wild kind of joy, relieved from the hours of anxiety and mad with the prospect of victory, assuaging his bloodlust and intent on putting his tormentors to the sword.

In ten bloody minutes, it was all over.

# Sixteen

## The Captain

If he was to be hanged, Kite thought as he paced the captured brig's quarterdeck, it might as well be as a sheep, not a lamb. Above him the Bourbon oriflamme fluttered in the breeze, superimposed by the British red ensign; astern of him the disabled *Spitfire* tugged at her tow-rope, Whisstock and two other hands left aboard to steer in the brig's wake. On their larboard side the yellow line of Formby Sands, fringed with low breakers, formed the north bank of the Mersey Estuary. Ahead of them the river was crowded with shipping, a cutter-rigged mail packet was tacking out towards them, her post-horn pendant at her single masthead, beyond her a pilot schooner was outward bound for her station off the Great Orme. Two coasters were, like themselves, inward bound, from Ireland, Man or, Kite thought with a leaping heart, Whitehaven, Silloth or Maryport on his native Cumbrian coast. Over on the Cheshire shore stood the White Rock Perch, and behind the beacon lay the low eminence of Bidston Hill, conspicuous with its windmills and the mast and spars of the lookout station. To starboard stretched the brown tidal flats of the Burbo Bank, beyond which rose the blue rounded hills of Flintshire. The dark peaks of a score of fishing boats, the paler sails of another pilot schooner and the square topsails of a cruising frigate dotted the horizon astern. It would be hard to make a more public entry on his return to Liverpool, Kite thought ruefully.

*The Conspiracy of Fate*, Kite had written in his journal the previous evening,

> has Ensured that I shall Return in what the World Considers as Triumph. Luck Delivered into our Hands a fine French Corsair Brig, *La Malouine*, of St Malo, which having Attempted to Take us, we Boarded and carried at the Push of Pike. We found our Advantage derived from her being Short-Handed on Account of the Success of her Cruise and her having sent away the Greater Part of her Company in Prizes . . .

Nor had their luck ended there, Kite thought, for among those on board Jones had discovered a Liverpool pilot named Farnell, who was much relieved to be delivered from his captivity. The unfortunate man had been captured in an outward-bound snow and retained on board by the corsair's commander, Capitaine Jean-Marie Guillermic, to advise him on navigation in the North and St George's Channels. Now Farnell stood beside the helmsman and conned them up the Channel as the young flood made beneath them.

"It is a small price to pay in recompense for my freedom," Farnell had said, waving aside any suggestion of a fee, "though I expect my wife would have been glad to see my stern for a while," he joked.

Below in his own cabin, Capitaine Guillermic lay a prisoner in his cot, his shoulder wound poisoning and his mind wandering in feverish distraction. In the brig's wardroom, under the guard of the boatswain whose face still bore greasy traces of his black mask, lay the rest of the wounded, including *Spitfire*'s own men. Puella and the cabin steward did what they could, but four Frenchmen and five of the *Spitfire*'s polyglot crew had already died of their wounds. The remainder of *La Malouine*'s company lay below hatches in the hold, one of their own guns loaded with langridge trained on the only access and a seaman with a lighted linstock standing guard over them.

The westerly breeze filled *La Malouine*'s sails, so that she made a brave sight inward bound, a white bone in her teeth as she swept up the Formby Channel on the flood tide. The lookouts on Bidston Hill had signalled the strange brig's arrival off the Mersey bar. A crowd had gathered on the waterfront as they entered the river proper, and the Cheshire bank closed with the Lancashire coast opposite. As the spires of Liverpool drew abeam, the upper yards were dropped, the forecourse was clewed up and Farnell ordered the helm over. *La Malouine* rounded into the tide and let go her anchor, the tethered *Spitfire* following her and trailing astern on her tow-rope.

"Well, Captain Kite," said Farnell as he confirmed the brig had brought up to her anchor, "I am much obliged to you, and the moment my gig comes off, I shall seek your immediate accommodation in the dock."

"That is kind of you, Mr Farnell."

"There will be a great deal of curiosity about your arrival, Captain, but I can assure you the Liverpool underwriters will be most grateful to you. This bloody Frenchman has been making a thorough nuisance of himself for some time now, but thanks to you and your schooner, well, I at least will be able to get my anchor down in the lee of bum island, eh?" Farnell smiled and held out his hand.

The distant boom of the noon gun marked the time, but it seemed to the euphoric and tired men aboard both the brig and the schooner to be a personal salutation.

Farnell proved as good as his word. By early afternoon another pilot came aboard *La Malouine*, with a second clambering over the battered rail of *Spitfire*. As the tide slackened and approached high water, *La Malouine* weighed anchor, and crabbed across the last of the flood, to breast the dock wall and warp round into the dock. A crowd stood on the dockside as the two vessels secured in their berths, a small band had been mustered and played the topical tune 'To Glory we Steer', much popularised the previous year in celebration of British victories.

As they slowly entered the dock, drawn forward by the men walking round the capstan and heaving the dripping head warp tight, Kite regarded the waiting assembly. On the quay Kite recognised Captain Makepeace, his wife and three children by his side; Makepeace was addressing the bewigged mayor and a party of aldermen gathered behind their mace-bearer.

"We are famous, it seems, Mr Jones," he remarked as the mate whistled his surprise.

"You're right, Captain. And to think I asked you to strike the old ensign . . . Deary, deary me." Jones shook his head ruefully.

"Don't reproach yourself, Mr Jones," Kite said cheeringly. "No man did more to secure our success than you and I hope that, in a day or so, I shall be able to help you."

Jones looked at Kite, his mouth opened in astonishment, but Kite remained studying the crowded quay. "Ah, there's a file of soldiers . . ." Kite's voice trailed off as he was seized by a sudden apprehension.

"To take care of our prisoners, I suppose," Jones offered.

Kite cleared his throat. "Yes . . . I suppose so." Kite swept the doubt aside. "Mr Jones?"

"Sir?"

"Be so kind as to ask Puella to come on deck."

"There's no need, sir."

"I'm here, Kite."

Kite turned. Puella stood in her fox fur, which she wore over a grey silk dress, her head held high, the nostrils of her broad nose flared as she breathed the chilly air, her eyes gleaming with pride. She looked every inch an African princess and Kite felt an enormous surge of affection for her.

"I have never seen you looking so beautiful," he said in a low voice. As *La Malouine* crept closer to her berth the crowd began to cheer. "This is a remarkable welcome. I expected nothing like this," he murmured.

"Captain Kite is a remarkable man," Puella said as a gangway was run aboard.

"Captain Kite is a charlatan," Kite muttered to himself. "And worse . . . oh, so much worse." Then he raised his voice and said, "I shall present you to the mayor as my wife, Puella, and you must curtsey. It is a formality expected of us."

"I understand," Puella responded, nodding.

Kite hitched the surrendered sword of Captain Guillermic on his hip and eased his shoulders under his best blue broadcloth coat. He had last worn it to dine at the Tyrells' and now perhaps, with the Frenchman's sword giving him a specious claim to gentility, he was aware that such hubris preceded a fall and that file of soldiers made him sweat. But Puella was ready and the mayor was waiting. Gamely, he led Puella ashore.

Her appearance descending the gangway caused a stir, but the polyglot crew of black, mulattoes, quadroons and whites who milled in the waist watching their commander were not unfamiliar to the citizens of Liverpool.

As Kite bowed to the mayor, Jones shouted, "Three cheers for Captain Kite of the *Spitfire!*"

The crowd joined in and it was some moments before Kite could hear the rather mumbled welcome from the mayor and accepted the dignitaries' compliments for capturing *La Malouine*. He half turned and presented Puella.

"My wife, sir, Mistress Kite." Beside him, Puella dropped a perfect curtsey.

"Charmed, ma'am . . ." The mayor's tone was condescending and beside him his lady stiffened as her husband quickly reverted to Kite. "You have been in the Antilles some time, Captain?" the mayor asked pointedly.

"I have, sir," Kite responded coldly, adding, "and my wife is expecting . . ."

Whatever further celebrations had been meditated by the mayor and corporation, these seem to have been abruptly terminated on the appearance of Puella and there was a general retrograde movement of the robed aldermen.

"Then she shall not be kept in the cold, sir. Come Captain, it is already twilight, allow me to offer my conveyance . . ." Captain Makepeace swept to their rescue. "Kite, Kite," he chuckled divertingly in a low voice, "all this and a new brig too . . ."

"I have to clear inwards at the Custom House," Kite protested mildly.

"Time enough for your jerque note tomorrow, Kite. Ride the crest of this wave while you may. Come, my coach is close by . . ."

"What crest?" Kite asked, a hint of bitterness in his voice as the mayor and corporation withdrew behind their mace-bearer and the band were marched off.

"The gratitude of the underwriters will, I am confident, be made manifest in due course."

A young infantry officer suddenly barred their way. "Captain Kite?"

Kite coloured. For one ghastly moment he thought that he confronted nemesis and that the subaltern had come to arrest him, but the young lieutenant smiled and languidly asked, "I understand you may have some French prisoners, Captain?"

"Yes, yes, I do." Kite turned and called out to Jones. The big mulatto ran up, a cutlass bouncing on his hip. Kite suppressed a smile at the mate's ostentation. "Mr Jones, deliver our French prisoners to the custody of the lieutenant here."

"Aye, aye, sir."

"What about the wounded?" Puella interjected, attracting the lieutenant's eyes.

"I'll attend to them too, ma'am," he said politely, staring with ill-disguised and insolent curiosity at Puella.

Kite nodded. "Very well."

"Come, Kite, come, Puella," Makepeace insisted, "it is growing cold."

Makepeace had a comfortable house in a new terrace on the rising ground above the river. He had schooled his wife well and she gave every appearance of sincerity as she welcomed Puella into their home, expressing concern for her condition. Mrs Makepeace was a thin, plain woman, some years younger than her husband, but she was well dressed and bustling, ordering her servants to accommodate her guests and admonishing her children as they stared with ill-concealed curiosity at Puella.

"Is she a slave?" her youngest son, a boy of about eight, asked in a piping query. It was an awkward moment, but Puella smiled.

"Mrs Kite," Mrs Makepeace explained with hurried resource, "is a princess from Africa."

"Does she sell slaves?" the boy went on, but Makepeace's oldest child, a girl of thirteen or fourteen, clapped her hand over her brother's mouth and said, "You must bow to a princess, Harry," and she dropped a respectful and diplomatic curtsey.

"Must I, Mama?" the boy Henry asked, wrenching his head out of his sister's grip.

"Most certainly, Harry," his mother said.

Henry sighed and pouted. "I have to bow to *every*body," he

protested, footing a jerky obeisance. Then he turned to his brother, a shy handsome boy of eleven. "Now, Charlie, *you've* got to do it."

Kite looked at Puella and saw the shadow cross her eyes. The coincidence of the boy's name to that of her dead child made her involuntarily lift her hand. Kite sensed she intended to distance herself from the boy, caught up perhaps by some primitive native instinct, but Charles Makepeace stepped docilely forward and taking Puella's hand, bent and kissed it.

"Your servant, ma'am," he whispered courteously.

To Kite's relief, Puella was charmed and the awkward moment passed. Makepeace ruffled the hair of his youngest son and remarked that he was a chip off the old block.

"And spoiled to boot," said Martha Makepeace, revealing a streak of severity that dominated her house when her indulgent husband was at sea.

Kite and Puella enjoyed a pleasant enough evening in the society of Makepeace and his wife. It did not compare for courtly elegance with the hospitality of the Tyrells on the far side of the Atlantic. Puella found Martha a cold and rather hectoring fish, but Mrs Makepeace for her part meant only kindness, informing Puella of the general state of affairs among her equals in Liverpool in a relentless manner. When the ladies had withdrawn, Martha intent on continuing her instructional monologue, Kite told Makepeace that he intended to lay his private ghosts and proceed to Cumbria at once. He hoped that there Puella would remain until she had given birth.

As for his fears, Kite explained, "The matter must be cleared up, don't you see, before I can see my way to settling here in Liverpool."

Makepeace nodded. "I entirely agree. You will suffer from too much distraction until you have discovered how the land lies and, if, God forbid, it runs ill for you, you must return here and ship out in command. God knows, you have enough vessels to chose from."

"I had not thought that far ahead; so, you do not think I should stand trial and clear my name?"

"I see no point in courting trouble, no. As you are innocent, it is surely proper to act in an easy and open manner."

Kite remained uncertain. "To run away once under the impetus of youthful fear is one thing, but to slip away now would be entirely misinterpreted."

"Ah, but if you were simply to return and go straight to sea, who would know?"

"Well, you and I . . ."

"Does Puella know anything of this matter?"

Kite shook his head. "No."

"And you do intend to marry her . . ."

"Yes. I do not want the child born a bastard."

Makepeace refilled his glass. "Kite, my dear fellow," he said, taking a deep draught, "you saw the interpretation put upon Puella's presence by my innocent children this evening, and you saw the, er, surprise evinced by his worship the mayor and his lady. Are you aware of the effect an extrapolation of such behaviour by society at large may have both upon you, and upon Puella?"

"And upon *you* and upon your business if it is associated with me?" Kite asked, colouring.

"Of course," said Makepeace reasonably, draining his glass. "Let us make no bones about it between ourselves. It is important that we understand each other perfectly, Kite. Surely you agree." Kite nodded reluctantly. "Very well. To Puella. She may in time be accepted, but it would be better to keep her as a mistress, if you must . . ."

"You have long known how I feel about Puella."

"Aye, Kite," Makepeace soothed, "and I know the pleasure to be had of a blackamoor, or better still of two," he jested, "but she is black and black wives are too much a . . . damn it, too much a novelty to be so easily shoehorned into society."

Kite shook his head and seized the decanter, filling his own glass to mask his anger. "Well, it is too late now. I have told her I intend to marry her and I have told the world that she is my wife. I am obliged to. Damn it, I want to!"

Makepeace sighed. "You always were a contrary fellow . . ."

"Look, Makepeace, I am beholden to you; no, damn it, I am *obliged* to you, I need your assistance and we are, or are soon to be, partners – unless you want me to withdraw . . . ?"

"No, I don't. There is a great deal to be made of our association."

"But Puella is an embarrassment?"

Makepeace shrugged. "Perhaps. The women do not like it. They suspect all manner of things, silly creatures, but the presence of a black woman as a legitimate, churched wife is unsettling. It uneases them to think a white man takes pleasure from lying with a blackamoor; it demeans them; it breeds jealousy and that is a contagious infection. They may take against Puella, conspire against her in some monstrous way. Damn it, Kite, the gossips will have their day. They are probably already embarked upon it as we speak, for you could scarcely have made a more public entry."

"That thought occurred to me," Kite agreed ruefully. "It is scarcely without irony."

"All will be forgiven if we prove profitable." Makepeace raised his refilled glass. "Let us drink to that. If you sail again and Puella sails with you, then matters will likely blow over in time. Nothing succeeds like success. If we sink, well, we sink and no one will be surprised."

"We shall not sink," Kite said firmly, raising his glass in response to Makepeace's toast.

"No, not if the auguries are correct. You will have added another ship to our fleet once the prize court has adjudicated, and as your letter of marque is valid they can do nothing but find in your favour. Fortunately there was no naval cruiser in sight, otherwise the Admiralty Johnnies would be claiming a share, damn them."

"Which brings me to the vessels," Kite said. "After I have cleared the *Spitfire*'s entry, there is the business of the deposition for the prize court."

Makepeace held up his hand. "For Heaven's sake relax, Kite. The prize court won't sit for weeks; as for the other matters, I offer my services as ship's husband. What, when she has been awarded to you, do you want me to do with *La Malouine*?"

Kite thought for a moment. "It will depend upon the condemned value, but I think we should keep her, she is fast and fit for, well . . ." He had been about to say 'slaving', but restrained himself. "Well, privateering, as we know. I should like her to join our fleet, though her name will need a change."

"What shall you call her, then?" Makepeace asked.

Kite scratched his head. "Well, to be truthful, we would not have taken her but for Puella . . ." Kite regaled Makepeace with an account of Puella's diabolical appearance and the affect it had on shifting the advantage to the *Spitfire*'s hard-pressed crew.

Makepeace much enjoyed the yarn, nodding appreciatively. "Then we must honour Puella's part in the action . . ." Makepeace paused for thought.

"*African Princess*," Kite said in a low voice.

"What's that?" Makepeace asked.

"What about *African Princess*?"

"By God, I like that, damned if I don't!" Makepeace said enthusiastically. "I like that and by Heaven, once the yarn of her part in the capture gets out, as it surely will, it might arouse the jealousy of the ladies, but by God she'll be popular among the men!" Makepeace slapped his thigh with glee. "The matter's settled then: *African Princess* it shall be!"

Kite smiled. "Good. And if you will allow her value to offset my capital stake then we may set aside the surplus for the crew, for they will have a lien against her condemned value as a legitimate prize." Kite paused. "If you agree, that is."

Makepeace nodded. "Yes. I agree. What of your mate, the mulatto fellow, Jones?"

"He's a prime seaman, but lacks schooling."

"If you appoint him agent for the crew, would they trust him?"

"And he would have you to act on his behalf?"

Makepeace nodded.

"If I was to advise it," Kite said, "I think he would accept it readily enough, as would the hands."

"Then we shall retain him as ship-keeper and see he is put to his books. He may acquire the rudiments of navigation while we await the court's ruling. I shall inform the Admiralty marshal of the matter. As for the *Spitfire,* we shall have to take her in hand and step a new mainmast."

"She is otherwise in excellent condition," Kite said, telling Makepeace of his meeting with Arthur Tyrell in Rhode Island.

"And did you meet his wife?" Makepeace asked with a salacious grin.

"I did."

"And what did you think of her?"

"Beautiful and temperamental."

"Temperamental?" Makepeace snorted. "Never!" He leaned forward, a little drunk, as Kite had seen him so often before. "Now if you were to take my advice, Kite, you would bide your time before marrying and then, when old Arthur has slipped his cable and run off to Abraham's bosom, you'd secure *that* little wench. By God, but she makes a man's bowsprit into a jib boom, there's no mistake!"

"That's as maybe, but . . ."

"You've Puella, I know, and you love her. I know that too. Don't think I don't remember throwing her at you that night. I suppose I've only myself to blame, eh?"

"I suppose you have," said Kite smiling wryly. "I hadn't thought of it like that."

"Well, 'tis pointless trying to make the world different. It tends more to profit to accept the world as it is. Now, listen, Kite, listen." Makepeace was speaking now with some care. The hour was late and it had been a long day. They ought soon to join the ladies, who had no doubt run out of things to chatter about long ago.

"You have my absolute attention," he said.

"Good. You, my dear fellow, must settle your mind, and then your . . . oh, damn it, your wife! Take my coach and go north tomorrow, after you have been to the custom house. Then you can leave the vessels to me. Go north. See your father. Publish your banns and marry. Return when you are content. I'd be obliged for the return of my coach in the interval, but I will send it back for you if you wish. If you want to return directly, then keep my fellow and the equipage up there. You can find somewhere to stable it for a night or two, can't you?"

Kite nodded, overwhelmed at Makepeace's kindness. "You are sure? Won't Mrs Makepeace object?"

"Of course not," Makepeace slurred, "of course Mrs Makepeace won't object." He rose unsteadily. "But come, let's go and make certain."

# Seventeen

## The Return

As Makepeace's carriage rolled north, Kite tried to share Puella's wonder at the passing countryside. Fortunately it was a fine day, a late February day when the winter still occupies the high ground but there are tiny hints of the coming spring in the lower-lying land. They spent the night in Lancaster, where the shadow of the castle sent a cold shiver through Kite. His change of mood did not go unnoticed by Puella.

"What is it, Kite?"

He shook his head.

"I know something troubles you," she insisted.

He smiled. "We have a saying, Puella, that one shivers when a grey goose flies over one's grave. It is just a premonition, a forewarning of our mortality. A reminder that one day we will die."

"That is like the spirit of the *obi*," she said, and Kite gained the impression that Puella was pleased to have found some metaphysical link between her culture and his.

"It is very primitive," Kite said without thinking, then recalled that it was unlikely Puella understood the meaning of the word 'primitive'.

"You are primitive, Kite," Puella said.

"Am I?" he said, unable to disguise his astonishment.

Puella nodded. "Very primitive," she said rubbing her enlarged belly. They rolled into the inn yard and jerked to a halt.

They crossed Westmorland next day. The long pale ruffled finger of Windermere lay between its eternal hills and Kite could scarcely believe he had been so long away and these mountains and lakes had remained as he saw them now, indifferent to him and his tribulations. They were in their stillness, he thought, as heartless as the hurricane had been in its furious, excoriating activity. His own existence was quite incidental to their own, his own concerns so petty that they had no meaning in the cold aloofness of the physical world. And yet he had a part in this physical world; he looked across the carriage to where Puella dozed. His child quickened in her brown belly and it too, God willing, would know these wild fells as its father had done. Kite found himself for the first time thinking of the child as a sentient being, individual and complete. It would have Charlie's coffee-coloured complexion, common among the children of St John's but not common here. He recalled all Makepeace's warnings, but looking at Puella now he wondered how could one not love her. She had, after all, drawn the venom from Sarah Tyrell. Surely all would be well . . .

But the anxiety of his own future gnawed at him. What would become of Puella and of her child if he was arrested, flung into gaol and brought to trial? Worse, what if, for all his wealth, he was found guilty and hanged? And once the Pandora's box of worry was opened, fearful suppositions poured from it. Makepeace was but a mouthpiece! The hellish jest taunted Kite; without his protection Puella and the child would be subjected to God only knew what ignominies and humiliations. She would be seen as a nigger, her child as a pickaninny! What had he done, bringing them here, so that the unfortunate infant would see the light of day within sight of the Hebblewhites' farm?

Panic seized Kite. He broke out in a sweat. Suppose he was seen as he entered the village? The arrival of a carriage, any carriage unfamiliar to the villagers, would arouse curiosity. Within minutes the news would be carried to the Hebblewhites and they would send word to the magistrates. By the morning he would be under arrest and on his way to Carlisle to await the Assizes.

And yet he had to see his father and Helen, for with them lay the only refuge possible to Puella if the worst was to happen to him. Kite gnawed his knuckle in an agony of indecision, staring at Puella asleep on the seat opposite. Almost maddened with terror, he stared at her long black lashes lying on her dark cheeks and her slightly parted lips. Why in Heaven's name had he fallen so hopelessly in love with Puella and her black and lovely body?

And then he knew with a painful clarity, as the carriage slowed at an incline and the hummocked summit of a hill drew into view outside the window, he had turned his back on these fells; they had not driven him away, he had fled them, taking his disgust with him. For he recognised now that it had been disgust at the sight of Susie's white and quivering flesh that he repelled him as much as the cretin she had born. Even as the breath left her body and she lay in so pitiable a state, Kite, her would-be lover, had experienced a powerful revulsion. Even now the thought of that moment made him sick.

Kite swore and mopped his brow. He was going mad! He let down the window and stuck his head out, gasping for air. The image of Susie, her legs apart with the monster between, slowly faded. He felt the breeze cool on his tortured face and the threatening waves of nausea subsided. The wind had got up and clouds swept in from the south-west, shrouding the summits of the old, familiar hills. Helvellyn rose to the east and the gleam of Derwent Water showed ahead as the road curved in its descent until they ran along its shore and crossed into Cumberland.

He drew back into the carriage and Puella roused herself.

"It is a small sea," Puella said yawning and leaning half out of the window.

"It is a *lake*," Kite explained, mastering his fears and settling back into his seat.

"Have you slept, Kite?" He shook his head. "Have we far to go?"

"No," he replied, wishing the drive could go on for ever.

A little later, as they came to a junction in the rough, unmade track, the coachman drew rein and asked Kite for directions. An hour later it was Kite who again leaned from the window. He recognised the spur of the mountain over the far shoulder of which he had fled the Hebblewhite brothers five years earlier. It seemed like the tensed back of an old and ossified beast, waiting to pounce upon him. Then he could see the valley opening up as the last of the daylight fell on the far side of the lake. The huge slope of broken scree still caught the sunset light as he remembered it, and the ebbing day threw the village into a premature twilight. He could see copses and farmsteads, and the tower of the church and . . .

He drew his head in and Puella, who had been dozing, jerked awake, staring at him. She reached out her hand and he took it, the white and brown skin almost the same tone in the gloom of the coach. We are one, he thought, she carries my child; after me, the child will live on.

"I will give you a son," Puella said, with uncanny prescience.

"How do you know my thoughts?" he said looking up at her, close to tears.

"I can see the spirits about you," she said, her hand clutching his as though she also understood his fear. He turned his head aside and saw the Hebblewhites' farm roll past, its whitewash grey in the dusk.

"Dear God . . ." he whispered.

The coach slowed. "Cap'n Kite, sir. Is this the place?"

Kite withdrew his hand from Puella's and dashed it across his face before peering from the window. It was almost dark, but not dark enough to obscure the sign above the door. He noted the paint was peeled and this reproached him even more than the legend: *Kite & Son.*

"Yes, stop here, if you please."

The coach jerked to a standstill. Kite opened the door, jumped out and lowered the step. He handed Puella down as the coachman dropped from the box with a grunt and stretched with a low oath.

"I will help with the portmanteau in a moment," Kite said. "Allow me a moment."

208

"Take yer time, sir," the coachman said obligingly, hoping for an easy day on the morrow. "Them nigger wimmin can't be hurried without a whip," he added to himself, unbuttoning and urinating against the offside front carriage wheel.

"Come, my dear," Kite said nervously, holding Puella's hand as she looked at the humble shop front. "Let us see who is at home . . ."

He tugged the familiar metal rod and heard the distant jangle of the bell. No light showed from within and for a long moment the place seemed to be deserted. Then a faint light swung obliquely through the windows of the shop, as someone approached along the passageway inside. A bolt rasped and the door opened; a woman, half hidden in a mob cap peered at them, holding a candle up to Kite's face.

"Is Mr Kite within?" Kite enquired.

"Who's asking, then?"

Thankful that he was not immediately recognised, Kite had anticipated this moment. He had no wish either to startle his father, or to announce his arrival. "I am from Liverpool and have letters for him."

"Are you from Master Frank?" the woman asked and Kite remembered his cousin. The thought disconcerted him. Had Francis learned of the arrival of a 'Captain Kite' with a captured privateer? Had Francis been among the crowd assembled on the dockside two days previously? He had not thought of that!

"Yes," he said hurriedly, seizing at a straw in the manner of a drowning man.

"Is that someone you have with you?" the woman peered into the darkness thrusting the candle further forward. "God Almighty! It's the devil!"

"It's my wife," Kite said sharply.

"Your *wife!*" The woman fell back and began to shut the door, but Kite pushed forward.

"Excuse me," he said. "Come, Puella." And taking Puella's hand he entered the passage and began to mount the stairs.

Behind them the woman screeched, "Missee! Missee! 'Tis the devil himself and his damnable missus!"

The smell of the house was exactly as he remembered, the dark stairs creaked at the fifth and the eighth step. As he reached the top of the flight and turned along the passage, the door of the small sitting room opened. The lamplight flooded out on to the bare boards, throwing out the shadow of another woman as she appeared in the doorway.

"What is it?"

"Helen?"

"Who is that?"

Kite recognised his sister's voice. "Helen," he said quietly, "it's William . . . Your brother . . ."

"Oh! My God!"

Kite stepped forward as Helen fell back in a faint and then he felt himself shoved aside as the woman who had answered the door passed him, having first pushed Puella out of the way.

"Missee Helen, Missee Helen . . ."

Kite followed the distraught creature into the room. Helen had subsided into a chair and the mob-capped woman bent over her in a fearful fluster.

"Is she all right?" he asked, and the woman turned, her face furious.

"What business is it of yours, you damned blackguarded devil!"

Kite's jaw hung open and he felt his own knees weaken. He leant back against the wall for support.

"Susie? Susie Hebblewhite? Christ, I thought you were dead!"

The woman haranguing him stopped, her face ugly and distorted. She was far younger than the first candlelit impression had suggested. "Who are you?" she asked. "Who are you? I know you! You are the devil . . ."

"That's William," a voice said, and Helen rose, taking Susie by the shoulders and soothing her. "That's William, Susie. Do you remember William, Susie?"

Susan shook her head violently. "He's a devil, Missee Helen, a devil and he's got Old Harry's wife wi' him! See! See!" Susan pointed, her stabbing finger trembling with terrified and pious indignation.

"My God!" Helen saw Puella in the doorway and Kite stepped forward to support the trembling, half-hysterical Susie in an attempt to reassure his sister.

"It's all right Helen, this is Puella, she is from Africa . . ."

But it was far from all right and it took some moments to calm the situation and restore a degree of equanimity to the two frightened women. But in due course Helen had ceased hugging him and had subsided to a genteel and decorous weeping while Susan, having poked Puella in passing, was finally persuaded to go down stairs and make some tea.

"I have nothing else, I'm afraid, William, we live simply."

"It is no matter, Helen. Is . . . Is Father . . . ?" He could not bring himself to finish the sentence, but left its uncertainties hanging in the close, lamplit air.

"He is out . . . Attending a sick woman . . . You will not know Mrs Sutcliffe, she is overdue and had been brought down with a fever, Old Mother Dole is with her." Kite remembered the midwife; she had been a dark and terrible presence the night his own mother died bearing Helen. "He may be back before long."

"And Susie," Kite said. "I thought her dead!"

Helen looked at him curiously and then at Puella. "Won't you please come in and sit down," she said. "I am sorry, this is all such . . . all so unexpected."

Helen stared with unconcealed curiosity as Puella entered the room and sat down. She had remained passively standing quietly in the doorway throughout this extraordinary proceeding. Now she smiled at Helen.

"Pray do not trouble yourself," she said, smoothing her skirt.

"She speaks . . ." Helen flushed and burst into a renewed flood of tears. "Oh, William . . . Who is she?"

"Come, Helen," Kite said laughing, "Puella is . . . we are betrothed. She is to become my wife. She speaks perfect English. She is an African princess . . ."

"And you," Helen looked up, her dark eyes sodden with apparent misery, "by all appearances, you are a gentleman."

"He is Captain Kite," Puella said insistently.

"*Captain* Kite? I don't understand . . ." Helen's confusion mounted, but Kite, suffering waves of relief at the sight of Susie Hebblewhite in the land of the living, if not quite of the wholly sane, yet still perplexed, sought to calm and question her.

"Helen, calm yourself, I beg. I shall explain everything but first tell me about Susie. I had supposed her to be dead . . . Did you ever get my letter? No, of course you didn't, Mulgrave died . . ."

"Yes, I did receive your letter. I recall it was brought me by a Midshipman Hope, who took the trouble to bring it all the way from Portsmouth."

"Good Lord."

"He was a pleasant man and we still correspond . . . Upon occasion," Helen added wistfully.

"But you did not correspond with me," Kite said reproachfully.

Helen shook her head and finally dried her eyes, pulling herself together with a muttered apology. "Father would not let me. We knew you thought Susie was dead, but Father said that if you thought that, and that you had killed her, you would make your own way in the world and, since he knew no other way in which you would be stirred to do so, he would not stop you."

"But I was innocent . . . I had no hand in her murder . . . I mean her injuries . . ."

Helen raised her hand to her lips as Susie came into the room with a tray of tea. "Thank you, Susie," Helen said. "Will you wait up until the master comes home."

"Of course, Missee Helen, I always does."

"Helen, I have a carriage and four along with a coachman outside. Would you have room for him?"

"Mrs Ostlethwaite'll have a room, Missee Helen," Susie said. She seemed calmer now and willing to help. "An' I'll send him up to the farm to stable the horses."

"That would be kind of you, Susie," Kite said, but Susie never took her eyes off Helen and she nodded. "If you would be so kind, Susie."

"I'll walk up with him, then," Susie said, throwing a quick glance at Puella. Kite heard her muttering as she left, and could hear her uttering imprecations as the eighth stair creaked under her weight.

"She doesn't appear to recognise me, or affects not to," Kite said.

"You are much changed, Will. I hardly knew you, but for your voice; your skin is so burnt . . ." Helen looked nervously at Puella.

Kite expelled his breath and Helen, colouring, poured the tea. "You know I never touched Susie, Helen," Kite said. "I came across her in the barn where she lay screaming and covered in blood."

Helen nodded. "She gave birth to a monster," she said matter-of-factly, handing a cup to Puella. "Philip Hebblewhite wanted people to believe you were the father and that that was why you had run away. Father was called to dress her wounds. He destroyed the still-born infant and heard her admit that she had never lain with you. 'Twas said that the child was sired by one or other of her brothers. Susie has been with us ever since but sadly the balance of her mind was disturbed and she will not recognise you, now you have changed so much." Helen shook her head and smiled. For the first time he properly recognised his sister.

"I see," he said, returning her smile. "But she was terribly wounded, Helen. Forgive me, but there was blood everywhere . . . The pitchfork . . . and," Kite frowned, "the child was *not* still-born . . . I am sure that the creature was living when I came upon her."

Helen shook her head vehemently. "Father would not lie," she protested, "he said the child was dead . . ."

"The child was dead, Helen, when I got there . . . But I did not tell you everything. It was not still born."

Kite turned and leapt to his feet. "Father!"

His father stood in the doorway, his old green coat about his thin shoulders, his face stubbled with his unshaven beard and furrowed with his careworn existence. "So the prodigal returns, eh? I met his coach and four seeking lodgings at the very farm this tragedy took place in."

"Father!" Kite repeated, nonplussed.

Mr Kite sighed. "According to the Scripture, I am supposed to welcome the prodigal," he said in his dry, remote tone.

"Will you not do so?" Kite asked, his voice thick with emotion as, with a delicate susurration of her grey silk dress, Puella rose with quiet dignity, her hands outstretched towards Kite.

"Who is that black woman in my house? Is she your whore?"

Kite shook his head. "No, Father, she is neither my whore, nor my slave. In fact, she is shortly to become my wife."

Mr Kite's face registered no emotion. "And what manner of man are you now, William? You look prosperous enough, but how do I know that your carriage and four is not hired?"

"If it pleases you, it is not mine. It was lent to me, Father, in order that I might come and see you . . ."

"That was good of you." Mr Kite's voice was richly sarcastic. "Five years is a long time . . ."

"For both of us, Father," Kite broke in, and Kite saw his father wince at the interruption.

"Well, you are here now. It is late. We shall talk of this again. I don't know where you are going to sleep, but your old room is still empty. Good night."

"He doesn't mean it, William," Helen pleaded as Kite turned back to his sister, his face angry and hurt.

"He has no idea," Kite said through clenched teeth. "Good God, he has absolutely no idea!"

"He knows, Kite. But he cannot say."

Kite rounded on Puella. "Oh, and I suppose you can see his familiar spirits," he said, his voice bitter with a vehement sarcasm that matched his father's.

"No," Puella said. "He has no spirit. He has given it all away to the woman who is having her baby."

Kite woke in the badly made bed to a howling gale and sheets of rain flinging themselves against the window. A pallid grey daylight filtered through the small panes and he rolled over to stare up at the ceiling. The same old cracks rambled across the plaster, making a rough map of an imaginary countryside which he had once peopled with warring kings and their armies, their castles and their cities. Mountain ranges and rivers and lakes intersected this chimerical landscape.

So, he thought as a gust struck the window and Puella stirred beside him, Susie was not dead. He had lived for five years with a fear as groundless yet as real as the kings and soldiers who had warred across his ceiling in their upside down and fantastic world. How cruel fate was, he thought; how like the cold rain that drummed upon the square of glass.

Slipping from the bed he tip-toed out into the passage and then descended the stairs, remembering to step over the creaking boards, only to discover that there were more now that gave under his weight in the silence of the night.

His father was in the warm kitchen, sitting at the old square table with its rough, scrubbed surface and the three rings burnt into its surface long ago by hot pots. Kite could remember the nights his distressed and recently widowed father struggled to cook for himself and his family at the end of a long day. The older man set down a steaming tankard and rose as Kite entered the low room and, for a moment, Kite thought he was about to withdraw, but instead he leaned over and lifted the kettle off the banked fire. Kite sat on the far side of the table watching his father fill a second tankard and push it towards him. It was filled with hot toddy.

"Thank you," Kite said as his father resumed his seat and stared into the glowing embers of the fire.

"We said the child was still-born," he said after a long silence, "to still any rumours. Old Hebblewhite knew you hadn't done it, though he had seen you enter the barn. He beat his louts when they returned after chasing you and thrashed the truth out of them. I think it was Philip who gave the thing its quietus and Philip, I think, who felt he had fathered it, but who knows? It was an unpleasant business."

"But she was . . ."

Mr Kite shook his head. "Unconscious and badly injured . . . Very badly injured. The pitchfork . . . You can imagine the filth . . . We drew stuff from her wounds . . . well, it was a nauseating business, but Old Mother Dole knew a few specifics and I was not entirely useless." A faint smile passed over the older man's face as he looked at his son. "She was no more badly punctured than had she been opened up for a Caesarean birth, for the pitchfork did not pass through her body. I think Philip was mad with fury; he was trying to stab the cretinous thing he had brought into the world and struck poor Susan. It was a foul affair."

There was a long silence, as Kite digested this information. Then he said, "Helen told me that you thought it better that I should be left to think that I had killed Susie . . . That even when I wrote you refused to let her reply . . ."

"What was the point? I could not afford to keep you." Kite's father looked across the table. "Well, Will, are you not twice the man now that you were then?" he asked.

"But . . ." Kite wanted to protest the cruelty of leaving him ignorant.

"Besides," his father went on, "you had run away. I assumed you were prompted by some guilt of your own."

Kite flushed. "Father, I never . . ."

"It is of no matter now. Tell me, that black woman you have brought with you. She is with child, is she not?"

Kite nodded. "Yes."

"Is this the first child?"

"No. We had a son, but he died of some form of infantile asphyxia."

"And where did this infantile asphyxia take place?"

"In Antigua."

"Is that in the West Indies?"

"Yes."

"And is she a slave, this black woman who is to become my daughter-in-law?"

"No. She was brought aboard the Guineaman in which I was serving, but I had her released and made free by an instrument of manumission."

"After taking her to your bed?"

"Father, do not think of me in the same way that you think of Philip Hebblewhite. Such an irony would be too much for me."

"But you wish me to take her into my house . . ."

"Only until our child is born and I have made provision for her."

"And where will this provision be made?"

"In Liverpool, where I conduct my business."

"In slaves and sugar, I suppose?"

"I have become a ship-master and a ship-owner, Father."

"Like Brocklebank of Whitehaven, eh? Well, well."

"I can much ease the circumstances of both you and Helen, Father. I can provide for your old age . . ."

"Do you love this black woman, Will?" Kite's father had turned towards him and Kite saw that the older man's reserve had cracked.

"I do, Father."

"And it is not simply lust?"

"No." Kite shook his head. Lust had inflamed him at Newport, but love for Puella had triumphed over that madness.

"And you lost a child, you said?" The import of the event seemed at last to strike his father. "I had a grandchild without knowing it."

"Yes, a boy," Kite repeated, "named Charles."

"And what is your woman's name?"

Kite explained, prompting his father to emit a low chuckle. "*Puella*, eh? Well, well. What a strange fancy . . . *Girl*, eh?"

"It seemed not so strange at the time." Kite paused, feeling the ice between them melting away. "Now I never think of the word as anything other than her name."

His father nodded and slowly rose to his feet. "I am growing old, Will, but I am glad to see you hale and well." He nodded. "Your Puella may stay here as you wish. Let us hope she and Helen tolerate each other and that she bears you another son." Mr Kite extended his hand and his son took it. "So, you call yourself *Captain* Kite, no doubt. What a conceit. Well, well."

His father went out in the direction of the latrine but paused in the doorway and turned round. His eyes twinkled and a mischievous smile played with the corners of his mouth.

"Puella, eh? Well, well. What on earth are you going to call your son?"

Kite followed his father as far as the doorway and leaned there, staring out at the dawn. The far ridge of the distant mountain's flank was as sharp as a sword-blade against the hard yellow light of the dawn. Long ago he had toiled up that steep and unforgiving slope of scree, in fear of his life with the Hebblewhite brothers in hot pursuit.

What a strange destiny had led him back. He stretched and yawned, shivering in the cold morning, the air tingling in his nostrils. The light was stronger now, sparkling on the frost riming the outbuildings, the wall and the fields beyond, yet throwing the fell into deeper shadow, its slopes, rocks, gullies and fissures hidden to him.

The freezing air invigorated him: suddenly the world seemed full of possibilities.

# The Privateersman

# Part One

## Death

# The Rice-Water Fever

The wind thrust him forward with palpable force, raising the capes of his heavy coat and pattering them across his shoulders with a strange fluttering insistence, so that he thought of black crows assaulting him, the frenzied beating of their wings just beyond his vision. The power of this image raised his heartbeat and made him fearful of the dark, stormy night. It was, he knew, populated with more than mere visions, for he could hear the whispers of the *obeah* women of the Guinea coast and the moans from the slave decks of a Guineaman sailing as swift as an arrow through the stunning beauty of a tropical night, a night whose perfection was marred by the sickly sweet stench rising from the gratings over her slave-rooms below.

Spiritually oppressed and instinctively wary, he hefted his heavy cane and gripped it like a club, half expecting to be attacked by footpads as he approached the corner, but the night was too foul for even those most opportunist of thieves.

He turned the corner and the thrust of the wind changed to a buffeting irregularity as it coursed up the rising street of tall and elegant houses. As the ground rose the wind came more directly off the River Mersey behind him and he felt its full force. A coach stood outside one house, a bright patch of light spilling from its open door, but the flaring torches of two patiently waiting link boys dissipated the domesticity of the scene, giving it instead a hellish aspect only added to by the figure of the coachman unmoving upon his box. The gale snatched away any noise of voices, giving it a detached, otherworldly appearance that was in accord with his mood. This was a night for death and dark deeds, not frivolous rioting.

He crossed the street rather than pass through that puddle of light and feel an irresistible compulsion to glance into the hallway. The lives of others had no part in his desperate fear and misery. Halfway across the cobbled carriageway the rain began, with a gust of wind that threatened to unseat his tricorne, and he hurriedly put his left hand up to its fore-cock to avoid losing it. The skirts of his heavy coat clung to his legs. He quickened his pace but the first sheeting squall struck him and drove at the nape of his neck with a chill sensation as if all the corvine birds in hell were flying to harry him. His heavy boots tripped on the uneven cobbles as he struggled uphill and he swore as he caught his balance, glancing behind him as if real crows terrorised him.

"You damned fool!" he hissed, forcing himself to stop and turn, to confront his primitive irrational fear with the cool logic of his solitude. Then the coach was coming up the hill behind him, its two lamps glowing like eyes and the black gleam of the straining horses' wet bodies presided over by the untidy black hump of the coachman atop the neat regularity of its swaying body. He watched it go past, blinds up and passengers oblivious to the drenching rain that in a matter of moments had turned the street into a hissing torrent of water. A footman on the box gave him a glance of commiseration and then it was gone.

The rain, almost horizontal in the little light escaping between the shutters, drove him uphill. The occasional sconced lamp only added to the desolation. Was it possible, he thought for one moment, to be *so* alone when surrounded by such habitations? But he already knew the answer: the presence of death isolated even those huddled now round their fires of sea coal in a lamplit atmosphere of familial conviviality. For cholera, like the tall and lonely figure, stalked the sea port of Liverpool.

By the time he turned the final corner, into a street that ran parallel to the distant river and whose houses thus afforded him a timely lee, his stock was sodden and the rain poured from the tricorne as if from three gutters. He clumped up the steps to the door and pulled the bell, turning to stare up and down the street as he waited, unconsciously pounding the step with his cane.

The door opened and he turned as the maid drew aside and bobbed a curtsy.

"Good evening, Captain."

"Evening, Bridget." He nodded at the Irish girl and stood in the hallway, the water pouring off him. "I'm sorry, m'dear . . ."

" 'Tis no matter, sir." She took his hat, cane and gloves and waited as he removed his greatcoat.

"Is there any news?"

"No, sir, nothing new . . ."

"Who is it, Bridget?"

" 'Tis the Captain, Miss Katherine."

As Bridget sank under the weight of his sodden coat he looked up to see Katherine Makepeace halfway down the stairs. The younger woman managed a wan smile. "Uncle William . . ."

"Kate . . . There's no change, I understand."

"No, no change."

"I am sorry."

"May I speak to you – please?" She indicated a door off the hallway, descended the stairs and, as he stood back, led him into the withdrawing room. A single candelabra burnt on a side table and the low light threw the young woman's face into stark relief. Growing fast beyond the age then considered as being marriageable, she was plain and almost severe in her looks, though her face lit up when she smiled, for she had perfect teeth. But she had nothing to smile about on this filthy night which rattled the sashes as the rain fell like a lash upon the windowpanes.

"What is it, m'dear?"

She drew herself up and faced him. "Uncle William, I fear the worst."

He nodded. "Yes, I understand. I know of no one who recovers once the disease has taken such a hold. You are taking those precautions that I advised?"

"Yes, insofar as we can."

"They must be most stringently enforced," he said, "with absolute authority, particularly so below stairs. It is imperative, Kate, or you, your mother and your servants will succumb."

"I have given instructions that all water is to be boiled and that they are to wash their hands when handling anything from the sick-room."

"Let us hope that is sufficient." Seeing the agonised look on the young woman's face, he added, "As I am sure it will prove." He touched her arm and smiled. "Bear up, Katherine, your mother will need all your help in the coming days."

"But –" she looked at him – "how did Father catch this disease?"

"It is everywhere, my dear, even up here," he suppressed any hint of irony, "and your father spent much time down in the docks and the lower part of town."

She was not listening and interrupted him, her eyes wide with concern. "Oh, forgive me, I forgot to ask after little William."

"He died this afternoon."

"Oh." The long expected news seemed to stun her. "Oh dear . . ." She hesitated, not knowing what to say. "I . . . I am so very sorry." The tears ran down her cheeks. "And it was the same?"

He nodded. "Yes, the rice-water sickness."

"And Puella?"

He shook his head and she heard the tremble in his voice. "I do not think she will last a month."

"She has the cholera too?"

He shook his head again. "No, but she has lost the will to live. I have seen her this way before; she withdraws inside herself and – " he sighed – "I am the author of her misfortune, hence my presence here, for I cannot remain at home this evening, though I suppose I must return later."

"You may stay here."

"No, that would be desertion and I cannot have that charge laid against me." He looked her in the eye. "I did have another reason for calling."

"About the ship?"

"Yes, I thought it best that your father did not know."

Katherine shook her head. "It is too late. Mother told him this morning. She was unable to prevent herself . . . I do not think my father took the news to heart, he was already in a high fever and seems unaware of anything happening around him."

"Well, there is nothing to be done. She is only our second loss in all these years, but it comes at a hard time."

"Uncle William, if – I mean when – Father dies, what will become of us?"

He looked at her and smiled. "Your mother will have a small fortune, my dear, a sufficient competence to sustain you and your two brothers. That is something upon which you may rest easy." He paused. "By the by, have your brothers been summoned?"

She nodded. "They are expected tomorrow, or the following day . . ." She seemed preoccupied and Kite asked if there was some other matter that troubled her.

"I have heard Father talking about money, fretting over some private matter, and Mother I know was anxious, so anxious in fact that she confronted him with the loss of the *African Princess* as though it was the summit of our calamities."

"I think not, Kate; that would be a gross exaggeration." He smiled at her again. "When the time comes I shall explain matters to your mother, and to you if you wish."

"Thank you."

But to Kite it seemed that this was no real reassurance. "Where is your mother now?" he asked.

"She is asleep beside Father, that is why I was anxious to know who it was calling at this hour."

"I am sorry, I really had no idea of the time."

"Oh no, I did not mind it being you. I was only anxious that it was not Frith. He will fuss so and pleads all sorts of excuses to disturb Father."

"Frith? You mean Samuel Frith?" He frowned.

"Yes."

"What business has Samuel Frith with your father at this time?" He tried to clear the fog of his own preoccupations away from his mind. Frith had called several times at the counting house to see Makepeace of late and the latter had dismissed his visits as being personal and not of much significance. "D'you know, Kate?"

She shook her head, a look of uncertainty crossing her face so that he was driven to dissemble. "Ah, I recollect," he said hurriedly, "I had forgot, your father offered him an interest in a Guinea voyage; nothing was concluded and I suppose Frith has grown anxious lest your father's illness interposed and stopped him participating."

"I do not much care for him, Uncle William."

"No, my dear, neither do I, and I should advise against either you or your mother entertaining him." This he said with perfect truth, adding, "I do not know why your father wished to solicit his interest."

Katherine looked at the floor. "Mr Frith had made Father a proposition regarding myself, Uncle."

"You?" Was this the personal nature of Frith's business with Makepeace? And was the opportunity to speculate on a voyage part of some proposed marriage settlement? Frith and Katherine were not likely bed-partners, though there were some advantages to be gained from the union commercially, and perhaps Frith might benefit from her embraces. He looked at her unhappy face as she confronted him.

"Yes." She shook her head. "I did not wish to accept, but . . ."

"Your father would not listen to you, I suppose. I did not know of this; but what was your mother's part?"

Katherine dropped her voice to a whisper, as though fearful of the very walls retaining her confidence. "She it was who proposed the union."

"I see." The ever-practical Martha's hand was not hard to discern.

"So," Katherine said, her voice hardening, "the death of Father will do nothing to loosen our bond with Mr Frith, rather it will be enhanced and Mother may feel compelled to unite our families in the interests of Charlie's and Henry's futures."

"For which you will be the guarantor."

"Yes."

"I see."

"Will you . . . ? Can you . . . ?"

"I will do what I can, Katherine," he said, wondering what on earth lay within the bounds of possibility. Katherine was entirely dependent upon her father, and if he died, Kite supposed her mother would have a greater influence upon the fortunes of her children. In the years he had known her, he had never entirely warmed to Martha Makepeace. Kate, however, was a sweet creature and not a marketable commodity. He tried to reassure her. "Thank you for your confidences; pray remember that you may rely upon me."

"Thank you, dear Uncle William." She leaned forward and kissed his cheek.

"I am not truly your Uncle William, Katherine, m'dear, but I hope you may count me a true friend. Now, if you will ring for little Bridget, I had better return to Puella."

"Poor Puella. You will give her my kindest regards." Katherine crossed the room to the bell pull.

"I shall. And please do you keep me informed of your father's condition. It were best, when the end comes, that you let me know first. Send Bridget; she is to be trusted, I think."

"I will." Their conversation ended as Bridget entered. "The Captain's leaving, Bridget."

As he left he turned in the doorway, a flurry of rain drove past him into the hall. "It is late," he said, "you should get some sleep."

# One

## Captain "Topsy-Turvy"

It was almost midnight when Captain William Kite reached his own house, buffeted by the gale against which it had been necessary to struggle. He went immediately to the bedroom, where the candle had almost burnt out. It seemed the only thing that had changed, for Puella sat in the darkness as she had when he had left, hours earlier. He stared at her, but she seemed unaware of his presence, staring straight ahead of her into the gloom, seeing at once the past and the future.

"Puella . . ." He called her name softly, but she did not stir, her handsome black features immobile, as though carved out of the ebony she so much resembled in the candlelight. He had removed his boots below and crept across the rich carpet to fish a new candle from the box she kept them in, for Puella hated the dark winter nights of these unfamiliar, hostile northern latitudes. Lighting it from the first, he replaced the old with the new candle and then lit another. Having reassured himself that Puella was beyond his contact, he left the room.

Holding the other candle he ascended to the upper floor, his heart beating heavily in his breast. He hesitated before entering his son's bedroom, then with a sigh, he turned the door handle and went inside. The candlelight fell on the body of the boy. The curly hair and the broad, flaring nostrils had all the beauty of his mother's, though the shape of his head was inherited from his father, as was the tall build and the line of his chin. "You would have been handsome, my darling buckaroo," he murmured, "like your beautiful mother and the brother that you never knew." He touched the boy's brow and the chill of the flesh still had the power to shock him, though he was no stranger to death. The finality of it had an absolute quality that was so at variance with the petty aspirations of his busy life; it mocked him with

10

a quiet, eternal jeering that was inescapable. Contemptuous of the solicitous intervention of priests, he felt again that solitary acquaintanceship with the ineffable and numinous power that bestrode the universe, familiar to seamen, hermits and the *obeah* women whose blood had so recently flowed in his dead son's veins. The sensation brought him no comfort, but with it came an unresentful acceptance. He, like his wife, bowed to the inevitable but in contrast to Puella he gathered himself again and in going on attracted her contempt and enmity.

Sighing, he rose and bid his son farewell. The dead boy would be buried tomorrow.

Kite softly walked down the stairs to his study where he picked up a blanket kept there for the purpose and made himself as comfortable as he could on the couch. When the spirits took a hold of his black wife, William Kite found it impossible to spend the night in the same room.

But he could not sleep alone either. The rain beat upon his window and the gale howled relentlessly, booming in the cold chimney and lifting the heavy curtains, so that he lay awake, tense and uneasy, as he had once lain in the cabin of the *Spitfire* as a hurricane attempted to dismember the schooner. With a monstrous effort he turned his mind from the cold body lying in the room above him and the immobile figure of his beautiful wife sitting with the past and the future gathered about her in the next room.

Grief over young William's death and a cold despair over his estrangement from Puella slowly ebbed. Instead his active mind reverted to the distraction of the evening, the situation in the household of his business partner, Captain Makepeace. Both had served in the slaver *Enterprize*, Makepeace as commander, and they had become joint shipowners in Liverpool towards the end of the Seven Years' War, men whose family lives were almost as interwoven as their business relationship. But what was he to make of Katherine's revelations about Frith?

Makepeace had never mentioned the matter of a liaison. Could his wife have been behind the match? That was a distinct possibility, Kite thought, sitting up. Martha Makepeace was a competent woman who in the years since her husband retired from the sea had lost some of her autonomy. By way of compensation, she had taken to manipulating other people. Kite himself had been relieved when she had, with every appearance of cordiality,

arranged matters between his sister Helen and Lieutenant Henry
Hope of the Royal Navy. But even supposing his conjecture was
accurate, surely Makepeace would have made some allusion to
it? He knew too much of the captain's past, of his flagrant
philandering on the Guinea coast, and this shady history linked
them so that they might have considered themselves confidants. In
the years of association in Liverpool their combined ventures had
drawn them closer, so that vexed asides about Martha's occasional
extravagances, the exasperations of fatherhood and the intermittent discord endemic in any household led him to the odd revelation. Surely, only a desire to conceal something from his partner
could explain Makepeace's silence on the subject of Frith.

Kite considered the matter further. In recent weeks, it was true,
Makepeace had been bound up with the purchase of a new vessel,
the *Pride of Galway*, but his preoccupation did not necessarily
conceal ulterior motives. Or did it? And had Katherine got wind
of something when she asked what would happen to her and her
brothers when her father died, as die he surely must? He would
follow his dead godson William Kite into eternity, for once the
dreaded cholera had induced its filthy rice-water flux there was
no hope of recovery.

"Christ!" Kite flung aside his blanket and rose to his feet.
He felt like death himself as he drew back the curtains. He
wondered if he had dozed, for it was light and the rain had
stopped, but he could see by the rigid winged flight of the
gulls above the chimneys that the gale blew with unabated
fury. The wind had shifted though, scouring the sky clear of
clouds.

"A north-wester," he muttered.

"Kite."

He spun round, startled. Puella stood in the doorway.

"Puella! You startled me . . ."

"I have seen into the future tonight."

"Yes," he said drily, "I thought you had."

"You will not be happy, Kite."

"That is scarcely surprising."

"Listen, Kite. Do not mock me."

"I do not mock you, Puella."

"You brought me to this terrible place, Kite."

He sighed, closing his eyes. He was too tired to remonstrate;
besides, it did no good. Puella was fixed in her views. As his old

father had observed long since, "she ploughs her own dark and incomprehensible furrow".

He bowed his head and when he looked up, she had gone. He followed her through into the bedroom. She lay on the bed, staring up at the ceiling.

"Puella," he began, sitting on the edge on the mattress.

She closed her eyes in dismissal and all he could do was touch her hand.

Puella refused to break her fast the following morning, or to leave her bed. She did not accompany him to the church for William's funeral, and the congregation was pitifully small. Katherine was there, as was his chief clerk, Jasper Watkinson, with Mrs Watkinson, and the assistant clerk Nathan Johnstone, whose wife had died in child-bed only two weeks earlier. Helen was in London with her husband, so poor little William had few to see him lowered into the cold earth. The gale only added a haste to the proceedings which Kite found deeply troubling as he fought to keep his balance in the buffeting wind.

Kite stood beside the priest as he intoned the committal. The man's surplice flapped with a furious distraction, like a flag, and his words were torn away in a mumbled incoherence. Kite's own coat remained sodden from the previous night and he felt the weight of it irksome. He was ashamed of this, guilt-ridden that it dulled the keen edge of grief, but the feeling of detachment was as much a consequence of his lack of sleep as was the gritty sensation in his eyes. Patches of sunlight streamed up the hill, over the distant masts and yards of the moored ships and the smoking chimneys, rising, it seemed, from the grey expanse of the Mersey, rather than emanating from the cloudy sky. The brilliant sunny patches were followed by deep, chill shadows, so that the change of temperature was as palpable as the unpredictable visitations of death itself.

Afterwards he stood and mumbled his thanks as Watkinson and his spouse awkwardly expressed their condolences. Johnstone followed, uncontrollably lachrymose, for the funeral too closely followed the burial of his own young wife.

"I'm so sorry, sir, so very, very sorry . . ."

"Thank you, Nathan," Kite said solemnly, wretched at the compounding of the man's grief.

Then Katherine was beside him, her plain face damp with tears. "I'm so sorry, Uncle William."

The paucity of words struck him: everyone was so sorry, as though they were apologising for their part in the sad little affair. "Thank you, m'dear," he said, touching her hand. "How is your father today?"

She shook her head. "My mother asked for you, but I did not like to distract you."

"I shall wait upon her later, Kate. It was good of you to come. Are you alone? If so I shall walk you home."

"No, no, that will not be necessary." She gestured unhappily to a figure whom Kite had not noticed before. Frith bowed.

"My condolences, Captain Kite, upon your grievous loss."

"Thank you, sir." Kite returned the bow. Frith had managed a different formula. It was more appropriate, but its uninterest was manifest.

"Your wife – is much afflicted, I don't doubt, Captain Kite."

"She is distraught, sir, as you may well imagine."

"Of course." Frith bowed again, then straightening up put on his hat and offered his arm to Katherine. Kite caught the glance that she threw at her honorary uncle and put his own hat upon his head. The priest was hovering for his fee. But as Kite walked towards that worthy he could not escape the slight hint of insolence in that small hesitation Frith had interjected to his reference to Puella. It was done by a man who knew of a secret power he had over his ignorant interlocutor.

Kite was seized with the conviction that Katherine, poor unhappy Katherine, had indeed got wind of something sinister. Returning home only to confirm what in his heart he already knew, that Puella had refused any food, he replaced his hat and made again for his door. He should, he knew, have invited the small funerary party back for some sustenance, but with the shadow of Puella's grief adding to the lugubrious morning he could not do it. Instead, he walked again to the Makepeaces' house where Bridget bobbed him her deferential curtsy and asked him to wait.

Mrs Makepeace came to him, red-eyed from weeping and watching at her husband's bedside.

"Oh, William, I am so glad to see you. He has not long now."

"Has the doctor . . .?"

Martha Makepeace shook her head. "He has gone." She paused, then added, "And he will not see a priest." The news did not surprise Kite, but he lowered his head in sympathy. He felt for Martha and her family, but his own situation continually overlaid theirs.

"I understand he was asking to see me, Martha," he said gently, and she nodded, recovering some of her old, familiar, brisk efficiency.

"Yes. Please forgive me. Come."

Kite followed her upstairs and into their bedroom. The curtains were drawn but Makepeace's pallid features were illuminated by a candle. His face was already cadaverous and immobile, the skin like wax, the lips all but gone and his mouth a dark hole through which he drew breath. His eyes seemed large, like a newborn child's, except that their rims were red and watery, and they fastened on Kite's figure as he loomed into the candlelight.

Makepeace lifted a hand and with a tiny gesture beckoned Kite, so that he bent to him.

"Makepeace, old friend . . ." he said, "it is Will Kite come to see you."

The dying man's lips moved and Kite bent to hear what he was trying to say, taking his hand and squeezing it gently. It felt like a scrap of discarded paper.

The words came out clearly, wheezed with long gaps between them, evidence of the effort that went into their enunciation. "You . . . must . . . forgive . . . me . . ."

Kite frowned and raised his head, to look Makepeace in the face. "There is nothing to forgive, old fellow."

But there was a blazing in Makepeace's eyes, a final desperate attempt to communicate, and then, quite loudly, just as Katherine came into the room, Makepeace said, "Forgive . . ."

"Oh, God." Martha was at the bedside on her knees as Kite straightened up and stepped back into the shadows. He caught Katherine's eyes and shook his head. She turned to the curtains, pulled them back and threw open the window. Then she went to the bedside and knelt beside her mother. Kite withdrew.

At the foot of the stairs Makepeace's manservant was waiting with Bridget.

"Your master is dead. You may send for me if there is anything Mistress Makepeace wishes me to attend to."

"There is no need to concern yourself, Captain." Frith's figure emerged from the side parlour. "You have troubles enough of your own, I imagine."

There was something unpleasantly insinuating about Frith's presence, Kite thought, but he merely bowed and took his hat and cane from Bridget.

"Thank you, Bridget," he said, noting the tears in her eyes.

Kite could not stay in his own house with Puella refusing to see him, and although he remained there for the rest of that day, and that night slept again in his study, he made for his company's chambers off Water Street early the following morning, calling for bread and coffee to be brought to him. A few moments later Watkinson entered the office.

"Captain Jones is here, sir, and asking to see you."

"Christopher Jones? Good God, how did he get here?"

"I have not asked him, Captain Kite, but he is clearly travel-stained."

"Ask him to come in."

A moment later Jones stood before him. He rocked a little, like a drunken man, but Kite could see the mulatto ship-master was exhausted. His blue coat was salt-stained and muddied, his breeches filthy and his shoes caked in mud. The stock about his neck was grubby and the deep rings beneath his eyes were purple on his honey-coloured skin.

"Sit down, sit down, Jones." Kite rose and motioned to Jones to pull up a chair into which the mulatto collapsed with a terrible sigh.

"A glass, Watkinson, and hasten that bread, damn it. Captain Jones is in extremis . . ."

Jones tossed off the glass of Jerez and rubbed a dirty fist across his eyes. He tried to say something, but only a croak came from his mouth.

"Take your time, Jones, take your time."

"I am sorry to hear of your loss, Captain Kite."

Kite nodded. "It is good of you to put the matter before your own tribulations, Captain Jones."

"I am sorry for those too, sir. I had not meant – I mean, I know the ship to have been of especial—"

"All our ships are special to us, Captain Jones. The loss of one is of no more significance than the loss of another." Even as he said the words, he knew them to be untruthful. The loss of

16

a ship with a valuable West India cargo was infinitely worse than one with two hundred tons of coal in her hold, but Kite could not add to Jones's obvious distress. He had been in command of the *African Princess*, the ship named after Puella, and Kite knew well that the wrecking of her had some mystical link in Jones's mind with the death of his own son and Puella's deliberate decline. His mixed blood placed him in part under the influence of such damning superstitions.

"How did it happen?"

"Bad weather, sir. Days of it. No glimpse of the sun, no sign of land till we struck. We were out in our reckoning, sir, way out, but if daylight . . . Well, sir, it wanted but two hours before dawn when Had we had just a little luck, a moon, or bright starlight . . ."

Kite waited. To relive that terrible moment when normality turns in an instant to chaos was clearly an ordeal. He could imagine it well enough: an hour or so before the first flush of daylight in the east; the ship running fast before the wind; an overcast sky and the night black as the devil's riding boots; then the sudden shuddering lurch, the parting of stays, the crash of topmasts, yards, sails, all going by the board and the splitting of the hull on the unyielding rocks. Perhaps, too, the sudden high loom of a cliff and then the struggle to contain disaster as panic-stricken men came up from below, screaming about water pouring into the ship, only to find the ordered deck a ruination of broken spars and a weblike trap of rope and canvas. Within moments the sea would be breaking over the wreck and the first men would be swept to their deaths; then the impossibility of getting out a boat and the quick descent from discipline and order to the anarchy of every man clinging on for dear life. Even in a moderate breeze, the scene would have been hellish enough.

Jones finally finished his account. They had struck on Cape Clear Island and the ship had gone all to pieces before the next morning. He and eight men had survived. He had the ship's papers and her log, and had saved a quantity of gold bullion from her, but that was all. Her muscovado had washed like honey out of her split hull, the rum had run out of its stove casks with a stink that had brought a score of indigent Irish onto the scene, and while these hardy men had risked their limbs and even their lives to save some of the cane spirit for their own enjoyment, Jones and his men had clambered ashore by way of the fallen mainmast.

Jones stood and fished in his coat-tails, his fists dredging up the bright glint of gold coin. "I could not sleep well while I carried this, no, nor tarry on my passage. We were a week on the island before the weather allowed us to get to Baltimore and then it was a long march to Cork where we took ship. It was two days before we left."

"We heard that the wreck had been reported by a military officer conducting a survey on the coast, Captain," Kite said. "He found the name board and her port of registry washed ashore near Schull and had thought the crew all lost. We received advice from Dublin to that effect. But surely no ship came in last night?"

Jones shook his head. "No, I have come directly from Tenby."

"That is the devil of a journey!"

"Aye, sir, it is, but I did not feel that I could anywhere rest easy until I had got rid of . . ." Jones gestured at the pile of coin glinting on the desktop.

"And the log and papers?" Kite prompted.

"I have them outside, sir," Watkinson said, indicating the door to the counting house, "and there is bread and coffee arriving."

Jones had arrived in Liverpool in 1760 as mate of the *Spitfire*, which vessel Kite himself had commanded. They had brought in with them their prize, the French privateer *La Malouine*, later renamed *African Princess*, and in due course Jones had been promoted into her as master. He had married and in the intervening eleven years had bred a family of four boys and a single girl between his voyages to the West Indies.

For some of that time Kite too had continued voyaging, taking command of a succession of the ships owned jointly by Makepeace and Kite: the *Salamander*, the *Firefly* and the *Samphire*. Puella had from the first steadfastly refused to accompany him, preferring to stay ashore and bring up their child. But in due time the strain of living alone, a black mistress in a household of white servants, had begun to unnerve her. She had trouble with a manservant and threatened to beat him; he raised a mob which stoned the house and broke all the windows. Kite had to abandon his sea-going and take up a desk alongside Makepeace in the company chambers.

Captain Topsy-Turvy, as Kite was known in Liverpool for

upsetting the conventions of the day, became a diligent ship-owner, well known and well liked in commercial circles, but his wife became an unhappy and increasingly resentful recluse. She rarely rebuked him, devoting herself to her growing son, refusing to allow Kite to send him to school, but insisting upon the employment of a governess and then, a few months earlier, a tutor.

Kite had acquiesced to all her demands, content that with his presence quelling any popular reaction to Puella's colour she seemed to have made a satisfactory life for herself. Their own moments of intimacy had become few and far between, but even this he could bear if he occupied his mind with the business of ships and cargo. Of the two business partners he, rather than Makepeace, was the more dynamic, and he had thrown himself into the work of acting as ship's husband. In this role he left to Makepeace much of the arranging of outward cargoes. His own superior handwriting and the contacts he had made whilst working for the Antiguan merchant Joseph Mulgrave occupied him with the business of concluding deals on the homeward cargoes. By this means he kept himself appraised of developments in the West Indies and in the American colonies, writing to his erstwhile fellow clerk Wentworth at St John's in Antigua, and to Arthur Tyrell in Newport, Rhode Island.

Gradually, as fewer and fewer people saw Puella, and Kite's presence on the dockside became a matter of daily regularity, people ceased to concern themselves with the anomaly of a rich black women in their midst. Liverpool was already a cosmopolitan town and, now unseen, Puella began to slowly acquire a kind of mythical status. That Captain Topsy-Turvy married a black woman worth, it was said, five hundred pounds a year in her own right, was seen by many as a mark of his financial acuity. By others it seemed to bear out the notion that in trade lay a fortune for all manner of people; if a black slave could earn her manumission and gain such a fortune, what might not a decent white person achieve?

Kite was oblivious to this widespread gossip. Makepeace, on the other hand, had been largely responsible for fostering it. After Puella's disastrous attempt to beat her manservant, he realised that not only was Kite's presence at his wife's side necessary, but that something must be done to protect his own fortune from any tainting by oblique association with the black woman. He had initially hoped that Puella would sail with her husband but when this proved impossible the only thing to do was to encourage a belief in the lady's native grandeur. It was not difficult to put about Puella's nobility. Strikingly beautiful in her tall, upright ebony way, she did not disdain to enter Liverpool's social life in the early days of her marriage. This had coincided with a popular print showing a native king trading with "some Liverpool masters". The print had shown a beplumed black chieftain attired, enthroned and surrounded by an almost Gallic splendour, while some homespun captains stood respectfully at the foot of the monarch's dais. To the right of the king's pavilion, the masts and yards of the white men's slaving ships lay at their anchors in the waters of a distant but unmistakably African river; to the left, a landscape of wooden barracoons were depicted spilling thousands of black slaves across a plain, like a dark stream which flowed towards the waiting ships. In the foreground a spokesman for the Liverpool masters, his hat in his left hand, his right foot forward in a bow, offered his right hand in a gesture of amity to that of a half-naked but lovely young woman descending from the dais at her father's bidding. To offset the Liverpool masters, a group of splendid negro spearsmen, courtiers and royal mistresses appeared to applaud what had every appearance of a secular marriage. The meaning was clear enough, spelling out the commercial benefits to both the merchants of Liverpool and the nobility of "Guinea", while few remained insensible to the implication inherent in the imagery. The print, known popularly as *The Cornucopia of Africa*, seemed to find genuine proof in the union of Puella and Captain Topsy-Turvy, for although it had become known that Puella had been shipped as a slave aboard Captain Makepeace's own slaver, the *Enterprize*, the story of her false imprisonment and sale by a tyrannical usurper was confirmed by the common knowledge of her independent wealth. Makepeace had added a couple of hundred per annum to the real sum, and entirely suppressed the fact that her annuity was the gift of a wealthy West Indian merchant named Mulgrave, now long since dead. People forgave her her beating of a worthless Catholic Irish manservant, admired her elegance when she went abroad and, as time passed and she became increasingly reclusive, slowly allowed her to slip from the forefront of their minds.

*    *    *

When Jones had gone, Kite called Jasper Watkinson into his office. "As you know, Mr Watkinson, Captain Makepeace's death requires that we review matters relevant to our joint business. I have not been a party to the late Captain's testamentary provisions, but it will be necessary to make a settlement in favour of Mistress Makepeace. I shall also have to determine what interest young Masters Henry and Charles are to take in our affairs, or whether they are simply to receive the benefits of shares; neither has to my knowledge evinced the slightest desire to go to sea, nor any interest whatsoever in the affairs of the company. I also purpose to ensure that Mistress Katherine is well provided for."

"Captain Makepeace has already made known to me much of his personal financial stipulations, Captain Kite," Watkinson said with his customary deferential efficiency. "In my employment as chief clerk to Captain Makepeace, you will understand that, pending the reading of his will, I should not wish to breach any undertaking of confidentiality . . ."

"Yes, yes, I understand all that, Mr Watkinson, your personal attachment to Captain Makepeace is well known, but that is precisely why it is necessary to raise these matters with you. The circumscribed manner in which Captain Makepeace made some of his arrangements means that his death leaves me at a disadvantage. I shall entirely rely upon you as I usually do."

Kite smiled at Watkinson, though there was a worm of unease uncoiling itself in his guts. Watkinson was, Kite knew, ambitious; his wife was a woman of social pretension, admirably so, as far as Kite was concerned, for he saw no advantage in keeping a good man in the shade. But he sensed that Watkinson was seeking to throw smoke in his eyes and confuse him, for some reason best known to himself.

"There is absolutely nothing to concern you, Captain Kite, at least until the will is read."

Kite leaned forward on his elbows and put his fingertips together. "You know, Jasper," he said dropping his voice, "there is much work to be done. The company will require a new partner and the opportunities for your good self are, well, limitless if matters should fall out that way."

"I understand, Captain Kite," Watkinson said turning for the door. In the doorway he turned. "I am sure, Captain, I can rely upon your good offices in my behalf."

"I see no reason why not, Jasper. Do you?"

"No, sir."

And yet he did. All that morning Kite's thoughts drifted off the ledgers from which he was reckoning the loss occasioned by the wrecking of the *African Princess*. The ship had carried her own insurance and her loss would be borne by the company in its entirety, but his train of thought would not settle in the rut of even so uncomfortable a furrow as financial loss. He should be weeping for his dead son, but poor Puella's irrational behaviour had, over the years, eroded his capacity to brood. William was dead and no power on earth could bring him back; Puella was killing herself in the manner of her people and nothing he could do would prevent her. Makepeace was dead and something was in train that he sensed had some direct bearing on the conduct of the company that was now his sole responsibility, notwithstanding the benefits in law which accrued to Mrs Makepeace and her family.

It was dusk when he finally brought himself to reckon up the losses of the *African Princess* and her cargo. The cargo alone came to over two thousand pounds, and there were the wages of the crew to determine. He sat back, unable to work any longer, procrastinating as his wandering and distracted mind thought again of Puella. Out of spirits and fearful of returning home, he considered eating out. Perhaps he should be pleasant to Watkinson, but the chief clerk had already left, making his excuses and saying he had to call upon Mistress Makepeace and did Captain Kite mind him leaving to attend to his private business? Captain Kite did not mind. The *Samphire* was nowhere near completing her lading and no ships were expected now that the fate of the *African Princess* was known. They should have news of the *Salamander* within the fortnight, but no, Watkinson was free to go.

Kite considered matters for a moment, then he rose and went to the window. Despite the rain and wind, the panes were grimy, but he could see the River Mersey and the masts of several ships anchored in the stream beyond the dock. He thought of poor Jones and the wrecking of his ship on Cape Clear Island, of the dreadful quality of calamity and how Jones looked like a broken man. It had been Kite who had insisted his former mate should study navigation and make himself competent to become a master; he himself had therefore initiated the chain of events that had led to Jones losing his ship. But he did not believe there was a real link between the loss of the *African Princess* and the death of his son. They had not occurred on the same day, let alone at the same time. He rose, went out to where Watkinson's desk overlooked the counting house and the desks of the three junior clerks and, striking flint on steel, coaxed the lamp into life as the evening gloom settled on the dusty office. He sat at Watkinson's desk and drew the log of the *African Princess* towards him. He already guessed what he was going to find and when he did so he sat back.

Young William had contracted the rice-water fever within the hour of the *African Princess* striking the Irish coast. It was an uncanny coincidence.

But that was all it was; a coincidence, two disparate occurrences taking place at the same moment, a quite fortuitous matter. Why, hundreds, thousands of things would have occurred at that hour throughout the world. How many coaches had shed their wheels? How many horses cast shoes? How many women conceived? How many plates been dropped, barns caught fire? And if a man fell from his horse did it signify if his wife pricked her finger with a needle at the same moment?

Kite cursed. Men and women were not such logical creatures that they could entirely throw off the notion that there *might* be a connection. He did not believe it implicitly, as Puella would when she found out, but the coincidence was strange. He looked up. The junior clerks were looking at him, and he wondered if he had unwittingly exclaimed, then they bent again to their work and he rose and retired to his own inner office, to gaze again out of the grimy window.

Of course he would not tell Puella of the curious coincidence, just as he would not in fact tell her of the loss of the *African Princess*. If she was determined to die, it would be quite pointless. But, he recalled, he was responsible for her situation too. She was going to die and he was doing nothing about it beyond accepting the ancient horrors of the spirits. He suddenly thought what life would be like without her; even Puella reduced by heartache and misery was better than no Puella.

Beyond the glass window the river shone like a sword blade in the last of the daylight. The wind was still blowing, though with far less violence than it had been, and the late gale was now no more than a strong breeze. A flat was running upstream against the ebb tide. In an hour the flood would be making, and the sailing barge would carry it far upstream into the country beyond. He came to a sudden resolution: with William dead he would take Puella to sea again. They would shut up the Liverpool house and go back to Antigua, shipping out as passengers aboard the *Samphire*. He could not leave her to die because she believed in silly superstitions, in the predestination of random occurrences and the power of the spirits to divine, determine and destroy.

She was capable of bearing another child, and if she did not wish to share his bed again, she could be saved from her self-inflicted death, diverted and made to live again under the warm sun of the tropics. What a fool he had been to have so immersed himself in his business that he had almost lost her! He had no interest in other women and had only given himself to work for the benefit of young William, exactly as Puella had sacrificed her own happiness to the success of their son!

He reached for his coat and hurriedly pulled it on, then clapped his hat upon his head and hefted his cane.

"Good night, gentlemen," he called to the clerks as they watched him go.

"Good night, sir," they called after him, and then stared at one another.

"You should have told him, Mr Johnstone."

"You think he will not know soon enough?" Johnstone replied, closing his inkwell with a loud snap, adding, "if it is true."

"Of course it is true, and when he finds out, it will be too late. Watkinson will have sewn the matter up . . ."

"That's what you want, ain't it, Nathan, Watkinson to sew it all up so that you can be chief clerk . . ."

"Be quiet!" Johnstone said, rounding on his two juniors. "D'you think I care about being chief clerk any more with the cholera taking my wife? Captain Kite has just lost his son. How can I be telling him things that we only suspect to be true?"

"You should warn him though, Nathan, or we may all pay for it once that Master Harry arrives to console his bosom friends and accomplices."

# Two

## A Speculation

Kite arrived home too late. He was greeted by his house-keeper, Mrs O'Riordan, with the news that the mistress was dead.

"It is not possible!" Kite was incredulous. Even in decline, Puella could not die in so short a space of time.

"Her neck, sir . . ." Mrs O'Riordan was finding it difficult to retain her self-possession. " 'Tis awful, sir . . . You see she asked that the chicken—"

"Neck? Chicken? What the devil are you talking about?" Kite looked from the woman's distraught face to the staircase. "Excuse me, Mrs O'Riordan."

He raced upstairs and flung open the bedroom door. The room was entirely in darkness and he bawled for lights, standing on the threshold, his heart thundering and his body trembling. At the noise of steps behind him he turned. Mrs O'Riordan, her body heaving with sobs and the effort of climbing the stairs at a run, held out the candlestick. Seizing it and holding it before him like a talisman, Kite entered the room.

The candlelight caught her eyes at once. Puella seemed to stare directly at him, a terrible accusatory glare that was at the same time piteous. Her head was flung back at an unnatural angle, hung over the edge of the bed so that her face was upside down. He moved towards her and, holding the candle above her, saw that she was quite naked. In the doorway Mrs O'Riordan gave a little shriek and he looked up at her.

"What happened, Mrs O'Riordan? Have you any idea?" He kept his voice low, under control, though a deep anger was rising in him.

Between sobs, the housekeeper explained. She had come, as the Captain had instructed, to offer food and drink at three in the afternoon. The Mistress had been sitting in her chair where, it seemed, she had been since poor Master William died. So she was all the more surprised when the Mistress asked for a live chicken to be bought and brought to her before it was killed in the house.

"It had to be live, sir, and it had to be killed in the house, sir, the Mistress was particular about that. And, begging your pardon, sir, but seeing the Mistress had her own ways like, I did as I was bid. I sent Maggie out to get a plump pullet . . ."

"What else did she say?" Kite asked, a cold sensation fastening about his chest like a rope lashing. "Did she ask for it to be cooked in a certain way?"

"N-no, sir, but to be truthful I didn't think much of anything else except that she'd be eating again, sir, and how pleased you would be at the news, though she did say as she was to be told when the chicken had been bought and she'd want to look at it to see if it was all right, sir, so I supposed that she would be telling me then how she'd want it to be cooked . . . She liked chicken, sir."

"Yes. She did." Kite leaned over her body and placed his hand beneath Puella's left breast. She was still warm but her heartbeat had long since ceased. "Go on," he commanded, his voice harsh with the effort of control.

"Maggie came back, sir, I took the pullet off of her and brought it up here to the Mistress . . ." Mrs O'Riordan paused and Kite looked at her.

"Was she still sitting in the chair?"

Mrs O'Riordan shook her head. "No, sir, she were lying on the bed. Like she is now."

"Naked, but not dead?"

Mrs O'Riordan saw the confusion she had caused. "No, no, sir, she wasn't dead but she was naked, sir, and that took me aback a little, though I have seen her that way before sir, as I think you know . . ."

"Go on, Mrs O'Riordan, please simply tell me what happened." He was breathing more easily now. The blind fury of anger had ebbed, and now, staring down at Puella, he was filled with regrets. If only he had come home an hour earlier, or fed her yesterday. He felt a wave of emotion surge through him, but he crushed it and listened patiently to his housekeeper.

"Well . . . Well, sir, she took the chicken and I supposed

she were going to feel it for plumpness, sir, but she kind of embraced it, sir."

"Embraced it?"

"I don't known how else to say it, sir, said like a prayer over it with her face all lit up, if you'll pardon me for saying so, sir, of a black person, sir, I don't rightly known how else to tell you, sir . . ."

"Casting a spell, perhaps."

"Oh, God, sir, that's terrible! That's wicked, sir, to be suggesting such a thing." Mrs O'Riordan crossed herself. "I know she was not quite a Christian, sir."

"Mrs O'Riordan, I respect your sensibilities, but you know there are women in Ireland as in England who make up potions for the shingles and the scrofula and they do so with incantations, do they not? So, was it like that?" He looked up at the woman standing, shaking on the threshold. "Well?"

Mrs O'Riordan nodded. "Aye, sir, I suppose that it was."

"And then?"

"She handed me back the pullet and said I was to break its neck quickly and to bring it back when she would tell me how to cook it. 'Twas no more than three-quarters of an hour ago, sir. I went directly downstairs, took the fowl and snapped its neck. I came back up the stairs and . . ."

"Please, Mrs O'Riordan, go on."

"She was like that, sir. Her neck all loose and – oh, God . . ." Mrs O'Riordan burst into sobs and fled.

Left alone Kite placed his hand beneath Puella's head so that he cupped her skull and gently lifted it. He was able to swivel it without resistance, for the vertebrae of the neck were detached from the remainder of the spinal column. As the chicken's neck had been broken, so had Puella's.

"I have never seen such a thing before, except in cases of extreme paroxysm among the insane," remarked Dr Bennett, taking snuff and dropping a considerable quantity down the front of his soiled waistcoat in doing so. Kite watched the doctor's huge nose wrinkle and sniff like that of a hound as it ingested the tobacco dust. An instant later Bennett's huge and ungainly body endured his own paroxysm. The pleasure thus engendered seemed to Kite to be of so suppressed a nature as to be merely an incomprehensible affectation, though he understood devotees claimed it to be beneficial.

"Of course rabies, in its final form," Bennett went on, "will bring on muscular spasms of such violence that small bones may break, but that the mere snuffing out of a chicken induces so dreadful a reaction in a human, even a black – begging your pardon, Kite – is much to be wondered at."

Kite grunted. The shock of Puella's death had passed, and he diverted his mind from dwelling on regrets. There were many hours yet until dawn and, given the unusual circumstances of Puella's death, he had felt it necessary to consult Bennett. The youthful experience of once, long ago, having thought himself under suspicion of murder had bred caution in him, but he was not surprised at Bennett's comments.

"You seem to reserve your own judgement, Kite. You know these people better than I; have you a theory?"

"Yes, and it may be more than a theory, for I believe there is a probability which I am unable to explain but which I have observed on more than one occasion, that the mind may be induced to release powerful agents. Such agents enable the physical being to do extraordinary things. I have heard of men leaping into trees to avoid lions, or of enduring terrible wounds in battle until some objective is achieved. The Africans of the Guinea coast place great confidence in the powers of the spirits they conceive to be all about us. They tap these in some way unknown to our more sophisticated and logical minds. It is perhaps a skill that we have lost through our greater leaning towards other things which, in the matter of our survival, we deem to be of a higher priority. They call these powers *obi*, or *obeah*. I do not understand the precise usage, but I know there are those who consider the magic not merely real but potent."

Bennett shrugged, his expression sceptical. "Then how do you explain the manner of her death? A kind of suicide?"

"Yes. She had nurtured a desire to die for several days following the death of our son. I had expected her to do this slowly, by starvation; she has acted in this way before when deeply troubled. I had in fact determined to stop her from this extremity, but thought that the matter was not one of urgency and it was perhaps better to allow her to grieve a little in her own way first." Kite pressed on, well aware that he was exculpating himself from a self-inflicted charge of neglect. "I myself have not felt much disposed to go on after William's death. But this afternoon I resolved to quit Liverpool for a while and to take Puella with me . . ."

"But fate intervened."

"No, Puella divined my intention. You must have noticed how married people oft times discover they have been thinking of the same thing when one opens a conversation and the other is already considering the same matter."

"You forget, I am not married, Kite. Who would marry a dropsical wretch like me?"

"You are not dropsical, Bennett, you merely eat and drink too much."

"It is the only pleasure available to an ugly man, but pray continue."

"She did not wish to continue her life and sought a means to end it. She disdained the knife, but needed only some means of tapping the *obi*, of reaching the agent necessary to induce, or release from her body, a last spasm, like your rabid or insane patient, so that she can twist and fling herself with such force that she breaks her own neck."

"But Mrs O'Riordan wringing the neck of a chicken—"

"Into which she had surrendered her own spirit, her own soul, Bennett, do you not see? If you can voluntarily pass into a trance, which is no more than a temporary and voluntary surrender of self, then you can do this with a finality, a last purpose to mobilise an effort of both physical and spiritual will which ends in voluntary death."

Bennett shook his head and gave out a great sigh. "Extraordinary," he breathed, "quite extraordinary."

They stood for a moment looking down at Puella and then the physician pulled the sheet over her. "She was very comely, Kite, that I must say. I have seldom seen so beautiful a form, black though it is . . ." He reached for more snuff, adding as he inhaled, "Love, I suppose, takes no notice of such things."

Kite stood a moment in silence. He had known Bennett for some years, knew him to be a man of integrity and intelligence, and a physician of no mean ability. "No," he said slowly, "but such things raise great barriers between persons, Bennett, even in death."

Bennett nodded and held out his hand. "You have so instructed me this evening, Kite, that I shall waive my fee."

"Will you join me for supper?"

"You don't wish to eat alone?"

"No, I do not." Kite knew that Bennett's presence would stave off the onset of a grief he felt he could not bear.

"And you will not serve me chicken?"

Kite was grateful for the black joke. "Mrs O'Riordan has a fine ham, Dr Bennett, and I can find a bottle or two, I dare say. To be candid, I should welcome your company."

"Very well. We should send Maggie out for the laying-out woman at once."

"Mrs O'Riordan has already called her, I expect she is warming her belly with a glass of porter in the kitchen below."

The two men descended the stairs and Kite made his wants known to Mrs O'Riordan, who had in part anticipated them. Over the cold ham, Bennett asked why Kite had called his wife by such an odd name.

"I never knew her native name. I could not bring myself to give her an English name, for though I purchased her from her enslaver, who happened to be Captain Makepeace, I never for an instant thought of her as my property. Calling her Nancy, or Molly, or some such seemed patronising in the extreme."

"Well, you had the wounds by then, I suppose," interjected Bennett, adding with his mouth half full of an enormous slice of ham, "the wounds of Cupid."

Kite nodded. "Yes. I was extraordinarily moved by her." He paused, lost for a moment in memories of Puella's love-making. "So," he resumed his explanation, "I simply called her by the Latin word for girl and to my mind the word came simply to signify Puella herself."

"Tell me, Kite, out of a clinical curiosity and availing myself of both my Hippocratic silence and the discretion of a friend, did you grow close to her? I mean by the question did you reach an intimacy comparable with your having married a woman of your own colour?"

"There are times," Kite said, "when I have observed considerable estrangement to exist between the partners in what I think you are alluding to in your inimitable way as a normal marriage. Certainly we had grown apart, as does any sea officer and his spouse, and this was made no easier for Puella by her being black and subject to some unkindnesses hereabouts. I was, of course, to blame for much of this and she never really understood how independent she in truth was."

"So she *did* have a competence of her own?"

"Such a sum as would keep you in snuff for about one thousand years, Dr Bennett," Kite said, smiling sadly.

"Oh. I had thought it mere jealous gossip."

Kite felt his spirits rally. Old Bennett was a shrewd mender of men and he warmed to his therapy. But they got no further, for at that moment the door to the dining room opened and a red-eyed Mrs O'Riordan stood bobbing her curtsy.

"What is it, Mrs O'Riordan? I thought you had retired long since."

"Oh, thank you, Captain, but I couldn't sleep and the laying-out woman has only just gone and now there's poor Mr Johnstone asking to see you, sir."

"Johnstone? What the devil does he want at this hour?"

"I'll be going, Kite." Bennett slipped a last slice of ham into his mouth and rose, revealing half a dozen new patches of grease on his coat.

Kite raised his hand without turning from the housekeeper. "No, no, Bennett, do you sit down, it is probably news of a ship, or some other matter." He raised his voice. "Come in, Mr Johnstone."

Johnstone shuffled in, revolving his hat in his hands. "Pardon me, sir, I did not know you had company, and Mistress O'Riordan has just told me that your wife – please accept my condolences . . ."

"Thank you, Nathan," Kite replied as Johnstone's eyes wandered to where Bennett, who had resolved to stay, was now hacking another slice off the savaged ham. Kite looked at the bereaved Johnstone and his pathetic, half-starved air. "You are hungry, sir. Pray take a seat, help yourself and then tell us your business. Mrs O'Riordan, another bottle and help yourself to a glass below stairs."

He smiled as the housekeeper bobbed a curtsy. She had already been helping herself, by the colour of her, but it was no matter.

Johnstone hesitated, made a half-heartedly self-deprecating gesture and then pulled out a spare chair as Mrs O'Riordan put a plate in front of him and fetched clean cutlery. Kite waited and watched; Johnstone literally drooled as he sliced the ham and placed it carefully upon the plate laid before him. For several minutes the two older men regarded the ravening of the younger. He did not look as though he had eaten for days and it occurred to Kite that he probably had had very little beyond some bread and tea. After a little, Johnstone recalled himself and, having drained a glass of wine, looked up at the others.

"I . . . I beg your pardon, gentlemen, I, er, I quite forgot myself."

"Please, take some more, but do tell us what brings you here."

Johnstone, who had already reached for the long-bladed carving knife and its accompanying fork, looked up as though paralysed. His eyes switched from Kite to Bennett and back again.

"Come, young fellow," put in Bennett, "what's the trouble? You have the look of a hare caught in a trap."

"Well, I . . . No, I cannot. The matter is confidential . . . between myself and Captain Kite."

"And you don't trust me not to blab your affairs all over Liverpool, eh? Is that it?" Bennett said with mock severity, laying his own knife and fork down with an air of genuine regret. "I am to be flung out of Eden, Captain Kite, by your damned clerk."

"I mean no offence, Dr Bennett," Johnstone responded with a swift anxiety.

"Ah, there's none taken," Bennett said rising with a low belch. "'Tis getting late and the ham will not sustain the two of us. Kite, I'm damned grateful to you for the fare and will leave you to your waterfront scuttlebutt or whatever evil nautical term you lay to your conversation." He held up his hands. "No, no, I'll see myself out, and I'll make sure Mrs O'Riordan leaves you in peace."

Kite sat again. "Good night, Bennett, and thank you for your company. I am obliged to you and greatly appreciate it."

"Good night, Kite. Think nothing of it. Good night, Johnstone."

"Good night, sir."

After Bennett had gone, Kite refilled Johnstone's glass. "Well, Nathan," he said, "the circumstances of this confidential visit must be extraordinary. Have you had news from Bidston of another ship in the offing, or news of a loss, or what?"

Johnstone swallowed the contents of his glass and stared at his employer. He was quite obviously mustering his thoughts and his courage, so Kite waited patiently. It was a night of revelations, he thought, but he had no desire to ascend those stairs again and see Puella, her eyes closed and her jaw bound up with a cloth.

"Captain Kite," Johnstone began, "I must ask you to believe that I have only two motives in coming here tonight. One is to protect my own interests. I mention this first if only to prove to you that I conceive my loyalty to you is not disinterested, and is thereby genuine. But added to that is a conviction that it would be wrong of me not to tell you that I fear something is afoot. Something, I fear, that is against your own interests."

He paused and Kite shifted uneasily. Was it not enough that a man should lose his son to cholera and his wife to the spirits of the *obeah* without a further visitation on top of the additional burden of the death of his partner and the wrecking of a ship? He thought of Watkinson's evasive and unsatisfactory conduct that afternoon, though it seemed like a lifetime ago. "Go on, Nathan," he said softly, sensing a further shadowy figure beyond the bounds of his present knowledge.

"I should perhaps have waited until something more concrete occurred, for I should not wish you to think of me as a conspirator or a spy of some sort . . ." Sweat stood out in beads over Johnstone's brow.

"How long have you worked for me, Nathan?" Kite cut in.

"Seven years, sir."

"And you have given me every proof of satisfaction. Now please, I beseech you, come to the matter directly."

"I believe you to have been cheated, sir. And I believe that further mischief is being hatched against you."

"By whom?" Kite asked. "To what purpose?"

Johnstone swallowed, held up his hand and shook his head. "Please, I beg you, sir, let me explain. 'Tis hard enough to comprehend, particularly as some parts of the matter are not clear, but I have fathomed out what I conceive to be a plan to dispossess you and over which the loss of the *African Princess* is but a fortuitous bonus to those who wish to encompass your ruin."

Kite could not imagine why anyone should wish to undertake so grievous a thing as encompass his ruin, but he suppressed his question and let Johnstone have his head. "Go on," he repeated.

"The *African Princess* was your own ship, sir, was she not, as the *Enterprize* was the personal property of Captain Makepeace? Your other ships were jointly owned in various proportions, some split with your own wife, some sixty-fourths being held by Mrs Makepeace, but the majority of the shares belonging to yourself and the late Captain. Is that not so?"

"Yes, that is so, though my wife and I owned the *Spitfire* entirely, while Makepeace and his wife wholly owned the *Salamander*."

33

"And in that way funds were laid aside to the principals in due proportion?"

"Yes, that too is so. And of course we shared the risks and any losses."

"Except where they were incurred by your own private property, so that you will personally bear the costs associated with the loss of the *African Princess*?"

Kite nodded. "But you are not suggesting that Captain Jones wrecked her deliberately, surely?"

Johnstone shook his head. "No, I am not. But did you know of the mortgages taken out on some of the bottoms?"

"Yes, we had remortgaged the *Samphire* to release some funds in order to speculate on a cargo for Spain . . . But you said bottoms; in the plural. To my knowledge we had only done it the once." Kite was frowning.

"And you were opposed to it, I believe? In the case of the *Samphire*, I mean. I speculate here, sir, but it does not seem likely that you would approve."

Kite nodded. "You are right. No, I did not like remortgaging a hull, just as I do not much like speculating in cargoes. I prefer that we offer a freight rate and let others pay. It is our business to offer tonnage and for others to buy and sell their commodities. I am a ship owner, not a speculator, a profiteer or a merchant. I do not have the aptitude or the interest for it."

"That is precisely my contention, sir. Nor did Captain Makepeace, but he became a victim and, well, I anticipate. The point is that most of your hulls are, in part or in full, remortgaged."

"I know nothing of this. It is inconceivable," Kite protested, then recalled Makepeace's last wish, his insistent desire for forgiveness, recollection of which had been driven out by the man's death and then the accumulation of his own miseries. He looked sharply at Johnstone. "So you are alleging that in proportion to the shares owned outside my own control, the vessels are not actually owned by Makepeace and Kite?"

"Yes, Captain, unfortunately that is just what I am alleging, and I am certain of it, for I have heard Watkinson discuss the matter with his principal."

The shadow moved out into the light. "Samuel Frith?"

"You knew!" Johnstone was astonished.

"I guessed. The man has made a proposition to Miss Makepeace."

"That is infamous!"

"Well," Kite said cautiously, unwilling at this stage to allow passionate emotion to obtrude, "it is perhaps not the most desirable state of affairs and Miss Makepeace certainly does not seek it, but as Frith is not married perhaps infamous is not quite the right word."

"But it is said, sir, that he has been Mrs Makepeace's lover!" Johnstone declared desperately.

"Is this more of your speculation?"

"It is common gossip, Captain Kite, that is all. But it may explain Miss Katherine's distaste for her own proposed union."

"Well, that is true, but what do you conceive Captain Makepeace has been doing with the funds Frith has been putting in his pocket? Has he been speculating in cargoes other than this shipment for Spain? I cannot recall evidence in any of our own ships apart from the *Samphire*, or those of others?"

"No, sir, that is where the remortgaging of the *Samphire* was clever. By making that known to you, and – though not without your own misgivings – your acquiescence in approving it being common knowledge, it signalled that Makepeace and Kite were not averse to the practice. Word of such matters spreads about the town while your personal suspicions would have been lulled for some time to come."

"Now that *is* speculation."

Johnstone nodded, then shrugged. "But if a man knows his wife has made a visit to the theatre in the company of a gentleman friend and does not object, he will not believe the rumours of adultery as quickly as will one who had never condoned such loose behaviour in the first place."

"That is somewhat sophisticated logic, Nathan."

"But you take my point?"

"Perhaps; but to what purpose? You have yet to tell me what is being done with the money raised by this remortgaging of ships."

"Master Harry spends, or should I say loses it, at the tables."

"You mean he *gambles* it?"

"Captain Makepeace was an indulgent father, or Master Harry a plausible liar. I gather Mistress Makepeace had frequent words with her husband, but then she had compromised herself and sought to secure her own future by marrying Miss Katherine to Frith."

Kite considered the matter for some moments and then shook his head, asking, "But why does Frith want ships? Tell me that. He is a wealthy man, for what possible reason does he want ships?"

"I am not absolutely certain, sir, but Watkinson is behind this matter, nursing his own ambition and guiding Frith. Frith I think has paid far less than the capital value of the ships. Makepeace was reluctant to dissemble directly, but content to leave the details to the chief clerk. Watkinson has undertaken much of the business to keep it from you, Frith has therefore not so much acquired ships as assets whose return far exceeds his own investment. I suppose Makepeace thought the sums advanced kept Master Harry out of trouble and might always be replaced, and that by securing Frith as his son-in-law the matter remained in the family and therefore in principle little had changed, since the ships would remain the property of the family!"

"Why could he not have acted openly?" Kite asked. "I could have disputed the matter and we might have divided the firm, but he could still have raised some capital in order to discharge Harry's debts."

"Because in the first place the matter of Master Harry's debts is serious; in the second place Watkinson did not want the size of the fleet diminished; and in the third place he wants you out of the way, pushed into the margins, sent back to sea as a mere master so that he can assume the powers of an active partner."

"Why does he so hate me?" But Kite already knew the answer and spared Johnstone the embarrassment of spelling it out. "Because I have lived with a blackamoor?"

"He would put it less charitably, Captain."

"Yes, I dare say he would," Kite admitted, considering all that had been said. "So now Makepeace is dead and Frith is already taking control both of the inconsolable widow and the wretched pawn of a daughter. But how would they rid themselves of me? Can you riddle me that riddle with your speculations, Nathan?"

"That is what I cannot reason out, Captain. Perhaps they will simply await your reaction. If you will forgive me for mentioning it in so indelicate a manner, the death of your wife will, in a sense, play into their hands, adding to your misfortune over the loss of the *African Princess* and making you vulnerable."

"Or perhaps very strong, Nathan," Kite said slowly. "You yourself are but recently acquainted with death. You have little to lose, I think, and risked my executing the messenger tonight, did you not?"

Johnstone flushed, then looked his employer in the eye. "I did say, sir, that I had every intention of protecting my own interests."

"Have you anything to keep you here, Nathan?"

"My late wife's mother, sir."

Kite leaned forward. "Would you be a conspirator, Nathan? As a partner, I mean?"

Johnstone frowned with uncertainty. "I should like first to know your mind, sir."

"Well, it is a little confused, but the *Spitfire* is expected soon and I have a mind not to tarry in Liverpool. Are you game for some more substantial speculation?"

"I have no money, Captain Kite. I, er, have never considered such a matter." He shrugged, clearly flustered.

"But you have an excellent brain, Nathan, and I might easily be persuaded to invest in it. Now tell me, what do you think their next move will be?"

"Well, sir, as I have said, and forgive my candour, but the deaths of both Captain Makepeace and your wife—"

"And the loss of the *African Princess* gives them an advantage, yes. I agree they will act soon while I am, so to speak, knocked down."

"Exactly, sir."

"Tomorrow?"

"I think it highly likely."

Kite thought a moment, then said, "We could, of course, transfer my own and Puella's shares in all our vessels clandestinely, as they have done, to Wentworth in Antigua. You could raise bills of sale and have the matter registered at the Custom House by tomorrow afternoon. I'd trust Wentworth with my life but—"

"You could be more subtle, sir, and avoid the risk of cutting off your nose to spite your face."

"Proceed . . ." And Kite listened while Johnstone explained his notion. Midnight struck as he concluded his dissertation and Kite smiled approvingly.

"You have given the matter some thought."

Johnstone shook his head. "No, sir, only a little in talking this evening."

"But tell me, how did you first become suspicious?"

"Well, it was not a matter of suddenly becoming suspicious, but Watkinson's manner towards me underwent a slow change. At first I was useful to him and I have to admit we were friendly, but then, when I married, I began to sense a distance growing between us. I thought at first it was that he wished to emphasise that he conceived his station to be above mine, but then I encountered him twice in deep conversation with Frith. Of course, I knew Frith to be a man of substance, but also a man of low morals. Mrs Makepeace was not the only woman his name was linked with. Moreover I heard he had been to London in company with Master Harry and shortly thereafter rumours circulated about Harry Makepeace's gambling here in Liverpool. At about this time Watkinson sported a new suit and cane, he appeared to be elevating himself in the world and his manner towards myself and the junior clerks underwent a slow but subtle change. I think he wished to conceal it, but he could not avoid a certain supercilious manner affecting himself.

"I should not have taken much notice, I suppose, had I not stumbled on him talking to Frith late one night. I had been down to the dock with a jerque note for Captain Matthews of the *Firestorm* and he had asked me to return some papers to the office. I did so and found Frith, Makepeace and Watkinson enjoying a bottle of wine in familiar ease. I'm afraid I listened. I heard sufficient. Your wife was mentioned in no very flattering terms, I heard an opinion voiced as to your judgement and your sense of trust. A little later Harry's name was mentioned by Makepeace and – this caught my attention particularly – both Frith *and* Watkinson spoke sharply to the Captain, as though they both enjoyed the whip hand over him. It was enough; I was about to leave when I heard Makepeace shout them down in one of his bellows. 'Damn you both,' he said, 'the *Samphire*'s worth more than that! I could mortgage her for a thousand,' whereupon Frith said in his cold manner, 'Sit down, Captain, you know perfectly well that to raise a mortgage on the *Samphire* you will need Kite's approval.' There was some movement in the inner office at this point and I fled."

"You were very wise to do so and I am grateful to you for your confidence." Kite stood up. "I have a melancholy night ahead of me, Nathan, one that you will have too recently experienced yourself. We may both be dead of cholera ourselves within the week, but we are not yet infected and may still confound our enemies. Tomorrow you shall be at your desk promptly, but not a word to a soul."

"You may rely upon me, Captain Kite."

"And my thanks to you for your speculation."

# Three

## A Great Sinner

Kite woke suddenly at dawn. He was cold and cramped but he rose and stretched stiffly, shivering miserably as he stared at Puella, where she had been laid out. From below he heard the first movements in the household, and as he touched the cold body with the tips of his fingers he felt a deep sense of guilt that his business with Johnstone overrode all other considerations. With an effort he went through to his study, rang the bell for coffee and hot water and wrote a letter to arrange for Puella's interment. She would be given Christian burial, of that he was sure, and would be laid to rest next to her beloved son. By the time Maggie appeared to answer his summons, his letter and instructions were ready. An hour later, improved in appearance if not in mood by a wash and shave, wearing clean linen and having broken his fast, he left the house. The straw strewn in the street to quieten the noise of passing wheels in acknowledgement of William's death had been dispersed by the gale, though wisps remained clinging to the cobbles where bird lime anchored it. He had ordered some more, and the windows of Puella's bedroom stood wide open, though he knew he clasped her *obi* himself and that she would not relinquish it to the Christian God.

He strode downhill, into the wind rising from the Mersey, towards the shipping office. Puella would truly understand the lifting of his spirits and he knew that in her death she had deliberately released him. Why, he wondered, had their love withered? Was that always what happened between men and women? Or had he really broken some ancient covenant, struck between God and mankind when the Ark grounded upon Ararat, that divided humanity into its disparate races?

If so, he thought, he had become a mighty sinner!

As he had hoped, he arrived before Watkinson, though

39

McClusky, the most junior clerk, had arrived to unlock the premises and Johnstone himself walked in some two minutes after Kite. McClusky evinced little surprise, for Captain Kite's habits were not regular and he was as likely to be late as early. He ran about tending inkwells and sharpening nibs with an impressive diligence. He would not yet know of his employer's bereavement, still less of the fact that before the day's end he would have elevated his station in life.

Kite caught Johnstone's eye, but the younger man looked swiftly away, a reaction that pleased him. A conspiratorial wink would have been scarcely appropriate, and a few moments later, as Peters, the other junior clerk, arrived, he saw Johnstone gather McClusky and Peters together, saw the involuntary twitches of their heads in his direction that betrayed the purpose of the impromptu conference: they were being told that Captain Kite was in mourning, though he wore no crepe about his sombre person.

It was exactly seven o'clock as Watkinson entered. He looked immediately at Kite; he, seeing that Peters was not then at his desk but came in a moment later, guessed that Watkinson had been informed of his bereavement. He affected to study some papers on his desk and then, just as Watkinson sat himself and gathered up some bills, rose and called to him.

"I do not know whether you have heard that Captain Makepeace died yesterday, Mr Watkinson."

"Yes, I had been informed, sir. I am most deeply affected and have sent my condolences to Mrs Makepeace."

"Very well. I understand the funerary arrangements are to be made by Master Harry when he arrives."

"I believe him to be already here, Captain Kite."

"If that is so, very well."

"And I understand, sir, that you yourself have suffered a grievous loss."

Kite fixed Watkinson with a stare.

"Please accept my sincere condolences."

"Thank you."

"She was a most gracious lady, if I may say so, sir."

"You may say so, sir, in my presence, though I hear that you say otherwise elsewhere." Kite smiled, watching Watkinson's discomfiture. He was thrown off balance and Kite struck. "Now that Captain Makepeace has passed the bar, Mr Watkinson, I

40

think it is time we dispensed with your services. You may leave at once."

Kite bent to his papers as Watkinson spluttered: "You cannot dismiss me! This is outrageous! I insist on knowing your reasons. I have done nothing to offend you . . . I may have made the odd joke at your expense—"

"Oh, Mr Watkinson, I do not care about the odd joke at my expense and my wife no longer cares about the odd joke at hers either, but I do object," Kite said, his voice rising as he looked up at the chief clerk, "to your selling our ships without reference to me."

"Good God, sir, I would never do such a thing! I have always obeyed the instructions of my employer. I did only what Captain Makepeace told me to do and acted scrupulously within the rights of Captain Makepeace as his agent for those numbers of sixty-fourths that the late captain or his wife owned."

"That may be true, Mr Watkinson, but the letter and spirit of my accommodation with Captain Makepeace was that I was to be informed of any such transaction affecting a vessel in our fleet."

"So I reminded Captain Makepeace, Captain Kite, and I am distressed to learn that he did not confide in you. I assumed he had done so. You agreed to the remortgaging of the *Samphire*."

"That is sophistry, Mr Watkinson, for you know I was opposed to it in principle." Kite sensed he was on slippery ground and losing his advantage. He had yet to draw Watkinson and the chief clerk was heady with indignation.

"That was a matter between you and Captain Makepeace," went on Watkinson, rallying, "to make me a scapegoat for your prejudice against a dead man—"

"I make you no scapegoat, Watkinson," Kite said vehemently. "Your prejudices are your own and as the sole surviving partner I have decided that I have no further need for your services."

"But you are not the sole surviving partner, Captain Kite. There is also Mr Frith . . ." Too late Watkinson realized he had stumbled into the trap. His triumphalism withered and he sought to regain his ascendancy. "I, er . . . I see that Captain Makepeace had not confided in you in that matter either."

"Tell me, Mr Watkinson," Kite said with steel in his tone, "that you knew nothing about Captain Makepeace's desire to conceal matters from me. Tell me you did nothing to encourage him to

make a secret of it. Tell me you did not advise Mr Frith not to
be open with me. Tell me you nurse no private ambitions of your
own to secure your own place as a partner. Tell me you have not
discussed all this with Mr Frith. Do please tell me all of these
comforting things."

Watkinson spluttered again, sensing a further entrapment,
yet eager to agree that all that Kite had suggested was true.
"Absolutely, Captain Kite, absolutely . . ."

"Tell me all of this and I shall call you a liar, sir, to your face
and, should you wish it, in front of witnesses, for there is one
thing you do not know."

"I – do not know?"

Watkinson's face was losing its colour and went a deathly
white as Kite smiled and said, "Yes, you are forgetting that I
was at Captain Makepeace's deathbed."

Kite held himself from elaboration; the impact of the information
stunned Watkinson. For a moment he stood swaying and then he
turned and made for the door and the counting house beyond.
Kite almost felt sorry for him as, at this moment and in evident
anticipation of circumstances being quite otherwise, Frith arrived.

Kite noted Johnstone look up and rise at the unscheduled
visitor, he saw Frith wave him aside, but then he saw a look
of swiftly suppressed consternation upon Frith's face as he saw
Watkinson's pallor. Kite moved swiftly round his desk and, even
as Frith advanced on Watkinson to see what troubled him, leaned
pleasantly from his inner office.

"My dear Mr Frith, you could not have arrived at a more
opportune moment, do please come in. McClusky! Tea!" Kite
ushered a reluctant Frith into his office and closed the door.
"Wretched business, Frith, wretched. I dislike dismissing a man,
but we cannot have untrustworthy clerks here. I daresay you
wouldn't tolerate an untrustworthy clerk, would you? Fortunately
for us Makepeace alerted me. Almost his dying breath, poor
fellow. You'll have heard, yes? Of course you have, you are
a close friend of the family, and, I understand, you have made
an offer for Katherine's hand. Well, well. Do take a seat. Poor
Makepeace was not terribly coherent and it is best that you tell
me yourself what the two of you have been up to. I gather Master
Harry . . . Are you quite well, Mr Frith?"

Frith eased himself into a chair. "It is not quite as black as
Watkinson has no doubt painted it, Captain Kite."

Kite chuckled. "Watkinson certainly wrecked any feelings of reliance I, and indeed many others on 'Change, may have as to your financial probity, Mr Frith, but I sense, as a good judge of character, that I may assume that Watkinson sought to save his own skin at your expense."

"May I ask what defamatory notions he laid at my door?"

"Defamatory isn't the word, goodness me, no. Well, that you sought to dispossess me, the means I confess seemed over-complicated to a sea officer like myself, and that you sought to take over all Makepeace's business and that, forgive me, Frith, but you would surely wish me to be candid; in fact that you were nothing less than –" Kite dropped his voice – "Martha Makepeace's lover. There was more, of course, for they say the greater the scandal the greater the chance of its belief, but there was also mention, preposterous though it is, that young Henry Makepeace was to stand for Parliament and that you were busy putting him in your pocket even while you ruined him at the tables.

"All in all it's quite a tale, Mr Frith, don't you think?" Kite shook his head as though bemused. "As I was the only person in the way of your progress, it seems that you were to discomfit me. Truth to tell," he dissembled with increasing private amusement, "I can scarce believe it . . ."

"Neither can I," Frith rallied. It was clear that, in the short term at least, Frith was preparing to toss Watkinson to the wolves.

"Of course," Kite said, his tone of voice no longer flippant, "it is so preposterous that it may all be true." He rose and looked down at Frith as he writhed in his chair, alarm writ large across his face.

"Come, Captain, you cannot believe—"

"Oh, I am a simple soul, Mr Frith, a mere nigger-lover, of no consequence, don't you know." Kite smiled, then bent over Frith as his voice became hard. "Now, sir, I shall not ask you what your motives are, only what you will spend to buy me out, lock, stock and barrel. Come sir, make me an offer and then you may have your heart's desire." Kite straightened up, opened the door and called out, "Mr Watkinson! Come here, sir!"

Watkinson appeared in the doorway and Kite motioned him inside, shutting the door behind him. As he did so he caught Johnstone's eye and gave the most cursory of smiles. Then he turned to Watkinson and said, "Mr Watkinson, I have offered all my shares in the joint-owned bottoms to Mr Frith. If he buys me out, I shall have no objection to you continuing your employment here. If the offer is not satisfactory, however, I am afraid your continuing presence will be undesirable. Now I dare say you will wish to discuss these matters between yourselves and I suggest you occupy Captain Makepeace's office. I shall absent myself for one hour as I have some matters to attend to following the death of my wife."

Kite then ushered the two men out in silence and watched them cross the counting-house floor to disappear into Makepeace's former private chamber. He was careful not to draw the attention of the junior clerks to any communication between himself and Johnstone, but left the premises and walked purposefully uphill towards Makepeace's house. He felt a surge of hubris, confident of the success of the intrigue. "Oh," he muttered to himself, "I am indeed a mighty sinner!"

Crepe and straw decorated the façade of his dead partner's dwelling. Kite was shown into the drawing room where, a few moments later, Katherine came to him. She wore a mourning gown which did not suit her, emphasising her lack of looks. He rose and bent over her hand.

"My dear, I am sorry to trouble you on this of all mornings."

"It is good to see you, Uncle William."

"How is your mother?"

"She is asleep."

"Good. May I ask you a question of the most offensive nature, for which I ask your pardon?"

"If it is about Mr Frith . . ."

"It touches him directly. Was he ever in any way connected with your mother?"

Katherine nodded. "He has long been an intimate in this house. When my father was at sea he was frequently a caller and sometimes I suspected that he did not leave, or returned late."

"I understand. Now, listen carefully. I am in the process of detaching myself from the company. Frith and Watkinson have been intriguing to gain control without my knowledge, a fact that I have become aware of. There is also a matter closely concerning your brother Harry, who is, I gather, being put up for a seat in Parliament. Frith, it seems, wishes to increase his wealth, standing and influence at the same time; Watkinson is his creature and you are no longer central to their plan. Now, my dear, the sad truth is that your mother would make a better wife for Frith and, if you refuse him, he will almost certainly propose to her. You have nothing to fear and I shall see that you are provided for before I leave."

"You are leaving us?" Katherine's alarm was touching.

"Yes, I must, but it is time that you left this place and had an establishment of your own. I shall install you in my own house and you may have Mrs O'Riordan, Maggie and the three men as your household. I will leave you an annuity and you will still benefit from the profits of the company. There, what do you say?"

"It is most irregular . . . What will others say?"

"Your mother will say you are ungrateful, Mr Frith will come to terms with it, the population of this town will say Captain Topsy-Turvy is up to his mad tricks again and you, I will lay five hundred guineas on it, will have half a dozen suitors paying you court within a month of my departure."

"But I cannot accept."

"But me no buts, my dear Kate, I need you to do as I bid. I cannot abandon Mrs O'Riordan, I do not want to lose my property, but Puella's death has ended my life here. You will not, I know, abuse my trust and I am anxious to restore my spirits."

"You are going back to sea?"

"I am, the moment the *Spitfire* comes in." He smiled at her. "Come now, I have much to do, let me know your answer by this time tomorrow. Will you do that?"

She nodded. "Yes, yes, of course, and thank you for your kindness."

"Tush, Katherine, I am not being kind, I am merely being pragmatic."

At his own house he learned from Mrs O'Riordan that Puella's funeral could be held the following morning and that she had sent Bandy Ben to arrange for a coffin maker to call. The rickety old fellow returned and knuckled his forehead to Kite, who wished him a good morning. Ben was a misfit and although Mrs O'Riordan never owned to it, Puella had discovered he was some sort of a relative of hers. But he was a reliable message bearer, and while he hardly ever spoke, Kite had discovered that he had a quite uncanny facility with figures. Such attributes made him uncommonly handy to a shipowner whose communications with the docks were frequent and often entailed quantities more than mere facts. Bandy Ben could recite an inward ship's draught, the tonnage of her lading, the dues payable and the wage bill for her crew without recourse to endless chits of paper. But he could not otherwise communicate, and stood in sudden solemnity while Mrs O'Riordan spoke for him.

"There now, sir, Ben wishes you to know how sorry he is about the Mistress."

"I thank you, Ben. You are a good man. You will see that she is tended well by the coffin maker, I hope."

Ben nodded vigorously. "Five feet six an' seven-eighths of an inch, Cap'n," he said, repeating Puella's height.

"I put a dress upon her sir, this morning."

"Thank you, Mrs O'Riordan. Now forgive me, but there are matters of business coming to a head and I have to return to the counting house."

He left Mrs O'Riordan to her head-shaking and her muttering about business being too important these days, and asking whatever happened to a decent wake. If ever a body needed a wake it was that of the black Mistress, or she herself was not Siobhan O'Riordan from the Cove of Cork.


Neither Frith nor Watkinson remained at the counting house when Kite returned there. He had half anticipated their departure, but nevertheless felt a sense of disappointment. Johnstone followed him into his private office and closed the door behind them.

"Forgive the presumption, Captain Kite," he said, "but the birds have flown."

"That is not altogether a surprise, Nathan. Were they in good spirits when they left?"

"Watkinson made a show of it, certainly . . ."

"Oh?"

"He smiled at me."

"Putting a brave face on it, or crowing?"

"Impossible to say, but I suspect the former."

"I think you might be more optimistic; after all it is not Watkinson who has to put up the cash. By the by, do McClusky and Peters have any notion of what is afoot?" Kite asked, seating himself and drawing towards him the sheaf of papers pertaining to the recent refit of the *Samphire*.

Johnstone shook his head. "No, sir. But I should not linger here, for it might arouse suspicions."

He had hardly regained his desk when Frith, disdaining to knock, marched into the office followed by Watkinson. Kite looked up. Both men wore expressions of neither triumph nor defeat, rather of grim determination. Frith made his offer; it was based on the overall sum of all shares owned by Kite or his late wife.

"As I expected, at three pounds per share you undervalue the ships."

"You are holding a pistol to our heads, Captain. It is a fair offer under the circumstances."

"It is as fair an offer as you are prepared to make, but wait a moment. Mr Watkinson, please call Mr Johnstone here a moment."

Watkinson did as he was bid and Johnstone came in and shut the door behind him. "Gentlemen? What can I do for you?"

"Johnstone, I have a small commission for you. I should be obliged if you would seek a valuation on my shares in our ships. It is my intention to sell out. You may start with Mr Bibby and then seek out Mr Brocklebank. Do you understand, Johnstone?"

Johnstone made a fair stab at feigning his astonishment. "Yes, I understand, sir."

"Don't be a fool, man," cut in Frith, "Bibby will undervalue once he knows it is a buyer's market, so will Brocklebank and the rest. If I put ten shillings on my price, will you not accept?"

"I will accept nothing less than four pounds a share," Kite said coolly.

Frith sighed. "Very well then. I agree."

Kite saw the gleam of triumph in Watkinson's eyes as he turned to Frith and nodded. He had not been wrong; Mr Watkinson had this day hiked up his station in the world. But, thought Kite, with that went his expectations too. He rose and nodded to Frith. "Very well, Frith. I shall not trouble you further. Let us conclude the business. I shall ask, er, Johnstone there to draw up the bills of sale and he can deliver them to Watkinson. Mr Watkinson, your fortunes today have been somewhat mercurial. I wish you joy of your new opportunities. You may draw up a deed for my perusal to detach my name from this company. As soon as these matters are concluded, I shall leave in the *Spitfire*. Mr Johnstone, you may grub me up a cargo for the Antilles, if you please."

And as he walked from their presence he thought again of the magnitude of his sinfulness.

*     *     *

The day of Puella's funeral was worse than that on which her son's had been held. The little group of mourners, consisting of Kite, Mrs O'Riordan, Maggie and Bandy Ben, with Katherine Makepeace, Johnstone, McClusky and Dr Bennett, stood under a downpour which fell in torrents from a sky of lead. The vicar rushed the committal, took Kite's *pour-boire* with a shifty manner that was so full of eagerness to be away that it compelled Kite to go back to the graveside and stand and watch while the sexton and his mate filled it in. He was conscious of his preoccupation during the last few days, a guilt which only compounded the terrible certainty that he could have saved Puella from herself and that the fact that he had not done so only attested to the fact that he had been neglecting her for a longer time than the last few days of the cholera outbreak.

Beside him the sexton coughed, waking Kite from his reflections. He gave the two men a guinea and, after they had gone, said his private and heartfelt farewell.

He and Puella had grown as far apart as man and wife can grow under the harsh, ineluctable and imperative circumstances of life; but he recalled her not as she had become but as she had been when he first set eyes upon her on the deck of the slaver *Enterprize*. He knelt, touched his finger to his lips and placed them on the ground. "Fare thee well, my dearest and only love."

Then he went home to where Mrs O'Riordan served tea and oporto to the desolate and dripping group. He moved among them, thanking them for their time and trouble, urging them not to linger in their wet clothes, coming last to Dr Bennett, who was talking to Katherine Makepeace.

"I was saying to Miss Makepeace, Kite, that your poor wife was as much a victim to the cholera as your son. You should console yourself with that thought."

"It is kind of you to ease my conscience, Bennett, but I am not sure that you are right. But tell me, is the cholera still rampant?"

"No, it is on the wane; why, I cannot tell you, but this week the numbers have dropped and I understand that this diminution is widespread, thank goodness."

Kite noticed Katherine shiver. "Come, Kate, we must get you home before you succumb to some fever. If you'll excuse me, Bennett, I'll see Miss Makepeace home."

"There is no need. I shall attend to the matter myself." Bennett offered his arm to Katherine, who took it with a smile. He leaned towards Kite and said in a low voice, "Miss Makepeace has confided in me your intentions regarding her. I think it most kind of you and have counselled her accordingly. I hope you don't mind my interfering."

Kite smiled. "I could never mind you meddling, Bennett, you are too old a friend."

Bennett chuckled and led Katherine off, then the others made their farewells. Johnstone hung back until last.

"Are you all right, Captain?" he asked solicitously.

Kite nodded. "Yes, thank you."

"And you wish me to continue as we discussed?"

"Exactly as we discussed."

"Very well. Then until I hear from you, I wish you farewell."

In the following few days, Kite put his domestic affairs in order, arranging a tombstone for the grave of Puella and her son, instructing Mrs O'Riordan of the arrangements which would come into force after his own departure and making financial provision for the running costs of the house and an allowance for Katherine. Until these were concluded he kept his own company, sending Bandy Ben off with his letters and patiently awaiting news of the arrival of the *Spitfire*. It occurred to him that should she fail to berth his case would be altered, but his fortune was not entirely bound up in his ships and his bankers held sufficient in deposits, private and Government stocks, to enable him to purchase a new vessel. He wrote to London, where he held funds with Messrs Coutts, to arrange bills of exchange and letters of credit, satisfied that these arrangements, some of which had been suggested by the shrewd Johnstone, would allow him freedom to exploit his capital to further his ambition. He also wrote to his sister Helen, his sole surviving relative, who was now married to her naval husband. Henry Hope remained a lieutenant on half-pay and he knew their circumstances to be straitened. In his letter he informed her of the deaths of Puella and William, and of his plans for the future.

*If Dame Fortune wills it,* he concluded,

> I shall Reëstablish myself as an Independent Shipowner and therefore in a better Position than hitherto to offer Henry a Post as Commander of one of my Vessels, if he so Desires. While I Appreciate his Reasons for Declining this Offer in the Past, I should not like him to Think it Withdrawn in its Entirety and, while it is Temporarily beyond my Means

at Present, it will not be long before I am again able to Make him such an Offer should he by then find that his Advancement in the Naval Service is Further Delayed.

Kite did not think for a moment that Henry Hope would abandon his naval ambitions, but it would have been unthinkable to abandon his brother-in-law, particularly as he might have need of some reliable masters in the near future. He thought too of Christopher Jones, and wrote to him, explaining his decision to quit the firm of Makepeace and Kite and leave for the West Indies in the *Spitfire* as soon as she had discharged her inward cargo.

A week later Jones was on his doorstep demanding to see him to explain that he had called at the company's offices and had seen that Kite's name was no longer on the sign board.

"I have no desire to work for a locker-full of grasping clerks, Captain. Will you take me as your mate again?"

"You would relinquish your entitlement to command, Jones?"

Jones nodded. "For the time being. Don't think I have lost my nerve, though God knows the memory of the wreck dogs me like the pox itself, but another opportunity will come and you are not the man to deny it to me, I think, Captain Kite."

"Do not have too good an opinion of me, Jones. You would not find it echoed within the hallowed precincts of . . . what exactly do they call themselves now?"

"Makepeace and Watkinson, sir."

"So, Mr Frith enjoys living in the shadows, eh? No wonder I rumbled him so much. I had not considered that."

"I'm sorry?" Jones frowned.

"No matter, Jones, no matter."

"I was sorry to hear about Mrs Kite, Captain. She was a sweet lady and as comely as they can ever be . . ."

"She could not stand young Will's death, Jones." Kite sniffed. The candour of his old shipmate was touching and threatened to unman him. He stared at Jones, whose woolly hair showed flecks of grey, though his coffee-coloured complexion could never be mistaken for mere windburn. He held out his hand. "I am damned glad to see you, Jones, damned glad! You shall stay here until the old *Spitfire*'s numbers are made and then we shall have some work to do!"

"Just like the old days, Captain."

"Aye, just like the old days."

# Part Two

Independence

# Four

## A Fall from Grace

In the month following the *Spitfire*'s arrival in the Old Dock and the discharge of her mixed cargo of sugar, indigo and rum, Kite and Jones laboured at her refit, an expense entirely charged to the account of Makepeace, Watkinson and Company, who still, as far as the outside world knew, were the agents for Captain Kite's vessel. The task was carried out with great thoroughness and without any hindrance. As Jones said with satisfaction as he, Kite and Johnstone conferred one morning in the cabin, it was precisely why the time had come to leave the employ of the company.

"Well," Jones had enlarged as Kite exchanged glances with Johnstone, "they might be able to determine betwixt a profit and a loss, but they have no one who knows the difference between a chess tree and a chestnut and that deficiency would soon render their other expertise null and void."

"You are only too correct, Mr Jones," Johnstone remarked as he put down a pot of small beer. "They will wake one day to the deficiency, but happily their self-conceit will obscure the facts for them for a week or two yet."

"Ahh," said Jones, "then you purposed all this?" He looked from one to another of them. Kite smiled, but Johnstone, now fully out of the shell of his former subservience, shrugged with mock modesty.

"Oh, we calculated that matters *might* fall out in this wise, yes . . ."

"You are too damned modest, Johnstone," Kite said smiling at the quondam clerk, "though I like you the more for it." He turned to Jones. "The fact is, Jones, that Johnstone here is the entire brains behind this enterprise, such intrigues being beyond the abilities of poor simple seamen."

"You do me too much honour, Captain Kite." Johnstone held out his pot as Bandy Ben, sent by Katherine Makepeace as manservant to Captain Kite, refilled it.

"Indeed I do, but it makes you an intelligent accomplice in my affairs, Johnstone." And in such a mood of convivial banter, the three men carried out the preparation of the *Spitfire* for her forthcoming voyage.

The *Spitfire* was a schooner, Spanish-built of mahogany in Havana eighteen years earlier. Limited in her capacity to carry much cargo, she was swift, armed and best suited as a small slaver or a privateer. As her ability to earn much by her lading was restricted, Makepeace and Kite had several times considered her sale, but although they had not taken part in slaving after his marriage to Puella, Kite had refused to sell her, arguing that another war with France or Spain would find her ample and rewarding employment. Her master, a young man named Moss, was eager to marry and had no objection to taking a voyage off, while the majority of her crew showed no reluctance to sign on again.

On a fine evening in the first week of June 1772, *Spitfire* warped out into the River Mersey and dropped downstream on the ebb tide, setting sail and standing to sea into the setting sun. Before dark she had crossed the bar and had laid a course north of the Great Orme, to double the Skerries and head for St George's Channel and the open ocean beyond. Thanks to the industry of Mr Christopher Jones and the hands, she was in first-class condition; thanks to the skill of Nathan Johnstone, she bore not only a quantity of blue and white chinaware for Jamaica, Antigua and Savannah, but the commercial mails for a number of mercantile houses whose principals were anxious about the increasingly fractious state of the New England colonies and eager to contact their agents and masters abroad. Captain Kite had made no secret of the fact that his ship was fitted out for any eventuality, that she was well armed and her magazines were full, for opinion in Liverpool was that the unstable condition of the Massachusetts was such that British goods could be at some risk, if the colonists lost their heads as they had already done in Boston. Kite's private agenda, concerted with Johnstone, had no warlike intent. He had simply equipped *Spitfire* to the best advantage, intending to sell her as a potential slaver in Cuba or Savannah and with the money purchase a ship better able to profit from the carriage of cargo, but there seemed no reason not to ride the wave of anxiety over the political troubles in New England, particularly as there were those who recalled Captain Kite's daring action in the last war when, greatly outnumbered, he had taken the French corsair *La Malouine*.

Kite himself had less faith in his martial abilities. His capture of the French corsair had been more a matter of luck than valour and owed more to the sudden appearance of Puella and the soot-blacked crew than to any spirit on the part of *Spitfire*'s commander. It had been these circumstances that had led to his renaming his prize the *African Princess*. But all that was in the past; the *African Princess* lay in pieces, strewn about the seabed off Cape Clear Island, and Puella lay in her cold, foreign northern grave on the hillside above the grey Mersey.

Kite felt a curious numbness over his loss. His slow estrangement from Puella made her death the more bearable, for the loss of young William had dissolved the one remaining bond that held them together. But he also knew that in the strange and self-inflicted manner of her death, she had bound her own spirit with that of her son while denying her body to Kite. On the one hand she took from him the sole means by which in time they might have come to a reconciliation, but on the other she set him free. He wondered to what extent she guessed he would return to sea, for he knew that one of the powers she possessed was a prescient sense that transcended mere female intuition. On those few occasions when they fought over their growing disassociation, she had once or twice flung at him the accusation that he would be happier at sea than in Liverpool, but when in desperation he had suggested that she accompany him again, she had always refused, arguing that she must remain in Liverpool and see their son brought up as a gentleman. Over the years he had made occasional voyages in command, partly to maintain his links with his trading associates like Wentworth in Antigua, and partly to run away from her unhappiness and the constant reproach of her presence. He felt his marriage had been the mistake many had prophesied it would be, and this had made him put a brave public face on it, extending its life against all probabilities. In her inimitable way, Puella had ended it by laying her ambiguous purpose on him like a paradoxical curse.

But while his crew hauled the *Spitfire*'s sheets aft and flattened her fore-and-aft sails as she stood west into the star-spangled night, he discarded his guilt. He was free of Liverpool and its festering cholera, he was free of all obligations beyond the bulwarks of the little schooner, and the pervading spirit of independence gave him an uplifting sense of hope, such as he had not experienced for years.

The schooner made a fast passage to the West Indies, during which she experienced fair winds and bright weather, reeling off the knots with an easy grace, her company settling into the pleasantly easy regimen of a ship's duty when the fates smile upon her passage. As they picked up the trades, Kite almost entirely threw off the megrims, troubled only by dreams which could be dispelled by a spell on deck and were easily diverted by his instruction of Johnstone in the vessel's navigation. It was soon clear to both Kite and Jones that, intelligent though he was, Nathan Johnstone did not possess those distinctive instincts of a natural seaman. He had no ability to act or to think swiftly, to react quickly enough to disarm even the most minor of problems, such as a kinked or fouled line which had been badly cleared for running. His mental skills, though gymnastic enough, were better employed in more orderly processes and he soon showed promise as a navigator, so that Kite recognised that he could easily outstrip Jones if it became a matter of necessity. As it was, he familiarised himself with the tabulated ephemeris and the manipulation of a quadrant, more to occupy his mind and to divert it from the incipient seasickness that dogged his first fortnight at sea than for any intellectual gain.

Jones, the mulatto mate, seemed not to resent his demotion. His respect for William Kite, both as a man and as his employer, combined with memories of his former status as mate under Kite's command to wind the clock back in his imagination. No man objects to reliving the happier periods of his youth, and the kindliness of the weather only added to the happiness of the illusion so that the pleasant voyage dimmed the horrors of wrecking the *African Princess* and drowning two-thirds of his crew.

The *Spitfire* warped into St John's a month later and that evening Kite and Johnstone sat at table with Wentworth and his plump wife, Kitty. She had once set her cap at Kite himself, but social convention and considerable wealth had buried the unpleasant little encounter, so that she acted as though it had never happened. Kite also sensed that Mrs Wentworth, who

had certainly not forgotten her abject lust and his humiliating
rebuff, derived some quiet satisfaction from the knowledge that
he had not profited long from what she considered his unnatural
marriage to his black mistress. Kite's misfortunes were not only
a matter of mild pleasure to Kitty Wentworth; they also proved
the rightness of her own opinion.

Wentworth had prospered mightily, having inherited a fortune from his late benefactor, Joseph Mulgrave. The house of
Mulgrave, Wentworth and Co. traded on its own account and
acted as agents for several plantations on the island of Antigua,
and elsewhere in the Antilles. On the bare hillside, where Joseph
Mulgrave's mansion had burnt down with a spectacular display of
cunningly laid powder trains, fuses and slow-burning matches, he
had built an extravagant villa fitted with every comfort. Looking
at his complacent host, Kite found it was impossible to recall the
fat and indigent clerk he had first known to inhabit Mulgrave's
waterfront counting house. Now Wentworth looked older than
his forty-odd years, corpulent and sweating, his face burnt brick-
red by the sun, his nose red-veined with excess. He had had three
children by Kitty, the oldest of whom, a boy, toiled as apprentice
to his hard-working father; for Wentworth belied his appearance,
being far from indolent and industrious in his pursuit of every
possible avenue of commercial profit.

The Wentworths' table groaned under steaming platters of
meats and bottles of wine for what was, in Wentworth's own
words, "a private and intimate supper". He would, he assured
Kite, be pleased to act as a proper host and dine Kite and his
"associate", as Kite had introduced Johnstone, in a proper and
fitting manner in due course. The evening's meal was, however,
to run over old gossip and to dispose in part of the more congenial
aspects of their business association, as well as to reveal to
Wentworth the extent to which Kite had detached himself from
his old involvement with the house of Makepeace.

As the cloth was removed and Kitty Wentworth rose to withdraw, she offered to show Johnstone the house and its immediate
grounds which had been prettily lit by flaring torches. "I do not
wish you to abandon my husband's table or his cigars or port,
Mr Johnstone, but I am sure that he and dear William will talk
so much of the good old days that it will bore you terribly . . ."

Johnstone looked, rather desperately Kite thought, from him
to Wentworth, but the latter waved airily. "I think my wife is

probably right, Mr Johnstone, as is usual. Do please feel free to take a turn with her if you are so inclined."

"Come, Mr Johnstone, it will be pleasant to hear of matters in England. I am so tired of the tedious doings of troublesome Yankees."

Johnstone bowed awkwardly to Wentworth and said, "If you will excuse me, sir, I have not had, hitherto, much occasion to smoke cigars and if my humble efforts at conversation will gratify your wife . . ."

"By all means, by all means." Wentworth waved them out, and as they left he slumped back into his creaking chair.

"The poor fellow has never, I think, been entertained in such style before," Kite said grinning and taking the offered cigar. "His fortunes have improved so rapidly of late that he can scarce believe it."

"You intend to make him a partner in this new shipping venture of yours?"

"Perhaps, if he wishes it. He has a shrewd mind and a better head for business than my own. Besides, I trust him."

"Well, he certainly seems to have declared his loyalty by making known to you this cabal against you. These rivalries," Wentworth expatiated between puffs of his cigar, "are bound to surface in any undertaking, and commerce is by its very nature conducive to the practice of trickery of one sort or another. By your account, though, you sound as if you might have succeeded in quietly ruining your own former associates."

"I doubt that it will come to that. But certainly, unless some unforeseen eventuality arises to support them—"

"Or they acquire a ship's husband or master mariner of sufficient acumen," Wentworth interjected with a knowing look. "There are a few such about in Liverpool, I dare say."

"Yes." Kite said, blowing smoke across the candleflames so that they guttered and turned the wraiths into strange forms. "But it was not my purpose to ruin them. I simply wished to extract myself once I realised the extent to which Makepeace had embroiled me. Johnstone saw a rather more tortuous advantage to be extracted and I had no objection."

"There could be one unforeseen event looming on the horizon to halt the decline in Makepeace and Watkinson."

"You are going to mention this trouble with the American colonists?" Kite said, smiling. " 'Tis true a few Liverpool ships have been taken up on charter as military transports, though most have come from London and a handful from Bristol, but I cannot see—"

"There is serious and seditious talk of rebellion, Kite. You heard no doubt of the massacre in Boston."

"Aye, but that was two years ago and it blew over. Besides, Boston, like many a sea port and like Liverpool itself on more than one occasion, has a rough populace given to excesses of one sort or another."

"You miss the point, Kite. You have been too long in England with all its comfortable certainties and ingrained misconceptions. I will do you the courtesy of not referring to them as prejudices, since I do not think that you native Englishmen can ever see your opinions in that light, but you and others like you would do well to listen to some of the grumbling coming from New England. I am not talking about any high-flown moral notions, but merely the pragmatic associations of men of business which will disintegrate if an open rupture is allowed to develop between New and Old England."

"Well, surely it is precisely because of those ties of commerce that there will be no rupture. I ask you, who will be the beneficiary?"

Wentworth shrugged. "Who knows? If it does come to open rebellion it will be easy for neither party."

Kite waved aside Wentworth's paranoia. "You are simply too fearful. Why, it would be like civil war . . . No, no, we have too much in common to throw away the advantages gained by the late war. Rest assured if there were any dissension, France and Spain would do their utmost to revenge themselves upon us for their recent humiliations."

"You prove my case, Kite. At the first spark of trouble they will fan the flames."

"Come, come, no one in New England could possibly want the French returning to Canada, for they would be into their own back yards inside a year."

"You don't believe there is a, what d'you sailors call it, a ground-swell of opinion, in favour of disassociation from the Parliament in London?"

"Perhaps by the very lowest who see in it some simple and superficial advantage to themselves. Only a fool would think the New Englanders capable of defending themselves without an army and a naval force."

"But supposing, Kite, there were men in New England who wished to be the new Whigs, the great landowners and nabobs of New England? Men who are excited by the thought of having their own parliament, their own rotten and pocket boroughs? Men who would apply the principles and practice of commerce to the principles and practice of government?"

"Are you telling me you consider such men exist?"

Wentworth burst out laughing. "Of course they exist!" He leaned forward and stubbed out his cigar, refilled his glass and shoved the decanter towards Kite. "Listen, Kite, you mentioned that damned massacre. Do you know what happened?"

Kite shrugged. "There was a riot, the military were called out, the Riot Act was read, the mob was intransigent, the soldiers fired to disperse the mob and some people were killed. A farce of a trial followed, men doing their duty were humiliated but the mob was unappeased. There, is that a fair and full summation, gleaned from English newspapers, which as any fool knows are bilious with prejudice?"

Wentworth nodded. "Well, that is a tolerably good recounting of the facts, but it misses the real significance of the event."

"Which is . . . ?"

"Enshrined in the fact that even you call it a massacre. You may, in your own mind, have put the word in quotation marks, considering it a mere matter of extreme exaggeration, but what would be your reaction if I said this incident was an unprovoked mowing down of innocent citizens by rolling volley fire of British lobster-backs?"

"I would say that it was an unpardonable exaggeration."

"You might be correct as a matter of veracity in its absolute sense, but you would not be believed in New England. In New England that is precisely how they regard the matter. Men and women living on remote farms and in small towns do not have the knowledge of the world that you have. They cannot conceive of any Bostonians, good people like themselves, as shouting incessant abuse at the military or pelting soldiers with stones. They cannot, I doubt, even imagine what a mob is, still less of what it is capable once it has coalesced into a monstrous hydra. All this, it has to be admitted, has been much helped by a mendacious engraving circulated throughout the province with every appearance of being a truthful and observed representation of what transpired. There was also some talk, I am informed, that the whole incident was cunningly fomented, since it started when a single off-duty soldier was seeking some work at a ropewalk and was taunted and provoked. Could this be established beyond doubt, you would find a conspiracy at the heart of it all, I don't doubt."

"And who are your informants, are they men of probity?"

Wentworth ticked them remorselessly off. "Oh, yes, Captain Hawkins of the *Dido*, Mr Wright, mate of the *Friendship*, Captains Douglas of the *Cleopatra*, Cracknell of the *Bostonian*, Greene of the *Emily and Jane*, Hubbard of the *New York*, and Maxwell of the *Lady o' the Lake* – all of whom except Hawkins and Maxwell are New Englanders or have been trading between here and the American coast for so long that they have forgotten they are British and have married and settled in the colonies. I rest my case."

"I see." Kite sat back and considered matters for a moment, then said, "Suppose I changed my mind and did not sell *Spitfire*, at least for a year or two, suppose I left Jones in her among the islands where he is happiest? I have sufficient capital to buy or charter a bottom."

"I'll come in with you if you sail as master. Young Johnstone can act as supercargo and learn the ropes." Wentworth put down his glass as if the gesture signified sudden resolution. "Yes, why not, what d'you say, eh? I'll go fifty-fifty with you on a bottom. You could pick up cargoes and trade up the coast and keep us wise to the gossip and the turn events are taking. The information alone will be helpful and you will see how best to exploit the situation if it changes." Wentworth paused, considering something. "I know of a ship, Spanish-built of good mahogany like *Spitfire*, but of four hundred or so tons burthen, the *Santa Margarita of the Angels* or some such Papist flummery. She's frigate-built and owned by a Spaniard in Maiquetia . . . Yes, she would do admirably."

"Maiquetia? That is on the Spanish Main, is it not?"

"Yes, but she is due here within a few weeks and I am certain we can acquire her. What do you say?" Wentworth was grinning like a schoolboy. "Come on, ain't you game?"

"I'm game, but let us take a look at her first."

"Done!" Wentworth rose. "Let us take a turn on the terrace and see what has become of Kitty and young Johnstone."

It was late when Kite and Johnstone walked back down the hill towards the harbour. They had eaten and drunk well and their bellies, unused to such rich fare, kept them quiet, or so Kite thought, as he struggled with a rumbling gut and thoughts of the projected new vessel. He did not want to break the news to Johnstone immediately, it being his habit to sleep on any decision. He knew the enthusiasm of the evening before could turn into regret when viewed in the colder light of dawn. It was some time, therefore, before he thought he ought to converse with his companion and broke the silence with a sigh.

"I hope this evening was not too intolerable for you. Old acquaintances can be somewhat self-absorbed, I am afraid."

"Not at all, sir."

"You ate well, anyway."

"Better than ever before in my life, sir."

"Good. And Mistress Robinson did not importune you, I hope?"

It had been intended as a joke, as a loose remark between men, to be taken as an irony, but Johnstone stopped abruptly. Kite, caught aback, had walked on a few steps before he realised what had happened and turned.

"What is the matter?" he asked.

"What did you mean by that question?" Johnstone asked, his voice tense.

"What did I mean by it? Why nothing; leastaways nothing of significance. If I meant anything, I meant that I thought you might have been less bored had you remained at table and that your manners did you credit . . ."

"She seduced me, sir," Johnstone said in a low voice through clenched teeth. "She made a fool of me . . . I . . . I thought you knew she had, that you guessed she might and that she had volunteered to take me into the garden out of lust."

Kite realised that, subconsciously, he had almost expected Kitty Wentworth to take the young man for her own pleasure. It occurred to him that perhaps Wentworth's children were not his own. His wife had been hot-blooded years earlier and although her figure had fattened, there was enough of the voluptuary in her to appeal to a young man in Johnstone's circumstances. The poor fellow had been deprived of his conjugal rights for several months now and his fall from grace was not surprising, except perhaps to himself.

"I did not think that, Nathan. But why confess the matter? Many men would have thought nothing of it."

"Because I am ashamed . . ."

"Did you not enjoy her? Did you fail to satisfy her?"

"That is the point, Captain Kite," Johnstone replied, his voice still low. "Of course it was pleasurable and she was hot for me. Or perhaps any man," he added revealingly.

"That we cannot tell, but why should you feel shame? Because your wife is not long dead?"

"Yes." It was too dark to see the expression upon Johnstone's face, but the enunciation of the word sounded as if he was being strangled.

"And you feel you have besmirched or betrayed her memory?"

"Yes," whispered Johnstone.

Kite stepped close to Johnstone and put his hand on the younger man's arm. "My dear fellow, you are no worse than the rest of us. I should be obliged if you would act discreetly while you are here, for if you have truly satisfied Mistress Wentworth she will most assuredly pursue you. Do not cause her to be bitter by taking another woman while we are here, simply do the gallant thing; we shall be here no more than a month."

"A month! I shall contrive to avoid the woman!"

"That would be ill-mannered of you . . ."

"But I have no desire to repeat my folly."

"Call it an indiscretion, Nathan. Consider it a privilege to have all your appetites satisfied in one evening, and a mark of good manners to have satisfied your hostess's wants too. Between us we have done well, for I have presented our host with something to divert *his* mind."

"That is most kind of you, sir," Johnstone said with a venomous sarcasm.

Kite laughed. "Oh come, Nathan, you should not have confided in me. I am not a priest."

"That you are not . . ."

"But I shall not make these facts public."

"I pray you will not, sir!"

"Come, Nathan, laugh at yourself. It will do you good, sir."

# Five

## The *Wentworth*

"**W**ell, what did you think of her?"

"She will not be fast, but she'll be weatherly enough and would stand more and heavier guns than the six miserable four-pounders that she bears now," Kite said, sitting opposite Wentworth in the cool of the waterfront office into which he had once stumbled what seemed a lifetime ago.

"And she is well built?"

"No question of it. Truth to tell, I prefer mahogany to oak, as I think it less susceptible to rot and, in these latitudes, the damned ship-worm."

Wentworth nodded. "Very well, I shall make Diego Galvez an offer."

Kite looked out of the window. The *Santa Margarita de los Angeles* lay off in the bay. He would change her name, though to what he had not yet decided. He would have wider yards fitted in due course, for her rig was too narrow for his taste and he thought she would profit from wider courses and topsails.

"We could send *Spitfire* down to Maiquetia . . ." Wentworth was saying and Kite came to himself.

"There is no need. Galvez is on board, on his way to Havana with his wife and daughter. Ask him to dinner. He is, as you know, eager to sell and would release the ship once he has reached Cuba. I think he intends to settle there, for he is past his middle years."

"What is the daughter like?"

"Pleasant enough in her manner. She speaks excellent English, but she is not handsome. Why, do you indulge in indiscretions these days, Wentworth?"

Wentworth winked and touched the side of his nose with his right index finger.

"It is the heat, no doubt," Kite remarked drily.

Wentworth chuckled and Kite thought that he had never seen anything less like a libertine than the rotund figure before him – but then, he reflected, Mrs Wentworth seemed the very epitome of matronly virtue and he knew that poor Johnstone had enjoyed her embraces on several occasions now.

"By the way, Kite," Wentworth said, breaking into his reflections and tossing a newspaper across his desk, "I received this from Holmes of the *Morning Star* which arrived after you had gone aboard the *Santa Margarita* – you are not intending to trade under that name, are you?"

Kite picked up the paper. "No, but what do you think? You own half of her."

"Which of the two of us owns the angels?" Wentworth quipped.

"Not I, I think."

"Then call her *Santa Margarita*."

"No, I do not like—"

"Call her *Wentworth* and be damned to it," said Kite, scanning the paper to see what it was he was supposed to be digesting. Then he saw the item and, as Wentworth smiled his approval at Kite's suggestion of the new name, he read the account of the burning of the *Gaspée*. Off the coast of Rhode Island, the British revenue schooner had been in chase of a local packet whose master was a suspected smuggler, and in chasing her into Providence she had run aground. That night boats from the sea port had approached the *Gaspée* and her commander, a Lieutenant Duddingston, had challenged them and forbidden them to come aboard. He was shot in the groin for his pains, whereupon over sixty masked men had boarded the vessel and she had been set on fire. A subsequent reward by the Colonial authorities of £500 had failed to tempt a single witness into giving information that would convict anyone involved in the deliberate act of piracy.

"If that is not an act of open rebellion, Kite, I don't know what is," Wentworth said.

"Yes, I confess that shocks me. You are right and the fact that no one will take the reward argues that it is men of influence who are behind all this trouble."

"They are indeed pirates; they should be hanged, all sixty of them. But in Rhode Island they are probably saying it indicates the unanimity of dissent, a general disaffection with Government and an indication of the loyalty of the populace to the ideals of liberty."

"And to hell with poor Duddingston."

"And to hell with poor Duddingston indeed, Kite. You will note that, unlike the so-called massacre at Boston, there is no mention of victims. Duddingston suffers as a proxy for the King and his ministers; not, of course, that they will care very much."

"No. But Lord Rockingham's government went a long way to redress the grievances of the colonists. If only he and not North were still in power."

"The impression here," Wentworth said, "is that North is the King's toady."

Kite smiled. "I think King's Friend is the correct designation of North's politics." He tossed aside the paper, a gesture eloquent with the dismissal of politicians in general and British ministers in particular. He stared once more at the ship beyond the window. "So, what do you say to *Wentworth*?"

"I think it makes her sound like an Indiaman and has an aristocratic ring to it, certainly. If you are to trade upon the Yankee coast it is as well that the King's late and conciliating minister should be so commemorated."

Kite frowned. "I don't follow."

"The Marquess of Rocking'm," Wentworth drawled the name as it was pronounced in London, "is Charles Watson Wentworth."

"Ahh. I had forgot. Then that is what she shall be," Kite said, standing, "and since I am intending to modify her sail plan I shall be satisfied with you having your name carved across her stern."

"Ah, you will trim her *kites*, then," Wentworth said with a chuckle.

"Very droll, Wentworth, very droll."

Captain Kite sailed from Antigua as soon as the sale had been completed and a cargo of sugar and rum had been loaded. He wished to be clear of the islands before the onset of the hurricane season and made first for Savannah with the last of *Spitfire*'s trans-shipped cargo of crockery. He had left Jones in command of the schooner and Wentworth had found employment for her trading between the islands. He had left Johnstone in Wentworth's counting house and Kitty Wentworth's bed. Johnstone was show-ing signs of tiring of his seemingly insatiable mistress, but he had not mentioned his liaison after that first, impetuous confession, nor had Kite raised the subject, for it was none of his business.

He was pleased to have established both Johnstone and Jones in posts from which they could profit. It had been essential to have them to help him refit *Spitfire* and leave Liverpool, but his desire for solitary independence had grown, prompted perhaps by the narrow society of St John's and the fact that much of the town was haunted by the ghost of Puella. He had never allowed himself to meander about the place; there had been no nostalgic wanderings off the track he had beaten for himself between the harbour, with its waterfront warehouses and counting houses, its sailmaker's loft and its chandlers' premises, the steps where the ships' boats picked up their officers, and Wentworth's villa. He went nowhere near the house which he and Puella had once rented and where their first son Charles had died, and he made a point of sleeping aboard either *Spitfire* or *Wentworth*, as the *Santa Margarita* was renamed with due ceremony.

It was never difficult to find a crew among the waterfront loiterers, and several of the ship's former seamen remained on her books. The matter of officers was more difficult, but Wentworth found a satisfactory first and second mate willing to serve and so Kite was able to sail in her as he had planned.

It was Kite's intention to trade on the American coast and to pick up a cargo of cotton from Savannah for Philadelphia or New York. He loaded a full cargo with an option to carry it to Liverpool, however, but before August was out he had discharged his entire lading of cotton bales at the Quaker city and then New York, somewhat relieved that he was not compelled to return to Liverpool so soon. In fact he picked up a part cargo of trans-shipped British and European manufactures, goods which ranged from fashionable gowns, millinery and a quantity of haberdashery, books, fine porcelain and glassware, cotton piece goods, silks and worsteds, to some fine guns and gentlemen's small swords. Although far from fully loaded, *Wentworth*'s part cargo when sold in Boston yielded the New York merchants a fine haul and Kite the high freight rate that Wentworth's agent had arranged.

"You see, Captain," this worthy had explained, "for some time now the Bostonians have not considered it fashionable to be seen purchasing goods from Britain. There is in fact what amounts to an embargo in that port. But of course, whether you are an ardent

Whig or a loyal Tory, you want the goods, so you quietly order them from New York and we ship them from here as though they are New York products."

"But that is ludicrous."

"It is also profitable, Captain, which as you know, overrides every other consideration in this life."

"But the *Wentworth* is a British ship; will that not raise a degree of this illogical prejudice?"

"No. The majority of the gentry purchasing your lading from the emporia of Boston will be Tory and therefore only careful not to excite attention in Boston itself. Most of the mob who are putty in the hands of the radical orators of New England will not know that the à la mode notions were carried in your vessel."

"But some of the mob will have discharged the cargo and will therefore know of its origins."

"Yes," said the agent with a trace of exasperation in his tone, "you are an Antiguan vessel and clearly have not come from England for most of your crew are negroes, mulattos or quadroons, with scarce a white face among them. As for yourself and your ensign, many British masters trade on this coast alongside their native Yankee cousins . . ."

And so for several months Captain Kite and the *Wentworth* were employed, mainly on the coast north of Cape Hatteras, until, with the onset of the worst of winter weather, Kite considered his plan of extending the *Wentworth*'s spars and sails. His experience of the ship convinced him that this was a proper course of action and he consulted his two mates, John Corrie and the forbiddingly named Zachariah Harper, a native-born Yankee.

"Well, gentlemen, what d'you think of my idea?" He looked first at Corrie, the senior of the two. He was a handsome man in his early thirties, but had lost most of his front teeth in a brawl and this detracted from his looks. He was married to a mulatto woman in St John's by whom he had had eight children and had proved himself a competent and steady man who knew his business both in working the ship and in the handling of her cargo. Corrie nodded his approval, his voice whistling through his broken teeth as he said. "It'll do no harm, Cap'n, none at all."

"Mr Harper?"

The second mate was a man with no claim to looks whatsoever. Indeed he was of such extraordinary ugliness that his face seemed to have no cohesion, being put together, as it were, from odds and ends of features. Neither eye matched its fellow, his nose was huge, his lips nonexistent and his chin jutted forward to a point upon which he grew a beard without a complementary moustache upon the upper lip. He had the large and pendulous ears of an old man and wore his hair excessively long. But he was powerfully built and Kite had more than once been glad to see him leading the hands aloft to tame a sail hurriedly clewed up in a squall. In short he was one of the finest practical seamen Kite had ever encountered and he waited to see what Harper would say.

"It is a good idea, sir," he said, "but we shall have to move the chess tree further forward and fit longer bumpkins over either bow to haul the tacks down, and that will necessarily govern the extent to which you can extend the yards."

"And the brace-leads will have to come aft," Corrie put in.

"That's less of a problem."

Kite nodded and then Harper asked, "Where will you have this work done, sir?"

"The only yard I have had personal experience of was at Newport, Rhode Island."

"Roberts's yard?" Harper asked. "I know it as a good place. I would not recommend New York, sir. There the prices are too high, they are so used to Government contracts."

"D'you have any objection to Roberts's yard, Mr Corrie?" Kite asked the mate.

"I have no opinion on the matter, Cap'n."

"Very well, Newport, Rhode Island it is. I shall write directly and see what we are able to arrange."

And as he sat at his desk after his mates had left the cabin, Kite felt a quickening of his pulse. Newport was the home of Sarah Tyrell.

Kite's knowledge of Roberts's yard in Newport, Rhode Island, had been a consequence of disaster. Several years earlier, while on his way back to Britain with the expectant Puella, the *Spitfire* had been severely damaged in a hurricane and he had put in to Newport, aided by Christopher Jones's local knowledge. Here the schooner had been repaired, her broken spars renewed and her hull thoroughly refitted. Here too he had bought Puella some warm furs for the transatlantic passage to an England lying under the frosts of winter. In so doing he had encountered Sarah Tyrell, the young wife of an older husband, Arthur

Tyrell, a merchant whose connections with Antigua were well established.

Mistress Tyrell had thought Kite louche in flaunting his black mistress, but had then made Puella's acquaintance and befriended the couple beleaguered by circumstances in Newport. Since then the house of Tyrell had been profitably associated with that of Wentworth in Antigua and Makepeace and Kite in Liverpool, and Kite had himself kept up a desultory correspondence with Tyrell, always asking that he be remembered to Mistress Tyrell and occasionally receiving reciprocal greetings, always couched in terms of absolute propriety.

There had been, however, an undercurrent to this exchange of pleasantries, for the physical attraction between Kite and Tyrell's wife had been mutual. It had amounted to no more than a brief exchange of veiled desire, a mere muttering of conventional pleasantries which had been charged with suppressed passion. In the ensuing years the possibility of their ever meeting again had grown increasingly improbable. But ever since he had read the account of the scandalous destruction of the schooner *Gaspée* off the Rhode Island coast, the possibility of again meeting Sarah Tyrell had quickened his heartbeat. Moreover, when the *Wentworth* sailed north from Antigua the thought of putting in to Newport had lain at the bottom of his consciousness. He had been half hoping, half fearing that, quite by chance, the ship would find herself loading a cargo for Rhode Island, but since this had not transpired he knew that fate was not going to oblige him. He could not wait to drift into what might add to his catalogue of great sins, for he knew he would not be surprised by the passion the sight of Sarah would arouse in him. He knew that he was being tempted, and that the notion of improving the *Wentworth*'s sailing qualities and the existence of Roberts's yard were perhaps in themselves fateful.

Well, it was no matter, he thought. He had no need to succumb to temptation like the unfortunate Johnstone. It would be pleasant to see both Sarah and her husband again, he told himself, and he ought as a matter of honour to tell Tyrell of the changed circumstances of the Liverpool firm that now styled itself Makepeace and Watkinson.

And so, after discharging his cargo in Baltimore, Kite succeeded in laying a few tiers of beer consigned to Rhode Island over shingle ballast and sailed for Newport.

\*     \*     \*

When Captain Makepeace, master and commander of the slaving brig *Enterprize*, had thrust the nubile and beautiful young black slave at the canting young Kite, he had intended merely to draw the poison of virtuous complaint against the slave trade by the poultice of lust. He hoped thereby to drown Kite's disapproval, to reduce him to the lowest common denominator of his kind, to take from him the awkward intrusions of decency, humanity and compassion. Makepeace had been annoyed that Kite, whom he had picked up in the gutters of Liverpool, should turn out to be a dissident spirit. The captain had no need of an abolitionist among his officers and so sought to encompass the youthful idealist's fall from his self-appointed status of moralist. But Kite and what Makepeace conceived to be his black whore had fallen in love. At the voyage's end Kite had purchased his "Puella" and set up house first in St John's and much later in Liverpool. In fact, though they had then been mutually hostile, Makepeace had by his fatuous act touched off a train of events which in due course had led to reconciliation, friendship, the virtual abandonment of the slave trade by the old Guineaman and the establishment of the prosperous Liverpool house of Makepeace and Kite. That single act of silliness on the part of Captain Makepeace had shaped Kite's future, as well as that of his old commander, though Kite himself had been wholly passive at its inception. He had often thought of it as a turning point in his life and ever since he had seen such moments clearly. Whilst young William's death from cholera was not such a pivotal moment, the sacrificial and accusatory suicide of Puella most certainly was, for it had persuaded him to return to sea and try his fortune elsewhere than in disease-ridden Liverpool.

The laying of the *Wentworth* on a course to the north-eastwards was his decision alone, despite the consultation he had had with his officers. That was for form's sake, a matter by which he could ease his conscience, for his determination to take the *Wentworth* to Rhode Island grew in him by the hour. He was motivated not by the public consideration of refitting his ship, but by the private desire to see again a woman who had once stirred him. The refitting of the *Wentworth* was but a means to another end and, as he came below and turned into his swinging cot while the ship lifted to the Atlantic swells off Cape Charles, he knew that he had set a match to a powder train. How violent the explosion at its end, however, he had no means of guessing.

The following morning Kite was awakened not by Bandy Ben but by Harper. The second mate was dripping wet, his tarpaulins glossy in the feeble light which filled the cabin. Beyond the cabin bulkhead Kite could hear shouts and he felt his cot jar and sensed the heel of the ship as Harper shook him.

"White squall, sir! And worse to come!" Then he was gone and Kite was tumbling out of his cot and reaching for breeches and a greygoe to pull over his nightshirt as the deck slid away from beneath him. It was the first bad weather he had experienced since leaving the Mersey and it came as a nasty, humbling shock. Fighting to keep his balance he felt the *Wentworth* stagger under the onslaught of a sea which slammed against her weather bow and set every part of her fabric a-judder.

He reached the cabin door and wrenched it open, propelling himself through it half by his own volition while, it seemed, the ship herself gave him a hand as the next wave struck her and, just as he reached the foot of the companionway, he was suddenly soused by a chilling deluge of cold water. He cursed with the shock of it and fought his way up on deck. As his head came clear of the coaming he was aware of a number of sensations. The first was the residue of water pouring across the deck, the second was the shock of it as the wind whipped it up and flung it into his eyes where it stung them with its saltiness. As he dragged himself to his feet by the stanchion at the head of the companionway, he could hear the shriek of the wind and the cracking and booming noise of the blown-out main topsail. Below that the mainsail had been clewed up, but the loose folds filled and bellied with wind, a pale ghostly thing expanding and contracting like some huge, revolting grey bladder. This threatened to carry away at any moment while further forward the watch were hauling on the clew garnets of the forecourse. A group of men were at the foot of the larboard pin-rail abreast the mainmast, hoisting themselves into the weather shrouds.

Kite reached the helm where a large negro seaman named Jacob held the wheel, his huge legs braced wide on the planking.

"Bad night, Cap'n!" he called. "Ship's head nor'-nor'-west, sah!"

"Very well, Jacob. Can ye hold her yourself?"

"Aye, sah, Jacob'd hold the horse of the devil!" The big man grinned in the gloom and Kite was suddenly glad of the sight of his wide grin.

"Good man. Where's Mr Harper?"

"Second Mate go forrard, Massah Corrie gone aloft to take in de main tops'l!"

Kite looked up and could see that the figures he had seen going aloft were now negotiating the futtock shrouds. Hauling himself up to windward, he edged forward. Beyond the ship's rail he could see the sea had been knocked flat by the wind and for the first time the extreme angle at which the *Wentworth* lay heeled. He thought of her lack of cargo below and hence a lack of positive stability, he thought of the likelihood of the shingle ballast shifting to exacerbate the delicacy of their situation. Anxiously he stared aloft, aware that he was looking nearer the horizontal than the vertical. Even as his brain formed the thought, the inevitable happened. The faint yet threatening thrumming of parting stays suddenly reached its brief and terrifying crescendo in a series of cracks, each of which was followed by a thunderous sound, like the vigorous beating of a muffled drum as first the fore topmast went by the board, then the forecourse blew out and the falling wreckage took the main topmast with it while this in turn carried away the mizzen topgallantmast.

Kite heard the shrill screams of the falling men, heard the dreadful, dull thump as one hit the rail, his body smashed in an instant, and heard too the thin reedy scream of a man fallen unhurt into the wake astern of the ship. For an instant he stood stock-still, stunned by the overwhelming power of the gust of wind, uncertain whether or not some rope or stay in his immediate vicinity might not strike him as it parted, and then he was beside Jacob, bawling at him to let go the helm and get a chicken coop overboard for the wretch in the water to cling to.

The wreckage lying over the leeward side dragged the ship's head round to starboard and the stern rose as it passed through the wind. Against a sudden patch of lighter cloud he saw Jacob hurl the chicken coop overboard to the pitiful objection of its occupants while the *Wentworth* swung round to lie wallowing, her starboard side exposed to the wind as she dragged the wreckage of her upper spars slowly to the south and east.

"Mr Corrie! Mr Harper! Muster your watches!" Kite bellowed.

Someone called out, "The mate's overboard, sir!"

Kite swore. "Who else is missing? Mr Harper, are you there?"

"Aye, sir, all my men are accounted for."

Kite felt a surge of relief as the hands came aft and assembled just forward of the helm. Harper was too good a man to lose. He cleared his throat: "Boatswain, call the mate's watch."

"Aye, aye, sir!"

After a few moments they established that in addition to Corrie there were three men missing, all able seamen who had gone out along the foretopsail yard with Corrie to pass the gaskets and secure the blown-out sail. Kite digested the news, then he passed his orders.

"The mate's watch to get axes and knives and start clearing the wreckage. Jacob, aloft into the mizzen top and keep your eyes open. I'll not give up on those men!"

"Cap'n Kite! I've found Nicholls, sir," a man shouted and there was a general move to the ship's larboard side where Nicholls had fallen. He had struck the rail and then fallen outboard, not into the water, but between the deadeye-irons and the bulwarks, his legs trapped on the chainwale, his broken body trailing overboard in a bloody mess.

"Christ Almighty."

"Let him go, sir?" asked the boatswain.

Kite nodded and one of the men called out, "Shame!" while another muttered a prayer.

"Come, men," Kite pulled them together, "we've work to do . . ."

As if the squall had been fatally conjured for their own especial punishment, the wind dropped rapidly and by the time the sun rose it was almost a dead calm.

Then Jacob bawled, "Ah see him, sah! Ah see Massah Corrie," and Kite looked up to see Jacob up in the mizzen top and pointing out on the starboard quarter.

"No, sah!" Jacob called, his voice high-pitched with excitement, "I see two men! Two men!" Kite looked at the boat on the hatch and was about to pass orders to clear it away when first Harper and then Jacob, having slid agilely down a mizzen backstay, were over the taffrail and swimming powerfully for the bobbing heads.

"Get some lines ready, Boatswain," Kite called, but the matter was already in hand.

Within half an hour, the second mate and Jacob had dragged

the two survivors alongside the wallowing tangle of spars, sails and rigging onto which half a dozen seamen had scrambled to drag all four out of the water. About an hour later, as all hands with the exception of the rescued and rescuers toiled to cut the *Wentworth* free of her encumbering spars, the freshening wind backed steadily round and blew again with a steady force from the south-west, whence it had come the evening before.

By mid-afternoon the *Wentworth* had resumed her voyage. Sails had been set on her fore and main yards, her fore topmast stay and a temporarily rigged forestay running to her bowsprit which, with her undamaged spanker, made her manageable. Kite stood Corrie's watch for him, while he was left to sleep off the horrors of his ordeal. Harper seemed reluctant to leave the deck and Kite ordered him below. Still the second mate hesitated.

"For God's sake go below, Zachariah!" an exasperated Kite ordered, but Harper shook his head.

"I'm sorry sir, that I didn't get the sails off her quicker . . . I felt something was wrong an hour or so before there was any sign of trouble, but I couldn't determine what it was. I thought at first it were the compass, which seemed to me to be oscillating too much, but . . ."

"You did your best, Zachariah," Kite said quietly. "No man can do more and many would have been entirely overtaken by events. You should not reproach yourself."

"But—"

"Go below and get some sleep. At least Mrs Corrie is not a widow tonight. You may console yourself with that thought."

Harper sighed. "I cannot sleep, sir. Not yet."

"Then tell me . . . tell me where you come from," said Kite, attempting to divert the young man from the lugubrious train of obsessive thought he seemed determined to follow. "And tell me of the troubles that seem to be fomenting against England."

Harper shook his head. "Why, sir, I come from New York, but as to the troubles I know little of them, being at sea. It seems that there is a popular feeling against England which is due to taxes and no places for us in Parliament, but I have read that we have in our Assemblies more powers to govern our own lives than you have yourself, if you'll forgive me for saying so."

Kite nodded. "That is true," he replied, choosing not to muddy the waters of debate by a disquisition upon the purchase of politicians such as young Harry Makepeace would like to become. He wondered what had happened to Harry, and his sister Katherine, but then he dismissed the thought as Harper went on.

"My father says that in God's good time these North American Colonies must of necessity become a self-governing nation because they are capable of infinite expansion west of the mountains. He served in the French and Indian Wars and has spoken to men who have been over the mountains and others who have crossed the Ohio, and they say that there is land there that stretches over mountains and plains beyond the Mississippi and it is a crazy notion that all this land can be ruled by the Tory ministry in London. He says it is against all natural law and precedent and that time will effect a parturition."

"But land without population is not a nation and these lands belong to the Indians."

Harper gave one of his slow, engaging grins which seemed, in some curious way, to transform his face into that of a gentle ogre. "Cap'n, them Indians ain't God's creatures. As for population, well, I reckon we Yankees can fill a city or two like you English have filled London."

"I have never been to London," Kite confessed.

"Well, Cap'n, if you'd seen London you'd say that there were enough people to fill the valleys of Kentucky and maybe that'd be a good place to put them, seeing as how there's no room for them in that smoky city."

"That is a thought," Kite conceded wryly. "But what does your father say to rebellion?"

"Rebellion?" Harper seemed genuinely astonished at the idea. "Why, nothing, sir. Why should he?"

"Because I hear there are men in New England who would stir up rebellion and seize power in the people's name but for their own purposes."

Harper nodded. "Yes, that may be true sir, and they all do chiefly reside in Boston, but there are enough redcoats in Fort William and on the Common to keep a few hot-heads in order."

"So men of your father's opinion do not think matters will be forced, then? Only that they will evolve by a natural process?"

"I think so, sir. My father says that England has had her civil war and that she knows the danger of another and will avoid it."

"But all men may not think like your father."

"Well, they'll soon see sense if a redcoat points a bayonet at their bellies."

"What is the temper of Rhode Island?" Kite asked.

Harper shrugged. "I don't rightly know; there was some trouble there a while back when they burned that English schooner."

"The *Gaspée*, aye, I heard of that."

"But nothing came of it and it blew over."

"I think that is what worries me," Kite said.

"What, that it blew over?"

"Yes. When a schoolboy is not chastised for a misdeed, he commits another, usually worse, just to ascertain the boundaries of restraint. Weak parents indulge such behaviour and laugh it off. But consider, if the youth is motivated by malice, or any species of personal gain, he will play this advantage to the utmost. Cunning is learnt early, d'you know, it is not a sudden acquisition of the mature."

"I see what you mean," Harper said slowly, nodding his head as he digested the meaning of Kite's words. "Well, men's names are mentioned from time to time, even in New York we have heard that of Samuel Adams."

"And who is he?"

"He dwells in Boston, I believe, where he was found involved with some embezzlement. I don't rightly know what it was, but they say it made him a great champion of what they pleases to call liberty and freedom from the tyranny of England." Harper shook his head. "My father says that they who sow the wind usually reap the whirlwind with interest thrown in."

"Your father is a sensible man, Zachariah."

Harper yawned. "I think I shall go below now, Captain Kite. And thank you."

"Thank you, Zachariah."

# Six

## Sarah Tyrell

"They say lightning never strikes in the same place twice, Captain Kite," remarked Arthur Tyrell as he rose and took Kite's hand. The years since Kite had last seen him in 1759 had bowed him; he was shrunken with age and rheumatism, yet his eyes were as bright as Kite recalled and his mind undimmed by time. "Yet you have come again to Newport as a port of refuge, William."

"That is not quite correct," replied Kite, smiling. "I was bound here from Baltimore with the intention of having my ship put in the hands of Roberts' yard to effect some alterations in her sail plan."

"Well, from what I saw of her yesterday as she came in past Dumpling's Rock, she is much in need of that," Tyrell joked, "but Sarah will be disappointed if she thinks that you had any purpose other than to dine with us."

Kite felt himself colouring involuntarily. "That is most kind of her, Arthur."

"She is a constant woman, William . . ."

For one humiliating moment, as a sensation of weak-kneed guilt flooded him, he thought he was going to faint; that the old man before him had some strange yet potent powers of divination capable of seeing into the depths of his soul to expose the potentially adulterous phantasmagorias which had haunted the margins of his sleep for the last few nights.

"Pray do sit down and I shall ring for some wine."

Gratefully Kite sank into an adjacent chair, vaguely aware that he should have made some polite acknowledgement of Sarah's constancy. "How is your wife?" he asked as matter-of-factly as he could.

Tyrell smiled. "Did you know that when you sailed, she

followed you on her horse, riding to Castle Hill to watch your schooner until you had passed out of Buzzard's Bay?"

Kite coughed awkwardly. "No, I had no idea . . . It was a long time ago."

"You made a profound impression upon her, William, and it has long been my hope that you would return to Newport. I heard that a Captain Kite was trading on the coast in a vessel hitherto unknown to me and I assumed it was you."

Kite, uncertain of the purpose of Tyrell's revelations and embarrassed to pursue them, took advantage of the opening and explained to the old man of his separation from what was now Makepeace and Watkinson. Tyrell listened in silence, his elbows on his desk, his finger tips neatly touching, and when Kite had finished he nodded approvingly.

"By your account, you have acted wisely," he said, "but tell me, what of Puella? She was expecting, if I recall aright, and Sarah will want to know all the details, though you may tell her yourself for I will not countenance any refusal to make our house your own while you are here."

"You are too kind, Arthur, but to the matter of your question, Puella is dead, as is the son she bore. He fell a victim to the cholera so prevalent in Liverpool, and she . . ." He hesitated.

"She took to her bed and died," Tyrell said, "yes, you will recall I spent some time in the Antilles and have seen such things before." He paused then said, "So, you are a free man."

"I suppose I am."

"William –" Tyrell rose to his feet and turned to look out of his window which overlooked the harbour – "you may think me foolish, but as the years passed and you did not return to Rhode Island, I confess I was pleased, though I knew Sarah wished otherwise."

"Arthur, I—" Kite began, but without turning round Tyrell raised his hand and he fell silent.

"I married Sarah after her betrothed had been lost at sea. She appeared inconsolable and there was foolish talk of her having lost her mind. It was all poppycock, of course, she was simply very young and completely infatuated. The young man was not particularly admirable, and probably much improved by an early demise; but those were my own cynical observations. In due course and as I had anticipated she spoke less of him and enjoyed mild flirtations with a number of other men younger than myself. You were among them."

Tyrell turned and Kite said, "Arthur, there was never a moment's impropriety between us . . ."

Tyrell smiled, "Come, come, William. Except that my wife struck you with her riding crop."

"That was nothing, a misunderstanding."

"A mark of her occasional ungovernable passion, William, behaviour that, though thankfully rare, once caused her mother to consider her dangerous. Look, my boy, I shall be frank. I am an old man and Sarah is a headstrong young woman. She pined for you after you left our shores and for years I feared your return. But as before what the sea takes, it takes completely. Now, however, the case is altered; I am glad to see you, for we live in dangerous times and I fear for Sarah's safety. New England is becoming lawless. Have you heard what happened to the *Gaspée*?"

"Yes; the bare facts revealed by a New York newspaper."

" 'Twas a terrible affair. Terrible. D'you know what happened to poor Duddingston, the commander? He had to plead for his life, writhing in agony at the feet of the villains with two pistol balls in him. And do you know what they did with the wretched man? They let him have a boat in order that he might proceed ashore as if it was the greatest act of humanity they could do him! God rot them all!" Tyrell paused, to catch his breath, so angry had he made himself by his tirade. "Oh, there are those who will tell you that Duddingston was a foul-mouthed villain, that he stopped every vessel without pretext or justification, that he allowed his men ashore to cut firewood upon anyone's property and that he swore that if the whole of Rhode Island was aflame he would not lift a finger, or suffer his men to do likewise, to extinguish the conflagration. Most of this is true, so far as it goes, but it does not go far enough, for the truth must embrace both sides of the affair and the truth was Duddingston had been commissioned to extinguish smuggling! And if he was an insolent agent of the British Admiralty, as foul mouthed, arrogant and ill-mannered as Admiral Montagu at New York, then these qualities were matched by the insolence, arrogance and mendacity – which is but another form of bad usage of words – of those against whom he had to contend, which included every fisherman in the province! Duddingston could not obtain firewood by purchase, since none would trade with him, neither could he land and requisition it without some holy patriot claiming ownership of the land and denying access. I swear to you, Kite, there has been abroad such a manner of spinning the truth that one scarce knows right from wrong, or the law from the lawless!"

"Did anyone know who perpetrated the piracy?"

"Oh, yes," Tyrell said vehemently, resuming his seat. "A gentleman named Abraham Whipple led the rogues. Their only motive was to extirpate the predatory efficiency of the *Gaspée* before her commander put an end to their own illegal evasion of duties. He was supported by sixty-four worthy souls, chief among whom was John Rathburne, a sea officer like Whipple. As for Whipple himself, it was he who answered Duddingston's challenge when the commander ordered the boats not to come alongside the grounded schooner, and it was Whipple who abused Duddingston in as foul a language as ever Duddingston abused any other man. At this point a desperado named Bucklin shot Duddingston, who fell back upon his own deck, and having boarded the *Gaspée* the brave Whipple taunted Duddingston and sported with him in a tortuous manner."

"But why were these facts not laid before the justices?" Kite asked, adding, "For I understood a reward of five hundred pounds had been offered for evidence against the pirates."

"Oh, there was a far greater commotion raised than a mere reward. That only produced a poor black slave whom no one believed. Although he imparted the names of Whipple, Rathburne, Bucklin and half a dozen others whom he had seen embarking in boats at the landing place, all believed he acted out of motives of greed! Ha! What a pickled irony lies there, William, and how cogently such a motive can be argued and then digested! Lost among all the argy-bargy are the little facts of the affair; the robbing of Duddingston's silver spoons, the concerting of the raid by the beating of a tattoo, which is certain evidence of a conspiracy, the shouted order that all who would have revenge upon Duddingston should meet at the house of Mr Sabin.

"But all this, indeed everything that happened that night, was forgotten! When the news reached London, the Attorney-General, Mr Thurlow, obtained a royal Order in Council commanding the authorities of Rhode Island to deliver up the culprits for shipment to England and trial for piracy at the Old Bailey. But in the first place no one could be found that knew a thing untoward had happened in Providence that night and then Stephen Hopkins, our now mightily revered old Chief Justice of the Province, refused to obey the command, refusing to sanction warrants for the arrests."

"So the names *were* made known to him?"

"Oh, yes . . ." Tyrell fell quiet a moment and then looked up. "I am an old man, William, and had I not had Sarah to worry about I should perhaps have stood up and declaimed the names of Whipple and Rathburne from the rooftops myself. But I was not in Providence and knew them only by hearsay, though that hearsay had all the authority of heroic praise! Instead I heard of a black slave who was witness to the affair and I sent for him. I encouraged him to give evidence to the commissioners, thinking that I might strike a blow for justice and give the poor man a means of purchasing his manumission under the protection of the authorities." He gave a short, self-deprecatory laugh.

"I reckoned without Hopkins, who proved as great a coward as myself and considered London to be too far off to bother us. He proved the shrewder judge, for astonishingly the matter blew over, hush-a-byed by Lord Dartmouth, who was at the critical moment appointed Secretary for the Colonies. It was said that his lordship received a letter from a self-styled friend of Great Britain resident in North America. This patriotic correspondent assured Dartmouth that protracted pursuit of the incendiary pirates of Rhode Island would result in the entire continent catching fire. Beside that threat the burning of a revenue schooner was set aside as of no consequence."

"And Duddingston?"

"He died in my house, raving with the pain of a gangrenous wound in his groin wide enough to place your fist into. A month after his death a letter arrived in which their Lordships of the Admiralty appointed him to the rank of master and commander."

"That you gave so unpopular a man some shelter argues against you being a coward, Arthur."

"Oh, it was not me; it was Sarah. She had some mad notion—" Tyrell recalled himself. "I should not have said that. Please forget I mentioned it. No, no, it is not fair . . . Sarah was compassion itself." He looked up at Kite, shaking his head. "I should not have referred to Sarah like that."

Kite leaned forward and touched the old man's hand as it lay trembling on the desk in front of him. " 'Tis no matter, Arthur, it was between ourselves; a confidence."

"Yes, well." Tyrell mastered himself. "Well," he said with a shuddering sigh that seemed to emphasise his physical frailty, "it brings me to the heart of this matter which is indeed between ourselves."

"Which is?" Kite frowned uncomfortably.

"William, I hardly know you, yet I liked you when I first met you and we have done business during the last thirteen years, and in that time I have learned that you are utterly trustworthy. You may think me foolish, but your arrival here today is mightily providential. I could almost believe that fate had stayed any inclination you might have had to revisit Sarah sooner, for I know you would not come to see me."

"Heavens, Arthur, I am here to see you now."

"Do not, I beg you, dissemble or misunderstand me. But now my mind is made up. She is yours, my boy, take her with you when you leave here, marry her when you can, for I shall not be much longer in this world. No, I am not given to moments of drama, William; but I recognise the fact and it is stupid to pretend otherwise. Lord Dartmouth may have prevented a conflagration sweeping the continent in seventy-two, but it will come this year, or next year. There will be some new outrage, engineered as the burning of the *Gaspée* was, by men whose own ambition is overweening. Already there is a new zeal abroad, and in every province there are now forming Corresponding Societies dedicated to uniting us in our resistance to acts of British tyranny such as were represented by Lieutenant Duddingston and his depredations hereabouts."

As Tyrell fell silent, Kite recalled his own analogy, expressed to Harper, of the bad boy pushing the boundaries of parental control until they burst.

"I am glad you have come, Kite," Tyrell said rousing himself. "And you *will* tarry at our house; I have much to discuss and arrange with you in the way of business." He rose, closed a ledger on his desk and carried it to a safe, the door of which stood open. He thrust the ledger inside and closed the steel door with a thud, turning the keys in the lock and then pocketing them. Turning, he confronted Kite, who rose to his feet. "Will you look after Sarah?"

"Of course, if both you and she wish it, I shall offer her my protection—"

"Then that is enough," cut in Tyrell with sudden resolution and, reaching for his tricorne, he added, "for the time being at least. Come, let us go home, I have need of my wife." And with this odd intimacy, he led the way out into the street.

Having divested himself of his hat in the hall of his house, Tyrell turned to Kite and gestured him to follow. "I do not wish to startle Sarah, William, so be a good fellow and wait for me to call you."

Kite nodded. He could hardly breathe and his heart was thumping in his breast. He felt ridiculous and eager, a paradox he could not reconcile as he stood behind Tyrell, who opened a door and went in search of his wife. Kite stared about him. He had a vague memory of the hall, of his arrival with Puella in her dress of brilliant red and yellow silk, and remembered the smell of rich food which is always a pleasure to a man inured to ship's fare. Now he heard Tyrell say, ". . . a surprise for you, my dear," and then he was being waved into the room.

She rose as he stood beside her husband and footed a bow. Her face was pale with astonishment and he thought for a moment she would faint. He stepped swiftly forward as she put out her hand and bent over it and as he straightened up she smiled, her eyes full of tears. "Is it really you, Captain Kite?"

"I should prefer it if you recognised me as William, Mistress Tyrell. It has been a long time and our former acquaintance was brief, but I recall we called each other by our Christian names."

"Yes, a long time." She retracted her hand with a gesture of awkwardness and dropped her eyes. "How is your . . . How is Puella?" she asked.

"Sadly she died. The air of Liverpool did not suit her and she died within a few days of our son, who was struck down by the cholera."

"I am so sorry. Was this long ago?"

Kite shook his head. "No, it occurred last spring, but it persuaded me to return to sea. I did not like an empty house. I resumed command of the *Spitfire* and having reached Antigua I purchased another ship. We arrived in her this morning, she is called the *Wentworth*."

"That is the ship with her topmasts missing?"

"The same."

"So you have come again to Newport for repairs?" She was laughing at the irony.

Kite half turned to her husband. "So everyone reminds me."

"My dear," Tyrell stepped forward smiling, "I have insisted that William stays with us while his vessel undergoes repairs. We have much to discuss and you will enjoy his company, I know. Now please do sit down and I shall order tea. William, do you write a note to the ship to have your effects sent up and I shall have it taken to the yard." Tyrell indicated an escritoire and a few moments later instructions were on their way to Corrie and Dandy Ben regarding Kite's location at the Tyrells' house and his need of a few necessities.

As soon as he had overseen this and the maid had brought in tea, Tyrell made his excuses.

"I shall take my tea in my study," he said to the maid, and then to Sarah and Kite, "I have some matters to attend to and I am sure you would like a some moments to yourselves."

For a moment the two sat in complete and baffled silence, then they both spoke at once and after a moment of foolish and constrained awkwardness Kite insisted that she continue.

"It is so good to see you, William," she said, her voice breathless. He thought he had never seen so handsome a woman. "I did not think we should ever meet again."

"I – er . . ." Kite hesitated, lowering his glance and stirring his tea with unnecessary vigour and concentration. He was at once confused and embarrassed, aware that after his earlier remarks Tyrell had left them alone to a purpose, yet unwilling to commit any breach of propriety that might be misconstrued. Simultaneously he was intensely moved by Sarah, eager not to let this opportunity slip past, impetuously anxious to say something which would adequately express his desire to establish that intimacy which had only previously existed in his own occasional, unfaithful fantasies. Distance and time gave no guarantee that Sarah felt any reciprocal emotion, only the strange illusion that it might be so, an illusion created entirely by Kite himself.

And yet he had left her that evening after they had all dined together long ago with pleasantries charged hot with innuendo. Moreover Tyrell had made no secret of Sarah's attraction to him, unless he had intended to exaggerate it in his anxiety for her future. For a moment the sudden intrusion of this thought had him stumbling tongue-tied, but he blundered on with an admission that not so much broke as smashed the ice between them.

"I had not intended . . . No, that is not correct. I had avoided coming here immediately I began trading on the American coast some months ago. At first I felt that it would prove awkward, that my association with your husband's business was not to be complicated by my own personal considerations and, since I was unable to pick up a cargo for Rhode Island, it seemed I was not destined to, but—"

"Then you were wrecked again, which must have struck you as uncommonly providential," she interrupted, her eyes uncommonly bright.

"You are laughing at my misfortune," Kite said smiling at her lightness of touch, "but that is not true either. In fact I *was* on my way here, quite deliberately intending to have some extensive work done to the ship. Then fate intervened and now has effectively extended our stay."

"Of that I am very glad. It has been so many years and much has changed." She paused, then added with an air of wishing the matter referred to, "I am sorry that you have lost Puella."

"Yes." Kite looked away. "I loved her, you know." An unaccustomed mist filled his eyes and it occurred to him that he had not wept over Puella until now, the moment when his feelings ran high for someone else.

"I know you did. But there was a strong attraction between us, was there not? All those many, many years ago."

Kite nodded, unable to speak. He sighed, cleared his throat and looked at her. "Yes, of course there was," he said thickly. "And it has not gone away. Time has enhanced your beauty, Sarah. It is a terrible thing to have been so moved by one woman and yet so sincerely love another."

"The distinction is usually between love and lust, is it not?" she said quietly. "I once thought I knew the first, only to discover that it faded and may have been no more than the latter."

"Your fiancé? Yes, your husband mentioned him . . . and what of Arthur?"

"Yes, it is love, of a sort. He has been very kind to me and I have not always been a comfort to him." She paused and smiled at him. "And what else did he tell you about me?"

"That you rode down to Castle Point and watched the *Spitfire* sail."

"He told you that?" She seemed astonished. "Yes, it is true. I watched the *Spitfire* until she was out of sight. And was that all, that and the intelligence that I had been betrothed?"

Kite shrugged. "He mentioned he thought that you regretted my departure."

"Did he tell you that I raged against my fate? Did he tell you that I was so furious that I nearly killed my horse and was gone into the back-country for three days? Or did he simply tell you that I was mad?"

"No, that he did not, nor do I think that you are. He did, however, express his concern for you in these troubled times and it is clear by his present absence that he wishes us to be friends."

"I hope that we are already friends, William."

"Of course."

"And I am delighted that you are here, truly I am."

"Sarah, I would not have you, or your husband, misunderstand. His anxieties are all about your future. As for myself, I am independent. Only the winds of heaven and commerce command me now that Puella is dead. I am at the service of you both."

"Most eloquently put, my dear William," said Tyrell, coming back into the room and closing the door behind him. "Unfortunately I am of the opinion that soon a stronger gale than that of commerce will be blowing; stronger and more irresistible than that of heaven's breath itself. I mean of course that of rebellion and war!"

"Come, Arthur, do not trouble yourself with these useless speculations, it will make you ill," Sarah said.

"Ah, my dear, circumstances will march past us if they have a mind to. God knows what the future holds, but I feel easier knowing that William is attached to you and is minded to trade on this coast. You are so minded, are you not, William?"

"Indeed, Arthur, I have no intention of returning to England while I may turn up a profit 'twixt North America and the Antilles."

"In that Arthur will be able to help you, I am sure, won't you, Arthur?"

"Of course, my dear. Now come, William, I will show you your room and your traps should be here within half an hour."

There followed six weeks of the most perfect harmony. Kite proceeded daily to Roberts' yard, discussed the work in hand with Corrie and Harper and then absented himself. Neither of the mates objected, being pleased to be left to get on without interference. From the yard it became habitual for Kite to walk to Tyrell's office, take tea or coffee with him, discuss cargoes and meet other ship-masters, agents and the like, and then return with Tyrell to his house for dinner.

In the afternoons when the weather served, he would go riding with Sarah. He was an indifferent horseman, but he improved rapidly once the livery stable provided him with a docile mare. They were too much noticed ever to indulge in the slightest intimacy, just as their behaviour behind the closed shutters of the house never infringed the generosity of Tyrell's hospitality. Neither of them wanted the pace of things forced, for they were long past the first, impetuous flush of youth. There was an unspoken, unacknowledged acceptance that things would not always be thus, that they would change and that the circumstances of that change would decide upon their mutual conduct. Paradoxically, yet perhaps not unsurprisingly, such restraint lent to their afternoons an unspoilt magic and a delight such as Kite had not thought himself fortunate enough to ever experience.

As was to be expected, there was some wagging of tongues. Kite was referred to as Mistress Tyrell's "English beau" and, unbeknownst to them, he excited some jealousy among a few men of Newport. But those rummaging for scandal of a more salacious nature could not persuade the Tyrells' servants to yield anything more than the honest truth. Sarah Tyrell slept in the same bed as her husband and the "English beau" slept by himself. After a few weeks this lack of adulterous news translated itself into a thoroughly satisfactory explanation. The English were mere milk-and-water shams, or worse, all public charm and private buggery. A red-blooded Yankee would have raised a cuckold's horns on old Arthur Tyrell's head long since! God knew, a few had tried! In this way the subject found a kind of equilibrium and then people forgot or ignored it, for there was a new subject to concern the gossips of Rhode Island. Rumoured news of a conciliating measure by Lord North's government had reached Newport; it was said that cheap tea was to be made available, and those who smuggled it to evade duty were concerned at a potential catastrophic loss of income.

None of these considerations impinged upon the happiness

of Sarah and her English beau as they headed north on their horses. Usually they took a quiet turn about the environs of Middletown, or up towards Portsmouth, but on one glorious day they rode hard, coming down to Howland's ferry and on impulse crossing the Pocasset River. On the other side Sarah whipped up her horse, Musketeer, with Kite in hot pursuit. She led him first uphill through trees which required careful negotiation so that she had soon lost the more cautious Kite, and he turned his mare back downhill to where, about a mile away, he could see the sparkle of sunlight upon water. As he came down onto the shore he saw on his left a few houses and, away to the south on his left hand, Sarah's Musketeer riderless at the water's edge. Fearing that something had occurred to her he dug his spurs into the uncomplaining flanks of his own mount and soon caught up with Musketeer. He reined in and turned about, calling Sarah's name, and then he saw her, coming down through the trees.

Catching Musketeer's reins up, he walked his mare towards her. "Are you all right?" he called and then he saw she was carrying her hat and limping, her hair dishevelled.

"No . . ."

"You fell?" he asked incredulously.

She nodded. "After pride," she said wincing, "which I have lost entirely."

Kite threw his leg over his horse and slipped down beside her and an instant later they were embracing in a welter of passion, all thought of injury forgotten.

# Seven

## The Tocsin

Kite cared not a fig for the debate on Lord North's Tea Act, which, it was maintained, threatened not only the smugglers of Rhode Island but also the china manufactories of Philadelphia and other native American industries. The measure that was presented by King George III's ministers as a conciliatory benefit to the American colonists was also intended to save the East India Company of London and to this cynical reason were soon attached numerous other attendant and incipient misfortunes which would, the propagandists insisted, bring ruin on America. It was argued that cheap tea would be followed by a flooding of every American market by cheap imports, Chinese porcelain being chief among them. This greatly alarmed the mercantile fraternity, and began to divide those hitherto firmly opposed to the lawless agitators of the radical party. This, aided by the alarm and despondency spread by the Corresponding Societies, steadily built up resentment against the eventual arrival of the cheap tea; resistance was increasingly referred to as patriotism.

While old Tyrell railed against these infamies and damned the King's ministers with incompetence, insensitivity and sheer stupidity, Kite turned a deaf ear. His relationship with Sarah had undergone a subtle shift since their intimacy in the woods on the shores of what Sarah had told him was known as Wanton's Pond.

"'Tis appropriate, is it not?" she had remarked that afternoon as they drew apart and bent their thoughts to returning home. Kite had gallantly denied it, hopelessly in love with the dark-haired beauty. But their rides had become less frequent as work on the *Wentworth* neared completion, and even the most innocent of their intimacies more guarded as they reconciled themselves to parting. Neither wanted passion to ruin happiness, nor wished to compromise or dishonour Arthur Tyrell.

90

But the old man seemed as robust as ever, apparently fired up by political events and given a new lease of life. "If only," he would say, "the ministry would remove all the tax from tea, instead of merely reducing it, then every objection to its import would evaporate, such is the slavery of every American to the habit of drinking it! But they will not, and thereby they put a torch into the hands of these damned self-seeking and self-styled Patriots and Sons of Liberty!"

As the work on the *Wentworth* drew to its conclusion, duty drew Kite to Roberts' yard and entirely disrupted the cosy routine he, Arthur and Sarah had established. Late one morning in early June, as he sat in his cabin drawing up his accounts, writing to Wentworth and Johnstone in Antigua and making arrangements to pay the shipyard, he overheard two caulkers working on a stage under his quarter gallery. They were clearly unaware that Mistress Tyrell's English beau had taken to spending more than an hour on board, nor would he have listened had not a familiar name cropped up.

"What? Tea-tax Tyrell? They say that the old fool has a warehouse full of the stuff."

"Aye, he's Tory to the core an' no mistake."

"They should make an example of him and burn his damned tea!"

"Hush your mouth, Jethro, remember who the skipper of this barky is."

"'Tis a shame and only adds reason to my arguments," the man named Jethro said, taking up his mallet and caulking iron again. The next moment the thud-thud of their labouring put paid to Kite's eavesdropping. Completing his work he gathered up his papers, placed them inside a leather wallet and rose from his desk. As he left the ship he avoided staring at the two men hanging under the starboard quarter and made his way towards Tyrell's offices on the waterfront to the south of the yard.

A small group of well-dressed men were assembled outside the adjacent newspaper office and one of them looked up as Kite approached them. He had clearly mentioned Kite's name because they all turned and stared at him, then as Kite made to pass them, they barred his passage.

"Well, well," one of them drawled, "if it ain't the English Cap'n."

Kite stopped and confronted them. "Gentlemen," he said coolly, "will you let me through?"

One of them whom Kite had seen frequently about the town stepped forward, ignoring his request. "I understand your ship is almost ready for sea, Cap'n Kite."

"She is, but you have the advantage of me, sir."

"I do, do I not, Cap'n? Well, well, that should not trouble you and nor will we if you sail soon."

"I shall sail when the work for which I am paying is complete, sir, and not a moment before."

"You are very bold, Cap'n."

"Aye, he is," added a colleague, arousing a chorus of assent among the group.

"If you will permit me to pass, gentlemen . . ."

"And if we will not, what then?"

Kite sighed. "Then I shall be obliged to walk another way."

The men deliberately stretched across the road. The little confrontation was arousing the curiosity of an increasing group of onlookers.

"Ain't you the nigger-lover? The man that Sarah Tyrell whipped when you first came to Newport, Cap'n?" one of them asked.

"She had some sense then," another added, and they laughed.

"And now you're cuckolding poor old Tyrell," the first man who had spoken went on. He was clearly their leader. He shook his head. "No principles, the English."

"That, sir, is a most offensive remark," Kite said colouring and aware that they had no intention of permitting him to escape without goading him to an extremity.

The leader leaned forward and thrust his face into Kite's. "And what are you going to do about it, Captain Kite? Call me out for satisfaction and meet me on the common tomorrow morning?"

"No, sir, because that is what you want."

"And you are afraid, you milksop."

Kite laughed. He had no idea afterwards why he did so, but the ridiculous provocation stung him not with the possibility of dishonour, but the folly of being led by such an obvious ploy. "Indeed, sir, I am afraid. Who would not be afraid of a combination of such bold fellows who would stop a single man and goad him with such puerile taunts? Heavens, gentlemen, only a fool would want to fight such gamecocks." And in the hiatus that followed, he pushed his way quickly through them and left them, walking quickly to Tyrell's office.

As he entered Tyrell's senior clerk looked up and Kite called him to the door. "Who are those men, Mr Borthwick?" he asked, pointing out the knot of troublemakers as they conferred. Borthwick removed his spectacles and peered up the street and then swiftly withdrew his head.

"Er, they are Captain Whipple's men, sir, officers and masters who associate with Captain Whipple."

"And the man in the bottle-green coat?" Kite pressed the nervous clerk, referring to the leader.

"That is Captain Rathburne, sir."

"So in short, Mr Borthwick, they are the men who burnt the *Gaspée*."

Borthwick drew in his breath sharply. "I could not possibly say, Captain Kite."

"Do you know why these men are assembled in Newport?"

"Good heavens no, sir!"

"Well, I shall have to be content. Thank you, Mr Borthwick."

"Thank you, Captain."

In Tyrell's office Kite told the old man of the conversation he had overheard between the caulkers and then outlined the intimidation he had suffered at the hands of Rathburne's gang. Tyrell listened in silence and then said ruminatively and half to himself, "I do not think the time can now be far off." Then he looked up at Kite and said, "I am sorry you have been thus treated, William, it is a crying shame."

"I had not meant to become embroiled in Colonial politics."

"I doubt you can avoid it," Tyrell said, then paused. "It is true I have some tea in the warehouse, but there is little of it left. The hypocrites have drunk most of it."

"Let me ship the balance; they will not be so particular in New York."

"No, my dear fellow. We shall fill you with ballast and perhaps some odds and ends of manufactures, piece goods, ship's stores and timber, but you must get the *Wentworth* down to Jamaica and load a full cargo of sugar and molasses. *That* I can sell, even to rogues, but hie you back soon, I pray you. Do not delay on any account. I shall have the bills and papers ready for you tomorrow."

"Very well."

"Go home now and make your peace with Sarah. Tomorrow, go aboard early and remain on board until you sail. We do not want another encounter with that fellow Rathburne."

Nor did it happen. Kite did not believe that his verbal riposte had warded off the provocative Rathburne, but he was offered no other insults and it might well have been that his keeping himself aboard the *Wentworth* as Tyrell had suggested was victory enough for Rathburne and his patriotic gang. His last afternoon with Sarah had been far from unpleasant, despite the fact that it was charged with their imminent separation. Both knew that, God willing, it was only for a few months and that their love could survive such an interval.

It was December before the *Wentworth* returned to Rhode Island, for she had sprung her new topmasts off the Florida Keys and Harper had discovered shakes hidden deep in the spars fitted at Roberts' yard that suggested someone in Newport had knowingly sold them defective timber, though it had passed the vigilant eyes of both the mates.

The thought occurred to Kite that his officers might have been bribed or even merely slack in their duty, but the consideration that the American-born Harper had been disloyal was too uncomfortable to contemplate, while Corrie seemed too straight a man to deliberately endanger his ship. Kite's own examination of the broken spars suggested that to all external appearances they had seemed perfect, but it was not impossible that, since there were two of them, a batch could not have been produced by some quirk of nature in the same stand of timber and their weakness had been known to the shipwrights and riggers of Roberts' yard. In the final analysis, however, Kite felt a lingering guilt himself. If he had been as assiduous as he expected others to be, the yard would not have dared to foist him off with damaged spars.

But although late, the *Wentworth* returned to Newport deep-laden and Kite entertained no apprehensions for the safety of Sarah or her husband during the ship's extended absence. During the voyage, he had encountered several Yankee masters newly arrived in Jamaica and from them had been reassured that matters in New England were much as he had left them. There were continuing fulminations against the proposed import of cheap Indian tea and a burgeoning fashion for publicly renouncing tea drinking, but no news of burnings or outright disorder.

*The Privateersman*

Relieved, Kite and his acquaintances amiably discussed the political situation over a pipe, a cigar or a bowl of rum punch. In these discussions with Americans and a few British masters familiar with the Yankee trade, all of whom were sober seafaring men, Kite began to perceive the other side of the American coin. Setting aside all the machinating, exaggerating and mendacity of the extreme Patriot faction, there were bold principles of libertarian ambition emerging in America. Some were not entirely foreign to a man used to working in Liverpool, itself no stranger to radical politics. Most intelligent men of commerce on both sides of the Atlantic argued that they owed no feudal respect to those who birth alone had placed over them, and Kite could see that the increasingly popular independence of American minds grew out of the vastness and opportunity of the country in which these men lived. The similarities with the vigorous commercial expansion of Liverpool and Manchester were obvious, and the aspirations of men in these two centres of shipping and manufacturing were suffering in like fashion. It was clear that if established British institutions were incapable of accommodating Liverpool and Manchester, they were even less able to approve the expansion all native Americans felt to be their natural, God-given destiny. In fact the Crown was wholly opposed to American expansion, forbidding colonisation west of the Appalachians for fear of further disturbing the Indian tribes and drawing British troops, for which the Americans were unable to pay, into costly wars of frontier protection. While King George and his ministers considered the Colonies had sufficient local control over their affairs in their Houses of Burgesses, Assemblies and Councils, it was impossible for Great Britain to relinquish title to the country and hence the right to raise a paucity of revenue.

But taxation without representation in the Parliament in London was a rousing war cry, while any measure taken by London could, by its incompetent nature, be laid before a suspicious and malleable population as out-and-out tyranny. Kite rarely argued with men who pushed this point of view, unless it was to caution them against the consequences of rebellion, or to ask them whether if they detached themselves from Great Britain they could protect themselves against the hostile rapacity of France? But this was all too often blithely countered by a smooth assurance that if France turned upon an independent America, it would not be in Britain's interest to stand by in idleness.

"Our two countries will always trade. That's a matter of common sense. So you see, Cap'n," he was told more than once, "heads we win and tails you lose!"

When the now familiar landmarks of Rhode Island came into view on a cold, crisp December morning as the *Wentworth* beat up into Rhode Island Sound, Kite went below and donned his best blue broadcloth coat, fresh brushed by Bandy Ben, who had also polished his silver-buckled shoes and now offered them to his master as Kite kicked off the old pair he habitually wore on board.

"I think boots, this morning, Ben, for 'twill be frosty ashore. Do you pack those shoes in the portmanteau with my other clothes and have it all ready for transport ashore when we berth."

"As you say, Cap'n."

"What d'you think of Rhode Island, Ben?" Kite asked as he settled the heavy coat on his shoulders.

"Not as much as you, Cap'n, and it don't compare wi' Liverpool."

"You want to go home?"

"In due course, sir. Yes."

"You miss the place?"

"Truth to tell I miss Mrs O'Riordan's meat pies, Cap'n, an' the useful jobs I used to do for ye."

"I see." It was the longest conversation Kite had ever had with the man and he resolved not to keep poor Ben as a mere servant, but send him home at the first opportunity. Perhaps, he reflected as he picked his hat off the hook beside the door, he should have left him in Wentworth's counting house with Johnstone.

On deck Kite found Harper standing at the lee main shrouds, levelling a glass at the coast. "Well, Mr Harper, how do matters stand?" He looked aloft. "I see you have the signal flying for a pilot."

"Aye, sir. But the damned wind's drawing ahead all the time and Castle Hill is dead to windward."

"Very well." Kite digested the unwelcome news, then made up his mind. "Nevertheless, you can clear away both bower anchors and get cables bent on them."

"Aye, aye, sir." Harper called his watch aft and passed the order while Kite stared ahead, at the narrows between Rhode Island and the adjacent Connonicut Island with its lighthouse situated on its seaward point, Beaver Tail. He could see the masts and yards of shipping anchored in the far distance beyond the strait, lying as he well knew off the waterfront wharves of Newport, and his heart beat at the thought of seeing Sarah again.

"So near and yet so far," he murmured, for it was all too clear that he had donned his best coat somewhat prematurely. He looked aloft again. The yards were braced sharp up and were bearing on the catharpings, the weather tacks of the courses drawn down right forward and the weather leeches of the topsails stretched taut by the bowlines.

"Damnation," Kite swore, raising his own glass and sweeping the shoreline as if he might discover Sarah sitting Musketeer upon its green sward

They beat fruitlessly all day, only working up closer to Beaver Tail and Castle Hill but unable to get a slant to pass through the narrows. Despite their signal no pilot boat ran out towards them.

"It's like the door being slammed in your face," Corrie remarked with a whistle through his broken teeth as he took over the watch at four o'clock in the afternoon. "They've given us up for today, I reckon."

"Yes," agreed Kite, but he still could not bring himself to admit defeat and go below and divest himself of the blue coat. All about him the hands glumly reconciled themselves to another night at sea, another night of beating back and forth, like a watchdog on a chain outside his master's door.

"Why, the damned wind even brings the smell of their confounded dinners down to us," he said pettishly, voicing his thoughts aloud.

"Aye, fate certainly enjoys rubbing our noses in our misfortunes," Corrie agreed.

Having spent so long refitting in Newport earlier that year, most of the men had, in the manner of sailors, made some friends or at the least established a presence in one of the several alehouses and taverns along the waterfront. Newport was famous for its distillation of rum and Liverpool men were famous for their ability to drink the stuff.

"And by the look of it, it's going to be a cold night to boot!" Kite added lugubriously as the red globe of the sun dropped quickly to the horizon through a sky untrammelled by a single wisp of cloud.

But as the sun set the strength of the wind died a little and, as darkness fell, the breeze backed sufficiently for them to lay the *Wentworth*'s bowsprit for the narrows. On the quarterdeck Kite saw the hands looking at him expectantly. He did not know that among them he had acquired a reputation, built on his past exploit of taking *La Malouine*, of being a lucky man. Only a lucky commander, they said, could have recovered men after they had gone overboard when a ship was knocked down by a white squall. So when he called out, "Keep her full an' bye! Call all hands! We'll stand inshore! Clew up t'gallants!" the watch on deck jumped to the fife and pin-rails with alacrity and even the watch below tumbled up with none of their usual grumbling.

"We'll not get through without beating, sir," said Corrie in a tactful reminder that they had no pilot, but Kite would brook no further delay.

"Then we shall have to tack in the narrows, Mr Corrie."

"And if the wind shifts again, sir?"

"Then we may have to anchor. Do you see to clearing the stoppers off the bowers."

"Very well, sir." Unable to raise any further objections to his commander's determination, Corrie went forward. A moment later Harper loomed up in the darkness, fastening the toggles of his greygoe.

"You're going in, sir?"

"Aye, I am; the wind's given us a slant. We may have to tack but do you go aloft and watch the land for me. I intend to stand close along the land under the Connonicut shore and then tack to gain ground to windward by poking our snout into Mackerel Cove."

Harper nodded. The inlet ran deep into Connonicut Island and would then give them clear water, past the Dumpling Rocks and Brenton's Point on the opposite Rhode Island shore.

"I'll watch out for you, sir."

With topgallants furled and courses clewed up, the *Wentworth* stood in for the harbour.

There are few things that compare with the taking of a calculated risk, Kite thought as he moved forward to take his station at the weather rail. Under shortened sail, the ship would handle quickly but not run away with him, while he could take tactical advantage of the entrance to Mackerel Cove and claw extra yards to windward before making a final leg into the anchorage beyond.

Kite put the *Wentworth* onto the starboard tack and stood across the entrance until, with the gleam of the lighthouse broad on the weather bow, he ordered the helm over and watched as the light traversed the bow. As Corrie yelled out the command to haul the main yards, he steadied the helm and laid the ship's head for the entrance. "Full and bye," he ordered and received the helmsman's repeated acknowledgement.

The breeze was holding steady and the *Wentworth* glided through the grey sea, the land lying dark on either bow. Slowly the loom of Connonicut Island grew closer and the orange fire in the lighthouse drew slowly abeam. The heel of the deck lessened as the ship came under the lee of the land and the hiss of the wash diminished to a chuckle as the *Wentworth* lost speed. Aloft the weather edges of the topsails lifted and fluttered.

Kite eased the helm a point, keeping the sails full, but giving ground to leeward. The long grey finger of Mackerel Cove opened up to larboard.

"She's luffin', sir!" the helmsman called.

"Keep her full and bye," Kite said, looking up to where the topsails shivered again.

"Wind's funnelling down the narrows," Corrie said, coming aft as the *Wentworth* paid further off to starboard and began to draw close to the Rhode Island shore.

"Aye, and I'll have to give her another point if we are to stay without coming aback," Kite muttered. "Do you stand by."

"Aye, aye, sir." Corrie went forward again and mustered the hands at their stations as Kite moved across the deck and stood beside the helmsman. "Free her off a point."

"Aye, aye, sir." It was Jacob, huge and reliable, who passed the spokes of the wheel from hand to hand, his black skin gleaming like ebony in the dim illumination of the binnacle light. Kite crossed the deck to the lee side. He could see the dark mass of Castle Hill climbing up against a background of stars as they gathered way, going faster now as they came clear of the lee of the opposite island.

"Deck there!" Harper's voice hailed from the foremast head. "Closing fast to leeward."

"Aye, aye," Kite called out, then asked, "Are you ready, Mr Corrie?"

"Ready, aye, ready, sir," Corric responded and Kite held his hand for a moment longer then spun on his heel. "Down helm, Jacob!"

"Down hellum, sah!" and before the words were out of his mouth, Kite felt the cant of the deck ease, saw the bowsprit rake across the sky ahead and then Corrie was holloaing and the men were casting off and tailing on the forward braces.

The ship came up into the wind, faltered a moment, then paid off on the opposite tack as the main yards followed the foreyards round and Jacob was calling out, "Full an' bye, starboard tack, sir."

Kite breathed easier as the *Wentworth* sped back across the narrows, heading for the entrance to Mackerel Cove, where he again put her about. Once more on the larboard tack, the ship headed up for the lights of the town but as she drew closer to the open water they had to weather Brenton's Point and it looked as though their leeway was such as to cause them to tack again. There would be little room at this most narrow part of the strait, and on the opposite bank rocks extended to seaward.

Aloft Harper was calling out their distance and Kite asked for the bearing of the extremity of Brenton's Point.

"Steady, sir," Harper called out, his voice clear in the darkness as not a man moved from his station, instantly ready to tack. Kite kept his nerve and stood on. A steady bearing presaged collision, but then, as they again came out of the lee of Connonicut, a slight increase in wind strength and their own speed altered matters.

"She draws aft, sir!"

The collective sigh of relief was loud and then they were clear and Kite ordered the helm eased. They wore round Brenton's Point, passed two anchored brigs to the south of Goat's Island, then he brought *Wentworth*'s head into the wind about three cables from the shore and half that distance from an anchored schooner. With the sails aback he ordered the larboard bower let go. It went with a splash and the cable rumbled out after it, sending a slight tremor through the ship.

"Very well, Mr Corrie, make a fist of it. I don't want the Yankees waking up in the morning to see a British ship that looks as though her company can't make a decent harbour stow in the middle of the night."

"Aye, aye, sir."

100

Kite could hear the lightheartedness in Corrie's tone of voice. He turned. "That will do the helm, Jacob."

In the waist the men busied themselves with clewing up the topsails and lowering the yards. At the mizzen three seamen were brailing the spanker and Jacob slipped the white sennit lanyards over the wheel-spokes. Kite turned and strode aft to stare at the spangle of Newport's waterfront lights. He still wore his best blue broadcloth and it was surely not too late to call away a boat and have himself pulled ashore. A clock began to strike and he wondered what the time was; ten, he guessed, or perhaps eleven. He began to count, but the clanging passed ten, then eleven, then twelve and he realised it was no clock but the persistent ringing of the church bell.

"Nice of them to make us welcome," Corrie remarked as he came aft to report the anchor brought up.

"Probably the pilots complaining we're trying to cheat 'em," Kite joked flippantly, but the worm of unease was uncoiling in his gut. A similar thought must have crossed Corrie's mind for after a moment or two he said, "It sounds like an alarm . . ."

Kite listened a moment more and then agreed. "Aye, 'tis a tocsin, all right, but why?"

"There's a fire, sir, see, there, along to the left." Harper joined them.

"Give me a glass," said Kite sharply, holding out his hand.

"I have mine here, sir," Harper fished in his coat-tails and passed a small brass telescope to Kite, who raised it to his eye and wrestled a moment as he focused it.

"That's odd," said Corrie reflectively, "but that fire's only just catching and the bell's been ringing for some time."

"Aye, but that's just due to the distance we are offshore. The fire may have been burning for some time," offered Harper.

"I think Corrie's right," said Kite, closing the glass with a snap. "Get the boat swung out, Mr Corrie. You're to stay aboard. Mr Harper, you had better come with me. I think that is arson and I think I know whose warehouse is afire!"

# Eight

## The Tea Deum

By the time the hands had got the boat swung off the booms and over the side there was no doubt that the fire had gained a firm hold of Tyrell's warehouse. As the boat pulled across the harbour, the clang-clang of the tocsin growing louder, it was equally clear to Kite that they were far too late, for the flames were roaring skywards, dissolving into upwardly flung sparks and completely consuming the tarred lap-straked building.

"There is nothing to be done, sir," Harper said as he sat beside Kite, one huge hand on the tiller.

"It's Tyrell's place," Kite said. "I am going to remain ashore. Do you go back to the ship and send the boat in for me at six in the morning. Keep watch and watch with Corrie, there's just the chance someone may have noticed our arrival and take exception to it."

"Aye, aye, sir."

Kite stared into Harper's face, lit by the glare of the fire. If he had entertained any doubts about the second mate's loyalty it was likely the next few days would reveal his political persuasion. Harper put the helm over and swung the boat under the overhang of the wooden wharf and up to a ladder.

"Are you sure you'll be all right, Cap'n?" he asked.

"Of course." Kite reached for the ladder, suddenly angry to find that he was still wearing his best clothes. As he hauled himself up on the planking of the dock he paused. He was unarmed and had not even brought a cane with him. As he looked along the waterfront he thought he might need one, for he was staring at a scene from Hell.

To the roar of the fire and the tolling of the church bell were added the shouts and whoops of a milling crowd. There was no sign of a single bucket of water, nor of distress, or even a sense that the fire might be out of hand and a threat to the surrounding buildings. It was obvious to Kite that he was witnessing arson, and arson committed by the entire community upon a single individual. Aware of someone behind him, he spun round nervously, relieved to see Jacob behind him.

"Massa Harper said I was to stay with you, Cap'n Kite."

Kite nodded. "Very well, Jacob. I'm glad to see you." He paused, undecided as to what he should do. He must get to the Tyrells' house, and he said as much to Jacob, but then he was distracted by an intensifying of the noise of the crowd.

It was a mob now, forming what looked like a ring about the landward end of the warehouse and baying for something with a cacophonous pulse that he could not comprehend. Then he caught the cadence with its alliteration.

"Tea-tax Tyrell! Tea-tax Tyrell! Tea-tax Tyrell!"

Kite began to move forward, a knot of anger and fear bunching up under his heart. He began to shoulder his way into the crowd which kept up their chorus.

"Tea-tax Tyrell! Tea-tax Tyrell! Tea-tax Tyrell!"

Into the light flung across the adjacent street staggered a terrible figure which Kite recognised instantly, though he was stark naked and glossy with a covering of tar. Around him, dancing with excitement, came a dozen youths. Some had bowls under their left arms from which, as if in some obscene sowing rite, they gathered up handfuls of tea with their other hands and flung them over Tyrell. The others bore flaming brands with which they beat the ground behind the old man's heels, making him dance obscenely, to the vast amusement of the shouting crowd of men, women and children. This was Newport's version of tarring and feathering, a ritual adopted by the "Patriots" to intimidate their Tory enemies.

Tyrell tried to ward off the tea dust, blinded by it and the warm tar his thin body had been daubed with. Even where he struggled against the press of the mob, Kite could feel the heat of the fire, and if Tyrell uttered anything from his opened mouth Kite could not hear a thing. He was outraged and his fury increased his activity. He began to elbow people aside so that he attracted attention and men complained, and then he felt his elbow caught in a strong grip and he was being dragged backwards. He half-turned, aware that Jacob was pulling him back through the crowd.

"Unhand me, Jacob, damn you!"

But Jacob hauled him clear and as Kite, his face suffused

with anger, began to berate him, said, "Look Cap'n!" Such was the insistence in Jacob's eyes that Kite turned. Now he could hear Tyrell's screams cutting through the yelling of the mob which gradually ebbed as the enormity of their collective act struck them.

The flaring brands borne by the taunting youths had set fire to the tar which covered Tyrell's body and now he blazed and danced a grim dido of death. Even as he did so the burning walls of his warehouse collapsed inwards with a climactic roar and upwards spray of sparks; then the noise of the fire died down. Even the church bell had ceased tolling the tocsin, and the almost sudden lessening of noise emphasised the terrible death agonies of the tormented old man. Children turned away and buried their faces in their mothers' aprons while the women themselves began to sob and cry.

Someone shouted out, "Shame!"

Another called out, "Murderers!" and few voices joined in: "Incendiaries!" "Bastards!" "Patriot scum!"

As Tyrell's dying body arched with a last spasm of pain and terror, the air was filled with the stench of his burning flesh. Someone vomited and the crowd began to melt away.

"Take heart, citizens!" A man's voice bellowed. "Better one old man dies that a people is enslaved!" A thin cheer from the die-hard Patriots greeted this short speech. "Death to all tyrants!" the ringleader went on, rallying his supporters. "Liberty, and damnation to the British!"

"Come, sah," Jacob persisted, "I promised de second mate I'd look after you, Cap'n Kite. There ain't nothing we can do, sah. The old man is burnt blacker than any God-damned nigra."

Kite caught one last view of Tyrell. The old man had given up the ghost and his corpse lay shrivelled and burned. Then, as Jacob pulled him forcibly into an alley, Kite called, "Wait!"

Obedience was ingrained in Jacob and he paused as Kite turned to peer from the partial cover of the corner. There had been something familiar about the voice of the ringleader. The mob had become a crowd again and this had almost dispersed. Only a small group of men remained at the site of Tyrell's humiliation. One stepped forward and, undoing his breeches, relieved himself over the corpse, adding the stink to the smell of roasting flesh.

"Allan," one of them remonstrated.

The man named Allan looked over his shoulder. "I'm putting him out," he joked, "don't let anyone say I let him burn."

"You'd do better waving that thing at his widow!"

"Happen I will before morning."

"She'll be glad to be rid of him."

"Go give her the news, John."

The ringleader shook his head. "No, we'll make her sing the Tea Deum in the morning," he said. At that moment Kite saw his face.

"Let's get out of here, Jacob," said Kite, shaking himself clear of the black man's restraining grip and leading Jacob up the alley.

"Where are we going, sah?"

"To call on a lady."

The Tyrells' house was in darkness as they approached. Through the dark window-glass on the ground floor Kite could see the internal shutters had been closed, and he feared for Sarah's whereabouts. Where had she been when her husband had been caught by the Patriot mob? He banged on the door and stood impatiently for some moments on the threshold. A silence had fallen now on Newport and he felt this was preternatural. It was broken by distant drunken laughter. He swore and beat on the door again, leaning forward to catch any sound from within.

"Dere's someone in dere, Cap'n," Jacob whispered. "I see the shutters move."

Kite stepped back and moved to the window Jacob indicated. "It's Captain William Kite, just arrived from Jamaica," he called in a low voice. "Let me in!"

Then the shutter drew aside and Kite started as he stared into the face of the Tyrells' housekeeper, Bessie Ramsden, her head swathed in a nightcap. He saw her turn about and a few minutes later heard the noise of bolts being drawn.

"Oh, Cap'n, I'm so glad—"

"Where's your mistress?" Kite cut in.

"I don't know, she went out looking for the master."

"Damnation! I beg your pardon, but where is she likely to have gone? Where did Mr Tyrell say he was going?"

"He never came home tonight, sir."

"From the counting house?"

"Yes, sir."

"And is that where your mistress is likely to have gone to find him?"

"Yes, sir. We had word that the Patriots were on the rampage after what happened over in Boston last night."

"What was that?"

"Oh, they threw all the tea into Boston Harbour, sir, all dressed up as Mohicans."

"Yes, yes, but is there anywhere else Mistress Tyrell might have gone other than the counting house?"

"Only the warehouse, sir; the master took a small consignment of tea out of a snow last week."

"Dear God! Have you a pistol and a sword, Bessie? Be quick!"

"Here, come in, sir . . ."

In the hallway Kite saw the servants all armed with muskets. He turned and gestured to Jacob. "Here, Jacob, arm yourself. We are going out after Mistress Tyrell, that old man's wife." Kite turned to the housekeeper. "Bessie, I doubt you'll be bothered until the morning, but if I find the mistress, I'm taking her off to my ship until this trouble dies down." He forbore saying more and took what he recognised as Arthur Tyrell's small sword and a brace of pistols from a manservant.

"They're loaded, Captain Kite," the man said. "D'you want me to come with you?"

"No, do you stay here and mind these ladies. If anyone wants to know now or later where your mistress is, tell them she left to find her husband and you haven't seen her since. D'you understand me?"

"Aye."

"Good. Now come, Jacob. We've no time to lose."

Kite walked swiftly back into the silent town. Ironically a clock now struck midnight, the chimes ringing out mournfully over the rooftops. A few lights still glimmered between the interstices in the shutters and from one tavern the incongruous noise of riot sounded raucously into the night as a door opened and a Patriot reveller made for the latrine. They came to the waterfront and the smouldering remains of Tyrell's warehouse, which still glowed as the breeze gently fanned the embers. In the area where once the carts had loaded there was no trace of Tyrell's body and Kite heard Jacob muttering.

"The white man is powerful bad," he said and Kite was

compelled to agree with him. At the scene of Tyrell's dreadful death and humiliation Kite paused and Jacob could scarce contain his unease, hopping from one leg to another.

"Where the devil d'you think the monsters have taken him?" Kite asked no one and then he turned on his heel and made for the entrance to the counting house up a side street. The upper end window was that of Tyrell's private office and looked over the harbour. It was dark, but Kite thought he could see a dim flickering within. Was that the start of another fire, or did it indicate some activity inside? If so, was it more "patriotism" or did it reveal Sarah's whereabouts?

He crossed the street and tried the door. It was locked and he bent to the keyhole. Again there was a that faint glimmer, like a single candleflame somewhere in the interior. He turned his head and pressed his ear against the door. He was almost certain that he heard voices and, keeping his ear against the door, he tapped it deliberately with his knuckles. The whispering stopped. He tapped again, then heard a shuffling as of someone approaching the door cautiously.

He swallowed, then placing his mouth near the key hole called in a low voice, "It is William Kite, master of the *Wentworth*, newly arrived from Port Royal, Jamaica."

There was a short pause and then a man's voice, tremulous with fear responded. "That is impossible!"

"Borthwick? Is that you? Let me in, I am indeed William Kite."

"How can I be sure?"

Kite thought for a moment, then asked, "D'you remember me asking who a certain man was when a gang of Patriots tried to waylay me?"

"Aye, if you are Captain Kite you will known whose name I gave."

"You told me the name was Rathburne."

"And who is the mate of the *Wentworth*?"

"John Corrie."

To his relief, Kite heard a key grind in the lock and the next moment the door was cracked open. He stood to show himself.

"Who have you there?" Borthwick asked quickly, shoving the door closed again.

"This is Jacob, Borthwick, my quartermaster from the *Wentworth*."

Again the door opened and both men slipped inside. "Where is Mistress Tyrell?" Kite asked quickly and Borthwick jerked his head to an open door. It led, Kite knew, to a bay large enough for a single cart, from which valuables were brought into a strong room within the counting house through heavy double doors onto the street along the side of the building.

"Cap'n!" Jacob stood wrinkling his nose, the whites of his eyes alarmed in the semi-darkness. Kite could smell the burnt flesh and swallowed.

"Wait here, Jacob."

In the loading bay stood a small flat-dray and on it, lit by a single candle, lay the mortal remains of Arthur Tyrell. Kite shuddered and retched, then saw Sarah. She stood pressed into a corner, immobile and staring through wide eyes at what had once been her husband.

Borthwick shuffled in beside him. He pressed a handkerchief to his nose and mumbled, "I have been trying to persuade her that she cannot stay here all night, Captain Kite."

Kite nodded. "Thank you, Borthwick, thank you. Do you leave the keys with Jacob."

"I cannot, sir, I cannot."

"Very well, then, wait with Jacob." Borthwick turned and went out, leaving Kite with Sarah. There was no obvious sign that she recognised him, or even knew he was there, and he very slowly moved towards her, his hands outstretched.

"Sarah," he called in a low voice. "Sarah, 'tis me, William, William Kite . . . Sarah?" As he drew closer her eyes never left the charred corpse, nor did she appear to blink, though her cheeks were wet with tears. Yet she sensed him looming over her, for slowly she sank down onto her haunches, one arm coming up to shelter her head as though he was about to beat her with a stick. A faint whimper came from her, but it was clear she was insensible to his identity, though he murmured both their names. He crouched beside her, but still she remained withdrawn and his one attempt to touch her resulted in a swiftly indrawn breath, so that he moved back, perplexed.

He stood and, looking reluctantly at Tyrell's remains, had a thought. A whip stood alongside the dray, leant against the wall by the last driver. Moving slowly he took it up and then moved closer to Sarah. As soon as she was within arms' length he swung the whip and knocked over the candle. It guttered and

108

went out, a moment later, as Sarah began to scream, he took her in his arms.

"Borthwick!" he called, aware that a flicker of flame ran along a wisp of straw on the board of the flat-dray. "Bring water, quick!"

"Oh, oh, oh . . ." Sarah was trembling in his arms as he gathered her up. Somewhere Borthwick stumbled and threw the remains of a jug of drinking water over the tiny fire and then in the next room the snap of flint of steel was soon conjured into a new light.

"Come, Sarah." With infinite patience, Kite led her out of the loading bay and into the main counting house.

"I should take her upstairs, sir, you can have some privacy there. I shall make some . . ." Borthwick had been about to say tea, but Jacob rose to the occasion.

"We'll make rum punch, sah. Do you light the cap'n up dem stairs, Massah Borthwick."

"Thank you, Jacob," Kite said as the clerk complied and he tenderly shepherded Sarah up the flight of stairs to Tyrell's private office. Here it seemed, she began to come to, blinking and looking about her, reaching out to touch familiar objects: Tyrell's inkwell, his tray of pens, the edge of a pile of papers. Slowly she made a circuit of his desk and then she looked up and seemed to see Kite for the first time, for she started, then stepped forward and, with her face a mask, raked her hand across his face.

"Sarah!" He staggered backwards, blood pouring from his cheek where her rings had cut him. It was a curious repeat of their first encounter when she had struck him with her riding crop. Into his outraged consciousness swam Tyrell's veiled allusions to his wife's high state of nerves, hints of instability, and now, he thought, of madness.

"Sarah!" He put his hand up to staunch the bleeding, and stared at her as she slowly realised what she had done.

"William? Is it you? It cannot be!" She began to shake, and tears suddenly poured from her eyes: not the suppressed weeping of her lonely vigil, but a full-blown and lachrymose collapse. Now she clung to him and slowly exhausted herself, voiding herself of the horrors of the night, as he leaned against Tyrell's desk and soothed her with soft, shushing noises, all the while stroking her lustrous dark hair.

At last, as though aware that the crisis had been passed, Jacob came up the stairs with steaming hot rum punch, leaving the jug with them as he retreated below again. "There was a boat, Captain," he said as his head reached the level of the upper floor. "I saw a boat tied up near where we landed. We can take that out to the ship when you are ready. There's no need to wait until the morning."

"Thank you, Jacob. Give us a few more minutes."

After a period during which Kite thought Sarah had fallen asleep, she stirred. "William?"

"Yes, my dear; it *is* me. We arrived this evening." He handed her a small tankard of the punch and she clasped it between both hands.

"Tonight of all nights," she said, sipping the hot liquid.

"Yes, tonight of all nights."

"The madness is an infection caught from Boston."

"So Mrs Ramsden explained." Kite took up his own punch and felt the warm glow expand in his guts.

"And Arthur would not lie low. Oh, God, do you know what they did to him, William?"

"Yes," he replied, "I do. I landed just as they finished . . ."

Kite wanted to make some excuse, to explain why he had not rescued Tyrell, but she went on.

"I saw it from this window. There had been muttering all day, after the news came from Boston. This evening a drummer went round the town, just like in Providence the night they burnt the government schooner. Arthur was restless and in the end he said he was going out. I begged him not to be foolhardy, but he insisted. 'All my life's work lies in that warehouse,' he said, and I argued that that was not only stupid, but untrue. His profits lay in the bank, in our house, in our property along the waterfront and our shares in ships at sea, but he would have none of it. 'It is a matter of principle,' he shouted. 'The law shall not give way to the mob!' and then he was putting on his cloak and hat and I said that I was going with him. He told me to stay, that you would look after me, that you had promised, but I said that whatever you had promised, you were not here . . ." She lifted the tankard again.

Kite said nothing; all that day he had been beating up and down outside the harbour in Rhode Island Sound, wondering why the confounded pilots were ignoring his signals. Now he knew why.

"After he left the house I followed him, catching him up before he reached Main Street. He was angry with me, then he took my hand and we came here. We were seen, of course. They were watching for us, I think. We heard them calling out.

"At first only a few of the waterfront loiterers followed us, but by the time we reached the door below there was a crowd assembling, and once we were inside and had found Borthwick Arthur made me promise to stay here. Before many more minutes had passed the crowd had become a mob. They were like animals, surrounding us and shouting their filthy abuse, people I have known all my life . . . Arthur was very brave; he opened the door and went out onto the step and asked them their business. They wanted him to open the warehouse and surrender the tea, so that they could brew it in the harbour as those others had done in Boston. I think that had he done so they would forgiven and forgotten his Toryism and have accepted he had changed his politics, but Arthur could not take the easy way out of this cruel dilemma and he refused to bow to coercion."

Kite remained silent, watching her and thinking how beautiful she was as she set down the empty tankard, her eyes blazing with indignation and her breast heaving with emotion. She drew herself up and her voice rose a little, cracking with the intensity of her feelings. "He had made me promise that whatever happened – *whatever happened* – I would stay here," she repeated, as though the knowledge exculpated and at the same time burdened her.

"He walked across the street with his keys to the warehouse, a great ring of them. I could see them gleaming in the lamps that people held up as they all fell silent. I wanted Arthur to throw open the doors of the warehouse and tell them to help themselves. The mob grew silent in anticipation, it seemed, of him doing this, but as they closed round him he drew back his arm and made to throw the keys over their heads into the harbour." She paused, shaking her head. "Then someone jumped up and caught them. John Rathburne, I think it was, and Arthur was pushed and shoved up against the door. The mob cheered and I lost sight of him, then I saw the door open and then close . . . It all grew silent again. I did not know what was happening until I smelt smoke. They set fire to the far end, the seawards end of the warehouse first. It was full of sugar. God knows what they did to him in there, but they stripped him . . ."

Sarah paused a moment, but she had control of herself now and went on calmly. "They stripped him and tarred him and in place of the chicken feathers they are so fond of they threw tea all over him and drove him back into the street and set fire to him."

"I saw the rest, Sarah . . ."

"But why, William? Why did they do that to an old man?"

"To unite them all, my dear. They are all complicit now, accessories after the fact, and though no one will ever be arraigned for murder, all their lives have been touched by the common crime."

"John Rathburne did it, he is their leader."

"I know, Sarah, and tomorrow we must take counsel, but tonight we must get you to a place of safety, the *Wentworth*. Come, I will send Borthwick home and he may let Bessie know you are safe with me. Let us get some sleep. Come."

He led her down the stairs and Borthwick put her cloak about her shoulders. Kite told the clerk his intentions. "If you can," he said, "return here for ten o'clock in the morning, but do not, I beg you, Borthwick, run any risks."

"I won't, Captain."

They stepped out into the now silent street. Smoke and heat still wafted across the street from the burnt-out warehouse and the dying embers glowed here and there, under the gentle impetus of the light breeze. Behind them Jacob emerged and Borthwick ground the keys in the lock.

"Good night, ma'am," he said, "good night, Captain."

"Ain't nothing good about it," mumbled Jacob, cocking the pistols. "Follow me, Cap'n," he said and led them obliquely across the street towards the wharves that jutted out from the waterfront.

A few minutes later Sarah sat in the stern of the stolen boat while Jacob and Kite each plied an oar. Answering the challenge from Zachariah Harper, they pulled alongside and with some difficulty in the dark Sarah was manhandled up the curving tumblehome of the *Wentworth*'s side. As they clambered aboard Jacob kicked the boat adrift.

"Nobody will know who took that boat," he said, handing the pistols to Kite.

"No, but they'll wake up to see an unexpected arrival lying at anchor in the harbour," Kite said.

Watching Kite escort Sarah to his cabin, Harper murmured, "Well, I'll be God-damned . . ."

"You'd better be for him, Mister Harper," Jacob said, "cos he's as angry as a five-legged hornet!"

# Nine

## Last Rites

K ite had left word that he was to be called at six o'clock and Bandy Ben found him wrapped in blankets on the deck of the cabin, his cot occupied by a remarkably beautiful woman.

"Cap'n, sir. Hot water."

Kite groaned; his body ached from lying on the deck. Then slowly the events of the previous day reinvaded his consciousness: the long hours of beating up and down off the Beaver's Tail, the tense passage of the narrows and then the terrible events beside the blazing warehouse culminating in Tyrell's scorched corpse and finally poor Sarah's ordeal.

At the thought of Sarah he threw off the blankets and rose to his feet. She lay in his cot like a beautiful but broken doll, fast asleep, her mouth slightly open, her hair tousled and her face and clothes fouled by sinister black smears. He caught the scent of her but it was impossible to avoid the smell of burnt flesh that hung about her dishevelled clothes and it occurred to him that she herself must have borne Tyrell's corpse into the loading bay.

He shook his head, turned to the hot water and shaved. When he had finished his ablutions he drew on his working clothes, the oldest of his coats that he wore at sea, and an old glazed hat which fitted tightly enough to withstand the odd gust of wind. Round his waist he buckled Tyrell's hanger and, bending a moment over his desk, scribbled a note for Sarah. Then he quietly left the cabin and encountering Ben told him to leave the lady until she woke and then to give her every attention.

"She is a person of importance, Ben; do you treat her kindly, for she has had a terrible experience." Ben grunted acknowledgement and Kite added, "While you wait for her to wake, be a good fellow and see what you can do to clean up my best coat and breeches."

113

On deck it was still dark. He found Corrie on watch and explained what had happened. The mate whistled through his teeth. "Zachariah said the fire looked bad, but I had no idea it was anything but misfortune . . ."

"Well, John, our consignee is dead, his warehouse is destroyed and his widow is asleep in my cot. I dare say we shall be able to sell our cargo to someone else and I shall attend to the matter later this morning. For now, however, I should be obliged if you will provide me with a boat as soon as possible. I have a mind to be ashore before the town is much astir. At ten o'clock send it back in for me. When Mistress Tyrell awakes, tell her I shall be back aboard at ten to take her ashore. I shall want Jacob turned out to accompany me."

"Zachariah wants to come with you, too."

"That's good of him, but do you not want him on board?"

"I can manage an anchor watch."

"I don't know how long we'll be, John."

"I'll manage."

"Very well."

Half an hour later, as the first glimmer of a wintry dawn threw the buildings of Newport into a sharpening silhouette, Kite stood again where he had witnessed the last moments of his friend. He walked into the charred timbers and heaps of ash that were all that remained of Tyrell's goods. Here and there embers glowed and the ash was still hot enough to warm his feet through the soles of his boots, but the sharp frost had cooled much of the previous night's conflagration. Smashed glass lay in piles, where bottles of wine and rum had exploded, while piles of barrel and cask hoops were all that remained of the large quantity of rum and beer Tyrell had had stored ready for shipping. Both were either distilled or brewed in the town and the incendiaries had damaged Newport's economy with a wantonness that shocked Kite. Of the offending tea there remained no trace.

Tyrell's warehouse was the last building on the waterside before it cut back in a dock, but on its far side rose the adjacent store owned by McFee, Browne and Kent. The nameboard announcing the owners was defaced by bubbled paintwork but, remarkably enough, it had not caught fire. A few buckets lay where they had been thrown at the end of the incident and the heavy frost that whitened the sloping roof showed where it had been thoroughly and constantly doused with water. There was no doubt that not only was the burning of Tyrell's warehouse arson, but it had been meticulously planned and carried out with great discipline.

A dog began to bark and somewhere a door slammed. Kite turned. A man was walking down the street that ran along the waterfront. He regarded the unfamiliar pile of ash and ruin that occupied the vacant lot and then noticed Kite and looked away. Standing still, Kite felt the heat burning through his boots and quit the site. It was too early to expect Borthwick to be at the counting house, but he checked, then walked off towards the Tyrells' house.

He found Mrs Ramsden a-bustle and obviously relieved when she opened the door to him. "Why, Captain Kite! Did you find the Mistress?"

"Yes, Bessie, she's safe aboard the *Wentworth*, but did you not hear from Borthwick last night?"

"We dursn't open the door to anyone if it wasn't you, sir. A man saying he was Borthwick came to the door, but I didn't reckon it was him, sir, and it was dreadfully late . . ."

"Very well, very well," soothed Kite, holding up his hand. "Pray do not distress yourself on that account, but I am afraid there have been terrible things happening in Newport."

He told her as sparingly as he could, but she was a curious and persistent woman, and despite the floods of tears and shrieks of dismay he could not, in the end, conceal the full horror of what had happened. By the time he had finished they had migrated to the kitchen and Mrs Ramsden felt the need for a tumbler of Tyrell's best rum.

"What are we to do, Captain? Oh," she went on without giving Kite the opportunity of replying, but dabbing her eyes with her apron and refilling her glass, "what a great mercy you came, sir! Had you not turned up, I don't know what would have happened to the Mistress, really I don't."

"No. The pity of it is, Bessie," said Kite, "that had I not met contrary winds yesterday I should have been in port twelve hours earlier and might have saved your Master."

"Oh yes, sir . . . To think of him being burned to death, oh, sir . . ." And she burst again into floods of tears. He waited until she had calmed down and then she repeated her first question. "What are we to do, sir?"

"I am not certain but I think we must see what transpires during the day. I hope the spirit of revolt will have had its fill of death and destruction, but it may not be so. There is, it seems, a very persistent faction in the town which is hell bent on mischief. Tell me, Bessie, what do you know of the man named Rathburne?"

"Oh, he is the worst of them, Captain, that I can assure you. John Peck Rathburne is one of Whipple's men – have you heard of Captain Abraham Whipple, sir?"

"I heard that he burned the *Gaspée*, yes, and I have marked him to be the ringleader of the active Patriots of Newport."

"Oh, he is, sir. The Master says— Oh, sir, forgive me . . ."

"That is all right, Bessie." Kite waited while she composed herself again.

"The Master," she went on, sniffling as she spoke, "used to say that he was the one man in Newport who was capable of real mischief. That was after the *Liberty* business."

"And what was that?"

"Oh, it was years ago, back in sixty-eight, I think, some business over a ship called the *Liberty* that belonged to Mr Hancock over in Boston. She had been taken by the Custom House officers for some problem over the duty that Mr Hancock should have paid or something. It was rather confusing, sir, seeing as how Mr Tyrell said, and I heard him say this, that the Crown officers were acting provocatively by strictly enforcing a regulation they had normally ignored. But Mr Hancock had annoyed them and I think they wanted matters done according to the regulation . . ." Mrs Ramsden had confused herself, but Kite could visualise the problem. It was probably waiving some procedure such as a strict entering of a ship for outwards clearance when the master cleared inwards at the Custom House. No doubt it had become a common practice to roll the two acts into one until, on this occasion, the Crown officers challenged the master of Mr Hancock's vessel, the *Liberty*, and accused him of not conforming to the letter of the regulation. Such things were done in Liverpool with a master who was a persistent problem to the authorities. But that, it seemed, was only half the story. "Go on," he said.

"Well, Captain, the Custom House officers used the *Liberty* like the *Gaspée* . . ."

"You mean they made her a revenue vessel?" Kite interrupted, incredulous at the inherent provocation of turning a seized vessel into a revenue cruiser.

"Yes, but all this was two or three years before the *Gaspée* business. Anyway, in the spring of the next year, sixty-nine that would be, the *Liberty* was lying here, off Newport. This raised a great commotion and they called a meeting and that John Rathburne was at the head of it, holloaing about Liberty being a matter for Americans and that it was all wrong for a ship with that name to be in King George's service and, oh, I don't known what all . . .

"Anyway, the upshot of it all was that they went out and burned her, said she wasn't British anyway. In fact I do believe that Mr Hancock himself came over from Boston and told them he didn't give a fiddle for the ship, what with him being the richest man in the whole of Massachusetts." Bessie Ramsden finished with a stout blowing of her nose which, Kite rightly concluded, signified she had overcome her moment of weakness. "So there you are, Captain, that's Captain John Peck Rathburne for you."

"A man with a fondness for burning things."

"Aye, quite." Mrs Ramsden pounded both hands upon her knees and rose to her feet. "And now, if you'll excuse me, sir . . . By the by," she asked, suddenly solicitous, "have you broken your fast? I'll wager not, and if you have it'll only have been that dreadful fare they serve on ships."

"Oh, 'tis not so bad when you've got used to it."

"Here, you sit down, sir, I've a fine ham, and we'll mash some tea and stir some porridge."

"And the condemned man ate a hearty breakfast," Kite murmured to himself as he relaxed, hoping that aboard the *Wentworth* they were looking after Sarah.

Kite reached Tyrell's counting house exactly as the church clock struck nine. Borthwick was already there but he shrugged his shoulders when Kite asked after his colleagues. "The word will have been passed to them to stay away, Captain."

"And you, do you wish to stay away, Borthwick?"

"I know the distinction between my duty and my inclination, Captain. Besides," Borthwick wrinkled his nose, "there is the matter of Mr Tyrell's remains."

"Yes, I have already considered that. I have been at the Tyrells' house this morning and before I left I sent word for a grave to be prepared for midday. Do you see that Mr Tyrell's attorney is summoned to the house with Tyrell's will and testamentary papers by two o'clock this afternoon. Now, before I leave you to go off to the ship again, I wish you to quietly see if there's a merchant who will take in three hundred and seventy tons of sugar and molasses, a small quantity of Spanish laces and similar wares."

"Very well, Captain, but they'll offer low prices."

"Then we'll sail for New York and sell it there."

Borthwick sighed and nodded. "This is a sad day, Captain Kite."

"Tell that to your fellow townsfolk, Mr Borthwick."

When he returned to the *Wentworth*, Kite found Sarah awake and dressed, sitting at his desk drinking chocolate. She rose angrily and accused him of abandoning her, but he swiftly responded.

"Would it have been proper to linger in the same accommodation as you, Sarah, beyond the time I had been called? Come, my dear, this will be a difficult day."

He watched her face soften. "I was frightened without you, William. When I woke I did not know where you were. Heavens, I scarcely knew where I was myself, until I remembered."

"Have you eaten?" he asked, swiftly changing the subject.

She nodded. "Yes, that odd little creature brought me hot burgoo and, as you see, I am completing my breakfast with this chocolate."

"That is Bandy Ben," Kite said, smiling for the first time, and she hesitantly smiled back. "You look better for your night's sleep. In fact," he said slowly, "you look uncommonly handsome."

She did not hear the compliment. "I cannot rid myself of the thought that with Arthur's death . . ." She hesitated, unable to bring herself to utter the words.

"Set those thoughts aside, Sarah, at least for the time being. Now, pray attend me and hear me out, for I have much to tell you."

It was odd, Kite thought afterwards, how events had conspired to throw them together, so that from the moment of his return to Rhode Island their fates had become inextricably entwined. There was never a formal proposal or any other of the regular conventions of courtship. She fell in with his plan not because he had assumed responsibility for her, but because it suited her and they were of one mind. For Sarah, outrage at the public murder of her husband, far more than the passion she felt for William Kite, made her aid and abet him. For Kite, friendship and respect for Arthur Tyrell obliged him to protect the dead man's helpless widow, while the commercial loss staring him in the face led him to acquire her help in solving their mutual problem. But both knew there was a distant objective behind this pragmatic union, and both knew that this governed the nature of their conduct upon that fateful day. It also enabled them to withstand the malicious intent of others who had already matured their own plan for the final disposal of the House of Tyrell.

Shortly before noon on the 19th of December 1773, the townsfolk of Newport were treated to a pitiful and dismal spectacle. A flat-dray, drawn by two nags and led by a huge black seaman wearing a cutlass, creaked its way up Main Street from the waterfront. Exposed on the dray lay what looked like a twisted and blacked log, such as one might pull out of a fire that had burnt out. It was scarcely recognisable as once having been a man. Behind the dray came a tall English sea captain in blue broadcloth, his cocked hat beneath his left arm, the glint of a silver-hilted sword at his waist and the scabbard-iron tap-tapping his gleaming hessian boots. He wore his hair unpomaded, his heavy clubbed queue bound at the nape of his neck by a black ribbon. He held his head up and his level grey eyes stared about him so that those who stood and watched dropped their gaze.

Upon his right arm walked Mistress Tyrell. Her voluptuous figure was set off in watered grey silk, over which she wore a black cloak whose hood was thrown defiantly back to reveal a cascade of hair tumbling about her shoulders. Like her escort, her head was also held high but she looked neither to right nor to left. Her eyes were fixed upon the disgusting sight of the black and shrivelled body of her husband which shuddered as the dray rumbled over the uneven surface of the street.

Behind Captain Kite walked Mr Borthwick in his common garb of black and grey, his arm supporting Bessie Ramsden, who was attired entirely in black. Four of the Tyrells' servants followed and the rear was brought up by a large and conspicuously ugly man, dressed in similar style to the captain, in a blue coat, apparel instantly recognisable to every person, man, woman or child in that seafaring place as the common clothes of a merchant sea officer. He carried in the crook of his arm a brightly polished blunderbuss, such as merchant vessels carry to deter thieves.

For the most part the people of Newport stood silently downcast, as though acknowledging their collective shame.

The men removed their hats, a number of the women sobbed silently and the smaller children peered from behind their parents' legs, scarce comprehending the grim sight. Only once, as the improvised cortege passed a tavern, was there heard an echo of the events of the previous night. A group of men, obviously appraised of the approach of the dolorous little procession, spilled out onto the street. Several had pots in their hands, others tobacco pipes and three wore their hats. Kite saw Rathburne standing slightly apart, hat on head and tapping his right boot with a cane. His face, a handsome one, Kite acknowledged, wore an offensive smirk and he stared at Kite quite unabashed. Kite felt Sarah's grip on his arm tighten. He held Rathburne's gaze until he could no longer do so without turning his head and he knew in that short period that he had made a mortal enemy. Sarah's grip eased as they passed clear of the group of men but behind them Kite heard the noise of exaggerated expectoration. Sarah grasped him again and he heard her indrawn breath.

"Steady, my love," he whispered and they slowly walked on.

In their rear a disrespectful murmur rose, then there was a laugh and as Kite guessed, having given offence as they intended, the gang withdrew inside the tavern.

There was only one person in the church other than the officiating incumbent, a man named Milton who, Kite was to learn later, was Tyrell's attorney. The funeral was short, swift and formal, spoken like the reading of the articles of agreement between a ship's master and his potential crew, Kite thought. Nor was the interment longer than was necessary, a circumstance hastened by a shower of snow driven in by a cold wind blowing from the north again. Afterwards, the little group of mourners slipped quietly away, traversing the back streets and heading out of the town towards the Tyrells' house. Here, irrespective of rank or station, Sarah had bid them assemble while some refreshments were served and Kite spoke.

"On behalf of Mistress Tyrell, I should like to thank you for your loyal support after the tragic events of the last few hours. It remains to be seen what the future holds for us, but I am certain that what provision can be made for you will be made."

"Thank you all," added Sarah, and she left the room, pausing only to address the attorney Milton. Kite saw the man nod, indicate his briefcase, pick it up and follow her. Kite joined them in the withdrawing room where he asked her, "Whom do you wish to attend, my dear?"

Sarah looked at Milton. "Mr Milton? What is your advice?"

"Besides yourself, ma'am, Captain William Alexander Kite, Mistress Elizabeth Jane Ramsden, Mr Solomon Lemuel Borthwick and Captain Thomas Edward Spenser Gray."

Kite called them in and they stood awkwardly about Sarah, who had sat on a single upright chair opposite Milton who was standing by a second. Kite recognised it as the one Tyrell himself favoured. "We seem to be one short," said Milton.

"Captain Gray is in the Antilles, Mr Milton, in the *Electra*," Borthwick offered.

"Then," said Milton drawing a sheaf of papers from his brief-case, "we shall have to proceed in his absence. If you would all be seated."

They did as the attorney bid them and an awkward silence fell. Borthwick coughed nervously, then Milton began to read. Kite looked from the window. It was the same one through which, less than twelve hours earlier, he had peered inwards at Bessie Ramsden in her night attire. He yawned, still tired after the exertions and turmoil of the night. The room was hot after the chill outside where the sky looked now like a sheet of lead. A soft and persistent fall of snow had begun to transform the landscape. Milton's voice droned over the testamentary clauses. The bulk of Tyrell's fortune had gone to his wife, as was to be expected, but there were special provisions for his housekeeper and chief clerk, who were both left two thousand pounds "for their loyalty and long and untiring service". Mrs Ramsden rocked as if about to faint, uttered a heartfelt, "God bless my soul!" and began to weep again.

Borthwick, by contrast, remained unmoved. He was charged with the conditional duty of advising Sarah "upon the disposal" of "the testator's commercial assets in their entirety, entirely freeing my wife from any encumbrance whatsoever". There was an exception to this, referring to the shares Tyrell had in various ships belonging to the ports of Newport, Providence and Bristol in the Colony of Rhode Island, which were to be made over to Captain Edward Spenser Gray, who was to enjoy or dispose of these as he saw fit on the sole condition that annually, or upon disposal, he paid five per centum of the profits raised thereby, net of all charges and taxes, to the trust mentioned in the next article.

Milton himself, in return for a legacy additional to his charges of one thousand five hundred pounds and an annuity of five per centum from an invested sum of five thousand pounds of which he and Sarah were the trustees, was "to advise my wife as to the best manner of drawing income from the residue of my estate". An additional provision was laid upon this trust, however, and at the mention of his name, Kite stirred from his brown study.

" . . . providing only," Milton read, "that this be in accordance with the wishes of Captain William Alexander Kite whom I charge with the duty, laid upon his honour as a gentleman, of ensuring as far as it lies within his power, of the future security, happiness and health of my wife . . ."

Milton looked up as the irrepressible Mrs Ramsden muttered in surprise and delight, expressing her pleasure and leaning forward and patting Sarah's knee before realising the unseemly nature of her presumption and flushing to the roots of her white hair. Sarah had gone deathly pale and had, Kite thought, been about to interrupt Milton and ask a question, but the attorney ploughed doggedly on.

"At the discretion of the said trustees of their heirs or successors, the funds shall be put at the disposal of any such children that my wife may have after my death."

Milton paused, then looked up. "Are there any questions?" he queried.

"When did Arthur sign that will, Mr Milton?" Sarah asked, her face pale, but her voice level and controlled.

"The day after Captain Kite sailed for Jamaica, ma'am."

"I see."

Milton folded the will and looked round. "I shall of course communicate with Captain Gray, Mrs Tyrell, as soon as that becomes possible."

"Yes, of course."

"May I ask something, ma'am?" They turned at the sound of Borthwick's voice.

"Of course, Mr Borthwick, what is it?"

"The question is to Mr Milton, ma'am, but closely concerns yourself."

"Well, sir," commanded Milton somewhat imperiously, "do go on."

"What is to happen about bringing the murderers of my late master to justice, sir?"

"It is a question that occurs to me too, sir," added Kite, lending weight to Borthwick's query.

"I think, sir, gentlemen, given the state of the country, we should find not a witness."

"But there were a hundred people . . ." Sarah breathed incredulously.

"You know it was Rathburne, do you not, sir?" Kite asked.

"I know only what I can get people to give as evidence in court, Captain Kite."

"I will give evidence in court," Kite said.

"I know, Captain, and perhaps, just perhaps, we might find another dozen brave souls to do the same, but you will find three times that number who will swear on oath that John Rathburne or any other person was at their house enjoying dinner or a game of faro."

"But what of the burning?"

"Oh, they will have seen a burning, they may have been among the numbers of men who turned out to fling buckets over the adjacent property to prevent the conflagration from spreading, but no one will admit to having seen Mr Tyrell, begging your pardon, ma'am, other than that he must have been within the warehouse when it caught fire and might himself have contributed to the ignition." Milton shook his head. "It will be the *Gaspée* affair all over again."

"So there is no redress?"

"You may try, Captain, but you will risk the most public and damaging humiliation." Milton looked pointedly at Borthwick and Ramsden. "If I might speak with you and Mrs Tyrell alone . . ."

"Of course, Mr Milton, I only wished to raise the matter out of respect for my late master." Borthwick rose, flustered and unhappy.

"That is quite understood, Mr Borthwick, and entirely to your credit. Your late master felt keenly that your loyalty was exemplary and he has provided for you most generously." It was a cruel and pointed dismissal, Kite thought, but if Borthwick felt it, he did not show it, as he led Bessie Ramsden from the room and closed the door behind them.

"I am sorry that Borthwick chose to raise the issue, ma'am," Milton said, turning to Sarah. "I was intending to touch upon the subject myself when we were alone. I have in fact some information that was laid before me this morning referring to this very fact." Milton shuffled the papers before him and lifted a single sheet of paper which had been folded as a sealed letter. "I shall not mince my words, for it pains me to be associated in any way with this sort of transaction, but this note," he held it up, "which is naturally unsigned, was delivered to me early this morning. It clearly states that any attempt to persuade the justices to pursue, and I quote, 'any line of enquiry which seeks to suggest the unfortunate death of the Tory merchant Arthur Tyrell was anything other than an accident, will not succeed'. As I said there is no signature, but there is a sub-scription which reads, 'By Order of the Committee of American Patriots of the State of Rhode Island', whoever, whatever and wherever that may be." He paused, then added, "By burying your husband, Mistress Tyrell, you have in part aided the Patriots' desire to have his death considered an accident. Now an inquest will be merely a formality, probably over within a few days and all but yourselves heartily glad of it." The attorney stopped again, allowing the import of his words to sink in.

Kite sighed. "It was my idea to have Tyrell buried immediately, the prospect of him lying—"

"No, it was not you, William. *I* wished it, you merely arranged it. That you anticipated my wishes is not important. This has been terrible, but I believe Arthur envisioned something like this occurring. Indeed," Sarah said, lowering her voice, "I might even consider that he precipitated it, for he was far from conciliatory to the radical faction."

Milton bowed his head in assent. "Sadly I think that is true, ma'am."

Sarah drew herself up. "Thank you, Mr Milton. There is much to be done. You will understand, I hope, that Arthur was aware that Captain Kite . . ." She held out her hand toward Kite and he crossed the room and took it, standing beside her as she confronted the attorney. "That Captain Kite and I are not . . ." She faltered, squeezing Kite's hand.

"Ma'am, I quite understand," Milton said hurriedly. "You and Captain Kite will forgive me if I say that few men could be immune from your attraction, Mrs Tyrell. May I congratulate you both."

"I'd be obliged if you will not fan whatever scandal is currently abroad, Mr Milton," Kite said. "This remains a matter of some delicacy, notwithstanding the provisions in the will which make it quite clear that nothing underhand was afoot behind Mr Tyrell's back."

"There is something more that I have to communicate with you, something of singular moment." Milton rummaged in his briefcase again and drew out a package wrapped in brown paper which he handed to Kite, who letting go of Sarah's hand took it, sat down again and reached into his pocket for his penknife. Cutting the sealed string, he noted the parcel was of a surprising weight and gave off a familiar chink. He began to unwrap it.

Inside the paper was a cloth which, once unfolded, revealed a small silver snuff box, two soft leather purses, one larger and heavier than the other, and a letter. Slitting the seal he unfolded and read Tyrell's neat and flowing hand out loud.

"'My dear Kite, you know the matter of which we spoke touching my wife, Sarah. I have given her into your charge because she' . . ." He paused and looked from Sarah to Milton.

"Would you wish me to leave, ma'am?"

Sarah shook her head. "No, I am not ashamed of having a witness. Do go on, William."

"Very well. 'Because she has long regarded you with more than mere affection and, now that you too are alone in the world, I hope that you will find it in your heart to make her happy. Should either of you not consider this reasonable or practicable, should some rift come between you, I only ask that you do not part in anger. For this reason, beyond binding you to her insofar as your advice may help her, I have made no special provision in my will. You are not without means and I should not wish to sully a friendship and a business relationship with fiscal coercion which would, I know, be anathema to yourself. I therefore wish you to have my snuff box. It was a present from Mulgrave and is supposed to have been fashioned by a Spanish craftsman out of silver from the Inca mines. You are also to have my cane, my small sword and my brace of Cranston pistols. They are for duelling, but I have never had to use them. God grant that you do not, but the times are growing troubled and respect for order is being drowned by men who declare themselves Patriots. You are also to have the accompanying sum of money in the larger of the two purses, which, like the Cranstons, you may need for contingent expenses and are passed to you for that purpose. The smaller purse is to go to Sarah, should she need funds separate from your own. I wish you both God's blessings, and deem myself fortunate to have met you and to have fallen in with a man of . . . ' I am sorry, I cannot read any more. Anyway, he signs himself off in a flattering and, by me, undeserved manner."

The three sat in silence for a moment, then Kite said, tapping his hip, "I have already availed myself of his hanger."

It was a lame jest but served its purpose. Milton rose, "I will put matters in train directly, Mrs Tyrell."

"Thank you, Mr Milton. William, will you see Mr Milton out?"

When the attorney had gone Kite went back into the withdrawing room. "I am at a loss," he said. "Quite overwhelmed."

Sarah sat quite still, staring into the middle distance.

"Sarah," he said quietly. "Are you all right?"

She looked at him. "What does it mean, William, to feel all right? I hardly know." The she seemed to shake her head. "You will stay here tonight, will you not? I could not bear to be separated from you again."

He nodded. "Of course I will stay, Sarah. But excuse me a moment. Zachariah and Jacob are still in the kitchen and I must attend to a few matters relative to my cargo."

"Of course. Please, ask Bessie for some tea."

In the kitchen Kite found a merry scene round the fire. Although not yet three in the afternoon it was as cosy as Christmas Eve, with Jacob and Harper occupying the fireside settle and Mr Borthwick, clearly the worse for a swift imbibing of rum, leaning across the table over which Mrs Ramsden presided. Kite's entry produced a swift and guilty silence, but he was tolerant of their relaxation.

"I am sorry to disturb you, but Borthwick, can you tell me if any interest has been shown in our cargo?"

The clerk shook his head. "No, shur," he slurred, rousing himself. "I only had time to try two houses, but I don't think we will find anything diff'rent tomorrow."

"Sell direct to the distillery," Kite suggested, but Borthwick shook his head.

"'Tis all shown up, shur," he went on. "The cargo's tainted goods . . . Shmells of the burning, shur. Take it to Boshton or New York."

Kite nodded. It was clear that he was going to make no progress tonight. He turned towards Harper and Jacob.

"Do you two get back to the ship. Tell Mr Corrie I'll be off in the morning."

"Aye, aye, sir." Harper rose, leant over and bussed Bessie Ramsden. "Thank you for the tea, Mrs Ramsden. You've a heart as big as my mother's, and no mistake." Jacob grinned widely and the two drew on their boots and coats. Then they left, a swirl of snow and cold air sweeping into the hot kitchen as they did so.

"Bessie, I don't think Mr Borthwick had better go home alone. Have we a bed we can put him in tonight?"

The housekeeper smiled. "Leave him to me, sir. Lord love you, sir, if the old master could see us now there'd have been some strong words said, and no mistake!"

Kite nodded. "Can you find something for us to eat? That ham was most tasty."

"You leave it to me, Captain Kite. You go and join Mistress Sarah and leave it to me . . ."

Kite rejoined Sarah in the withdrawing room, where he unbuckled Tyrell's hanger, laid it on a chair and made up the fire, waving aside Sarah's admonition that he should call one of the servant girls. "That isn't necessary, Sarah, I was making up fires before I even blacked boots."

"We are going to have to leave this place," she said, looking about her. "I do not want to stay here."

"No, I can understand that. I think the best course of action we can take is to try, once I have discharged this cargo, for a lading for Antigua. We will be close enough for the mail to allow us to settle your affairs here, while being away from all the fractious trouble that is brewing in this unhappy part of the world."

"Milton will sell the house; he may even buy it himself. He always admired it and told Arthur he liked it."

"There will be much of that sort of thing if people are terrorised for remaining loyal. Milton and his fence-sitting fraternity will pick all the cherries hanging in the garden."

"That is a quaint fancy," Sarah said.

"That is the first time I have seen you smile properly today, and I am very glad for it."

"And I am glad you are here, William. I keep trying to imagine what it would have been like without you."

And from the memories of the past hours they bent their thought to the future, making plans amid the strange circumstances of their present lives. They had adjourned to the chilly dining room to address the rump of Mrs Ramsden's ham when the pounding came on the door.

Kite opened it to find Jacob on the doorstep, his eyes wide with alarm.

"Sah, come quick! They am beating that damned drum again and Massah Harper says there will be more trouble!"

"Hold hard, Jacob!" Kite said, restraining the black man as he made to run off into the thick snow. "What is it to do with us?"

"We had just got to the wharf, sah, when we saw groups of men hanging about and smelled trouble. Mister Harper, he say, 'What's this? More trouble brewing?' and a man overheard him and told us, hadn't we heard, that damned English captain, he was going to get his come-uppance in real Rhode Island style. Mister Harper, he said that was one helluva good idea and nodded to me and I understood that I was to get back to you, sah."

"The ship," Sarah said, coming into the hall behind him. "They mean the ship, William. First the *Liberty*, then the *Gaspée*, now the *Wentworth*!"

Kite paused a moment, thinking fast. "Come in a moment, Jacob," he said, closing the door behind the negro, who stood dripping on the wooden floor. "Sarah, get me those pistols of Arthur's. Now, where did I put that sword?" He dashed into the withdrawing room, picked up the hanger and buckled it on. Emerging again into the hall he took his coat from the peg and drove his arms into it. "Where is the second mate now, Jacob? D'you know?"

"I reckon he'll be awaiting for us, sah."

But just then a knocking came again at the door and Jacob opened it to reveal the figure of Zachariah Harper. Even in the lamplight Kite could see the blacked eyes and the contusion about his face. Harper grinned. "There were three of 'em, sir. Only two ran away."

"There will be hell to pay if you've killed one of them," Kite said, then asked, "Any news?"

Harper nodded. "Yes, I'm afraid it looks as though they're assembling several boats. I think they're going to take the ship."

"God rot them!" Kite swore, jamming his hat upon his head as Sarah ran back down the stairs with the pistol barrels in her hands, offering him the butts.

"I've loaded them, William."

"Thank you." He took the pistols, checked the pans, closed the frizzens and stuck them in his waistband.

"Be careful, for God's sake," she said, but he bent and kissed her.

"I can't promise to be back, but lock and bar all the windows and doors. The password is 'Wentworth'." He turned to the two men. "Come, my lads!" he said, then opened the door and led them into the falling snow.

Sarah stood at the open door for a moment until they had disappeared into the swirling darkness. They she closed the door and locked it. Leaning her back against it for a few moments, she stilled her beating heart. The pace of events was overwhelming, but no one, neither Kite, nor herself, nor Bessie Ramsden, nor Borthwick, Milton, Jacob or the singularly ugly man named Zachariah, seemed to question what was already a fact: Captain Kite and the Widow Tyrell were already as one.

# Ten

## A Ship for Rhode Island

They stumbled through the thick snow almost blind, glad of its concealment, yet uncertain of their way, until Harper called for them to halt and they heard some drunken shouting which, in ten minutes, led them to the waterfront. Earlier, among the score or so of craft moored along the wharf, Harper had spotted a small rowing boat, too small for the gangs of Patriots that, if the noise was anything to judge by, were already pulling through the soft snowflakes towards the anchored ships.

"At least there will be no lack of warning," Kite said anxiously, as the other two scrambled down into the little boat.

"Aye, but John Corrie might think they're only revellers, sir," said Harper as he sorted the oars. "Christmas is not far off."

"Christmas?" queried Kite, pausing as he turned to step from the ladder into the wildly rocking boat. "I had forgotten about Christmas."

"We're ready, sir," Harper said. The second mate and Jacob had settled themselves on the two thwarts and each pulled a pair of oars.

"Very well, then let's cast off." Kite turned to get his bearings. The boat had no rudder and he would have to set their course from memory. "Give way together . . . Pull starboard . . . Now . . . pull evenly."

A moment later it was as if the world had disappeared. The boat surged along, floating on jet-black water in a tiny circumscribed area which was limited by the cold, pale and falling snow. As each white flake touched the surface of the sea, it vanished, but Kite took no interest in this. He was looking over his shoulder, trying to keep track of the wake and correct its deviation from what he tried to judge was a straight line in the direction to the ship. Somewhere ahead of him he could hear the noise of the Patriots and after a few moments he commanded: "Oars!"

Harper and Jacob raised the oar blades and held them horizontally as the boat carried her way through the water. Kite listened intently, trying to divine the direction of the *Wentworth* from any commotion, but the Patriots had fallen silent themselves.

"They'll have strung themselves out in a line abreast," Harper offered.

Kite nodded. "Just what I was thinking." They glided on in silence for a moment, his anxiety increasing with every passing second. Then, quite distinctly, they heard a shout which confirmed their supposition.

"Here she is!" the voice called, and there were several shouts as each boat identified its relationship with the locator of the *Wentworth*.

Kite was galvanised. "Give way! Pull starboard hard!"

Harper and Jacob laid back on their oars and the boat leapt through the water, the bow rising under the power of their strokes, with Kite in the sternsheets leaning forward as if he could impart impetus to their advance. Then he suddenly sensed something was wrong. A second later there seemed to be a huge black hole in the white curtain of snow as the hull of a vessel loomed out of the night. An instant later they struck her bow-on, the violence of the collision tumbling Jacob and Harper off their thwarts onto their backs. Kite was catapulted onto his knees in the sternsheets, striking his head on Harper's vacated thwart. The second mate lost his oars, and the boat's stem was sprung, so that as they ceased swearing and settled themselves again, Jacob exclaimed, "Boat's leaking, Cap'n!"

"God damn!" Kite said, but a voice above their heads interrupted.

"And what in tarnation may all you noisy buggers be up to running into this ship when any self-respecting Yankee would be tucked up in the lee of bum island?"

Kite settled his hat and looked up. A man's face stared down at them out of the darkness and a moment later another next to him held a light over the side. The assumption that they were part of the general uproar abroad on the waters of the harbour that night caused Kite to recollect himself. "We're looking for the English ship, the *Wentworth*."

"And what have the poor buggers over there done to upset your precious susceptibilities, then?"

"They're defying the Patriot Committee's regulations on the imports of tea."

"Are they indeed," the man drawled. "Well, well, and is that a lynching offence in Rhode Island? Well," he went on, not waiting for a reply, "she's not half a cable away on my larboard beam . . . I should hurry if I were you." The seaman nodded and they looked down to where a dark swirl of water, lit by the glimmer of the lantern, was just beginning to cover the bottom boards.

"Shove off, Jacob. Give way!"

They worked their way clumsily off the strange vessel's side. Jacob stowed one oar and he and Harper carried on with one oar each. Kite looked back and called out his thanks, recognising the schooner next to which he had anchored the *Wentworth* hours ago. As they rounded the bow with Harper holding water, they heard the noise of the attack. There were shouts and a pistol cracked in the darkness. Someone aboard the *Wentworth* was ringing the ship's bell rapidly as an alarm while above the uproar Kite clearly heard Corrie's voice calling all hands.

"Pull, damn you!" he shouted, but their progress was hampered by the rapid increase in the boat's weight as it filled and steadily lost buoyancy. Kite stared ahead, but could still see nothing beyond the white curtain and then, away to the left, he caught sight of a flash and a second gunshot sounded above the hubbub.

"She's filling fast, sir," Harper grunted between tugs at his oar.

"I know," Kite snapped and then he sensed the loom of the ship and hissed, "Hold water!" Over their heads raked the *Wentworth*'s bobstay, and as Harper and Jacob dug their oars into the sea Kite reached up and tried to stop them. The deceleration caused the water in the boat to rush forward and Jacob groaned as it rose round his legs.

"Up you go, Zachariah!" Kite commanded as he clung to the chain bobstay. Harper dropped his oar and Kite turned away as the second mate's feet momentarily kicked in his face and then disappeared into the darkness. "Now you, Jacob!"

Kite followed the quartermaster as the three men scrambled aboard over the bow and paused for a moment by the bitts to gather their wits. They could see the fight in the waist was already over. The Patriots had easily overwhelmed the

*Wentworth*'s anchor watch. They, and the rest of the crew coming sleepily on deck at the summons for all hands, had been shepherded into a confused and disconsolate huddle by the mainmast. The Patriots not guarding the *Wentworth*'s crew were busy assembling lanterns and Kite could see Rathburne's face lit by one of these as he confronted John Corrie, his drawn sword scarcely an inch from the unfortunate mate's breast.

"Pipe down, the lot of you, and no harm will come to you," Rathburne was saying as Kite, drawing his own hanger, stormed aft and shoved his way through his cowed crew.

"Put up that weapon, Rathburne!" Kite brought his own sword blade up and his men surged forward. But his sudden emergence made no impression upon the imperturbable Rathburne, who merely held up his hand to stop any precipitate action by his own men. Calmly he turned his head to Kite and smiled. The next moment Kite felt the jar of sudden impact and the sword was struck from his hand and he, and not Corrie, was menaced by Rathburne's sword-tip.

Kite flushed with mortification as Rathburne rapped out his orders. "Get this mob into two boats and take them ashore. You may go with them, Captain Kite, and count yourself lucky that I am only seizing your ship."

"You have no right, damn you!"

"I have every right, Kite!" The rhyming remark produced a laugh from the Patriots, who immediately began to herd the *Wentworth*'s crew over the side. The lantern light jumped erratically from one face to another as Kite felt a rising tide of furious impotence.

"You cannot treat these men with such inhumanity, Rathburne – let them at least take their personal effects!"

"We will send what we do not require ashore in the morning," Rathburne said dismissively, sheathing his sword. Then he bent and quickly picked up Kite's sword, grasped the blade in both hands and snapped it smartly across his knee. Holding the two parts out to Kite he said, "You should not carry one of these unless you can use it, Captain Kite. It is a gentleman's weapon."

Kite kept a level head. "I shall ask you formally, Rathburne, by what right and for what purpose have you boarded my ship?"

"I am not answerable to you, Kite. I am requisitioning this ship for Rhode Island."

"What? Does Rhode Island have a navy?" Kite scoffed.

"It does now, Kite. Now get over the side while I still have my temper and thank God that you are a man of small significance."

Stung to the quick by Rathburne's cool arrogance, Kite said, "You are a murderer and a pirate—" But he bit his tongue as the tip of Rathburne's sword raked his cheek.

"There, sir, is a mark for you, where once Mistress Tyrell struck you to the amusement of the townsfolk. You may tup her, *Captain* Kite, as the pleasure takes you, for she is as mad a bitch as ever came on heat. But every time you shave, sir, you will recall how John Peck Rathburne fucked you! Now get over the side!"


It had stopped snowing when Kite woke and the humiliations of the night crowded into his recollection. A brilliant sunshine shone through the imperfectly pulled curtains and he sat up, his cheek drawn and scabbed from Rathburne's sword cut. Touching it he groaned with discomfort that was more moral than physical.

"You are awake." Sarah turned from the dressing table where she sat before the mirror in her satin robe, brushing her luxuriant dark hair.

"I am ruined," he said shortly, trying to recall the extent of their intimacy the previous night and then, seeing the blood-soaked shirt and neck linen thrown over the back of a chair, remembering his abject homecoming. He had been exhausted and, having had his wound cleaned up, for the intense cold had stopped the bleeding, he had been helped to bed and recalled only falling into the softness of Sarah's mattress before oblivion claimed him.

"Oh, God . . . They have the upper hand so completely . . . They have taken the ship, Sarah." He ran his fingers through his tangled hair. "What the devil are we to do? We are besieged here, damn them."

"John Rathburne sent three men here this morning about an hour ago. They have brought a portmanteau full of your effects. Your man Ben is below in the kitchen with that ugly fellow Zachariah, the negro and another man named John."

"Corrie?"

"Yes." She skilfully wound her hair into a tight knot and, lancing it to the top of her head, began to assume the cool and

134

elegant poise that he so admired. "The rest of your men were put into a barn for the night."

"That is most kind of the Patriots," Kite said with a vicious and hopeless sarcasm. He threw off the bed sheets and rose, fumbling behind the sidescreen as he urinated into the chamber pot concealed behind it.

"I will send for hot water," Sarah said.

"We must go to Antigua," he said, emerging from the screen, "but first I would lodge a formal complaint with the Governor."

"That will do little good," Sarah replied. "Listen to me. I have been up most of the night and have considered our situation in the wake of what has happened and what I know of matters hereabouts. We have no place here, the Patriots will see to that. It would not matter that we declared ourselves the most ardent admirers of Sam Adams and John Hancock, that we hated King George and drank daily to his damnation, they would never believe us. What titles we have in law will be overturned the instant they begin the rebellion."

"They are intending to *rebel*?" Kite paused as he tucked his shirt-tails into his breeches. It was as though the actual import of what he had been involved in had only just fully occurred to him in the aftermath of the taking of the *Wentworth*.

"You think all this is some kind of childish prank?" Sarah asked in astonishment. "For years these people have committed acts of provocation to one purpose, to goad the authority of the Crown. Today, tomorrow, who knows when? Oh, William, you know perfectly well what this is."

He nodded reluctantly. "Yes. Yes, I do now. In the abstract, as touching the lives of others it was of no great personal moment but now . . . now it is very different."

"And do you wish the seizure of the *Wentworth* to be a *casus belli*? I do not want the murder of my husband to tear this otherwise pleasant place apart!"

"Have you no thoughts of vengeance?"

"On the few, yes. But not on the many. For those who like sheep baaed at Arthur's terrible end I have only contempt, William." Her eyes blazed as she regarded him, half turning on the stool before the dressing table. He was almost choked by the intensity of her passion and her beauty. Moved, he held out his hands.

She rose and came towards him. "We will take our revenge in due course, at a time of our own choosing, William."

He nodded and looked down at her. "I have not been very gallant, have I?"

She shook her head and took his hands. "No, sir, you have not," she said, her mood suddenly lighter. "You wallowed in my bed and this morning, you rose and took a piss in my jordan as though you had every right to be in my bedchamber." She was smiling. "In fact, Captain Kite, your behaviour has been monstrous and you should hang your head in shame."

But he could not match her flippancy. "Oh, Sarah, I have far more than you know to hang my head in shame over. I was disarmed by that man Rathburne on the quarterdeck of my own ship in the most humiliating manner."

"So, sir, your own loss of honour is greater than mine, is it?" she asked with mock severity.

"That is not what I mean."

She put her finger on his lips. "I know, my dear, but please right one wrong before you seek a more conspicuous and public satisfaction. You have only to ask . . ."

It took Kite a moment to comprehend her innuendo and then he threw off as much of his megrimmed mood as he could and dropped to his knees. He looked up at her. "It is too short a time for either prudence or convention, Mistress Tyrell, but what has convention to do with our present situation? You must therefore forgive me all my monstrous presumptions, I beg. Will you therefore consent to do me the honour of becoming my wife?"

She drew him up and they kissed. He felt the urgent pleasure of his arousal and pushed her backwards towards the invitingly rumpled bed, but she drew away smiling broadly, his blood smeared across her cheek. "Not now, William. You forget I have ordered you hot water."

"I am sorry, I had indeed forgot."

And as if she had been waiting outside – and perhaps she had, thought Kite – Bessie Ramsden knocked and brought in a large ewer of piping hot water. After she had gone and Kite bent over the steaming bowl, stripped to his waist and luxuriating in the perfume of Sarah's soap, he heard her say, "We may publish our banns in Boston, William, and marry there."

"After which we must go to Antigua." Kite said, picking up

a razor laid out for him, a distant look in his eyes. "That is our only chance."

"And shall we live in Antigua? I am not certain that I want to live in the Antilles. What shall you do? Go to sea and leave me alone in a strange place?"

He broke off shaving and looked at her, as though suddenly having to encompass her in his plans which were still full of revenge and the longing to obtain redress from Rathburne. "If you are right, my love, and rebellion breaks out in New England, much ill may befall us. You yourself said we have no place here, and we could return to Liverpool." He rinsed his razor and wiped his face, straightening up and turning towards her. "Sarah," he said, "it may be unwise to marry in Boston, or indeed anywhere . . ."

"But why?"

Kite reached for his shirt and wrinkled his nose at its soiled state. Sarah rose and, her face set, opened a drawer and drew out a clean shirt and stock. "Please, use these. But why should we not marry? I have just accepted your proposal," she concluded flatly.

"Because I would not make you so soon a widow twice."

She picked up his dirty linen and rounded on him angrily. "For God's sake, do not play games with my heart! Why should that be so?"

"Rathburne may kill me."

"Then he would have to kill both of us." Sarah said with finality.

"Come, Sarah, that is not logical."

"If I were to come to sea with you it would be perfectly logical."

"But you do not know what you ask."

"Puella accompanied you, did she not?"

"Yes, at the beginning."

"Well, we are at the beginning and I cannot play the role of passive wife any longer in these turbulent times. Think what being Arthur's spouse has meant to me, William, these last thirteen odd years. I am but four and thirty."

"Beg pardon, my love, but the sea life is nothing like anything you have experienced. Besides, having you with me will deprive me of my spirit, for I will be constantly anxious about your safety."

"Are the anxieties of being master of such a dimension? Why, I know of wives in Newport and Providence who accompany their husbands to sea. They are strong women, full of courage, but I do not think them my superiors in spirit."

"But you are a lady, Sarah, and besides . . ." Kite tailed off, taking up the clean crisp linen that had been Arthur Tyrell's.

"And besides," Sarah prompted, "you are concealing something from me."

"No, I have not yet revealed it to you."

"Then do not prevaricate. What is your purpose in returning to sea, if not to trade?" And then the thought occurred to her and she asked frowning, "You cannot mean you intend to seek a commission in the King's service?"

"Join the Royal Navy? No, no." Kite sat and pulled on his left boot. Then he pulled on the other while Sarah put her hands on her hips and shook her head.

"For God's sake, William, tell me what is on your mind and which, it seems, you are too terrified to admit for fear that I will faint, or something. I assure you that I shall not. I have learned to have a strong stomach, one that I venture to suggest may even tolerate the perils of the deep."

Kite stood and stamped his feet into his boots. "Very well, Sarah. But you must understand that if you wish to delay our marriage as a consequence . . ."

"Tell me, confound you!"

"I own another vessel, the schooner *Spitfire*. Do you recall her?"

"How could I forget," Sarah murmured.

"She is in the Antilles and, should matters go as we anticipate, there is every possibility of fitting her as a—"

"A privateer. Of course. I should have thought of it myself. They will issue letters of marque to put an end to Colonial trade and if you do not fit out your ships as privateers you will have lost all chances of profit, for you will not be trading with rebellious colonies tomorrow any more than rebellious colonies will trade with you today!"

Kite nodded. "I see you understand me perfectly. As for yourself . . ."

"But you do not understand *me*, William. I shall come with you in *Spitfire*. I can acquire such skills as may make me useful. I shall be an apt pupil, I promise."

Kite paused in the act of drawing on his coat. It no longer had any pretence at being smart, but it would have to do. "There is no doubt in your mind, is there?"

"None whatsoever. Our souls were linked long ago, William, when our fates were intertwined. This is but the outcome."

They embraced and Kite asked, "And shall our bodies find a compatibility of such a niceness, Sarah Tyrell?"

"Only while our minds remain in such perfect harmony," she breathed, adding, "but not yet, William, not just yet. I must shake the dust," she paused, "and the ashes of this place from my feet."

"To Boston, then. Milton may find us there with his papers and deeds. Shall you have him sell this place?"

"Yes. Or Rathburne's Patriots will burn it."

"I think not. Rathburne's ambitions may be such as to tempt him to sequester it. In the name of Patriotism, of course."

"Of course."

# Part Three

Vengeance

# Eleven

## A Cargo of Flour

"My dear friends," Wentworth said, smiling broadly and bending over Sarah's bosom until his wife's disapproving eye burnt into his back, "I have excellent news for which I know you have been waiting these past weeks."

"When is she due?" Kite asked, leaping up at Wentworth's awaited arrival.

"Patience, patience." Wentworth settled himself in his chair and accepted the tea his wife passed him. "'Tis unpleasantly humid today, don't you think, Mrs Kite?"

"I think, sir, that were you sitting as close to my husband as you are to me you would judge it to be getting hotter by the moment."

"Oh, you do treat me so damnably bad, Mrs Kite," Wentworth said, pulling a face.

"But not as badly as I shall, sir," remarked Mrs Wentworth with as much forced humour as she could muster. "Nor as badly as Captain Kite," she added looking up at Kite.

"And do you sit down, Kite, please. Matters are very trying at present, with all the uncertainty in Boston; I pray you don't add to my troubles by standing up and waving your arms about in that remonstrating manner."

"I am not waving my arms about, Wentworth."

"No, but you look as though you might be in a moment or two."

"For God's sake, Wentworth, what is the news of the *Spitfire*? When is she due?"

"Sit down, and I shall tell you!" said Wentworth brightly.

"He is teasing you, Captain," Mrs Wentworth explained. "He is like a child when the fancy takes him. You have no recourse but to excuse him."

143

Wentworth turned to Sarah. "Do you think me like a child, Mrs Kite?"

"*Very* like a child, sir."

"There," sighed Wentworth, "then I shall sulk like a child."

"And Captain Kite will have to beat you like a child," Mrs Wentworth added, not without a hint of glee, as if in expectation. She nodded at Kite, who had sat down but remained poised expectantly on the edge of his chair. The banter was amusing to a degree, but the long weeks of waiting in Antigua had not been an unblemished pleasure and the constant presence of Captain and Mrs William Kite had strained relations with Mrs Wentworth. Her husband did not greatly care – whether he noticed anything amiss is to be doubted – but Sarah seemed to have swept down out of a New England winter with an overwhelmingly cool elegance that even the heat of Antigua could not melt. The round of social engagements with which Mrs Wentworth had at first encouraged them to occupy themselves had palled once it was obvious that the men of St John's, and in particular the officers of the garrison, were profoundly sensible of Mrs Kite's wonderfully voluptuous charms. Having been herself a garrison lady during her first marriage, Mrs Wentworth began to perceive that she was eclipsed by Sarah. This, and other petty differences, all of which demonstrated the plain fact that the two wives had absolutely nothing in common, produced a coolness between them.

Kite himself was sick of idleness. At their departure from Newport, he had not thought the months would have passed so slowly nor so little have been achieved. Having seen Sarah and those of her servants who wished it removed into Boston, he had paid off the *Wentworth*'s crew from his own private funds, obtaining a half-hearted promise from a few of them that if and when he returned there in the *Spitfire* they would rejoin him. He had told them he would be pleased if they did so but, so uncertain were the times, he urged them to look after their own interests first. He had other matters with which to preoccupy himself and Sarah; his return in *Spitfire* seemed to be too distant to worry about.

The settlement of Sarah's affairs, and the winding up of her interests in her late husband's business, proved a long-winded matter. Twice they had had to leave their lodgings in Boston and ride back to Newport to sign documents at Milton's chambers, a trip that was far from pleasant, given the inflamed mood of the countryside.

To their more personal satisfaction and dispensing with the prolonged tedium of formal mourning, they had published their banns in Boston and married quietly, sustained by their self-preoccupation as lovers through the tedium and imperfections of their long-enforced exile. Neither of them liked Boston, nor did they enter into society in any sense, though Sarah had several friends among the town's population with whom they occasionally dined. The newly-weds were in no position to reciprocate, nor did they feel moved to foster acquaintanceship amid the prevailing atmosphere of uncivilised disorder that dominated Boston. The majority of the citizenry inveighed by one means or another against British tyranny, with broadsheets, newspapers and street-corner gossip everywhere encouraging civil disobedience against the authority of the Crown. Evidence of this was produced at every turn, but centred chiefly upon the troops bivouacked on Boston Common. Such winter quarters contrasted badly with the cosy homes of the Bostonians, and while their officers managed to secure lodgings the common soldiers shivered in their tents, for it was as much a matter of principle for the Bostonians to refuse tea, as to refuse payment for billeting private infantrymen.

Kite had seen Samuel Adams once and had thought of seeking a confrontation with him over the *Wentworth*, but he had been prevented by Sarah, who counselled caution and inconspicuity until they again better controlled their own affairs. Nevertheless they once dined with Governor Hutchinson through the agency of a friend of the Tyrells', and Kite laid before him the circumstances of the illegal seizure of the *Wentworth*. Hutchinson promised "to see what could be done", but Kite soon realised that the man was losing his powers thanks to the damaging effect of revelations from his private correspondence, which had fallen into the wrong hands and had been maliciously circulated by the Patriot party during the previous year. Moreover, rumours were circulating that Hutchinson's civil authority would soon pass to General Thomas Gage, the military commander, and in May these predictions came to pass when it was known that Hutchinson was to sail for England.

To add to their personal uncertainty, it soon became clear that no one in Newport was going to bid for the Tyrells' house, as Kite had guessed. Though unwilling to do so, he and Sarah decided to offer it to Milton at a peppercorn rent, to prevent it falling into the hands of Rathburne or his ilk. With what Kite afterwards described as "a touching display of affected reluctance", the attorney finally agreed to taking a lease on the property in November and Mrs Ramsden had agreed to stay on in the house pending Milton's decision as to whether to remove himself into it or to acquire suitable tenants.

As for the Kites, having spent Christmas of 1773 trudging the streets of Boston seeking lodgings, they were in more comfortable circumstances a year later. Inviting some company to join them in a modest dinner party in their lodgings, they repaid some of the kindness and hospitality they had benefited from themselves. Kite had written to Wentworth, outlining his intentions, but he had replied that until a state of rebellion broke out, "a circumstance I very much doubt will occur, such a thing being so contrary to good sense and so damaging to trade", he could and would employ the *Spitfire* in a profitable manner. "She is not a vessel of any great capacity, but her speed makes her useful," he had added, concluding his reply with the remark that, "there is such a great deal of money to be made at the moment that I should be reluctant to relinquish the vessel and in view of your loss of the uninsured *Wentworth*, it would not be in your interest to curtail her useful voyages for three months at the earliest."

The remark had raised no apprehensions in Kite's mind at the time. He had become reconciled to frustration; inertia begets inertia and he had discovered great pleasure and diversion in Sarah's love-making. Nor did she seem unduly troubled; for her the long years of devoted but lacklustre marriage could at last be set aside and she found Kite a man of consistent and pleasing energy. Otherwise, to combat ennui and to wipe out the shame of his disarming by Rathburne, Kite had taken fencing lessons from a rather indigent army officer who, for a little private income to fund his habit at the gaming tables, gave private tuition. Most of his clientele were Tory gentlemen aware that a nodding acquaintance with self-defence might come in handy in the coming months. Under this tutelage Kite had rapidly improved his elementary technique, learned as a boy with a single-stick.

It had been late March before the transactions were concluded that terminated the business enterprise of Tyrell and Co. The residual property and assets had been transferred to Borthwick, Borthwick and Co., established by Tyrell's chief clerk and his brother, a sea captain from Providence. Kite, having managed to make himself useful to the extent of acting as agent for a number of Boston merchants who were anxious about the future, was at last ready to leave for Antigua and had secured a passage aboard the brig *Savage*. He had carried south to the West Indies a number of commissions undertaken on behalf of several parties, carrying letters of credit to Wentworth and others in Antigua, and securing measures to prevent losses if and when a run on the banking houses was precipitated by the breakdown of order which most now foresaw as inevitable.

Once at sea and caught up in the familiar routine of shipboard life, Kite wondered why he had delayed so long, swiftly forgetting the interminable wait for correspondence referring to all the complexities of Sarah's affairs. In the manner common to attorneys, Milton proved unused, even resistant, to haste. Nor did Sarah wish to leave until every possible knot had been tied and she could depart free of regrets or obligations. After a week enduring the agonies of seasickness, Sarah had found her sea-legs and began to take an interest in her new surroundings. Kite, having nothing to do, had taken the opportunity to school her in the business of the ship, the principles of navigation and of elementary sea lore.

Free of the frenetic atmosphere of Boston and her nausea, the *Savage*'s passage south had proved a congenial hiatus for her. At Antigua, however, further and seemingly interminable enforced idleness combined with anxiety and uncertainty to erode her belief in a future and in Kite's purposeful equanimity. Such had been the pressures of their existence in Boston that she had assumed that once they reached the Antilles a new existence would unfold. He assumed matters would move ahead swiftly, but he learned to his chagrin that *Spitfire* had only just departed and would be gone for many weeks. Having learned this he had at first made no further enquiries, reconciling himself to another wait and explaining matters to an increasingly impatient Sarah. Neither of them now enjoyed a rootless existence, and while their sojourn in Boston had been endured as a finite exile spiced with the novelty of their intimacy, they were irked by their life in Antigua as "guests" forced upon the Wentworths' hospitality.

To these irritating circumstances came the exacerbation of new uncertainty with the news from Massachusetts concerning the events of the 19th of April 1775. British troops sent out from Boston to seize illegal arms caches in Concord township had been opposed by militia drawn up on Lexington Green. The redcoats had dispersed the inexperienced "Minutemen" and marched on, but they had found little in the way of arms at their destination and having spoiled quantities of flour and other alleged "military stores" had began to march back to Boston. This proved to be a very different ordeal, and their return had been harried by highly effective sniper fire from every building on their long route, a profound humiliation for a detachment of British infantry.

For the Patriot party, the day marked not simply a victory over a British "army", but the long-awaited spark to the assiduously laid powder train of popular rebellion. For the men who had harried the British soldiers had not all been radical fanatics, but solid Americans for whom the British excursion into the countryside had been an outrage. In the ensuing weeks such men were coming in from far and wide to dig entrenchments cutting off Boston and transforming the town from the hot-bed of rebellion, to the beleaguered centre of royal authority in New England. Such news arriving in St John's only made William Kite grind his teeth in impotent frustration. He resumed his fencing, taking as a partner Nathan Johnstone who had been mysteriously absent on their first arrival.

Kite had had his first opportunity of speaking confidentially with his former clerk one afternoon as they had rested after a practice bout in a cleared area in the counting house where once as a young man he had lodged. Prompted, Johnstone revealed his own adventures. "I grew tired of Kitty," he said, "and somewhat ashamed of my conduct with respect to Mr Wentworth, who is a decent enough man when all is said and done."

"How did you detach yourself from Mistress Wentworth?"

"I spoke with her husband and suggested that I shipped with Captain Jones to better learn the ropes and see Havana, Guadeloupe, Basse-terre, Jamaica, St Kitt's and so forth." Johnstone smiled sheepishly at the recollection. "He jumped at the notion. I rather think he knew all the time what I was up to – the lady is insatiable, if you'll pardon me for saying so, but it is so undignified in one of her years – and perhaps he had sharpened his own appetites after a period of fasting . . ."

Kite laughed. "Yes, I recall she tried to seduce me once."

"Besides, I had become something of a laughing-stock among the garrison," Johnstone confessed.

"Ah, that I can imagine."

"Well, I removed myself into the schooner for some time, sailed with Jones and visited most of the islands while I have become a tolerable seaman as well. Then I acted as Wentworth's agent in St Maarten until –" Johnstone shrugged – "well, I returned here, delighted to find you back and, if I may say so, sir, so pleasantly circumstanced."

"I think you will find me a less tolerant husband than Wentworth."

"Captain Kite," Johnstone said hurriedly, "please believe I am not that devoid of honour that I would ever, in any circumstances . . . well . . . I mean to say, the matter is unthinkable."

Kite looked archly at the younger man, who had changed since they had last met. "Come, Nathan, let us lay on and see who first scores five."

" 'Twill be you, sir, you have the art to a nicety."

They came *en garde* again and the scrape and clatter of their buttoned foils filled the still warm air of the tropical afternoon.

Such diversions, though pleasant enough, were not satisfactory to the impatient Kite. The mock victories he achieved over Johnstone he wanted translated into real success; the defeats he suffered at Johnstone's hands became small, prickling reminders of Rathburne's unopposed run of luck. He wanted no proxy wins, he wanted blood and ruin to descend upon Rathburne and his vile gang of murderers and incendiaries and this perverse lust began increasingly to fill his being as the weeks dragged by during the long wait for news of the *Spitfire*'s return. It was for this reason that he grew so agitated when at long last that hot afternoon Wentworth walked up from the harbour and announced that he had at last received news of the *Spitfire*.

In that impatient moment he was far from considering Mrs Wentworth's suggestion that he beat his old friend as a joke. "By God, madam, that is a capital idea!" he cried. "Come now, Wentworth, cease your damned games."

Wentworth bent as though cowed. "Oh, oh, help, help," he pleaded in a squeaky voice, "please, Captain Kite, don't flog me!"

"Wentworth . . ." Kite cautioned, an edge to his voice and his face far from seeing the ridiculous and amusing side of Wentworth's conduct.

"She's just come into the harbour," Wentworth announced in a sudden rush, recovering his dignity.

"*What?*" roared Kite. "You have taken all this while to tell me she is already here?"

"Hold hard, Kite, I have asked Jones to come up to the house the moment he has completed his clearances, so you will have to wait an hour or so longer. Sit down, for pity's sake, and possess your benighted soul in patience." He turned to his wife. "Is there perhaps another cup of tea for a thirsty and abused messenger, my dear?"

Wentworth grinned at Kite, then leaned towards Sarah. "Do, I beg you, Mrs Kite, soothe the ingrate," he implored mockingly.

Wentworth's reference marked the strain in the relationship between the two men. Kite had known for some weeks that the delay in *Spitfire*'s arrival had been caused by Wentworth having sent Jones out on the last of several slaving voyages. He had promised Puella he would never again personally profit from such an enterprise and he was exceedingly angry that Wentworth had done so on his behalf. Untroubled by moral considerations of this delicate nature, and bowing only to the imperatives of the market-place, Wentworth had waved aside his objection, justifying his act on the grounds that Kite had "distracted himself on the American coast with no very clear indication of his intentions relative to the *Spitfire*". This, he had claimed, left him free to employ the vessel in the manner he deemed most profitable to the *Spitfire*'s owner. Since the voyage had proved highly profitable, he was unable to comprehend how Kite felt he had the slightest grounds for complaint. He had no idea that Kite would suddenly want his vessel back "on a whim". Kite did not argue; it was enough that she was safe and would be at his disposal. Indeed his principal preoccupation was what he would do with Captain Jones, now that the man had regained his self-confidence along with the habit of command.

In the event, this problem never arose. Jones had made sufficient money to take a small house into which he installed a handsome quadroon with whom he declared he wished to "relax, at least until the coming hurricane season was past, and perhaps for longer".

" 'Tis the languor of his tropical blood," Wentworth had explained with a singular lack of insight and a good deal of prejudice. Kite was not disposed to argue the point. Instead in a burst of released energy he hastily removed every trace of the *Spitfire*'s slaving voyage, constantly aware that in the mahogany-built *Wentworth*, Rathburne and the Rhode Islanders had, as they might themselves say, "gotten themselves a tarnation fine little man-o'-war at a real Yankee bargain price". Refitting and rearming *Spitfire*, he made of her not merely a private ship of war, but a privateer bent on a most private mission.

He received assistance from an unexpected source, Nathan Johnstone, who volunteered to join the ship.

"A privateering voyage," Kite explained, "is in the nature of a speculation. I cannot afford to pay you."

Johnstone waved these considerations aside. "I shall, if you will permit me, venture a little capital and ask that you take me as a gentleman volunteer. I have no desire to remain longer among the islands and to serve with you for a few months will take me north to –" he shrugged – "who knows what?"

"Very well," Kite agreed. "I shall make you gunner. You may take charge of the arms chest, the powder and the shot, along with the guns."

Johnstone nodded with satisfaction. "That seems a very sufficient inventory for a clerk," he said, smiling, as the two men shook hands.

"Now I suppose I must show you the principle of a magazine."

"It might be of use, certainly."

In the last few days of refitting the schooner, Kite felt a mild sensation of panic as the news arrived from Massachusetts. The investment of Boston by rebellious Americans was, it was claimed, of such a provocative and forward nature that General Gage must soon evacuate the town or utterly defeat the rebels. British fortunes in New England now hung, like the Damoclean sword, by a single thread. It was enough. Shipping a quantity of powder and shot and placing it in Johnstone's prepared lazaretto, Kite loaded *Spitfire* with rum and a consignment of imported flour, and on Wednesday the 17th of May 1775 the schooner sailed from St John's, heading for New England.

"I cannot pretend that I am not glad to see them go, my dear," Kitty Wentworth said pointedly, slipping her arm inside that of her portly husband and falling into step with him as he took a turn on their terrazzo as the sun set. "We can enjoy our own and the island's society again now." She paused, threw him a quizzical look and observed, "Your friend Kite is much changed, and not for the better, I am afraid."

Wentworth stopped and turned to his wife. "I fear the same must be said of *his* friend Johnstone. Come, my dear, tell me if you love your husband. Do you?"

"Of course I do," she replied coyly.

"Come then . . ." He took her hand and led her hurriedly into the house, shutting the chamber of their bedroom door and swinging round on her. "Come, madam, I have an urgent need of you!" he said, taking off his coat and kicking off his shoes.

"My dear, you are all haste, surely a little tenderness . . ."

"Devil take it, you have been hot for him for weeks! Ever since you quenched Johnstone." Wentworth advanced on his wife who backed towards the bed, half alarmed and half acquiescent. "Now let me show you what manner of man I can be when my wife is aroused . . ."

"Oh, sir!" she exclaimed, laughing, seeing his engorged state spring from the confinement of his breeches as she fell back upon the bed and lifted her skirts. "It has been some time!"

"Aye, madam, and we shall be glad of their visit if only for this moment . . . of – rapture at – their – departure . . ."

Kite and his wife found Boston a very different place from what it had been but three months earlier. It was now a town under formal siege, with rebel positions straddling the narrow isthmus of the Neck and cutting off communications with the rest of New England. The harbour, overlooked by Dorchester Heights in the south and Bunker and Breed's Hill in the north, was full of shipping. A handful of Royal Naval cruisers, a number of military transports and numerous merchant vessels, both American and British owned, all lay at anchor below the commanding heights.

If Boston had seemed to be full of soldiers before, it was now stuffed to overflowing, British troop reinforcements having arrived during Kite's absence. The contrast was marked by more than a mere increase in numbers, for where before the troops had tended to distance themselves from the hostile townsfolk, now this augmentation seemed to empower the troops, so that they were less self-effacing and conducted themselves with a certain swagger. Kite marvelled at this, particularly among the young subalterns, seeing that since the colonists had so effectively chivvied the British infantry back into Boston after their sally towards Lexington and Concord in April, and had since then prevented them from repeating the exercise. The besieging of Boston by a hay-seed army of militia seemed to him to be a humiliation to which the gay young officers seemed indifferent. Moreover, he soon realised that Boston was short of every necessity and was filled with more than the hungry mouths of several thousand extra soldiers. In fact Boston's political colour had been changed dramatically, for men and women too terrified of the Patriot party to remain in the surrounding countryside had come to seek refuge under the bayonets of the King's soldiers and this wretched population now optimistically awaited the exertions of General Gage and his army to restore them to their homes.

Making his way to the Commander-in-Chief's headquarters after attending to the usual inward formalities at the Custom House, Kite reflected upon the increasingly desperate situation. At the Custom House the Collector's clerk had brought the newly arrived ship-master up to date with the situation and then assured him of a profitable sale of his cargo, particularly if he permitted his own brother to act as agent in order to avoid the painful consequences of government requisition.

"I do assure you, Captain Kite, that between ourselves there is an eager market with payment in ready money for flour, but you must not delay. Once your inwards clearance is processed you may well have to surrender the lot for a pittance."

"Tell me," Kite countered, "have letters of marque and reprisal been issued against the rebels?"

The clerk looked astonished. "No, sir." He dropped his voice to a confidential tone. "There is a marked reluctance on the part of General Gage to admit that a state of open rebellion exists, let alone war!"

"Good God, sir! You mean to tell me that these hostile preparations don't signify?"

"No, sir, they don't. Only two days ago, on the twelfth, the General issued a proclamation offering a free pardon to every person in the province with the exception of John Hancock and Samuel Adams."

"Which fell on deaf ears, no doubt," Kite commented drily.

"Indeed it did, Captain. But if you wish to dispose of your cargo . . ."

"Yes, yes." Kite frowned, thinking for a moment and then asked for directions to General Gage's headquarters. With an assurance to the Custom House clerk that he would let him know directly about the disposal of his cargo he hurried out into the street.

There was an appearance of military activity outside Province House, Gage's headquarters. The open doorway was guarded by two sentries, both wearing the tall caps of men from a grenadier company, while two orderlies held the nervous heads of five officers' chargers. Just as he approached, one of these men grabbed the reins of a sixth horse as it galloped up and its rider slid to the ground and threw them to the orderly. The young scarlet-clad officer fumbled in his saddlebags as the brilliant June sunshine twinkled off the silver crescent of the gorget at his throat. Having drawn out of his saddlebag the bundle of papers he had brought to headquarters, the young man strode up the steps two at a time. Kite made to follow but one of the sentinels barred his way with his musket.

"I have dispatches for General Gage," he lied, adding with more truth, "I am Captain Kite, master of the schooner *Spitfire*."

The soldier looked at him and the briefcase that contained his inwards clearance papers. "Where are these despatches from then, Captain?" he asked with a truculent and suspicious air as his fellow sentry came over, but a voice behind them interrupted.

"Good God! Is that you, Uncle William?"

Both sentries snapped to attention as the officer who had preceded Kite into the dark interior of the requisitioned house retraced his steps. Kite looked from the unco-operative visage of his interlocutor into the good-looking and sunburnt face of Harry Makepeace.

"Good God, Harry! What the devil are you doing here? I thought you had taken a seat in Parliament."

"Long story, but come in, come in." Makepeace waved the sentries away and led Kite through the hallway and into a withdrawing room given over to acting as the ante-room to the adjutant-general's office. "I heard the names 'Kite' and '*Spitfire*' and well, here you are . . . Do you have despatches for the General?"

Kite shook his head. "No, not exactly, but I'd like to see a senior military officer, if you can arrange it. I dare say your own mission warrants a quick entry . . ."

Makepeace laughed. "These?" He held up the papers from his saddlebag. "These, dear uncle, are the daily returns from my regiment. They represent the extent to which military duty is entrusted to a mere captain of infantry in Boston these days," he said ironically.

"I did not know you possessed any great military knowledge capable of more fitting employment, Harry," Kite responded with equal irony and a smile.

Makepeace assumed a serious face and like the Custom House clerk an hour earlier dropped his voice. "Even a young fool just out from England with reinforcements for his regiment and a purchased captaincy knows it is utter folly to allow those damned rebels to dig themselves in and surround Boston. Why, they'll be up on Dorchester Heights and Bunker Hill before Gage—"

"Captain Makepeace!"

"Sir?" Makepeace turned. An officer had opened the door of an inner room. He wore the lace of a major and his outstretched right hand was ink-stained.

"I am waiting for your battalion's daily muster *again*!"

"Major Hayward," Makepeace said with plausible aplomb and turning to indicate Kite, "this is Captain Kite of the schooner *Spitfire*; he has urgent business with the adjutant-general . . ."

"Not as urgent as yours will be if you don't hand over your papers."

"Come, Hayward," said Makepeace, winking at Kite as he handed the papers over, "there is no need to be unpleasant just because you owe me twenty guineas."

"I shall whip your arse at the cart's tail if you are insolent, Makepeace. This is an army headquarters, not a gaming house."

"More's the pity, but what about Captain Kite here?"

"*What* about Captain Kite?" asked Hayward, looking down and studying the muster lists Makepeace had given him.

"I want a letter of marque and reprisal for my schooner, sir, from the Commander-in-Chief in his capacity as Governor of Massachusetts," put in Kite boldly.

"You have twenty-six men sick in the 59th, Makepeace." Hayward looked up at him, ignoring Kite's interjection.

"Some sort of flux, sir. Nothing serious, the surgeon says."

"Fat lot he'll know about it," Hayward said, looking at Kite for the first time and frowning. "What did you say?"

Kite repeated his request adding, "I've a cargo of excellent flour that I shall be pleased to trade for such a commission."

Hayward started, grasping the import of Kite's words. "You want a commission for your schooner to act as a privateer in exchange for your cargo, is that correct?"

"You have it, sir. She was very successful as a private man-o'-war during the last war."

"I can vouch for that," put in Makepeace helpfully.

"I wouldn't, if you wish to render Captain . . ."

"Kite, Major Hayward."

"If you wish to render Captain Kite any kind of service." Hayward sniffed and looked at Kite. "I can simply requisition your cargo, Captain. It would be a lot easier."

"I can be of considerable use to the government, Major Hayward, and I would not advise you to requisition my cargo."

"Why not, pray?"

"I could weigh anchor and go and sell it, along with the gunpowder and shot I have laid by, to the rebels."

"That would be a treasonable act."

"But your taking my cargo without recompense would be another action to discredit His Majesty's name in Massachusetts and I have already lost a ship and my wife has lost an entire business, all of which was taken by the rebels without any compensation from either themselves or His Majesty's Government."

Hayward turned away. "I cannot enter into any discussions about your personal misfortunes," he said over his shoulder as he retired to the inner room.

"Major Hayward," Kite called after him, "you may have a hundred tons of flour for a letter of marque and fifty guineas to clear the pestilence of debt from your shoulders."

Hayward spun in the doorway, his face colouring. "You would try to bribe me, sir?"

"'Tis the way business may be done, sir," Makepeace interjected quickly. "Captain Kite is a man of capital good sense, Major, and means you no affront. Allow me to wipe out your debt, sir, for a letter of marque."

Hayward hesitated. "I shall see what can be done."

"Today, sir," pressed Kite.

"Before I see you at the tables . . ." Makepeace added.

Hayward looked from one to another of them and then, drawing himself up said coolly, "Damn the pair of you. You may discharge your cargo, Captain, and Makepeace, you can pass word to the QMG."

"My pleasure, Major Hayward," grinned Makepeace, saluting the closing door. "Well, Uncle," he said as they strode out into the sunshine and he shook his head at the orderly, "let us take a glass of wine before I return to my battalion. I am intrigued, you said 'my wife' – was that all a fabrication?"

"No, Harry, I remarried. A lady from Newport, Rhode Island, named Sarah Tyrell."

"I was sorry to learn about Puella. And young William."
Makepeace paused and eyed his adopted uncle. "I gather it was
your bereavement that decided you to quit Liverpool and dissolve
your business association with us."

"Yes. That and the fact that Frith was not a man I had any
sympathy with."

Makepeace turned and ducked into a tavern, where he called
for a bottle and sat himself down.

"I am sorry to hear that. I have always found him congenial
enough."

"I am sure you have, Harry, and I am sure he went to some
trouble to be so to you. I found him otherwise."

Makepeace poured the wine and left Kite to pay for it. He took
the opportunity to drop twenty guineas onto the table.

"I thought the sum was fifty," Makepeace said, picking up the
gold coins.

"I do not have that sum with me, and in any case I only
mentioned fifty to Hayward. You expressed satisfaction with
the repayment of his debt."

"You have lost none of your shrewdness, Uncle." Makepeace's
tone was dry.

"Thank you," Kite replied. "I was sorry to hear you are still
gambling."

"Oh, don't be censorious. To be truthful there is so little else
to do. We sit here day after day waiting for God knows what. The
enemy seem to possess at least as much military competence as
we do, which isn't saying much. There was some muttering about
the seizure of the southern heights at headquarters yesterday."
Makepeace sat back and stretched out his legs. "Alongside such
incompetence, a night's gambling seems a small enough sin."

"What are my chances of getting Hayward to comply with my
request?"

"If I remember, a letter of marque is a complicated document,
ain't it?"

Kite nodded. "But it legitimises my actions and I have my own
accounts to settle. If the rebels won't do business our way, I shall
do it theirs."

"Gage has done everything possible to appease them; I cannot
see him making an exception for one merchant master."

"Then my money is wasted."

"I fear it may well be. What will you do?"

"Keep my own counsel."

"You don't change, Uncle William."

"A man only has his character, Harry. It may prove his best friend or his worst."

"Ah, now you sermonise."

"What's the news of your mother and Katherine?" Kite asked, changing the subject.

"They are well, despite your abandonment," Makepeace responded without malice, "though you were kind to sister Kate, I own. She prospers and is engaged to Dr Bennett . . ."

"Ah, that is good news and it does not entirely surprise me. And your mother?"

"She has married Frith. I thought you knew, from your earlier remark."

"No, but I suspected it. And Charles?"

"Ah, my sober and upstanding brother. He has come down from Cambridge with an eye on chambers in Lincoln's Inn and a seat in the House." Makepeace paused. "Truth to tell, Uncle, he would make a better fist of it than myself."

"And what of you? Will you follow a military career?"

Makepeace shook his head and refilled his glass. "Frith thought military experience would stand me in good stead at the hustings so, here I am, eager to serve my King and Country."

"That is very good of you, Harry. I hope his Majesty appreciates your devotion."

Makepeace grinned. "*I* hope that General Gage gives me something useful to do, otherwise my invaluable military experience will consist entirely of gambling, wenching and drinking. Which of the three would you recommend?"

"Ah, there you have me, Harry. I have only ever gambled in business, when I came out evens over all, I suppose. As to wenching, I did little of it, taking up with Puella and remaining faithful to her until her death. Now I have Sarah."

"Whom I must meet. Where is she now?"

"Calling upon friends."

"And of course you don't drink."

"Not to the excess that qualifies me for an opinion, no."

Makepeace drained his glass and stood. "You are dull, Uncle William, but rich and therefore admirable in your own way."

"I am not rich, Harry, I have lost a great deal in America." Kite stood and faced the young officer, holding out his hand.

"I shall remember that when I lead my soldiers to attack the confounded rebels," he said as they shook hands. "Which I suppose we must do eventually."

"I am content to seek my own revenge, Harry."

"I am sure you are, Uncle Will, but do not let that famous character of yours mislead you. Remember your stout masts break in a storm while the gull wafts away to leeward."

"Most poetic, Harry," Kite said smiling and putting on his hat as Makepeace led the way out into the hot sunshine.

"Most philosophic, Uncle Will," Makepeace corrected. The two men were about to part when Makepeace hesitated. "There is something . . ."

Kite noticed a troubled look cross the young man's face. "Yes? What concerns you?"

Makepeace looked straight at Kite. "I had every reason to dislike you, Uncle William. Frith was strong in his language when referring to you, but Kate said his opinion was prejudiced, so I am entrusting you . . ." He drew a signet ring from his right hand and handed it to Kite. "Give this to my brother, will you? There's a good fellow."

And then he was gone. Kite stood a moment watching him return for his horse. He felt a chill despite the heat of the sun and shuddered. Then he admonished himself for falling foul of the spirits Puella would have said hung about the young man's departing figure.

Looking down at the ring he slipped it into his waistcoat pocket. "Bloody fool," he muttered of himself and, turning, went in search of his wife.

# Chapter Twelve

## Boston

During the next two days Kite waited in vain for his letter of marque. Despite Hayward's remark that he might discharge his cargo he waited upon events, in case he might yet require its value as a bargaining counter. He called daily at Gage's headquarters at Province House but never succeeded in seeing Hayward again, despite sending in messages. Nor did he catch Harry Makepeace bringing in the muster lists of the 59th Foot and he gradually gave up any hopes of legitimising his meditated vengeance. On the morning of the 16th of June, having spent the night on board *Spitfire*, he had himself pulled ashore and landed on the Long Wharf at the foot of King Street. Instead of making for Province House as had become usual, he turned right and headed for the lodgings in Hanover Street where he had installed Sarah so that she might enjoy a little society while he fretted about the vessel.

Breaking his fast with her he announced his mind was made up. "I am growing weary with waiting, my dear. I do not wish to languish twice in this godforsaken place and am considering acting entirely on my own account." He looked across the table at her, anxious to know what she would say.

"*Entirely* upon your own account?"

He nodded. "It seems I must. The rebels have made of this a civil war and I am not minded to let them cruise in the *Wentworth* without doing something about it. Today I am intending to sell the cargo to the highest bidder, for it is clear that the military have forgot all about me."

"Well, I have some news for you, William, which I think you will account good."

"Oh? Please, do tell me."

"Yesterday evening, after you had left me to return to the

*Spitfire*, I received this letter. You have the knack of inspiring loyalty, Captain Kite."

"I do?" Smiling at her, Kite took the paper Sarah held out to him and read it.

> Dear Madam,
>
> Having seen Notice of the Arrival of the Spitfire, Schooner, under Your Husband's Command and having made it My Business to Acquaint Myself of Your Lodgings, I should be Obliged if you would Make Known to Captain Kite that I and Six or Seven other Stout Fellows are Desirous of Joining Him should He find Employment for us. I shall say no more save that a Matter Touching Your Recent Misfortunes is Known to Me and that, Notwithstanding any future Acquaintanceship or Employments, I am Most Desirous to Make Known certain Facts to Captain Kite or to Yourself. Please send Word at Your Earliest Convenience to, Your Humble Servant, ma'am,
>
> Zachariah Harper.
> At the Sign of the Bear, Fish Street, Boston
> Nine of the Clock Post Meridian, this 15th of June 1775

"Well, well. Zachariah Harper. I had almost forgotten him. He speaks of six or seven stout fellows. I shall send word for him shortly, but I must first settle things with you."

"I know what you are going to say, William, but I am not going to be left here in Boston. You have just called it a godforsaken place and I do not think it will improve; rather otherwise, I guess, so I wish to make it quite clear that nothing is going to persuade me otherwise than to keep my word and accompany you wherever you go. My happiness is not to be found anywhere other than by your side."

"I am overwhelmed."

"I have not been idle these past two days. I have not told you before because I knew we should dispute the matter, but now it is too late for disagreement. You have no option but to fall in with my wishes."

"I have no wish to quarrel, Sarah."

"That is as well." She smiled at him and he was moved by the radiance of her expression. "I have almost completed my trousseau and will be ready to join you this evening."

161

"Your *trousseau*?" Kite was utterly puzzled. He had long expected that Sarah would not sit supinely ashore and, truth to tell, he had no great desire to leave her behind. The strategy had not worked with Puella and was even less likely to do so with the headstrong Sarah. Besides, he would rather she threw her lot in with him entirely, for he had ceased to think of life as a preparation for tomorrow, but a matter for today.

Sarah shrugged. "Perhaps I should say my traps, or my dunnage. I forget the nautical noun. In any event I have acquired some boots and breeches and will look as pretty as these British subalterns I see mincing about the streets . . . By the by, have you noticed there is a lot of activity in the streets today?"

"You mean military activity?"

"Yes."

"I cannot say that I noticed, but perhaps you are right."

"Well, you will fill your head with freight rates and stowage factors, so I suppose I cannot expect you to be observant as well."

"I have been filling my head with other matters, but I suppose today I must think of obtaining ballast." Kite drew the napkin off his lap, wiped his mouth, rose and leaned over his wife. "Do you see if you can buy a dozen bottles of oporto, a decent cheese or two, a dozen laying hens and do the duty of a wife at least for today before you pull on breeches."

"Very well," Sarah said, rising in a susurration of silk, "though they will cost a great deal."

"No matter."

"Very well. I shall be ready to leave before sunset."

"I shall try and come for you myself, otherwise the boat will wait by Woodman's wharf."

"You may send Zachariah. I should like to see his misshaped countenance again."

"Then I must go and seek him out."

Zachariah Harper was not at the Sign of the Bear, so Kite took himself to the Custom House and found the clerk who had performed his inwards clearance.

"I think you are too late, Captain," the man responded when Kite raised the issue of discharging his cargo.

"What d'you mean?"

"Would you care to borrow the long glass, sir." The clerk indicated a large telescope resting on a rack secured to the wall.

Kite picked it up, went to one of the several windows that overlooked the harbour and levelled it on his schooner. A lighter lay alongside and, conspicuous in the sunshine, the scarlet uniform of a British officer told its own story.

"They have requisitioned it, by God!" he exclaimed, lowering the glass and turning to the clerk, who nodded.

"I did emphasise the necessity of acting in haste, Captain," he observed dolefully.

Kite closed the glass with a snap and returned it to its resting place. "A plague on both your houses," he said, half to himself.

"I beg your pardon, Captain?"

"No good will come of any of this, you know."

"Any of what, exactly, Captain?"

"Civil war," he said.

"D'you think it will come to that?" the clerk asked, his face no longer wearing the bland expression of bureaucratic time-serving, but the concern of a Crown official in a position of obvious and potentially unpopular faction if the rebels took Boston.

"It's my experience that it already has," Kite said, picking up his hat.

He was about to leave when the clerk asked, "Would you care for your outward clearance now, Captain? It might help you later."

The appeal for help, laying Kite under at least a technical obligation to aid the clerk if and when events warranted it, was transparent. But the offer also played into Kite's hands. "Very well," he said, waiting impatiently while the clerk made it out.

He walked from the Custom House in a fury at losing his cargo, but his boat was nowhere to be seen and he recalled he had sent it back to the *Spitfire*, intending to remain ashore until after noon. Now, unless he hired a boat, he was marooned while the military authorities seized the cargo of flour for their own purposes. He calmed himself. The troops had been pushed to the limit of their endurance in Boston and he should not so far forget his own humble origins to begrudge them their daily bread. Besides, it would be utterly futile to protest against the removal of his cargo and while he wondered, for a self-deluding instant, if Hayward had actually organised the drawing up of a letter of marque, he doubted it. In short, he wished for no further delay. Calming himself he decided to accept the fact that he could not

easily reach his ship. There were no obvious boats plying for
hire and he recalled the authorities had been busy requisitioning
them too, so he abandoned any notion of rushing out to the
*Spitfire* and involving himself in a tedious row he could never
win. Having met Hayward and his military methods, he believed
that like the situation he had found himself in at Liverpool, it
was sometimes better to cut and run, keeping a distant but more
important objective in mind. Suddenly resolved, he headed at a
brisk walk for the Sign of the Bear.

Harper was not at his lodgings but, just as he wheeled away
to seek a cargo of shingle for ballast, another familiar face hove
in sight.

"Jacob!"

The big negro turned and recognised his old commander. "Cap'n
Kite! Why, sah, 'tis wonderful to see you." His grin was heartening.
"Massah Harper has all the men mustered and we was thinking
of taking a boat out to your little schooner. Why sah, she look
damn fast!"

"Well, Jacob, she schoons with the best of them, that's a
certainty." Kite smiled and nodded his pleasure at seeing Jacob.
"It is good to see you. Tell me, where is Mr Harper now?"

"He sent me back here to the tavern, to pick up his portmanteau.
He's with the other men at Hutchinson's Wharf."

"Has he had any success at finding a boat, Jacob?" Kite
asked.

"Seems to be some difficulty, sah, but if you stand fast but a
moment, Cap'n, I'll be right back . . ."

The sun was hot on Kite's back as he waited for Jacob to
return. Sarah was right, there *was* an increase in military
activity this morning. Some of the boats from the men-of-
war anchored off the town, the *Glasgow*, *Somerset* and *Lively*,
were assembling in the dock south of the North Battery, as
though some movement were being meditated. Kite stared south
across the sparkling waters of the harbour to where Dorchester
Heights rose. Was Gage intending to occupy the elevated position? Was that why all the boats were being requisitioned? It
made sense, of course, for if the rebels raised batteries upon
the eminences, they would command the anchorage and thus
reinforce the besieging works about the town. Boston and its
harbour would become untenable and what that meant to the
position of the Crown authorities was unthinkable. It was surely

something to be avoided at all costs, even by the appeasing Gage.

"Captain Kite!"

Kite turned to see Harper approaching, his hand held out and his ugly face cracked by a smile of genuine pleasure.

"Zachariah!" They shook hands and Kite said, "I thought you were at Hutchinson's Wharf – I have just met Jacob."

"Ah, well there are no boats to be had, so I thought that I would come back here and save Jacob the labour of carting my gear."

"I have my own boat coming alongside in an hour or so," Kite explained, "so we can take her, but tell me how you are."

They exchanged pleasantries and Kite learned that although most of the *Wentworth*'s crew had dispersed, the passage of time had brought half a dozen back to Boston, all of whom were willing to ship out again with Captain Kite.

"Why me, Zachariah?"

"They trust you, sir, and the experience of being kicked out of the *Wentworth* has turned them against the rebels. Besides, most have no life ashore here, being from the Antilles or Liverpool, and seek only employment afloat."

"Come," said Kite, "let us walk a little and I will explain our situation." The two men walked along the quays, heading north along Fish Street, in the direction of Ship Street and the North Battery. Kite explained his failure to obtain a letter of marque but his intention to attempt the recapture of the *Wentworth*, the presence of Sarah and Johnstone as gunner, and his need of men willing to risk their lives in their commander's interests. "I make no bones about it, Zachariah, I want only willing volunteers. I have yet to put this proposition to the men on board, but I would be obliged if you would tell me whether you think your men will serve under such terms."

"If you take the *Wentworth*, sir," Harper asked, "she will be restored to you. What then is the inducement for the men?"

"Good pay for four months and a bonus if I take the *Wentworth*."

"We could be adjudged pirates . . ."

"I think not, unless by the rebels in some court of their own creation. I am willing to risk that."

"You have every confidence in your enterprise."

Kite stopped and confronted him. "I may fail, Zachariah, but I shall not give up because the British Governor of this province has not the wit to protect the rule of law." He paused, then asked, "Well, what about you yourself?"

"Me?" Harper looked surprised. "Oh, I'm your man, sir. Don't fret, I'm certain the rest will be too, but I'll sound them out."

"And try and be discreet. I doubt we can keep the matter secret in this place. It would be better if we wait until we are all on board."

"Aye, aye. I shall see to it."

"Very well," said Kite, satisfied. "Now, do you bring your men to Woodman's Wharf while I shall try and find a cargo of ballast and I will meet you and your volunteers there in, say –" he looked at his watch – "an hour."

Kite had no luck in securing any ballast. The siege had halted all outward trade and although some of the ships lying in the harbour had secured ballast, many still required it before they would be able to sail to seek a homeward cargo elsewhere along the coast. The chances of this were diminishing daily, for the news arriving in Boston by every hour indicated that, far from the rebellion being confined to New England, there were signs of colonial truculence everywhere. In short the normal flow of American exports was falling off. This further frustration only served to worsen Kite's temper when he returned to the rendezvous where he found Harper and his men waiting.

Explaining the situation to Harper, he expressed his annoyance. "It puts paid to a swift departure," he said.

"We can get our own, sir."

"I had thought of that, but any landing hereabouts will attract the attention of the rebels."

"Then we can land on one of the islands in the outer harbour."

Kite looked at the ugly face of the American. He was grinning and Kite laughed and slapped him on the shoulder. "Damn me, Zachariah, why in God's name did I not think of so simple a solution?"

Harper shrugged. "Don't ask me, Cap'n."

"By Heaven, you've quite restored my spirits!"

"Where there's a will, there's a way, they say."

"And they are damn well right!" Kite cheered up, particularly as at that moment he saw the *Spitfire*'s longboat picking her way through the anchorage, her oar blades flashing in the brilliant sunlight.

During that afternoon Kite and the schooner's company took little notice of events elsewhere. The sudden withdrawal of lighters, which brought an abrupt halt to the discharge of the cargo of flour, served as a welcome relief by withdrawing the gang of wharf-labour, rather than alerting them to impending military events of any great significance to themselves. The rumours that Dorchester Heights were shortly to be occupied by the British seemed so sensible, and the operation so overdue, that it was dismissed as a matter for the authorities to be getting on with. Kite and his men had other fish to fry.

To his satisfaction, Kite discovered that no one had any misgivings about serving aboard the *Spitfire* and that all were willing to enter into formal articles, to be signed the next forenoon, binding themselves to a four months' term of service during which the recovery of the *Wentworth* was to constitute their chief objective. At the termination of that period, they would either be re-engaged or discharged with their pay in Boston, New York, or St John's, Antigua.

On the passage from Antigua to Boston, Kite had shared the watches with the *Spitfire*'s mate, her former slaving mate, Hamish Lamont, with Johnstone standing a watch alongside Kite to gain experience. Now he appointed Harper as his second mate and Jacob as an additional quartermaster, drawing up a watch bill with the customary stations for sail-handling and action. He would rather have had Harper as his mate, but Lamont was a quiet, competent enough officer whose only fault so far had been to allow a young subaltern sent out by the Quartermaster General's office to persuade him to open the schooner's hatches in order that the army might seize the cargo of flour. Lamont was apologetic, but Kite waved the incident aside and as the lighters were withdrawn the matter blew over.

Once Kite had consulted Lamont over the watch bill, the two men set to drawing up the orders for the regulation of the *Spitfire*. At sunset Harper was sent ashore to pick up Sarah as arranged. When she arrived, Kite left her in the cabin to settle herself and took a turn on deck. The evening was warm and in the waist some of the men had gathered to smoke and sing songs. Over the almost windless waters of the harbour the stillness of the night settled, and the anchor lights of the men-of-war, the merchant vessels and the military transports joined the lamps and lanterns in the houses and taverns along the waterfront, their reflections long tongues that flickered on the black water.

Kite sent for Harper and when the second mate joined him he asked, "In your letter to my wife you mentioned, if I recollect the phrase aright, that you knew something about a matter touching my misfortunes. I presume that you referred to the loss of the *Wentworth*. Was I correct?"

"Indeed, sir, you were. I happened to ship in a snow owned in Boston but trading with Rhode Island. I found myself among men of the radical persuasion and dissembled to the extent of not disagreeing with their sentiments. Fortunately none of them knew me and we encountered none that did so, since we generally called not at Newport but at Providence. Anyway there is great agitation in Rhode Island and the representatives which they have sent to what they term their Congress have been charged to form a rebel naval force. The names of Whipple and Rathburne are much talked of as being men fit to lead such a squadron either in the name of Rhode Island or of the United Colonies. Whipple commanded a privateer called the *Gamecock* in the last war and is thought to be a capable man. Of course I listened when they mentioned Rathburne, and upon enquiry as to whether this navy would have any ships, they said that it already had, Captain Rathburne being in command of a fine frigate-built ship, the *Rattlesnake*. Admitting that I did not know of her, and enquiring what was her armament and so forth, I was told that she had only lately been acquired, that she had been a British vessel named the *Wentworth*. Now she is armed with eighteen guns and fitted to cruise against British trade anywhere between Halifax and New York. I dropped the matter after that, and kept my own counsel."

"That was wise of you."

"I had little option, Cap'n. They made other remarks regarding their collective smartness in outwitting the dumb fools aboard the ship . . . You can guess I had no choice but to pipe down."

"Of course."

"I shouldn't be sorry to wipe the smiles from their faces, though," Zachariah said. He stifled a yawn. "If you'll forgive me, Cap'n, I must get my head down. I've the anchor watch at midnight."

"Not at all, Zachariah. And thank you for the intelligence. It's a long stretch of coast, but who knows what tomorrow will bring."

# Thirteen

## Bunker Hill

Kite woke in the night and lay in the darkness listening to the faint noises of his schooner. The vessel lay almost motionless in the still, calm water, with only a faint creaking coming from the rudder stock as it moved slightly, constrained by the sennit-work beckets looped over the tiller on the deck above. Beside him the faint sound of Sarah's breathing came to him, and as though aware of him being awake, she turned uneasily. He felt supremely happy, as if neither the night nor the future held any fears for him, though both were pregnant with possibilities.

He pondered this, for such a grim hour was usually filled with unbidden horrors and apprehensions. Yet the feeling of well-being persisted and he realised that for months that had run into years he had never felt any sense of tranquillity. Even though the prolonged period of sadness following the death of Puella had ended with his marriage to Sarah, the seemingly interminable difficulties of settling their affairs and the unsatisfactory sojourn in Antigua had given him no fulfilment. Indeed the difficulties seemed to him to be fate's recompense for the joy of his love for Sarah. For although this had always seemed like an oasis in a desert of desolation, like an oasis it could only be left for further travail through the wilderness. Now, however, all seemed different. He felt a sense of purpose that had begun to form as he had undertaken the simple task of assembling his crew and drafting his standing orders to them. This and the satisfaction of reassuming full command of the *Spitfire*, free of the constraints of consignees' demands, had been crowned by Sarah joining him, throwing in her lot with an abandon that stirred him. He turned towards her.

It was already growing light and he could see the detail of her beautiful face on the pillow beside him. A wisp of hair drifted over a cheek and he looked down over her body as it lay under the light coverlet.

"You are awake." Her voice startled him and he looked at her face again, bent and kissed her. She drew back the sheet. "Come," she said, and he moved over her tenderly as the dawn flushed the eastern sky.

Afterwards they fell asleep and it was late when Bandy Ben woke them with news that the whole place was in uproar.

"Why is that?" Kite asked, reaching for his breeches.

"Because the rebels are here," Ben said with a confusing lack of accuracy.

"You had better go up on deck, my dear," Sarah urged, thinking like Kite that the Americans had attacked Boston itself.

On deck in the brilliant sunshine of mid-morning, Kite found the entire crew lining the rail. He joined Harper and Lamont, who had their telescopes trained on Boston.

"What the devil's going on?" Kite asked. "Are the rebels in Boston itself?" he asked, his tone full of incredulity.

"No, sir," said Harper turning and handing over his glass, "take a look above the North Battery."

From the position of the anchored schooner, the North Battery formed the visible extremity of Boston. Beyond, on the far side of the entrance to the Charles River, was a low hill, marking the end of the Charlestown peninsula. The hill rose to a greater height known as Bunker Hill which, from Kite's vantage point, lay directly above the nearer North Battery. On both hills could be seen swarms of men, the brown scars of earthworks under construction and the occasional brief flash of a swung pick or shovel catching the sunshine.

"Well, I'm damned."

It was quite clear what had happened; either as a matter of coincidence or of pre-emptive initiative, the rebel commanders had decided to occupy Bunker Hill on one side of Boston before the British claimed Dorchester Heights on the other.

From beyond Boston, unseen in the Charles River, came the boom of gunfire and Kite noticed a small brown shower of earth fly up, as one of the warships pitched roundshot into the rising entrenchments.

"This will set the cat among the pigeons," Harper remarked. "General Gage will have to do something now," he added, to which Kite could only agree.

"There's a flood-tide running," Lamont said, "and high water is about two o'clock this afternoon; surely they'll not try pulling barges and flat-boats across the Charles River with the ebb under them."

"It will take time to muster the troops, though," said Kite, recalling his own brief military experience in the taking of Guadeloupe years earlier, "and they'll need artillery to dislodge the rebels."

They could hear the distant rattle of drums beating and, perhaps more imagined than perceived, though it seemed real enough in their recollection afterwards, a buzz rising from Boston itself. Like a disturbed hive, the town would be swarming with troops and citizens. Some would be eager for the moment of decision that seemed now to force itself upon the reluctant Gage, some fearful of the outcome. Kite could guess that many of the military would be all agog to drive the insolent rebels from their position on Bunker Hill, while a few more perceptive souls might regard the task with some concern.

"May I see?"

Kite turned at the sound of Sarah's voice. She wore her grey silk day-dress and her hair was loosely caught up at the nape of her neck, so that the light breeze caught it, while the sun shot lights through it. He thought her very lovely as she steadied the glass against a stay and levelled it on the distant hill. For a moment they remained contemplating the rebel activity, aware that the crew were equally fascinated by the turn of events, then Sarah asked, "Should we not do something?"

"Do?" Kite said, frowning. "What can we do?"

"Well, we cannot just sit here like the audience at a play, surely?" Sarah lowered the telescope.

Kite was nonplussed. "Is it our business to do anything?" he asked, looking at his two officers, as though seeking some reassurance from them as men in the face of this odd, female notion. Both men shrugged and shook their heads, then Johnstone asked, "What do you mean, Mistress Kite? Have you an idea in what way we might prove useful?"

"General Gage will send his army across the river to attack the enemy, surely," Sarah said. "And if so, may we not assist?"

"They will go over in flat-boats, harbour lighters such as the one which took part of our cargo yesterday, and the boats of the men-o'-war—" Kite began, but Sarah interrupted him.

"Well, we have a longboat they can use."

"Yes, but they will not require our help," Kite assured her.

"And we have some guns," she persisted.

"Sarah," Kite responded, a hint of exasperation in his tone, "the *Somerset* has a broadside of over thirty pieces."

"And you don't have a letter of marque," Sarah riposted quickly.

Kite saw her logic. "You think that by helping Gage we will ingratiate ourselves to the extent of the General issuing us with a letter of marque?" He laughed at her. "I am sorry to disappoint you, Sarah, but I think this will occupy the General's mind with rather more important matters than a letter of marque for a would-be privateersman."

"Maybe your wife has a point, Captain," said Lamont, "not so much in respect of the letter of marque, but we may be able to assist a little and the benefit to the men of firing the guns would prove useful."

"That is a point, sir," Harper put in.

Kite vacillated. It was true that they might be able to do something, but they might equally get in the way and incur the displeasure of the authorities. Then the second mate added, "It would not take long to weigh and work our way across the harbour."

Kite felt himself being boxed into a corner. On the one hand he was reluctant to get involved. He had a lingering feeling that to do so would compromise the clear and happy intent with which he had woken in the early hours of that same morning. On the other hand he was aware that to act in a manner offensive to the rebels was long overdue, both personally and nationally. At the same time his rejection of an entreaty from Sarah, coming so soon after their love-making, seemed an unkind and dismal response and Sarah, as if divining his train of thought, came to his rescue.

"There will be wounded if there is fighting," she reasoned.

"Aye, we could do something there," Lamont said.

At this point Johnstone rejoined them. He had been studying the fortifications on the hills from the forecastle and Sarah turned to him as to an ally, asking him for his opinion.

"Well, I'm no strategist, but I suppose that it is better to be involved than to sit here and watch."

"Very well, then," Kite said, "man the windlass and the halliards."

An hour later they anchored again some three cables east of Moulton's Hill. To the south-west of them, lying in the narrow strait between Boston and Charlestown where the Charles River debouched into the outer harbour, the *Falcon*, *Lively*, *Somerset* and *Glasgow* lay, their guns firing at the rebel positions ashore. Both Bunker Hill and the lower eminence in its front, known as Breed's Hill, now bore well-defined entrenchments and they could see the white and grey of the rebels' shirts as they continued to ply pick and shovel to the grassland. Over on the Boston side a battery at Copp's Hill was opening fire on the rebel positions while on the placid waters of the harbour, which sparkled under the hot noon-day sun, a flotilla of some thirty or so boats began to slowly cross the Charles River, heading for Moulton's Point.

The brilliance of the day added a fairground aspect to the occasion. The sun danced not only upon the water, but upon the oar blades of the boats, and twinkled on the bayonets of the soldiers crammed into them. Up on the hills, whose altitude though not great was now more obvious to the observers aboard the *Spitfire*, they could see the rebels not as remote dots, reflecting points of light, but men preparing for battle. Yet despite this, there seemed no great drama in the moment, for it was too pretty to be the prelude to slaughter. Even the gouts of earth and stones sent up by the guns of the warships and Copp's Hill seemed mere theatrical tricks.

Staring through his telescope, Kite raked the shore of the Charlestown peninsula and noticed the works which extended off the flank of Breed's Hill, a stone wall that ran to the foreshore and was surmounted by a rail fence. He pointed it out to Lamont and Harper.

"They are manning it," he said without removing the glass from his eye, "and I think it might be in range of our long chase guns. We have our colours hoisted and at least as legitimate a reason for engaging the rebels as they have of threatening us; shall we try a shot or two?"

"I have no objection, Captain Kite," said Lamont.

"Nor I, sir," added Harper, grinning. "We shall have to close the range, though. If we get the anchor a-trip and let the tide carry her upstream a little?"

"Very well," said Kite closing his glass with a snap. "Lying to the flood like this, we shall need to clap a spring on our cable and manhandle the starboard bow chaser into a midships port, but let us see what we can do."

The casual consent of the commander set the Spitfires into action. Since the order had been given to shift their anchorage they had been in excited anticipation that they would be up to some form of mischief before the day was out. Now they turned-to with a will. Harper led a few men forward to haul short the anchor cable and let the schooner drift closer in, while a second party of seamen eagerly slipped the breechings of the starboard six-pounder bow chaser and dragged it aft. A third group ran the smaller four-pounder out of its port and a fourth hauled a rope from the starboard quarter, outside the schooner, and made it fast to the anchor cable as Harper veered this and brought *Spitfire* up to her anchor again. This, the spring, was then adjusted so that by sharing the schooner's weight between cable and spring the *Spitfire* was slewed across the tideway allowing her six-pounder to be brought to bear. By manning the helm, she was held more or less steady while the six-pounder was laid on the rail fence and the line of militia behind it.

By this time a column of redcoats could be seen advancing from Moulton's Point, parallel to the shore towards the rail fence. It was clear to Kite that the British intended to attack along the low ground and envelop the higher position on Breed's Hill and that his gunfire might indeed prove of some use to the advancing infantry. To what extent this was true he was never to know, for the six-pounders moving forward with General William Howe's light infantry companies had been supplied with roundshot for twelve-pounders. Moreover when they loaded grape to clear the enemy, the boggy ground prevented them from getting close enough to be effective.

On board the schooner Harper insisted on laying the *Spitfire*'s six-pounder, and he judged the matter to a nicety, his first shot ploughing up the ground in front of the rail fence with a fine feather of earth and pebbles. Kite saw the fall of shot quite clearly, as he did the second where it struck a perceptible shower of stones up and threw a few men back out of the rebel line. He was equally ignorant of his target, who were Colonel John Stark's New Hampshire infantry, but his shot, though it wounded a few men, actually fell on a second rail fence thrown out in front of his main position by Stark to encumber the British approach. Thus his action only stiffened the resolve of Stark's soldiers so that, as the British advanced on them and Kite was compelled to hold his fire, they were as steady as regular troops.

Kite and his company watched in dismay as the rebel volley fire, controlled by Stark and other officers who were familiar with British musketry drill from their own experiences in the Indian Wars, stopped the advancing column. Despite pressing forward again, the British were met by a second volley, and then as they tried to clear the farmers' boys from their positions with a rapid bayonet charge, by a third.

For a few moments the disciplined order of the column dissolved. As the smoke from the volleys of the rebels rose in clouds, the British infantry milled about in front of the rail fence, firing piecemeal in a furious, frustrated response. To Kite, watching intently through the glass, memories of just such a moment on Guadeloupe flooded back. His heartbeat quickened and a lump rose unbidden in his throat, for then the men with whom he had impetuously charged had carried the field, but he was now watching brave men on the edge of defeat. Even as the realisation came to him the British infantry began falling back, then he could see beyond them another column, which had struck across higher ground towards the American positions, also in retreat.

"Open fire again!" he yelled, lowering the glass, but the tide was turning and it was some moments before the spring had been adjusted and his gun's crew could again lay their weapon upon the rail fence. By then General Howe's men had reformed and were advancing again, the greater portion of the British heading not for the rail fence but the redoubt which crowned Breed's Hill. The light infantry, however, persisted in their attack upon Stark's position and were received and driven off in the same manner.

Watching the British infantry on the higher ground Lamont exclaimed, "They are wearing their knapsacks!" They all stared as the distant waves of redcoats toiled up the hill. "Why in God's name would they want to do that in this heat?" he asked, looking round, but he received only shrugs in response, for it was clear that the rebel position was not going to fall to the British regulars as easily as they had anticipated. As the second attack crumbled and the red-coated infantry fell back again, more boats were seen crabbing across the Charles River from Boston, bearing reinforcements to join a large body of soldiers from the earlier attacks who now massed on Moulton's Point, where they were dumping their knapsacks. Amid these men, the observers aboard *Spitfire* could quite clearly see wounded soldiers being borne down the hill, while lying in front of the rebel entrenchments small, individual red dots told their own story.

"It is not going well," Sarah said, her voice half questioning, as if seeking assurance that, on the contrary, it was all some dreadful ruse which would produce victory in a few moments.

"No, my dear," said Kite, his own tone harsh, "it is not going well. In fact it is damnable."

"There are dead and wounded on the hillside."

"Yes, there are."

"If we sent away our boat, William," she said in a low voice, as though her earlier suggestion had been responsible for all this death and destruction, "we might be able to offer them some help."

"Yes," said Kite hurriedly. "It is infinitely preferable to pitching shot . . . Get me the apothecary's chest." He turned to Lamont. "Bring the longboat alongside, Mr Lamont, and have her manned."

He was halfway to Moulton's Point, urging his boat's crew to pull as hard as they were able, when Howe launched the third attack, straight up the hill in the hot afternoon sunshine. He watched the red lines waver as the rebels held their fire and knew in a moment of insight that they were picking off the British officers. Their gorgets would sparkle bravely in the sunshine as the sun westered, inviting targets to young men used to bowling over rabbits and coneys at fifty or sixty yards. As the longboat pulled into the landing area the noise increased and they could smell powder, mixed with the rank stink of sweat and smoke, for beyond the milling troops Charlestown was ablaze. The foreshore was a litter of boats and bodies. Many regimental drummers were acting as stretcher-bearers and the wounded lay in writhing rows, the crimson of their coats and the white breeches disfigured with bloody stains and gouting wounds. Blood ran over the ground and was soon soaked up by the thirsty earth.

Kite bent to his task. The son of an apothecary, he had a rudimentary knowledge of medical matters and had once acted as a surgeon aboard ship. No one challenged him as he sent the longboat back to the *Spitfire* for fresh water and some linen for bandages. It was clear that the military authorities had made little effort to provide a field dressing station at such short notice, and he was filled with a sense of rage at this neglect. It was all of a piece, he thought as he bent with needle and thread and closed a flap of flesh over a sword wound, with the inefficiency and the misplaced preoccupations of men like Major Hayward.

For the most part the men lying in the sun were officers, and many of them had been hit by musket balls. Aimed low, these had driven deep into their soft bellies or their thighs, causing fearfully painful wounds; many were mortal but few were quick in their fatal effect. Kite did what he could to ease these men's suffering with a little water when the longboat returned, but the majority were almost bled white by the time they had been brought to the foot of the hill for treatment. He bumped into a regimental surgeon who filled the air with a thick torrent of profane oaths, aimed at the bumbling incompetence of which he himself was a part. The man was drunk, but he drove his probe remorselessly into an officer's lower abdomen until the wretch was dead. Next to the surgeon Kite had more success. He dug out a ball which had flattened itself against the femur of another officer and was delighted when no gush of blood followed the extraction.

"You are lucky," he said to the young man, holding up the offending lead projectile. The youth was already pale and rolled his eyeballs as he passed out. "Poor devil," muttered Kite as he turned to the next man.

"Help me hold him," the drunken surgeon muttered as he readied his saw and laid it across the wounded man's left leg. The knee was shattered and, as Kite bore down upon the man's shoulders, he recognised the face staring up at him.

"Harry!"

"Oh God!" It was as far as Harry Makepeace got before his teeth were bared in a grimace of extreme pain. A moment later he had passed out and Kite turned to look at the surgeon. It was already too late. The cauterisation of the arteries was imperfectly done, the fumbling was fatal and blood ran from Harry Makepeace as from an insurance company's fire-hose.

"Damnation!" The drunken surgeon swore and moved on to the next casualty, leaving Kite beside the dying son of his old friend. It was soon over and after the death of Makepeace it seemed to Kite that the afternoon dissolved into one interminable series of bloody wounds, each of which confronted him with a mounting sense of abject failure. He had no obligation to be kneeling on the foreshore tending the remnants of Gage's assault force, yet he could not tear himself away. He felt himself bound to grovel amid the dust and the blood and the vomit, surrounded by the groans and cries of anguish and pain, and to do whatever seemed possible. It was little enough, for he had little equipment, nothing in the way of those unguents with which his father had insisted a wound might be kept clear of infection, only a handful of torn sheets for bandages and pledgets, and only water from the harbour to clean open wounds. As for drinking water, there was insufficient of this to ease more than a few men, and most died with a raging thirst to add to their last agony.

Kite was dimly aware that Sarah and Harper had joined him and were moving among the wounded with water and a kind word here and there. Sarah collected messages, last-minute wishes to be communicated to wives and sweethearts, fathers and brothers. A few other kind souls from Boston had arrived to help, so they were less conspicuous among the military scarlet as the afternoon drew to its close. News came down the hill that Howe had finally forced the rebels from their positions and chased them back up Bunker Hill and beyond. This raised pathetic little cheers from the wounded and dying men.

As the sun set, Kite, Sarah and Harper were relieved of their self-imposed duties as the dead, dying and wounded were taken back across the river to Boston. Kite gathered the others on the beach and waited for the return of the longboat from Boston, whither she had taken a number of the wounded. They stood in complete silence, unable to meet each others' eyes in the deepening twilight. At last Harper announced the approach of the boat and they were just waiting for it to close the beach when a young and dishevelled officer ran up to them and bowed to Sarah.

"Madam," he said breathlessly, "I bring you Lord Rawdon's compliments and thanks for attending him. He asks who was his ministering angel?"

Sarah looked at Kite and stretched out her hand. Her fine eyes were filled with tears and he could see her swallow. He took her hand and squeezed it, nodding his approval. She said with a cool dignity, "I am Mistress Kite, sir, from the schooner *Spitfire* of which my husband here is the commander."

The young officer turned to Kite and made a short bow, taking in the sodden state of his garments which reeked of gore. "His Lordship is obliged to you, madam, and to you, sir, and," he added, seeing Harper standing there, "to you too."

"It has been a bloody day, sir," Kite said without expression.

The young officer nodded. "Indeed it has, sir, but at least it is ours."

"At a cost," Kite responded quickly, "and one which I doubt you can sustain. Pray give our compliments to Lord Rawdon and wish him a speedy recovery and a better victory than this over the rebels."

"I shall drink to that, sir." The young officer made a final bow and turned on his heel just as the forefoot of the longboat drove onto the beach beside them with a crunch.

"You were too hard on him, William," Sarah murmured.

But Kite shook his head. "Such a victory is a greater evil than defeat," he said.

"Then why wish him another?"

"Because if the British troops fail to smash these rebels quickly, there will be an infinity of scenes such as the one which we have just witnessed." He paused and added, "This is a war, Sarah, not a shooting party."

After they had regained the *Spitfire*'s deck and Sarah had gone below, Kite lingered for a moment or two. Two men had not returned in the boat from Boston and he wondered why Johnstone and one of the seamen had gone missing. It was no great matter, he thought, staring at the hills which he could now barely make out in the darkness. He felt the weight of the day cling to him like the stench of powder, blood and dust that clung to his coat. The spirits of the dead and the damned seemed thick in the heavy night air and then he felt a faint but purifying zephyr gently fan his face.

A faint trace of the dawn's optimism inexplicably slowly stole over him. He felt the dreadful affair of Bunker Hill slough off him and knew that Puella's shade and the spirits of the *obi* kept him close company.

Puella's generous spirit had led him to make love to Sarah that morning and suddenly he felt fate's benediction with relief. Others had been destined to die on Bunker Hill that day; for William Kite there was still a tomorrow.

# Fourteen

## A Moth Drawn to a Candle

The discovery that Johnstone and one seaman had landed in Boston from the longboat the previous evening to assist with the wounded had caused little concern on Kite's return to the *Spitfire*. Although the boat was sent back in for them, neither had materialised by midnight and such was the confusion in the town that Jacob, who had been acting as the boat's coxswain, had decided to return to the schooner without them. Long before Kite received the news of Johnstone's absence Sarah had removed her fouled clothing and fallen into the sleep of exhaustion. He too was dropping with fatigue and was more concerned with divesting himself of his own filthy clothing. Hearing Jacob's report of the state of Boston, he thought that Johnstone had most probably become so involved with the removal of the wounded that at the late hour at which he was free to return to the ship he had been too tired, and had found lodgings ashore.

The following morning he ordered the schooner prepared for sea, passing word that the longboat should be sent ashore again during the forenoon to pick up the two missing men. Meanwhile the empty water casks were hove up on deck and Lamont supervised their stumming, prior to sending them ashore for refilling, the rigging was rattled down and overhauled, and the final preparations made for their cruise. The morning, being almost windless, persuaded Kite to hoist *Spitfire*'s sails and check them over, allowing them to dry out after the night's dew and for some new cringles to be worked into the bolt-ropes of the foresail and fore topmast staysail, the neglect of which might cost him his prize if he ever got sight of her.

Attending to such details absorbed him, temporarily driving out of his mind the concerns he had for locating Rathburne, and entirely wiping from his mind the two absent men. The events

181

of the previous day had, however, cleared from his mind any lingering doubts about his intentions. The British "victory" at Bunker Hill had not merely been Pyrrhic, it was an illusion. Kite knew that the stand the Americans had made had come as a profound shock to the British officers, for he had overheard enough comment while tending the wounded. That it had been brushed aside in that laconic off-handedness that characterised the casual attitude of the young blades did not fool him: he was himself Briton enough to recognise the underlying worry.

An eighteen-year-old ensign who while having a bullet wound in his upper arm dressed drawled that "brother Jonathan is a tough nut to crack, by Jupiter" had proved himself courageous enough. But his shuddering frame could not hide the impact of the enemy's action, which had struck deeper than his flesh wound. Such bravado, Kite knew, was a requisite quality among these stupidly brave young men, for no one could doubt that they had driven Jonathan from his entrenchments by raw courage and sheer persistence. Admirable though these qualities were, they were limited and could not win a long war. It was this consideration which had stirred Kite from sleep and occupied his thoughts that morning. The rebels had had it all their own way and he felt that he *must* strike at Rathburne. To translate that resolve into action meant locating Rathburne with all the advantages of surprise on his side, for he was in no doubt at all of how tough a nut Jonathan was to crack.

It was while Kite scoured his schooner for defects that the lighter approached with a hail of *"Spitfire* ahoy!"

"What d'you want?" Lamont queried.

"The rest of your requisitioned cargo, if you please," a man dressed in the blue uniform of the Customs Service responded with mock civility. As the lightermen shipped their sweeps, the barge bumped alongside and the lines were thrown, the Customs officer stood and looked up at the schooner with her sails hanging loose in the hot summer air.

"You shifted your anchorage, Captain. Not thinking of leaving, I hope?"

"I most certainly am. I've my outward clearance, mister," Kite declared, "but that was not my intention by moving our anchorage. That was to do what we could to help the army."

"I'm sure it was," the Customs officer replied with flat ambiguity.

"Had I wished to leave, I should have already done so," Kite answered with some asperity.

"I don't doubt it, Captain," the other rejoined, his voice suspicious as he made for the rope ladder thrown over the *Spitfire*'s side. On deck he held out his hand and added, "Come, sir, things have been all topsy-turvy of late. We abandoned your discharge the day before yesterday for military reasons and now have a greater reason for wanting your lading ashore."

"Things went ill, then," Kite asked, pretending ignorance. The Customs officer shrugged his shoulders and looked away. "We were close inshore, we saw a great deal," he added.

"Well, 'tis true that the cost of yesterday's victory was somewhat excessive, but the chief worry is the fact that Boston is isolated. Without supply from the sea our position here will deteriorate."

"Then you are welcome to my cargo, but you would be well advised not to antagonise too many shipmasters. We are a tediously fractious breed."

"So I observe, Captain."

"Almost as intransigent as Custom House men," Kite said with a grin, seeing the signs of anxiety on the native-born colonial's face. The officer relaxed and wiped his hand across his sweating face. "Come below for some refreshment. My wife has some lemonade aboard."

Sat in the cabin with a glass of the cool drink in the easing presence of Sarah, the Customs officer unbent to the extent of revealing that rumours of evacuation were beginning to circulate among the tense and overcrowded drawing rooms of Boston. "Things could go very ill for us," he said, referring to the loyal portion of the population. In response, Kite briefly outlined the mauling he and Sarah had endured at the hands of the party calling themselves Patriots. Leaving the Customs officer to fulminate on the perfidy of such men, Kite offered him some rum, which he drank with as much eagerness as he had the lemonade, so that he manifested no surprise when Kite asked if he had heard of John Rathburne.

"Oh, indeed I have, Captain, indeed I have. He is one of those men most implicated in defying the levies and duties placed upon trade, not to mention a man tainted by criminal acts. You'll have heard of the *Gaspée* affair?" Kite nodded. "A noose is too good for that fellow," the Customs officer went on. "Truth to tell," he said, leaning forward with an air of confidentiality, "the man is a pirate and deserves to hang in chains betwixt high and low water. My God, Captain, along with Whipple and a handful of others, mostly from Rhode Island I might add with due respect to y'r wife, such a fate would be too good for the dogs – begging your pardon, ma'am."

"Please don't worry, sir. I am entirely of your opinion."

"Are you aware that he is at large in an eighteen-gun ship named the *Rattlesnake*?"

The Customs officer nodded. "Indeed. I heard he was at Salem or Marblehead."

"But," said Kite, rising, pulling a chart out of a folio and spreading it on the cabin table, "that is not far away!"

"Not at all, Captain; why, the man is as bold a devil as any. For all I know he was in that redoubt yesterday. Yes indeed, I should not be at all surprised if he was."

"Well, well." Kite tapped the chart thoughtfully then, suggesting his visitor relax until the cargo was discharged, excused himself. "I must go on deck for a moment. Sarah, my dear, do please entertain our guest for a while."

Running up on deck he began to pace the starboard side of the after deck, ignoring the fine cloud of white dust that settled over everything. Such was his preoccupation that he failed to notice Lamont trying to attract his attention. After about twenty minutes he suddenly stopped and spun on his heel.

"Mr Lamont?" he called and the mate emerged from under a whitening fold of the mainsail that hung almost to the deck from the dipped gaff above them.

"Captain?"

"What news of Johnstone?"

"None, sir, I'm afraid."

"Damn! And how long until that confounded flour's out of the ship?"

"Another hour, two at the most."

"Very well."

But the lightermen stopped for dinner and the two hours dragged on into the afternoon so that by the time the lighter bore all the *Spitfire*'s cargo the Customs officer was dead drunk and Kite sent the barge ashore without him, ordering two men to pitch the inebriated official into Johnstone's cot.

"By God, sir," Harper remarked with a broad grin, "these recruiting methods are worthy of the Royal Navy."

"Believe me, Zachariah," Kite responded, warming to the second mate's drollery, "I have no intention of shipping that wastrel in place of Nathan Johnstone. Now," Kite went on lowering his voice, "do you know any reason why he should still be ashore?"

Harper dropped his eyes to the planking on the deck. He was a poor dissembler and his awkwardness was almost palpable.

"Zachariah?" Kite prompted.

"Well, sir, he was ashore with Carse, sir . . ."

"And? Is this significant?"

"Well, sir . . ."

"Come on, Zachariah, spill the beans, damn it."

"Carse is a Bostonian, sir, and, er, he has an uncommonly pretty sister."

Kite was aware of Jacob grinning as he coiled a rope within earshot. "Well, Jacob, is this true? What do you know about it?"

Jacob hung the rope over a belaying pin and confronted Kite. "Well, sah, all I can say is that Massa Johnstone is drawn to de wimmin like a moth to a candle."

"D'you know where this Carse lives, Jacob?"

"I do, sir," Harper admitted. "His parents run a boarding house. I stayed there between voyages."

"Very well, then. Let us have the longboat manned. Zachariah, do you come with me. Hamish," he turned to the mate, "secure the deck in my absence and get her ready for sea. We'll pick up ballast from one of the islands tomorrow."

"Aye, aye, sir."

Kite went below to consult Sarah and a few moments later he scrambled over the side.

Even almost a day after the affair on the slopes of Bunker Hill the streets of Boston fairly seethed. There was an air of nervous expectation about the place after the long months of complacent inactivity. The few troops on the streets had a slightly battered and hangdog look, and yet there was a typically British disregard for disaster in the attempt by all parties to continue with everyday affairs as though nothing of note had occurred.

Carse's boarding house stood up an alley off Ship Street and an enquiry from Kite soon revealed that Johnstone was indeed in the place. It was clear from the attitude of the serving-girl that his presence was a matter of some amusement as she rolled her eyes at Harper with a giggle.

"Damned wenches," muttered the big American.

The two men were shown into a tawdry parlour whose whitewashed walls were ochre with tobacco smoke. Harper sat down and stretched his long legs out in front of him while Kite stared out of a grimy window. A few moments later Johnstone came in. He was in his shirt-sleeves.

"Ah, Captain Kite."

Kite turned from the window and regarded him. "Mr Johnstone," he began formally, "for your absence from the schooner yesterday, I put your motive down to humanity."

"Indeed it was, sir."

"But it seems that this is no longer the case."

"Carse and I were very tired, sir," Johnstone began.

"But I am told that you are probably late abed for purposes other than sleep."

Johnstone grinned and looked from Kite to Harper and back again, seeking a measure of understanding from two fellow males. "Well, sir, I have formed a sincere attachment—"

Kite broke in. "You know, Nathan, when you first agreed to sail with me you were a grieving widower, as was I."

"And you have married again, Captain Kite," Johnstone interrupted sharply, "pray do not forget that."

"I do not even consider it, Nathan, but do not forget that you are engaged to be gunner aboard the *Spitfire*."

"Well, sir, I wish now to break that engagement and establish another." Hostility and determination were clear in Johnstone's tone.

Kite frowned. "You wish to stay in Boston?" he asked incredulously.

Johnstone nodded. "I do, sir. I intend to marry, sir."

"And what of the rumoured evacuation? What will become of you then?"

He shrugged, a trifle smugly, Kite thought. There was no point in pressing the matter, though. "Very well. I presume you wish to gather your personal effects. Will you come off with us now?"

"I will come out in an hour, Captain."

"As you please. And you may keep your prospective brother-in-law with you."

"That will not greatly trouble him, Captain Kite."

"It will not greatly trouble me either."

Kite and Harper returned to the ship in silence and it was only when they regained the schooner's deck and Kite noticed with satisfaction that Lamont had had the crew refurl the sails that Harper caught his sleeve. He turned.

"Beg pardon, sir, but I couldn't say anything in the boat." Harper spoke in a low voice.

"Well?"

"It's Carse, sir . . ."

"Go on."

"I think he's attached to the Patriot party, sir. I surmise that Johnstone may be falling for the other side."

"Johnstone's to become a rebel?" Kite asked with astonishment.

"The movement is widespread, Captain Kite. If their rebellion succeeds it will mean new opportunities and Nathan's an ambitious man."

"He's certainly a changed man," Kite said grimly, adding, "damn him." Then reflecting upon what Harper had said he asked, "And what happens if their rebellion doesn't succeed, eh? Tell me that?"

"It may well do so, sir. This is a big country and the British army cannot hold it all." That was true enough, Kite thought ruefully, thinking of the clumsy attempt to hold Boston, let alone the whole of Massachusetts. "There is land west of the mountains, sir. The rebels will retreat there like the Israelites into a land of milk and honey."

"Indians and swamps, more like," said Kite with a sudden bitterness. Then he looked sharply at Harper. "And what about you, Zachariah? You are a born American; if the Patriots win, what will you do?"

"I don't know what I shall do if they win, Captain, but for the time being you may rely upon my loyalty. I will fight with you as long as you will have me."

Kite looked hard at the big man. It was a curious world, he thought, damnably curious when a man who owed him much deserted him, and a man who owed him nothing protested a touching loyalty.

"You have my hand and my word on it, sir," Harper said, holding out his paw.

Kite took it and instantly regretted it, for he felt the pressure in the big man's grip. "I shall take your hand and your word, Zachariah. All that I ask is that if your loyalty wavers you will leave me and not deceive me."

"There would never be any question of that, sir."

"Then I am content," he said as Harper released him. "I do not wish to know when Johnstone comes off to recover his gear. He will get a surprise to find a King's officer lying in his cot. Pray put both of them over the side with the ship's garbage," he said over his shoulder as he made for the companionway and the society of his wife in the cabin below.

He was dozing in a chair when the knock came at the cabin door. Sarah laid aside her needlework and went to see who it was.

"It's Mr Johnstone," Sarah announced as Kite stirred and rubbed his face.

"What?"

"It's Mr Johnstone, my dear."

"I don't want to see him."

"I think you do, Captain Kite," said Johnstone gently, forcing his way into the cabin with an apology to Sarah. Kite was awake now and rose quickly to his feet, alarmed at Johnstone's insolence in view of his changed political sympathies.

"Damn you, Nathan! I know you have turned your coat by your intended union with Miss Carse, but you will gain nothing from me."

Johnstone held up his hand in a pacifying gesture. "Captain Kite! Please! Pray give me a moment of explanation, I beg you!"

"Sir, the so-called Patriot party have given me much cause for deep and lasting grief, so you cannot suppose that I wish to debate New England politics."

"I know that, Captain Kite! That is precisely why – Mistress Kite, can you not intercede? I know you of all people have no reason to sympathise, but pray give me a moment."

"William, perhaps," Sarah began, her lovely face marred by anxiety, "you might heed Nathan for a moment."

"Please, Captain!"

"Oh damn it. Very well."

"Thank you. I make no bones about this matter –" he looked from one to the other of them – "and I know that I owe you, Captain Kite, a great debt for your kindness. That is why I come with a proposition."

"A proposition!" Kite expostulated.

"William!" Sarah bade him to instant silence and he clamped his mouth firmly shut.

"I confess that I behaved badly in remaining ashore, but Miss Carse is a most agreeable girl, not at all the type of daughter one would suspect of a common tavern-keeper. It is true that her father and three brothers are radicals. I have had long discussions with them – that and not dissolution was the reason for my sleeplessness – and I am convinced that despite all the horrors and excesses of the mob that presently calls itself a party of patriots, there is much to be said for the libertarian instincts of these Americans. Furthermore, Captain, I believe that were you not so circumstanced, and were you not laid under so deep a grievance, both you and Mrs Kite must agree that much justice lies in the claims of the radicals. I cannot, nor would I wish to, plead their cause with you now, but I will say that there is a movement particularly advocated by the Rhode Islanders to form a naval force on behalf of the United Colonies. You cannot pretend to avoid what this implies and I wish you and your enterprise well, for in the personal you deserve your vengeance. To this end I will tell you that I know that Captain John Rathburne's ship *Rattlesnake* presently lies in Marblehead harbour."

"I already know that, if that is your proposition."

Johnstone shook his head. "No, it is not, and it eases my conscience somewhat that you already have intelligence of Rathburne's whereabouts. No, my proposition runs as follows: if this rebellion succeeds it is my intention to found or ally myself with shipowning interests in New England. Sooner or later Great Britain and America must re-establish relations, and while this might be politically strained, commercial pressures will prevail and a trade between, say, Boston and Liverpool will be revived and will flourish again. Such a trade will profit those ready to exploit it and I would have it that both the names of Johnstone and Kite were reunited under such happier circumstances. You must see, Captain Kite, that I am a rootless man unless I seize those opportunities that providence offers me. There is nothing to draw me back to Liverpool, though I own a personal attachment to your own person. Therefore, as long as you have your property in Liverpool I shall know where to find you."

"And if your rebellion fails, what then?"

"Judging by yesterday's events, I do not think it will, Captain Kite, but if it does, the revival of trade will be necessary and those who first re-establish it will first profit from it."

Kite looked at his former clerk. "You astonish me with your audacity, Nathan," he said quietly, turning to his wife. "Have you an opinion, my dear?" he asked. "You are, after all, an American."

"It is a bold notion, William, and since Nathan's fortunes lie beyond the compass of our own plans, not without merit whichever way matters come to pass."

Kite nodded. "I do not like the manner of its inception, for it goes against the grain."

"Commerce, William," Johnstone said boldly, sensing the softening in Kite's mood, "is of primary importance in this world, that you and I both know, as does Mistress Kite. Let us part as the friends we have hitherto been." He held out his hand.

Kite looked wary, then took the outstretched hand. "You and I shall both pursue our private goals and subject ourselves to the caprice of fate, Nathan, but whichever way the cards fall, and always supposing we shall both survive, let us hope that we may again shake hands in amity. Very well, I agree."

When Johnstone had gone Kite poured two glasses of wine and, handing one to Sarah, asked, "Do you despise me, Sarah?"

She took the glass and sipped at the wine, staring at her husband over its rim. "No," she said when she had swallowed and lowered the glass, "for such rifts will occur throughout the Thirteen Colonies if this civil war becomes general. Besides, you two will not act in concert until after this present matter is resolved, and in the aftermath men of goodwill must come together. But that will not be for a long time."

"Aye," Kite nodded, "and there is many a slip betwixt the cup and the lip."

"And we have a private matter to attend to."

"Whatever justice Nathan conceives to lie with the Patriots cannot lie with John Rathburne. He has passed beyond the law."

# Fifteen

## Beacon Island

The *Spitfire* sailed from Boston harbour the following morning under the influence of a light breeze and her headsails, slipping easily between Governor's Island and Castle William, above which flew the bold colours of the British Union flag. Passing through King Road and doubling Spectacle Island, Kite brought her up to her anchor close to Long Island. Having before sunset established the fact that he might ballast the ship from stones and shingle on the shore, he made arrangements for the hire of three local boats and some labour the following morning.

For almost a week the crew and a few local farmhands and fishermen not otherwise employed toiled at the tiresome business of loading stones and shingle into baskets, placing these in the longboat and the local craft, pulling them out to the anchored schooner and transferring the contents into the hold. Here the ballast was shovelled out into the wings and forward and aft throughout the length of the hull, to stiffen the schooner and render her stable. Long acquaintance with the *Spitfire* had determined the draft and trim at which she sailed best on all points, though this was inevitably something of a matter of compromise, and Kite made frequent observations at bow and stern. Despite a gnawing anxiety to get away and nail Rathburne in Marblehead before he escaped – and he could not rule out the strong possibility that Carse would reveal his intentions – he was nevertheless determined not to act precipitately. That *Spitfire* should be as carefully prepared as his forethought and endeavour could make her remained his paramount consideration; he had been too long at sea not to know that one should leave as little to chance as possible.

"Providence," he explained to Sarah over dinner one day, "is a false goddess unless a proper and deferential sacrifice is first

191

made to her. She lends her support only to those who prepare themselves."

Such a sententious proposition would have seemed a pomposity had not they witnessed the fighting on Bunker Hill a week or so earlier. As it was, the terrible effects of military bungling lent a creeping purpose to their activities, and while the crew grumbled about the fossicking of their commander they admired his taking of pains, particularly as he was not averse to joining in with them as they worked. For Kite, such physical involvement was in part a panacea to his impatience, and in part a need to hasten things as much as he could, for he was aware of a smouldering agitation in Sarah, whose docile acceptance of the circumscribed life of a ship-master's wife was, he knew, a temporary expedient. While the Spitfires and their hired help scrabbled and dug up the foreshore of Long Island, she went for walks across the island, wrapped in her own solitude.

In due course, however, the task was completed and Captain Kite pronounced himself satisfied with his vessel. The final layer of ballast was left in its wicker baskets on top of the dusty deposit in the hold. Next morning, the decks having been washed off, the hatch battened and the longboat hoisted inboard and placed on her chocks, the men went cheerfully forward to man the bars of the windlass. As they did so to the rousing chorus of a shanty, Sarah appeared on deck. She wore breeches, boots and a man's shirt and bore in her arms a cascade of brilliant red, white and blue silk. Calling Jacob to help her she bent the large pendant to the mainmast head flag halliards and had him run it aloft. As the breeze lifted it, it streamed out revealing its motto, red letters on a white, red-edged ground: *Spit-Fire and Seek Revenge*. On reading it, or having it read to them, the men raised three cheers and in no time at all Harper was calling out that the anchor was a-trip and the main and foresail halliards were manned. Ten minutes later *Spitfire* was heading for the north point of Long Island and the open sea of Broad Sound beyond.

There was no sign of the yards of the *Rattlesnake* in either Marblehead or Salem, though Kite stood as close inshore as he dared. He then stretched out towards Cape Cod, thinking Rathburne would cruise there on the chance of taking British merchant ships making for Boston. But here too he was disappointed and he set course for Halifax, an alternative cruising ground for a man intent on damaging British trade. Kite spoke with every ship he could bring-to in the hope of receiving news of his enemy, but the trail had turned cold.

"Or you have been deceived," Sarah said as they ate one evening with the coast of Nova Scotia grey on the northern horizon. "Put back for Boston," she added sharply, "that is where the focus of rebellion lies."

"I should like to think your tone was bred of certainty," he said smiling. "But I suppose he may well have gone to cruise in the Irish Sea."

" 'Tis too far from the seat of events, William. Think, we speak of a man who seeks every possible advantage from rebellion. Would you go far from Boston if you were such a man?"

"You are persuasive."

"Say rather that I am intuitive." Sarah paused and then added, "And we have wasted three weeks on this fruitless quest."

Kite considered the matter for a moment and then nodded his head and rose from the table. "You are right, my dear. I shall go on deck directly and put the vessel about."


"Well, Zachariah, what d'you make of her?" Kite's voice was tense with expectation and he went so far as to remove his eye from the spyglass and turn and contemplate his second mate impatiently, as though he could worm from Harper the answer he wanted by fixing him with a glare. The big American was not to be hurried.

"Look at those yards, man; they are the *Wentworth*'s, or I'm a Dutchman!" Kite said.

"They are certainly longer than one would expect on such a vessel," offered Lamont helpfully.

The *Spitfire* was close-hauled under fore and aft canvas, her square topsails furled and her sheets hauled aft as she thrashed to windward in a stiff breeze under a grey sky. It neither felt nor looked like a July day, for the overcast was mirrored in the sea and the wind drove the spume off the wavecaps in wicked little gusts that sent it over the weather bow with an intermittently vicious hiss and patter.

"Well, sir?" Kite asked, again staring through his glass as the schooner bucked under them. Harper lowered his own glass and confronted Kite. "I'm not certain, sir, I cannot be sure."

"Oh damn you, why 'tis as plain as that damned great nose on your face!"

"Well, we shall know in an hour or two, when we come up with her."

"If this wind remains as strong as it is, or strengthens further, she will have made Salem or Marblehead long before we come up with her," Kite said disconsolately.

"Then we will blockade her, or cut her out," Lamont said cheerfully.

Kite shut his glass with a snap and took himself below, while Harper and Lamont exchanged glasses, the mate raising his eyebrows. "Is he often like this?" he asked, and Harper shook his head.

"No, but then I have never seen him in such circumstances before. I am reasonably certain that ship is, or was, the *Wentworth*, but to raise his expectations would be foolish. We have to recall that if it is the *Wentworth*, the vessel was once his own property. It cannot be easy to see your own property so flagrantly used by another man."

Lamont grunted. "Like finding your wife abed with a neighbour."

A strengthening wind and nightfall failed to resolve the question for them, and Kite hove-to rather than drive to windward in the darkness. They reduced sail, hauled the headsail sheets to windward and lashed the tiller so that the *Spitfire* bobbed easily into the seas, her decks now dry. A tolerable if not a comfortable night now lay in prospect for them all. In the cabin, Kite pored over his charts. The strange sail had been on their lee bow and was clearly not intending to double Cape Cod, which suggested she was bound for Boston, Salem or Marblehead. Heaving-to was not likely to lose them their quarry, if quarry she was, for she must tuck in somewhere or stand across their bow during the night and, if she did that, she must surely be seen, for she would have to pass close while the wind lay in the west-south-west.

Writing up the *Spitfire*'s log he was convinced the ship they had seen earlier was indeed the former *Wentworth* and, bracing himself against one of the schooner's more violent curtsies to the oncoming seas, he recorded as much in the wide right-hand column of the log-book under the heading *Observations*. By the time he had sufficiently composed himself for bed, Sarah was already asleep. Staring down at her for a moment before he doused the lantern, he marvelled at her ability to stay cool. That she had a temper he had ample evidence of, but it seemed to have lain dormant for many weeks under a paradoxically seething calm.

He blew out the lantern, bent and kissed her, murmuring her name into the darkness.

He was on deck again at dawn, but now the wind had dropped and the sky had cleared so that the visibility extended for miles and he could see the blue line of the shore from Cape Ann in the north to Cape Cod in the south, with the faint outline of New Hampshire beyond the former. Only half a dozen sails were in sight, but none of them even remotely resembled the old *Wentworth*. He swore under his breath, walked forward and hoisted himself into the foremast rigging. He climbed with slow deliberation until he could throw one leg over the topsail yard and then he scanned the horizon again, but it brought him no satisfaction.

"Well," he muttered, "we shall have to start again."

Regaining the deck he found the watch had been roused and were anticipating him passing orders. "Very well, Mr Harper, let fly those heads'l sheets and let us lay a course for Salem. Full and bye on the larboard tack. Then you may set those topsails and the flying jib." The tempting smell of coffee rose from the cabin skylight and he was about to disappear below when he added, "And keep a sharp lookout."

"Aye, aye, sir."

By noon they could see there was nothing of comparable size to the *Wentworth* lying in either Salem or Marblehead, so the helm went over again and they stood south on the starboard tack, heading for the cluster of islands known as the Brewsters that lay off Boston and between which the two safely navigable ship channels wound. Kite was bitterly disappointed, the more so since he remained convinced that it had been the *Rattlesnake*, the former *Wentworth*, that he had seen the previous afternoon. In this despondent mood he went below in search of a light meal. Within an hour, however, his mood had changed and he was roused from the doze into which he had fallen by a hammering at the cabin door and the intrusion of Harper's ugly but happy face.

"It's her, sir. I've no doubt of it!"

Kite was on deck in an instant. The afternoon was now bright and sunny, the wind a steady breeze which offered the *Spitfire* her best chances, while in the lee of the distant land the sea was negligible. He recorded these details automatically; his attention was entirely engrossed by the ship to windward of them, some three miles away.

"She suddenly emerged from Nahant Bay," Harper explained, "and she carries no colours . . ."

"Meaning she wishes to conceal her intentions." Kite completed the sentence. But as if prompted by the schooner to leeward, a British ensign rose to her spanker gaff, matching the one at *Spitfire*'s own main peak. Kite registered a bearing along with the fact that they were sailing faster than the *Rattlesnake*. He was reluctant to give up the leeward position from which Rathburne might escape, but wished to be certain of his quarry before bringing his enemy to action. On his present course Rathburne looked as if he was going to make for the north ship channel, and pass inside the North Brewster Island before hauling round and beating up into Boston harbour. Perhaps the rebels had taken up more positions in their absence, or perhaps Rathburne was intending to raid shipping in the outer roads; either way he could afford to give a little ground.

"Let us also play the innocent, Mr Harper," Kite ordered. "Do you put her on the other tack and let us cross his stern. When you have done that pass word that the men are to muster at their general quarters. Have Mr Lamont report to me, but do everything without ostentation."

"Aye, aye, sir."

As the *Spitfire* came up into the wind and the watch hauled the topsail braces and shifted the headsail sheets, Kite kept his glass trained on the *Rattlesnake*. He could see the small form of two figures on her quarterdeck and fancied he recognised Rathburne, but he knew it for a foolish assumption and concentrated on the hull of the ship. It was the work of a moment to recognise the stern decorations of his own vessel, for all the emblazonment in new gilt letters of the name *Rattlesnake* upon her transom timbers. Jumping in the lens of his glass he could see a man staring back at them through a long glass. It was impossible to identify the person at such a range and, even if it was Rathburne, the sight of the *Spitfire* would mean nothing to him, unless Carse had betrayed them. Mercifully, however, whoever it was could not possibly read their name, while schooners such as the *Spitfire*, despite her Spanish origins, were sufficiently common in New England waters as to excite no suspicions. Kite explained all this to Sarah, who had come on deck and, as was her custom when her husband was handling his ship, stood quietly beside the main windward rigging.

"Captain Kite?"

Lamont, rubbing the sleep from his eyes, reported himself as required and Kite said, "That is my ship, Mr Lamont, and I intend to retake her. At the moment I am playing the innocent and attempting to pick my own ground. Have the men go to quarters quietly and prepare the guns. Double shot them but do not run them out through the ports until I pass the word."

"I understand, sir."

As if it was the most natural thing in the world Kite ordered the schooner round onto the starboard tack again and stood after the *Rattlesnake* a cable or two to windward of her track. "If he is making inwards to Boston, as I think he surely must be," he said to Sarah, "I shall try and cut him off and catch him inside the passage, where his draught and the trickiness of the navigation will hamper him."

"You think he intends to raid shipping in the roads?"

"Yes, that would seem to be very possible."

"Might he not decide that we are a suitable prize?"

Kite shrugged. "Possibly, but we are only a small schooner and he may be after larger craft." He stared ahead and out over the starboard bow. "If you'll excuse me, my dear, I must slip below for a moment."

Having steadied on her new course, he went below to consult the chart. Picking it off his table he rolled it up and took it on deck where he gave it to Sarah to hold. Then he turned to Harper and relieved him of the conn.

"I'll take the ship," he said formally.

"Very well, sir. Full and bye, starboard tack, course sou'-by-west and we're overhauling our friend."

"Very well. Now Zachariah, I'm intending to slip between Deer Island and Niches Mate, and to avoid the reef off Deer Island we must wait until Castle William lies clear between the two. It will require a tack or two, but we will arrive in the roads before our friend, as you call him, and may well pin him against the islands when we offer battle."

Harper nodded; the bigger and deeper *Rattlesnake* would almost certainly run down inside the Brewsters and join the south ship channel, entering Boston harbour by way of Nantasket Road. The action of both vessels would be seen as perfectly usual and Rathburne would not compromise his approach for fear of losing the initiative he so clearly thought he possessed.

For the next half an hour the two ships parted company, the *Rattlesnake* continuing south, leaving Kite to concentrate upon making the lead of Castle William in the distance lie between the southern point of Deer Island and the northern point of Niches Mate. He then tacked in along the lead, the *Spitfire*'s square topsails clewed up and the schooner handling under fore and aft canvas like a yacht of the Cumberland Fleet. An hour later, inside Long Island a mile from the anchorage where they had loaded their ballast three weeks earlier, they hove to and awaited the *Rattlesnake* driving up from Nantasket Road.

But after the passing of yet another hour she was nowhere to be seen, and it was Harper who, clambering aloft, reported her yards with the sails clewed up, bearing roughly south-east.

"If you ask me he's anchored, sir," Harper said as he regained the deck and reported to Kite. Kite asked Sarah for the chart and unrolled it. Harper leaned over his shoulder and laid a finger on the paper. "About here, I'd say, Captain. Near Great Brewster Island."

Kite looked up then sang out, "Helm hard over! Let fly the heads'l sheets and let fall those topsails! Brace the yards round for the starboard tack!"

The *Spitfire* gathered way and Kite steadied her for the run down Nantasket Road, stamping up and down the deck with impatience as the schooner raced to the south-east, the wind broad on the beam and the white wake flying out astern of her. It was an exhilarating half an hour as the shores of Long Island to starboard and first Gallops and then George's Islands sped past to larboard. Soon they could see from the deck the upper yards of the *Rattlesnake* over the islands and, as they cleared the southern extremity of George's Island, Rathburne's intentions became clear.

The *Rattlesnake* had been brought to her anchor close to the south of the Great Brewster Island and her boats were plying between off-lying Beacon Island, one of the so-called Little Brewsters, and the anchored ship. Beyond the anchored *Rattlesnake* lay a schooner.

"Well, I'll be damned, they are going to damage the light-house!" Kite announced, closing his glass. "Well, let us see if we can frustrate their plans!" He raised his voice. "Run out the guns!"

In fact, unbeknown to Kite, the schooner had been on the scene for some two hours and the work of destruction was far advanced by the time *Spitfire* arrived to contest the matter. Nevertheless, clewing up the square topsails, they approached the anchored rebel vessels with Sarah's pendant streaming from the main truck. Running past the *Rattlesnake*, they fired a broadside into her, taking her completely by surprise but apparently effecting little damage. Continuing past the *Rattlesnake*, Kite ran very close to the rebel schooner and fired into her also, shooting away her main gaff, wounding both her masts, beating in a portion of her bulwarks and lodging a few shot in her hull. Gybing, Kite stood back towards Beacon Island and threw shot into the cluster of boats, then put up his helm and ran past the eastern flank of the island, firing at the parties of men ashore. He was now compelled to break off the action and work round the island, to beat up from the south before engaging the *Rattlesnake* again.

There was little doubt that the *Spitfire*'s gunnery had damaged the rebel schooner, whose name Sarah said was the *Concordia*, but Kite was conscious of having thrown away the chance of overwhelming the *Rattlesnake* by surprise. However, he knew that had he concentrated upon her, the *Concordia* would have undoubtedly engaged the single schooner and overwhelmed them, so he was not too dispirited as he passed south of the island. He did not need a glass to see the rebel party on the island as they bore off stores and equipment from the lighthouse, nor to guess why shortly afterwards a curl of smoke became a raging fire where the rebels burnt the wooden parts of the pharos.

"Sarah, my dear," he said turning to his wife, "do you bring up the small arms with Ben, my pistols and the like."

She smiled and, her eyes wild, ran below.

As the *Rattlesnake*'s anchorage opened up again, Kite ordered Jacob to put the *Spitfire*'s helm over, then told Lamont to double-shot the guns of both batteries and to withdraw the breech quoins.

"I shall pass close across her stern," he announced. "You may fire at will, but make certain every shot tells. Any man not at a gun may take up a pistol or musket here, aft of the mainmast. You may knock heads, not hats, off."

Heading north, Kite ordered the main and foresails triced up, slowing the rate of advance, though he kept the headsails drawing. "I'm intending to tack on his quarter, Jacob, where he has no gun to bear upon us, and then run back across his stern and fire the larboard guns. D'you follow me?"

"I follow you, Cap'n Kite!" The tall negro bared his teeth in a wild grin and Kite caught the infection of excitement in that wild, fearless moment. As they closed the enemy, he saw the schooner was making sail, having cut her cable, and escaping to the north-east; then they were swiftly approaching the *Rattlesnake* and her stern began to loom over them. Forward the first gun fired, then the second, and the boom of the discharges rolled along the *Spitfire*'s side in a series of concussions that echoed between the two hulls. A musket shot struck the rail beside Kite and he saw the pale blur of a face behind the open sash of one of the stern windows. Sarah, her hair blowing in the breeze, her arm outstretched and steady, levelled a pistol and as a musket barrel emerged she fired so that the barrel was hastily withdrawn. Beside her Bandy Ben passed her another loaded pistol and she pinked a figure that leaned over the taffrail.

As the *Spitfire* drew off on the quarter an after gun was fired, but the shot flew wide and then Kite ordered Jacob to put the schooner's head through the wind, exposing her stern to the enemy who fired a number of muskets and a swivel gun into her cabin windows. One pane of glass shattered noisily.

The second pass across the *Rattlesnake*'s stern was at a greater distance than the first and the enemy had mustered more men with small arms in the cabin and at the rail. Aboard *Spitfire* a man at a midships gun was hit, another had his hat knocked off and several holes appeared in the schooner's sails, but she drew clear little the worse for her audacity. What damage she had inflicted on the *Rattlesnake* Kite was uncertain, for the smoke from the schooner's guns drifted slowly to leeward and blocked their view, but it was clear that the rebel ship had sent most of her crew ashore and was actually as vulnerable at that moment as she would ever be.

"I shall run directly alongside," Kite called out, motioning Jacob to put the helm over again and warning the men at the sheets to tend them as the schooner gybed. But he got no further, for there was a shout from forward and out of the smoke blowing to leeward came the bows of two boats which thumped alongside and then men were swarming over the side yelling like banshees.

"We've run into their bloody boats!" Lamont yelled, as he grabbed a boarding pike from the rack. Kite suddenly realised that he bore no arms, but then Bandy Ben yelled, "Captain!"

and threw him his sword. He was aware of Sarah beside him, a pistol in one hand, a sword in the other, and he lunged forward as the guns' crews rose from their pieces and thrust rammers and sponges at their assailants.

"Jacob," he roared, "ease the sheets and get her before the wind!" Then he plunged into the fray, slashing and thrusting as the Spitfires prevented the boarders from forcing their way further aft. To his left he caught sight of Harper hacking right and left with a tomahawk, and beyond him the masts and hull of the *Rattlesnake* as they glided past. By an irony, the presence of the rebels on the deck of the *Spitfire* prevented the rebel gunners left aboard from firing into the schooner as she swept by Kite felt a man cannon into him as Sarah withdrew her sword and an American voice yelled that the boats had gone and that they were being carried away. In a moment the fight ended with the attackers diving over the side and swimming back to their ship or to the two boats bobbing in the wake of the *Spitfire*.

As they drew clear, Kite took stock. One man lay dead, a pair of his own crew sat between the guns nursing broken heads, while another had a cut arm. At the foot of the foremast, Harper had pinned a single rebel, a youth of about sixteen whose feet barely touched the deck.

"Who is your commander?" Harper demanded.

Half choking the young man gasped out the name "Rathburne" and Harper let him go. Slumping onto the deck, the boy strove to regain his breath before getting unsteadily to his feet. "You can swim back to your ship, or stay a prisoner," Harper said as the boy stared astern at the growing distance between the *Spitfire* and the *Rattlesnake*.

"I surrender, sir," the youth gasped and Harper conducted his prisoner aft to where order was re-establishing itself as *Spitfire* stood out to sea.

Kite crossed the deck to the dead man. It was the rebel who had fallen heavily against him and whom Sarah had thrust through the shoulder. He had a head wound from which the blood still oozed, and a pistol ball had smashed in one eye to penetrate the brain. He nodded to two seamen.

"Throw him overboard," he said, then turned to the mate. "Secure the guns, Hamish." He smiled at Sarah, who appeared undaunted by her encounter with the enemy. "You have despatched one of them," he said, "though they drove us off, I fear," he added ruefully as Sarah, Lamont and Harper gathered round the pitiful boy who represented their sole trophy.

"Brother Jonathan is a tough nut to crack, Captain," said Harper, and Kite looked at him sharply, momentarily forgetful of where he had heard the phrase before and disproportionately fascinated by the long shadows cast by the setting sun.

"What's your name, son?" the second mate asked his prisoner.

"Joe Paston, sir."

Harper looked at Kite. "His commander's name is Rathburne, sir."

"I see," said Kite, recalling himself at this news. "We had better lock him up in the gunner's cabin."

"I'll see to it," Harper said, pushing the lad towards the companionway.

"Wait," said Kite. Turning his full attention to Paston, he asked, "Where was your Captain during the fight, Joe?"

"He was ashore, sir, a-burning the lighthouse."

"He wasn't in the boats, then?"

"No, sir."

Turning aft, Kite pulled his glass from his pocket and levelled it astern. Against a flaming sunset he could see the hummocks of the islands and the tall stone lighthouse tower from which a column of smoke still rose into the air. To the north, in silhouette against the brilliant sky, the sails of the *Rattlesnake* showed her heading north, towards Marblehead.

"Brother Jonathan is a damned tough nut to crack," he muttered and then he felt Sarah by his side.

"I failed to retake my ship," he said, taking her hand and turning towards her.

"You are not a natural killer, William, but you shall succeed at the next encounter."

"I wish you were not so certain," he said miserably, bowing under the weight of obligation.

# Sixteen

## The Gun

Having withdrawn offshore, Kite hove the *Spitfire* to again and the schooner lay that night upon a placid sea. He went forward to tend the men wounded in the action and found them merrily bragging over their scratches and bruises. The mood among the hands was one of elation, because they did not share their commander's sense of failure. For most of them it was their first taste of action and while firing the guns and enduring an enemy's return of fire blooded them, the short but physical encounter with the American boarders was a more satisfactory affair. In this their little victory was incontrovertible, and their pathetic prisoner evidence of their triumph.

Kite came aft again. Lamont and his watch had the deck and Kite paused beside the binnacle. He stared round the horizon. The night was moonless and the almost cloudless sky was dotted with stars; Arcturus blazed above them while the steady light of Saturn lay close to their southern meridian. Lamont coughed and Kite looked up as the mate approached until the dim gleam from the binnacle lamp showed the features of his face.

"What d'you propose doing now, sir?" Lamont asked.

Kite shrugged and shot a glance at the man at the tiller. Whatever he said would be carried below and it would be churlish to withdraw and whisper in secret.

"Well, Hamish," he said with a confidence he was far from feeling, "we roughed them up a little, but we have lost the initiative and they will know our identity now. If they rumble that we are neither a naval schooner nor a revenue cruiser, which is not very difficult, they will make enquiries. One way or another, bearing in mind the situation regarding Carse and Johnstone, our friend Captain Rathburne will soon know that the *Spitfire* is involved in some personal crusade. With half the enemy ashore burning the lighthouse, we didn't effect much . . ."

"Oh, come on, sir, that's a gloomy view, we did a wee bit more than rough up that schooner!" Lamont protested. "We knocked the tar out of his deck seams."

The helmsman grunted his agreement. "I see I am out-voted," Kite said wryly.

"I've been thinking," Lamont went on, "if we had a few more men and one heavy long gun . . ." The mate left his sentence unfinished and watched his commander's face. But Kite was unpersuaded. Where could they come by either a long gun or more men willing to join in a forlorn and private revenge?

"Well, if you can think of where we can come by a gun, I'll consider the matter," he said. He could smell something like a stew filtering up from the cabin below and he felt suddenly famished. He smiled at Lamont. "For tonight I shall wish you a good night. Keep a good lookout and call me if you are at all concerned."

"Aye, aye, sir."

In the cabin Ben served supper, and after he had cleared away and Kite had written up the log, Sarah came and stood beside her husband. Pushing her hands through his hair she ruffled it playfully.

"You are too serious a man, William."

He looked up at her and put his arm about her. "Who would not be, with a wife as lovely as you?"

She pulled a face at him then she bent and kissed him. He rose and they embraced, then Kite tore off his coat and blew out the candles. The cabin was not in total darkness, for not only did the starlight throw up a pale reflection from the dark water but the easy motion of the schooner, in troubling the surface of the sea, stirred up a phosphorescence that illuminated it with a numinous light. Lit by this cold glow, they both unrobed and stood naked before each other before coming together in a sudden and overpowering passion. Afterwards they lay together on the deck in a tangle of limbs and a disarray of clothes and blankets.

"You must have made love to Puella in this place," Sarah whispered.

"I did," Kite replied, "but you should not—"

She placed a finger on his lips. "I am not jealous . . . She was a sweet person whom I wronged, and sometimes I fancy she still sits in the shadows, keeping me company when you are on deck."

"I have never thought of her as a ghost," Kite said.

"If she is, she is a friendly one," Sarah said contentedly, "and she believed in the spirits."

"Yes, she did, and I am certain that her spirits linger here."

"And she bore you a child."

"Sarah, it is not important."

"But I am with child, William, and I think Puella's shade is not displeased."

He was incredulous, then delighted, and in the quiet of the night he reckoned the matter out. Sarah must have conceived the night before Bunker Hill, the night he had felt so optimistic about the future.

At ten o'clock the next morning the senior of the two lighthouse keepers on Beacon Island off Nantasket Point took the spyglass from his junior colleague and levelled it at the schooner just then dropping her sails and hoisting out her boat after having come to an anchor.

"No colours," the junior keeper observed nervously to his principal.

"Another damned rebel, then," the other replied.

"I thought perhaps she looked a little like that man-o'-war schooner that intervened yesterday," the junior offered, reigniting a stale argument.

"That weren't no government schooner, Jim," the senior keeper said firmly, "she was more like a privateer with some private pendant flying, I noticed . . . Hullo, there's a boat pulling ashore."

The two men watched the boat's oars catch the sunlight as her crew plied them, propelling the schooner's longboat in towards the landing place. In the stern sat a man in a cocked hat; beside him was what appeared to be a woman.

"Well, I have no idea what this is all about, Jim, but get them scatter guns. After yesterday, I don't trust no one." The principal keeper remained on the wrecked parapet of the tower as his colleague scrambled below. The previous day had been a terrible shock and he feared worse was to come. He stared again through the glass. Was the "woman" a ruse? A seaman dressed in a gown? The fact that the lighthouse had escaped total destruction the previous day had been entirely due to the timely arrival of a strange and unidentified schooner, but the rig was common, and in the outrage of the rebels' looting of the lighthouse neither of the keepers had taken in any details of the intervention on their behalf taking place a mile away. As it was the rebels had burnt the wooden parts of the lighthouse, removed all the lamp-oil and the gunpowder for the fog signal gun, stolen the hay and a thousand bushels of barley from the island's barn and terrorised the little community. They had departed swearing to come back and complete the job after they had dealt with the intruding schooner. When they had made off, they had taken the two pulling boats which belonged to the island, leaving the keepers and their families isolated and fearful. Was the arrival of this schooner the promised threat of further destruction, or the return of the friendly vessel?

There seemed to be a great deal of activity in the waist of the schooner, which suggested some intention which could only be hostile. The older keeper watched the boat approach the landing then turned for the ladder leading below. The rebels had burned the wooden staircase and he swore volubly. He was no longer a young man and the staircase had been bad enough, but negotiating the temporary ladder his colleague had rigged up made his rheumaticky limbs creak with effort.

At the open door at the base of the tower the junior keeper handed him a blunderbuss.

"Thank you, Jim," the principal keeper said as they waited for the party to come up from the landing place. They could already see the boat pulling back to the schooner having landed its passengers. The principal keeper felt his stomach twisting with apprehension: there was something unnaturally threatening about all this and he was too old for more excitement. A moment or two later the two keepers were approached by a middle-aged man in a dark blue coat, white breeches and boots. He appeared to point something out to his companion, though what this was neither keeper could decide, but the stranger wore no sword and appeared relaxed and smiling, while at his side, her hand resting upon his arm, walked a woman in a bottle-green riding habit. Beneath the hem of her skirt polished boots gleamed intermittently in the sunshine and as they came closer the two keepers could see that, far from being a seaman in disguise, her feathered tricorne shadowed an uncommonly beautiful face.

"Good morning," the blue-clad gentleman said, doffing his hat and smiling. The two keepers kept silent, their blunderbusses held across their chests. "You suffered no casualties in yesterday's attack, I hope?" he enquired.

"Would it have mattered to you, if we had?" the principal keeper asked truculently.

"I am Captain William Kite," the gentleman said, ignoring the affront and replacing his hat. "I am commander and owner of the privateer-schooner *Spitfire* . . ."

"We don't wish to treat with any damned rebels, Captain, nor do we want any trouble. We are here for the benefit of mariners."

"My dear sir, we are not rebels," Kite expostulated. "I was hoping that our intervention yesterday afternoon prevented the rebels inflicting much damage upon your station." He looked up at the smoke-marred tower. "But I see that has not proved to be the case."

The two keepers exchanged glances, seemingly mollified. "They did enough," the older man said, "and threatened to do more. If you were willing, would you take word of the attack into Boston? The rebels stole all our stores, oil and powder, not to mention our boats. Perhaps General Gage will send us a garrison."

"Yes, I will do that if you wish to draft a despatch, but I have first to ask a favour of you."

"Oh, what is that?" The principal keeper narrowed his eyes suspiciously.

"I wish to take on board your signal gun. I see the rebels did not take that. It is a twelve-pounder, I believe."

"It is an eighteen-pounder," the younger of the two keepers said, but the older held up his hand.

"I can't let you do that. 'Tis a signal gun to be fired in case of fog."

"I have a need of it," said Kite, "and you said the rebels stole your powder. Besides, you could pretend that the rebels took the gun as well."

"They did try and spike it, 'tis true," said the junior keeper.

"Hold your tongue!" his senior snapped and then, screwing up his face and looking from Kite to his wife, he asked, "Why would you be wanting an eighteen-pounder?"

"Because I have a particular desire to engage that ship that landed her crew here yesterday."

"The *Rattlesnake*?"

"The *Rattlesnake*," Kite agreed, "formerly the *Wentworth*, a vessel not long since owned by myself and seized as an act of piracy by a Captain Rathburne."

"John Peck Rathburne, eh? God, I know that bastard – begging your ladyship's pardon."

Sarah graciously excused the principal keeper with an inclination of her head. "Do you know him?" she asked sweetly.

The principal keeper nodded. "Aye, I am originally from Rhode Island. I should have recognised him! I recall him now," he turned to his colleague, "he was that bugger in the brown coat, d'you recall? He led the incendiaries . . ."

"He is very good at burning things down," Sarah said, her voice suddenly harsh.

"Ah, well, I wish I'd a-known . . . Not that we could have done much, just the two of us with our wives and a few children, but still."

"Could you not say that he made off with your eighteen-pounder?" Kite repeated.

"He stole off everything else!" the younger keeper exclaimed. "He'd have taken the gun if he could have! But for your arrival he might have done just that!"

"Without powder, you can't use the thing to defend yourself or warn any ships of fog, can you?" Kite persisted.

"No," the principal keeper said ruminatively, "but what will you do for shot? We have none here."

"We shall manage," Kite said, "and I can offer you gentlemen a little money by way of smoothing matters with your superiors, whilst adding my evidence that we saw the rebels bearing your gun away . . . You may write all this in your despatch which I will send into Boston at the first opportunity."

"I am not much of a hand at the writing."

"I can write," said his younger companion.

"Aye, but you'd not know what to say."

"Perhaps," put in Sarah, smiling benignly, "while my husband and his men shift the gun, you and I can sit down and compose your despatch."

The principal keeper rubbed the side of his nose with a grubby finger. "How much would you be thinking of, Captain?"

"Would fifty pounds between you be a sufficient—"

"Sixty," interrupted the junior keeper.

"I told you to hold your tongue."

"Don't squabble, gentlemen," said Kite gently. "To be truthful fifty is as much as I can reasonably afford and sixty is out of the question, but shall we say, for the ease of division, fifty-four gold sovereigns? Twenty-seven pounds each must surely exceed your individual annual emoluments."

"Fifty-four pounds is fine, sir," said the principal keeper hurriedly, watching as Kite, fishing in his coat-tails, drew out a purse.

"Shall we withdraw into the pharos," he asked amiably, "and conclude our business in private?"

The eighteen-pounder weighed two tons, and although it proved possible to move it some way towards the landing on its carriage it was clear that the path was too uneven to facilitate the matter properly. This eventuality had been foreseen, however, and Harper and most of the *Spitfire*'s crew arrived ashore with spare spars, some timbers and a quantity of cordage and blocks, permitting the rigging of two pairs of sheer legs. By erecting one pair of sheers directly over the gun, it was lifted off its carriage and then lowered onto short billets of wood, made largely from dunnage and toms brought ashore from the schooner. By securing lines to the trunnions a combination of men and a pair of small horses hired for the day from the farm on the island worked the gun further towards the landing, the sheers being moved to assist over the roughest of the ground.

By sunset, aided now by the downward slope of the land towards the beach, the gun reached the high-water mark. Kite was unwilling to lose an instant, and so he sent off to the schooner for a pot-mess, fed the men round an open fire on the beach and then urged them on to complete their task. Under the stars the men of the *Spitfire* toiled on into the night.

While Kite, Harper and the greater part of the *Spitfire*'s company concentrated on dragging the gun down from its position near the lighthouse to the place selected for its embarkation, a smaller party of seamen under Lamont worked on board the schooner. Their task had been to construct a raft from materials on board and some taken off the island. A number of water casks were emptied and placed inside a rough framework of lashed spars, held together within this structure by a net to which they were individually lashed. The whole structure was then covered with a storm trysail of heavy-grade canvas, folded in half for additional strength and stretched by means of a rope lacing. This extemporised raft was then dragged ashore and anchored in water reckoned deep enough to float it even when loaded. At about nine o'clock that evening the relocated sheer legs lowered the heavy gun onto the contrivance. It bore the two tons of dead weight well and by ten o'clock, the men having wearily pulled the two boats towing their cumbersome burden back out to the anchored *Spitfire*, the gun lay alongside the schooner. The foresail throat halliard had been overhauled and shifted from the fore gaff jaws to the end of the fore boom and this was topped up with the sheet, unshackled from the deck, left on it as a purchase. By this means the eighteen-pounder was finally deposited upon the *Spitfire*'s deck, inducing a slight list. By midnight the carriage had followed and the hands were piped below, orders being passed to turn out again at daylight.

The following morning, having obtained additional stout timbers from the roof of a partly burned outhouse adjacent to the lighthouse keepers' dwellings, Harper and Kite began to fashion an extempore barbette just forward of the main hatchway where the longboat usually nestled on her chocks. They had compensated for the additional weight of the eighteen-pounder by striking four of the small broadside guns down into the hold, simultaneously clearing the larger weapon's field of fire. Before securing the hatch, the deck was shored up from below to take the weight of the heavier gun. Having completed bolting the necessary beams to the deck, a traversing slide was built on the barbette. This was liberally slushed with tallow and linseed oil and topped by the gun's carriage, shorn of its wheels. Finally, twenty-six hours after Kite had opened negotiations with the keepers to acquire the gun, all forty hundredweight of the large iron weapon was laid on the carriage, the cap squares were closed and pinned, and the men raised a ragged but spontaneous cheer. Before sending them to dinner Kite ordered a practise firing. A charge of powder was brought up on deck, wadded home and, with the gun pointed away from the island, fire was applied to the touch-hole.

As the charge in the chamber exploded, the gun carriage recoiled satisfactorily along the slide, though the whole ship shook with the reverberations of the thunderous discharge. But the gratifying concussion brought smiles to the faces of the men and two of them executed an excited little caper, to the delight of their watch-mates and the general merriment of all hands.

"Belay that bloody dido," Lamont said with a laugh. "Larbowlines away for dinner," he ordered and with the larboard watch sent below for their midday meal, the starbowlines manned the windlass and the halliards. Half an hour later the two keepers on the parapet of the wrecked lighthouse stood and watched the schooner as she disappeared behind George Island and headed towards Nantasket Road, heading for Boston.

"These are strange times," the principal keeper remarked philosophically, his fingers jingling the gold in his pocket.

"Aye, they are," concurred his colleague with a laugh.

"She was a handsome woman, that Mistress Kite . . ." the older man said wistfully.

The younger man nodded enthusiastically. "Aye, she was that. And she knew all the right words to say to explain matters."

"Aye, and she had to help you with spelling some of them words, too."

The older man smiled at the recollection. Then he stirred and said, "We had better put that money safe away; I don't want them dirty bastard rebels getting their greedy paws on it if they come back."

"No," the younger man said, grinning, "not like they took the fog-signal gun."

The two men laughed and congratulated themselves. "Not a word now, Jim lad, not even to your sainted mother."

Kite hardly dared to suppose that his luck had changed when he met a naval cutter in the King Road. If he could pass to her commander the task of informing General Gage of the attack on the lighthouse, he could the sooner be about his own affairs. He gave the schooner's waist a quick glance: the eighteen-pounder lay concealed under a tarpaulin and looked like a pile of deck cargo. They had also taken Sarah's pendant down while the displaced longboat was under tow astern, making the *Spitfire* look even more like a merchantman than she really was.

To attract the attention of the outward-bound cutter, Kite had a bow chaser fired to leeward and then hove to and hauled the longboat alongside, ordering half a dozen seamen into it and leaping in to take the tiller himself. He felt his spirits lift as he clasped the despatch largely dictated by Sarah and painfully written out by the junior keeper of the Brewster lighthouse and the boat danced across the wavelets towards the cutter which was in turn heaving-to. Scrambling up the little vessel's side Kite raised his hat and introduced himself.

"Captain Kite of the schooner *Spitfire* of Liverpool."

"John Gilbert, lieutenant-in-command of His Britannic Majesty's cutter *Viper*, at your service." The two men shook hands.

"I am on passage, Lieutenant Gilbert, but have been in contact with the lighthouse on the Brewster. They were making signals of distress having been attacked yesterday by rebels. We did what we could, but the lighthouse has been damaged and its stores completely looted. The keepers are anxious for the continuing existence of the pharos, not to mention their own safety, for I understand the rebels threatened to return. I have here their report of the incident."

Gilbert took the offered packet and nodded. "We were on our way out there, Captain Kite, having heard some rumours from the village of Hull on Nantasket that smoke had been seen rising from Beacon Island."

"Forgive the presumption, sir," Kite said, "but the faster a garrison is placed on the island, the better. I believe the keeper's report to be comprehensive, having urged him to write it to secure the prompt response of the authorities, and it may well be advantageous to convey it directly to Boston rather than waste time merely confirming the details. General Gage or the admiral will need to put troops or marines ashore as soon as possible in order to deter a further rebel descent on the island."

Gilbert considered a moment and then nodded. "Very well, Captain. My thanks to you. I will see what I can do. Tell me, where are you bound?"

"To Halifax, sir. I cleared outwards from Boston a couple of days ago, having discharged a cargo of flour from Antigua."

"Very well. And thank you, Captain."

The two men took their leave. As he put back to the *Spitfire*, Kite had the satisfaction of seeing the cutter swing round and her sails trimmed for a return passage to Boston. He wanted to escape all entrapment and involvement, and the encounter had been fortunate. Besides, a report brought by a naval officer would have more impact than one brought by a mere merchant master, so the meeting with the *Viper* was to the advantage of all parties anxious to defend the rule of law.

Both Lamont and Harper wore anxious expressions as they met him at the rail. He scrambled back over the *Spitfire*'s side and the longboat was passed astern again on its painter.

"Well, gentlemen, that was the cutter *Viper* and Lieutenant John Gilbert proved most obliging. I think the coast is now clear for us to proceed, so let us work out clear of the islands and thereafter lay a course for Cape Cod."

"You are going in chase of the *Rattlesnake*, then, sir?" Harper said.

"Why, Zachariah, what else should you suppose I would do?"

"Nothing, sir, but . . ."

"But we need to be certain, Captain Kite," interjected Lamont, "so that we can better prepare ourselves."

"Indeed, I agree. We shall dine together once we have sufficient offing, in order to do just that. But for now let us work out clear of the Brewsters."

"Aye, aye, sir."

And hauling round herself, *Spitfire* headed again for the passage between the islands and the open sea beyond.

# Chapter Seventeen

## Nantucket Sound

That evening the light in the cabin burned late. Hitherto the cabin had been Kite's private quarters, but that night, leaving the deck to Jacob, Kite entertained his two officers in formal state. This was not entirely a disinterested matter, for he had formed a liking for both men and they, it seemed, rubbed along together very well.

"We all need a good night's sleep, gentlemen," Kite said, as Ben cleared the dishes and Sarah made to withdraw at least from the table. "Stay with us, my dear," he said, restraining her, "for this whole affair touches you as much as the rest of us and we should welcome your opinion, should we not, gentlemen?"

Lamont and Harper both concurred; Mistress Kite was a woman whose society it was difficult to avoid enjoying and besides, Captain Kite's hospitality, rare though it was, proved lavish enough when he dispensed it.

"I think ye've earned a place at our council, Mistress Kite, and a welcome one, if I may say so," Lamont said, "if your conduct in the late scrap with the rebels was anything to go by."

"Hear, hear," said Harper as Ben completed his task, drawing the cloth and setting a decanter of Madeira on the table. Kite drew the stopper and passed it first to Lamont.

"Now," he said, clearing his throat, "I am certain that our friend Rathburne has retired to Rhode Island to refit. I am equally certain that he will be back to raid the Brewsters again and, one way or another, that he knows who and what we are. He is not a man, I conceive, to let matters drop. On the contrary he is likely to come looking for us so, if we are to regain any initiative, we must fight on our own terms and for this the eighteen-pounder gives us our best chance." Kite paused and looked round the table. "Zachariah, you are looking troubled; what is the matter?"

"Sir, I heard you talking to Hamish here, and saying that we could make up langridge and may even find some rocks in the ballast to charge the big gun up with, but if we could threaten him by implying we have a heavy calibre weapon capable of battering him from a distance . . ."

"I have thought of that." Kite leaned forward eagerly. "The bore of the eighteen-pounder is a little larger than the sheaves in a number of the heavy blocks on board. We have several spare blocks in store, and by fitting rope grommets we can match the bore. A few pairs of these with bolts such as we keep for the channels between each of the sheaves will make good bar shot and my plan of attack is this . . ."

Carefully, and in some detail, Kite explained his intentions, concluding: "So it does not greatly matter in what circumstances we encounter the *Rattlesnake*, only that when we do so, the gun crew acts with absolute coolness. I am therefore going to order you, Hamish, to handle the eighteen-pounder. Pick your men carefully and impress upon them the absolute necessity of following the plan." He paused and stared at Lamont, letting his import sink in.

The mate nodded. "I understand, Captain."

"Good. Now, Zachariah, I am depending upon you to take the forward guns and the headsail sheets, while I shall handle the after guns and the ship herself. Both of us will be prepared either to lead the boarders or, if matters go against us, to defend the ship. To that end I shall require you to see that all the men not selected by Hamish for the eighteen-pounder have weapons prepared and to hand. We will issue small arms tomorrow morning and, depending upon how long we have to wait for Rathburne, draw charges and renew them every morning or after any rain or excessive spraying. Is that understood?"

Lamont and Harper both nodded.

"Good. Now, since it may be some days before we find our quarry, we will divide the ship's company into three watches. I will prepare watch bills tomorrow forenoon and we will commence the three-watch system at noon."

"You mean to keep a watch, then, Captain?" Lamont asked.

"Yes. When we meet Rathburne, we will require all our men to exert themselves to the utmost and by this means we can all benefit from the rest." Kite paused again, judging the impact of his words. "Finally," he said at last, "while I do not intend that we commit ourselves to a useless fate and I am confident that this will not become necessary, if events do go against us I shall not willingly submit. This man has done me and mine," he paused and looked at Sarah, whose expression was one of rapt attention, "a deal of harm. I am not out for revenge, but for the only form of justice that men of Rathburne's stamp comprehend." He stared round from face to face. "Now, any questions?"

Lamont shook his head.

"Beg pardon, sir, and you, Mistress Kite, but what of your wife, sir?"

"I shall fight," said Sarah simply, speaking for the first time since the council of war had started.

"But is that wise?" Harper asked, colouring so that Kite wondered if he knew, or guessed at, Sarah's condition.

"No, it is not wise, Zachariah," Sarah said coolly. "It would be wise to retire quietly to England with my husband," she reached out and placed one hand over Kite's as he leaned forward clasping his glass, "but then I am an American and I am not much given to wisdom, Zachariah, much like yourself." She smiled with such charm that the three men all laughed.

"Well," said Kite, raising his glass, "here's to our next encounter with the *Rattlesnake*."

After the two mates had gone, Harper to his cot and Lamont to take over the watch on deck, Kite turned to Sarah. "Zachariah has a point, Sarah. Does he know of your condition?"

"Certainly not!" she exclaimed with a laugh, tossing her hair in a charmingly youthful motion. "As for Zachariah being right about my lack of wisdom, you know my sentiments. My child will not wish to be born an orphan and I would rather die at your side than survive to be at Rathburne's mercy, whatever happens to you."

Kite laughed. "You might lack wisdom, my love, but you certainly do not lack honesty!"

"Come," she said rising and matching the gentle roll of the *Spitfire*. "If you are keeping the morning watch, we should get some sleep."

They cruised for a day or two in Rhode Island Sound without success. Outside his own watch, Lamont and a pair of

216

seamen he had selected for the big gun's crew carefully prepared the extemporised ammunition for the eighteen-pounder, while Harper, in his watch below, prepared the small arms, made up cartridges, checked the knapping of flints and the edge on cutlasses, tomahawks and boarding pikes.

After a while Kite set the *Spitfire*'s bowsprit east from Block Island, cruising the shores of Buzzard's Bay and Martha's Vineyard, nosing into New Bedford and scouring every inlet along Nantucket Sound. They sighted fishing boats and the occasional coasting vessel, as well as two Royal Naval frigates and a sloop of war, but *Rattlesnake* had vanished, or so it seemed. Kite held to his theory in the face of an increasing if gentle and well-meant disagreement with Lamont.

"You have put too much trust in your judgement of the man, Captain Kite," Lamont argued. "It is all right for you, with a single objective, but Rathburne, for all his hot-blooded temper, is only a part of the rebel movement. He may well be subject to orders."

In the end Kite had to admit that the mate's opinion that Rathburne had retreated, not to Rhode Island, but to the coast of New Hampshire, or perhaps that of Maine, was probably correct.

"If they are meditating another descent on the lighthouse," Lamont continued to argue with increasing conviction, "they will waste little time and could have dropped into Plymouth or Portland before returning to raid the Brewsters again."

Kite capitulated with a good grace and once again they doubled Cape Cod, this time heading to the northwards, standing inshore towards the Brewster Islands. But here they saw the red dots of British uniforms ashore, and signs of men working on scaffold boards around the lantern of the lighthouse tower. Beyond the hummocks of the islands they could see too the masts and spars of two vessels lying at their anchors. One appeared to be a man-o'-war cutter and Kite thought her the *Viper*.

"Well, the lighthouse seems secure enough from further attack," Kite said gloomily, tucking his glass away and giving orders to put the *Spitfire* about yet again. He leant his weight to the tiller as the sheets were trimmed and the men milled expectantly in the waist. They were enjoying the relaxed regimen of the three-watch system, but the delay in bringing their enemy to book was beginning to grate. It was almost noon and most of the ship's company were on deck, either idling in the sunshine or waiting to relinquish or relieve the forenoon watch. He turned and regarded Sarah, Lamont and Harper, bracing themselves as the schooner swooped over the waves and ploughed through intermittent patches of brilliant sunshine.

Kite frowned uncertainly. He remained convinced Rathburne must return to Rhode Island sooner or later and decided that he might more certainly be induced to do so if word reached him that Rhode Island itself had been attacked. And suppose that he had never left Newport at all? Suppose all this time Rathburne, aware that the British were repairing and fortifying Beacon Island, had betaken himself quietly home? What a fool he had been to think that by simply trailing his coat up and down outside the entrance Rathburne would fall for his foolish enticement! Damn the man! If the *Rattlesnake* was in Newport Road, then it was time he was made to feel the weight of his enemy's wrath. Moreover, he thought with sudden resolution, it was the one way he could recoup almost all the initiative he had lost by his earlier encounter off the lighthouse.

"I intend to go back to Rhode Island," he said suddenly. "We will enter the harbour and attack any shipping we find there." As Lamont opened his mouth to venture an opinion, Kite added "But me no buts, Hamish. I am resolved."

"I was not going to argue, Captain Kite, only to suggest we could the more quickly attack shipping in Salem or Marblehead."

"Damn Salem and Marblehead," Kite said with a sudden ferocity, "I have no quarrel with either place."

"No, nor I," put in Sarah, stepping forward and uncharacteristically thrusting her opinion into their debate, "but I have a strong reason for returning to Newport!"

"I have no argument with your proposition, ma'am, nor that of your husband. Besides," Lamont added wryly, "perhaps Master Rathburne has been there all the time."

"Exactly what troubles me!" concurred Kite.

"What about you, Zachariah?" Sarah asked, staring at the big American.

"Where you go, ma'am, Zachariah Harper will follow. But he will the most willingly follow you back to Newport."

Sarah smiled. "I am obliged to you, sir," she said, bobbing him a flattering curtsy on the canting deck, and Kite and Lamont grinned as Harper's ugly face flushed brick-red.

\*     \*     \*

On their return they beat through Nantucket Sound under a grey sky that fitted the grimmer mood aboard the schooner. Word had been passed among the crew that they had abandoned their hunt for the *Rattlesnake* off shore, and that Captain Kite was determined to attack any vessels lying at anchor off Newport. The plan found no dissenting voice on board, for all were by now spoiling for a fight, emboldened by their action with the rebels on the 21st of July and intent on inflicting greater damage on the enemy. Whispers of acquiring a prize or two began to circulate, following rumours of Captain Kite's need of more money to sustain his vendetta against John Rathburne. There were more rumours, said to be facts though the source was never revealed, that the *Rattlesnake* was known to be lying at anchor there.

Passing between Nantucket Island and Martha's Vineyard on the afternoon of Monday the 31st of July 1775, *Spitfire* lay down under reefed canvas as a summer squall passed over her, her decks darkening under the onslaught of driving rain as she ran her lee scuppers under. Astern the longboat tore along in her wake as the white water rushed out from her stern with a wildly seething hiss that Sarah, sitting reading in the cabin, exclaimed was like the noise of a snake.

The realisation that she had spoken out loud made her start. She was alone, Kite having run on deck as Harper raised the first alarm of the approaching squall.

"What foolishness," she murmured, staring about her, but her heartbeat had increased and the hairs on the nape of her neck were standing up in a strange sensation, like the excitement before love. "Was I so lost in my book," she asked herself, "and so roused from my abstraction?"

The strange, almost concupiscent feeling did not diminish as the moments passed, but her heartbeat remained strong and her breathing light and hurried so that she placed an involuntary hand on her breast and rose, braced against the extreme heel of the deck, her other hand steadying herself on the deck beam overhead.

"Puella . . . ?" she whispered, dropping her book and staring into the dark recesses of the cabin. "Puella? Are you there?"

And it seemed to Sarah that in the hiss of the sea, the shriek of the wind in the rigging above and the creaking of the labouring hull as it accelerated through the sea, that Puella answered her in a voice that was audible, yet could not be heard.

"Puella," Sarah whispered, no longer frightened, but highly excited, "shall things be well with us?"

And again the word came without sound, but full of conviction and certainty, so that Sarah sank back into the lashed chair. Gradually her pulse subsided and she was flooded with a great joy, like the afterglow of love. Her hand strayed downwards from her breast to her belly, as if seeking the life growing within her, and at this sensual moment the wind dropped. The heel of the schooner's deck eased suddenly, and a patch of sunlight fell about them, illuminating the wake that rushed like a millstream out from below the windows of the cabin.

Five minutes later Kite, his cloak and hat running with water, came through the cabin door, his face split with a grin. "My God, Sarah, but did you feel the old girl *go*? Why, damn me, I think she is spoiling for a fight!"

He helped himself to a drink from the decanter nestling in its fiddles against the cabin bulkhead and turned to her, glass in hand. She shook her head. Seeing one hand upon her belly and recalling her condition with sudden contrition, Kite crossed the deck and dropped to his knee beside her.

"Sarah, forgive me, but are you well?"

She looked at his face and smiled, placing her right hand reassuringly upon his arm, whilst leaving the other on her quickening womb. "I have never been better in my life, my darling," she said.

Kite shook his head. "You must not fight, my dearest," he said, "you must not exert yourself."

"Shhh." She placed an admonitory finger on his lips. "I have put two fine flints in your Cranston pistols and shall do as I promised, William. Not even you are going to come between me and the man who murdered Arthur."

"Sarah . . ."

"But me no buts, as you are fond of saying to others. I do not love you any the less, but Arthur has no other champion but me."

"That is not true," Kite began, but Sarah overrode him.

"You are my new and happy life, William, but my old one is not quite over. Providence is never quite as tidy and accommodating as we should like her to be."

"I am anxious for the child, Sarah."

"Rest easy on that score, my dearest William."

"But you cannot be certain, and it would be foolish to take risks . . ."

"Shush! I *am* certain. Don't ask me why, but I am."

And although he pressed her no further, he involuntarily stared about the cabin, as though searching for something.

By passing south of Martha's Vineyard, it was Kite's intention to deceive any watchers on the shore and to look as though he intended to make a passage to New York. But after dark, when the wind had dropped to a light westerly breeze, he headed the *Spitfire* north towards Rhode Island. His plan was to pass the Narrows at dawn and descend upon the unsuspecting ships anchored off Newport in the first hour of daylight. He had therefore arranged to be called an hour before his watch commenced at four in the morning.

Harper called him at three and he eased himself from his bed-place trying not to wake Sarah.

" 'Tis six bells, sir," Harper said in a low voice, "and the wind has fallen light."

"We are not yet close up to the Beaver's Tail, then?" Kite queried.

"No, sir."

"Damn! Very well. I'll be up directly." Kite reached for his breeches and boots. The first flush of dawn showed the panes of the stern windows as pale rectangles, giving him just sufficient light to find his clothes. He must shave and dress carefully, for he would be in action later and knew that he must compose his mind in order to concentrate on taking *Spitfire* into Newport Road. At least the delay gave him a little more time.

He was tying his stock when the door burst open. "What the devil—?" he began as behind him Sarah stirred and Harper's figure loomed in the doorway.

"Sir! It's the *Rattlesnake*!"

"*What?*"

"She's coming down the coast from the east—"

"From the *east*?" Kite grabbed his coat and hat. "Come!" He paused only to call Sarah: "It's Rathburne, Sarah! Wake up!"

But she was already awake and he caught sight of her legs as she swayed to her feet. An instant later he was pounding up the companionway behind Harper.

# Eighteen

## Point Peril

They were closer in than Kite had supposed when Harper had warned him the wind was light. The lighthouse on Beaver Tail was broad on the larboard bow, with Brenton's Key almost ahead. Price's Neck and Coggeshall's Ledge stretched away to the east, grey against the dawn sky. And there too was a ship, running down from the east, no more than five miles away.

"The wind's changed," Kite said, fishing for his glass.

"It was in the east at midnight, sir. Hamish said it went right round at about six bells in the first watch. I've called all hands," Harper went on, and Kite was aware then of men milling in the waist. "I'm certain it's the *Rattlesnake*, sir," he added as Kite levelled his glass.

Kite needed only a moment to recognise those extended yards. He shut his glass with a decisive snap. "So am I."

He strode forward to stand on a gun truck, one hand holding the main shrouds. "My lads!" he called as the men's faces turned towards him like the features of ghosts in the dawn. "My lads, that ship is the *Rattlesnake*. You all know she is the vessel we have been searching for. I do not know why we have not encountered her before, but now that she has so obligingly appeared I urge you all to do your duty. Follow the orders that I or Mr Lamont or Mr Harper will give you and we shall prevail. Remember, we have justice on our side. Good fortune guard you all! Now take up your battle stations!"

"Three cheers for Cap'n Kite!" someone yelled, and as the cheers died away the *Spitfire*'s company broke away for their quarters.

Lamont and Harper came aft and there was a brief moment of conference. "Well, do you recall the plan?" Kite asked anxiously. Both men nodded. "Good luck then." They shook hands and as

222

Kite turned to Jacob on the helm and passed orders so that the schooner swung round towards her foe, Sarah appeared. She wore breeches and an old coat of Kite's, cinched in to her waist with a seaman's belt from which the butts of her two pistols protruded. On her head she wore the tricorne with its ostrich feather. He could not suppress a smile.

"You are a veritable pirate, my love," he remarked.

"You forgot your sword," she said, producing the weapon from behind her back.

"The devil I did! I'm mightily obliged to you, Mistress Kite. Will you give me a kiss for luck?" Their lips touched and then he said quietly. "Do take care, Sarah. Would that I could, but I cannot watch over you."

"I would not have Captain Kite become Nanny Kite. You have your task to do and I shall do mine. All will be well."

Kite brought the *Spitfire* hard on the wind, which was growing with the daylight. As soon as he had steadied the schooner on her course, he ordered Harper's men to let fall the square topsail to close the distance as rapidly as possible. As the men on deck toiled at the halliards, Sarah ran up her red and white battle flag with its legend, *Spit-Fire and Seek Revenge*.

In the waist Lamont had cleared away the eighteen-pounder and its prepared ammunition was being brought up from below.

"Where is our prisoner?" Kite asked Jacob, into whose charge Joe Paston had been given.

"He's below, sah."

"Bring him up on deck, Jacob," he ordered, taking the helm and leaning against the heavy tiller. He had forgotten what hard work steering was, particularly with the *Spitfire* going to windward hand over fist like this. He stared ahead. The *Rattlesnake* was slightly inshore of them, on their lee bow, and Kite guessed what Rathburne would do as they came up and he recognised their hostile intention. The thought quickened his heartbeat, but brought a vicious little smile to his face as a cold resolve fastened itself around his innermost being. He had dodged this arrogant Rathburne's parries for so long, made a clumsy riposte off Beacon Island some eleven days earlier, and now he was intent upon a fatal reprise.

Returning his attention to his own deck he called out, "Mr Lamont! Are you ready?"

"Ready, sir!" came the mate's response.

"Mr Harper?"

"Ready, aye ready, sir!"

"Very well. Mr Harper! The moment I luff, I want the square topsail off her!"

"Aye, aye, sir!"

"Mr Lamont! You may first train to larboard. You other gun captains, the larboard battery will be the first to engage."

A chorus of acknowledgement greeted his instructions and at this moment Jacob reappeared with an ashen-faced Paston. "Master Joe," Kite addressed the boy, "how are you this morning?" Paston mumbled something and Kite went on, "Do you keep my wife company. She will look after you. We are about to engage Captain Rathburne, as you can see." He looked at his wife. "Keep an eye on the boy, my dear. He'll make an admirable shield. Oh, and Joe, don't try any tricks, or someone might have to shoot you dead."

Paston shuffled miserably across the deck towards Sarah. He was shivering with cold and fear and looked quite incapable of any form of trick.

Grinning, Kite looked ahead again. The *Rattlesnake*'s ensign was hidden from him by her forward sails, but if he was in any doubt as to whether the approaching ship knew of their own identity this was now removed as a great pendant rose to her main truck and suddenly fluttered out to leeward. Kite raised his glass and had no trouble in reading the inscription: *Don't Tread on Me*, which wound alongside the undulating image of a rattlesnake. He glanced up: above his head Sarah's pendant matched the rebel banner and he felt a surge of ridiculous elation thrill him. Behind him he could hear the snap of the British red ensign as it flew from the main peak.

"That is *my* ship," he growled, unconscious that he spoke at all as the two vessels closed the distance between them and he studied the *Rattlesnake* through his spyglass. And equally unconscious, he raised his voice so that the sound of it quelled any chattering between the men as they crouched or squatted at their stations, or soothed the nerves of those for whom these last minutes before action were filled with the awful anticipation of death.

"Steady, boys, steady . . . She's coming down like a lamb to the slaughter just fine and dandy-oh . . . Steady, Jacob, keep her full and bye, full and bye . . . That's fine . . . Soon now he'll bear up and try . . . Soon now . . . Soon . . . Now wait for it . . . Come on, Captain Rathburne . . . Come on, now . . .

*"There she goes!"*

The *Rattlesnake* suddenly altered course as Rathburne bore up, hauling his yards, crossing the *Spitfire*'s bow and exposing his starboard broadside. Kite lowered his glass as the points of yellow light rippled along the *Rattlesnake*'s side to be extinguished an instant later by grey smoke which drifted off towards them in a lazy cloud. Then the balls whistled past, two passing through the square foretopsail, several plunging into the sea alongside, the rest whistling away God knew where as the deep and shocking rumble of their discharge reached the approaching *Spitfire*.

"Hold your fire, my lads, not yet," he called, "not yet. Mr Lamont, shift your gun to starboard, shift to starboard! Keep it laid upon the target!"

Lamont waved acknowledgement and his crew shoved the heavy gun so that it traversed across onto the starboard bow. Aboard *Rattlesnake*, Rathburne had backed his main yards, stalling his ship almost dead in the advancing track of the schooner and prepared to rake the approaching *Spitfire*. This would be the moment of their greatest trial.

"Steady, my boys . . . Stand this and you will stand anything . . ."

The distance between the two vessels was closing fast. Just as the second broadside twinkled along the *Rattlesnake*'s side, Kite called out, "Starboard guns, hold your fire until we come under his stern! Marksmen, make ready! Mr Lamont, when you are ready!"

And then the thunderous impact of the *Rattlesnake*'s shot was among them. A ball struck an after gun, tumbling it off its truck with an echoing clang followed by the rending of the carriage as it split apart. A man jumped clear, but fell over and struck his head on an eyebolt while a shower of wooden splinters exploded into the air and caught another member of the gun's crew. A second ball flew through the topsail and a hole appeared in the foresail, while a third and fourth struck the hull forward, one passing through the bulwark and carrying off the leg of a man waiting innocently to clew up the square topsail.

"Larboard a half-point," he said to Jacob and raising his voice, roared, "Clew up that topsail!"

They were rushing down towards the *Rattlesnake* and her higher freeboard began to loom over the starboard rail as the *Spitfire* struck back. The obstruction of the larger ship's hull killed the breeze as the schooner passed into the wind-shadow, but

Jacob coolly ran the *Spitfire* close under the *Rattlesnake*'s stern. Choosing his moment, Lamont jumped back from the breech of the elevated eighteen-pounder. The big gun belched fire and thunder, the smoke of its discharge streaming back over Kite, Jacob, Sarah, Paston and the men at the after guns. All about him, Kite could hear the crackle of musketry, hear the shouts and the cries, but he ignored them, intent upon the task in hand, standing rigid beside Jacob and as they came out into the wind again under the *Rattlesnake*'s larboard quarter. "Hold her steady, Jacob . . . Now! Down helm! Headsail sheets, there Zachariah!"

The *Spitfire* swung round onto a course approximately parallel to that of her enemy, but as the starboard guns opened fire and the air was again filled with the ear-splitting concussion of the broadside, Kite noticed Rathburne was hauling his main yards round to catch the wind. As *Spitfire* drew steadily ahead, *Rattlesnake* also began to gather way and move forward, but Lamont had the eighteen-pounder fire again, then again, and Kite was aware of only an intermittent response from the larboard guns in the *Rattlesnake*'s broadside.

As the two vessels moved ahead, the smaller schooner was now on the larger ship's windward bow. Kite realised that for a moment or two he had a decided advantage, for only the forward guns of the rebel ship bore, while the traversing eighteen-pounder could sweep the waist and quarterdeck of the *Rattlesnake*. But Rathburne was equal to the occasion and in the face of this withering fire, tacked his ship through the wind in an attempt to rake the *Spitfire*'s stern, extend the range and re-engage with his starboard broadside. "Down helm! Lee-oh!" Kite roared as the more responsive fore-and-aft-rigged schooner conformed, to take station again on the *Rattlesnake*'s windward bow and resume her destructive cannonade.

Suddenly the full force of a double-shotted broadside swept them and Kite felt the enemy balls strike the *Spitfire*'s hull, sending up showers of splinters all along the bulwarks and dismounting a second gun forward. A man screamed with pain and another fell stone dead beside the mainmast, while one of Lamont's gun crew slumped slowly to the deck, leaning on his rammer.

"Keep up the fire, my lads!" Kite shouted, looking about him for Sarah. For a moment his heart skipped a beat as he saw her stand up, her shirt soaked in blood. Then she caught his eye and smiled bravely and gestured at the still body lying at her feet: the blood was another's and Sarah had been comforting the dying man. "Is that Paston? Where's Paston?" he called, casting about him and fearing the dead man was in fact the American prisoner, but the boy was crouching between the guns, released from duty as Sarah's shield by her sudden concern for the dying seaman.

The two vessels were now close hauled, standing to the east-north-east and exchanging fire. It was clear that Lamont's fire was having its effect on the larger ship, for while he could no longer throw anything remotely heavy at the enemy, the loose canvas bags of langridge were having a devastating impact on both the *Rattlesnake*'s personnel and its rigging, slowly but surely robbing Rathburne of his ability to manoeuvre his ship. Lamont's ammunition consisted of canvas bags into which all manner of odds and ends of metal junk, nails, broken bolts, shackle pins, broken glass bottles, stones and musket balls had been sewn. To these horrific missiles he added short lengths of chain, old off-cuts from the schooner's bobstay and her yard slings and other rubbish which habitually littered the carpenter's shop on any vessel. At a short range, thrown on a high trajectory, the latter sliced through rigging and sails, while on a lower path the former swept the enemy deck or flew in through the open gun ports. It occurred to Kite in a prescient moment that Rathburne's ship's company was under-strength, that the imperfect response from the *Rattlesnake*'s larboard guns was evidence that they were not fully manned, even by men crossing the deck from the starboard battery. Perhaps he had landed men somewhere, and this had had something to do with his apparent disappearance and his present attempt to reach Rhode Island.

Kite looked about him. His own vessel was in a state, but she remained manageable and, though riddled with holes, her sails still drew. As the two vessels continued to exchange fire, he grew increasingly alarmed at their position, for beyond *Rattlesnake* the higher land was falling away to a river valley. He looked astern; already Seakonnet Point was behind them while up ahead the land curved round across their bow towards Point Peril and the Old Cock and Hen Rock. They were working their way into the bay into which the Coakset River debouched into the sea and this neglect of navigation by Rathburne, a man familiar with the locality, convinced Kite that his enemy was in trouble.

"His fire's faltering, William," Sarah called, and Kite, sensing the same thing, was truly puzzled. Amidships, Lamont continued to pour his fire at the enemy, while the larboard broadside guns which remained in action still threw their shot at *Rattlesnake* with unabated fury.

"What's that you're saying?" Sarah suddenly asked Paston, calling out, "William!" to attract her husband's attention and pointing to the boy, who was watching the *Rattlesnake* with a grin. He suddenly looked up at Sarah, realised he had been speaking his thoughts out loud amid the prevailing thunder of the guns, and shook his head. "What did you say, Joe?" she said, one hand going to a pistol butt in her belt.

"Come here, boy!" Kite ordered and as the trembling youth came close, he hauled him up onto the rail. "What is it, eh?"

"Nothing, sir."

"Tell me, damn you!" Kite shook the lad. "Tell me!"

He could feel Paston shuddering with terror and then, as the guns barked and shot flew past him, endangering him from his friends' fire, the lad stuttered, "The lobster pots . . . the Two Miles Rock . . ."

For a moment Kite failed to understand, but then he saw the flags on the light spar buoys marking the lobster pots around the rock lying in the middle of the bay. Did Rathburne intend to run his ship aground? Or had Kite's manoeuvring unwittingly driven him into a position from which he could not escape?

Just then one of Lamont's seamen ran up to him. "Sir, the mate says he has only three rounds left, sir!"

"What?"

"The mate . . ."

"Yes, yes!" Kite waved him aside and raised his voice, aware now that he was hoarse with shouting. "Cease fire! Cease fire! Jacob, down helm, put her about! Mr Harper! Headsail sheets! We're going about!"

As the schooner turned and her big main and foresails shook with a rattle of blocks as she passed through the eye of the wind, Kite watched the islet that formed Point Peril track across the *Spitfire*'s bow, then he spun round and stared astern. A few shots followed them, as the schooner's vulnerable stern was exposed, but the risk betrayed the truth: Rathburne had shot his bolt and even as Kite realised that the storm of raking shot was not going to follow them he saw the *Rattlesnake*'s foremast shudder and then crash forward in a tangle of falling spars and torn sails.

"She has struck the Two Miles Rock," he said flatly. Then, turning forward, he called out, "Secure the guns and ease yourselves, men. You have done well. Mr Lamont and Mr Harper, do you lay aft, if you please!"

"William, look!"

He spun round and stared to where Sarah was pointing. Extending his glass and raising it to his right eye he could see, just beyond the *Rattlesnake*, under her stern, a pair of boats in the water, men lying on their oars. Had they come from the shore, or had Rathburne's slackening fire meant he had diverted his men to lower the boats from the waist? Then he saw the wooden davits that Rathburne had erected under the mizzenmast since he had stolen the ship: their falls trailed in the water. Rathburne was abandoning his ship. Kite was furious. "I knew it had been too damned easy," he said, turning with a sudden cold anger at what he knew Rathburne was about to do. The telescope closed with a metallic snap.

"What is it?" Sarah asked, seeing the terrible expression upon her husband's face.

"That *bastard*," Kite bellowed, though it came as a cracked roar from his strained throat, "is going to burn *my* ship!" He strode forward. "Get back to your guns and load 'em! Boarders are to be ready! Second Mate! Headsail sheets! You men amidships, veer that fores'l sheet! Jacob, up helm! Lamont, load that gun of yours with all the shit your can lay your hands on!"

"Up hellum," intoned Jacob.

Kite turned aft, kicked Paston and called to Sarah, "Come you two, help me veer this mainsheet." Then, raising his voice again, he shouted, "Stand by to gybe! Overhaul those sheets now . . ." Bending, Kite, Paston and Sarah tended the big mainsail as the *Spitfire* cocked her stern up into the easterly wind. "Watch there! Watch there!" Kite called out and then to Paston and Sarah he warned, "Be careful when she gybes . . . Now! Heave in!"

Frantically they hauled the sheet so that when the wind caught the other side of the huge mainsail above them and carried the heavy boom across the deck with a murderous swing they checked it with the sheet before it had gained an excess of momentum. The moment of dangerous flurry over, the sheets were trimmed, and with her men once more at their battle stations the *Spitfire* stood back into the bay towards her enemy.

Kite was frigid with anger. The concentration of nerve and

judgement necessary to the handling of the *Spitfire* in the action had not yet drained him of his reserves of energy, while the realisation that he might yet lose his rightful property induced a terrible, cold rage. It was directed against Rathburne not solely as a man, but against him as an agent of that capricious providence of which Sarah had so recently remarked. To receive another blow to his fortunes argued that fate had, after all, a grudge against him, and this he could not yet fully contemplate, though the notion lurked on the edge of his sensibility. For the moment, however, he was a thing of sinew and bone, of blood and a raging desire to level with the pirate who, under some illusory banner of assumed rectitude, had merely exercised the ancient tyranny of might.

"Train to larboard, Mr Lamont, I'm coming alongside his starboard gangway! D'you have some lines ready fore and aft! Gun captains, remove your quoins and double-shot your pieces! Boarders make ready! We'll storm her after the first discharge!"

Kite stared ahead as they approached the *Rattlesnake*. She drew more than the schooner and, though he had given the matter little thought, he guessed they might lie alongside her without themselves touching the reef. He could clearly see figures running about her waist, and men staring in their direction, then a gun was fired, followed by a second. He was vaguely aware of the tearing sound of the passing shot, felt a dull thump somewhere and heard someone scream in agony, a noise that subsided into a whimper. One could ignore that, he thought callously, it simply spoke of a soul in agony. He moved closer to Jacob.

"Set up the main and fore topping lifts, and stand by all halliards," he called. He watched with mounting impatience as the seamen threw the coils off the pins and singled up the turns ready to drop the heavy gaffs and the two headsails. He must keep way on the schooner enough to carry him directly alongside. More guns were fired from the *Rattlesnake*, but this was no concerted broadside, thank God!

Kite chose his moment. "Lower all! Handsomely with that foresail now!" Dropping his voice and sensing Sarah by his side, he muttered, "It would never do to smother Lamont with falling canvas at the crucial moment." Then he turned, and his eyes falling on Paston beside his wife, he motioned to him. "Come here, boy!" he ordered and as the trembling youth came close he thrust him forward. "Get up onto that rail and let those rebel dogs see you."

"William . . . !" Behind him Sarah protested, but he was not listening. With her sails lowered, the *Spitfire* was losing way, but her jib boom was only seventy yards from the *Rattlesnake*'s side. "Put the helm over, Jacob!" he sang out as the thunder of six or seven of the *Rattlesnake*'s guns fired, but now the balls passed over their heads and, with the *Spitfire*'s sails doused, it no longer mattered if they cut away a rope or two.

Forward, the jib boom fouled in the wreckage of the *Rattlesnake*'s foremast where it hung over the side in the water. Her swing was arrested, but several of the gun captains had anticipated this and were busy spiking their guns round as Lamont, traversing his with far greater ease, set his linstock to the eighteen-pounder's touch-hole. The gun fired with a tremendous roar, confined as the noise was by the proximity of the *Rattlesnake*'s side, and then Kite drew his sword and called the boarders away.

He scrambled up the old *Wentworth*'s remembered tumblehome and over the bulwark onto her deck.

The scene that met his eyes could scarcely be believed and, as the wave of boarders followed, it seemed they paused in shock. Their shot had dismounted no guns, nor had it much damaged the sturdy fabric of the *Rattlesnake*'s upperworks, but the stones and nails, the old bolts, copper rovings and odds and ends of metal and glass had driven in through the open gun ports and swept over the rail to wound and maim. Men lay twisted in the agonies of painful death, lacerated and bloody from a score of flesh wounds. Many still groaned as their life drained from them and a few, the least wounded, dragged themselves painfully about, withdrawing from the enemy just then heaving themselves over the rail with a muttering of oaths and slithering in the slimy mess that ran across the once clean decks of the West Indiaman. Somewhere someone was sick and behind Kite, Sarah stood on the rail astounded at the horror before her.

In that instant of stunned hiatus Kite smelt the smoke, and a moment later, as though playing some hellish trick, like a madly sinister and deadly jack-in-the-box, a score or so of men poured up from below, armed to the teeth. "The incendiaries!" He lunged forward to strike at the nearest man. "You bastards!" he said, almost losing his footing in the gore. Then, recovering his blade, he parried the man's sword thrust, and riposted swiftly, running the fellow through.

A few feet away a man stood his ground at the foot of the mainmast and beside the binnacle. "Captain Kite!"

Kite recognised the figure in his brown coat. "Rathburne, you dog, surrender and give up my property!"

"You shall never have her, Kite! She is bilged and burning!" But as Kite sought to get over a pile of three tortured bodies, he felt a hand grab his ankle and, looking down, slashed at the mortally wounded rebel who sought to encumber him. Breaking clear he looked up in time to see Rathburne spin round, drop his sword and clasp his upper left arm.

"Remember Arthur Tyrell!" Sarah shrieked from the rail, from where, without advancing a foot, she had shot at Rathburne. Then Kite closed the distance between them and had Rathburne up against the mast. "I should kill you, you dog, and would do so if it would not lower me to the level of a pirate like yourself . . ."

But Rathburne spat in his face and as Kite jerked back and wiped his eye, Harper was beside him, his face pale under its covering of powder smoke. "Get back to the schooner, sir! They've fired her with trains to the magazine! Look, see where they run!"

Kite was aware of the rebel seamen rushing aft to clamber over the taffrail and down into their waiting boats. Two men turned at the stern and shouted for their commander: "Cap'n Rathburne!"

But then they saw Kite, his sword drawn and its point against the familiar figure backed up against the mainmast. Behind the vicious-looking Englishman were more men, including a large, ugly-featured fellow brandishing a tomahawk who stood above Rathburne and the English commander. Both rebels turned and threw themselves over the side.

"You will burn in hell yet, Rathburne, like you burned Tyrell . . ." Kite said, his sword point an inch from Rathburne's face.

"Damn you, Kite, damn you!" Rathburne, his face contorted by the pain of his broken arm, glared defiance at his persecutor.

"Come, Zachariah," Kite said, getting an arm about Rathburne, "help me get this bastard aboard." As they rose unsteadily, with Rathburne between them, he called breathlessly to the immobile Sarah, who seemed rooted to the spot by the terrible scene before her. "Sarah! Go back aboard. Tell Lamont to hoist the sails!"

The fire had already taken hold of the *Rattlesnake* and was burning fiercely below as they struggled across the deck towards the *Spitfire*, shouting at the boarding party to retire and fall back. Reaching the rail they lowered Rathburne down to where a few seamen helped them, then Harper was running forward along the *Spitfire*'s deck, shouting orders and hacking at the ropes securing the two vessels.

Dumping Rathburne beside the binnacle to which Jacob swiftly cast a line connecting it to the wretched man, Kite leaned on the tiller. "Bear off forrard!" he yelled, but Harper was already hacking at the tangled jib boom and, his leg against the *Rattlesnake*'s forward channels, was thrusting with all his might as more men joined him, taking alarm from the column of smoke and flames roaring up out of the *Rattlesnake*'s hold.

But the wind pinned them against the larger ship's hull, and although Lamont had some men toiling at the halliards they could not shove the schooner's head clear. For a moment Kite thought the game was up. Any second he expected the whole world to be rent asunder in an immense and terrible explosion as the *Rattlesnake*'s magazine blew the ship apart, but the minutes passed. Very slowly, they began to drop astern, grating all along the *Rattlesnake*'s side, with Harper and his men managing to shove them clear of the worst of the obstructing channels so that little real damage was done to the *Spitfire*. Then her stern was clear of the stern of the *Rattlesnake* and Kite could see the rebel boats pulling ashore where a small crowd had gathered. Finally drawing away, the *Spitfire* blew round broadside to the wind, her jib boom pointing ashore as her sails filled and she began to gather way.

"Sah," warned Jacob, "it will get too damn shallow inshore, sah. Don't press revenge too hard, sah!"

"What?" Kite was vaguely aware of the increased rhythm of the oarsmen ahead of them as the fugitive enemy tried to escape.

"Jacob's right, William," said Sarah beside him, and he looked round into his wife's eyes. He would never forget her appearance, for she looked like a corpse, her beauty oddly stark, drained of colour yet not of form. She would look like that when she died, he thought, shocked at the awesome revelation. "Don't pursue vengeance any more. We have done enough slaughter for one day and have Rathburne a prisoner."

Suddenly Kite relinquished the tiller. "Jacob," he said unsteadily, "take the helm and put her about."

"Helm's a-lec, stand by to tack ship!"

Slowly the schooner began to turn up into the wind. It seemed to Kite that they must at any moment run ashore, but then the long strand of Hen's Neck beach with its grass-covered dunes was swinging past the bow, followed by the burning *Rattlesnake* and then the hummock of Point Peril and the Old Cock and Hen Reef beyond. A few minutes later, her sails trimmed, the schooner *Spitfire* stood out to sea, the embroidered pendant still streaming from her mainmast head.

Kite looked at his old ship. The mainmast rose like a flaming tree and deep red flames flared within the roiling column of smoke that poured up out of her burning hold. "She has not exploded," he remarked to no one in particular.

"She was bilged," a voice said, and Kite looked down to where Rathburne had propped himself against the binnacle and stared astern. "The water," Rathburne gasped with an effort, "must have flooded the magazine." The sweat stood out on Rathburne's forehead as, gritting his teeth, he concluded his explanation: "Before the fire reached it." The two men looked at each other. "You . . . you are a lucky man, Captain Kite."

"No, sir," Sarah breathed venomously, "you are a lucky man, Captain Rathburne, for you deserve to be as dead as my late husband!"

Rathburne merely looked at her with contempt and then, with an effort replied, "Perhaps, Mistress Tyrell, if you had been a good shot, I would be."

Sarah drew in her breath smartly, but Kite put up his hand between them and then beckoned Paston over and ordered him to make his commander comfortable on deck by bringing some blankets and a pillow up from below.

"What, have they got you too, Joe?" remarked Rathburne with a brave smile at the frightened lad. "Well, well. I thought I had broken my promise to your mother."

And Kite, staring at the two of them, wondered why he felt so little except an immense and wearying sense of loss.

# Nineteen

## Rathburne

K ite straightened up. "There," he said, holding the pistol ball up in the forceps, "that is what did the damage."

On the cabin table Rathburne relaxed and Jacob let go of him with a sigh of relief. It had been a long probing and the American was soaked in sweat, but he lay quiet at last, the extraction complete. He opened his eyes and looked at the lead ball.

"Give it back to your wife," he whispered.

Sarah lent over and wiped his face, ignoring the remark.

"Now, Rathburne, I have to suture you," Kite said. "You have lost a deal of blood, but the wound is clean. Infection and dirt are close companions, so I think you have little to fear."

"I fear nothing, Kite . . ." the wounded man hissed, trying to sit up, but Jacob seized his shoulders and forced him back on the table.

"We know you for a brave fellow," said Kite abstractedly, holding a needle up to the light coming in through the stern windows and drawing thread through it.

"So very brave," added Sarah, "especially with flint and tinder . . ."

"Damn you . . ." But Rathburne carried his diatribe no further as Kite bent over him again.

The American commander remained silent for the next quarter of an hour as Kite, having cleaned and closed the wound, bandaged his arm, then stretched and splinted it. When he had finished, they laid him on the cabin deck, where a seaman's palliasse had been laid as a temporary bed.

"Well," said Kite washing his hands in the basin Ben brought in for him, "that is the last of the wounded. How many of them were there?"

"Two rebels, Captain Kite, four slightly wounded of our own, three severely wounded and one mortally," Ben answered without hesitation.

"Mortally? Ah, yes, Dodd, the stomach wound . . ."

"And six dead, sir," Ben added, completing his computation.

"Thank you, Ben."

"I will wash down the cabin," Ben said, indicating the blood-soaked table top, the stained deck beneath it and the bucket full of bloody rags.

"Let us have five minutes' peace, Ben." The rickety-legged man nodded and, picking up the bucket, left the cabin.

"He is a treasure," Sarah remarked as Kite turned and drew the decanter from its fiddles, pouring three pegs of rum and handing one each to Sarah and Jacob. "And thank you both for your assistance."

Sarah had sunk into a chair and the tall negro stood and leaned against the forward bulkhead. Both drooped with fatigue as Kite too eased himself into a chair. "Come, Jacob, sit down." Kite indicated a vacant chair, but Jacob shook his head and merely buckled his legs, his back sliding down the bulkhead so that he sat upon the floor. Before any of them had finished their rum, they were asleep, unaware of Ben slopping out the cabin round them.

On deck Hamish Lamont and his watch slumped at their stations as, battle scarred and exhausted, the ill-tended *Spitfire* sailed into the night, her head to the south.

Kite woke to find himself in his bed with Sarah alongside him. He could not recall how he had got there, nor what the strange noise was that had woken him. Raising his head he peered about him in the darkness. He could see nothing, but then thought that perhaps he should have been on deck, on watch. Had they been below to call him? Had he drifted off to sleep again? He threw his legs from the cot and then, as he stood unsteadily on shaking legs and felt the strain of yesterday's exertions, the events of the preceding hours came back to him in a rush. In the next instant he almost stumbled over Rathburne's groaning form as the wounded American turned uneasily in fevered sleep. So that was the source of the strange noise!

Kite stooped and placed his hand on Rathburne's forehead. It was hot, but that was to be expected, and he eased the blankets into which the unconscious man had twisted himself. Then he rose, dressed quietly and went on deck.

Harper had the watch and straightened up from the binnacle as Kite appeared. "Good morning, sir," he said formally, testing Kite's mood.

Kite grunted acknowledgement and Harper, after a moment's hesitation, slumped back over the binnacle.

"What o'clock is it?"

"Six bells has just been struck, sir, about ten minutes ago."

Ten past three in the morning, Kite thought as he fell to pacing the deck. And what was he going to do with the day that would shortly dawn? For weeks, no months, he had set his mind to the problem of recovering the *Wentworth*, and now that objective had been wrenched from him he was at a loss. Instead he had Rathburne lying below, a liability and a burden to him. Why in God's name had Sarah not shot him through the heart and put paid to the wretch?

Kite seethed with fury at the notion of having to tend him. Yesterday, as he had looked after the wounded, he had not thought much of the matter. Rathburne was just one of those who required attention after the fight, and as such he had had his just share of Kite's imperfect skills as a surgeon. Now, however, his mind was on a different tack and, as the first faint trace of daylight began to edge the horizon under a sheet of grey overcast, he realised something else. The utter loss of the *Wentworth* meant a severe reduction in his fortunes, for while he had a chance of recovering the ship he had not let his mind dwell on the outcome of her irretrievable loss.

He was not a poor man, it was true, but there had been considerable outlay in fitting the *Spitfire* and since then the costs of her running and manning had made severe inroads into his capital. Moreover, he now had Sarah to support and, God willing, her unborn child. He felt the prickle of sweat break out along his spine. The coast under his lee, perhaps by now all of it, was hostile while Sarah herself was no longer in the first flush of her youth. How was the child after the horrors of yesterday? He recalled the way she had looked, drained of all colour, like a bloodless corpse. What physiological changes wrought that effect and did not have an impact upon the foetus in her womb? Great God! But why was the world so full of unanswerable questions?

He paced the deck in an agony of indecision and loneliness, his tousled hair, half escaped from its ribboned queue, swept by an impatient hand as he flew up and down the deck muttering to himself. After half an hour of this wild abstraction he went below again, leaving Harper and his watch to heave a collective sigh of relief.

Two days later, still trailing her longboat astern, but with no ensign at her peak, the schooner *Spitfire* stood in towards Newport Road between the Beaver Tail and Brenton's Key. From her mainmast head flew a large white flag, fashioned from one of the few bed-sheets on board. Standing well up amongst the anchored shipping the schooner was hove to and her boat hauled alongside. A crowd of observers had congregated along the waterfront once the word went round, and the crews captive aboard the ships watched as the *Spitfire*'s boat was manned. Word went round that a body was being lowered into it and that this was followed by the figure of a blue-coated gentleman and a woman in a green riding habit wearing a feathered tricorne. The boat shoved off and headed for the shore; in its bow a boat-hook was raised and from this a smaller white flag, made from a table napkin as it happened, hung limply as a sign of truce.

As the boat approached the wharves and headed for a slipway, a group of the more curious of the male onlookers moved towards its intended landing place, their voices querulous as to the purpose of this strange event. Fifty yards off the landing the strange oarsmen rested and the blue-coated gentleman stood up in the boat's sternsheets. Without removing his hat or giving any sign of courteous salutation, as the rebel newspaper the following day reported sniffily, the sea captain called out:

"I am Captain William Kite of the British privateer *Spitfire* of Liverpool. I have here Captain John Peck Rathburne, a native of Rhode Island . . ."

At this intelligence, the newspaper afterwards stated,

> a murmur of incredulity and anxiety ran through the assembled populace whose strong feelings were mitigated when they learned from the British commander that Captain Rathburne was not dead, but merely wounded in the arm, a wound which, we are pleased to be able to assure our readers, will soon mend and enable Captain Rathburne to further the noble cause to which he has espoused and for which he almost gave his life.
>
> "Captain Rathburne's ship, a frigate of this Free

Province of Rhode Island, the *Rattlesnake*, having run
aground after an action with a ship of the Royal Navy,
had been burned and Captain Rathburne wounded in
the action. Captain Kite, we are assured, was employed
to provide safe passage for Captain Rathburne. Having
landed its precious burden, the British boat withdrew.
Captain Kite is rumoured to have had some interest in the
*Rattlesnake* which, readers will recall, was most gallantly
carried off this port some months ago by a boarding party
under Captain Rathburne.

"Reports have also been passed to the Editor that with
him in the boat, Captain Kite had a lady not unknown
in Newport which delicacy forbids us to dishonour, but
who, having been but recently widowed, has cast aside
hor proper weeds to become the whore of a British
seaman. To such low ends must all who cling to the
Tory cause reduce themselves . . .

And thereafter the Editor relieved himself of a good deal of
bile at the expense of truth, all of which was of inestimable value
to the cause of "Continental Union".

Pulling back to the *Spitfire*, Kite managed a grim chuckle.
"I wonder what they will make of that?" he asked Sarah,
adding, "Not to mention your presence. Do you think you were
recognised?"

"Oh yes," Sarah replied. "I was pointed out by several of the
ladies on the wharf."

"An' not a few gennelmen noticed you, ma'am," remarked the
seaman pulling at stroke oar.

"I am notorious, then," Sarah said with a smile.

"Undoubtedly." Kite smiled back.

In the two days since the action, they had done much to restore the
damage to the *Spitfire*'s upperworks, but she was leaking badly
and the men had to spend an hour at the pumps every watch,
for which labour Kite maintained the three-watch system and
made for Halifax. Here he spent the remaining days of August
1775, emptying the schooner of her ballast, hauling her down
and effecting permanent repairs to her two shot holes and the
split strakes that admitted water in a dozen places. The stoutly
built schooner had stood up well to the early gunnery of the
Rattlesnakes, for this had proved the most deadly.

During his brief period on board, Rathburne had recovered sufficiently to give them an account of his side of the affair. This had not been a matter of weakness, for he was fiercely anxious to know why so inferior a vessel as the *Spitfire* had taken his "frigate".

Having given them an account of the first attack on what he called "the Boston lighthouse" which had been led by himself and Major Joseph Vose and during which the only thing they had not carried off had been the fog-signal gun, Rathburne had made a second descent on the night of the 30th and 31st of July. In the interim the *Rattlesnake* had been in Plymouth Harbour, sailing at dawn on the 30th with a number of whaleboats in tow and having embarked a detachment of three hundred New Hampshire troops under Major Benjamin Tupper.

The troops had overwhelmed the garrison of thirty British marines under two officers with the loss of only two men, and then captured a dozen carpenters and bricklayers working on repairs to the lighthouse and its outbuildings. All, including the two keepers, their wives and families, were withdrawn by Tupper, and Rathburne had returned to Plymouth, where he had completed negotiation for the purchase of a British vessel from her captors. Like the *Wentworth*, she had been illegally seized, and a party of influential Rhode Islanders, desirous of forming their own coast guard, had offered a sum of money to acquire her. Rathburne had accordingly placed half of the *Rattlesnake*'s company aboard, to refit her and bring her round to Newport, which accounted for the parlous state of his own ship when she had engaged the *Spitfire*.

"She was not your ship, Rathburne," Kite had said gently, as he sat at the side of his enemy, "she was mine."

"You lost her and I acquired her by force of arms." Rathburne's eyes glittered with passion as well as fever.

"Is force to justify everything in your new country, Captain?" Sarah asked, her hostility to the man who murdered her first husband unmitigated by the catharsis of action.

"Why did you not shoot me through the heart, madam?" Rathburne turned his eyes on her.

"Because I wished to see you suffer."

Rathburne looked at Kite. "Your wife is mad, Captain Kite. I wish you joy of her."

"I am not mad, Captain."

"Hush, Sarah, he is still fevered—" Kite began when Rathburne interrupted.

"Feverish but sane . . ." he said, breaking off to chuckle mirthlessly. For a moment the trio remained awkwardly silent, then Rathburne turned to look at Kite with a sudden intensity. "That midships gun of yours, where did you get it? Was it from the lighthouse?"

Kite inclined his head and Rathburne murmured, "Of course," and turned away, closing his eyes.

"It was my wife's idea," Kite said quietly, taking Sarah's hand.

"She *is* mad," Rathburne added in a low voice and without opening his eyes, "Quite, quite mad."

The decision to land Rathburne conspicuously was Kite's. He had no wish to take the man prisoner and, despite his assurances to his patient, had no idea whether he would yet survive. But on the morning of his departure from the *Spitfire* Rathburne was fully lucid, though still weak.

As the longboat approached the landing place, Kite bent over him and spoke to him for the last time.

"It would seem that the entire populace has turned out to welcome you, so I shall wish you a full recovery and have done with you."

"No, Kite, you shall hear more of me. You too are mad, like your wife and all your foolish countrymen." Rathburne's tone was low and intense in its vehemence, but Kite had grown weary of the American's bombast and straightened up as the boat glided towards the waiting crowd.

The *Spitfire* sailed from Halifax at the end of the first week in September. The eighteen-pounder had been struck down into the hold along with all but four of the smaller carriage guns, and on top of them Kite had loaded a full cargo of timber. Her stability thus secured, the men made their final preparations for sea. Kite offered any that wished to take it their discharge. Four seamen availed themselves of the opportunity of remaining in North America; the rest, having been paid and permitted leave to enjoy a short debauch ashore, rejoined for the transatlantic passage.

Battened down, her longboat once again nestled in its amidships chocks, her sails and rigging repaired, the schooner had stood bravely out to sea at first light on Saturday the 2nd of September, to run east towards England before the equinoctial gales.

# Twenty

## The Return of Odysseus

K atherine Makepeace looked up at her husband. He stood by the unshuttered window against which the wind dashed the rain.

"Bennett, my dear, do close the shutters and come and sit by the fire . . ." Dr Bennett grunted but continued to stare out into the dark street. "Are you waiting for a summons?" Katherine asked, fearful that some inconsiderate and ailing soul would deprive her of her husband's society on this foul night.

"No," Bennett replied.

"Don't tell me that Milton wishes to pay a call?"

"No."

"Then why do you stare out of the window?"

"To be truthful, my dear, I do not know, beyond the fact that I am entertaining an apprehension."

"Ah . . ." Katherine nodded. Her first guess was correct and her husband was dissembling. She had come to learn that her husband's "apprehensions" were apt to precede some cataclysmic event occurring to one of his patients. She bent again to her needlework, a little irritated but resigned.

Then Dr Bennett suddenly closed the shutters, crossed the room and rang the bell. He remained standing until Mrs O'Riordan entered the room.

"Siobhan, my dear, do please warm the bed in the back bedroom."

"Captain Kite's old room, Doctor?" Mrs O'Riordan's face bore an expression of astonishment.

"If you please."

"Are we expecting company, Bennett?"

"No, we are not *expecting* company, Kate, my dearest, but I apprehend it may arrive." The doctor bent, threw out his coat-tails and sat down while the two women exchanged glances. Having rolled her eyes to heaven, Mrs O'Riordan bobbed her habitual curtsy and swept from the room; Katherine looked at her husband, but the doctor had closed his eyes and clasped his hands contentedly across his portly belly. She resumed her sewing with a sigh.

The two sat in silence until Bennett broke it with a gentle but persistent snoring. Katherine looked up again at her husband; he had been called out at five o'clock that morning and had a right to doze in the warm room, she concluded charitably. He was a good man as well as a good physician, attentive without being demanding, and she had long since despaired of having children. It was a shame, though no child of hers would carry on the Makepeace name and, with Harry dead, all hinged now on Charlie. Nevertheless, she would have liked children and flattered herself that she would have made a competent mother. Her train of thought strayed now to Harry, her poor wastrel brother, who had thrown up his chances of a political career, annoyed his stepfather, upset his mother and bought himself a commission.

"I shall make a name for myself in North America," he had declared with a laugh to his sister on the eve of his departure when he had appeared resplendent in his scarlet coat and his powdered wig. His battalion had been embarked in one of Makepeace and Frith's vessels, for war transportation was proving lucrative to the shipowners of Liverpool, despite the downturn in general trade with America. Poor Harry had made no impression upon America; on the contrary, the continent had made a fatal impact upon him. Bunker Hill! How could so beautiful a creature as Harry Makepeace die on the slopes of so prosaic a place? His mother had wept for a week, inconsolable over the loss of her favourite child. They had had a letter of condolence from Captain Kite, one of several he had written since he had left England, saying that he had met Harry in Boston before the battle and had learned afterwards that Harry had been "among the fallen".

Here her reverie was abruptly ended as her husband jerked awake with a start. "Here they are!" he exclaimed.

"My dear," she said gently, "you are confused by a dream. There is no one."

"I heard the bell!"

"No, Bennett, you heard nothing."

"There it is," the doctor said, his face beaming as, from the hall, the sound of the front door bell jangled.

"Good Lord," exclaimed his wife, growing pale.

"Well, well," muttered her husband, getting to his feet and walking to the door. "I shall have to see who it is at this hour."

As Bennett left the room, Katherine laid aside her work and rose to her feet. From the hallway she heard her husband's voice raised in surprised welcome.

"Good God, William, is that you? Well, well, and you have a lady with you . . . Ah, there you are, Siobhan, look who the gale has blown to our door . . ."

"Why," Katherine heard Mrs O'Riordan say as she primped her own hair, her heart beating, "Captain Kite, sir, what a pleasure!"

"Kate!" Bennett called and she joined the merry confusion in the hall. "Lo, Odysseus has returned," he said with a delighted laugh, "and brought Penelope with him!"

Katherine looked at the strange woman who was slipping off her cloak, catching a glimpse of dark hair and a face of astonishing beauty which smiled magnetically as it caught her eye. Kite bowed over her hand then Bennett ushered them into the drawing room, where Kite introduced his companion.

"My wife, Sarah . . ."

Dr Bennett bowed and Katherine nodded, welcoming her new guest while Bennett drew up chairs and invited Kite's wife to seat herself. Katherine studied her with interest, noting enviously that though her own senior by several years, the new Mistress Kite was indeed a woman of outstanding beauty, with fine dark hair, a fair unblemished complexion, clear eyes, even teeth and a sensuous mouth. Her riding habit, though worn and stained, seemed a little small and though graceful in her movements, Katherine formed the suspicion that she was pregnant.

"Well, well," Bennett said from a side table where he poured oporto into glasses, "a warm welcome to you both. When did you berth?"

"We arrived this morning, before the wind got up," Kite said, "and were fortunate to berth directly on the tide." He took the offered glass and expressed his thanks. "There were the customary delays, but I was determined that Sarah should not spend another night on board." He reached out and took his wife's hand. "She is expecting . . ."

"I knew it," Katherine said, smiling and clapping her hands with pleasure.

"You see, my dear," Bennett said, "I told you I had one of my apprehensions."

They explained the uncanny presentiment of arrival that Bennett had experienced and Sarah said, "You are very kind. I hope we shall not put you to too much trouble."

"Who else should you go to, my dear lady?" Bennett replied enthusiastically. "The house is yours and I am entirely at your service professionally and as a private person."

"Thank you, Dr Bennett."

"Dear lady, please call me Joshua." He leaned forward conspiratorially. "It would give me exquisite pleasure, for my wife denies me the intimacy and insists on calling me 'Bennett'." He pulled a face and sipped his wine, " 'Tis such a damnably *dull* name, don't you think?"

"Oh, I don't know; I have heard it used as a Christian name in America."

"Ah, but not by Christians, surely. By Red Indians, I suppose?" Bennett's eyebrows rose quizzically over the rim of his nearly empty glass.

Sarah laughed. "Of course by Christians." She turned towards Kite. "Shall we call our son Bennett, William?"

"If it please you, my dear Sarah, though I fear William Bennett Kite is something of a mouthful."

"William Arthur Bennett Kite," Sarah corrected, adding wistfully, "I should like Arthur to be thus memorialised."

"As you wish," Kite said, smiling indulgently.

Katherine asked: "Who is Arthur?"

"My first husband. He was killed by the rebels."

"Oh, I am so sorry," said Katherine awkwardly, quickly adding, "so was my brother Harry . . ."

"Lord, Katherine, I had forgot," began Kite as Katherine shook her head.

"Do not worry, William, the time for grief is past and you were kind enough to write at the time. Besides, this is a cheerful occasion and not one on which we should dwell on death. Pray tell me what you would like to eat." Katherine turned to Sarah. "I know little of ship's fare beyond the fact that it is distasteful. What would you like?"

Sarah shook her head. "You are very kind, Katherine, but I am not hungry. We had a fresh pie brought aboard from the shore and did not intend to put you to any trouble."

"It would prove no trouble at all."

"Well, I shall have another drink," put in Bennett, "and I doubt not that you will join me, Kite, eh?"

"Obliged, Bennett."

"You'll be glad to be home then, William?" Katherine said. She added pointedly, "And we must find alternative lodgings, Bennett."

"Eh, what's that?" Bennett said, looking round from the side table. "Oh, yes, my goodness me, we must, we must."

Kite held up his hand and shook his head. "No, no, it is not our purpose to evict you, though I should like us to remain here until after Sarah's confinement."

"As I said, dear lady, this is the very place for you in your condition." Bennett handed Kite his refilled glass. "There is ample room for us all and we had anticipated your arrival, for the bed is airing as we speak."

"Your forethought does you credit, Bennett," Kite said. "But in all seriousness, we shall need some time, for I have my fortune to repair and I do not think this war will benefit us here, in Liverpool."

"War? What war?" Bennett looked up, halted in the very act of resuming the comfort of his chair, his face transformed by incredulity.

"Why, this war in America . . . The war in which Harry was killed," Kite said with an air of bafflement.

"But though Harry was killed, Bunker Hill was a victory for the King's arms and surely it has put paid to all notions of outright rebellion?" Bennett was frowning.

Kite and Sarah exchanged glances and Kite shook his head. "My dear Bennett, Bunker Hill was only the beginning, and Harry lost his life not as some unfortunate but necessary consequence of the military art. There was little artful in the attack on Bunker Hill and Harry, in common with some ninety-six other infantry officers, lost his life largely through incompetence."

"Oh!" exclaimed Katherine, her hands to her mouth. "That is too cruel!"

"Not necessarily his own, Katherine," Kite temporised, "but that of General Gage and General Howe."

"But how d'you know all this?" Bennett asked, throwing an anxious look at his wife.

"We were there, Bennett, among the wounded when the first two attacks failed. It was no brilliant military exploit but a hard-fought battle in which the rebel yokels stood their ground and repulsed our infantry like heroes."

"Damn it, Kite, that is treasonable!"

"Oh, Bennett, pray do not take up the stupid opinion that likens admiration for an enemy to some form of treachery. It was widespread among the officers in Boston before the battle and they thought if they took brooms to the summit of Bunker Hill they could sweep the farm boys out of their entrenchments. Now I understand that the defeated hay-seeds have fortified Dorchester Heights and the talk is increasingly of our evacuating Boston."

"*Evacuating* Boston? Good God, is this true?"

"It is all too true, Joshua," said Sarah, "and on another occasion, I shall tell you how my first husband lost his life and how my present husband fought the rebels at sea."

"Good God, Kite, you have resumed privateering, have you? I had not heard that letters of marque and reprisal had been issued."

"Nor had I," remarked Kite drolly, "but the whole matter has gone beyond such touching niceties, Bennett. Believe me, we are at war and will have a hard time of it before it is over."

Bennett blew out his cheeks and nodded. "Aye, I can see that, and if we become preoccupied with our misguided transatlantic cousins, I would lay money on the French trying their luck against us."

"I should not wonder if the Americans will not seek an alliance with them," Sarah said, "though they may make strange bedfellows, to be sure."

Katherine looked at her sharply, astonished at her presumption.

"No, nor I," agreed Kite, seemingly unruffled at his wife expressing her political opinion so frankly. "And if so, we shall have to consider our personal position most carefully, though we have left Nathan Johnstone behind; you will remember him as my clerk—"

"Oh yes," said Bennett, "I recall him; a widower."

"Now remarried, I shouldn't wonder, to a rebel lass and intending to settle in Massachusetts."

"Good Lord, what will become of him after the rebellion?"

Katherine asked, emboldened by Sarah's candour. "Will he not hang for a traitor?"

"If we win," said Kite, "do you suppose the King's ministers will order every rebel hanged? There are thousands of them. Besides, it presupposes our troops will prove victorious."

"And you do not think they will be, do you, Kite?" Bennett asked, his voice sober with concern.

Kite shook his head. "No, not in the end. They will have their Bunker Hills and declare them victories, but in the end I think the task too vast. The country is enormous."

"Well, what do these rebels want?"

"Independence – a new country . . ."

"A new England? I thought they had that."

"No, something entirely different," put in Sarah, "a country where any man may rise and not concern himself as to how he does it."

"A republic, then?"

"Yes."

"And a man like Nathan Johnstone can change his nationality in this rebellion, and emerge as an . . ."

"American," offered Sarah coldly.

"Well, well," said Bennett, digesting the news. "Well, well."

They sat in silence for a moment, the gulf of different experiences lying between them, then Kite recalled something.

"Kate, my dear, it is remiss of me," he said, reaching into an inner pocket of his coat. "I seem to be forgetting everything important this night." He held out a small paper package sealed with wax. "It is Harry's ring. I think Charles is to have it, but I do not intend to wait upon Frith, so perhaps you would deal with it."

Her hand shook as she took the little packet and broke the seal. "How did you come by it?" she asked.

"I was with him when he died. It was quite circumstantial."

Kate looked up from the ring which lay in its crumpled square of paper. "You never said so in your letter."

"No. There is always much one does not say in such letters."

After they had retired for the night, Kite was unable to sleep. Beside him Sarah's even breathing told where she had sunk into the unbelievable luxury of a feather mattress. He recalled another homecoming, when he had taken the expectant Puella north to his native Lakes and how he had come down the following morning and been filled with such optimism that it seemed the whole world must be imbued with the same sensation of hope. But so much had happened since that bright moment of expectation. Puella and her son were dead, killed by the cholera for which this place was notorious, he had all but abandoned Liverpool and as the world moved on the fortunes of men rose and fell. He thought of Johnstone in Boston hitching his fate to the apparently rising star of Yankee republicanism, of Wentworth and his unfaithful wife in St John's and of the late Captain Makepeace's widow now in her marriage bed with Frith, her former lover. He thought too of John Peck Rathburne in Newport, and the Rhode Islander's defiant declarations; would they ever meet again? He sought an answer in the darkness, but there was no sense of Puella's presence. Perhaps she slept at last, and then he recalled the odd little yarn of Bennett's "apprehension" of their arrival tonight.

Well, well, how strange. Puella had killed herself in this very room and yet he felt no terror at the thought, only a profound sadness for her unhappiness and a vast gratitude at her act of manumission to himself. That her *obi* approved of his new wife he was in no doubt, but he was not a man of sufficient self-conceit that he could content himself with such a thought, even as Sarah lay breathing evenly beside him. No, William Kite, the self-declared privateersman, had murdered a hundred men on the deck of a ship he conceived to be his own property wrongfully taken from him. What had happened to the apothecary's son who had once splinted the wings of birds and bound up the wounds of pet dogs?

The terrible image of the carnage upon *Rattlesnake*'s deck filled his mind's eye; the writhing bodies, torn to pieces by the ragged, homespun and extemporised weapons of death, the stink of blood and shit, mixed with the smoke coiling out of the ship's hold. He shook off the haunting thought and Rathburne returned unbidden in its place, Rathburne defiant even in his pain, telling him his wife was mad.

No, Sarah was not mad; they were all mad! Poxed with insanity in all their vain endeavours! And he, William Kite, was adding to the world's overflowing portion of folly, for he had fathered another human life even now quickening in his wife's belly.

What would become of his third child? Would he or she survive? Would cholera revisit his family and take the infant? Was that how nature revenged itself upon the ludicrous creatures that called themselves humans? The sensation of panic rose in him and he was aware that Puella's spirit had gone now, leaving him alone and frightened in the darkness. How quickly a man's mood swung!

He eased himself from the bed and went to the window. Peering through the curtains he watched the grey daylight grow over the rooftops of Liverpool and felt his own apprehensions recede. He must not linger here in Liverpool to expose either Sarah or her child to the dread rice-water disease, despite Bennett's offer of himself as man-midwife. He must take all possible care of them both, for fate had given him a new lease on a life he had once thought finished and such opportunities came to few souls.

Having resolved the matter, he returned to the bed, careful not to disturb the sleeping Sarah. He lay quietly for a while and then, as the sun rose, he slipped into a dreamless sleep.